FAR AFT A̶  ̶̶N I LY

EXCERPT FROM CHAPTER VI.....

A half nautical mile off our port quarter, a huge warship sliced through the waves of a cobalt blue sea at more than 30 knots! The hybrid battlecruiser-aircraft carrier looked menacing and powerful. Her entire profile was dramatically displayed as if she was posing for the ship's postcard photograph. In the clear sea air her peacetime light gray paint scheme was illuminated with an almost painful intensity by a sun standing tall in the sky on a gloriously clear day.

Due to the high speed of her massive 40,000 tonne bulk, a steep green wave crowned by white foam was piled up at her prow, only to be cleft in two and swept aside by the widening steel hull, curling over while angling off to port and starboard. Only the very tip of the battlecruiser-carrier's bow protruded beyond and through an obscuring curtain of dazzling white spray, there it hung seemingly dislocated from the rest of the ship.

As if great fists of smoke and fire beat upon its surface; the sea beneath her six big gun muzzles, I observed; was violently concussed. Where, with every flash of flame heralding the eruption of a full salvo, it vibrated like the tympanum of a gigantic drum that instantaneously produced vertical tendrils of white vapor.

The *Johan de Witt* was shooting very rapidly. Dense black smoke belched out of her port stack fleeing aft. Her stark almost white hull and upper-works contrasted sharply with the gloomy background pall of funnel smoke and chocolate brown billows produced by her massive artillery.

Barely visible at the battle-carrier's masthead the deep horizontal red, white and blue bars of the Netherlands' tri-color could be made out, snapping stiffly in the slipstream. High up in her air operations control tower a message was being tapped out by Morse lamp, its intense bright eye blinked out coded instructions to the observation planes circling aloft.

Far aft on her flight deck; I was able to discern that a large air group was being prepared for launching. The sunlight created multiple points of bright reflection where it encountered clear Plexiglass canopies, spinning steel propellers and polished duralumin. Around and amongst the waiting aircraft swarmed ant-like; the tiny white clad figures of men........

EXCERPT FROM CHAPTER XXIII.....

At once a burst of power dragged the fighter forward. It charged down the long deck towards me. In a flash the barrel like body of the Brewster F2A hurtled past the island with blue flames firing out of its twin exhaust pipes. The first combat mission of the day was off the deck, Monday morning at 05:08hrs December 08, 1941. The weapon had been unleashed.

I looked up into the early morning sky. An approaching weather system had disturbed the atmosphere but offered as compensation a rich combination of blues, yellows and red pastels. I jammed a *Gold Tipped Imperial* into my lips, lit it behind my cupped hand, and took in my first deep inhalation, flooding my relieved system with rich calming nicotine.

Far to the east towering thunderheads were already forming over the South China Sea, one of which now colored by the dawn was entirely pink and shaped exactly like a gigantic human skull! The startling formation seemed to peek around from behind a mushrooming billow of yellow and orange highlights, from where it leered horrifically downward, casting its great shadow onto the sea across the course of my fleet!

Death it seemed was at hand, hungry and hoping for a morning banquet! It hovered gluttonously over the sea and with toothy jaws agape it waited, preparing to gather up all the young slaughtered souls!

Could it be that only I noticed this cumulus monstrosity? Frozen for a moment I watched in horror as against this unsettling backdrop, moving across its face, there seemingly crawled and wiggled in the air currents maggot like, the tiny silhouettes of the Task Force Combat Air Patrol fighters as they clawed for altitude. I shuddered and prayed that some wind would hurriedly dissipate this unnerving spectacle!

Now blowflies were added to its face, and became starkly silhouetted or illuminated to shine with a wet green yellow or pinkish metallic hue, as squadron after squadron of bombers and fighters left the decks of the two battlecruiser-carriers and climbed into the dawn. The air throbbed with the power and effect of tens of thousands of kilowatts driving their propellers, whose steel blades beat the heavy moist air of the young day with innumerable blows.

EXCERPT FROM CHAPTER XXVIII.....

"The old Light Cruiser *USS Dixie CL-14* swept bravely up our starboard side, with two gigantic Stars and Stripes Battle Flags streaming from her fore and main masts! With the tune; Bonnie Blue Flag blaring from her loudspeakers she led the nine *old four pipers* of *Desron 5* against the armored might of the Japanese Battle Squadron. These hulking monsters could now clearly be seen approaching with unaided vision through the intermittent breaks in the smokescreen at a range of only 17,000 meters, their dark sides alive with the flashes of gunfire. As the antiquated American warships; with all their little guns popping away furiously charged forward and began to vanish one by one into the smoke, I saw them raise up to their main mastheads the old Confederate Naval Ensign! A lump came to my throat for I knew the fearless reputation of their crews, and that I was looking at these brave little ships for the last time!"

FAR AFT

AND

FAINTLY

Mark Klimaszewski

ISBN: 978-1-4834-3957-0 (sc)
ISBN: 978-1-4834-3958-7 (e)

Library of Congress Control Number: 2015916754

Lulu Publishing Services rev. date: 06/09/2016

Contained herein are more than fifty
never before seen declassified maps,
drawings and photographs of WW 2
in the South East Asia Theater, relating
to the First Battle of the South China Sea
on December 08, 1941.

A NOVEL BASED UPON THE JOURNALS,

MILITARY PHOTO COLLECTIONS AND

THE FIRST PERSON ACCOUNTS OF THE

OFFICERS AND MEN WHO SERVED WITH

THE BATTLECRUISER – CARRIER FLEET

OF THE

ROYAL NETHERLANDS NAVY

1936 - 1942

DEDICATION

To my brother Matthew; for the faithful support of all my endeavors, for

five decades of good cheer and the many shared moments as hobbyists.

To my nephew Michal for his unwavering comradery, honesty and sense of humor.

Lastly, to my father; Kazimiez Franciszek Klimaszewski - 1914-1997:

Born to the sound of German artillery bombarding Warsaw. A Survivor

of: The Great War of 1914-1918, the Russian Revolution: 1917-1919,

The Soviet-Polish War: 1919-1920, the Spanish Influenza Pandemic 1918

-1919, the Polish Civil War of 1926, the Great Depression: 1929 to 1939,

World War II: 1939-1945, captivity as a POW in Nazi Germany 1939-

1944. A Horse Artillery Soldier, a combat veteran, and a driven man who

overcame great obstacles, so that he may live in freedom, raise a family and who

worked tirelessly for fifty years to see his beloved homeland free once again.

Cover Art By:

James Flood - Maritime Artist

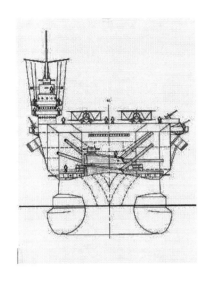

TABLE OF CONTENTS

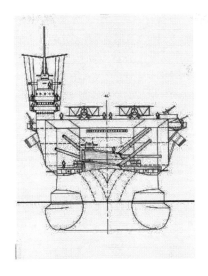

EXCERPT FROM THE INTERROGATION OF THE JAPANESE GENERAL TOSHIRO OMITU OF THE IMPERIAL JAPANESE ARMY AIR FORCE, STAFF OFFICER TO THE SIXTH AIR ARMY; BY THE ALLIED MILITARY COMMISSION; TOKYO – MARCH 1946.

VOLUME XXXIII, CHAPTER XVII.

QUESTION:

"General Omitu; what was the significance, if any, of the Battlecruiser-carrier Squadron of the Royal Netherlands Navy to the planning of the Japanese Aggressive Military Campaign in South East Asia from 1941 to 1942?"

GENERAL OMITU:

"Prior to the arrival of the Netherlands Battlecruiser-carriers in South East Asia, the Dutch Fleet, was merely a handful of small surface ships possessing such limited offensive power as to be inconsequential, and were therefore not discussed in our strategic planning. The RNLN had however deployed a sizable force of submarines in the Far East that we had to consider. But as these were older boats and had a short range, we felt that once their bases were destroyed they would present a limited threat that could easily be dealt with by our antisubmarine aircraft, and sub hunters."

"The Dutch Admiralty, did however introduce a 'Strategic Element' into the South East Asia region with the deployment of their Battlecruiser-carrier Squadron from Europe to their East Indies Colony in 1939, a move which came as a great surprise to us, as we believed these major warships, and their escorts would not leave Dutch home waters, with an aggressive re-armed German state sharing a common border."

"The three Battlecruiser-carriers of the RNLN, on occasion loaded more than 250 planes for an operation, half of which were fighter aircraft. In addition to the considerable capability of such a large concentration of military aircraft, all three warships were outfitted with powerful artillery; six pieces of super heavy guns each; which when combined, was more than that carried

by a Battlecruiser Division of the Imperial Japanese Navy! The Navy Intelligence Section, had for planning purposes; assigned the three Dutch battle-carriers, when operating as one unit; the equivalent strength of two first line fleet carriers with a battlecruiser in support; a powerful force. The Battle-carrier Squadron also had their own dedicated escort of a cruiser squadron of two or three divisions, and one or two flotillas of destroyers."

"Since the Imperial Japanese Navy was vastly superior in strength to the Royal Netherlands Navy, we surmised that the Dutch Admiralty in Batavia, would assume a defensive posture. Their fleet would deploy within the ring of Army Airbases, and the Naval Air Stations numbering more than forty locations on the islands of Borneo, Celebes, Java, and Sumatra. The Battle-carrier squadron could move thousands of kilometers east to west on the Java, Flores, and Banda Seas and equally great distances south to north from the Java Sea to the Celebes Sea through the Strait of Makassar, and do so with considerable air support at all times."

"These hybrid warships therefore were not only difficult to locate, but difficult to attack as a bomber fleet first had to fight their way past the cordon of enemy fighter aircraft raised by those airbases screening their route of attack. Then having done this, our bombers were faced with the Battle-carrier's fighter umbrella which was at least the strength of a Hikosentai (air regiment). In addition to these airborne obstacles the vessels of the Dutch Battle-carrier Squadron were equipped with very powerful anti-aircraft batteries, which had to be overcome to deliver a successful air attack."

"The Japanese Army Air Force strategists, agreed that in order to avoid a long air campaign of attrition, it would be necessary to lure the enemy Battle-carrier Squadron from its protected nest with tempting targets, and then destroy it. So yes; the Dutch Battle-carriers immediately became a strategic factor in the planning of Japan's South East Asia Campaign".

QUESTION:

Would you be able to expand on that?

GENERAL OMITU:

"Well for several reasons: the first being that soon after the successful attack on Pearl Harbour by the Imperial Navy, we believed that a crushing blow had been dealt to the Americans, even though three fleet aircraft carriers were still at large somewhere in the Pacific, having escaped the destruction. General Doolittle's raid on the Japanese mainland by carrier borne bombers clearly revealed, to our High Command; that aircraft carriers; and not battleships would dictate the course of the war."

"In January 1942, our naval intelligence services discovered through its agents in Europe that the British were planning to return to the Pacific Region in force by the spring of 1942. The Royal Navy began to assemble a fleet at Aden under the command of Admiral Somerville, to operate in the Indian Ocean, from the base at Trincomalee, on the east coast of Ceylon. The heart this force was to be composed of the Battleship Warspite, four 'R' Class battleships and three modern aircraft carriers. There was now a great threat that this British fleet, would combine with the Dutch battle-carriers and the surviving American aircraft carrier force to give the enemy a nucleus of nine flight decks in the Pacific, from which they could operate as many as 900 to 1000 aircraft! A force that could, at least on paper, equal the entire 1st Air Fleet of the Imperial Japanese Navy! The Americans *could then reinforce this with elements of their Atlantic Fleet, as many as five aircraft carriers, giving them a decisive superiority."*

"We therefore resolved never to allow these widely separated enemy forces to concentrate. We had to keep them divided, then destroy them piecemeal. The Battle-carriers of the Dutch Navy therefore became an important target, as they were located in the center of these widely dispersed forces, at the bullseye of the target, if you will."

"Secondly; our military campaign in South East Asia, depended upon the rapid capture of those enemy territories that contained the strategic materials that Japan required to pursue victory; primarily tin ore, the oil refineries and rubber plantations of the Dutch East Indies. The Army planned to do this with seaborne troops. But amphibious operations could not begin without first gaining complete air and sea superiority, over the beaches, lest the operation face undue risk."

"The enemy Battle-carrier Group was capable of steaming 700 miles in a single day, in any direction, and could therfore introduce unexpectedly, at any location, such a heavy concentration of aircraft and surface weapons that it could easily dominate the air and sea locally and destroy any amphibious operations underway by the Army. Until the Dutch Battle-carriers could be eliminated; the only way to negate them; was to carry out simultaneous landings that were separated by great distances. If they managed to destroy one, the other landing could be carried out successfully. But this could only be done at great risk, and with the heavy use of our very limited oil resources because at the time, the American Oil Embargo against Japan was in place. The Dutch Battle-carrier Force for these reasons represented a grave threat, and had to be factored into our strategic plans for conducting the war."

QUESTION:

"In your opinion, why did the Japanese Sixth Air Army Operation: Nezumitori (Mousetrap), fail to destroy the Dutch Battle-Carrier Fleet, in the South China Sea, as planned on the morning of December 8, 1941?"

GENERAL OMITU:

"The first error of the plan was strategic in nature. Certain high placed generals in the Japanese Army and Army Air Force, completely underestimated the capabilities of the Royal Netherlands Navy, as well as the powerful nature of their battle-carriers, which were still an unproven ship type, and unwisely held them in complete contempt. This is evident in the name that they assigned to the operation; Mousetrap! I argued without success that those planners of 'Operation Nezumatori', did not understand their enemy, and would benefit by reading the naval history of the Dutch, whose symbol is a Golden Lion. To catch a Lion, I argued; you must set a Lion Trap, which is exactly what we did at New Guinea, one month later. The single Hikodan (Air Brigade) of four Hikosentais (Air Regiments), commited to Operation Mousetrap was just not up to the task assigned to it. I argued that the entire 17ᵗʰ Hikoshiden (Air Division) was required to destroy a fleet that may have as many as 100 aircraft defending it!"

"The planners of 'Operation Nezumatori' were confounded by a major failure in naval intelligence. They had prepared to attack a Dutch Task Force whose strategic ships; the two battle-carriers normally carried one fighter squadron apiece, each of 21 fighters. What the planners failed to account for was two additional fighter squadrons landing aboard the battle-carriers on the evening

of December 07, 1941, and the next day as the airbattle was raging, the Dutch Fleet was supported by an Dutch Army Heavy Fighter Group of some 30 machines. So instead of our air regiments battling their way through two enemy fighter squadrons they were fighting six, with two more land based fighter squadrons shuttling forward and available from Kendari airfield later in the day! The enemy dive bombers operated without fear and consequently decimated the Malaya Invasion Convoy of General Takaguchi!

"The second error was the complexity of the first day of our operation. The JAAF High Command selected too many enemy targets for destruction on the first day. They knew that the Dutch Fleet would sail east from Singapore of December 07, 1941. Statistical probability suggested they would steer for the Java Sea where our submarine cordon would attack them. But during the night they changed course northwards, picked up two extra fighter squadrons, and entered the South China Sea. It wasn't until, the morning of December 08th that this was confirmed and by that time our Sunburst Convoy was well committed and in grave danger!"

"The third error; was tactical in nature, but still of great importance. The poor performance of the fighter aircraft of the 123rd Hikosentai based at My Thoa Airfield in Cochin China. That fighter regiment was the closest unit to our Malay Invasion Fleet Sunburst at the time of the Dutch air attacks, yet they failed to continue in action against the enemy after their first unsuccessful contact. This was a critical factor, and was the primary cause of the desruction of General Takaguchi's Malya Invasion Force. The 130th Chutai was badly shot up by the Dutch Navy fighter escort, while the remaining two intact squadrons; the 131st and 133rd had mistimed their sweeps and failed to intercept the unescorted Dutch heavy dive bombers on their second strike against our Invasion fleet. These errors resulted in the sinking of practically the entire formation including the dreadnoughts Kumamoto and Kagoshima and killed General Takaguchi. For these repeated failures, honor demanded that the commander of the 123rd Hikosentai commit seppuku."

"The fourth error, was a shortfall in airfield equipment. The new bomber air bases that we recently constructed in French Indo China, lacked equipment to repair the airstrips after they had been bombed. The heavy earth moving machinery which should be part of an operational airfild's inventory had been stripped away to support ongoing amphibious landings. Our follow up operations from those airfields which had been bombed by the Dutch that should have been prepared within a few hours, instead took more than one day. Consequently the Royal Dutch Army Airforce attacks using their obsolete Glen Martin medium bombers, enjoyed successes during the first three weeks of the war far beyond what they should have achieved."

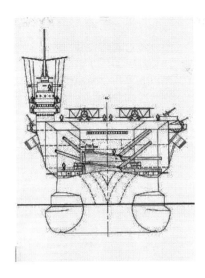

PROLOGUE

This book journey began for me in 1981 with a casual meeting, which turned into a friendship, which produced a promise, then a broken promise, and finally redemption. The story that you are about to read is one of war as it came to South East Asia in 1941. It is a not my story but that of an old gentleman from the Netherlands, Mr. Maarten Sweers who I encountered one day in Beacon Hill Park in Victoria, B.C.

I sat in the shade of a 300 year old juvenile Douglas Fir Tree on a comfortable wooden bench by the bank of a large pond and waited for my father. Seated to my left was an old man, quietly engaged in feeding the water fowl with bits torn from a loaf of old bread. In short order I struck up a casual conversation with my bench-mate. I discovered that he was a Dutch Naval veteran of the Pacific theater in WW2, now living in Canada. He became much more open and talkative when my father, himself a veteran of that War joined us.

I was soon left out of the conversation as the old veterans chatted, which was only proper as I was not yet thirty, and knew when to keep quiet. The old fellow, actually a generation senior to my father was in fact a retired Admiraal in the Royal Netherlands Navy and to me at least he was living history. As I looked at the frail old gentleman it was hard to imagine him as the vigorous warrior sailor of his recollections. After listening to these august men chat for five minutes I noticed that the conversation was winding down. At that point I interjected and informed the old gentleman that I had a great interest in naval history and prevailed upon him to capture his experiences on cassette tape. After a moment's consideration, he shrugged and said "why not?"

Over the course of some three weeks of conversation; the history of the Dutch battlecruiser-carriers; Task Force *Popeye* and *Olive* and their struggle to defend the Dutch East Indies against Japanese aggression from December 1941 into 1942 unfolded to my astonished ears. The sheer volume of historic and technical detail contained within the old sailor's narrative was incredible. After I had spent many pleasant evenings with the aged veteran, I told him that I would like to write a book on his experiences. He agreed to help me do this. At the end of September he left to winter in the Mediterranean, but prevailed upon me to apply myself to the project as he would return in the spring. I bid Mr. Sweers safe journey, not aware it was the last time that I would ever see him.

The next month a small wooden crate arrived from Amsterdam, it contained a large amount of Maarten Sweer's war papers, photographs, several diaries and an introductory letter for the book, reminding me that I had promised him a hardbound copy of the first edition. The work began and for several weeks he was available by telephone to clarify and sort out areas of confusion.

Some six months after his departure the Canadian economy began once again another of its wild swings. Unfortunately at this time it toppled into a deep bust and I was forced to concentrate all my efforts on trying to make a living. The book; a chancy long term prospect at best was put on the *back burner*, and then forgotten in my all consuming quest for a paycheck.

Now reader; we fast forward twenty years to a time when I had abandoned all hope of a home, steady employment and family life in Victoria. Instead I have discovered a new life style, one that I share with sixty million other North American men: the varied joys of the *NAFTA post-industrial transient temporary worker*. A brave new career that provided endless rounds of new office proceedures, retraining, travel, hotel living, job interviews, application forms, security checks, long hours, tight deadlines and the blurred memories of a hundred *hello-goodbye* friendships. As the century prepared to close, the book project had almost completely been forgotten.

On the last Monday of September 2001, I found myself standing on broiling sand flats amongst desiccated scrub brush, and wrapped in a cloud of fine white clay dust, some five miles southeast of Brownsville Texas. The overheated earth slowly cooked my feet through the gum rubber soles of my suede *desert boots*. The heat worked its way around my ankles and climbed up my exposed legs. Huge beads of sweat were continually being drawn out of my overheated flesh to form multiple rivulets which coursed down my torso, soaking my cotton shorts. The effect of the noonday sun was a physical force that pressed heavily upon my shoulders crushing me downwards, and evaporating my will. The slightest movement would result in folds of heated clothing re-contacting my body to momentarily sear my skin.

After the six hour drive from Houston into the Rio Grande valley, I was required to endure this self-imposed torture as I was no longer a youth, and had to stretch my legs to work out the numbness in my buttocks. What a cursed land I thought as I checked my wristwatch. I had an hour to wait before my interview at the Amfels Shipyard; a facility situated near the Mexican-US border, several miles inshore from the Gulf of Mexico, at the head of a canal connecting it to the sea. In that year, as I recall, it was a wholly owned Chinese company. New Amfels was a renowned yard for new construction and repair that serviced the Gulf of Mexico's offshore oil and gas industry. Nearby was the scrapyard that had a contract with the US government to recycle old warships. The yard was one of the few facilities in the U.S. designated to safely handle the removal of dangerous materials found in old ships. In reality it was a huge opportunity for Chinese Engineers to study warship construction. Even an old warship contains a vast storehouse of valuable structural engineering information, and a huge quantity of high quality reusable bronze items and equipment, for a nation that only in recent years has decided to build its first true blue-water navy.

I decided to drive along the dirt road skirting the artificial salt water basin and dredged channel that served the shipyard and several ship breaker operations in the area. Herein always lay a variety of fascinating vessels riding quietly at anchor in the brackish green waters awaiting either the yard's careful attentions, or the rude assault of the ship breaker's torch and shears.

I returned to the hot confines of my Lincoln Town car, started the engine then switched the AC unit to the coolest setting and its fan to full blast. In a few moments the temperature within the sedan dropped to a comfortable level and with relief I reached for my water bottle for a swallow. Then engaging the transmission, I drove carefully along the faintly marked dirt road to keep my dust cloud manageable.

Proceeding down the sandy track, my eyes wandered over the ships in the basin; their type, paint scheme and age providing a hint of what must have been a fascinating record of maritime trade. The fading grey paint, now almost bleached white, of several rafted groups indicated that these were ex-naval vessels demobilized from the several US Maritime Administration (MARAD) ghost fleets located around United States waterways. These at one time were made up of more than 2000 decommissioned warships and coast guard vessels, mostly of post WW2 vintage but the odd one close to 100 years. Any paint scheme, other than gray would usually indicate a commercial vessel, in need of repair or scrapping. Here the 'grand old ladies' congregated, resigned to their fate, waiting out their last few quiet months of a long life, now at an end.

Only two years earlier, the yard had cut up a flat boxy like barge, and sent its old bones to the smelters in China. Three weeks later an excited group of forensic naval architects and officials from the Smithsonian arrived at this very spot, only to discover that their quest had ended in tragedy. The vessel that had been cut up was an ancient rail car ferry that had been serving on the Mississippi River, which however in her recently discovered previous life had been the *USS Chickasaw*, a river monitor from the American Civil War.

I came abreast of the fabrication area of the shipyard located three hundred yards across the other side of the dredged basin, from where the banging of hammers, the clatter of chippers, the growl of metal grinders and bright winking electric welders heralded that a new vessel was being born; a floating offshore drilling platform.

The huge floating structure stood upon four massive splayed legs, all standing on a great square frame of huge tubes that made up its base. When completed it would tower some forty stories above the surface of the sea, while below; its long steel tentacles and hardened alloy bits would be lowered to the ocean floor, where they would grind their way through miles of rock to suck out the black gold buried deeply within mother earth. The stupendous floating steel structure was a veritable *planet harvester,* an awe inspiring statement of man's ingenuity and his unquenchable thirst for energy.

Here now was something quite unusual; a very old vessel, its low superstructure twin raked funnels, and three raked masts revealed, a miniature of a Titanic style liner. How, I marveled; had this once *grand old lady of commerce,* born perhaps around 1910 managed to eke out a profitable career that must now be close to 100 years? The raised steel lettering on her stern, had been painted over in black to match her hull color, but due to heavy rusting and the angle of the sunlight I could read her original name; *Thames,* after the river in England. But below this, and painted in white was the name under which she had labored on for many more decades, far beyond her designed life cycle; *Rio de La Plata,* her port of registry; Liberia. What a contrast to the new construction going on at the shipyard!

My gaze now wandered further down the basin to other ships, Hello! What was that? To sort out what had focused my vision, I drove on for a few minutes. The silhouette which had confused me resolved itself into the profiles of three vessels. The first was a USN fleet general cargo liner, with a single stack surmounting a short superstructure located amidships. Located to forward and aft of this were cargo holds and three separate pairs of masts, and their associated cargo booms laying down in their deck chocks, this was a typical naval auxiliary vessel produced during WW 2 to move armies, and their equipment. The accommodations for the troops were located amidships; the zone of easiest motion, while the varied cargos were stowed fore and aft.

Behind her in the next basin lay an old light aircraft carrier of WW 2 vintage, and of the type built on cruiser hulls. I could still make out the fading paint of the hull numeral on the bows of the compact little warship; CV 28, that would make her the *USS Cabot,* I believe. A tough little ship, she bled to ensure America's freedom, too bad that she was ending up here. I recalled a few of her wartime photos; afire, wreathed in smoke, guns spitting fire as she fought the Kamikazes off Okinawa. I studied the little ship, sadly; unremembered, just sitting there in the scummy dust covered water, listing a few degrees to starboard, now powerless and awaiting her fate. I turned away.

The next basin held an unusual vessel, causing me immediately to knit my brow as I pondered what lay before me. She was rather large and voluminous with a great deal of space enclosed in a massive boxy superstructure. She looked at first like a car carrier, but the tall mushroom vents sprouting out the top of her upper-works and along their full length made me pause, was she an old cattle carrier, or a sheep carrier?

Her hull was quite distinct structurally from that which was constructed on top. At one time the sides of that hull had full rows of portholes, now plated up. She was an impressive ship, in her day. The hull portholes would suggest that she was an old liner, cut down and rebuilt from the main deck up. But her hull, was very unusual, an effort had been made to widen the hull by what looked like torpedo blisters, a very expensive and unusual modification to any vessel and normally reserved only for very important classes of warship! The mystery hulk was an old warship, and a very large one.

How unusual I thought. With the exception of old battleships, the American industry seldom produced that type of work, being usually very wealthy they preferred new construction. Only a nation interested in extending the life of a useful hull would so modify such a large vessel; she must have originated either from the British, the Italians, the Japanese or the Dutch….my thoughts drifted. As there seemed to be no gates or workers on duty, I drove a bit further to obtain an unobstructed view of her profile. What the devil, I muttered under my breath.

The ship breakers had already been aboard I suspected, as large portions of her upper-works side plating had already been cut out, a practice of the business to bring in light, dry out the interior and ventilate any pockets of lingering dangerous gases. The original foredeck was now exposed, and some of the arrangements were unusual. The vessel; it was now revealed was not so heavily rebuilt; as it had been rather; *plated-over.* Three drum like tanks, perhaps 28 feet in diameter, had been exposed on the foredeck. Also evident were five *plated-in* ports in the forward structure. Wait a minute, those structures were not tanks, they were barbettes, upon which sat at one time; turrets for very large pieces of artillery! While the plated in ports could only be *old pattern* secondary battery mounts. The cast wrap around *British Admiralty type* open hawser chocks along the hulls shear line were the giveaway. This was a dreadnought of pre-WW 2 vintage, and one built to Royal Navy standards.

Upon hearing the muffled approach of vehicles, I looked to my left and saw a small procession of cars wreathed in dust. I retreated to my Lincoln to let them and their cloud pass, when to my surprise they halted just somewhat past my location. My fingers sought out the handle of my Colt Model 1917 .45 cal. service revolver located beneath the driver's seat. The warm steel, and its weight gave me comfort. Strangers encountered in such a remote location as, in this part of Texas, I knew from experience should wisely be considered as dangerous as their weight in rattlesnakes!

The dust drifted away over the water to reveal three large automobiles out of which climbed with some difficulty a group of elderly gentlemen; six Caucasian and five Asian. They looked for a long time at the ship which I had just been studying. A discussion began, and a considerably animated one; white crowned heads together under straw sun hats, lots of pointing. Some of them had cameras, and those that didn't returned to their cars for them. The ship obviously meant something of importance to these old fellows, and they may have the answer as to the identity of the strange ship.

I now became so caught up in the moment that I, decided to take a big risk and intrude upon their conversation. I cracked open the door of the Lincoln and got out, then quickly closed the door with a noticeable bang and advanced cautiously upon their party some fifty to sixty feet away. I checked my watch and still had at least half an hour before I should leave for my interview at the yard, so there was time.

I approached slowly so as not alarm them, a clipboard on my left arm and a water bottle in my right hand. In a moment one of their party noticed my presence, and they all turned to watch the approach of a much younger and powerfully built 280 lb. man.

This being the Mexican American border, the old fellows had come prepared for any eventuality. When still some twenty feet away from their group, six turned to faced me squarely and revealed that all had holsters for small automatic pistols fixed to their trouser belts. I smiled and raised my hands in the open palm gesture, and introduced myself, what I was doing in the area, and explained that I was unarmed.

I asked them if they were old sailors that had come to say goodbye to their ship; and I pointed to the sad *USS Cabot*. The question visibly relaxed them and they waved me closer exhibiting an immediate friendly deportment. Upon introduction, they were indeed found to be old sailors, but upon querying them on their unusual accents, I discovered that they were all former sailors, but of the Royal Netherlands Navy. I voiced the opinion it was my guess that they were veterans of the war in the Pacific. It was then that I caught their full attention with; "Have you veterans ever heard of a Dutch Admiraal; Maarten Sweers? They abruptly became very serious, then a tall gaunt fellow; Rudy Keppler asked me: "What do you know of Vice Admiraal Sweers," young man?

I then revealed to these men that some twenty years previously, I had an opportunity to meet an elderly gentleman in Victoria, British Columbia, Admiraal Maarten Danielzoon Sweers of the Royal Netherlands Navy (retired). After a short conversation with the old Admiraal, I realized that he had been part of incredible events, whereupon I prevailed upon him to please wait upon me, until the next day, so that I may prepare to record his story on cassette tapes.

Then Mr. Keppler continued; "Just so that we may understand you completely, would you perhaps be able to recall some of the names of the ships that the Admiraal may have mentioned?" I replied at once without the slightest hesitation; "Admiraal Sweer's flagship was the *Cornelis de Witt* and her sister ship was the *Johan de Witt*. Then there were some cruisers; the *Golden Lion*, and the *Amelia*, and the *Draak* and the *Prins te Paard* to name a few. There were many more but I cannot recall exactly due to the passage of time." These revelations brought a serious expression to their faces. I now imagined that up to this point, they thought that I may be part of some sort of elaborate deception!

The men lapsed into their native tongue, and conversed excitedly for a minute or two, until another fellow; a Mr. Jan Steen, said; "This is very important, where are these cassettes you spoke of?" To which I replied, "Within my storage locker in Victoria B.C., not Victoria, Texas." I explained that I had started to compile the tapes and a lot of his sketches into some order to understand exactly what his story was, but was interrupted in these efforts, as a series of severe and lengthy, back-to-back economic recessions then engulfed Canada during the 1980's and 1990's.

My life had once again became transient in the constant pursuit of work, and this singular preoccupation, had put a stop to all my plans to compile his story. Mr. Steen explained that they would very much like to have access to these; to listen to and copy. I explained that it was impossible, as the locker was half a continent away, and the tapes were packed up somewhere amidst six cubic meters of personal belongings, and I saw no opportunity in the near future to return to it.

Mr. Steen then said, "Did you know that Maarten Sweers passed away in 1987?" I replied that I had not and at that moment I recalled the promise that I had made to the nice old fellow. Another *bust* to add to the long list I thought, I always talked too freely in those days.

I revealed to them that it had always been my intention to write a book based on these tapes when I found the time, but life for me, at present was rather hand-to-mouth. A quick glance at my wristwatch compelled me to break off the conversation. I told the old sailors that I must present myself at the yard in half an hour for a job interview otherwise I would love to spend time with them. I scribbled my address down, tore off the paper from the pad, passed it to Mr. Keppler and prepared to part their company.

Mr. Steen seemed somewhat crestfallen with this answer, then placing his hand in the crook of my arm, and visibly brightening while nodding in the direction of the ship basin while at the same time he said; "Yes Mark; you were correct in your guess young man, we did come today to look at our old ship, for the first time it is possible for us, in sixty years! If you look hard at that great sad hulk, resting quietly over there, and if you have a good imagination, you may be able to distinguish what remains of the original hull of the once great Battlecruiser-carrier; *Cornelis de Witt*!

At this statement I halted as I was in the process of turning away, but stopped and looked with more concentration. The strange qualities of the hulk vanished, the modern steelwork evaporated in my mind's eye, as I now recalled the neat sketches the old Admiraal had made of his ships for me and I was able to recognize the original structure.

I was looking at the last Dutch Battlecruiser-carrier, itself born out of the earlier original vessel the *HMS Lion*, a battlecruiser, one of the *Splendid Cats* built for the RN in 1909!

Alas, more than twenty five years have passed since my last exchange with Admiraal Sweers and twelve since my conversation with the eleven old sailors. Those few surviving members of the RNLN Battlecruiser-carrier force, who had congregated from all corners of the world, would now hold a lonely wake for their great ship, and its thousands of ghosts amidst the swirling dust of the ship breaker's basin at Brownsville.

How long did the old men linger in that desolate backwater I wondered? Having finally found her, I knew they would faithfully keep a quiet vigil, as their ship; made to refine young men and wander the oceans, was torn, sliced and cut apart by rude tools in uncaring hands, its spirit; draining away, expiring bit by bit in the hot dry dust, longing to break free, to feel the wind over her flight deck, and to dip her bows once again into that glorious world of sparkling blue, that hangs beneath the sky!

Mark Klimaszewski,
Medicine Hat, Alberta - 2015

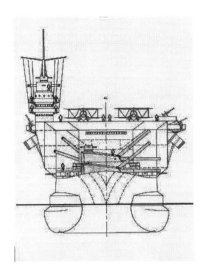

FOREWORD

My name is Maarten Danielzoon Sweers. I was born in 1894 in a colony of the Netherlands called the Dutch East Indies, in what is known today as Indonesia. My family lived on Biliton Island in the west Java Sea, where we enjoyed a prosperous happy life on our ancestral home; a sprawling palm nut oil plantation called *New Eden*. The family operated several other related businesses which included a spice orchard, a small mahogany timber operation, and a shipping line of four coastal steam ships ranging from 300 to 600 tonnes. These supported the immediate needs of the farm but also handled profitable tonnages within the colony each year. Our family had lived at *New Eden* for three centuries, and had created the neat palm groves and manicured lands from the raw jungle with our ingenuity, sweat and with the aid of a native workforce.

I obtained my senior matriculation at the age of seventeen, and had arrived at that great moment when all young people first point their toe towards the path that will become their life. As I always had an interest in the comings and goings of our plantation's little fleet of ships, it was natural for me I suppose that I developed an interest in the sea. After talking it over with my parents I applied for the 1911 fall semester to study Naval Architecture and Shipbuilding at the *Technische Hoogeschool van Delft*, (Technical University of Delft) in the Netherlands. I was accepted and my father chose to accompany me on the long voyage from Java to Europe, to ensure that I arrived safely, and was set up properly, as the world in those days was considerably larger and more dangerous than it is today. There were no such things as airlines. People had to travel by sea to undertake such long journeys, a considerable portion which in 1911 was still done under sail!

We boarded a steamer the *S.S. Borneo* a modern passenger liner of 6,000 gross registered tonnes in late July and after a voyage of some 20,000 kilometers and 38 days we arrived in Rotterdam. My father and I took the train north to Delft where we spent the evening in a Hotel. The next day I was enrolled in the University, and we found a small comfortable apartment. Then having ensured that I was properly registered, and accommodated, my father took me to the bank and set up a modest account for me which I was to use for school and living expenses. We returned to my small furnished flat on Spiekmanstraat, only one kilometer north of the campus. He gave me a firm handshake, a hug and warned me sternly not to embarrass the family but study very hard. We then parted as he had a great deal of purchases to make for the plantation. I now for the first time felt loneliness and a profound appreciation of the great distances that separated me from my family.

My studies went well and I showed a good grasp of the principles of naval architecture and shipbuilding. Every year I completed with honors, graduating with my Bachelor of Engineering in 1915.

The Great War had begun, and I was soon approached by the navy who promised to pay for my advanced degrees if I would sign up. So it came about that I joined the Koninklijke Marine Nederland (KMN), the Royal Netherlands Navy and began training as a junior commissioned officer in the hastily expanded facility in Den Helder Noord Holland. I took to the service, made it my career, and rose to prominence.

My doctorate in Naval Architecture soon propelled me to Flag Rank and the head of the Warship Design Office. Our office was contracted to build new warships for the Argentinian Navy, and I undertook the design work. But politics intervened and I traded my office in naval base at Den Helder for the deck of a Battlecruiser-carrier. I was soon after deployed to the Dutch East Indies, and it was happy to return to my home plantation. But war swept everyone up and changed everything.

The buildings in which the Naval Headquarters had been located in Batavia on the Island of Java were heavily bombed by the Japanese Army Air Force (JAAF) and set afire. Similarly; back in the Netherlands, many of the naval records once held at Den Helder Noord-Holland were incinerated by the Luftwaffe bombings in May 1940, with the remainder captured by the German Army when they occupied the naval base. Most of these documents were packed off to the Kreigsmarine Naval Intelligence Headquarters in Wilhelmshaven, and there they remained, until completely destroyed by a series of massive RAF night bombardments in March 1944.

Not only were the engineering files and drawing vaults of the Naval base in Soerabaja, destroyed, but many of the action reports and much of the intelligence data was lost. Whatever captured Dutch military documents that were stored there, and any Japanese military or police records that remained after the surrender, were subsequently burned.

I must relate events now long past, some almost five decades old. I therefore ask that the reader forgive me for any errors in dates, or precise locations and names that I may unintentionally introduce into this retelling. Time has worked on my memory; much as rust inevitably eats through the toughest armored plate. An accurate recounting of the all the warship histories is made difficult as the log books of most of the battle-carrier squadron were never recovered. An effort, to record those events at this time will be further hampered as I no longer have all of my private journals covering my military service for the years 1939 to 1942. Although these were once quite extensive, now only a portion of these remain in my possession. They have suffered the ravages of time, and climate as does all delicate mortal material such as flesh and paper. In addition, the activities of Government archivists, professional journalists and amateur researchers, although well intentioned, nevertheless have eroded my files over the ensuing decades.

One must also remember that my journals were written at the time when these events occurred, mostly during a period of strict secrecy, and general confusion, and were therefore composed only from what information was officially sanctioned for release.

The record is raw and has not been sifted, polished, or buffed for the last fifty years to make it less controversial, and attitudes which were once widely accepted as normal, today may offend.

It is from these greatly diminished sources that I will attempt to reconstruct an accurate narrative on the short-lived history of the KMN Battlecruiser-carrier force. A unit; with which I was so intimately involved during its creation, its deployment to the Far East, and subsequently its operational activities as the Second World War expanded into the Netherlands Oriental Colonies. I may on occasion include too much technical detail in this narrative for the layman, but remember that this is a record of technical triumph as well as human drama and I am a man whose diverse occupations were entirely involved with those varied applied sciences one employs while executing the professional duties of a naval officer, a naval constructor-architect, and a naval pilot. I am an admitted amateur however, when it comes to the research of such histories and its serving up.

The time period of interest; which encapsulates the history of the Battlecruiser-carrier force spans only ten short years; from 1932 to 1942, a service which involved at one time or another some 19,600 naval seamen and flyers who rotated through the Battlecruiser-carrier division during this period.

The Japanese were defeated militarily, but their idea took hold amongst the native populations of the Dutch East Indies. As there was no Allied Army within the Dutch East Indies for the Japanese army to formally surrender to, the situation was very dangerous to all whites.

Within a matter of days after the final surrender of the Japanese Armed forces in the Dutch East Indies in September 1945, there was a power vacuum as there was no Allied Army within the region. The Nationalist Leader *Sakuro* seeing an opportunity; seized power and declared the Republic of Indonesia. His followers having availed themselves of both surrendered and captured Japanese Army weapons began a campaign to obliterate all documents relating to Dutch ownership of property. In this way they hoped to prevent a return of the Dutch Colonial Administration, and make a bid for independence.

The revolutionary population now completely without conscience, turned upon the emaciated and defenceless white inmates that were released from the Japanese Prison camps and began to slaughter them; men, women and children without mercy, in a final ruthless attempt to rid themselves of Colonial Rule. Consequently, the Sweers family never returned to *New Eden*. The plantation, which we nurtured and developed for more than three centuries was lost to us. A home in which every acre of land was clawed out of an uninhabited raw jungle, and every palm oil tree was planted by the hand of my forefathers or by the hands of those in their employ. To have attempted to reclaim our property in 1945, after the defeat of Japan would have resulted in our immediate deaths at the hands of the natives.

The great library of my home, with more than 11,000 volumes, many of these being three centuries old, and its vast store of nautical records, and ancient relics was burned in the widespread *anti-Dutch ethnic cleansing* that followed the surrender of Japan.

Imperial Japan had planned to create an *Asian Empire for Asians* called the; *Greater East Asia Co-prosperity Sphere*, by simply replacing the former European Colonial Administrations of the newly conquered territories, with their own. The Japanese were defeated militarily, but their great plans for the Dutch East Indies were not an entire disaster, as Dutch Colonial Rule could never be re-established.

I feel comfortable in predicting that Japan's great ambitions for the region, ambitions that cost me my home, the land of my birth, and the Netherlands its great East Asia Colony will eventually come to naught. Japanese industry took several decades to fully recover from its total obliteration in WW 2. These were followed by only two decades of limited market success for their goods in the former *Co-prosperity Sphere*. However these markets will never reach *full flower* for Japan before good quality and low cost Chinese products supplants them. Today for an example, *New Eden Plantation* is owned by a Chinese cooking oil conglomerate!

The eight European Empires are all gone now, and have been for two generations. Many of their former colonies are in far worse shape than they ever were in my day. One reason for this is the disastrous economic pairing of inept local leadership with misguided financial aid from an overly generous United Nations!

I look forward to the completion of this book you now hold, a presentation of my recollections of naval service during my involvement with the KMN Battle-carriers, those great ships; the unusual hybrid cross; half battleship, half aircraft carrier.

The world of the 1930's, was a very different existence than today, it was a time when there were still many distant horizons yet to be explored. The world held a promise of high adventure. I was young and strong and full of optimism, with pride in our service, and a fierce warrior of my Queen.

Vice Admiraal Maarten Danilezoon Sweers (Retired)
Koninklijke Marine Nederland, (Royal Netherlands Navy)
Commander 1st Battlecruiser-Carrier Squadron – 1939 -1941
Amsterdam, NL – 1981

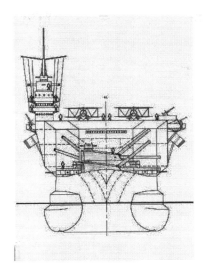

CHAPTER I

DEN HELDER NOORD-HOLLAND

By the mid-1930s, the nations of Europe, including its two remaining Empires; the British and the French were mired in a deep global economic depression which had stolen the hard earned wealth and dreams, of a half a billion people during the last five years. The defrauding of the population by the *Captains of the Economy* following only ten years after the vast sacrifice and bloodletting of the Great War 1914 to 1918, then immediately followed by the devastating Spanish Influenza Pandemic, left the hard pressed populations embittered, cynical and impatient for a return to an ordered prosperous existence. Tragically, this was not to be, as the devil was only taking a breather.

In the Asia-West Pacific region great political and economic pressures were also boiling over. The resource starved new industrial powerhouse of Imperial Japan flexed its muscles, searching for new horizons and sources of raw materials for its factories. To her south; lay the rich French, British and Dutch colonies, and the American administered Philippine Islands. Beyond the Sea of Japan to her west extended the coastlines of the great ramshackle Empire of China, and the gigantic seething cauldron of the Soviet Union.

Japan had been conducting trade negotiations with the Netherlands for several years now to purchase raw material from our East Indies Colony. Her delegates were particularly interested in oil, rubber and a number of rare earths. However the negotiations had not been going well. Nippon was becoming frustrated, and dictatorial as we refused to give them the broad unfettered access to our island's resources at the low prices that they demanded. Japan's aggressive posture towards us made it ever clearer that we must bolster our military forces as soon as possible to provide the necessary deterrent that may well head off a potential war.

Seeking a swift solution to her needs; Japan invaded China in 1937 to acquire the territory and the resources that she coveted. For the Netherlands of the 1930's; a diminutive nation, there was a well-founded fear for the security of her remote Dutch East Indies Colony, situated as it was so close to the expansionist minded military power of Japan.

In three centuries of colonial rule, the Dutch people had explored and developed the natural resources of that colony. By introducing agriculture, harvesting rare spices and sinking mines into the earth's mineral pockets, they had developed products from these great islands which were then marketed to the world, using the roads, railways, and shipping that they had built. The Dutch East Indies Colony had become the *Jewel of the Netherlands*. Time would reveal that it was a jewel that many coveted.

In the year 1936, certain conditions developed for me personally that would gestate into the history contained within these pages. For our diminutive navy, the spring months produced a singularly momentous event: the birth of the Royal Netherlands Navy Battlecruiser-Carrier Squadron and its planned deployment to the Far East, to deter possible Japanese designs on our vulnerable East Indies Colony. By the stroke of a pen the KMN had received funding that transformed it from a handful of little vessels into a service of such strategic significance that it would be rated as a regional naval power. The part that I was to play in the magnificent metamorphosis of our navy from a few little herring into a lethal pack of wolf toothed barracuda, began in the late spring of that year.

Oddly enough; now that I am in my eighties, it is a particular smell or song that initiates the clearest recollection of those far off days. On occasion if I pick up and study a once very familiar object; my thoughts may also be easily transported. I seem to vividly recall one particularly fresh, clean and brisk sea-breeze morning. I kissed my wife and children good-bye and I began my daily walk to work.

Clambering down the staircase of my third story apartments on *Prins Willem–Alexandersingel* I exited the five story red brick building, turned my face to the new dawn and set off at a good pace along the south side of the canal on the first leg of my four kilometer walk to the expansive naval facility of the *Koninklijke Marine* at Den Helder, Noord Holland.

At forty two, I still felt twenty. I was serving as a commissioned officer in the Koninklijke Marine Nederland (KMN). The previous year, I had obtained my broad stripe and first star when I was raised to the rank of Commandeur (Commodore). I was the officer in command of the warship design desk at the (KMOB); Koninklijke Marine Ontwerp Bureau or Royal Naval Design Office in Den Helder; a highly prized posting.

My career was advancing rapidly, my children were healthy, I had a beautiful, loving wife and my overseas businesses in the East Indies Colonies seemed to be slowly growing, despite the harsh economic conditions of a world in its seventh year of *The Great Depression*. The lives of my family were full of promise; I was in all respects that spring of 1936, a healthy and happy sailor.

The white and pink blossoms had now vanished from the cherry trees which grew along the stone walled canals of the Old Dutch trading port and naval base. These were now exhibiting their early wine colored leaves, tinged with green. Yet some of the flower's perfume still lingered on the early morning's damp heavy air. The sound of the hard leather heels of my black military issue shoes on the brick lane echoed throughout the masonry canyons of the still slumbering neighborhood.

Quite suddenly, like a series of cuckoo clocks at the top of the hour, doors and shuttered windows began to open. The narrow lanes which partitioned the brightly painted stone and terracotta roofed multistoried homes quickly began to fill with people and the sounds of domestic activity that morning in late April. It soon grew from the first creak of a door hinge to a muted cacophony. I checked my watch, then turned south entering *Somebastraat*, making good time.

Perched atop the steep slate roofs of the *Tillerman's Hotel*, located on the other side of the street resided a recently arrived group of *city roosters;* three bothersome gulls had moved into the neighborhood and had become the self-appointed trash monitors of the hotel's kitchen scraps. I don't mean to imply that the staff of that business did not properly handle their trash, quite the opposite. However, the nighttime foraging of an equally disreputable gang of furry masked little bandits always exposed the offal. The seagulls were always ready to deal with their leavings, when the graveyard shift ended.

On this otherwise fine morning, these gulls had become loudly engaged in a squabble, perhaps critiquing the menu choices made by the patrons of the hotel's dining room on the previous evening? Or perhaps the raccoons had not left the table quite as expected? Nevertheless their shrill protestations rose as each sought to drive home their particular point of view over the rude interruptions of their fellow connoisseurs. At one point a crescendo was attained, one that reminded me ever so much of a certain strutting, overly dramatic *Chancellor* and his crowd that had recently captivated the minds and souls of the powerful bemused nation of our German cousins to the east.

That's what they are alright, I murmured to myself, glancing up at the noisy seabirds with a private chuckle, the big one is obviously Goering, the little one with the ratty feathers and damaged leg is Goebbels and the one always squawking, flapping and puffing-up is Herr Hitler! Why the entire Nazi elite is nothing more than a trio of trumped up *Stront Haviken*! (Shit-hawks)

The neighborhood's female folk now turned out, opening windows which had been shuttered for the night. They moved briskly, with a rustle of starched cotton house dresses; out onto the brick cobbled canal embankments to greet their neighbors and engage in some type of good natured verbal jousting, whatever the mood of the day. The ladies busied themselves with the arrangement of colorful flower boxes which hung from the window sills of their homes or carried water cans to the similar potted glories which hung from the street lamp brackets. Still others washed brickwork or swept up the winter's dried detritus from in front of their doors, their voices, blending together to sound remarkably like small wavelets lapping against old wooden wharfs.

Here and there the old men congregated in little knots and enjoyed a pipe and conversation with their first coffee of the day and exchanged comments on the news items in the morning paper. Still other white haired senior gentlemen drifted towards these groups carrying the odd tool or sporting a half carved piece of wood. The mere presence of these items on their person, seemed to suggest that at any moment work may spontaneously commence, so… there was no real need to *rush into it.*

A breeze carried the aroma of freshly baked bread to my twitching nostrils and I immediately dreamed of hot scones with fresh butter, and toyed with the idea of starting my walks a little earlier in order to include a bakery stop each morning. But I shook off the idea, as I neither required the extra calories for the duties that I now held, nor wanted to arrive at work with the odd crumb adorning the carefully brushed deep blue naval tunic.

Each morning as I strode from my house along the canal to the Naval Dockyard I received pleasant greetings from these happy industrious citizens. Some called to me by name or simply nodded while still others gave voice to optimistic plans in anticipation of a lively business season. In all I sensed their underlying nervousness and the unvoiced question; will we have peace or war? Across the street; old, arthritic Jakob Polder was winding up his huge ornately carved *De Carillion*; a massive wagon sized street organ, common to Holland. I greeted him, and being a retired merchant marine seaman, he straightened his posture and casually saluted my one star, then continued tapping the inverted bowl of his pipe against the hard oak breast of an elaborately carved mermaid; one of a group that decorated the vertical posts of his instrument.

My uniform and senior rank carried with it a responsibility to keep close watch on the spoken word. Even a casual comment could be interpreted any number of ways. I managed well enough with polite nods and confident smiles. My daily, repetitive and unhurried walks seemed to contribute a certain air of safety or added perhaps a certain quality of balance to their day. The subtle signs of a population under stress were everywhere if one chose to look closely; an absence of young couples arm in arm for example. These affairs were on hold as the young men were now involved in army maneuvers. Sadly, war worries dominated, crowding out the more pleasant thoughts on these lovely spring days. The gloom of the citizenry was much the same as those in our armed forces; for the Netherlands held very large Far Eastern colonies of vast wealth, yet our military power was quite modest. There were added security measures now in place, due to my rank I was a potential target and had to be watched. Although I was aware of this, it only became obvious to me on my most recent walks to and from work.

I knew my neighborhood and its faces. Now it seemed; there were added a number of new faces that I was quick to notice. Young, very fit looking men who seemed always to be unusually idle, yet did not pay much attention to the young women. These fellows; constantly kept me under observation. They were always present, wherever my route passed the entrance of a shadowed alley, any series of sharp corners in lanes or open warehouse doors. As they openly nodded to me whenever I encountered them and made no attempt to hide I assumed that they were naval security. I had, it seemed; become a valuable asset!

On April 24th at approximately 09:00hrs I was summoned to the Admiralty building for an unscheduled conference with Admiraal A.K. Van de Velde, senior to the few Four Star Lt. Admiraals in our modest fleet. He was the officer in command of Asset Procurement for the Royal Netherlands Navy; and my immediate superior officer. I set aside the longitudinal strength calculations that I had been painstakingly graphing for a new class of destroyer, donned my tunic, checked my uniform in the mirror, locked the drawers to my desk, informed my adjutant of my destination, then hurried down the slate paved lane *Rijkszee en Marinehaven*. It was but a short walk to the large grey stone, five storied building of 17th century vintage, which held the offices of our most senior officers.

I was a little frustrated at being interrupted at this point in my work. After weeks of detailed calculation and precise plotting I was very close to completing the moment curve on the 'wave profile bending diagram' for this long thin warship. If the weather should change and the atmosphere became damp in the next few hours, the friction on the surface of the drawing paper would alter. Only a slight variation in this would

4

adversely affect the rotation of the many finely machined delicate parts that fed data to the mechanical computer within the device and completely invalidate days of effort!

The *Stanley Intergraph;* (a mechanical computing device and instrument) was a product of British ingenuity and craftsmanship and was a marvel to behold; when in operation. A precision combination of wheels, rods, gears, springs, and tapered shafts formed the heart of the device, mounted in a sturdy open frame. The entire mechanism was lovingly executed in machined polished bronze and nickel steel, and resulted in an instrument, which was easily the equal in precision and workmanship to the finest Swiss watches to be found. It represented the ultimate in drawing office instrumentation, and one of the most impressive marriages of mathematics and mechanical engineering possible for its day. As the operator moved the device's pointer, tracing along the shear curve for the ship (which had previously been plotted on paper), the *Intergraph* performed mechanically the mathematics of integration while the instrument's arm with pen attached drew the results of these calculations; the bending moment curve. Once completed it was simply a matter of determining the point of maximum amplitude indicating where the greatest stresses occurred along the hull.

I had waited for the perfect day, one that had the correct humidity to start this work, and therefore had initiated some tedious directives by way of preparation. I requested base maintenance to block those roads adjacent to my building to all motorized transport to eliminate vibration. No kettles were to be boiled on my floor to make coffee and all of my staff was cautioned not to drop a book or slam a door, and the instrument had been thoroughly calibrated and cleaned by a naval instrument technician rated to service Stanley equipment. Everything was prepared and the ideal circumstances required to operate the device were at hand, I had completed a brief finger and wrist limbering exercise and had just begun when I was summoned to an unscheduled meeting with my Commander! As the conditions were perfect I reluctantly delegated this *Intergraph* work to Lieutenant ter Zee 2e Klass (Lt. Commander) Versteegen. I was a little annoyed but then my thoughts left the world of calculation and focused on the curious.

Upon my arrival an Adjudant Onderofficier (warrant) officer of de Velde's staff ushered me into a long corridor illuminated only by a single window at its end. Then he departed, silently closing the heavy door made of thick, age-blackened oak behind him. The location, with which I was quite familiar had a peculiar effect; in that it tended to agitate me and on occasion transported my thoughts to those boyish days when I too often occupied a hard wood chair outside the office of our strict humorless Quaker school master, and awaited in discomfort to be summoned within to answer for some transgression.

I had arrived a little early and so had a few minutes on my hands before being admitted into the Admiraal's conference room, I seated myself on an ornately carved oak bench of some ancient ancestry and allowed my eyes to wander the always interesting structure of this quiet, secluded corner. Perhaps three hundred years old; the hall was constructed mostly of ballast stone, heavy timber beams, shrunken and split by time, supported by masonry walls covered in thick plaster now yellowed by the many years. The high ceiling contained massive age-darkened fir and oak timbers, well fitted and artfully decorated with fantastic carvings of mythical sea beasts. There were a number of redundant blind socket joints exposed in the sides of the great beams, an unusual feature which indicated to me that these timbers may once have supported part of the main gun deck of a very large *East-Indiamen* galleon. One that having out-lived its usefulness had been dismantled, with its ribs, deck beams and wood art preserved to be lovingly incorporated it into the building. The edifice as it now stood was at once both an architectural and archeological treat as well as a fine testimony to Dutch frugality and the faithful devotion of my people to our proud and glorious marine tradition.

Our East Indies Colony presented us with a major security dilemma. India has often been referred to as the Jewel of the British Empire. The Netherlands also had a similar jewel in our Sea Empire, and that was the Dutch East Indies. This huge colony lay north of Australia, and was composed of a chain of great islands; Sumatra in the west, then Java, Bali, Lombok, Soembawa and finally Flores for the great islands, followed by a chain of smaller islets running to the great island of New Guinea, a distance of some 5000 kilometers. Above these were to be found two more great islands; Borneo and Celebes all totaling three million square kilometers of land, rich in natural resources. The nautical lexicon of today contained the popular phrase; *The Seven Seas*, which refers to the famous seven seas that divided and surrounded these aforementioned islands namely; the South China, the Java, the Timor, the Flores, the Banda, the Molucca, and the Celebes. The colony was home to many tens of millions of slightly built Javanese natives, Chinese and Indian contract workers, but with only some 60,000 Dutch citizens, other than those serving in the military, or engaged in the administration of the colony. The East Indies presented a colony of tremendous opportunity for the Netherlands, and offered our diminutive nation the limitless horizon and personal challenge that all young men need if they are to discover their full potential.

My mind then quickly readjusted itself to discover the reason for this rather unexpected summons and to the collection my thoughts. I must quickly suppress my agitated attitude at being taken away from the work that I loved. I would soon be called upon to provide clear precise answers for any type of questions relating to the projects that my design team had underway. These ranged from the development of a revolutionary submarine *surface breather* apparatus that would allow the running of the diesel engines while the O-boat was submerged, to assessing floatplane launched torpedo stabilizer modifications allowing for the attack upon targets that lie in shallow waters. What was the nature of my summons…..?

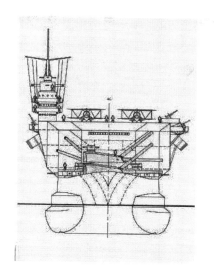

CHAPTER II

THE FLEET ADMIRAAL

Four Star Lt. Admiraal Adriaan Kannegieter Van de Velde; to many officers in the Royal Netherlands Navy, was an intimidating figure, being a giant of a man, two meters plus in height and weighing some 185 kg. Raw boned, ruddy complexioned, square jawed with unwavering blue eyes all topped off by a thick shock of white neatly cropped hair. That was my commanding officer; the very image of a heroic figure right out of the 17th century. All that was missing to complete the image was the old costume, the quarterdeck of a fighting galleon, a long wig and cutlass!

The Fleet Admiraal was a renowned yachtsman and owned an 18 meter gaff-rigged yawl on which you could find him on Saturday mornings, and if not on her deck; at the dockyard. He was a devoted scholar of the old manuscripts in the museum which contained mountains of old logbooks and mercantile records, accumulated over the centuries of the far-flung explorations which made up our rich marine history. Although of a very old family of singularly historical distinction; he had little patience with elitist minded officers, being simply a highly professional sailor who felt a considerable attachment to the lower ranks.

The door to naval officer's cadet college stood wide open for young Adriaan. But like Czar Peter the Great who preferred to learn shipbuilding by beginning at the bottom as a common shipwright's apprentice, the young De Velde joined the Royal Netherlands Navy in 1892 as a "seaman aspirant", at the tender age of 13! This inspired act caused his mother to swoon and his father; a shipping line owner; to slap his knee and chuckle. To him, the most senior and respected Admiraal in our service, the *common sailor* was the very backbone of the navy. Woe unto any officer, family connections not withstanding; that neither trained his crews thoroughly nor treated them with the accorded respect as contained in the modern naval regulations. In his mind there were no bad sailors, just unimaginative and incompetent officers. He held deep concerns for the welfare and progress of the naval rating, not just at the beginning of their service; as enthusiastic energetic youthful assets, but also at the end of a career. He felt that the old hand, crippled with arthritis, ravaged by tropical disease or maimed by wounds received in action and subsequently released from duty, as an asset of limited value to the navy, must be adequately provided for. He increased the retired naval seaman pensions as well as expanding the medical coverage due the naval invalid. For these reasons, and that he had risen from the lower deck every sailor loved him.

Many of our sailors admitted to a lack of confidence in our service, as most of our warships were generally small with many quite dated. The moral crisis came to a head aboard the *De Zeven Provicien* off Sumatra on Feb. 5, 1933. Her crew had received their pay packets, and were soured to discover that their wages had been reduced due to budgetary constraints! The ventilation system in the old ship's engine room then packed it in a few hours later, and in short order below decks the temperature soon soared to lethal levels. The mixed crew of Dutch and Indonesian sailors rose in mutiny and seized the ship. They held it for six days and surrendered after the vessel was bombed and twenty seven crew killed. For years the stingy members of the government resisted Admiraal de Velde's urging for reform. However, only after the mutiny aboard Hr. Ms. *De Zeven Povincien*, did the government grasp the gravity of the situation and release the funds to improve the lives of the sailors in Her Majesty's Navy.

The Fleet Admiraal had championed improvements to the habitability of our warships. Air-conditioning was installed on all vessels in tropical service, vastly improving the health for those afloat. He was in many ways a legend in his own time, and the very rudder of our modern service. The Admiraal not only revered the *old ways of the sailing navy*, but was a major driving force in the development of modern technical training programs for our sailors. To him any success that the twentieth century navy may expect to have in action, relied heavily upon the quality of its noncommissioned officers, marine trades and technical specialists. All of these by necessity; had to be of the highest order.

One minor way that the extent of his interests in our naval traditions was revealed was his frequently observed habit of tying and then untying seaman's knots. It was a purely meditative preoccupation, almost a reflex action, which allowed him to concentrate on the solution to any involved problem. One obvious aspect of his continual tying and untying activity was the heavy use of the arm and shoulder musculature. His hands and forearms had developed into truly simian proportions. Van de Velde did not practice these cordage exercises with mere parcel twine but with a two meter length of 20 mm diameter rough hemp rope. I recall that I observed him on one occasion tie up his rope into one huge tight ball. Then he dug his thick fingers into the cordage and proceeded to work the knots free. I asked the reason for this as the ball of rope represented no useful knot. "Strength Maarten," was his simple reply, "strength of the fingers, wrists forearms and shoulders, it was the key to the superiority of the Dutch sailor in the old days of sail. Our sailors also hardened their broad backs in the labors on the herring fleet; having spent many an agonizing hour with knees against the bulwarks and hauling in the nets with the power of their backs, or on the long sweeps propelling their heavy craft over the sea. Those men had to free knots in even frozen cordage and do it quickly, this required fingers like steel. For a sailor working high aloft with heavy, wet, wind-whipped canvas a strong grip was at times all that stood between him and death. Ultimately of course there was combat. Fighting the enemy; hand to hand. Powerful hands were needed to crush throats and break wrists. For sailors, some things never change; life aboard ship or ashore in the beer hall or worse" he said with a wink; "fists like sledge hammers for any young sailor in port ensures comely women, and your own table in a tavern!" Yes, I can now admit in good humor, after so many decades; that my Commander was at heart; a bit of a pirate!

At fifty-five he was still capable of astounding feats of strength which were sometimes unexpectedly revealed. I recollect on one occasion when I was walking in company with Admiraal de Velde across the parade grounds of the naval dockyard during the annual navy day open house display of 1933. The citizens and off-duty naval personnel with their families in tow had come to our facility to view our museum and take in the various demonstrations of traditional seamanship performed by our sailors for public inspection and enjoyment. We were strolling past a reenactment of a gun drill performed by naval cadets while standing on an "off-balance" wood platform, which simulated a moving deck. The Admiraal's critical eye had been observing the performance when quite impulsively he stepped forward and interrupted this drill to demonstrate to the young cadets and the assembled people; the proper stance to use on a heaving deck when handling an artillery round. At the same time he gave to the junior Lt. who was commanding the drill such a glare that I swear it could have removed varnish! The young officer swallowed then visibly blanched, and backed off the deck.

To enhance his explanation the elderly Admiraal had snatched up a dud shell and then explained how to cradle the tip of the heavy object on your left forearm while palming the base with your right and followed this by showing how to quickly switch grips from the left to the right crook of the arm and the footwork that a gunner had to master to serve the gun while standing on a wet, possible debris-covered heaving deck. The attentive crowd clapped at the old seaman's dexterity, then, having completed the demonstration, the Admiraal nimbly dismounted and with only the slightest hint of being winded slammed the heavy object's base onto the sod with a heavy thud. The slack jawed and wide eyed young cadets were completely astounded by all this as the shell which Van de Velde had casually snatched up with his great paw and handled with an apparent ease wasn't part of the drill equipment, but an old museum item that happened to stand nearby. The shell was a British 9.2" diameter shell of the Great War, an item which even without charge or fuse weighed at least 150 kilos! I then considered, (but only for a brief moment) that my Admiraal may have revealed a suppressed inner desire for a career in the theater until it dawned on me exactly what it was that he had held in his hands, and I paused with a more serious reflection.

I could only imagine the awesome physical power that had once been his to wield some twenty years ago and which I am sure that he did, for it was well known in naval circles that Van de Velde had worked his way up from the *lower decks*; where, as a common sailor he revealed a wild side, and had acquired the reputation of being a notorious head buster, a trait that age had not completely cured him of. I was beginning to appreciate the unease that all felt while waiting an audience with the Fleet Admiraal and the dread evident on the face of the gun drill junior officer.

I recall a story of the Admiraal's early service. As a common seaman; de Velde, still a boy at the age of 17 did not entirely begin to appreciate his own power until it was revealed to him in an unfortunate occurrence. During an off-watch period aboard the old armored cruiser *Princess Elisabeta*, he was engaged with his shipmates in a comradely game of *Cockleshells*. A game which originated centuries earlier; during those long idle periods when the great galleons found themselves becalmed in the horse latitudes, and the men did anything during these periods to break the monotony. This entirely moronic activity involved some miscreant junior sailor, standing but bent forward, with his head locked firmly between the knees of a sitting bosun. The burly senior rating while clamping his knees painfully tight on the head of the unfortunate lad also reached over his back to clutch the backside of the victim's canvas trousers, which he pulled tight to remove any wrinkles and to prevent any escape backwards. The other crew members would line up with glee to participate, by administering only one, open palm smart smack to the defenseless buttocks, which slowly became tenderized under the unrelenting assault of many hands! The unfortunate sailor of course was not completely trapped, he could earn his freedom simply by correctly identifying the sailor who delivered any of the blows, and then that man would take the captive's place and assume the position. However as warships of that size usually accommodated some 550 men, and the victim's posture deprived him of sight; correct identification seldom happened. At some logical point the Bosun would terminate the punishment, as he neither wanted to shame the lad nor have him report unfit for duty. Quite often he replaced him with any shipmate that exhibited an excessive glee when inflicting his slap!

During one of these events it became seamen de Velde's turn to strike, he did so with such force that he had fractured his shipmate's pelvis with his open palm! Fortunately the lad healed, but he was subsequently released from duty. This was a sobering experience which greatly distressed the young Adriaan and introduced him to the actual costs associated with seeming harmless activity. An appreciation that began immediately with the wearing down of his own posterior by his shipmates when he took the place of the sailor that he had injured. However, life in the *tween decks* contributed greatly to the rapid maturing of the young man and had produced a fine sailor. Somewhat later he was able to get a small relief from his sense of guilt for unleashing such a heavy blow. Adalbert; his injured shipmate, had later explained that his release from naval service had worked out for the best. Being a lad himself, he had recovered the full use of his leg completely. He did not miss the carefree life of a sailor as he was now able to marry his sweetheart and be taken into her father's business of marine chandlery, where his sea and naval training experience made him most useful!

I began to speculate further on the reason for being summoned to this meeting. There had been rumors circulating among the senior command that Argentina had missed a few progress payments to the Dutch shipyards converting two large warships for their navy. As the design work for their modifications had been the product of my office, I became concerned that a technical problem may have arisen. Perhaps there had been a major political development? Even a new crisis! The fascist dictators Hitler and Mussolini had recently announced their intention of aiding the Spanish Army in toppling the democratically elected government of that nation and replacing it with a fascist military dictatorship. The response of the League of Nations members to this gauntlet being thrown down at their feet; was anemic at best, the occasional scowl for press photographs, and furious shuffling of paper, but little else. Political tensions were further compounded by the recent withdrawal of the Japanese delegation from the League of Nations. These two events although played out half a world away; were still in close proximity to either the Netherlands or her colonies, and were enough to remove the cobwebs from the eyes of the majority of our politicians who had long opposed the heavy expense of a naval expansion. But then, even the most myopic of these old men must have been able to see the looming threat to the treasure house that was the Netherlands East Indies.

There may be another announcement regarding the long overdue expansion of our little navy, a palpable tension was in the air, something was in the offing, of that I was certain. Beginning in the late 1920's our military focus became increasingly preoccupied with the defense of our sprawling Pacific Colonies. The strategic planning section of the Koninklijke Marine conducted numerous *Naval Battle Studies* and *War Game Exercises*, to prepare for the defense of these possessions from air and sea attack. Our perceived adversary in all these studies was the mighty *Rengo Kantai* or Imperial Japanese Navy. The growing might of that force was rapid, and its ships and service demonstrated great technical capability and professionalism respectively. At the outbreak of the World War Two the *Rengo Kanti* had; in my opinion actually eclipsed the British *Royal Navy*; certainly in naval aviation, perhaps in raw battleship big gun power, and arguably even numerically in modern effective ships. Of course at the time I developed these opinions I was unaware of secret and powerful new weapons which the British then had under development. Ship and Airborne radar for example gave the RN an ability to attack an enemy fleet in the darkest of nights using guns or radar equipped bombers. A capability unimagined in 1935!

A click of the door mechanism returned my thoughts to the present and made me glance across the room just as the young warrant officer smartly opened the heavy door, came to attention and asked me to join the officers within the next room. The atmosphere within the room was not as I expected, all the officers present seemed to be in good spirits; ranging from buoyant mood to suppressed excitement!

Fleet Admiraal Adriaan Van de Velde stood beneath an enormous gilt framed, oil on canvass painting depicting the Battle of Texel; (the Dutch naval victory over the combined Anglo-French fleet back in the 17th century). He towered over the other senior officers gathered about him who were engaged in muted conversations. The man, like the painting seemed the stuff legend. Like a great Admiraal from the past, Martin Tromp he had risen from the ranks, and was known to the enlisted seamen as one of their own; a *dekzerls* (tarpaulin), he held the respect of seamen of all ranks. He was to most in that room the very embodiment of our country's naval traditions, with the spirit of a Tromp or De Ruyter, but sadly, with only a miniscule fleet at his disposal. The Fleet Admiraal turned at my entrance, smiled and casually motioned to me to approach while he introduced me to the group of Admiraals, then he directed the group to take their seats around a massive eight-legged polished oak table black with age. The conference I soon discovered was to be relaxed and informal; and it soon proceeded in an entirely unexpected direction!

Occupying Van de Velde's great desk were rolls of drawings and stacks of bound documents which were the center of all the attention. I instantly recognized these as one of my earlier submissions to his office, by its light blue accordion folder. The folder contained a unsolicited proposal; a solution to the (RNLN) Royal Netherlands Navy's long promised but sadly neglected new vessel program; The *Kapital Schip Verwerving*

Plan of 1933 (KSVP33) (Capital Ship Acquisition Program of 1933). For those readers who are not familiar with the term; *Capital Ship*, it was one applied to only the most powerful types of warships afloat. Therefore a very important name for it was chosen; usually the capital city of a nation or province. In a variation on this; the names of an ancient pagan God, a King, or victorious battle were sometimes substituted. The term *Capital* remained, attached to this ship type, on down through the centuries.

Admiraal Van de Velde called the meeting to order, then began his presentation with a brief summary of the current situation as it affected our ship building program and security of the Empire. He then began, a briefing of recent naval developments that would change the future of all seated in the room, and move our little navy from backwater insignificance, to that of a strategic naval power. I was soon to discover; that our service would, for the first time in centuries, have modern Capital ships, the weapons of a global naval power; weapons that allow a nation the opportunity to shape the course of its history.

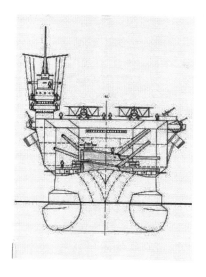

CHAPTER III

THE BATTLECRUISER-CARRIERS

The Fleet Admiraal continued; "On many occasions comic parallels have been drawn; equating our current Empire to an open pasture packed with billions of guilders, all tied in neat bundles and piled up in great stacks on the grass. The pasture is bounded on all sides by busy roadways, from which any passerby has a clear view of this great treasure. The field has no protection, other than a low wire fence, with an old guard sitting on a rickety chair by the chain link gate. He has been given the responsibility of securing this wealth, but the tools that have been provided for this great task consist entirely of a whistle and a broom!"

He then continued, "The Royal Netherlands Navy, is that *old man* gentlemen! We all know that our little navy; whose heart is great, has but a few small ships leaving it woefully under-equipped for the tasks imposed on it by the Nation. Yet we must provide for the common defense, and secure the commercial sea lanes of a great many far flung maritime colonies, a number of which contain a vast potential wealth in natural resources that are coveted by our neighbors. Some of these resources, I remind you, have vital military ramifications as the raw materials are *strategic* in nature: oil, rubber, tin, copper, chromium and rare earths to name just a few of these."

"Our allies in the Far East at present; are the likeminded colonial powers of Great Britain, France and the Republic of the United States who all hold the common opinion that any future naval alliance designed to counter the power of Imperial Japan must be based on a multi-national fleet of warships that will be capable of operating large combat air groups as their primary weapon. Only aircraft carriers have the capability to operate across the vast regions of the Pacific. In 1934 the American Naval Attaché attending a social occasion hosted by our Secretary of Navy proffered the unvarnished opinion, *"that the paltry Dutch naval contribution to the security of the Pacific region was wholly inadequate, and its weaknesses actually invited aggression, and would inevitably prove a catalyst for future Japanese military action."* The Netherlands, they hoped, in the near future would contribute a fleet of larger, more capable vessels to a *Far East Alliance;* than the light cruiser squadron now on station at Java."

"To our credit the RNLN had based a large fleet of submarines in the Far East, and our government had long maintained that these O-boots (Onderzeese boot) represented the; *RNLN Strategic Asset* in the theater. However, given the vastness of the Pacific, our allies countered that these submarines were seen as anti-shipping assets only and were inherently incapable of fleet action, as they were slow, suffered from supply problems and could not be coordinated as a unit to handle the shifting conditions presented by a modern, high speed and far ranging sea battle."

"The British, French and Americans do however recognize the value of our submarines to conduct commerce warfare against the Japanese. But this type of warfare would require a lengthy campaign before its results would have delivered a significant impact upon the enemy, and could not force a quick decision, that a decisive naval battle could."

"Our allies would only place top value on weapons that could win naval battles, any one of which could bring swift victory. If the Netherlands is to maintain its position as an equal partner in planning the defense of South East Asia with the other *Colonial Powers,* then she would have to substantially strengthen her navy to protect that status."

A huge smile came across the Fleet Admiraal's face as he revealed, "Gentlemen it is my distinct pleasure to announce that on Wednesday of this week the *Tweede Kamer* (parliament) had approved a rapid, far reaching and generous rearmament program for the navy! We had been given 100% of funding for KSVP33!" This remarkable development elicited broad grins from all the officers in attendance. Such happy faces; this office had not seen in a year!

"Contained within this emergency program are substantial appropriations for two and possibly three Capital ships for the Royal Netherlands Navy, six new light cruisers of the De Ruyter class, two high speed oil tankers and two high speed support ships. These vessels would be designed for extended service in the tropics, primarily the defense of the East Indies Colonies, with duty in our Caribbean Colonies on occasion."

Although this news was exceptionally good for all those assembled, there still remained the same internal conflicts within our service regarding the type of Capital ship to obtain. If anything this announcement would *fan the flames,* and the two camps of pontificators would form up to deliver their oft used battery of verbal salvos. The *big gun advocates* would undoubtedly push for high speed heavily armed battle-cruisers, while the *naval aviation group* countered with the construction of aircraft carriers. Both camps however held the opinion that as finances had now been made available; time had become the biggest obstacle that we must overcome, regardless of whatever we decided to build.

All present understood that ships of either type would take at least five years to design and construct with a completely unified effort, while our service remained sharply divided as to the ascendant weapon of the future; big guns, aircraft or the submarine.

Our senior naval officer corps contained powerful cadres for each camp, and they could not agree on what type of ship would best serve the future needs of the RNLN. All held the common fear that; if we built the wrong type of ships they would be unable to defend our interests at sea, and disaster could befall the Empire. There was no magical crystal ball into which we could gaze that would allow us to peer fifteen or twenty years into the future so that we could negotiate through this era of rapid technical advancement and obsolescence.

"Gentleman", began the Admiraal, "as you may recall; under paragraph fourteen of the 'exemptions sections', subsection (II) of the Washington Naval Treaty of 1926 dealing with the disposal of major warships to minor non-signatory nations; signature powers of the treaty may dispose of no more than five of their surplus ships to any one of those countries classified as *'minor powers.'*

Accordingly, Great Britain, with by far the largest fleet, sold many surplus warships this way in customers on the Continent of South America, specifically, Chile, Argentina and Brazil, who on occasion have become locked in their own Continental conflicts, including the most recent turmoil."

"Bolivia and Paraguay share an arid plain within the interior of that Continent called the Gran Chaco desert, which makes up a large portion of both their two countries. There; now for several years they have been engaged in a bloody territorial dispute over the desert region's extensive oil resources. The fighting had expanded to a point where it seemed that an Argentine occupation of the Bolivian sector of the Gran Chaco may be in the offing, a development which would have been viewed as an ominous threat to Brazil's security within the region."

"Argentina; which had been preparing to enter the fray and aid Paraguay; realized that she may as a consequence be faced with Brazil as an opponent. Suddenly she faced a big problem. The flagship of the Brazilian Navy the *Rio de Janerio* was a Battleship-carrier hybrid, a unique type of warship that her naval department maintained would pose a serious threat to Argentine maritime commerce."

"The Argentinean Minister of the Navy Miguel Cardonna, concerned with the current weakness of his nation's fleet as you all remember, had contacted the Dutch Government who handed off his requests for aid to the naval designers of RNLN for ideas to expand their navy. Our design office, headed up by Maarten here," he nodded in my direction, "then proposed a solution; the Argentine Navy should acquire two warships for conversion into battle-carriers, and thereby check the threat posed by the Brazilian Battleship-carrier. The vessels Commodore Sweers selected for Argentina were the ex-RN Battle-cruisers; *HMS Lion* and *HMS Princes Royal* of Great War fame. The decommissioned hulls were in good shape, as they had been sitting in a semi-freshwater estuary in a partially dismantled state from 1927 to 1933." Mr. Cardonna accepted and the project undertaken with urgency.

"However the war in the Gran Chaco came to a sudden conclusion in the fall of 1935, when the chief operating officers of the US oil companies that supported the territorial rivals settled their differences, some say on the outcome of a golf match held on the manicured links of the Oakmont Country Club."

"The Argentinean Government reacted with favor to this shift towards peace, then reversed its course, stood down from its planning for war, and stepped back from the brink. In the following year, in a move designed to further reduce political tensions and raise some cash; it sought to down sized its naval forces with the sale of its two almost complete Battlecruiser-carriers. So from all this volatility has come opportunity!"

He continued with the announcement that he had been granted complete authority by the Minister of Defense Erik Deckkers to choose whatever type of Capital ship was best suited to our needs and to acquire or build these ships under the single proviso that they must be in commission no later than the summer of 1939!

This last bit of news was a shock to all assembled as the three year timeframe essentially ruled out any new design-build. Therefore the Admiraal had focused on the purchase of any existing foreign warships or those already under construction and modify them as may be required to satisfy our technical needs while keeping strictly within the timeframe.

Admiraal de Velde had subsequently investigated what warships were available or building internationally and had made his choices. He concluded that the only option still open to us given the time constraint was to purchase the yet incomplete Argentinian battle-carriers. There would be no time to redesign these ships to more closely suit our needs. We would have to go with what the Argentinians had settled on if we were to have any chance of completion. The material orders had been placed and there was no going back at this late date. "So I approached them with an offer," he announced.

"Naval Minister Cardonna, accepted our proposal. The work of the conversion having being undertaken by Dutch shipyards of the Amsterdam Schipwerke in late 1934 is currently underway. You men all have a massive amount of work to complete in the next three years gentlemen. "His steely gaze had fallen upon me at the conclusion of that statement.

The Fleet Admiraal continued; "Thus, the timely intersection of certain events had created an opportunity for the RNLN that was seen as the last possible chance to redress the bleak naval situation that faces us in the East Indies. We are now going to up-grade our diminutive status by acquiring a fleet of new ships of such size and power that the KMN will be able to contribute in a major way to the aggregate deterrent forces provided by our allies in the region upon which our security in the Far East relies!"

The new hybrid ship type of great potential was the Battlecruiser-carrier, which provided a multi-role capability that seemed to receive positive comments from both naval schools of thought in the RNLN; naval gunnery vs naval aviation.

The concept of big guns with a large compliment of attack aircraft combined on one hull was at least a decade old, but was still considered as radical. Nevertheless the potential of the Battleship-Aircraft carrier division as a strategic deterrent to the ambitions of Japan was fully accepted at the highest levels.

A major concern of the Battleship-Aircraft carrier type lay in that it was untested in combat. This perhaps was also its greatest strength. Fear of the unknown is a common enough human trait. Experienced old Admiraals were no exception. I held the positive belief that any *Rengo Kantai* war game of the future in which a squadron of Battleship-aircraft carriers was a chess piece would wrinkle the most experienced brow, raise doubts and create a nagging feeling of unease. The *fear of the unknown* was an ally upon which the RNLN might have to rely upon one day.

The correct choice of weapons is something that Government officials and military men spend a great deal of time agonizing over, as bad choices usually mean defeat in war and the destruction of one's society. On top of this war is a chancy thing, and naval warfare even more so. These were the worries of the various Netherlands officials that had cause such a delay in the modernizing of our navy; worry over ship type.

The RNLN Admiralty was galvanized into immediate action, by the opportunity presented and the fear that our long vacillating government may once again find an excuse to withhold funding. The navy certainly did not want resurgent inter-service bickering to provide a platform for the more timid politicians backpedal. Consequently, an order was then issued to the effect; *that all future open discussion on the topic of guns vs carriers was to cease at once, and it could only be revisited during the planning of combat applications.* Every officer must openly support the decisions of the high command.

The Fleet Admiraal was determined that the *Tweede Kamer* would have the entire senior naval officer corps united behind the task at hand. Consequently he issued a warning to those at the table before him, "pass this message along gentlemen: *for those officers who choose not to immediately obey my direct order to close ranks and support the official position, and who instead continue with the debate on the various merits of ship types, they will do so at great peril. The fate for any officer involved in such a discussion, may include to start with;*" at that moment, Van de Velde paused, and caught everyone's eye for dramatic effect, "*having me personally filleting the offender like a Cod fish with a rusty saw blade! An experience that I guarantee the offender may later have cause to look back upon with fondness, before I am through with him!*" The faces, of even those very senior sailors of long acquaintance with the Fleet Admiraal, became pale and deadly serious.

The Fleet Admiraal explained to the assemblage that the technical documents and calculations before them had formed the design and construction package that the Argentines had purchased from us in 1934. The Fleet Admiraal then directed me to summarize for the assembled officers the basic highlights of the two battlecruiser's conversion, now underway in our shipyards.

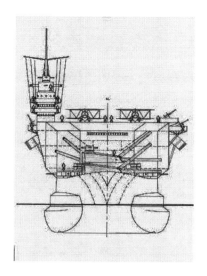

CHAPTER IV

THE TECHNICAL BRIEFING

I searched through the drawings on the table until I had located the Outboard Profile, and the Weather Deck Plan drawings. Several officers then rose to assist me in unrolling these long sheets which we carried to the wall, and tacked in place. With a shuffling of chairs the remainder of the assembly rose to better view these and approached the hanging blueprints, then all eyes were once more turned in my direction with complete absorption.

I then started; "Sirs, the Outboard Starboard Profile Drawing reveals the modifications undertaken to a Great War era British Battle-cruiser of the Lion Class which transforms it into the much more versatile ship type; the Battle-carrier. The vessel had been lengthened, by adding a 32.5 meter long mid-body. The after main battery turret was removed, and 'C' Turret shifted forward where there are now grouped three main battery turrets; from forward to aft; A, B and C, housing two 343 mm (13.5") guns each. Aft of these, another accommodation deck was built above the original main deck, on top of which sits the lower aircraft hangar, then above this the upper aircraft hangar. Upon the flight deck sits a small deckhouse to facilitate air operations. The hull will have multiple torpedo protection systems incorporated within it, including extensive lengths of crushing cylinder and deep torpedo blisters. The ships have been converted to burn oil instead of coal and the turbines have been replaced to provide more power and rapid acceleration. Hundreds of men whose duty was to labor in the filth and darkness leveling coal bunkers or shoveling it into the boilers, will now be replaced by some 700 highly skilled aviation technicians and airmen of an air-group that will be about sixty to seventy aircraft." (See Appendix A&C)

The next drawing to be tacked up was of the Flight Deck Plan View and below it the Main Deck Plan view, which revealed that the main gun battery control tower was situated between 'B' and 'C' heavy gun turrets and was connected to the aircraft hangars by a continuous flight deck that extended all the way aft and overhanging the stern. The firing arcs of the main battery were illustrated, the antiaircraft batteries, their fire-control optical housings, as well as the location of the twin aircraft elevators, located one forward and one aft along the ship's centerline.

I picked up a pointer and ran it along the length of the first drawing indicating the underwater portions of the hull which had been modified by the addition of massive torpedo bulges. Turning to the seated officers, I explained; "The Argentinian Minister of the Navy; Senior Cardonna; being a man of keen appreciation of modern naval technology, held a justifiable great fear of the torpedo and the threat it imposed to even the largest of warships. The hulls of their new ships were therefore given additional defenses with anti-torpedo bulges similar to those on the Battlecruiser *HMS Repulse*. This improved transverse stability, but increased the molded beam by 4.5 meters. The lengthening of the hull required us to add a third rudder to allow the longer ship to retain the reasonable tactical diameter of the original hull. Most of this work will be accomplished using electric welding, which is still a new process, only two decades old. However the savings in time, material and weight over riveted construction would enable the shipyard to meet the project timetable set by the Argentine's."

"The Naval Engineers of the *Regia Marina* (Italian Navy); have conducted underwater destructive testing on hull of the *S.S. Brennero*. The large freighter had its coal bunkers cut out and within the resulting available space; were constructed the experimental torpedo defense system known as the *Pugliese Crushing Cylinders*. Senior Cardonna had been favorably impressed by the results of these experiments and asked for these to be included in the design."

I then introduced about another promising torpedo defensive measure; the *Ferranti Triple Bottom*. This last system was pioneered also by the Italians who correctly calculated that recent developments with magnetically sensitive exploders would enable torpedoes to detonate just under a ship's vitals which sat atop unarmored hull bottom structures. A torpedo detonation under this part of a warship would have a more devastating effect than a hit to the sides of a warship which were usually armored.

The latter system which required the construction of an entire new lower hull beneath the existing bottom shell. It provided additional fuel oil tanks 1.8 meter deep that were particularly useful volumes for the storage of the highly flammable 100 octane aviation fuel, it also gave the vessel additional buoyancy. The new structure allowed us to work in some dead rise, a slightly smaller prismatic coefficient, while improving the metacentric height and offering a longer range of stability.

The ships had been cut in half just aft of transverse frame number 160. The two halves which had been made watertight in way of the cut, were then floated off their keel blocks when the Dry-dock was flooded, and the hull sections floated apart. The shipyard divers then repositioned the existing keel blocks, under the new location of the two halves, and the water was pumped out until the two hulls settled. Once this had been completed, a new 32.5 meter Mid-body hull section was constructed in between to connect the forward and aft sections of the original vessel. The lengthened hull provided the added buoyancy that the redesigned vessel needed, and the lengthening assisted the vessel achieving the contracted 31 knots design speed.

Minor additions were also made to the bow to improve the waterlines forward and flare was added to improve sea-keeping. These changes provided increased flight deck area, and achieved the required aircraft hangar space. There was now sufficient internal volume for the crew's quarters and messes for the additional 700 men of the air operations, with adequate machine shops for an air group that was set as a minimum for these ships; sixty three planes, which could be expanded by one squadron if required.

The old coal fired boilers had been removed and replaced with 24 Yarrow oil fired Small Tube Destroyer boilers to allow for the rapid accelerations required for aircraft launch and retrieval operations. These boilers provided the power to achieve her design speed in the fully loaded condition, at a displacement of 40,000 tonnes.

The propeller shaft turbines had been replaced with the latest Brown-Curtis; All Geared Model Cruiser turbines rated at 24,000 kilowatts each. The propulsive machinery and boilers were chosen for maximum reliability and cost, as their weight-to-fuel efficiency ratios were somewhat technically inferior to what the Italians or the Americans could have designed. The propulsive machinery package price offered to the Argentineans was so low that it reinforced some earlier suspicions, about the British intent. (On the eve of the Great War of 1914-18, Britain seized the Turkish and Brazilian dreadnoughts under construction in their yards to bolster the power of the Royal Navy.) But in hindsight I have concluded that it was just a very good price, performed at cost that would allow the company to keep its skilled labor.

The flight deck was to be of transverse, tongue and groove 150 mm thick Canadian Douglas Fir planking over steel transverse web frames incorporating steel deck longitudinal beams. The strength deck of the new design remains the battlecruiser's original armored deck, so the flight deck and aircraft hangers incorporate four watertight expansion joints. There are two new superimposed aircraft hangar decks, each of 30 mm armor accessible by one aircraft elevator forward and another aft. The upper space being the largest measured out at some 136 meters in length by 33 meters in width and efficiently house bi-plane air groups totaling some forty machines.

Tests and data from the U.S. Navy involving wooden flight decks revealed that damage could be quickly repaired at sea with the most simple of tools to allow continued air operations. By comparison a steel deck, although of lighter construction deformed due to bomb damage in such a way that it could not be as easily repaired at sea, moreover the flames and sparks of the welding equipment and cutting torches represented an additional serious ignition threat to a damaged vessel with aircraft and hoses full of high octane aviation fuel. A further factor influencing material choices was the revelation that damaged steel plate torn to razor sharpness by explosions had a remarkable ability to slice apart fire hoses stiffened and weighted with water. These time consuming material characteristics would delay repairs and the recovery or launch of aircraft.

The section of the flight deck over of the citadel was composed of 75 mm armor had a section of removable flush mounted planks to facilitate the servicing of B turret. The flight deck *duck bill* extension; (installed on the *Cornelis de Witt* only) at the front of the citadel had been specially designed to resist blast from the main battery while minimizing air turbulence.

The conversion of the ships was not so far advanced that it prevented us from under-taking whatever modifications that the RNLN may require to the aircraft hangars to accommodate more capable aircraft in the future. I had limited faith in the current air groups chosen by the Argentines. Some like the Blackburn Baffin torpedo plane were still very useful although quite a dated design, but other choices were made up of discarded, or obsolescent British aircraft types, some having the most lamentable performance.

One type; unloaded on the Argentine Navy was a horrendous looking monstrosity called the Bison. This lumbering, ungainly reconnaissance biplane was the single machine in which the team of designers had finally managed to incorporate onto one airframe all of those unique characteristics that made that aircraft design firm what it is today; a memory.

The fighter-bomber the Argentines had acquired for their flagship; was the Fairy Sea Fox MK I. Initially, in 1932 it was considered a good design, but by 1936 it was already inferior as a fighter; poorly armed, and an antiquated formula, at the end of its development cycle. As a bomber it possessed a payload of a paltry 100 kg. By comparison several contemporary American naval aircraft types were far more robust, had a greater operating range, carried more than twice the payload, and were generally some 75 kph faster.

The American Curtis Model 77 *Helldiver* dive bomber for example carried a 227 kilogram bomb but also served a duel role as second line fighter. If we were so fortunate in the future to obtain *Helldivers* each of our new ships would enjoy an air umbrella of some 60 aircraft if facing a very heavy air attack.

I returned again to discuss the main gun battery located on the foredeck. These heavy weapons were a requirement of the Argentineans, retained to oppose the big guns aboard Brazilian Navy's Flagship. There were several very good design and operational reasons at the time to retain the heavy battery, the logic was not lost on other navies as both the American and the Japanese, each of whom armed their largest aircraft carriers with a battery of heavy artillery. To remove the three forward gun turrets, barbets and their associated machinery, all together some 4,000 tonnes in weight from each ship at this stage would have required a total redesign and a further two years of work. Time for us; was a luxury which we didn't have in 1936.

The 'big gun theorists' within the RNLN (and all navies had them) had been championing the drive to have constructed three new battle cruisers rather than two large aircraft carriers. These 'big gun' senior officers maintained the position that carriers were too fragile for their size. They always referred to our battle study: Fleet Problem 6; where a raiding force of enemy heavy cruisers, using their high speed, screened by our many islands, and aided by the dark of night or foul weather to cloak their movements, attack our lightly-escorted carrier force and smother it with a long range heavy guns. They further maintained that this raiding force would enjoy a heavy superiority in gun power over a light cruiser escort, and could, with rapid long range concentration of 203 mm gunfire bring down such a heavy volume of shells that it would quickly, destroy the flight decks of any aircraft carriers before a defensive air group could be prepared and launched to counter them. Then with their flight decks destroyed, the aircraft carriers would be defenseless. It was further advanced that neither the expected return gunfire of the carrier's screening light cruisers nor the torpedo attacks from her destroyers would be able to prevent the destruction of these expensive assets.

Under these surprise conditions; the large and very expensive aircraft carriers would succumb to cruisers one quarter their displacement they argued, where as a combination of airfields and all big gun battle cruisers would not. The senior officers who supported the 'big gun ship' presented an argument which was valid and had several good points, except that the enemy could simply employ even heavier gunned ships and as many as it took to overcome a single battle-cruiser division composed of two or three ships.

One had to consider that the fixed airfields could be neutralized by bombing, subject to attack from land, or as all save three were adjacent to the sea, shelled at night by warship. Such attacks would be far more difficult to undertake against a highly mobile airfield, one which had the ability to be elusive and protect itself with aircraft, big guns and armor plate.

The Imperial Japanese Navy had a large number of heavy and light cruisers available to deploy for any such a theoretical adventure, while the Netherlands had only a small force of light cruisers and destroyers on hand. The Royal Netherlands Navy now unfortunately found itself at last in a position when there was no more time for further debate, no more time for checking and rechecking our options. The time that remained for us to redress the impossibility of our position required one final, complete, irreversible and unswerving commitment. Build the ships. Build them now!!

With all these broad considerations notwithstanding, dire predictions forced the issue and the commitment was made! The government imposed a truly political solution: *the Bureau of Naval Constructors must acquire multi-role ships, with both a heavy gun capability and which could carry a large air group having the potential to launch a heavy air attack against land or sea targets; provide a two capital ship minimum, three if possible and deliver the completed ships, with escorts of six light cruisers and twelve destroyers within three years.*

It was clear that our Fleet Admiraal's selection of these two Capital ships was a compromise combining features of the aircraft carrier and the battleship. A choice it was hoped that would eliminate the weakest feature of each type while retaining the strongest. Therefore the retention of six heavy guns per ship aided by modern optics and range calculating computers formed half of the solution, while a battle squadron that could also operate 120 to 160 aircraft having well-balanced capability formed the other. The escorting vessels presented us with no critical time issues. The navy placed orders immediately for repeats of the *De Ruyter* and *Tromp Klasse* light cruisers, and twelve new units of the *Zeeland* and *Perseus Klasse* destroyers. As the shipyards were repeating ships that they had already delivered, estimating, planning and procuring was accomplished very quickly and the keels for the first of the new ships were laid within two weeks!

The new vessels' aircraft would give the 'desired strategic air capability' in the Far East, a fact which was of most importance as far as the government was concerned, for it allowed the Netherland's an equal seat at the political table with the 'big boys' in the area; Great Britain, France and the United States.

In order for the layman to comprehend the power that the heavy guns; (largely a kinetic energy weapon) gave to the fleet, one must be aware that a single 343 mm; 610 kilogram shell; delivered some 210 million joules (140 million foot pounds), an energy greater than that of a full eight gun broadside of a modern heavy cruiser such as the Royal Navy's *County Class*! Theoretically one of the big gunned battle-carriers could match artillery power with seven of the largest and most modern heavy cruisers then available to the *Rengo Kantai*! In addition to this power, these large ships were comparatively heavily armored; with up to 230 mm over the vitals. Protection beyond the capability of any Japanese heavy cruiser's guns to deal with. Our big ships could absorb multiple 203 mm gun hits, without being mortally damaged while just one solid hit from a 343 mm shell, could spell disaster for a heavy cruiser.

One may be able to appreciate then what confidence the big guns aboard these warships inspired in our naval gunnery sailors. When these weapons were combined with the striking power of our aerial bombs, (which are primarily potential energy weapons due to the relatively low altitudes of release for sea-battle), numbering in their hundreds, the new battle squadron was revealed to be a very tough nut to crack, in anybody's book.

It must be stated that the design rational for this ship type held that the units were not best employed in the 'offensive gun platform scenario.' However should a situation arise for our carriers where their aircraft were preoccupied or unavailable due to damage, and a surface attack by a heavy force of cruisers developed the six 343 mm guns of each ship acting with its screening vessels would provide a powerful defense, whereas the escorts of light cruisers and destroyers by themselves could not. Should enemy battleships launch a surface attack, the Battlecruiser-carriers had the speed to stay outside the range for a duel between heavy guns, while still pounding the enemy with bombs.

Finally, in conclusion I discussed the secondary battery and the anti-aircraft defenses. The retention of the 102-mm casemate forward battery by the Argentinean Navy was meant as a temporary measure only as their armament industry had been working on a new dual purpose 130 mm naval gun of advanced design, one which they had planned to introduce in two years. Had the design proved successful it would have been install-ed on their cruisers and as the secondary battery for all battle-carriers.

The Swedish armament firm of Bofors, was working on a project which would have equipped our navy with a similar weapon by 1941- 42. So at that time it was decided to leave the 102mm guns aboard as a temporary measure since they had the necessary range and still provided a useful if somewhat limited anti-torpedo boat/destroyer capability.

Shipboard air defense was provided by twenty two pairs of 40 mm Bofors Anti-Air-craft (AA) automatic cannons, a seemingly very powerful outfit at the time. These fine weapons were supplemented by sixteen 20 mm Oerlikon light auto-cannon AA guns, which proved very useful at the closer ranges. However as events were to prove, the absence of a long-range AA weapon in the 125 mm size was clearly revealed.

"We are gentlemen however facing construction timetables laced with critical items that simply do not allow for much rework. We need to get these ships to sea as soon as possible in order to begin the very complicated training associated with the integration of a completely new ship type into our navy. We also anticipate a complete change in aircraft types within two or three years. By that time we should have completed all other shipboard operational training and be able to devote all efforts to training on the new planes. This concludes the general technical overview of our new warships." With that I seated myself. The meeting then turned to other non-related topics.

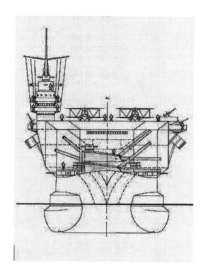

CHAPTER V

MY SECOND STAR AND SEA DUTY

Admiraal de Velde having dictated a unity of opinion amongst the KMN senior naval officers, advised our politicians long tasked with taking positive action on naval matters, that it was time to act. Prime Minister Beerenbrouck gave his approval, the funds were released to the Argentinians and he ordered the KMN to proceed without delay to obtain these types of warships!

The RNLN Admiralty had always suspected that our Government's approval of the new warship building program was not entirely genuine since it was considered technically impossible to achieve in the time allotted. The great fear that those in the room shared with me was the political game. The government of the Netherlands would be seen as trying to protect the nation without really having the money spent or by doing so offending Germany. But the political developments in Argentina now offered us the absolute last real chance to obtain these big ships and in doing so bolster our fleet.

Prior to training at sea the air groups and flight deck crews of the battlecruiser carriers had already spent three months training with their aircraft as guests of the Royal Netherlands Luchvarrtafdeling; the (Army Air Force) large training complex at Soesterberg, just north of Utrecht. A portion of that military airfield had its runways painted to duplicate the relatively small flight deck area of the ships and modifications included a mobile wooden deckhouse, this island was towed into position to simulate the ship's layout and training would continue. The mobile island was constructed with all the equipment required to allow the aircraft to operate. Deck crews in turn practiced how best to concentrate air groups on the deck while leaving enough runway room for launchings and recovery. Other shipboard electro/mechanical aircraft landing equipment included arrestor cables and crash nets of US Navy pattern.

Those experienced pilots of the Royal Netherlands Army Air Force, upon becoming acquainted with the purpose of the new painted boundaries on their concrete runways, would push their garrison caps onto the back of their heads and whistle with their eyes bulging when they contemplated from the air the seemingly tiny decks from which the navy pilots would have to operate. When they factored in the moving deck, smoke from the ship and the unforeseen air currents the Army pilots soon developed a deeper respect for their blue-water brothers.

All our officers and ratings soon came to believe that an effective offensive/defensive capability for the capital ships had been achieved and they felt that their great battlecruiser-carriers to be the most powerful warships afloat. In truth the day that the war in the Pacific started the three capital ships in the Battlecruiser-carrier forces under my command were fully capable of engaging any two of the most powerful aircraft carriers, out to three hundred kilometers away, or in a gun action; a squadron of heavy cruisers from any of the best navies of the world at that time.

A fierce pride was evident in their crews and a great many sailors sought billets aboard, in numbers far surpassing the capability of the ship's to accommodate them. Naval recruitment leapt upwards and we had no difficulty in finding the 20,000 personnel required for the expansion.

The Battle-carrier conversions were completed within twenty-six months for a total sum of 30 million Guilders including the cost of the air groups. In March of 1938 both Battle-carriers passed their sea trials and were commissioned into the Royal Netherlands Navy. The former battlecruiser *HMS Lion* was commissioned as the battlecruiser- carrier *Hr. Ms. Cornelis de Witt*; fleet flagship, and the former battlecruiser *HMS Princess Royal* became the battlecruiser-carrier *Hr. Ms. Johan de Witt*. These names taken from Holland's past; were selected to honor those two most famous sons of the city of Dordrecht, for their successful naval action that humbled the haughty British delegation and brought them back to the negotiation table to end the second Anglo-Dutch War in 1667 with the Treaty of Breda.

Johan De Witt a statesmen holding great influence at a time in the powerful merchant faction of government planned to attack the English Fleet where it lay at anchor at the mouth of the Medway River. He knew that the English sailors had not been paid for a very long time and that their moral was low. So he directed his brother *Cornelis* to take a Dutch battle-fleet across the channel and attack the English fleet. The plan worked perfectly the Dutch warships sailed up the Medway River. Displaying masterful seamanship the Dutch sailors overcoming hidden sandbars and shifting currents to destroy the English Fleet and make-off with its flagship; the new three decker the Royal Charles!

At the acceptance ceremony for the new battlecruiser-carriers the Crown presented the ship with her commissioning pennant, and the officer's with a fabulous Sterling silver dinner setting for their wardroom. These sets for three hundred plus places represented in weight some 900 kilograms each in sterling silver, and were the artful creations of the famous *Van Kempen & Zoon* the Royal Silver Smiths in service to the Crown of the Netherlands. These gifts to the ships, from our beloved Queen represented a fabulous treasure and were received with great pride and humility by the ship's company.

Five days later on the 15th, at the evenings commissioning dinner/ball which had at least two thousand guests Admiraal de Velde rose to make a speech and read a long list of promotions. When he announced my promotion to Rear Admiraal I didn't even hear it as I was listening to a muted side comment by Kapitain De Langeboom. So I just politely started clapping and looking around for which sailor had been honored. Everyone was

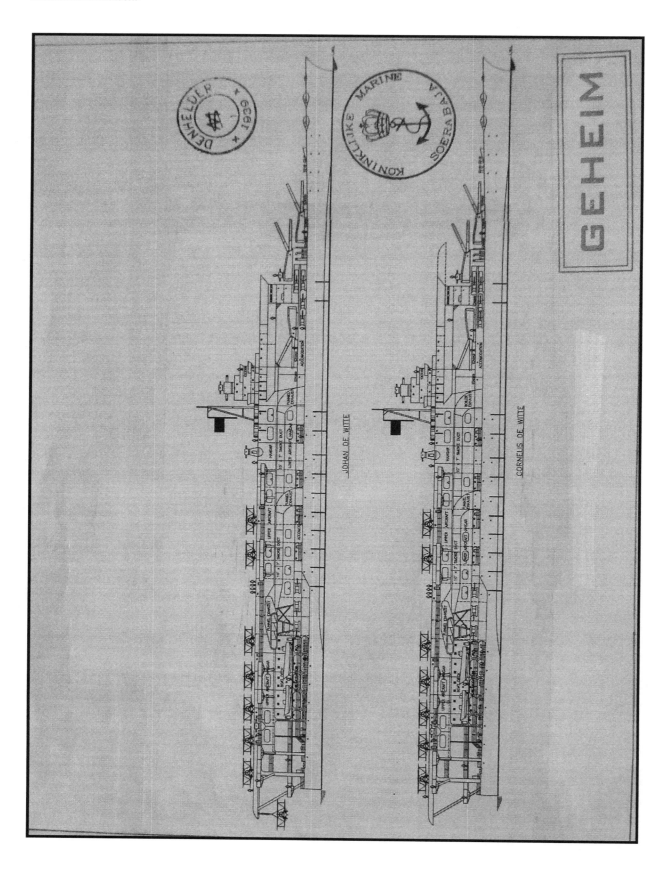

looking at me for some unfathomable reason and all at my table were laughing and congratulating me, until Karen, laughing tearfully said, "Didn't you hear Maarten? You've made Rear Admiraal, you have your second star!" In a few moments her light hearted spirit changed to one more solomn when she realized that periods of long separation would once again enter the marriage.

Two days later my new assignment came through; the command of the new Battlecruiser-carrier squadron! This was a truly an unexpected development as there were many officers in the KMN having more sea time and who had commanded cruiser squadrons. The largest vessel that I had commanded was the light cruiser *Sumatra.*

The Admiralty board were not concerned with this so much as all our warships up to this point were of the smaller variety. They did look with great favor on me as I had recently obtained my wings as a naval aviator, and the fact of having qualified both in fighters and single engine bombers weighed heavily in my favor as I was the only officer of Flag Rank in the KMN to have done so!

In addition to this the Battlecruiser-carrier design conversion was my brainchild alone, and represented the single cost effective solution that the KMN had been searching for, these past few years. I was in their minds the most logical choice for such a position.

My Naval career, was now set on a new course once again; back to the sea, from the theoretical, designer/builder, to operational Commander of a battle squadron! There were literally a host of new tasks to undertake from the selection of my staff officers to the development and implementation of all new combined ship tactics.

I had to consider for example; all aspects of the supply and sustenance of the new fleet, and be prepared to undertake any mission; months in advance. I must become intimately acquainted with every major port city of the world, so that I may succor my ships under any circumstance or location, as a diplomat or battle commander. Quite suddenly the task seemed very challenging.

But the new duties which lay ahead, give back to me that which is closest to the heart of every land locked sailor; a return to active duty aboard a fine ship. For only at sea will a sailor discover his inadequacies, and correct them in order to truly perfect his trade. As a cadet, only a few of my shipmates suffered from my errors. However as the new commander of this battle-carrier squadron, thousands of lives were in my hands.

Lastly the sense of limitless freedom and opportunity that is conveyed to a young man, when gazing forever at a distant blue horizon. All apologies to my dear wife, but it was with a high heart that I looked forward to a reunion with that most alluring and seductive of mistresses; the sea!

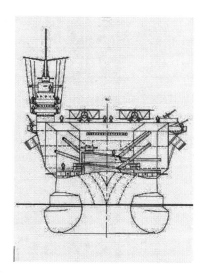

CHAPTER VI

TRAINING CRUISE

My new command; the 1e Slag-Kruiser Lucht Schipvloot (1st Battlecruiser-carrier fleet) departed the naval dockyard at Den Helder, Noord-Holland, on August 14, 1938 at 06:00hrs, to begin a one-month training cruise in the Baltic Sea and the Atlantic Ocean, the first of several.

FLEET COMPOSTION:

1st Battle-Cruiser Carrier Division:

The *Cornelis de Witt;* (Vloot Vlaggeschip) and its sister ship, the *Johan de Witt.*

The 3rd Cruiser Division;

The *Gouden Leeu;* (Eskader Vlaggeschip), *Aemilia, Prins te Parrd* and *Oliphant.*

The 4th Torpedobootjager (destroyer) Flotilla:

Consisting of the Eendraagt (Flotilje leider), *Zoutman, Piet Heyn, Draak, Bulhond, Jakhals, Gelderland* and *Zeeland.*

The specific Battle-carrier training was to include tactical exercises in the following; naval gunnery, anti-torpedo tactics, refueling at sea from fleet tankers, and from battle-carrier and cruiser to destroyer, damage control management, structural damage repairs at sea, firefighting, towing of damaged ships and tactical maneuvering of the battle-carriers to verify physically a number of the hull's characteristics arrived at through calculation, such as her tactical diameter, with reduced power and less than four shafts. Air group training consisted of; torpedo attack and defense, bombing attack and defense, fighter air umbrella development and coordination. In a final training operation, and the one that most of the ship's crew looked forward to, had the fleet split into two equally balanced forces that would hunt each other, in a mock naval engagement.

The cruisers and destroyers that had been assigned to screen the battle-carriers contained 30% experienced men of long service and were well drilled units in their own right. Therefore the emphasis of this training cruise was to develop the procedures for correctly utilizing cruisers and destroyers with a battle-carrier division, which processed a wide range of capabilities. While the RNLN had operated bombers and torpedo planes from naval air stations for fifteen years, ship borne air groups, were a completely new weapon.

The escorting vessels under my command must develop an instinctive understanding of battle-carrier operations so that they may anticipate the maneuvers of the big ships well in advance in order to avoid a collision. They must be far enough away to allow the big ships all the maneuvering room that they needed, while remaining close enough to provide effective screening and anti-aircraft support.

The morning of that first training cruise, aboard the battle-carrier *Cornelis de Witt*, I will always recall as a picture-perfect day. An off shore breeze of five knots, slightly ruffled the Noord Zee, with little wind currents snaking across the surface of the water creating shifting patterns of a royal blue, and tossing off sun diamonds from the wavelets. The sea conditions at present were mild so I decided to exercise the engine room crews somewhat earlier than expected and create a little drama in those spaces. Turning to Kapitein Voorne; I ordered him, upon the fleet reaching the open sea to sound; *"beat to quarters, all hands take up their battle positions,"* then ring up for 320 revolutions on four shafts and make for the exercise area at flank speed. Voorne saluted, I then returned my binoculars to its case and began my morning inspection, selecting random paths through the ship.

Exiting the ship's command bridge on the No. 2 deck in the gunnery citadel, between 'B' and 'C' Main battery mounts, I collected my assistants, two Lts. ter Zee 2nd Klasse (Lieutenant), who were both attached to my staff. They were to grub around for me as required; crawl into tanks, unbolt W.T. plates, and lift heavy hatches for me in addition to recording my comments. Grabbing their notepads, they quickly fell in behind me as we made our way aft to the diminutive armored door through the 50 mm thick after bulkhead of the navigation bridge. We passed through it, continuing aft down the corridor, which spanned over 'C' Turret of the main battery, which connected the bridge to the upper aircraft hangar. We then came up to the 50 mm armored door in the forward blast bulkhead of the hangar, passed through this, and then down a short bulkhead mounted companionway to the 30 mm armored deck.

Here I paused for a moment to don the faded blue overalls that I had rolled up and under my left arm, I then tucked my Admiraal's cap inside over my heart before buttoning it up to the chin. The two junior officers retrieved similar apparel from the bulkhead hooks, and grasping my intentions made themselves as equally inconspicuous.

On this deck were housed thirty-one bombers and seven fighters. We threaded our way through the aircraft and dodged nimbly around a group of engine mechanics with their tool boxes, spare parts and other various *overhaul detritus* lying about. Some seven meters above us; the deck head held suspended the light yet bulky items; spare sets of wings, rudders and ailerons which could quickly be retrieved and installed to a machine by the airframe mechanics, keeping the damaged machines airworthy.

We continued aft until reaching aircraft elevator 'A'. I indicated to my aids that I intended to go up onto the flight deck. While one of my officers manipulated the elevator control I glanced over to a group of engine mechanics working on a *Hawker Sea Fury Mk II's* of the fighter group. The group of air technicians with their backs to us, had not turned at the sound of the elevator's motion horn, and so they did not notice the junior officers or the presence of their Admiraal, as the overalls gave my group sufficient anonymity. It was a ruse which I sometimes employed to make useful observations. I preferred to view my crew, engaged in their duties, rather than seeing them always standing stiffly at attention.

The verbal exchanges interwoven with creative curses that I caught from this group of artificers, were of the same sort all working men are apt to make, when a certain level of frustration is experienced. Lieutenant Stoop; an air officer, was going to chastise them, but I shook my head for him to forget it, as I didn't want to blow my intentional *incognito status*.

Lieutenant Van Nyees, then noticed me glancing at three other *Sea Fury* fighters parked nearby. Here I discovered, that under the engine of each, and slung by a thin wire was a cut down canned food tin being utilized to catch the drippings of lubricant which oozed slowly from the bottom of the engine oil pan gasket. The can moved slowly with the soft rocking of the ship, mostly doing its intended job, but still missed the odd drops, which lightly spattered the steel deck. I told the young officer to enquire of the air maintenance officer the reason for the fighter planes to be leaking the valuable engine lubricant.

Lt. Van Nyees, responded that he had made this enquiry earlier of the men, and had discovered that it was the tolerances of the oil cooled engines of the fighters. The machine bolts were difficult to keep tight as their lock washes lacked sufficient *spring* and the gaskets seemed to be made of an inadequate material that did not expand fully back from the compression due to heat tightening of the engine casing. They lost over time their resilient quality and slowly oozed oil, a condition that was further aggravated by extended periods of engine vibration, and by cooler weather. Our mechanics were somewhat less than happy with them and they much preferred to work on the excellent Bristol Pegasus air-cooled radial engines. I enquired further of my Lieutenant if this default was common, and had other fighters exhibited this characteristic?

The aircraft elevator arrived at our level with a screech and a bump. We hopped on and the Lt. replied that this was unfortunately the case. Our air operations people, he explained; were in the process of drawing up a standard maintenance form, on which they intended to record for the coming exercises, those time consuming mechanical repairs, directly attributable to the leaky engine gaskets that would be responsible for delaying the turn-around time of a fighter after a mission.

There was a feeling that torpedo operations against enemy shipping may be hampered as the Swordfish torpedo bombers would experience a delay while waiting for their fighter escorts on each turn-around. Apparently this was due to the time required between missions spent on the annoying task of re-tightening various bolts on the Sea

Fury fighter's oil pan. A condition, which would progressively erode as the number of missions, climbed.

Arriving upon the flight deck I dismissed the two junior staff officers and sought a few moments for myself to reflect. I looked up at the masthead where my Rear Admiraal's long; single point pennant; of blue bunting blue with two gold stars snapped in the stiff breeze. I had waited my whole life for such a moment, it was with a deep sense of satisfaction that I made my way aft down the starboard side of the deck and looked astern to my fleet as it cleared the *Engelschmangat* narrows separating Texel and Vlieland Islands. I reached for my cigarette's, checked my wristwatch and waited for a few moments.

Off went the trumpet call for general quarters, and the ship started to rumble with hurried activity. Within the hull, hundreds of watertight doors were being slammed closed, and the hundreds of deadlights in both hull and superstructure were closed then dogged down. The ship echoed to the sound of thousands of racing feet pounding the steel decks as the men responded.

In a few short moments I felt my body sway and I steadied myself, as deep within the bowels of the ship the frantic engineering crews opened valves to connect more boilers. The terrific potential energy of the pent up superheated steam was released and it slammed into the turbine blades, dragging them around with a demonic fury. The great ship slowly began to accelerate.

Approximately 400 meters abaft the flagship, and to port steamed our sister ship the *Johan de Witt* looking quite impressive. Stretched out in her curving wake came the light cruisers and destroyers. They looked to be a very distinctive group of vessels in their smart white, with black trim paint scheme. The trumpet; *call to arms* from the other warships carried faintly to me across the waters.

Commandeur (Commodore) Konrad van Speijk commanded the second squadron aboard his flagship the Battlecruiser-carrier *Johan de Witt*. Her gunnery officer; Kapitein Lt. ter Zee Wiliam Visser te Hoofer; was an expert in his field, and perhaps the best at that activity in entire (RNLN) Royal Netherlands Navy. Four years ago his ship, the cruiser the *Tromp* won both the Fleet Gunnery Cup and the Queen's Pennant. He was by nature; a fierce competitor and was determined that the marksmanship of all the artillery, regardless of caliber aboard his battlecruiser-carrier would surpass that performance. He passed up the Captaincy of a light cruiser, to transfer to the new Battle-carrier as her Senior Artillerie Officer, thereby fulfilling his life-long career ambition of commanding a battery of massive naval artillery!

While studying the Battlecruiser-carrier *Johan de Witt,* through my binoculars, I detected that Kapt. Lt. te Hoofer was conducting some type of preparatory test, as from the half nautical mile that separated our ships I could make out that the three turrets of the main battery trained first to starboard and then to port while the long muzzles of the big 343 mm kanon alternately; rotated, depressed and then elevated to their maximum of 40 degrees.

The RNLN had experienced many frustrations in the previous fifteen years, having had several requests for three modern battlecruisers for the fleet being repeatedly shelved. Indeed the RNLN hadn't had a battleship on force since the *Koning der Nederland* of the 1890's, an old turret vessel mounting four 281 mm guns. There was a small old coast defense ship in the East Indies; the *De Zeven Provicien.* But, as she mounted only two obsolete 280 mm guns, and sitting at 6,500 tonnes displacement it was by the twentieth century, hardly a capital ship!

During the 1930's the concern for obsolescing equipment was widespread throughout the RNLN; whether you were a common sailor or commissioned officer. Seamen of all ranks worried that in the case of a future war they would wage it with old weapons and would be called upon to make the *ultimate sacrifice* while floundering around the sea in useless ships, and wasting their lives to make a futile gesture!

The entire fleet was looking forward to the main caliber exercise that would herald in the new reality for the rebuilt navy. The *main battery shoot* for the both Battlecruiser-carriers was to be evaluated on two levels; first the gunnery training and second the assessment of the effects of blast and recoil on the ship; its motion, its structures, the aircraft and overall flight deck operations.

The detailed calculations notwithstanding, some officers still had concerns for longitudinal whipping as all six big guns were concentrated forward in the first third of the waterline length on a riveted ship, one which had been already lengthened by some 30 meters. However the addition of the massive torpedo blisters port and starboard, the added double bottom of the Ferranti torpedo protection would negate any ill effects due to the lengthening, as the hull girder section modulus had been greatly increased over that of the original ship.

The fleet support vessel *Zuidercruis* rendezvoused with our force at 10:00hrs bringing with it a number of towed wood and canvas targets for the gunnery exercises. The targets were handed over for the actual firing practice to the destroyers *Gelderland* and *Zeeland* who would handle the high speed tow.

The battlecruiser-carriers would practice shooting at targets moving at the high speed associated with an enemy warship. The targets were therefore to be towed by the assigned destroyers, as the *Zuidercruis,* at best an 18 knot vessel was not up to the task. She would instead return to Den Helder to bring up the additional targets required for the swordfish torpedo planes and light bombers.

I took up a position on the battle bridge of the citadel to observe the gunnery exercise. There were fifteen officers on the battle bridge, all with binoculars at the ready waiting expectantly. Excitement was in the air. Kapitein Voorne turned to me and said, "Admiraal, the targets are in position and making 25 knots. Both of the capital ships are ready to begin the gunnery exercise and await your orders.

Kapitein Voorne, barked an order down his chain of command. "Hoist the Black pennant." He then turned in my direction to address me, "Rear Admiraal, navigation reports that the fleet has arrived at the firing range."(Many nautical charts have marked on them, large areas of the sea that are reserved for warship exercises). Glancing at the bulkhead mounted Battle-clock I replied, "Kapitein, it is now 10:58hrs. Make to the *Johan de Witt* to commence and then open fire when you are ready." I was expecting my Vlaggeschip to demonstrate a superior performance and the Kapitein was aware of this, as I had already ordered a trophy case for the officer's mess from the ship's carpenters. Voorne then turned to his officers and passed along my orders. I braced myself against a bulkhead frame with bent arm and turned to the window. Now I would see, firsthand how sturdily these great ships were built. Would the tremendous recoil energy released by the main battery six gun broadside, calculated at 1.26 Billion Joules (420,000 foot tons) be effectively dissipated into the surrounding ship structure, or would the battle-carrier start to come apart, rivet by rivet as each broadside shook the great ship testing the integrity of its new configuration; from its masthead to its keel plates?

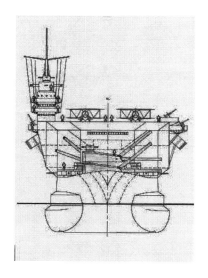

CHAPTER VII

GUNNERY EXERCISE

The three great 343 mm gun turrets of the *Cornelis de Witt,* began to slowly traverse to starboard, as the starboard barrels of each mount elevated to 35 degrees, and the port tube to 25 degrees. For a moment these reminded me of the questing antenna on the head of a giant insect, which then froze as the range was received by the guns. The firing gong sounded three times followed by a short heartbeat of silence, then the great guns erupted with a flaming ferocious blast! Immediately the ship began a noticeable roll to port and at the same time the bow was thrown a meter in the same direction, a movement; however that was quickly corrected by our experienced helmsman.

Despite the crew's many preparations, a variety of objects were still hurled to the deck, and some officers were staggered. Several of them who had been leaning with their elbows against the 51 mm steel of the curved blast shield had the shock of the recoil transmitted to the long bones of their arms, and the pain was evident in the pallor of their faces. Well, I thought; this danger had been well covered in training, we mustn't let the excitement of the moment, make us careless.

Straining to balance myself, I struggled to keep the target within the field of view of a pair of 200 x 80 Zeiss pedestal mounted binoculars, as I mentally counted down the remaining seconds to the impact. There, they rose; six tall geysers of dazzling white spume, one hundred meters high at least, three beyond the target, and three below it, but right on for deflection!

Immediately the fire control computer, that automatically solved the calculus problem of the related rates of change, began their adjustments to update the guns, and the naval range finding method, referred to by the Germans as; *walking the ladder* had begun in earnest, with no salvo taking longer than 30 seconds. The process involved the port side elevated barrels in the three turrets correcting the range downward, while the less elevated three barrels in the starboard side of the turret corrected upward until both guns were on target. Once the range was found the big guns would be worked furiously to maximize the rate of fire.

I was amazed at the advanced automation of the British heavy gun's breech mechanism and their loading operations in general. The Armstrong Whitworth system was almost entirely automated; with smooth hydraulics and mechanical rammers. Only one gunner handled the entire loading process at the breech, with a great lever actuated polished steel mechanism, that drew the huge shells from the cavernous magazines, deep within the bowels of the ship, then up and rammed into the gun's breech, to be followed by 160 kilograms of cordite. Another gunner stood at the port side of the breech and operated a hand crank that quickly completed the locking of the mechanism preparatory to firing. These great masses of polished steel machinery, being entirely motivated by only a few kilograms of human effort, displayed a smooth symphony of motion and were a wonder to behold.

In contrast, the reloading mechanisms within the 14 inch gun turrets of the US Navy, were by comparison astonishingly quite primitive. More gunners were involved; one had to manually open and lower the massive breech block on its hinge, while others gunners had to manually manipulate the 1400 lb shells. These arrived vertically from the magazine up an armored tube, where men then had to grasp the projectile's tip, and somehow lay it down on its side onto a dolly. The dolly and shell were then wheeled to the open breech, where the ¾ tonne projectile was hand rammed in place, followed by the three one hundred pound powder charges. When loading was completed, the gunner had to squat and dead lift the breech block, to swing it forward, up and into the gun's breech, then lock the interrupted screw mechanism. He was aided in this task by getting an assist from below where two gunners with poles heaved upwards. It was all rather heavy work, very cumbersome, dangerous and would undoubtedly result in early crew fatigue.

I did in time begin to develop deep reservations regarding the ability of the USN Battlewagons to fight a prolonged big gun duel with the heavy units of the Japanese Battle-fleet, whose gun mechanisms followed the much more advanced British design.

After two minutes of this activity, the *Cornelis de Witt's* gunners operating the range-keeper called out; straddle…straddle, then the first hit coming at three minutes. This was immediately confirmed by radio from the destroyer *Gelderland* engaged in towing our target. Her gunnery team had been instructed to assist the *Cornelis's* fire control center by reporting the fall of shot.

In truth I had expected more, as the battlecruiser-carriers had been outfitted with the very latest American artillery fire control computer then available in 1938. The mechanism was a union of two components; the Ford Mark 38 Range Keeper, a device installed within a second device; the Ford Mark 38 Gun Director. These were the finest instruments of the day in the opinion of Kapitein – Lt. ter Zee (Commander): Tieler Van Riper, our chief Gunnery Officer. These mechanisms had been selected by the US Naval Constructor, over mechanisms of British and German, manufacture. The Ford mechanism had been installed aboard the powerful Battleship *U.S.S. Colorado*, and had successfully withstood the full broadsides of the Mk 2, 16 inch guns, awesome weapons which generated twice the recoil of the guns of my flagship! Then after a few moments of reflection I chided myself for my impatience, being afterall the first time that my gunnery crews had discharged this artillery!

Once the first hit had been registered, the *Gelderland* had orders to maintain this initial course and speed for five minutes, then increase to thirty knots and introduce a slight zigzag to the her course to confuse our gunnery, much as any vessel may attempt when under accurate fire, employing the well-used avoidance tactic of; steering to the last fall of shot.

To assist with the long range spotting of a weaving target; the Vlaggeschip's air operations officer; Hoof Officier Vlieger Konrad Van Braekel had ordered the launch of a Fairy Sea Fox light bomber, to radio-in the accuracy of *Cornelis de Witt's* shells.

I then decided to relocate, and chose to observe the launch from the deckhouse flight control position on deck 06. I wanted to note how quickly the flagship was able to check fire, turn into the wind, launch an aircraft, then return to her base course, to reacquire the target and resume shooting.

Captain Voorne turned to me and said, "Admiraal the observation aircraft is standing by to launch, I will wait for your signal from the island." Followed by my two staff shadows I quickly made my way to the companionway leading to the deckhouse. Upon reaching the upper deck within the structure, I picked up the telephone and told the Kapitein to *check fire* then turn into the wind.

At the leading edge of the flight deck a valve was opened to emit a small cloud of steam that immediately whipped down the deck to starboard. The so called; *steam sock*, acted as the wind direction indicator that allowed the air operations helmsman to steer the ship into the wind, a direction which best suited the aircraft. Once the steam was flying down the very center of the deck the ship was steaming directly into the wind. The combined speed of the natural wind added to that generated by the ship's own velocity optimized conditions that would allow heavily laden aircraft to be launched.

In ten or twelve seconds conditions were ideal. The Sea Fox revved up its 642 kilowatt *Hispano Suzuia* engine and lumbered down the wooden flight deck. With almost fifty knots of wind *down the wood* the plane needed only to travel some twenty five meters before it lifted off, banked to port and began to climb for altitude.

Once this was accomplished the air operations helmsman signaled to the battle bridge that he was turning the helm over to them. The *Cornelis de Witt's* big balanced spade shaped rudders bit into the water at 30 knots, heeling her over several degrees as she slewed around to starboard. Then steadying up on the old course, she raced to catch up to the target that had used the opportunity to flee as was to be expected by any overmatched opponent.

I watched as the main battery rangefinder, located six meters above me rotated until it had found the target. The whole launching process had taken a remarkably short period of only two minutes! When I heard the firing gong's warning I opened my mouth, covered my ears and braced myself for the painful concussion. The gun turrets, now rapidly being fed both the range and deflection of the target, were releasing full six gun salvos. The blast experience on the island was nothing less than cataclysmic, as I stood in a rather exposed position not more than 25 meters from the twin muzzles of 'C' Turret!

The noise measuring instruments at my position I noted, were recording a sound rating of 187 decibels at each salvo! Our medical evaluations on the *limits of the human body* equated this to standing five meters from a stick of dynamite as it detonated. I decided that I would not stay at this location for too much longer, as I felt some of the fillings in my teeth had actually loosened! The main battery drill was generating powerful shockwaves, I noted that the bulkhead instrument mounted for the tests recorded an air pressure increase of some 0.6 kilograms per square centimeter, which was very close to what I had calculated would result when nine hundred kilograms of cordite propellant was ignited and the energy vented in such close approximation.

Perched as I was; up on forward upper platform of the air operations deckhouse I studied the effects of shock and extreme vibration on the ship's structures. The duck-bill, the leading edge of the flight deck, was an extension designed to aid heavily loaded monoplanes take-off, from an overcrowded or damaged flight. The 'bill' extended out over the roof of 'B' Turret. It was a twin boomed cantilever configuration and of substantial steel plate construction, carefully arranged as to dissipate the considerable muzzle blast of the heavy guns, while minimizing air turbulence over the flight deck.

The flight deck area between the cantilever booms utilized heavy removable planking 150 mm thick, that allowed the dockyard crane access to 'B' turret's service well. I could now distinguish that the blast had shifted some of these planks, an occurrence that I hurriedly scratched into a note book which contained my observations for the day. I also made notes to provide some sort of blast shielding, in lieu of the current handrail for the air operations island to reduce the exceedingly uncomfortable effect of the concussion, the worst part of which created a brief sensation of having giant fingers inside ones skull, that squeezed your eyeballs with every blast.

Turning my attentions once again to the gunnery exercise, I raised my binoculars to locate the target, but the optical distortion hid it in a seemingly tumultuous horizon, as the range was close to 28,000 meters with the sea conditions now turning misty. I therefore relocated to the rear of the A.O. tower where I prepared to observe the main caliber shoot of the battlecruiser-carrier *Johan de Witt* for a few minutes. I now chose to view the warship through one of the many pedestal mounted, high power *Zeiss* binocular sets used by seamen on look-out duty. Through these, our sister ship loomed huge, with every detail standing out in crisp relief due to the powerful light gathering ability of the 200 mm diameter objective lenses. The associated *depth of field effect* produced by the refraction, seemed to enhance this optical impression.

Half a nautical mile off our port quarter; the big warship sliced through the waves of a cobalt blue sea at more than 30 knots. The hybrid battlecruiser-aircraft carrier looked menacing and powerful. Her entire profile was dramatically displayed as if she was posing for the ship's postcard photograph. In the clear sea air her peacetime light gray paint scheme was illuminated with an almost painful intensity by a sun standing tall in the sky on a gloriously clear day.

Due to the high speed of her massive 40,000 tonne bulk, a steep green wave crowned by white spume, was piled up at her prow. Almost immediately it was swept aside where it collapsed and curled widely to port and starboard. Only the very tip of the battle-carrier's bow protruded beyond and through an obscuring curtain of dazzling white spray, there it hung seemingly dislocated from the rest of the ship.

Behind and over this shifting curtain loomed the massive blast shield of the armored hanger and gunnery citadel complex at the base of which I could make out the huge gun turrets of the main battery. The great ordinance I could discern were trained to starboard. From out of their long tubes erupted immense dark roiling clouds of cordite smoke crowning the flash of a huge yellow fireball. The regular salvos blasted out with an incredible rolling thunderclap effect.

Immediately following this auditory assault there was carried to my ears with each salvo; a loud and prolonged ripping noise, like the tearing of huge linen sheets. This was due to the passage of the heavy shells, which being ejected from their muzzles at 850 meters per second literally shredded the atmosphere. I might have heard this similar effect from our own heavy ordinance, had not my senses been so completely overwhelmed by the blast effect of *Cornilis's* shooting.

As if great fists of smoke and fire beat upon its surface; the sea beneath the *Johan de Witt's* gun muzzles, I observed; was violently concussed. Where, with every flash of flame heralding the eruption of a full salvo, it vibrated like the tympanum of a gigantic drum, to instantaneously produce thousands of vertical tendrils of white spume.

The big battle-carrier was shooting very rapidly. Dense black smoke belched out of her port stack fleeing aft. Her stark almost white hull and upper-works contrasted sharply with the gloomy background pall of funnel smoke and dark brown billows produced by her heavy guns.

Barely visible at *Johan's* masthead; the deep horizontal red, white and blue bars of the Netherlands' tri-color could be made out, snapping stiffly in the slipstream. High up in her air operations tower; a message was being tapped out by Morse lamp, its intense bright eye blinked out coded instructions to the observation planes circling aloft.

Far aft on her flight deck; I was able to discern that a large air group was being prepared for launching. The sunlight created multiple points of bright reflection where it encountered Plexiglas canopies, spinning steel propellers and polished duralumin. Around and amongst the waiting aircraft swarmed ant-like; the tiny white clad figures of men.

Suddenly I was overcome by the inspiring sight, and felt hotly flushed with a fierce pride! These magnificent weapons of steel would protect our ancient far flung empire! The great guns would speak with their awful voice, our long aerial torpedoes would strike deeply into the enemy's submerged vitals, and the bombs would rain down from out of the sky to smash the enemies of our Queen!

The huge warship presented an impressive spectacle, a balance of controlled raw power and graceful beauty, one that I had visualized many times in my mind's eye while developing the design. Now, here was my creation, dream to reality after some six years of intense but enjoyable effort! I experienced a deep sense of satisfaction that I had carried out my duty and completed this task as directed: to deliver these powerful warships to my motherland in the briefest possible time period, within cost and without sacrificing technical quality. The RNLN's battlecruiser-carriers would provide a considerable deterrent to any Japanese ambition against our East Indies colonies, especially when we were standing resolutely shoulder to shoulder with America, France, Great Britain, Australia and New Zealand!

The main battery exercises had concluded very successfully. The heavy guns and their associated equipment was shown to be a delightful combination of reliability and accuracy, truly a fine example of British ingenuity; a technology far ahead of its time.

The modifications we had carried out to the turret roofs and gun mountings allowed an increase to 40 degrees of elevation, had proved their worth. The contracted range of 30,000 meters was achieved with 1,800 to spare and with an acceptable *spread* of shells in the salvos. On a day of average visibility and at the reasonable battle range of 26,000 meters the 343 mm three gun salvos, under the new Ford Fire Control Computer, allowed the ranging men to find the target within two minutes of opening fire. Once having achieved this, the six gun salvos would obtain a minimum of one hit every one and a half minutes in moderate seas, which was better than 8% of shells fired. For our first exercise I was satisfied with this result although the *Johan de Witt* I was soon to discover had been able to score slightly better! Verdomme!

To the layman this score may appear to be ridiculously low. But it must be remembered that the training was for a naval battle, and not for howitzers shooting a stationary target on terra firma. In a naval shoot, the shells are being released from a ship moving at 15.5 meters per second horizontally, towards a point on the sea some 450 meters ahead of the target also travelling at a similar velocity. The shells travel horizontally, vertically and laterally, for thirty seconds through air of varying densities and moisture content, perhaps even rain, to descend toward that point at which it is hoped the target ship will arrive, at the precise moment. The target ship all the while has continually maneuvered so that the ship shooting at her will with only great difficulty be able to calculate her true range and speed, and approximate her exact location some thirty seconds in the future.

Air Operation experiments were conducted while maintaining *a course to suit the guns*, and not turning into the wind to suit the launching aircraft. Our fully loaded biplane aircraft had little difficulty in taking off, even with the reduced wind over the deck. Cross currents however, were more frequent, being a particular danger to these aircraft with their lightly loaded wings.

The Sea Fury fighter aircraft, and the Sea Hart light bombers, with the ship at full speed needed only 25 meters of deck to become airborne. During a main battery shoot, the pilots were required to launch within the thirty second lull between salvos. The Hawker biplanes required less than four seconds to become airborne, and their air groups could be launched over the gun turrets and get clear of the blast in plenty of time, the frequency of the launches, was nevertheless very closely controlled. The Swordfish torpedo planes, however required a little more time and fifteen meters more deck to get airborne due to their heavy loads under ideal circumstances. However due to their painfully slow takeoff speed, they needed a total of twenty seconds to get clear of the effect of the main battery blast.

The concept of maintaining *a course to suit the guns* was operationally possible with the current British aircraft due to their lightly loaded wing surfaces. They provided an operational flexibility to the ship in a crisis. I then speculated that after the inevitable changeover to faster aircraft this option may not be possible due to insufficient flight deck length. Turning into the wind to obtain maximum air velocity over the flight deck to launch aircraft would become our standard operational procedure.

The effects of blast, roll and wracking on the ship's structure, were among those items closely studied with regard to air operations. The ship's vibrations due to main battery gunfire would throw down toolboxes in the hangars and cause aircraft in the forward part of the ship to jump in their restraints.

The ship's new structure, that steelwork added during her extensive conversion from battlecruiser to battle-carrier, had stood up well to recoil and concussion caused by the firing of the big guns. The new command center/citadel proved to be a robust structure but this was to be expected as the bulkheads were fabricated largely of 51mm Krupp cemented armor, under a 75 mm armored section of the flight deck. The flight deck *duck bill* extension had been installed on the *Cornelis* only, was a test structure and needed to undergo further evaluation in its exposed position, to record how it withstood the blast effect of the main battery. Several of its deck planks had come loose, but it was later discovered that they had not been properly fastened. The main mast whipped excessively due to recoil but this was corrected with additional bracing. The loose contents of the forward messes and cabins were much tossed about. The aircraft mechanics had requested that sail makers manufacture for them special canvass cushions to support their tool boxes and loose parts. These simple innovations kept the items from flying around.

The ships were gradually brought up to 90% efficiency, during this first cruise. The battle-carrier crews now instinctively braced themselves upon hearing the firing gongs. Certain equipment foundations had to be strengthened. Leaking pipe systems were identified and modified. Packing and repacking of items resulted in a minimization of the blast effects on the ship's stores. In any case a torpedo or bomb hit would be a much more powerful event. Adapting to the blast and recoil of the big guns was merely part of the training that any crew of a battleship would have to master.

The Armstrong Whitworth MK VIII model 102mm gun, of the secondary battery, was the vintage 1909 original outfit; and had been retained for expediency. The guns were scheduled for replacement within three years but this did not prevent us from conducting a thorough series of exercises. The weapons were found to be quite robust, easy to handle, simple to maintain and accurate at their extreme range of some 11,000 meters, one which was useful but by 1938, rather weak for a secondary armament on such large ships. Anti-torpedo boat exercises carried out against two remote controlled 40 knot boats targets, showed that these older guns were still effective although the manual traverse was cramped to operate and it soon exhausted the men trying to track such small fast moving objects. To offset the MKIII gun's deficiencies against high speed boats, we relied on our Bofors guns. A surface target that dared to approach to within than 6,500 meters of a Battle-carrier would be subjected to a massive barrage by the twenty two 40 mm Bofors guns of its Flak battery mounted along each side. If the target continued to close, to under 2000 meters, then the general purpose 20 mm Oerlikon automatic kanon would also contribute to surface defense. These combined weapon systems, it was felt would be adequate to fill the dual purpose of air and sea combat and suffice until the installation of the modern secondary battery which we had planned for 1942-43.

The Anti-Aircraft training for gunners serving the Bofors 40 mm, and Oerlikon 20 mm automatic kanon batteries consisted of a Swordfish-towed canvass target, streamed at a variety of speeds, elevations and ranges depending on the weapon in use. These exercises were constant, and allowed the gunners to become proficient in the use of their weapons. Individual Flak batteries were assigned sectors of the sky to defend, as well as combined battery fire, where all guns that could bear would be controlled by one director. Air defense control would assign targets, and transmit orders through the battery commander's headsets. But the quadrant system of defense initiated by a *quadrant on* command or abandoned with an *independent fire* command allowed all port or starboard AA guns to engage just one target. Each four-gun Bofor battery, had one pair equipped with a gun camera. The crews of both AA gun calibers, found that they were able hit well when the target was towed at optimal ranges and at the speed of 300 kph. All targets were destroyed with ease at these speeds yet modern aircraft velocities were much above this, so the air gunners had to adjust their lead on a target, a task made much easier as every fifth round in the magazines was a tracer round. The cameras confirmed this with their film. Common to all warships, the bow and stern AA defensive fire are weak, compared to that of her sides, the battle-carriers were no exception. Two days of live AA fire against towed targets at *Swordfish-speeds* were alternated with one day of high speed training with more modern aircraft of the army.

The Luchvaartafdeling (Dutch Army Air Force) contributed to our naval AA training. The army carried out simulated high speed strafing attacks on the Battle-carrier division with thirty Fokker G.1 twin engine fighters. These training operations were designed for the Army Air Force, to suppress the ship's anti-aircraft defense by shooting up the optical range finders and AA guns and crews in the tubs mounted along both sides of the flight deck. The Army's, Fokker Heavy Fighter, a twin engine monoplane was well suited to this type of attack as it carried eight machineguns in its nose battery. These modern Army aircraft were similar in performance to the first line types we could expect an enemy to employ against us. Training with these high speed aircraft became a sobering experience as it was revealed how much more skill was required to track these aircraft and keep them in the gun sites for a minimum of the three seconds or so, required to get hits.

The Oerlikon guns; although a far less sophisticated weapon than the Bofors auto-kanon were much lighter, and therefore could track the Fokker fighters more easily when *close in*. The overall evaluation of our AA defense was concluded. The air operations and gunnery officers, the ship's Kapiteins and Admiraal's aboard, all were in agreement that our current Flak batteries were capable of defending the ship from five air targets, coming from each side, at the same time, but out to medium ranges; 3500 meters only and against aircraft types that were soon to be obsolete. Our after training analysis revealed, that a larger caliber Flak weapon of greater range would soon be needed to properly complete the big ship's air defenses. The weapon must be equipped with a powered tracking system, capable of engaging the more modern and generally swifter aircraft out to 10,000 meters.

There were seven *Afstand Zoeker* (stereoscopic optical range finders) on the ship. The big 7.60 meter model, which incorporated the *Ford Fire Control Range Taker* was dedicated to the big guns but could be slaved to the secondary battery.

There were six 3.90 meter *Zeiss* rangefinders. One, which was mounted on the top of 'B' turret was dedicated to the primary and secondary battery only as a redundant set. The other five could be slaved to the secondary battery, or to the two models of AA guns with which the ship was outfitted. These five 3.90 meter range finders had an electrically powered traverse and elevation mechanism capable of tracking fast aircraft. Air defense control could track five air targets and dedicate up to four pairs of Bofors guns and four Oerlikon guns to each target.

However I concluded that the individual Flak battery commanders needed to improve their abilities of identifying the most threatening targets. The excitement of action had to be mastered, with further training to prevent an aircraft being overlooked resulting in a penetration of the ship's AA fire envelope.

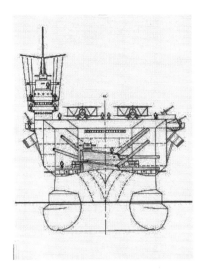

CHAPTER VIII

AIR GROUP TRAINING & FIREFIGHTING

The air group training for conducting anti-shipping attacks, began in the second week of the cruise in mid-August. The aircraft we had aboard at that time were the machines purchased by Argentina and which we inherited when we acquired the ships. Each battle-carrier had aboard one squadron of fifteen Fairy Swordfish Mk 1 torpedo planes, one squadron of fifteen Fairy Sea Fox fighter bombers and two squadrons of fifteen Hawker Sea Fury MK II fighters each. The training was organized to evaluate the capabilities of our air groups in locating and attacking shipping while maintaining an adequate air umbrella defense for the battle carriers. The aircraft were difficult to form into balanced complimentary groups, due to the great differences in their ranges.

If a target was located at a distance of one hundred and fifty miles out we could attack it with torpedoes and bombs. If the air strike was intercepted, the Sea Fox fighter bombers could jettison their bombs and defend the torpedo planes. However if a target was located from two hundred miles to even four hundred miles out we could attack it only with up to thirty torpedo planes.

The lumbering and slow Swordfish bombers operated at ranges far beyond that of our navy fighters and were incapable of defense against any fighter opposition. While the torpedo groups were engaged in very long range missions, the ship's bomber air groups were still capable of launching an attack with thirty Sea Fox out to a range of one hundred and fifty miles and these planes were capable of self-defense, being second class fighters. The Hawker Sea Fury MK II was a well-balanced fighter design, being nimble, reasonably armed and fast for a bi-plane, but with the exception of their range. They were only capable of seventy minuets of flight compared to the seven hours duration of the Swordfish! Consequently they were dedicated to the air umbrella defense of the battle carriers and their screening vessels.

The ship's fighter air umbrella provided the Battle-carrier squadron's long range shield against air attack. Accordingly under war conditions it was the only air group operating continually, regardless of whether there were any strikes planned for the torpedo planes or bombers. The air umbrella may involve all sixty Sea Fury fighters from both ships in emergencies. However, during peace-time operations *condition blue*; we normally deployed only two three plane fighter sections at any one time to cover the entire squadron. The *Cornelis* group would be replaced by a *Johan* group and so on. In this way any section of fighter pilots had seven hours between flights and the aircraft mechanics were able to service the problematic oil cooled engines.

Early on into the air group training we realized that our equipment was at best, a miss-matched lot. Our fighters were unable to escort the strike groups to the battle distances, one associated with an of air-sea battle. Our dive bombers lacked sufficient range as well, and their single little bomb of 100 kilograms was hardly worth the effort, although their speed, guns and agility when *light* gave them some protection from purpose built fighters.

The air groups were originally chosen by the Argentinean Navy, whose strategists envisioned the role of their battle-carriers as weapons to attack enemy harbour and coastal installations with their big guns and bomb coastal shipping and targets inland. Their naval thinking extended only as far as attacks against an enemy's merchant ships and submarines, but not his surface warships, which were considered too fast, and hard to hit. The RNLN, on the other hand must be prepared to seek out and attack all types of shipping including the fast and powerful warships of Imperial Japan.

The Air Group training continued with attacks against two old destroyers and two merchant vessels which were radio controlled from their support ship or from its float plane. The floatplane's altitude gave it a perfect perspective from which to carry out maneuvers to defeat the targeting efforts of attacking planes. In the short time of two weeks we obtained our first hard information on carrier air group operations, what our groups were capable of, and what further refinements were still needed to achieve maximum effectiveness.

The pilots now faced firsthand those simultaneously occurring problems encountered when landing on a small moving deck that both pitched and rolled, as did the aircraft handlers who soon came to fully appreciate the restrictions it imposed on their operations.

The airmen of both battle-carriers found that their operational capability was greatly enhanced when conducting joint operations. By having two flight decks and four service elevators, continual strikes could be launched then recovered, rearmed, refueled and redeployed at a rate which allowed more than just a doubling of the capacity of two widely separated ships.

Once a certain level of efficiency was reached; the next strike missions involved more aircraft, with shorter rotational periods until it was noticed that the men were under pressure to perform the tasks. Then the level of training was held to that point until efficiency was once again attained. In this way we ensured that everyone was capable of safely carrying out their duties.

In order to obtain the most realistic information on the capabilities of our new battlecruiser-carriers, we had to have some system of evaluation that went beyond groups of umpires arguing over the results of an exercise. Unfortunately, we discovered with the *Umpire System*; that the accurate evaluation of results, tended to defer to rank. I therefore had to develop a more realistic system, one that went beyond *Gold-Braid Opinion*. The training aircraft using the new system would now attack our ships with non-exploding bombs and torpedoes to produce *visibly identifiable* hits on the target.

The naval ordinance group had been charged with developing an *Opleidings Torpedo* (training torpedo). It was equipped with an external yellow dye marker in a crushable ceramic warhead that when ruptured against the target's steel hull, shut down the compressed air to the torpedo's turbine, while releasing the dye into the sea and forming a yellow patch on its surface of some 1000 square meters in area. In this way we effectively eliminated any argument as to whether or not a torpedo hit had occurred. Actual hits could now be accurately registered without rupturing the hull of the target or damaging the torpedoes. It was in all respects; a simple and effective solution. We deployed a flotilla of six 15 meter torpedo recovery vessels available for this training, three, stowed aft on each Battlecruiser-carrier.

I was forced to accept the severe limitations of our Sea Fox bombers. The single 100 kilogram bomb while useful against submarines and freighters were not warship killers. Until a replacement bomber could be found we evolved tactics to fit this reality. The Sea Fox fighter bombers would approach a warship and attack with five aircraft releasing their little bombs simultaneously. The fighter bombers would always achieve at least one hit with this method. The theory being, if we could at least damage a warship, its capability would be reduced, and make it vulnerable to torpedo attack. It was a very weak rationale and the casualty rate for this type of attack was estimated as severe. In reality they could come under serious AA fire while employing this method but at the time it was argued that the forward fire of their twin machine guns would suppress the enemy ship's air defenses.

The practice bombs that these light bombers employed was also of a hollow shell configuration, of fired ceramic construction. They were designed to fracture upon impact with a light steel structure and would not rupture if just dropped into the sea. The practice bombs when fractured released a large volume of chemical smoke mixture that indicated a hit.

The training against remote controlled freighters required a means of establishing theoretical damage. We graded the damage in the following way; a freighter if hit by one practice bomb; was assessed to have its speed reduced by half. If hit by two bombs; the speed was reduced by 75%. The engines were then stopped if a third bomb hit. These were designated as *crippled ships*, and left to be sunk by submarine or torpedo plane. In this way the most effective use of the torpedoes was discovered.

The dangers are of course too great to drop even non-exploding practice bombs on crewed target ships. Therefore we employed old German torpedo boats taken as war reparations after the Great War. These were fitted with remote radio control instruments in the wheelhouse and engine room, with the ship maneuvering controlled from an aircraft. These made excellent real life targets for our bombers, which much more accurately demonstrated the true skills or shortcomings of our airmen.

Warship targets were considered to be a much different matter than merchantmen. The warship's large and highly trained crews would have damage control parties, making them a much tougher nut to crack. For small warship targets we allowed a 25% drop in speed for two bomb hits, 50% drop for four bomb hits and so on until eight 100 kilogram bomb hits were required to stop a small warship of destroyer size. There was a time limit on this condition of only an hour, in which she could be finished by torpedo, as its crew would repair their ship and be underway again.

Naturally we did not intend to employ this method against a battleship as an entire cluster of 100 kilogram bombs against that type of ship would cause only the most insignificant damage and probably result in the loss of half of the planes. A strike against a major warship would see the bombers and fighters employed as a diversion only, to cover a determined torpedo bomber attack. The reality was, our bombing capability using the Sea Fox machines against an enemy fleet was rated as 10%. Of course the Swordfish could carry much larger bombs, but could be used only in high altitude level attacks, as they were so vulnerable to Flak. The results of these attacks were far less than the accuracy they achieved with torpedo. While their great wingspan did not allow them to execute high speed diving attacks, or employ effective evasive manouvers.

The Swordfish torpedo plane proved to be our most effective weapon for attacking ships. Coordinated multi-plane attacks could achieve hits on fast targets such as destroyers, although a high expenditure of torpedoes, usually six were launched to obtain one hit. This result was unsatisfactory as our battle carriers followed the established American practice when it came to the ship's magazine inventory, we carried only two torpedoes per torpedo plane!

The battle-carriers now experienced their first war game with our shore based, Fokker T-8 naval torpedo float plane squadrons. These large, twin engine monoplanes were; very modern, and although a bit slow at 285 kph, they carried either a 610 mm torpedo, or 600 kilograms of bombs internally, and possessed a very good range, of over 2700 kilometers. As the Battle-carriers were intended for Dutch East Indies service, our fleet would always have this type of torpedo plane support from our many Naval Air Stations in that colony. Most of these fine machines had been deployed to the East Indies, before the Netherlands defeat in May 1940.

The battle-carrier squadron was some 1100 kilometers out in the Atlantic Ocean one morning when it underwent a massed training attack by thirty of these aircraft! Only my staff knew of this part of the exercise, as it was meant to introduce the element of surprise the men. There were a number of our training flights aloft the time the attack came in, and the *Air umbrella* of seven Sea Fury Fighters didn't raise the alarm immediately as they assumed the T 8's were from our ships. The twin-engine Fokkers aircraft managed to get within ten nautical miles before they were properly identified, and therefore would be within launch range in four minutes!

When Flag Captain Voorne realized that an aerial attack was developing he transmitted a squadron alert to all ships and aircraft aloft. He then rang up the engine room telegraph for maximum revolutions, and began evasive maneuvers. The first torpedo bomber attacks were launched from the port and starboard bows simultaneously.

Three flights of five aircraft were approaching from each side, at a very low altitude almost wave hopping. These ignored the escorting ships and went straight for the battle-carriers which were only making 17 knots on eight boilers connected with four on stand-by. In an effort to economize; the Captain ordered that twelve of these remain unlit, and consequently; were completely cold.

The T-8's were also armed with the *practice torpedoes* of the type that utilized the yellow dye marker crushable warhead. The crushing warhead dissipating the considerable

46

kinetic energy built up by the torpedo's velocity so there was no danger to the side plating of large steel ships, where even the unarmored areas at their thinnest was 20 mm thick. However there was a minor chance of slight damage to the ship propellers, through the nicking of a blade. I could live with that, however as I felt that these exercises were necessarily realistic, and the best way to forecast accurate battle damage.

All the escort vessels now generated smoke and raced to position themselves between the attackers and the capital ships. The *Cornelis de Witt* was belching smoke and maneuvering as she attempted to increase her speed. Of course only a passive defense was available to the ships of the squadron. The fighter umbrella, without ammunition could only buzz the incoming torpedo bombers to distract their aim, but smoke and evasion was all that the ships could really do in peacetime.

However, the attacking T-8'S had gotten in too close, and there was no time for the huge battle-carriers to build up speed and evade effectively. Nevertheless the escorting destroyers strained to protect the big ships. There was also a seven knot wind blowing which tended to dissipate the smoke screening efforts.

The *Johan de Witt*, which had been executing its tactical diameter at best speed, slammed her helm over to port in an attempt to comb the torpedoes. The *Cornelis de Witt* at the same time chose to steam directly downwind at fifteen knots. Now, the vast pall of black funnel smoke generated by the ship, rather than blowing clear, hung about the vessel, and grew to such a volume that it enveloped the entire ship. Although this soon was to become of supreme annoyance to all aboard, I could see what Kapitain Voorne was hoping to achieve; the complete shrouding of his great ship within a smoke cloud.

The escorting vessels, fully cognizant of the ruse, had kept the Vlaggeschip informed of the progress of the torpedo attacks by radio. A number of the torpedo planes had launched their weapons against the still visible *Johan de Witt* and then departed at their best speed. The *Johan* had evaded most of the torpedoes aimed at her, but it was discovered that she was trailing yellow dye from both sides; evidence of at least two simulated hits.

All that could be seen of the Vlaggeschip was her wake trailing out behind a vast grey-brown cloud that slowly drifted across the surface of the water. Therefore the remaining torpedo planes denied a clear target by the smoke chose to simply run up its wake, and launch their weapons. Having accomplished this they flew off. Immediately informed of this development by the escorting vessels, Kapitain Voorne decided to order *all stop* on the turbines, and continued with *way on* only, and rudder amidships coming out of his turn to port.

The *Cornelis de Witt* ceased the generation of the smoke screen, and the battle-carrier majestically drifted clear of the pall. The crews in the transom mounted Bofors Flak battery reported that they could spot no *yellow dye* in our wake. Yet one of our Sea Fury fighters, looking down through the cloud from above, informed us that there was a clear patch of sea visible in which he could identify at least one yellow stain of in our wake.

The Battle-carrier division had been caught with its pants down, and both capital ships had taken hits from slow unescorted torpedo planes. A sobering lesson had been learned; hostilities against our ships may commence at any time and without being proceeded by a formal declaration of war. During the 1930's this had become an increasingly common tool of diplomacy used by both of the Axis Pact States of; Japan and Germany.

However many officer-fliers and Flak Battery commanders agreed that the attack could have been completely stopped if the Anti-Aircraft batteries and fighters had been armed and prepared to defend the vlaggeschip! They made a good point, but I could not agree with it completely as, opening fire on a target is not the same as stopping an attack. It was a case of their assumptions vs the yellow dye in the water. The successful results of this type of air attack, were of course still debatable.

The destroyer; often referred to as the *Greyhound of the Fleet,* is a small warship that has powerful propulsive machinery which consumes fuel at a high rate. These characteristics when combined with the volume limitations of the type, having only a twentieth the displacement of a Capital ship, does not allow for the carrying of sufficient fuel for long voyages. Consequently, they seldom engaged full power, for any length of time.

Destroyers are often occupied in ship to ship refueling, from tankers preferably, but also from other warships which carry large quantities of fuel oil, such as battle-carriers and on occasion even the light cruisers. All the warships of the Battle-carrier fleet practiced the necessary skills of streaming the fuel lines to these ships, coupling and maintaining station while refueling. Refueling at sea operations from warship to warship proved to be a cumbersome and time consuming exercise, although a vital one. During for our peacetime cruises the fleet would travel with the high speed tankers and supply vessels specially built to support this squadron. The 22 knot; 20,000 tonne sister fleet tankers *Groningen* and *Utrecht,* the 22 knot, 16,000 tonne, munitions ship *Nijmegen* and the 22 knot, 18,000 tonne, supply ship *Arnhem.*

In 1936, our naval attaché in Washington; Kapitein Rien Brongers arranged at my request; for a RNLN technical mission to the famous American aircraft carrier; the gigantic *USS Lexington,* the longest class of warship in the world at some 900 feet! She was a vessel approximating the size of the Empire State building lying on its side!

As the lead Naval Architect of the RNLN, I headed up our operational study of this aircraft carrier. An exercise which proved to be of great assistance to our design and commissioning efforts. It was during this technical mission that a minor event occurred, but one which nevertheless illustrated the level of that ship's versatility, and experienced seamanship.

One afternoon, returning to the Philadelphia Naval Yard after conducting a major flight operations demonstration, Captain Bledsoe; the Lexington's Commander, was informed that the tug assigned to his 300 meter long ship had suddenly began to develop thrust problems, and was not under control, his reaction was immediate and effective!

The huge carrier not under its own power, in a very confined space and with its towering profile, was at the mercy of the light breeze. Responding with characteristic professionalism to a potential crisis; Bledsoe gave orders to the standby crews of six prepositioned aircraft parked on the flight deck.

Three fighters up forward and three aft had arranged athwart ships, with the machines firmly lashed down and had their wheels blocked. Their standby crews; being all *aircraft taxi qualified* tradesmen, occupying their cockpits had the engines of these six machines running and warm. The aircraft's combined power of 5,400 hp and variable pitch Hamilton propellers enabled the Captain to gently move his huge ship completely sideways into her berth as carefully as a mother putting her child into its crib! An impressive example of men and material in action!

The tug which had lost its propeller, was drifting dead in the water was entirely helpless. In the modern world of the 1980's, many similarly large ships are equipped with underwater bow and stern thruster propellers aligned athwart ships. But this was how it was handled back in the 1930's.

The only US crewman who was *up in arms*, over this display was the *"Lady Lex's"* aircraft maintenance officer; one, Lt. Commander Dexter Arbuckle. He took the opportunity to remind the ship's captain of the extra wear put on the precious engines, which did not have the cooling benefits of air traveling past their cylinder cooling vanes at 400 kph.

Upon recalling these events, I then hatched an idea to conduct an experiment using our own equipment, but in a slightly different manner. Given the tremendous power of aircraft engines, I wanted to determine what speed the ship could obtain with a group of our aircraft lashed down on the flight deck. In this way I hoped to add to our tactical flexibility. For this test I told Kapitein Voorne to assume that the *Cornelis de Witt* had lost all power for steaming due to damage, and therefore I ordered the placement of twenty planes aft on the flight deck having a total of 9,600 kilowatts combined. These were lashed down, aft of 'B' Elevator, facing forward and blocked. The Engine room was signaled to cut power to the shaft turbines. The propellers would slowly rotate as the ship proceeded under momentum alone. The aircraft's engines were started and warmed up. Conscious of the threat of overheating the engines, of this test I laid hoses forward to create a fresh water mist which the propeller would pull over the cylinder vanes, cooling the engine.

I retrieved the technical manual for the ship from shelving in the Command Center, and flipped through its pages. The ship's propulsive data revealed that the kilowatt utilization curves indicated that a speed of 11 knots was achievable with 9,600 kilowatts. The *Cornelis* which had been making 17 knots gradually lost way until it hovered at a speed of 10 knots! And an attempt to steering the ship using the aircraft rudders alone actually worked although with almost imperceptible slowness!

I was very pleased with the ship's response to the thrust of her aircraft's engines. I soon became aware that my senior aircraft maintenance officer Lt. Commander Vanderlay standing close by my right elbow, and was watching the demonstration with unease. He then addressed Kapitein Voorne in a loud voice, "Sir, I understand the source of this exercise, but it would be worth to recall that the *Lexington's* aircraft were equipped with air-cooled engines, and we are using some aircraft that are oil cooled." Voorne replied, "Your point is well taken Lt. Commander, but on any training cruise, like a commissioning cruise, equipment may be *tested to destruction*, so that we may discover our total capability."

Fifteen minutes of this experimentation had passed, and the aircraft engines were maintaining a reasonable temperature due to the cooling effects of the fresh water misting. The *Alternate Propulsion Experiment*, had produced results that had satisfied my curiosity. I turned to Captain Voorne and told him to resume normal steaming, and return the aircraft to their hangars. I then complimented the relieved Lt. Commander, on his well-maintained aircraft engines, and explained that the experiment had just demonstrated that the engines of the ship's *combat cripples* may one day just save it. He seemed content with this, as all traces of concern vanished from his face.

The firefighting training on the battle-carriers was especially intense. Our big ships used a combination of inert gas to flood the compartments and fuel lines, and both salt and fresh water sprays to fight fires throughout the carrier. Within the aircraft hangar spaces, large asbestos impregnated, isolation curtains were employed. These divided the large aircraft hangar spaces into five zones for the upper hangar and three, for the lower hangar to isolate any fires. The gravity deployed, deck head mounted asbestos fire curtains had a few problems. When deployed they occasionally landed on aircraft which prevented complete atmospheric isolation of the compartment. They were also extremely heavy after wetting down and took a lot of time to dry out before repacking. Nevertheless they worked sufficiently well in containing the fire and when used in conjunction with the CO_2 gas and the water misting system the flames were quickly extinguished. For these events; all the damage control teams were issued with a special carbon particle filtered breathing apparatus to protect them from the deadly fumes and smoke generated by fires as well as the lethal fumes of the CO_2 gas firefighting system.

The utilization of fresh water sprays and mists aboard aircraft carriers were unique to the RNLN. The purpose was to use it to fight fires in the hangar decks where salt water corrosion would damage our expensive aircraft. Then as now; an aircraft carrier's planes cost almost as much as the ship itself! Aboard each of the battlecruiser-carriers there were two freshwater tanks of 800,000 liters to supply this service, one located in the forward and one aft in the triple bottom tanks. They were filled at dockside, but in a good rainstorm they were filled from the flight deck scuppers as were all the non-potable water tanks. The ship's condensers were seldom overworked, as distilled water for the boilers was easily supplemented by rain water run-off, from the huge flight deck.

When I evaluated, how much we had learned about operating air groups at sea in the brief time of that first month long cruise. I had sober reflections on how skilled the naval aviators and air technicians of our rival navies must be, who like Great Britain and America have trained with naval aviation for close to twenty years!

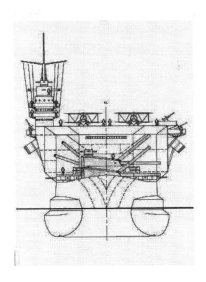

CHAPTER IX

BATTLE-CARRIER WAR GAME

The final portion of this first training cruise was the highly anticipated simulated carrier group vs. carrier group engagement. The squadron was divided into two task groups, of equal strength. During the night each group made away at high speed in a separate directions. At dawn the two groups of vessels were to seek out and attack one another.

For this exercise, ship to ship communication was limited to Morse lamp. Air to ship communication generally involved a series of short coded radio signals, at specific times. While aircraft location, involved the use of Radio Direction Finding Loop Antenna (RDF), and triangulation.

The squadron having the *Johan de Witt* as flagship was under the overall command of Luitenant Admiraal Konrad van Speijk. Escorting the *Johan* were the cruisers *Gouden Leeu* and *Aemilia* supported by the destroyers *Zeeland, Gelderland, Jakhals and Bulhond*. My Command; the *Cornelius de Witt*, was supported by the cruisers *Prins te Paard, Oliphant* with the destroyers *Eendragt, Zoutman, Piet Heyn* and *Draak*.

Both of the Battle-carrier Swordfish Squadrons were, for this exercise, armed with the same type of practice torpedo as used by our Fokker T-8 torpedo bombers, those having the '*Yellow dye marker charged, Crushable warhead*'. The training of these pilots was as close to realism that we could make it, short of engaging them with our Flak batteries, and they utilized the same attack methods for crewed or unmanned targets.

However, the Sea Fox fighter-bomber's 100 kg practice bombs; that were so effective when used on unmanned stationary and radio controlled targets could not be utilized on a *manned ship* for obvious reasons. A manned target required totally different equipment for the bombers.

To simulate a load they were limited to a maximum speed of 227 mph. The dual role of these aircraft as fighters found them equipped with gun and belly cameras to evaluate the effects of the plane's machinegun fire and bombs. To claim a bomb hit the pilot would fly over the deck of the target select the belly camera button, snap a few frames then expel a one liter bladder of yellow dye through a small port below the cockpit. The photographs were developed and then evaluated with any physical evidence of yellow dye droplets on the target's decks to determine if a hit was obtained. The limitation of this improvisation was that it did not provide an immediate and unchallengeable result like the chemical smoke bomb. Umpires had to search for dye stains on ships which resulted in delays tallying simulated bomb hits. Although the method worked, it nevertheless still seemed a bit crude.

At 20:00hrs, in the first opening move; the two groups of vessels, which had been steaming some ten kilometers apart broke away from each other and made off at 25 knots. The success of this type of exercise depended upon who could get in the first air strike on the other squadron's carrier. The tactic of choice was to launch a reconnaissance air group at first light, have them locate the enemy, radio in their position and then launch the attack. Logic dictated that, if I could somehow maintain contact with the enemy, following the initial separation, we could avoid the *search phase*, and launch our attack immediately at first light. Accordingly, I detached the destroyer *Draak* to seek out and establish contact with the enemy, shadow until dawn then radio their position, and if the opportunity existed, launch an independent torpedo attack against the opposing battle-carrier.

The *Cornelis* launched a Swordfish torpedo plane at 10:30hrs, to track the enemy squadron by its phosphorescent wake. These versatile aircraft could fly a search pattern for nine hours without the weight of its torpedo. Conditions were ideal; being partially overcast and quite dark, the wake was not too difficult to make out. The torpedo plane, having located the enemy force, located the *Draak* with the assistance of the destroyer's infrared Morse lamp. Flying low over its deck, she dropped a message buoy, equipped with a faint blue light. In this way the vessel received the information, without breaking radio silence. While these operations were underway I speculated on what methods would be employed by the *Johan Group* to locate my squadron and how we could defeat them.

At 02:00hrs the clouds dissipated and the sea lay like mercury under a harvest moon. The *Draak* was clearly visible to the Swordfish flying a search pattern eight nautical miles away. The wakes of the *Johan's* squadron of ships could no longer be seen in this light, so the torpedo plane, departed on a dead reckoning course in an attempt to locate the *Johan Group*. After flying for 60 nautical miles on this heading the ships were identified moving at moderate speed to the south west.

The plane then returned to the *Cornelis* and by 04:00hrs the battle-carrier had worked up to thirty knots, closing the distance to the target. A strike group of 12 torpedo planes and 15 fighter bombers was being prepared for launching. Captain Voorne expressed a feeling of jubilation, as these aircraft making up the first attack left the ship.

Lt. Commander Drebble received a transmission from his flagship locating the *Johan de Witt's* squadron. He then calculated that an unexpected surface attack by a lone destroyer coming from the dark side of dawn, had a chance of success. The *Draak* was therefore committed by her commander to a defiant gesture; a lone suicide attack against the ships of the *Johan group*.

Accordingly, the destroyer had been closing at 33 knots since 02:12hrs. Now at 4:30hrs against the ruddy dawn of a new day the target ships were visible at a range of some 25,000 meters, moving in tight formation, at a speed of no more than 10 knots.

Lt. Commander Drebble at the time felt that there was something unusual about this formation. There was sufficient light for the carrier to operate her air umbrella, yet no aircraft could be discerned in the sky. The escorting vessels should have been picketed out at least a nautical mile from the battle carrier, yet they were all bunched together. Commander Drebble, then decided to take advantage of the excellent target they presented. He ordered all torpedo tubes prepared for launch, and with her bow buried in foam and producing a stern wave that rose a meter above the after deck, the *Draak* turned bow onto the target and closed the range at flank speed.

The operator of the 3.0 meter Main battery stereoscope; Chief Petty Officer Rangefinder; Hanns Stoope, located above the wheelhouse in a small lightly armored tower stared through his high power glasses at the target and slowly called out the decreasing ranges. He now noticed a change in the course of the largest vessel still silhouetted against the dawn. The ship was turning to port exposing her entire beam, and distinctive silhouette for the first time to the attacking destroyer, now only 12,000 meters away, and still undetected. Within the darkened confines of the Rangefinder compartment the phosphorescent glow from the instruments painted P.O. Stoope's face in a soft green. With his eyes fixed to the rubber cups of the stereoscope his broad grin soon transformed into one of astonishment and then disgust! He hailed the bridge and reported; with ill-concealed disappointment evident in his voice to Commander Drebble that the intended target appeared to be a large factory whaling ship with her attendant fleet of hunting vessels!

Completely exasperated; Commander Drebble immediately broke off the attack and informed the *Cornelis de Witt,* with rapid 'PQ', a prearranged Morse signal; that the target had been misidentified. The *Draak,* now slowing quickly approached the fishing vessels at 10 knots. The ship which had been mistaken for the *Johan de Witt* and its escorts, was in fact the Norwegian factory whaling ship *Vulcania,* a large vessel of 15,000 tonnes and her brood of six fast hunting vessels of 700 tonnes each. These were clustered around the factory ship; engaged in dropping off of whale carcasses for flensing and butchering. A thousand gulls must have been in attendance gorging on the offal. Even at half a mile their angry greedy cries carried across the water. The whaling men, subjected to such a racket and busily plying their trade hadn't yet become aware of the *Draak's* approach.

The receipt of the *Draak's* disappointing information caused a minor panic in the air operations center of the *Cornelis de Witt.* My squadron was easily identifiable now as the sun was well up, and we had no idea where our opponent was. We had to consider that our ships by this time may have already been located by *Johan de Witt's* scouts. Everyone went into high gear as we expected an air attack to develop at any moment. There were seven Sea Fury fighters up already, and the remainder were prepared and launched.

The *Cornelis's* strike group was now some forty nautical miles out and heading for a false target! The Sea Fox fighter bombers, due to their relatively short range were immediately recalled. The Swordfish torpedo planes having seven hours of duration at full load, were ordered to begin a search pattern to the west at high altitude.

Commander Drebble allowed his ship to move slowly towards the busy fleet of whaling craft as he felt very much exposed. His destroyer of 2,200 tonnes was not that much larger than the whale hunting vessels, and each was equipped with harpoon cannon on their foc'sle decks. The whaling operation generated a huge offal bloom with the blood and bits of whale flesh attracting thousands of sea birds. The *Draak* drifted into this patch of rich nutrients and quickly attracted hundreds of these creatures seeking refuge from the multitude of sharks. These, drawn by the blood in the water, snapped automatically at any object including the waterfoul.

The seabirds that wheeled about her, settled thickly on the *Draak* and hid her features under their bodies, camouflaging its identity quite effectively from the air. The drone of aircraft engines could be heard faintly over the gulls. Lookouts reported to Commander Drebble that aircraft were preparing to fly over the whaling ships. He located the aircraft with his glasses and concluded that these aircraft, were definitely British model fighters but couldn't be from the *Cornelis* squadron. As these planes closed he could distinguish their red painted engine cowlings marking them as coming from the fighter umbrella of the *Johan de Witt* which meant that she was close by.

The two Sea Fury fighters attempted a close inspection of the whaling ships but the huge cloud of seabirds kept them at a distance. Not wanting to risk bird hits on the aircraft, the pilots after a few attempts at observation circled back towards their battle-carrier squadron.

The aircraft's radio frequency was quickly located by the *Draak's* radio officer and the fighter's transmissions reported these vessels as a whaling operation. They had completely overlooked the *Draak* as she was lying close in among the group of hunting vessels, with her features effectively distorted.

To the west and low on the horizon could be seen the smoke and ships of a squadron. Over these vessels several aircraft could faintly be discerned wheeling in formation. The *Johan de Witt* and her escorts had been located, and they were closing his position rapidly.

Aboard the *Johan de Witt* Luitenant Admiraal Konrad van Speijk was enjoying a feeling of confidence. The *Cornelis de Witt* had been spotted at 04:07hrs and seemed unaware of that fact, as her fighter umbrella had not attempted to engage the lone reconnaissance swordfish. That plane, like all involved in the exercise, had an assigned sector to patrol. By knowing its speed and the flight time elapsed, its signal located her position for her carrier. The air-gunner/radio operator sent a very brief signal which positively located the *Cornelis Group*.

The attack group of planes already fueled, armed and waiting on the flight deck was rapidly prepared to be launched. When the last plane had flown off at 04:20hrs, the remaining attack groups were being brought up out of the aircraft hangar on 'B' Elevator, loaded with practice torpedoes and bombs. The planes were rolled to their assigned positions on the flight deck and had their wings unfolded.

The *Johan de Witt* was making her maximum speed and heading directly for her target some 140 nautical miles distant. It was the intention of her commander; Commodore Bronckhorst to close the distance and meet her returning air group which at this time should be within visual range of their intended victim. The sky was devoid of enemy planes, and off the port bow at 18,000 meters there was a cluster of ships which her fighter umbrella had identified as a large whaling factory ship surrounded by seven hunting vessels busily engaged in dropping off the carcasses of their kills for processing.

05:30hrs aboard the *Draak* Commander Drebble couldn't believe his luck. His headlong charge to attack the perceived enemy squadron had resulted in a high expenditure of fuel, only to discover a whaling fleet. Now in a total reversal of fortune the desired target was approaching his position at high speed!

The big-battle carrier and its escorts were now no more than 7,000 meters away and appeared to be on a course that would take the flagship less than 2,000 meters from the whaling ships. Aboard the destroyer, six practice torpedoes were in their launch tubes and all was in readiness to fire. The *Draak* by utilizing her twin screws with skill managed to hover just 200 meters behind the bow of the large factory ship hiding itself from close observation by the battle-carrier's range finders. Commander Drebble intended to launch the first six fish at 4,000 meters a distance which should at the combined speeds of target and torpedoes result in hits within two minutes. Upon immediate reloading the remaining six torpedoes would be launched in two groups of three at wide dispersal on bearings that would approximate the position of the flagship if it attempted to evade the first torpedo group to port or to starboard.

The approach of the huge battle-carrier and her escorts so close to his whaling operation, eventually got the attention of the captain of the big factory ship. The proximity of the small unknown vessel obviously a warship laying close to his vessels increased his interest as a number of his officers raised their binoculars to scan the approaching fleet and then alternated to observe the *Draak*.

The captain of the factory ship lifted his binoculars to view the bridge of the small warship lying close off his starboard bow. At 150 meters distance, even the faces of its crew were easily distinguishable. A few moments ago the naval officers had been waving in his direction good-naturedly. Now he could observe all of them intently observing the rapidly approaching group of warships. Suddenly, now in his powerful glasses the naval officers could be observed barking soundless orders and to his amazement the vessel began to launch its torpedoes!

The captain of the *Vulcania*, came to the realization that he might be occupying a front row seat at the expansion of the hostilities still raging in Spain, a limited conflict, but one having gigantic international repercussions! But whose ships were these? The approaching fleet had a huge warship at its center and was obviously therefore a British Royal Navy formation. The smaller warship still lying motionless off his starboard bow was unidentifiable as its flag was hanging limply at the masthead. Aboard the small warship obviously a destroyer or torpedo boat of an unidentified navy could be observed the highly animated crew rapidly reloading the torpedo tubes for another attack. A slight breeze shifted the flag so that the captain thought that he could distinguish the red and white of the Soviet naval ensign! The Captain of the whale factory ship, raced to the conclusion that the Soviet warship was going to attack the British ships, and his whaling operation may be viewed by the British as assisting in the attack, after-all the little torpedo boat was sitting motionless close by his attendant fleet of 700 tonne whale hunters, and looked almost indistinguishable from them.

05:33hrs aboard the *Johan de Witt* Kapitein van der Hulst was observing the whaling fleet some 3,000 meters off his starboard bow. A great plume of black smoke began rising out of the single stack aboard the big mother ship as she was forcing her boilers to raise full steam obviously in preparation to get underway. He quickly realized also this was a very unusual activity for the whaling factory ship as she was girdled round with whale carcasses awaiting processing. At that moment he noticed a Morse lamp signal flashing from the bridge of the large whaling ship; *To RN aircraft carrier and escorts approaching my ships, from Norwegian whale factory ship M.V. Vulcania; are you at war? Unknown destroyer; (believed Soviet), located behind my flotilla has launched torpedoes at you!*

Kapitein Van der Hulst, obviously startled, turned to his air operations officer; Kap. Lt. Jan Florisz, and ordered his planes to take a closer look at those whaling ships. Florisz replied that he would order it but cautioned, that to get too close to the whaling ships risked the downing of the aircraft from collision with any one of the thousands of seabirds circling overhead. Van der Hulst then turned to his executive officer; Kap. Lt. ter Zee Arnold Mussert, and ordered him to dispatch *Jakhals* and *Bulhond* to close the whaling ships and investigate the report of an unidentified warship behind the whaling vessels. At that moment Van der Hulst received a further signal from his aircraft informed him that the air umbrella reported six torpedoes, in the water, wide dispersion approaching the starboard bow at a distance of 500 meters. Kapitein van der Hulst ordered an immediate turn to port to comb the missiles although he knew that he only had perhaps fifteen seconds before impact, nevertheless his ship making 30 knots, he knew, was reasonably maneuverable for its size.

Meanwhile the commander of the light cruiser *Gouden Leeu*, in a suicide attempt to screen his vlaggeschip, raced up the battle carrier's starboard side and took two torpedo hits indicated by the yellow dye patches growing on the surface of the sea. Two other torpedoes passed astern of the cruiser, between her and the flagship which was now 90 degrees to her original course, while the remaining two torpedoes slammed into the *Johan's* rudder area. An umpire stationed on board the battle-carrier in a transom mounted AA Bofors gun tub reported two hits on the flagship's rudders and propellers. The *Johan de Witt* continued on with her hard a port maneuver, but was forced to slow and was parallel to her original path but on the opposite course when three more torpedoes slammed into her port side.

The exercise umpires aboard the *Johan de Witt* having recorded five torpedo hits on the battle carrier, eventually declared it to have a condition of heavy damage, with an assumed list sufficient to suspend air operations, with a loss of steering and all engines stopped, and out of action for three hours. To me this was an overly generous appraisal, *out of action and in a sinking condition*, would have been more to the mark! The umpires on board the *Gouden Leeu* declared her: *heavily damaged, out of action and in a sinking condition*, which I agreed with. If the *Cornelis's* planes would have found the *Johan de Witt* at that time, the exercise would have been concluded in our favor in short order.

The officers aboard the *Draak* seeing the cruiser and battle-carrier slow and then stop realized that they had achieved an exceptional success, and as two enemy destroyers were approaching, Commander Drebble ordered a withdrawal at high speed keeping the whaling ships between the enemy and herself. Shortly after the *Draak* steamed clear of the whaling operation and its blanketing clouds of seabirds, the *Johan's* fighter umbrella identified the assailant and persued but as they carried only machine guns and they were theoretically unable to score any points against her.

Commander Drebble, realizing that there were no enemy bombers or torpedo planes visible, with only the *Johan de Witt's* fighter umbrella able to oppose his retirement, felt that he had every chance of success if his ship could outrun the enemy destroyers now in hot pursuit. Commander Drebble's final significant act in the day's drama was to radio the exact location of the enemy fleet to his Admiraal and inform him of the successful attack of his ship which crippled the enemy battle-carrier and one of her escorting cruisers. Commander Drebble marveled at his success, looking aft he observed his pursuers. Smoke belched from their stacks and their bows were buried in white foam as they piled up huge bow waves, running at flank speed. They were determined to bring the *Draak* within the range of their guns, at which time they could assume theoretical hits based on mathematical probability and accumulate at least some points for their squadron.

While that action was concluding the *Johan de Witt's* first attack group fell upon the *Cornelis's* squadron. The aggressors were composed of twelve Swordfish escorted by five Sea Fox bombers flying light and acting in the fighter role. The *Cornelis* had all fifteen Sea Fury fighters up, alerted her bomber groups that were just starting to arrive back at the ship. These bombers having expended less than half of their fuel were immediately ordered to abandon their bombing mission, revert to fighter status, assume CAP duty and attack the enemy swordfish formation. Initially there was some confusion as the bombers tried to sort out the situation, as they were trying to distinguish the enemy aircraft by silhouette, which were the same machines as their own! But as soon as *that kicked* in they realized that the *Johan's* aircraft had red noses, they were fine. (All of *Cornelis de Witt's* aircraft have yellow painted engine covers and cowlings.)

The alerted battle-carrier already conducting evasive maneuvers at 30 knots, began generating large quantities of black smoke as did her escorts. Nothing more could have been done so every effort was made to spot the launch of torpedoes or their wakes and steer the ship to avoid them.

The torpedo planes from the *Johan de Witt* now divided into two groups and chose to approach the target at right angles to one another. The attack was skillfully carried out across the *Cornelis's* bows, and was intended to form a large grid pattern through which the ship could not avoid steaming. The depth control on the torpedoes were set at 8 meters and intended to pass under an escorting cruiser. The Swordfish came on relentlessly wave-hopping to the target. At 1,000 meters the aircraft began launching their torpedoes with at three second intervals between each fish. In this way the anticipated grid would be quite large and unavoidable.

The escorts of the torpedo bombers positioned themselves some 100 meters above their charges and weaved back and forth. The *Cornelis de Witt's* `fighter umbrella now swollen to about thirty aircraft made repeated head on runs at the attacking formation. As this was only an exercise, there was of course no shooting. The tactic commonly known as *playing chicken* was never the less distracting as it was quite deadly if an error in judgment was made. The last torpedo having been launched the attacking formations departed, continually under assault by our fighters.

Kapitein Voorne, at this time was heavily inundated with numerous reports flooding into his command center, from aircraft aloft, the anti-aircraft batteries, and the engine room, while at the same time he attempted to guide his massive vessel through the area of danger. The helmsman, an experienced hand calmly followed his skippers instructions, and spun the polished steel wheel first to port and then to starboard. Everyone in the citadel battle bridge held on as my big ship twisted violently and danced across the sea. Miraculously the determined torpedo attack generated no hits on the *Cornelis de Witt!*

One of the attacking Sea Fox bombers engaged in attacking the battle-carrier found himself almost in collision with the island structure. The pilot released dye and snapped a few pictures from his gun and belly mounted cameras. During de-briefing this pilot claimed that he could have crashed into the air operations platform of the *Cornelis* in a suicide attack. Initially his claim was discounted but when his aircraft's film was developed and some dye stain was located on the deckhouse his claim was upheld and the *Cornelis* was assessed to have sustained serious upper works damage that degraded further efficient air operations.

At 05:57hrs the *Draak's* message describing its successful attack was received by Kapitein Voorne and passed on to me. I ordered him to transmit the location of the enemy squadron to our lingering torpedo squadron and to continue the attack on the crippled *Johan de Witt* and the crippled cruiser. By 06:00hrs these orders had been acted on and our planes some 100 nautical miles from target were closing to launch an attack in one hour.

At 06:30hrs the flagship received a weather report from Naval Headquarters in Amsterdam that very heavy weather was moving in from the northwest and gave data on the potential of the storm. I ordered a transmission to all ships and aircraft that the exercise was terminated. The fleet was ordered to reform on the Vlaggeschip and all aircraft were to return to their ships, and the fleet was to concentrate, rig for very heavy weather and make for home.

September 17, 1938 the 1st Battle-carrier Division passed into the naval base at Den Helder, Noord Holland, after battling to windward in a Force 10 gale for most of two days. The entire squadron had performed well in their role of screening the battle carriers during air operations, in seamanship, especially the cruisers and small destroyers in such heavy weather.

The first training cruise had obtained much valuable data that would form the basis of our future operations. In the competition between battlecruiser-carrier squadrons the *Cornelis de Witt* beat out the *Johan de Witt* in overall points as it was considered that her strategy of shadowing the *Johan* with a ship and aircraft was the decisive strategy leading to a victorious action. The *Johan de Witt* was considered *best battle-carrier at tactical operations* as her air groups were first to locate and attack her opposite and she had also won the gunnery competition. The overall *Outstanding Ship Citation* went to the destroyer *Draak* and her skipper Lt. Commander Eelke Drebble. His inspired location and attack on the *Johan de Witt's* squadron, an action; had it been carried out under war conditions, would have been regarded as most daring and highly successful.

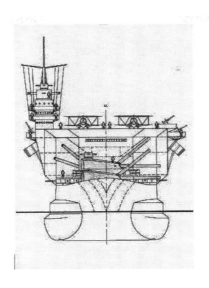

CHAPTER X

THE DUTCH NAVAL CRISIS OF 1939

The spring of 1939 brought with it no sense of freshness or renewal that one would expect from that change of season which issues in new life. Quite to the contrary; the stink of injustice and evil in Europe was like the foul odor of a dead rat under the kitchen floorboards, and one which grew ever stronger as the weather warmed with the passing of weeks.

Many Europeans could not understand why America and Great Britain; the *self-proclaimed champions of democracy*, had seemingly sided with the Fascist invaders of Spain? The American and British news services sidestepped any serious investigation into the great question of WHY? How could little Spain, an impoverished nation of some nine million souls pose a threat to these two super powers, who with their combined great wealth: fully half that of the planet, and having a total population with that of their colonies numbering close to one billion souls? After all; the government of Spain was only a very weak coalition, cobbled together from many parties such as the Barber's union, the Railway union, the Miner's Union, the Peasant's Union and such. It had come to power through democratic elections and it was recognized by the League of Nations as entirely legitimate. Yet America and Britain had, with the aid of Hitler and Mussolini, placed a naval blockade on Spanish ports. They allowed Nazi troops, weapons and munitions to enter, destined for the Fascist Armies of the Rebel General Franco, and the German and Italian expeditionary forces, while at the same time denying basic aid to the hard pressed Spanish population defending its first taste of Political power. Could it be that these two *great democracies* feared a *true democracy*, and the simple idea that the socialist leaning political parties of the most humble citizens could come to power? Were they really that afraid of the example that Spain had set for their own disenfranchised millions, still suffering after long grueling years of depression? I personally held the opinion that the American and British Governments' complicancy in the crushing of the young democracy of an enfeebled small country, was a dishonorable and foul undertaking for two such highly respected and powerful nations.

The individual must know his place in this world, and determine where his loyalty lies if he is to survive and prosper. I was after all an officer in the navy of a nation that was governed by a Monarchy which was a Colonial power, yet my heart was with the struggling Spanish Republic and its tattered civilian militia. The daily news from *Espania* had become appalling, with the brutalization of the non-combatant population. However by 1939, the fourth year of Civil war; the *great moral issue* of that struggle had been decided. The Nazis had triumphed, and had broken the back of Spain's civilian army. Wealth, privilege and military power trumped the rights of the common citizen to determine his or her own fate by democratic election. For the working men and women of Spain, 1939 was the beginning of the end, as the revolution wound down to its tragic conclusion.

But another political crisis was reaching a flashpoint at the other end of Europe. The Netherland's Office of Political Intelligence; *Polticke Inlichtingendienst I* (PID), was able to predict with a 97% chance of certainty that Poland, was the next on Hitler's list, and that nation would be attacked by Germany in the late summer of 1939! Both the *Eerst Kamer* and *Tweed Kamer*; (First and Second Houses of Parliament) were briefed on this intelligence. Such an act would initiate an all-out war on the Continent. There was no doubt that the proud and martial Poles would resist, and a conflict would begin, one which many believed would draw in Britain, and France, thereby precipitating a second global conflict. Indeed, this clash soon became unavoidable as in August of that year, both France and Great Britain had guaranteed Poland's freedom, in exchange for vital cryptographic hardware. The vitally important equipment was developed by engineers working for Poland's Secret service, which was able to decode German Top Secret Military Transmissions. (Known as *Enigma*, this was the greatest military secret of WW II, and was only declassified in 1979!)

In another ominous development, the Dutch Crypto Service; *Codedienst* (CD), had intercepted information through its contacts in Germany, and was able to discover that the Fascist Dictator General Franco, had ordered all Italian military forces, and the German *Kondor Legion* (a Luftwaffe Bomber unit) *to be out of Spain by the end of March 1940, to avoid a diplomatic incident with France.* Interpreting this with other data CD forecasted with a 93% level of certainty; that Germany was preparing to launch an attack against France. Their invasion would come along the traditional route; that being west through the *Low Countries*, to skirt the end terminus of the Maginot Line and into France. The date; no later than May 01, 1940! Both the Eerst Kamer and Tweed Kamer were briefed once again, and their members finally accepted that the Nazis would respect no border of a European nation, and that the Netherlands freedom hung on the mere whim of Hitler.

Therefore plans were formulated to allow the Netherland national identity to continue abroad. It had been decided that the vast and rich colonies of the Dutch East Indies, would become the Netherland's new cultural, political and commercial heart until the tides of war had ebbed. There in that Pacific paradise; new centers of administration and finance would be established, remote and secure from any European conflict.

Great Britain; had anticipated close cooperation in any future maritime strategy with the forces of the Netherlands to contain Nazi Germany. During the last two months, beginning in February 1939, the Netherlands had begun to receive entreaties from Great Britain suggesting that the RNLN may want to consider using the RN's Scapa Flow facility as an alternate base for the bulk of the Dutch fleet. The First Lord of the Admiralty had consequently directed that a dormant section of those extensive facilities at that naval base be reactivated for the anticipated arrival of our ships. There was great logic behind this; as the Netherlands had no strategy to combat Germany, with our fleet based easily threatened in Den Helder Noord-Holland. Whereas the remote location, of Scapa Flow in northern Scotland was seen by the RNLN as a safe haven in case of Germany striking west.

Great Britain, we came to believe; considered that our navy's main base in Den Helder, was impossible to defend and were fearful lest our ships fall into German hands, whereupon these would be commissioned into the *Kriegsmarine* and be employed to sail against Great Britain and her Colonies.

The Prime Minister's Office however was not keen on the British offer and held the opinion that; *"If our fleet was relocated to Scapa Flow, it would at best be well positioned to put in place a naval blockade of Germany, and conduct convoy escort, only to bolster Great Britain's strategy, her centuries old formula for dealing with an aggressive continental power. Our ships would be under British control, as they would now become dependent upon them for supply. In the worst case scenario of a military crisis, the ships may be seized, then used as England required to safeguard her Maritime empire. While the Netherlands enjoys good relations with Great Britain, we have not built up our Navy to protect the British Isles or its Empire, but to protect our own far-flung Colonial interests, and the well-being of the Dutch people."*

The British nevertheless kept pressing this proposal with a regularity that became annoying; as their entreaties also tended to become increasingly less diplomatic, as the tense weeks of 1939 ticked down. It soon became clear to our strategic planners that the fleet must make a move out of Den Helder, as the proximity of our naval vessels so close to the German border, was a tempting prize, which must now be viewed by Whitehall as a strategic threat to British security.

Many Britons viewed the Dutch as close cousins to the Germans, and were a people that had in the past, been a formidable foe of their Island Kingdom, all of which in fact was true. These factors contributed to certain nervous uneasiness in the minds of the British people, and raised questions of what choices the Netherlands may make when confronted if the German move westward?

In recognition of a possible threat against our fleet coming from Britain, the Netherland's Naval Intelligence Service; *Office Van Zeeinlichtingen* (OVZ), in the hope of conveying the urgency of the situation to our Government, and thereby forcing them to act, presented them with a scenario, which they labeled *Dreeigend Gevaar;* (Imminent Threat). Outlined very briefly; the following theoretical scenario; *Localized surprise attacks by parachutists against key targets behind the Dutch frontier, would undoubtedly precede a full scale attack westwards by the Wehrmacht. There would be no declaration of war by Germany. One of these targets would certainly be the Dutch Fleet in Den Helder. A tethered mine field could be laid nocturnally by torpedo boat and U-boat in the shallow waters of the Waddenzee off the entrance to the naval base, and Texel Island. A battle group composed of naval marines and parachute troops could in fact paralyze Den Helder naval base, trapping our fleet and preventing its escape to the open sea. Should the unthinkable happen, and the fleet be captured intact, then Hitler would now possess an additional strategic weapon to use against any transatlantic convoy operations.*

Both the Kreigsmarine and the Royal Navy understood this danger. Logic would dictate that each service had drawn up contingency plans, and had by now presented these military operations to their respective Governments. One plan being enabled to acquire a great prize, while the other; designed to prevent this from occurring. Our first suspicion that such a plan had been prepared was a certain nervous tension noticed in the deportment of a contingent of Royal Navy officers sent to further press us with their earlier proposal designed to move the fleet out of Den Helder. The frankness evident in straight forward talk of these senior officers led us to believe that they were desperate to avoid some alternative military action viewed by them as appalling.

The OVZ scenario had been estimated as 87% probable! Both the *Eerst Kamer* and *Tweed Kamer* (the upper and lower houses of parliament); although thoroughly convinced of the danger, still viewed the fleet's move out of Den Helder with extreme reluctance, and countered with; *"Such a redeployment of the fleet to Scapa Flow would be seen as an ominous development, one which may be twisted by the German Propaganda Ministry and turned back upon us to look like a provocation to Hitler. There would be further consequences in that such a move would create a sense of abandonment by the people, compounded by an unavoidable devaluation of the Guilder!"*

The procrastinations continued however, with a great wringing of hands. Too many bloody businessmen in Government these days I told myself! The OVZ, kept insisting with urgency, and the PID backed their position, and informed the Defense Minister Deckkert; that reliable contacts in London now feel certain that several sections in the British Admiralty are operating in a top secret crisis mode regarding the RNLN! The PID operatives interpreted this as evidence that the RN would adopt preemptive action immediately following a German attack westward, and would involve a strike by British Air and Sea forces to destroy the Dutch Fleet, along the lines of the OVZ scenario, thereby denying it to Hitler!

The Dutch Government; was now presented with a *threat assessment* that was backed by both of the OVZ and PID intelligence services, and was forced to accept that the time for action was at hand. Our fleet could neither remain much longer at its main base in Den Helder nor was it desirable to sail to the reactivated facilities in Scotland, and so the decision was made.

Then one day, it was noticed that in a very quiet low key manner, the exodus of the key Netherlands government offices and financial institutions had begun, to the perceived security of Great Britain, Canada and the Dutch East Indies. In March 1939, the Netherlands informed Great Britain that it had the intention of moving most of its naval forces not to Scapa Flow, but to the Far East as a deterrent to a resource starved and increasingly martial Japan. The departure of the fleet was set for early June 1939. To dispel any rumors regarding this deployment, it was decided a have a *big bash send off* for the fleet, a brave show was planned, complete with radio coverage, news-reels, pomp, gaiety and military bands. The ships were to look immaculately clean, fly the colorful bunting of warships *fully dressed,* there would be cheering crowds, waving flags and smiling faces. The bravado was to be delivered with an upbeat commentary emphasizing an; the all is well confident attitude of: *Off to the colonies for an extended tropical cruise!*

The sense of relief coming out of British Admiralty was surprising. Our decision; it now became obvious, was one that had relieved the Royal Navy of some plan of action, a burdensome duty which they found most distasteful. The positive attitude now displayed by Whitehall towards our announcement seemed to confirm our worst fears, and the timeliness of our decision. One can only reflect on what this action may have been when seen in the light of subsequent events in June 1940, with the defeat of France. The very powerful and modern ships of the French Mediterranean Fleet, being completely intact following six weeks of war; now presented Great Britain with an even more severe dilemma, than the presence of the Dutch Fleet, just across the channel, once had the previous year.

The stage was now set for yet another tragic affair, a small part of the greater drama yet to unfold as *the crumbling ruins of Old Europe*, teetered along inevitably towards an unavoidable collapse. Due to the gravest political and military miscalculations of its ministers at the highest levels, Great Britain now faced after the fall of France, the might of Nazi Germany alone, and on her doorstep.

Desperation then gripped the British Government, as evident by a number of remarkable acts. One of these was the removal of all the Gold Bullion from those bank vaults on British Isles, loading it aboard a six inch cruiser, and dispatching her to Montreal at flank speed! While another was perpetrated against the French Navy, in an attempt to prevent its possible use by the Germans. One must remember that Germany had not demanded of France that she surrender her navy, and it remained under French control, secure in fortified bases that were located more than eight hundred kilometers from the German occupied territory! I truly believe however; that the tragic fate that befell the French Fleet, was the outcome of a resurrected plan of action, one originally formulated to solve the problem of the Dutch fleet located in Den Helder Noord-Holland, under similar circumstances.

To the strategists of the Royal Navy; the modern battleships, cruisers and aircraft carriers of the French fleet could not under any circumstances be allowed to fall into enemy hands. If by some means these vessels were employed to bolster the navies of Germany and Italy; the Fascists would be able to challenge the power of the Royal Navy on more than equal terms, compromising the entire Empire and drastically devaluing the Pound!

The French Government, still in a state of shock from the totality of their military collapse did not fully appreciate the nightmare scenario now developing for Great Britain, nor did it entirely appreciate that the pending strategic crisis demanded a British solution by a '*Resoudre par la force!*'

Tragically, within days of the French defeat, and the signing an Armistice with Germany; the British Gibraltar Battle Fleet; designated Force H, fell upon her hitherto unsuspecting former ally; the French Mediterranean fleet where it lay, in its North African base at Mers el Kabir. Admiral Somerville, the commander of 'Force H' was handed the dreadful task of conveying Great Britain's terms to the French Admirals. The French Fleet had been given only a five hour time limit to surrender and sail with the British or scuttle itself! If it did not accept these terms by the deadline, it would be destroyed!

The French, who had just concluded hostilities with Germany, could not join the British Fleet as it risked a renewal of German attack for violating the terms of the armistice. The

French Admiralty could not scuttle its fleet under such a threat as it was in their eyes dishonorable. 'Force H' opened fire against a fleet still tied to its wharfs. It was a slaughter; *like the shooting of fish in a barrel*, Daniel Peacock a Royal Marine Officer, manning 'A' Turret of *HMS Hood* sadly admitted. Casualties among the French sailors were heavy; with some 1400 dead! The rashness of the act caused an undeclared war to break out between France and Great Britain, and diminished the relationship between these two nations for many years after World War II had ended.

Soon after the conclusion of this action, the French Government stung to strike back, asked for clarification from Hitler if he would allow the Forces of France to retaliate against Great Britain without violating the recently concluded armistice. Hitler gave his consent, and a within hours the French Air force was bombing the British Base at Gibraltar!

Britain had weighed her options and accepted; *as the lesser of two evils*, the consequences of her action which proved to be enormous. Many nations condemned the action, and it was felt that Great Britain had become as dangerous an aggressor nation as Germany. In America as well; public opinion now became very anti-British. However, President Roosevelt, looking beyond the tragic act now believed; that for the first time in half a decade; Great Britain had displayed some backbone, and he sensed the depth of resolve of the new government formed by Winston Churchill.

Prime Minister Churchill had accepted this stain to Britain's honor in order to ensure that regardless of fate or circumstances these vessels could not be used against her. The inglorious act, following a series of such acts; the facilitating of Hitler and Mussolini's three year war against Spain of 1936 to 1939, the serving up of Czechoslovakia to Hitler in 1938, ignoring its treaty obligations to provide military assistance to Poland in 1939, when that nation was invaded by Germany, had greatly tarnished Britain's reputation in those years.

Indeed many of her people at home and many millions of the citizens of her colonies had begun to wonder; into what was type of nation was Great Britain transforming? These stains to the British honor were shoveled down the throats of an undeserving nation by those in high office, who had long neglected their duty. Yet it was largely through the copious shedding of blood, the self-sacrifice of the common servicemen and women, and of the civil volunteer, that after six years of planet wide war; Britannia's honor; was fully and completely redeemed!

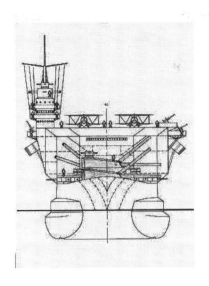

CHAPTER XI

DEPARTURE FOR GIBRALTAR

The British Admiralty held the opinion that the Netherlands' *powerful if not ideally balanced* naval squadron, would be a most welcome ally in the Far East as; His Britannic Majesty's forces in that part of the Empire were *rather thin* to put it bluntly. As a consequence, England made every effort to assist RNLN with the transit of our fleet through her strategic regions, in the interest of a common defense. All Royal Navy bases and their facilities along our route to the Dutch East Indies were to be made available to the RNLN. These services rendered to our squadron with efficiency and generosity greatly aided us in surmounting the innumerable logistical headaches on our long voyage ahead.

In keeping with our commitment made in March, most of our naval and a substantial part of our air forces in the spring of 1939 began to redeploy to the East Indies. The naval contingent included the battlecruiser-carriers; *Cornelis de Witt* and *Johan de Witt*, the light cruisers; *Gouden Leeu, Aemilia, Prins te Paard* and *Oliphant* supported by the destroyers *Zeeland, Gelderland, Jakhals, Bulhond, Eendragt, Zoutman, Piet Heyn* and *Draak*. The fleet train followed with the 22 kt. 20,000 tonne sister fleet tankers *Groningen* and *Utrecht*, the 22 kt. 16,000 tonne munitions ship *Nijmegen* and the 22 kt. 18,000 tonne supply ship *Arnhem*. The last ship added to this fleet was the new 30,000 tonne liner *Willem Usselinx* just recently converted to a 2300 bed hospital ship. The attachment of this last vessel to our fleet auxiliaries lent a sense of foreboding to the otherwise colorful departure.

June 10, 1939 the harbour of Den Helder prepared for the departure of nineteen warships and 11,500 personnel of the Royal Netherlands Navy, the largest peace time deployment in a century. The Queen bid farewell to the fleet from her Royal Yacht the *Piet Hein* anchored just outside of the harbour's mouth. While crowded long the wharfs of Den Helder base and along the shoreline of the *Waddenzee* were gathered some 50,000 family members and spectators *seeing-off* the ships, the precious sons and husbands. The deployment was to be of four years in duration. The spectacle; though gaily presented;

seemed to confirm the reverse, that the ominous clouds of war were coming ever closer, and that the *great storm* was soon to break.

The ships closed up for the sea voyage, tugs nudged up smartly to our towering steel hulls, the mooring buoys were cast off and we were finally underway. Many of the officers and men alike on that chilly grey morning feared but dared not to put into words the conviction that they would never again see their country or families in this life.

The saluting of the departing ships and men, began spontaneously with the firefighting tugs as they engaged their powerful pumps and sprayed long graceful arcs of seawater from their fire monitors as a way of saying; God's speed. Then the merchant ships, lining the jetties got into the spirit of the event, soon these were joined by the fleet auxiliaries and the fishing vessels who all began enthusiastically saluting our departing lads with their many and varied steam horns. It was touching moment as our nation's heart has been long bound to the sea and its many traditions.

I passed along the order that all ships may return the good wishes and our executive officer Kapitein Lt. ter Zee (Commander): Luis Van Rooten quietly pulled the steam horn's cord and my Vlaggeschip; *Cornelis de Witt* exhaled four sad deep prolonged bellows that carried across the shallow waters of the *Waddenzee* and far into the Island of Texel where the citizens of the towns of *Den Burg* and *Oudeschild* halted what they were doing, perhaps for a moment of sober reflection. In short order the other warships followed suit in saying farewell to their country.

Once clear of the mole, the warships one by one, came abreast of the Royal Yacht *Piet Hein,* each of which then fired off a twenty-one gun salute. Thousands of seamen lining the rails smartly snatched off their caps with their right hands, and holding them aloft gave three loud hurrahs for Her Majesty. Then each ship's band broke into a lively rendition of the tune; *De Jonge Prins Van Friesland,* reserved for such occasions, which carried by the ship's own loudspeakers so that even in the remote bowels of the ship, sailors on duty could share in the moment.

The ship's steam horns and barking light caliber salvos were answered by an increasing but intermittent roar of fifty thousand throats, their cheers and farewells modulated and made infrequent by the variable winds, which brought home to all of us that our contact with Holland was already fleeting.

The off-duty seamen went to relax along the railings, to watch as the low hills of Texel Island slipped past, then the flat grassy plain of Noorderhaaks Island loomed up to starboard and then fell astern and were soon lost in a lingering morning mist. The value of this last glimpse of home, even of a grass covered sandbar or a black stretch of tidal mud flat could not be underestimated in its value to the men. Finally clear of the sand bars and safe from the shallows; the tugs made off to return to other duties. Deep within the engine rooms of the ships, the main steam valves were spun open releasing the pent up fury of the boilers into the turbines. The ship's sharp stems were pointed to the open sea as their propellers began to revolve ever more rapidly, threshing the waters under their counters to a hissing white froth.

Once the *Noorderhaaks* had fallen astern, the small flotilla of pilot boats approached close to port to picked up their man from each vessel and cast-off. For many of our warships crew this was the last physical tie with the land of our birth. The fleet was underway at last. For the thousands of young sailors aboard; their dreams of exotic adventure and the beginning of an exciting naval career was at hand.

The warships had been steaming in single file through the confining waters of the dredged ship channel, but once out in the *Nordzee* it took up the open water cruising formation that was to be used for the entire voyage; leading the squadron; three destroyers abreast at one kilometer spacing between ships, trailing these at 500 meter intervals the flagship *Cornelis de Witt* followed by her sister the *Johan de Witt*. Behind these, also in *line ahead* the two new high speed tankers, followed by the hospital ship, the two supply ships and lastly the munitions ship joined the fleet from her obscure location and took up its station some five nautical miles behind the fleet.

Half a mile to port and starboard of the Vlaggeschip a cruiser was stationed. Trailing these and astern of the last tanker, came the remaining two cruisers. Half a mile outboard of the cruisers, and abreast of the *Cornelis de Witt* were two more destroyers, each followed by three more, equally spaced down the length of the battle squadron's steaming formation.

Upon the flight deck of each battle-cruiser carrier along the starboard side securely lashed down and covered with tarpaulin were fifteen Fokker D. XX1 monoplane fighters destined for our army air bases at Batavia on the island of Java.

The cruising speed of the squadron was set at the economical 17 knots, which brought us without incident to *the key to the Mediterranean,* the strategic fortress of Gibraltar on the clear morning of June 13th. The harbour pilots came aboard our ships and guided us to the reserved anchorages, we soon picked up our respective mooring buoys and the entire squadron was by 11:00hrs swinging gently around to point their bows southeastward, and into a hot late morning gritty wind sweeping in from the sand wastes of North Africa! Many a lad aboard, took a moment to sniff the new breeze, which this morning had a very faint hint of figs.

Our ships were positioned one and half kilometers out from the city near the first corner of the harbour's great outer break water. The area contained within the seawall of the naval harbour was not really that large; perhaps only two kilometers square. Nevertheless it was efficiently laid out and a large proportion of the British Mediterranean Fleet was visible over the stonework of the mole.

The tripod masts of two 'R Class' battleships were visible. I could also distinguish that a battlecruiser was riding at buoy bow on to us; either the *HMS Hood* or *HMS Repulse*. To the north; the upper works of a big County class 8 inch cruiser could also be made out. All were lying quietly under their sun bleached tropical awnings. Many more warships were at moorings outside the sea wall, and in our company, most notably the distinctive profiles of the aircraft carriers; *HMS Furious* and *HMS Eagle*. Numerous small naval cutters and auxiliary vessels cut through the blue waters, crisscrossing the harbour with their wakes, all the while engaged in shuttling material and white clad sailors, back and forth between ship and shore.

Arrayed along the wide top of the stone mole, at a distance of a kilometer or so, a large Royal Navy Band was rehearsing. Shimmering in the heat, they became a disconnected blur of precision movement, white uniforms and polished brass as they practiced marching and rehearsed their instruments. Then to my ears, came faintly, and in snatches brought on the breeze, a lively rendition of a favorite Royal Navy tune; *Heart of Oak*!

Half a kilometer beyond the military band, and further down the wide stone breakwater a detachment of Marines outfitted in their sand colored 'tropical short' uniforms was conducting a bayonet drill, the blades on the end of their Lee Enfield Rifles flashed in the sun. An unusual amount of glare from those bayonets, I thought, and with the white webbing, I concluded that they must be a ceremonial unit.

The seagulls dipped and dived around my great ship, making the most of what the turbulence of the many propellers in the harbour had brought to the surface. Their excited calls mingling with the putt-putt-putting of the little single stroke engines of the many cutters that criss-crossed the confined waters. The sunlight reflecting off the wavelets had covered all the vertical plating and the underside of the flight deck overhang of the *Cornelis de Witte* with a beautiful shifting pattern of illuminated mottling. All these visual and auditory delights, unique to a harbour experience, are of the type that have been drawing adventurous fellows, for millennia, like magic; to the sea.

I now studied each of my ships through my personal binoculars. All were riding safely at their moorings. I could see various work parties breaking out the canvass awnings, and winding open the mushroom ventilation trunks on the decks. These were always deployed on stationary ships in tropical waters to shade over the entire length of the ship's hull. The awnings when used in conjunction with the deck mushroom vents would lower the temperature in the accommodation spaces below by as much as 40 degrees, and allow the crews a restful sleep. All seemed well. A fleet under my command had entered its first foreign port on our voyage to South East Asia!

Our generous hosts; The Royal Navy, ever mindful of seafaring traditions had all their warships in our vicinity turn out their crews, earlier in a salute to our arrival, which was a very nice touch indeed, and made us feel quite welcome.

My ships now lay under the guns of the great Rock of Gibraltar. The morning sun whitened that gigantic limestone crag. Discernible; far up the slopes perhaps at an elevation of 300 meters or so were visible the dark mouths of innumerable deep caverns carved out of the solid rock. There in lay the hundreds of pieces of artillery and AA battery mounts that made this base unassailable from either the army of fascist Spain or from an attack by the sea or air.

Looking back into the harbour, I observed that numerous supply vessels were clearing the varied jetties and making their way or being towed towards my squadron. These carried oil fuel for the ships, 100 octane gasoline for the planes, crated aircraft parts, tools, and lube oil for the battle carrier's air groups, fresh water and food for the men.

In that short passage from Holland, the fleet commissary units had already supplied the crew with victuals for some 103,500 meals! Many of which were enjoyed twice of course, especially by the news media people aboard as we crossed the Bay of Biscay, often known for its roughness. Twice; once down and once up! Ha!

At Gibraltar my two battlecruiser-carriers were to receive, as contracted with the British Government, some eighteen replacement aircraft for those lost or worn out due to the attrition of this last year of accelerated training. But in this we hit a snag. Due to the heightened level of invective coming out of Nazi Germany's propaganda factory, Britain was becoming increasingly alarmed and consequently more cautious when it came to the release of armaments that other nations had contracted her industry to supply them.

As her production of military aircraft had been long neglected, and was far behind schedule, it had been decided by His Majesty's Government to retain all of their military aircraft, regardless of type and cancel the transfer of those to be delivered under all previous foreign contracts. The immediate benefit of course, was that it; more rapidly redirected aircraft into the burgeoning RAF training programs and newly created squadrons, a development which now affected my battle squadron directly, and caused great inconvenience.

The warships and fleet auxiliaries of my convoy were moored to naval buoys, which by the 1930's were commonly equipped with telephone connection to land lines and other ships in the harbour through the naval base telephone exchange. The supply barges had been rafted up to my ships and replenishment of the fleet was well underway when a good friend from my early days at sea; Captain Edward Hawke, the current Commander of the aircraft carrier; *HMS Furious* telephoned me. He greeted me warmly and requested when he may visit the flagship at my convenience, to discuss the *replacement aircraft situation*. After a short pause, I replied; "lunch, 13:00hrs aboard the *Cornelis de Witt*." Setting down the phone I pondered upon his phrase; for until that moment I did not know that there was *a situation*, relating to the replacement aircraft that I expected to take aboard today.

Putting that issue aside, as an item to be raised later, I was looking forward once again to seeing my old friend *Eddy*. We had both served as junior officers in South East Asia, twenty years ago! The last three years from spring 1936 on had been so busy for me that I had allowed my personal correspondence to lapse. However, as I later learned from Captain Hawk, he sympathized with my plight, as his command also had imposed upon him a similar fate. He would later intimate to me that *big things were afoot*, and that the Royal Navy just as the KMN was working its ships, equipment and most experienced men ragged.

Even back in 1936 our naval planners had anticipated that there would be a problem obtaining replacement aircraft from Britain for our two battle-carriers. In fact it was a central argument of those officers who advocated the 'big gun' concept, when we debated; big gun ship vs aircraft carrier. One option open to us for acquiring aircraft, I had mentioned earlier; involved the Americans who were planning to replace all their naval bi-plane carrier aircraft with higher speed monoplanes, so that the USN may keep pace with similar developments within the Rengo Kantai (Imperial Japanese Navy).

Accordingly; the Netherlands had sought to purchase the entire surplus bi-plane air groups from the USN carriers *Saratoga, Lexington* and *Ranger*. The sale also included 100% of all the replacement aircraft for these ships along with all their associated tools and spare parts. The decision to avail ourselves of this fantastic opportunity now saved us, for by November 1939 the U.S. Navy had already delivered eight shiploads of crated Grumman and Curtiss naval aircraft, with their tools, engines and spare parts to the remote Dutch East Indies; Naval Air Station Mendado, located at on the north east peninsula of the large island of Celebes!

In addition to this source, there was another. While the US Navy had been blockading Spanish harbours during the Civil War, to prevent war supplies from reaching the war zone, the Grumman Aircraft Corporation, with the full cooperation of the US Government, had set up an Aircraft Manufacturing Plant in Port Arthur Canada. Grumman then began to supply F2F fighter aircraft covertly from that remote facility, to the same Spanish forces that the US Government was officially blockading!

With the surrender of the Spanish Government to the Fascist Rebels on March 28, 1939, the aircraft plant in Port Arthur Ontario began redirecting its sales to the French Navy, to supply aircraft to their fleet carrier *Bearn*. These fighters were stockpiled in Puerto Rico, along with Curtiss model 77 Helldivers, and there they waited the arrival of the French aircraft carrier.

For a time, the Grumman Aircraft Corporation still produced their stubby bi-plane fighters at the Canadian plant. The unexpected rapid collapse of France in June 1940, prevented her aircraft carrier the *Bearn* from picking up these machines, and the entire lot was purchased by the KMN, and were subsequently delivered to several naval air stations in the Dutch East Indies. By the outbreak of war in the Far East there were, in addition to those machines at sea; at least 90 Grumman F2F-1, F3F-1 or F3F-2 biplane fighters and 176 Curtis Helldiver biplane dive-bombers on the naval inventory of our airbases as squadron replacements, secured in secret underground revetments.

A decision was made by the RNLN to drop the Swordfish torpedo bomber as a seaborne weapon when we began to switch over to the American planes. The great range enjoyed by each type of our torpedo planes allowed them to operate from any one of the many airfields and Naval Air Stations that we had established among the islands of our East Indies Colony, and made ship board deployment unnecessary. Their air umbrella was so extensive that our battlecruiser-carriers were always under it even at the extremities of our designated operating areas!

Additionally the torpedo planes were not only very slow but were quite large aircraft and we could store three Helldivers below deck in a space occupied by two Swordfish. The carrier's air operation's magazines limited the Swordfish to only two torpedoes each while the Helldivers were each allotted sufficient 225 kilogram bombs for twenty sorties.

Bombs having this mass were lethal to all vessels with the exception of battleships, therefore an *all dive bomber* outfit for each battle-carrier was considered at the time to be the most logical choice. The Curtis Modell 77 Helldiver, a swift aircraft, would allow the battle-carriers to attack a target with five times the explosive tonnage of a Swordfish squadron in the same time period. An additional bonus gleaned from the Helldiver was its capability as a Class 2 fighter. The machine was very agile without bombs, and could defend itself if attacked by enemy fighters, while at the same time as a substitute for the Swordfish; they would provide the fleet an extra defensive punch of fifty six 0.50 Cal. heavy machineguns.

Therefore it was decided that torpedo attack duty was to be handed over entirely to our naval land seaplane bases located strategically throughout the Netherlands East Indies. The two carrier Swordfish squadrons would operate in the same role as our Fokker torpedo bomber squadrons.

The navy was expecting a lot from the very modern Fokker T- 8 torpedo planes. They were very powerful steady aircraft of pleasing proportions. Fitted with robust floats the bomber was not tied to a base, it could land in any cove. To take advantage of this ability twenty small camouflaged shore based naval air depots had been supplied and equipped for war. There were six ten tonne high speed replenishment craft attached to these units just to shuttle around air and ground crews from location to location.

Captain Hawke arrived aboard my ship from *HMS Furious* with a large group of his officers. At the top of the gangway he faced aft to salute our naval ensign and then requested permission to come aboard. Once granted; his party was led forward along the main deck then up onto 02 deck, where we greeted each other underneath the massive 343 mm gun barrels of 'C' Turret. (See Appendix G) (See drawing Page 26)

"Congratulations Maarten! A fleet commander, no less!" he said keenly, while quickly gazing around at my great flagship. "A lot of blue water has passed under both our keels since we took the Chinese pirate junk *Green Dragon* together eh, and put an end to that old scoundrel Hong Shou (Red hands)?"

"Yes indeed, it has old friend" was my reply as we shook hands firmly; "I see that your *cutlass hand* has not lost its grip," I blurted out jokingly, as we both sought to crush the others hand, much we used to do as young men.

Great Britain's greatest hero; Admiral Lord Nelson had often stated: "Duty is the great business of a sea officer" and the *Aircraft Situation* was to be dealt with first. I then placed three of my officers at the disposal of our Royal Navy guests who may have wished to tour the ship, then invited Captain Hawke and his much reduced, small select group of officers to join me in my day cabin to discuss the business at hand. In anticipation of the subjects to be covered I also had in attendance Kapitein Voorne and my Chief of Fleet Air Operations; Hoof Officier Vlieger (Commander Flier): Konrad Van Braekel.

I started with introductions, and moved quickly to a summation of my Battlecruiser-carrier squadron's pressing need for eighteen replacement machines, their spares, and equipment. I then handed a letter to Captain Hawke, formally requesting that the equipment listed, now be supplied to my ships at this time under the terms of the Anglo-Dutch Naval Technical Agreement of 1938. Captain Hawke replied that he officially acknowledged the receipt of my request, and handed my letter to his adjutant. Turning to me he said; "Rear Admiraal, it is with deep regret that I must inform you that current supply shortages in our own service will not allow HMG to re-supply your squadron as requested, and I do not know when this situation will improve."

I replied; "My battle-carrier division is short of eight Swordfish torpedo planes, and ten Sea Fox bombers, while six of our Sea Fury fighters need replacement engines. Tensions with Japan are increasing. You know their history, I may be sailing into a war zone in the Pacific, and this unfortunate development places my ships in a very vulnerable situation!"

He reiterated that Great Britain was desperately short of military aircraft, aircraft engines, and especially the Swordfish. There were no aircraft available for export at this time. I then reminded Captain Hawke that all these replacement items had been paid for. Nodding in acknowledgement of this fact he informed me that if the political situation improved, exports would recommence and most aircraft parts would once again be obtainable. Captain Hawke understood that the replacement aircraft had already been paid for, and he deeply regretted the great difficulty that this recent development would impose upon my ships, but the aircraft that we had contracted for had already been delivered to RAF Coastal Command. HMG was prepared to generously compensate the Dutch Crown.

In order to somewhat offset this unpalatable situation; all the facilities of His Majesty's naval bases were to be placed at our disposal to support our fleet's voyage to the Far East.

Fuel oil may be obtained for the voyage at no charge, the cost of which would be offset against the monies already paid for those aircraft and spares, if I wished. In addition he would have six engines for the Sea Fury fighters delivered today to redress the shortfall from the stores of his own ship.

I replied, "very well, I find this compensation of value and I would take the fuel oil and supplies offered, but would leave the final settling of the accounts to those branches of our respective Governments."

Captain Hawke was more than a little surprised at how mild my reaction was to his bad news. But we had by that time the secure knowledge that aircraft much better suited to our needs would soon be in our possession and for a only a fraction of the cost of replacement British machines. At this time the RNLN aircraft arrangement with the Americans was still very much a secret. God Bless America, I thought, that nation would undoubtedly become *freedom's factory.*

For two decades following the Great War, Great Britain had gambled on peace and downsized all branches of its military services. This proved to be a dreadful miscalculation. One could argue in her defense that she simply had chosen to invest in society rather than weapons, like any civilized nation would. *Guns or butter* was the popular phrase of the British Press. If that was indeed the case, then why did; *there is precious little evidence of the bloody butter,* also become part of the nation's vernacular? Nevertheless there was one bright spot that I knew would warm the cockles of the British heart; the peerage seemed to be managing.

Unfortunately, other nations would now begin to pay the price for Britain's folly, today it was the turn of the Royal Netherland's Navy. Symptomatic of a chronically unprepared military was the increasingly desperate situation with the passage of time, necessitating draconian measures that HMG now implemented, in order to redress the large shortfalls of all types of weapons, in all her branches of service. Many of these *solutions* lacked the typical British finesse, and it was left up to fine officers like Captain Hawke to suffered the embarrassment of having to personally communicate the bad news at the last possible moment, leaving some customers in the lurch; often facing an alarming situation.

Now that our official business was concluded; I could interact on a social level with my old friend. I suggested a tour of my flagship and then some lunch. Captain Hawke was one of the best carrier commanders in the Royal Navy and I earnestly wished him to view my flagship, to have him see our hangar deck arrangements and hear his comments.

The big-gunned aircraft carrier was a novel, and still very controversial type of warship and Captain Hawke was similarly interested to gain a firsthand understanding of the positive and negative aspects of the marriage of super heavy artillery with the operation of aircraft. In order for him to do this I had instructed our officers to assist our Royal Navy guests touring the ship, and to allow them to ask any question of our naval and air technicians.

The tour involved a walk-through of both the upper and lower aircraft hangers, and the aircraft machine shops. In the upper hangar he stopped to look at a group of Fairy Sea Fox light bombers, a craft completely outdated in 1939. He seemed then, to really grasp the feebleness which our air group represented. Turning to me he said with great earnestness; "Maarten, I will do everything possible to get you some replacement aircraft." Then we made our way forward, exiting the main aircraft hangar and out onto the mid-ships weather deck, near to where he had come aboard and under the 343 mm gun barrels of 'C' Turret.

Captain Hawke, a professional officer of great experience knew his warship types well and walking around the barbette he studied the arcs available to the big guns and nodded in approval and said; "a generous arc indeed, at least as good as that of HMS Rodney's 'C' Turret." Then he asked me to outline the most difficult aspects of the vessel's metamorphosis and how we solved them.

In one hour we concluded the tour and adjourned to the officer's wardroom for a meal. Here I announced Hawke and his party and then after applause we were seated. Lengthy informal discussions now ensued, regarding warships of the rival navies and their qualities. Cpt. Hawke did express his admiration for the way we had managed to add fangs to our fleet. Although of an unproven type; our battlecruiser-carriers were nevertheless very powerful warships indeed. He also expressed his opinion that the workmanship of the reconstruction, evident during the tour seemed to be in his view; first rate, while the aircraft hangers seemed to be well ordered and laid out.

Captain Hawke concluded that our battlecruiser-carrier's combination of big guns and aircraft certainly filled a void in our navy, and provided a surface defense solution to an attack by heavy cruisers, even though our big ships could not be employed in a line of battle for obvious reasons. The battle-carrier had undoubtedly powerful weapons capable of offensive and defensive operations in the air and on the surface.

In any event he felt that our ships were the right weapon at the right time for the RNLN. Both the American and Japanese navies obviously valued the concept as their very largest aircraft carriers were armed with a full heavy cruiser's battery of 203 mm guns. In Captain Hawke's estimation, the Battlecruiser-carrier was an unnecessary warship type for the Royal Navy. It did not need multi-role warships such as these, for she had on strength plenty of big gunned ships, five carriers and enough cruisers to counter any enemy. He trusted in the concept of proven highly specialized warships, rather than investing heavily in an untested hybrid. The Royal Navy, he felt would never choose to develop the type.

In recalling that one statement I cannot help but chuckle, for Captain Edward Hawke, would find himself in about three years hence, the new commander of *HMS Colossus*, the flagship of a fast Battleship-carrier Task Force! She was the sixth unit of the King George V Class battleship, redesigned, at the direction of the Prime Minister into a hybrid, following the loss of Force Z off the coast of Malaya due to lack of air support. At 15:00hrs the Captain Hawkes party, having concluded its business and touring the ship, departed for HMS Furious.

HMS Colossus had been lengthened by some 160 feet with a new mid-body inserted just aft of amidships. The A and B, main battery mounts were retained forward in their original location, leaving her a six 14 inch guns of the original ten. An aircraft hangar of some 700 feet long by 100 feet wide had been constructed, replacing the original upper works, to house some 110 modern Barracuda, and Sea Hurricane fighter aircraft. At some 900 feet in length over all, retaining all her battleship armor, and displacing some 46,000 tons, the new Battle-carrier was a *Colossus* indeed!

There are few diversions for me aboard a moored warship more relaxing, than inviting your officers for an evening cigar and a whisky under the awnings, to enjoy the evening breezes. In lieu of traditional awnings we had, the shaded area under the flight deck, and had rigged a canvas curtain on the starboard side to block the low rays of the afternoon sun. On this occasion; of this first night in Gibraltar Harbour folding canvas chairs set up under the long gun barrels of 'C' Turret, for my Chief of staff and senior officers. The chief steward had the portable bar rolled out and set up discreetly behind us, and brought us a tray of pipe tobaccos and cigars. The men and I would take an hour to enjoy the evening.

Here we sat quite informally and chatted, smoked and exchanged our thoughts for the days ahead, while enjoying the bustling harbour view. Visible over the mole, and against the brown smudge of the African coast a huge White Star Liner could be made out exiting the Atlantic, perhaps bound for India via the Suez. Now, outbound from Gibraltar a much smaller Blue Star cargo liner, with *the bone in her teeth* was on a heading into the open ocean, her bows already dipping into the long swell! Both ships were highly illuminated as they were prepared to steam just outside Spanish waters, an area that was still classed as a war zone.

The evening breezes that played softly across the teak decks and gently bellied the canvass curtain, had started out hot and dry but transformed with the angle of the sun into ever more cooler caresses, even bringing a hint of chill. Slowly across the great expanse of the naval base and the city, lights began to come on, as did those of all ships on mooring or riding at anchor.

Gibraltar was known for spectacular sunsets, and Africa on this evening did not disappoint us. The dust carried up to the stratosphere, by the massive updrafts of the open desert created an immense panorama of shifting golds, pinks reds and blues, which we enjoyed for more than an hour until the great orb finally, sank into the Atlantic.

Tonight I thought; I will forsake my bed, and break out my *sea rig* by the open deadlight. I wanted to swing in my hammock to the gentle rocking of the ship. I studied the stars as I puffed on my cigar, and enjoyed a rare moment of complete relaxation; as content as a babe in its mother's arms. Across the dark harbour waters there floated to our ears band music and snatches of faint laughter from *HMS Eagle,* one of the RN aircraft carriers.

Both Gibraltar naval base and at Malta were, I knew, somewhat infamous for its social extravaganzas, apparently even more so when the aircraft carriers were in. I have on occasion heard it said that many a newly commissioned young Officer in His Majesty's warships met his *bride-to-be* at one of these events. Unfortunately, not all were happy unions. A worldwide depression was reality, and the steady Navy pay packet meant that *life* could begin for many a young lady with some security and as equally important it was a ladder to higher society. Any naval cadet, even one of humble origins, did upon graduation and with the receipt of his commission, obtain the status of a *gentleman* and his wife therefore officially became through the institution of matrimony; *a lady* with one foot firmly planted upon the bottom rung of the social ladder. British Society in those days had many social barriers, but a military commission was one of the very few conduits that would allow a commoner to rise to great heights.

There was, as I subsequently discovered through casual conversation with RN Officers; *a regular shuttle service*, that could be magically activated to transport prospective young ladies from mother England to all the fleet social occasions, through-out the other Royal Navy bases in the Mediterranean: Malta and Alexandria. (Field Marshal Alexander of

Tunis once referred to it in jest as: *an operation, of such organization and complexity, that it rivalled the Allied invasion of Sicily!)*

On the following day my squadron second in command Commodore Konrad Van Speijk Bronckhorst and I went ashore to meet with Admiral Sir David James Hardwicke the commander of the Gibraltar naval base. The Admiral welcomed our squadron into his naval station and offered us its every facility. His strategic base located where the Mediterranean Sea meets the Atlantic was in the process of a rapid upgrade, in preparation for hostilities, which seemed imminent.

Admiral Hardwicke had naturally a great interest in the capabilities of the Italian battle fleet and air forces as these could be foes with whom he must deal with in the near future. He asked my opinion as a naval architect of their warships. I had replied that one should expect them to be absolutely first class, as one had only to look at their well-documented maritime history;

The Venice Arsenal by the 16th century was the most advanced center of Naval Architecture and ship construction in Europe, its most ancient and the original facility, from which all other training establishments including those of Great Britain had sprung. Indeed; the English King Henry VIII, who had traveled to Rome in the hope of obtaining the Pope's blessing for his most recent marriage stopped in Venice to visit the famous Arsenal. The Venetian navy; in honor of the English King's visit had planned to build a 600 ton galley for their navy, as a demonstration of their shipyard's ability. In the time it took King Henry to dispose of the banquet; the Arsenal works had in a few hours assembled the warship from thousands of entirely pre-fabricated parts! A feat which was quite astounding as the traditional ship building methods of Europe would have at required at least four months to construct such a ship! The British Monarch was so deeply impressed that he dispatched his ship-wrights to the Venice Arsenal to learn *the art and science of shipbuilding*. English shipwrights up to that time had been constructing ships largely by scaling up wooden models, leaving symmetry to the eye and engineering to the old rule of thumb. At the Arsenal they would learn the specific mathematics of Naval Architecture.

I offered the opinion that Italian craftsmen strive for absolute perfection in all their wide engineering and artistic abilities. It is evident in everything that they put their hands to, with shipbuilding being no exception. When one thinks of craftsmanship, one immediately thinks of Italy, a reality that is as true in the late twentieth century as it was 2500 years ago!

It didn't seem logical to me that the Italians would rebuild the *Regia Marina* into a service that contained some of the swiftest and most powerful cruisers and destroyers in the world, and then have as its very nucleus a squadron of slow 22 knot battleships, as reported in that famous military bible; Janes Warships! As a naval architect I suspected that their ships were first rate, and I told the Admiral as much, and to expect the *Cesare Class* to be much swifter, and unusually powerful for their displacement. In reality; the reconstructed WW I era Italian Battleships were among the smallest of their type of all the combatant navies during World War 2. Yet remarkably; with their modernized main battery guns, they had more than twice the firepower of the big new German battlecruisers of the *Scharnhorst Class*, ships some 10,000 heavier! One must also expect that their men were equally capable and their training thorough.

Admiral Hardwicke knew that the passage of our fleet through the Mediterranean would bring out the Italian Fleet to show the flag of *Regia Marina*, a bravado type of display that the IL Duce (Benito Mussolini) seemed quite fond of in those days. In his position Hardwicke couldn't make the outright request of us to compile intelligence on the Italian fleet for him. But he did enquire as to the possibility of putting five of his officers, each equipped with a 16 mm movie camera aboard my Battlecruiser-carriers as observers in order that we may *begin cooperating in air operations training,* and then disembark this group in the Aden. I saw a benefit in this and in any event, I knew that the British were as just as keen to nose around and film the new ship type that the *Cornelis de Witte* represented as they were with the filming the modernized *Regia Marina* at sea! Accordingly, I allowed ten RN personnel; five naval pilots and five sea officers to board my flagship from the carrier *HMS Furious* prior to our departure for Alexandria.

One of my younger officers had earlier brought it to his Kapitein's attention that there were one hundred British army nurses originally destined for Singapore but currently stranded in Gibraltar. Their troopship it seems had struck an uncharted rock and had been delayed while undergoing repairs in the *Queen Alexandra* dry dock. I then offered Admiral Hardwicke the services of our spacious and comfortable new hospital ship the *Willem Usselinx* to transport this *rather delicate supercargo,* in the interests of efficiency and cooperation between our respective navy's medical specialists. The Admiral thanked me for my generosity, but had to decline the offer from the RNLN, as on this occasion he had already managed to find them temporary duties in Gibraltar. Perhaps the thick pipe smoke hovering about Hardwicke's balding head had played a trick on my sight or did I notice a slight twinkle in his eyes over the rim of his tea cup?

Later that evening; Admiral Hardwicke invited my senior officers and I ashore to the base naval mess for a delicious dinner. My party showed up at 1900hrs and included four Admiraals, twenty captains and Commanders. Captain Hawke raised the first toast welcoming our ships and men to Gibraltar. I rose to reply, and keeping in mind that it was a Friday I asked all to raise glasses with the appropriate RN toast of the day; *"To a willing foe and sea room",* one which elicited boisterous good cheer and clapping from our tradition conscious hosts. Here in this good company, could be found the very heart of the Empire's true strength, a most implacable foe; the servicemen of the Royal Navy.

Much later in the evening, Admiral Hardwick asked me to join him in his private library to look at a rare original journal from the Napoleonic Wars that he had obtained from an Egyptian bibliophile. We donned pairs of soft white cotton gloves, then he retrieved the item and handed it to me for my inspection. He then leaned against his fire place and felt for the ornate key with which he began to wind-up the mechanism of a magnificent Egyptian Sphinx style pendulum clock rendered in polished slate that sat on the marble mantle over the firebox. I turned the pages of the tome, noting their excellent state of preservation. While so engaged, Admiral Hardwicke incautiously put out feelers on my opinion of the *Polish situation.* I must admit that I was still somewhat put out from the earlier revelations of the *aircraft situation* from Captain Hawke. Still Hardwicke seemed unusually comfortable with me when he asked; "How do you personally feel about the Poles Maarten?"

"Well I replied, if attacked they will fight, as they are very stubborn and proud. Throughout their long history they have exhibited a certain reckless success in all their many great military victories. They possess a characteristic boldness that has served them well on many occasions. They are after all the only nation to ever conquer Russia and place a puppet Czar on its Throne."

Hardwicke, then said "I believe that the Nazis will definitely attack the Soviet Union if he sees an opportunity, although Poland does stand in his way." "Possibly" I replied, "but Hitler would have to be a complete idiot to contemplate undertaking such a task. One has only to consult an Atlas to grasp the immensity of such an undertaking. My family has traded with Russia for more than two centuries, and I have heard many stories from my elders on that region and its people. What would be a very rough day for a typical German is a holiday occupation for your average Russian. Remember what happened to Napoleon's *Grande Army*? Those soldiers, drawn from all the countries of Europe in 1812 were much closer to the land and much more hardy than the largely city bred German of the 1930's, yet they perished! No, in my opinion Hitler cannot be even remotely considering an invasion of the Soviet Union. I believe that he wants to defeat a Continental European Empire such as France or the Netherlands, and then later at the peace table he will demand rich colonies as tribute. These lands are populated only by more easily managed native peoples. With this last statement I concluded my views on the topic and we rejoined the others.

The Netherlands like many of the other smaller Continental European nations did not have an island retreat, like the British, but were wide open to aggression, from the massive land power of Germany. Consequently we were much more concerned with creating a united firm coalition of states to confront aggression.

Admiral Hardwicke thanked me for my sincere views and apologized for his seemingly casual regard for a political situation which many thought was a looming life or death crisis for the people of Europe. He admitted that he privately agreed with me, and had come to similar conclusions on the prospects for the near future.

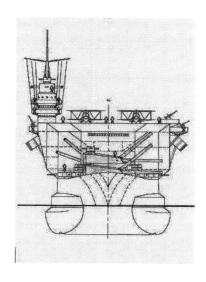

CHAPTER XII

CROSSING THE MEDITERRANIAN

At 04:00hrs June 15th, I gave orders to the ships of my squadron to light boilers in preparation for getting underway, and provide steam for cruising speed. Within two hours the entire squadron was preceding eastward in an extended formation, at an economical speed of 17 knots.

Our destination was the other end of the Mediterranean Sea, and the British naval base at Alexandria some 1700 nautical miles and five days away. The warm sunny weather of these waters was a pleasant change from the cold and misty sea conditions of the North Sea and North Atlantic. Many of the crew found time in their off duty hours to stretch out on the flight deck and work on bronzing their skin in preparation for the climates ahead.

Our air groups were to provide on a rotational basis; a Combat Air Patrol (CAP) and Anti-Submarine Patrol (ASP). The fleet, from that day forward was to maintain for every day it was a sea, an umbrella of six Sea Fury MK II fighters on CAP and three Sea Hart Bombers on ASP. These minor operations were complicated due to the restrictions imposed by the clutter of the flight deck cargo of crates and planes.

The problem of replacement aircraft had now come home to roost. Essentially the British were telling us that we were on our own and War was looming ever closer. As the squadron commander I would seek to provide aircraft for my ships, and bend a few rules on this voyage, if I had to.

Accordingly I ordered *Senior Air Ops* Van Braekel to uncover one of the Army Air Force new Fokker fighters from the *Cornelis de Witt's* deck cargo and evaluate it for flight testing. I prevailed upon him to select our best pilot to begin takeoff and landing experiment. All these efforts being preliminary to me requisitioning the new aircraft for my fleet operations!

The British had always tried to adapt their aircraft designs to serve both on land and at sea. The Royal Air Force was in control of all new aircraft design as the naval air arm was a much smaller organization. Inevitably designs suited for land based operations were produced. The RN then tried to adapt these to aircraft carrier operations. A major problem that they encountered when converting the aircraft for sea duty was its undercarriage, as these were all structurally inadequate to withstand the rough bumping of a carrier landing.

The Royal Netherlands Army Air Force Fokker D XX1 fighter had an unusually tough simple fixed undercarriage and I wanted to determine if these planes could be adapted to my carriers. The D-XX1's speed and engine reliability were quite superior to our Sea Fury. The Bristol Mercury radial engines of these Dutch fighters were very similar in design to the Bristol Pegasus radial engines powering the Fairy Swordfish. Captain Lt. Van Braekel my senior air operations officer assured me that our air mechanics would have no difficulty servicing these planes, and he suggested we outright steal them!

We were now approaching those waters considered as strategic to the Italians. The Italian Dictator Benito Mussolini often referred to the Mediterranean Sea as *Mare Nostrum* (Our Sea). In my mind; why not? Great Britain after all claimed to be the mistress of all our world's seas and oceans, while the American policy of *Manifest Destiny*, held that the entire western hemisphere was American strategic territory. Mussolini had not expressed any ill will towards the Netherlands, and did not see the Netherlands as a threat to his nation's progress. I felt no threat cruising in these regions. The ships of Holland had been trading in these waters for five centuries and we would continue to do so.

If either the *Regia Marina* or *Regia Aeronautica* made a show; I for one would be glad to see either force turn up, just for the spectacle. All the Italian warships were known to be an exceptional combination of beauty and power. Their aircraft were similarly advanced technically, having won many international competitions.

By 10:00hrs of June 17th, the ships of my extended convoy had rounded Cape Bone Tunisia and were passing south of the island of Sicily when the *Regia Aeronuatica* made its grand entrance. From the airfields dotting that island, large formations of bomber and fighter types began over flying our fleet.

The formations flew at such a low elevation that we had no difficulty in recording the individual squadron insignia. The bombers which formed up in groups of fifty, seemed to be the of the three engine type Savoia Marchetti SM-79. The fighters were single engine monoplanes with retractable undercarriage of the types Macchi MC - 200 and also the very similar Fiat G 50.

The Italian fighters escorted their bombers regiments, in squadrons of twenty. Both those fighter types were similar to the Fokker fighters stowed on our flight deck under tarpaulin, but were more sophisticated craft and slightly superior in speed and weaponry. Also evident were modern bombers with fixed undercarriages, escorted by the venerable line of Fiat CR 32 and CR 42 biplane fighters. These latter squadrons did not require prepared airfields due to their sturdy fixed landing gear. Any open virgin land would do.

What had started off as an interesting spectacle; evolved into a foreboding show of Italian air-power. The seventy plane formations flew over our squadron for over three hours! We counted some 1,400 aircraft on that day. In the face of such a force our fighter umbrella of five Sea Fury Mk II machines was a humbling experience!

The Royal Navy's guest officers, magically produced 16 mm movie cameras and shot several reels of film. I felt that the men of the Royal Navy had often expressed a bad habit of *talking down* rival navies. Many of them believed that the Japanese were an inferior race incapable of night vision due to their narrower eyes! The Italians similarly were referred to as "ice cream merchants" or "spaghetti benders." After that demonstration of air power, however I noticed there were far fewer such comments about the sons of New Rome.

Il Duce's demonstration was not yet over. Toward the end of the air spectacle the *Regia Marina* showed up. My convoy went on to a speed of 22 knots, the maximum, as we had passed the island of Malta some 20 miles to port and 40 miles astern when our air umbrella reported a fleet of warships coming down the from the heel of Italy, these having most likely sortied from the naval base at Taranto.

By 16:00hrs the Italian warships approached our port side and closed to within 300 meters of our destroyer screen. We identified the battleships *Cesare* and *Conti de Cavour,* which were escorted by four heavy cruisers, ten light cruisers and thirty destroyers.

All were elegant and very modern looking vessels. Even the old battleships which were pre-World War I reconstructions, and of the same vintage as my battlecruiser-carriers had a very pleasing appearance and seemed to present a well-balanced and efficient design in every way.

After the surrender of the Italian fleet in 1943, the Royal Navy set up a technical mission in Malta to study these two battleships. Upon completion of an extensive survey of these modernized warships they discovered to their surprise that many of the armor arrangements were actually quite superior to British standards, and the Italian shipyards had replaced practically all the riveted steel hull structure with the exception of armor, hull castings, internal decks and bulkheads for an incredible total of 60% of the structural steel. The *Cesare* and *Dulio* class battleships were for all intents and purposes; completely new battleships!

The British naval reference book 'Jane's Warships' for 1938, recorded the *Cesare* class battleships as having only 22 knots maximum speed after their reconstruction. A speed which carried the implication that they could be easily dealt with by the largely slow but more numerous battleships of the Royal Navy.

Naturally these subtle, but crucial bits of data had widespread ramifications. The inaccurately reported speed of the Italian Battleships placed them in the nuisance, rather than the threat category. An *obscure inaccurate estimation* that had the huge effect of keeping marine insurance rates down on British shipping, and at the same time made a review of the Royal Navy's capability at a time of great financial restraint, unnecessary.

However; these inaccurate records, generated a false sense of security. The Italians, had planned for their fleet to have within a few more months four such, heavily modernized battleships capable of a high speed. These would in fact, for a short period of time and in theater of the Mediterranean Sea alone, be a strategic weapon! Their 27 to 28 knot speed would enable them to operate beyond the reach of the bulk, if not the entire battle fleet of the RN, an Italian capability which the British government was loathe to consider.

It must be stated that the unmatched professionalism of the Royal Navy could indeed offset some deficiencies in equipment, that its reputation was legendary and its history so spectacular that it did indeed have the effect of a mild sedative for the British people. For these qualities that were able to overawe an adversary were also capable it seemed; of sedating those in Government whose duty it was to provide the weapons needed to defend Britannia's planet-spanning Empire from a host of envious nations.

However during the 'lost-decade' of the Great World Depression, how can one find fault with a government whose preference was for butter instead of guns? The British fleet had been reduced drastically in size following the Great War. She found herself twenty years later with only three 'heavy-gunned ships' capable of bringing the modernized Italian battleship squadron into action! Only one of these three ships, the *Hood* was a fast battleship. She enjoyed a hefty 25 % superiority in main battery firepower, over a single Italian battleship of the rebuilt type, and a two to three knot advantage in speed. But her armor although a little thicker, was not as well arranged. The *Hood* however, would be quite overmatched if fighting two of the modernized *Cesare* or *Duilio* Class fast battleships.

The other two British ships the *Repulse* and *Renown* were battlecruisers similar in gun power to the Italian vessels but with a dangerously skimpy system of protective armor. In my opinion, as a naval constructor; those two battlecruisers, were, ship for ship; somewhat inferior to the reconstructed Italian battleships.

One had to consider the following theoretical scenario; did the Royal Navy's three swiftest capital ships the *Hood, Repulse* and *Renown* have the speed to catch the Italian fast battle squadron composed of the small battleships *Cesare, Cavour, Duilio* and *Doria*, and having done so, did they have the raw fire power to sink them? Let us look at the mathematics of such a theoretical encounter:

Question:
Would the combined firepower of the Royal Navy's three Battlecruiser's twenty big guns be able to dominate the forty big guns of the four ships of the Regia Marina's fast battleship squadron?

Fact:
In one minute the 381mm heavy guns of the three British ships could fire forty shells having a combined of weight of 35,500 kilograms, while during the same period; the 320 mm heavy guns of the Italian ships whose guns were lighter, but enjoyed a higher rate of fire, could deliver eighty to one hundred shells, having a combined weight of 63,000 kilograms, and due to the mathematical principal of probability; strike twice as often!

The British 15 inch heavy guns were far superior weapons compared to the 12.6 inch artillery mounted on the Italian ships in that they were almost twice as powerful and more accurate. Both of these heavy pieces were originally manufactured by the same British Industry, Armstrong Whitworth for the 15 inch, and Woolich Arsenal for the original 12 inch and 12.6 in rebuild, both subject to rigid British Admiralty standards, the technical quality was equal. While the 15 inch gun with a range of 35,000 meters outranged the 12.6 in gun by some 4000 meters, the Italians had increased the elevation of their big guns to compensate for this somewhat, and battle ranges were normally some 25,000 meters, well within the capability of both weapons.

Nevertheless the outcome of such an encounter would have been far from certain for the Royal Navy, when one considers the historical inability of British battlecruisers to withstand heavy gunfire. In truth, recent history and the mathematics would indicate that the British would most likely have been defeated in such an encounter.

The comparison that I have made is uncannily like a comparison between the ships under Admiral Beatty's command and those of his opponent; Admiral Hipper at the battle of Jutland in 1916. The Italian ships have very similar proportions and statistics to the German battle cruisers, although even more powerful. While the British ships do not show any radical new improvements, in armoring that would enable one to say with any confidence that they would not explode under fire like their predecessors.

Of course, even if such an engagement had ended in a resounding victory for the Italian Fleet, that would not have been the end of it. The British Royal Navy had a huge fleet, and in 1939 could bring many resources against the *Regia Marina*, until their total defeat was assured.

The modern world appeared to be drifting towards another major confrontation. In such a case the Royal Navy would have to depend once again; upon the quality of its men and their unmatched professionalism to make up for hardware shortcomings, a legacy from decades of cost cutting to the military budget.

As a naval architect I understood the design concept of these rebuilt Italian battleships completely. I planned a little experiment in the hope to reveal their actual speed and provide a wake-up call for many of the complacent British.

I ordered the destroyers *Gelderland* and *Zeeland* to stay with the fleet train and maintain course at 22 knots for Alexandria. The destroyers *Jakhals* and *Bulhond* were sent forward, then I ordered all ships with the carrier division to make preparations for 30 knots.

The Italian warships prefer to cruise with their main gun barrels elevated to the maximum which created an impression of power and aggressiveness, which were good qualities for a weapon of war. Mussolini had produced numerous propaganda newsreels displaying the power of his reborn military, including a very modern fleet, with ships of groundbreaking design.

I had the pleasure of meeting Admiral Riccardi in 1937 at the International Naval Review at Taranto naval base in honor of the Silver Jubilee of King Victor Emanuel II. He commented to me, that for him the elevated gun barrels on a warship at sea communicated an aggressive posture, much like a gladiator's salute with raised *gladius* (short sword).

Admiral Riccardi now commanded that impressive fleet cruising off our port beam. I knew that he would be studying our ships intently through his binoculars, and guessed how he would react to my plan to make him reveal the flank speed of his rebuilt battleship division, as no spy had yet been able to confirm anything speed above 22 knots.

I ordered all ships to elevate their main battery guns to maximum, as a challenge to his ships. The big 343 mm guns could impress anyone and I ordered them to elevate to thirty five degrees (five short of their maximum). The chief engineer reported revolutions for 30 knots was now possible. The flagship always sets the squadron speed and all our ships had to match our rate of acceleration, which was not difficult as we were so much more massive. All ships of our squadron designated to participate were signaled with code to prepare for 30 knots. I ordered the *Cornelis* and *Johan* to make 320 revolutions or better. Immediately, I felt the increasing acceleration and the great ship surged steadily forward.

The Italian Admiral took up the unspoken challenge and his fleet responded in kind. Our speed rose and 25 knots was quickly achieved, then 26 with the Italians still keeping pace 27, 28, and then 29. The battle carriers were heavily loaded and over their design displacement by at least 1000 tonnes and could only make 29 knots. The *Cesare* and *Cavour* were making heavy smoke as they forced their boilers but maintained the pace for half an hour after which time their stack emissions were much cleaner, which indicated that their boilers could handle the load. Ever so slowly the *Cesare* and then the *Cavour* dropped back by a ship length. I turned to Kpt. Voorne and loudly ordered the speed of the Italian battleships entered into the log as 29 knots! A fact not lost on our guests; the supercargo from the RN, now crowding my navigating bridge.

I had the information that I wanted and ordered a gradual reduction of speed to 17 knots thereby allowing the fleet train to catch up. Shortly after this the Italian fleet veered away to port still at high speed and sailed north. The RN officers aboard were impressed and expressed surprise at the speed of the Italian battleships. An observation that I knew would be communicated to their superiors.

During the contest of speed between the ships, the Italian air fleet had passed on into Tripolitania and Cyrenaica. By 17:30hrs the fleet train had rejoined the battle squadron, and the ships had resumed their original cruising positions on a heading for Alexandria.

We had an eventful day. The last rotation of the fighter umbrella was launched for the day from the *Johan de Witt*, five Sea Fury fighters took to the sky, looking ever so fragile and antiquated, only a nine year old craft. In the hectic pace of aviation design in the thirties and forties, most aircraft showed their age after only three to four years of service.

Oddly enough, some twenty years later while visiting Rome, I was standing by the famous Trevi Fountain with my wife when an Italian gentleman offered to take a photograph of *the tourist couple*, standing together before this famous marble treasure of his beloved city.

I struck up a conversation with him, to be polite and practice my Italian. The gentleman; one senior Giuseppe Fabricanti as it turned out; had been a naval officer during the war. I discovered to my great surprise, that he had served as a 'Tenente di Vascello' (Lieutenant) on board the heavy cruiser *Trento*, a warship of the Italian Fleet which had participated in that short contest of speed with our Dutch battle squadron as it transited the Mediterranean Sea that spring of 1939.

I told him in my broken Italain, that I knew of his ship, I considered her a very graceful vessel and that I had taken a photograph of her at sea in 1939. The revelation aroused quite a bit of curiosity in Giuseppe. When I replied to his query; on how I had known of his beloved cruiser, he was astounded to learn that I was the Admiraal in command of the RNLN squadron that day. *"Admiral al Commando? Comandante della Flotta Olandese en ese dia?"* he exclaimed in disbelief!

Well that was it; he embraced me as a long lost brother, tears were streaming down his brown cheeks and called out loudly to his lovely wife Asunta who had been talking to Karen to hurry and telephone home to the daughters to start cooking and begin preparations to receive honored guests!

Indeed there had seldom been any animosity between our two nations, or services and so we could exchange stories without the worry of offending each other. Karen was for it, so off we went. It was a very pleasant day so we walked the two kilometers to his nice three story stone house bordering the lovely little park of *Villa Borghese* in Central Rome.

Giuseppe commented, "But Admirale! I read in the Rome newspaper that all your squadron was completely destroyed in a terrific naval battle with the Japanese in 1942,

I am so happy that you are alive!" *"Mae sembro di stare bene"* I replied pointing to myself in denial, (I seem to be fine.) Then he burst out laughing. "If I may return the sentiment; Tenente di Vascello Fabricanti, I am also glad that you survived the *Trento's* encounter with the British Mediterranean Fleet!"

Senora Fabricanti had ordered an elaborate meal to be set up in the garden courtyard of his villa under a beautiful pergola heavy with grape vines. Four of his lovely dark haired daughters were introduced to us and they continually smiled as they prepared a sumptuous meal of great variety. Zoof, the chilled pumpkin soup was a delightful discovery; and was a tasty dish designed to cool the body core!

Giuseppe then tapped the last barrel of wine put up by his late father. We ate and drank and talked of our lives, our service and our ships. What wonderful people they were, soft sophisticated conversation, laughter, music in the warm evening outdoors in the scented garden, heavy with natural perfumes and lit only by candles. This was how life is meant to be…as I took and squeezed Karen's hand.

I remarked to my host, on how impressive his fleet looked that day, and that the warships of the Italian Navy were considered by most professional seamen as the handsomest of all the fleets of the world! He visibly swelled with pride at my compliment, then told me that our battle-carriers were ships of great interest to the *Regia Marina* as they had also been studying the battleship-aircraft carrier concept.

In fact one of the design variables considered by their naval architects was the conversion of the two *Cesare* class into battleship-aircraft carriers while retaining five 320 mm guns, in the forward pair of turrets. The work would have been undertaken after the delivery of the last of the new 381 mm armed *Roma Class* battleships. But the air strike at Taranto and resulting damage to the fleet derailed the program, as Italy's shipbuilding industry was not prepared for war and its capacity, initially at least, was limited.

Giuseppe, revealed that; *Supermarina*, the (Italian Naval High Command) was fully aware of our plans to transit through the Mediterranean Sea and wanted to take a close look at my ships. Everyone aboard his cruiser was impressed by how huge and swift my battle-carriers were, with the big guns elevated forward and flight decks packed with aircraft.

Giuseppe Fabricanti was very proud of the way the *Regia Marina* had stood up to the much more powerful Royal Navy, giving as good as they got. Indeed many allied vessels lay strewn across the bottom of the Mediterranean as a testament to their capabilities. When the conversation drifted along political channels we both tried to avoid further wartime reflection. The orange, after all has sweet flesh until you bite into the seed.

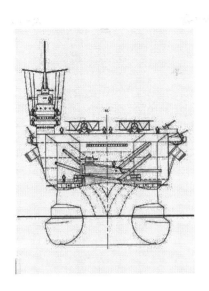

CHAPTER XIII

ALEXANDRIA, GHIZA, THE SUEZ

The battle-carrier squadron passed through the east entrance of Alexandria harbour at 08:10hrs June 20th. We were directed to mooring buoys within the bend in the five mile stone seawall. Closer towards the city were moored the battleships and aircraft carriers of the British and French Mediterranean fleets. Three aircraft carriers were present. One of them I recognized as the French carrier the *Bearn*. There were also two short, compact looking French battleships of the *Courbet* class and two *Queen Elizabeth* class battleships.

The great harbour also held perhaps twenty destroyers and six cruisers, representative of the British, French, Greek and Turkish navies all gleaming in white livery and sleeping under their sun bleached canvas deck awnings.

There were several large liners getting underway and a host of general cargo ships lying along the great wharfs outside of the naval basin. I glanced behind me at the six officer candidates at their station, a great chart table. Behind them on the shelving were some eighty volumes, containing every bit of data on all the registered ships of every shipping line in the world, and similar books which covered all warships.

These officer aspirants aged 14 to 17 were doing their *sea time* rotation away from the Naval College. It was their duty to identify and record in their log every ship that was visible, their entries were to be supplemented by a standard map of any harbour, in which we stopped, and they would indicate the location of each ship as best they could, and enter the date and time on this drawing when it was completed.

Normally you would see them, with noses down in the ship recognition books while, the senior in the group with binoculars raised would be trying to distinguish vessel characteristics. This for them was a pleasant duty while at sea, as vessels would only occasionally be encountered. Otherwise they were free to choose observation positions, in the wings of the structure.

Kapitaine Voorne, caught my glance. His *Adelborsts* (midshipmen) had today been performing this duty, and in such a busy location, they did not have even one minute to take a pause, while on the bridge, especially in the presence of the Fleet Admiral! Now, all were gazing out the windows in silence at the exotic sights, completely lost in the moment.

"Vooraanstaand Adelborst in Scheepvaart Versteegen!" Kapitaine Voorne called out sharply in a deep voice. Leading Midshipman Versteegen, jolted as if coming out of a sleep; snapped to attention, clutching his binoculars hanging by its lanyard and looked at the Kapitain. *"Please identify for me that ship preparing to cross our bows, and provide all it principal particulars"* Voorne said, pointing at a large liner, *"the one making for the harbour entrance."*

The young aspirant, quickly raised his binoculars and reamed off the following information; *"Cargo-Liner, off starboard bow, bearing green one zero, range 400 meters, three funnels; painted black, with one white band, hull; light brown, white upper works, two raked masts, with cargo derricks fore and aft, company flag"*; he paused for a moment, then called, *"white burgee with red star in center"* Lowering his binoculars he looked at his commander and reported; *"Cargo Liner of the Red Star Line Sir; it must be the steamer Belgeland; about 20,000 tonnes, 25 knots I would say?"*

Versteegen had looked at his group of more junior officer aspirants, to supplement his statistics, when one of them spouted out; *"Steamship Belgeland; 22,000 tonnes displacement, three oil on coal fired steam turbines, triple screws, 38,000 shp, speed 25 knots maximum, crew 76, passengers 750, built in Le Havre in 1927! – Red Star Line, Registered in Antwerp."*

I then turned back to the table and addressed the most junior cadet; fourteen year old; Joos de Momper. *"Adelborst, explain to me the difference between the Italian Mercantile flag and the Italian Naval ensign?"* The startled cadet officer aspirant snapped to attention, and fear slightly altered his expression, as the 'Fleet Admiraal' had addressed him directly! But the lad mastered his fear of failure and spoke up quickly; *"Both are quite similar Admiraal, having the Coat of Arms of the Royal House of Savoy emblazoned on a central vertical field of white that is bounded on the left by a vertical green field and the right by a vertical red field, with all fields of the same width. The naval ensign however has the added Royal crown of Italy in gold over the Arms of Savoy."* I replied, *"Thank you, Adelborst, stand easy, and …feel free to breathe."*

Kapitaine Voorne, looked at me with ill-concealed satisfaction, and then to Versteegen, he said; *"Thank you, Adelborst, I will look forward with great interest to the review of your harbour drawing at the end of your watch."* I smiled inwardly and nodded, the 'Adelborst in Scheepvaart'; Versteegen; and the other young 'officers in training' had not shown any slackness, and had made their Kapitein very proud!

The *Cornelis* was riding on a mooring buoy some two kilometers north of that fabled city of antiquity; Alexandria, and no more than 500 meters off the ancient Egyptian seawall. The old causeway terminated at a small island on which the first Greek Governor of Egypt; Ptolemy I had begun the construction of the great harbour beacon of Alexandria, around 250 B.C. The stone tower at 140 meters tall, was once considered as the 4th *of the Seven Wonders of the Ancient World!*

Upon the top of that soaring structure, a huge stack of palm logs was erected, inside a gigantic bronze saucer, itself more than eight meters across. These, were then soaked in oil, and set afire at sundown, and the great pyre kept fed with fuel the entire night. This flaming beacon provided a navigation reference to the ancient mariners as far as fifty miles into the Mediterranean! The laborious task of hauling some twenty tons of logs and oil up the 700 stone stairs was performed faithfully every night, without fail; for 900 years!

The structure became unsafe to use in 641 A.D. due to cracked masonry, and collapsed into the sea during an earthquake in the 14th century. Except for the great pyramids of *Kheops* and *Khafre*, at Ghiza, men would not build above its height for eighteen centuries, not until the construction of the soaring twin spires of the great Cathedral in Cologne, Germany.

If time permitted, I had intended to take my cutter over to the ancient seawall and skin dive down onto the tumbled masonry of the tower which lay at a depth of only two fathoms. I longed to look into the stone face of the Cleopatra Sphinx, lying on her side, she has gazed dreamily for thousands of years into the turquoise gloom. Perhaps, I may even retrieve some small artifact to bring the ship luck!

Accompanying me ashore was my chief of staff; Kapitein–ter–Zee (Captain): Derik Van Klaffens, the squadron's second in command Commodore Van Speijk, the battle-carrier Captains; Voorne and Van der Hulst, my cruiser squadron commander, Commodore Lius de Kroon and his Captains; Van der Lay, Van Galen, Scheltema and Schiedam and lastly my destroyer squadron commander Kapitein den Otter.

We were met on the naval jetty by William van der Rijn of the Netherlands Embassy who was tasked with seeing to our needs. Three long black Mercedes 6x4 staff cars waited to receive us, whereupon we were whisked off amid a swirl of dust to the cool shaded grounds of our embassy.

Mr. Van de Rijn had confidential fleet documents for me, a rather gloomy intelligence update, mail for the fleet, crew rotations, canal transit forms and many of the other details one would associate with a fleet deployment.

Finally, national business was concluded and I told the embassy officials to prepare a plane to take myself and other interested officers on a day trip to Cairo one hour by air from the harbour. I had promised myself that someday I would stand before the Great Pyramids on the El Giza plateau, and given the deteriorating International situation, I felt this possibly was to be my only opportunity.

The embassy drivers then negotiated the narrow chaotic streets of the old city, to drop our party off at the British Admiralty to pay our respects and discuss recent developments. At 11:00hrs we arrived at the headquarters of Admiral Sir Archibald Ismay-Fairfax, C in C of the British Mediterranean Fleet. In attendance were several of his more senior staff officers, his senior captains and Contre-Amiral Michelet of the French Mediterranean Fleet (who was later killed at Mers el Kebir in 1940 while under bombardment by the Royal Navy). The ten British officers who had come ashore with us had long since gone on their own separate ways to a debriefing.

Introductions and greetings having been made all around, Admiral Ismay called for opening of his bar and he came forward to greet us, carrying an ornate Cedar humidor which contained excellent cigars. An informal exchange of information and opinions followed. I related to him, the deep impression made upon my crew and I by the fly over by the *Regia Aeronautica*. I presented our observations on the numbers and types of aircraft that we had encountered their heading and from which bearing they seemed to have originated from.

We then speculated on the possible existence of a major airbase deep in Libya that would allow the *Regia Aeronautica* to fly over the Sudan to Italian Ethiopia or Eritrea. The possibility of the Italians shuttling air armadas from Europe to the Red Sea Gateway to the Indian Ocean came as a shock.

If this was indeed the case, then Mussolini could effectively render the Suez Canal useless by total domination of the Red Sea from the air not withstanding their naval forces in East Africa. I then revealed that we had been escorted by the major ships of the *Regia Marina*. I gave a description of the encounter and clearly emphasized the fact that the Italian battleships could maintain 29 knots. A fact which Admiral Fairfax was initially disinclined to accept as that made the *Cesare* class battleships 5-6 knots faster than the British flagship; the *HMS Warspite;* the swiftest of the three battleships in his squadron!

A speed advantage of such large proportions that it rendered his battleships totally ineffectual unless operating with the support of aircraft carriers which were capable of damaging the Italian battleships and slowing their speed at which time the British battleships could close and engage.

I pointed out that the same performance could be expected from their *Doria* class battleships which would soon be joining the *Regia Marina*, and these should prove if anything more modern and capable than the first pair.

Admiral Fairfax then enquired as to our schedule and if it would be possible to transport a squadron of Sea Gladiator fighters to Singapore for them. The fighter planes were replacements for the air groups starting to deploy to fortress Singapore over the next two months.

I informed him that I would be able to take aboard only those numbers and types of the aircraft that were now due my squadron from the Royal Navy's stores. Otherwise we would be unable to accommodate him as we already had thirty extra fighter aircraft aboard destined for our army air force on Java and that further use of the flight deck for parking his crated Sea Gladiators would deny us planned flight operations. I informed Fairfax that the re-supply of my ships would be completed today and that the squadron would depart for Port Said and the Suez Canal at 05:00hrs of June 22nd.

Business concluded, the Admiral invited all present to the officer's mess for a delicious brunch. I informed Admiral Fairfax that I had planned to give the off-duty crews an eight hour pass to this historic city if he approved, a favor which he readily granted. I explained that a number of my officers had hoped to find the time to fly to Cairo to see the Pyramids.

The Admiral's Chief of Staff; Captain Winthrop a student of Egyptology and his aide Commander Speke who spoke Dutch, graciously requested to be our guides, which I happily accepted. Admiral Fairfax said that we were being left in good hands but he had to beg off joining us as he had seen El Giza many times.

Captain Winthrop placed two of the Royal Navy's excellent Short Singapore MKIII flying boats at our disposal for the trip. In this way we could be picked up right at the flagship and landed on the Nile only a short drive from the great Sphinx and the great pyramid monuments of *Kufu* and *Kafre*.

07:00hrs June 21st, our excursion party of eight officers gathered on the port bow gangway awaiting the arrival of the two large seaplanes that could be observed wave hopping across the harbour from their jetty some two kilometers to the southeast. We disembarked to the *Cornelis de Witt's* ten meter launch and approached the yellow and brown camouflaged biplanes now taxiing towards us. Our shore party then divided into two separate groups and boarded the seaplanes. The launch, shoved clear and I settled into the closest seat to the cockpit and strapped in. Captain Winthrop was already aboard and greeted me cheerily while Commander Speke was attached to Lt. Admiraal Van Speijk's party in the other seaplane.

Our pilot adjusted the pitch of the aircraft propellers to swing the nose of his ship past the looming bow of the battle-carrier and into the wind. Once this had been accomplished he revved up the four 610hp Rolls Royce Kestrel engines. The seaplane accelerated rapidly and with the engines droning loudly I was pressed back into the creaking wicker seat as the plane bounced across the harbour. Through the view port I saw the spray leaping from the hull. Then suddenly all became still, the jostling ceased, a creaking was heard when the wings took the weight of the ship as we became airborne. We climbed above the harbour, over the city, then leveled out at 2,000 meters and flew south across the great green garden of the Nile's delta.

Shifting my location I looked to starboard and had my first view of the Nile from the air. I could discern at least six major tributaries converging towards Cairo. The Nile delta I was able to gauge; appeared to form a huge triangular fan roughly a 175 km. per side. It was revealed by our advantage of elevation to be lush, well-populated and patterned with a great variety of agricultural endeavors.

The numerous waterways were rich with avian life and dotted with a multitude of tall white triangular sails. The river deltas were carpeted by vast expanses of papyrus, while the banks hosted cool groves of date palms under which were evident many trim white buildings. Out of the starboard side-light I could gaze out over the seemingly endless gray-yellow sand and barren stony desolation. I beheld an incredible contrast.

Straining forward in my seat, I obtained a pilot's view through the cockpit wind screen of what lay ahead. I was able to make out the silver ribbons of multiple waterways converging to form into the mighty Nile. Of the City of Cairo, I could see nothing, but even at 150 kilometers the three largest pyramids at Ghiza could be distinguished etched by the sun and rising above a blanket of grayish red haze. The ancient lands of the Bible! Regardless of my present duties I would make time and see these wondrous edifices, still considered by many to be man's greatest works.

The pilot, looking back over his right shoulder, yelled out over the drone of the engines that we would be landing in twenty minutes. Captain Winthrop called out to the pilot as he fumbled with his Kodak box brownie and asked him to make a complete circuit of the Ghiza prior to landing. Addressing me he said "with your permission Admiraal." Glued as I was to the port light he did not actually expect an answer.

The seaplane banked into a shallow starboard turn. Everyone shuffled for a better view as we circled the pyramid site at an elevation of 700 ft. Then shortly after executing a lazy *figure-eight* the aircraft descended towards the river, touched down gracefully and taxied towards a small beach upstream of the site's wide wooden dock.

Three sedans in army sand paint scheme were parked under the palms and a large 6x4 infantry lorry with twenty troops awaited us under a grove of palms by the riverbank. Cairo in those days, was seething with intrigues and conspiracies, and the Royal Navy was taking no chance in providing for the safety of our party.

In addition to the regular troops we had assigned to our party, were six gigantic black men of incredible physic and fine looking features. These men, referred to locally as *Cavasses* were professional guides and interpreters, and members of an old respected guild that held service contracts with the British Government going back generations. Only through them were we to interact with the Arab natives.

Their leader Ahmed Abu Ali was a gigantic Senegalese with an easy smile but a very officious disposition. His party was strikingly attired in the most fantastic of outfits imaginable. These it seemed could have been costumes right out of a theatrical production of *Arabian Nights*. Each one the *Cavasses* looked the part of a wealthy Sultan or Prince.

Ahmed was very proud of the fact that his men had the exclusive contract with the British Embassy to provide these escort services. I did observe that they seemed to take their positions as somewhat of a license to be rather heavy handed at times with the locals; however it was after all; Ahmed's world.

Accepting the offer of a lift, my party boarded the military vehicles and were transported up the gentle six kilometer slope to the site. The first stop was at the Sphinx. In those days just the head and neck protruded from the sand.

I walked completely around the huge stone head, checked my light meter, and snapped a number of photographs with my Lica camera. I then halted and studied the sculpture directly from its left side. Having up to that time only viewed photos and artist sketches of the effigy, I now experienced a singular revelation. The defacing done to its nose, could not hide the fact that the profile clearly revealed the visage to be that of a young black woman or adolescent black male!

Given the egoism displayed by the ancient Pharaohs of Egypt, it did not seem sensible to me that their art would reveal the edification of a black individual on such a grand scale, unless that person actually existed and held a powerful position within their society. Either the black race played a far greater role in the history of Egypt than had hitherto been guessed, or the Sphinx came from an earlier period, perhaps an age where a dominant black culture predated the pyramids? The written records of which were undoubtedly lost in the mists of time, perhaps lying in the sands, just under our feet, patiently awaiting discovery.

Indeed there was some historical basis for this last theory. At a time when the black race was generally discounted, one may do well to recall the books of the Roman historian Livy; in which he wrote of the ancient pyramid fields of Merowe, laying within the black kingdom of Kush on the upper Nile. He claimed that these edifices predated the pyramids of the Egyptians by several millennia, yet their stonework was greatly superior! One must also consider the writings of the Roman historian Tacitus, who provides a further glimpse into the fragmented culture of the ancient black race. He describes the impression made by the Nubian Queen *Imane Sheketo* on the Romans as she beguiled then crushed their army which had invaded her realm in 23 B.C.

Gius Marcus Severus, the commander of a Cohort in the 6th Legion who witnessed that debacle related the following tantalizing gem to the senate of Rome; *"The Nubian Queen led her massed army against us in a chariot that seemed to be of brightly polished steel. Although it was quite large, carrying four spearmen, it was drawn by only a single horse, yet it moved swiftly over the deep sand, for it had no wheels but hung in the air on a blanket of smoke! Our*

Spanish legionnaires; seeing the strangeness of the craft became unnerved by its evil nature, and being very wary, saw this as a bad omen. Our mercenary soldiers panicked, and broke formation, then the enemy were upon us. I managed to cut my way back to the barges with a handful Roman legionnaires and saved the Legion's Eagle standard."

This passage is a startling kernel of ancient history indeed. One made even stranger by the passage of more than twenty centuries, to a time when science would make the description of the Nubian Queen's chariot technologically comprehensible!

I then walked to the head of the Sphinx and placed my hands on the warm stone and closed my eyes. My fingers sought in vain for the chisel marks long gone now for several millennia, and ran my palms along the joints between the blocks. Under my skin lay one of the first titanic works in masonry undertaken by our species. Clearly to me there was a greater mystery here, than one first may suspect. The world contains so many hidden wonders. The story of man is ancient and lost in time. How many cycles have come and gone already? Civilizations take hold, grow in size, prosper, then become perverse, bloated, top heavy and finally collapse. How many times has mankind dragged itself up from bestial barbarity, one thinking mind at a time to unimagined heights of refinement; only to have it all topple in a steep swift fall into ignorance? Is man's imperfection the cause of his own demise or do cataclysms of nature account for these cycles? Will modern weaponry and war put an end to ours as well, or will it be greed, sloth and disease? Putting these musings behind me I took my leave of the Sphinx.

Then it was on to the pyramids. I had studied their dimensions and was familiar with many of the statistics associated with the site. I knew how many blocks were theoretically contained within the great structures, how much they weighed and that their foundations were only 1/100th of an inch out from a perfectly level plane, after the passage of 4500years! But now standing before those hand reared mountains of cyclopean masonry I was silenced and overawed by the gigantic scale of the work. It is no wonder that primitive tribes developed a belief in giants when they wandered for the first time into these regions that contained such works. It is hard to even fathom their undertaking, unaided by twentieth century engineering. Keep in mind that as a builder of ships, themselves great objects, I was a man comfortable with colossal objects. Simply stated, the most stunning fact for me was this; there is enough quarried, cut and dressed stone in the three largest pyramids at this site to construct a wall; 3.5 meters thick and 10 meters high that would extend from Portugal to Hong Kong, a distance of more than one third of the way around the planet!

Being a designer and builder in wood and steel I envied the durability of stone construction. If a mason built in heavy granite blocks; his creation could be discernible for five thousand years! My works in steel sitting in a salt water environment would seldom last for more than several decades, executed in wood perhaps a century. Considering the pace of 1930's technology, my proud ship's would soon become obsolete and not long survive in their present form; perhaps fifteen to twenty years maximum, before being scrapped and melted down to provide new plate, and structural steel.

However, these titanic piles of masonry, testaments to an era of organizational ability, engineering fundamentals, absolute authority and of devotion to one's God, would be quite beyond the capability of today's society. Few contemporary nations contain the necessary elements of cohesion to create such works; to organize and finance such a massive effort that must be sustained for generations.

To the Egyptians equipped as they were with mathematics, muscle power, bronze tools and knowledge of the wedge, how much more gigantic must the task have seemed and yet they remained undaunted. Physically, the work could be considered perhaps one hundred times as difficult if undertaken today. Try to imagine the will of those vanished people! I am afraid that their like does not walk the earth today. They certainly couldn't be found in the modern hash reeking Kasbahs of Cairo.

I was then seized by a mad compulsion to climb the great pyramid of Khufu, but I restrained myself only with some difficulty. It would certainly have been a major undertaking in this heat. The impulse was to be frowned on by a naval officer having such responsibilities as I had. I had nineteen ships and 11,500 people under my care. The battlecruiser-carrier squadron represented my country's hopes of deterring a war in the Far East. To attempt the climb on an impulse would have been seen as ill considered, and my government wouldn't long trust this treasure to an officer of an unpredictable temperament!

Our party then proceeded to enter an ancient breach in the side of the Khufu pyramid to view the mysteries of its interior. The coolness of its depths, were a welcome benefit. Immediately upon entering, we smelled a cook fire and came upon a group of grinning local men roasting several chickens for lunch and boiling water for tea. Greetings were exchanged between these and our Cavasse escort. Then I noticed with horror that the cook fire was kept fuelled from a stack of desiccated mummies retrieved from the interior of the pyramid! The Cavasses, seeing our displeasure, and believing that they in some way had allowed a breach of protocol to occur, immediately fell upon these *brigands* and by means of administering a frightful beating and an avalanche of curses and kicks dispersed them all with a great lamentation. Ahmed, seemingly satisfied that he carried out his duties, turned to my men and told us that these men were *filth and were nothing*, whereupon he sat down with his men upon the stack of mummies and began to devour the abandoned meal!

The irreverence displayed by these natives in the dastardly treatment of their own ancestor's remains deeply shocked and saddened me. My state of mind was further agitated when Ahmed explained to me that the local railway had been using the mummies as a supplementary fuel source for forty years and that an Anglo-Egyptian fertilizer company had been grinding up the mummies and shipping them to England for use on little old ladies rose gardens since the 1890's! An incredible defilement of millions of graves! To this day I am unable to fathom it!

I explored the pyramids on the *El Giza* plateau for three hours after which I took some light lunch of melon and relief from the sun under some palms and in the shade of the slightly smaller pyramid of *Khafre*. Captain Winthrop seemed the only member of the party besides myself still having some enthusiasm for exploration, the remainder of my party being done in by the heat and the lack of novelty, for they had been stationed here for several years. I told Winthrop that I would like to return to Alexandria harbour and skin dive off the ancient breakwater. If they would just drop us back at the *Cornelis de Witt* the other officers had to return to duty.

I returned to the flagship at 13:40hrs. *Air Ops* brought me a report that a major storm was driving south out of Europe and could hit our area within a day. The meteorological data indicated that potential wave conditions and high winds would make it difficult for our ships to enter the head of the canal.

My battlecruiser-carriers with their high profile would find it particularly difficult to maneuver in the narrow confines of the canal under high wind conditions. Accordingly I decided to depart for Port Said and the mouth of the canal forthwith. The squadron was ordered to raise steam.

The *Cornelis's* steam horn, a mechanism of some eight tonnes; bellowed out in its deep throated voice that carried twenty kilometers, a message to all ashore; *return to ship*. A signal repeated by the distinctive horns of the rest of my ships and recognizable to their officers and men. All ships in my convoy then lowered their boats with parties of marines aboard to assist in the collection of the crew.

Alexandria harbour saw the still afternoon sky marred by the multiple towering columns of black smoke growing out of the stacks of our ships. Admiral Ismay-Fairfax had earlier requested that his observers continue on with us to Aden. Our ten Royal Navy officers therefore hurriedly rejoined the battle-carriers and with steam up our squadron cleared Alexandria by 16:00hrs.

Port Said and the entrance to canal was reached after a five hour steam. The British always efficient, held all traffic at both ends of the canal and the *Bitter Lakes* upon receipt of our request to transit a soon as possible. Our squadron remained at anchor for two hours until the last ship an up-bound a Greek tanker had cleared the canal and entered the Mediterranean. Other up-bound ships that would have taken too long to make Port Said had to moor in *the lakes* to allow our squadron to pass through.

The transit through the desert would be very dark so all ships prepared their searchlights to illuminate their way. At 00:40hrs four destroyers raised their anchors and entered the canal, followed by two cruisers, two battle-carriers, the fleet train, the remaining two cruisers and these were followed by the last four destroyers the last ships to enter.

The first 100 kilometer leg of the Suez Canal took the squadron twelve hours as a speed of six knots was the maximum possible, as waves generated by the higher speeds eroded the banks of the canal. Although the Netherlands was not at war, I still felt very uneasy. The squadron was extremely vulnerable in the narrow confines of the canal, and that the maximum depth only existed for one third of the 143 meter width at the surface.

The two battle-carriers had to proceed on the outer pair of screws alone. Our ships loaded with explosives were vulnerable to submarine mines that could be set to go off under their keels.

Look outs were stationed at key locations throughout all our ships. They were briefed to watch either bank, and report the sighting of any object or group of men at the water's edge or any vehicles approaching from the desert that may look suspicious. Aided by high power glasses to sweep the canal banks and radio headsets they were kept constantly on duty for the transit. The lead destroyer *Gelderland* had taken aboard a skid from the munitions ship *Nijmegen*, which contained cases of army hand grenades which the crew dropped off the stern at regular intervals.

Perhaps this measure seemed unusually dramatic but this short transit of the Suez Canal was considered the most dangerous part of the whole voyage. War tensions that summer of 1939 were running high and thoughts of sabotage were foremost in our minds.

The *Bitter Lakes* on the canal is actually one lake roughly twenty miles long by five. If the foul weather had overtaken us it was my intention to keep the battle squadron at anchor on the lake. To enter the narrow canal would necessitate a reduction in the speed of the squadron and risk damage to the ships propellers from the wind driving them up against the canal banks.

However by the time the squadron reached the southern end of the lake the effects of the storm, although evident had not made the remaining distance impossible. The Gulf of Suez and open water being only three hours away I decided to complete the passage and our ships transited the short lower canal.

We entered the narrow waters of the Gulf of Suez by 23:20hrs on June 22nd, when my ship's dropped off their pilots, I felt very relieved having cleared the most dangerous part of our journey. At any time a number of old freighters could have been scuttled in front and behind my squadron rendering it totally *Hors de Combat!*

The squadron resumed its open water cruising formation, and increased speed to 17 knots. I would not feel at ease in these confining waters as I had little room for maneuver. We churned south, through the night, and the ship's speed giving us relief from the heat, thereby allowing us to reduce the strain on our air conditioning plants. Our next port of call was the strategic British naval base of Aden located in Yemen at the southern entrance to the Red Sea. There we would refuel the squadron in preparation for the long leg to the British naval base of Colombo in the Indian Ocean. With the Suez passage now behind us I chose to relax a little. I retreated to my cabin for a night of rest, happy to be ahead of schedule. There, while resting on my bed beside the open deadlight, I revisited in my thoughts the memories that I had collected from my all too brief time in Egypt.

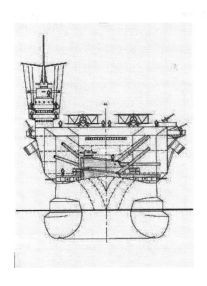

CHAPTER XIV

THE RED SEA INCIDENT

I awoke from a deep renewing sleep, to a fresh breeze blowing across my berth from two partially open sidelights in the portside plating of the compartment. I vaulted out from under the bedclothes to begin my routine of isometric exercises. These were soon completed, whereupon I quickly donned a white cotton collarless shirt and white shorts then entered my day cabin. I opened the gas tight door in the ship's side, then proceed out onto the *Admiraal's Walk* for a lungful of sea air. My accommodation spaces were located on the port side of my Vlaggeschip's towering aircraft hangar structure, at the *opposite-hand* to the air control deckhouse, below the flight deck, between No. 2 and No. 3 anti-aircraft batteries, and some 17 meters above the sea.

Here I enjoyed a magnificent view of the morning and an invigorating breeze. My steward handed me my first cup of coffee and brought me my cigarettes. So equipped I took a mouthful of the hot brew, lit up a coffin nail, and took a deep drag off of the *Balkan Sobranie*, then placing both of my forearms on the teak rail I leaned here to relax. The morning of June 22, 1939 was now revealed as having a clear sky with excellent visibility. I noticed with some considerable relief that the fleet was in the process of clearing the Gulf of Suez, with the land falling away on rapidly, as we steamed towards the entrance to the Red Sea, where the waters appeared as a steel gray slowly transforming into a royal blue. Studying the surface of the water, I estimated the winds to be from the southeast at twelve knots, creating one meter swells.

As the dangerous confines of those narrow waters were behind us, I felt exceptionally refreshed and was eager to face the day. My stewards prepared a substantial breakfast of scrambled eggs and cheese, bacon, toast with English orange marmalade, half a grapefruit and a pot of coffee. My uniform had already been laid out and a small pile of status reports from the fleet and the Intelligence Section, sat on the corner of my desk, and awaited my attention. I was in good appetite and polished off the whole lot, then asked my chief steward to take the coffee and pastry tray to the bridge, for the men.

I dressed quickly, whistling as I did my tie, then with a clap of my hands, grabbed my cap, quickly scanned through the messages and launched myself out of my quarters and headed out down the passageway, taking the steps of all the companionways that I encountered on the way down; two at a time, to the forward end of the lower aircraft hangar deck. There a young 2nd class marine un-dogged the 50 mm thick steel armored door in the hangar's forward blast bulkhead and shoved it open for me.

I stepped out, over the door's high coaming and onto Deck 02 weather deck, just under the long barrels of 'C' Turret, and beneath the shelter of the flight deck, one of my favorite locations aboard. Here I could best feel the ship's characteristic motion through the soles of my feet. All was in order. Moving to the port rail, I paused for a moment to watch the new sun begin its climb. Just then; with the sound of rushing air, and the snarl of a powerful radial engine overhead caused me instinctively to start as a fat bi-plane flashed into view; flying low from starboard to port over the flight deck and heading east.

Looking up at the underbelly of the aircraft some 60 meters above me, I could see that it was one of our precious Grumman Duck float bi-planes. She dipped her port wings and began to circle in preparation to land aboard. These floatplanes were highly prized as they could take off from the flight deck, land on the surface of the sea, and return to the flight deck, as their large central float held retractable landing gear. Generally, they were our first and last connection with land. Her small cargo hold as usual would be stuffed with two or three crew replacements, official communiqués and the mail for my small floating city. On any lengthy sea voyage of the early 20th Century, mail and personnel were forwarded to the British, French, ports of call along the route by long range flying boat. The *Ducks* would then be dispatched to pick up these cargos and land them aboard ship.

The pilots regularly rotated to the Ducks during peacetime, and these were the most sought after duty by all the pilots aboard, for it allowed them time away from ship. On occasion while waiting for the mail and the replacements; the connection required as much as half a day in port for the pilot. On occasion it occured, that the young pilot with time on his hands, achieved another type of *connection* during these short missions, one that generally required medical attention and the viewing of a little film regarding the dangers of careless living.

Still watching the graceful motion of the aircraft in her turn, I slowly covered the thirty meters to the massive 50 mm thick armor plate door in the rear bulkhead of the conning tower. Although a small aperture; the door weighed a quarter metric tonne! A marine standing on duty un-dogged it, and slowly swung it open on its two heavy hinges. Passing through I ascended the steep companionway up into the bridge, where I observed, that all seemed to be in order.

Kapitein Lt. Daniel Voorne who had been leaning on his Captain's chair and sweeping the seas ahead with his binoculars, turned at the noise of my entrance, then greeted me with an obviously buoyant spirit. "Good Morning Sir." He smiled, and then offered me one of his exotic *Russian Gold Tipped Imperial* cigarettes that he had recently picked up in Alexandria, and reported; "All is in order Admiraal. The fleet has passed the night without incident, all ships are on station and maintaining the squadron speed of 17 knots."

I settled onto a pedestal-mounted, red leather padded oak chair located in the port wing of the compartment and accepted the exotic looking cigarette; charcoal paper tube with a one inch long gold paper encased filter. At the same time I waved to Kap. Voorne to feel free with the coffee service which my steward was laying out on a desk top adjacent to the chart table. I picked up the bulkhead telephone and hailed the air command center to request the Chief of Air Operations to join me in the battle bridge.

Having cracked open the large square window of the bridge port wing, just in front of my chair to get a bit of the breeze I struck a match off its bronze frame and lit the black papered stogie. I sucked in a huge lungful, held it for a moment and then exhaled an impressively large cloud of the pungent Turkish tobacco smoke. "Kapitain, *Bloedige Hel*! This is almost as serious as those *Mahorka* cigarettes that the Polish Aviation Engineer from the PZL Aircraft Co. smoked!" Then with a shake of my head and a blink, I held the smoke at arm's length looking at it with exaggerated caution, while squinting at the Kapitein, "Are you sure that these are…entirely legal?" I exclaimed, at which point Van Braekel chuckled.

The '*Mahorkas*' were a strong peasant's smoke. Poland was in those days a poor country so the farmers blended their expensive tobaccos fifty-fifty, with a variety of local agricultural fibers, including hemp, one of their most common industrial crops. Nevertheless, the 50-50 blend *Mahorkas* were unusually popular. I rapidly gulped a couple of mouthfuls of the strong sweet coffee.

The Air Chief arrived shortly, and greeted me. Returning his greeting, I added, "It seems that the mail plane, is right on time. The fuel stop in Gaza seems have worked out very well for it. I do hope that she carries only good news in the men's mail and in the general dispatches." To which Van Braekel, nodded in agreement and added; "Yes, Admiraal, that would be nice for us all."

Air Operations officer Van Braekel, had kindly employed his photographic intelligence department to undertake the following training exercise; *Developing the Fleet Admiral's Ghiza Plateau Film*. He handed me a thick manila envelope containing my black and white photographs. These I studied with a critical eye, some of which even *approached the artistic*, I privately mused while savoring the heavy tobacco blend, and sipping the hot coffee. Then, I returned the photos to their envelope, crushed out my butt, tossed it into the brass shell casing that served as an ash tray and began to work.

I asked Van Braekel how the progress was going on preparing the Army's Fokker monoplane fighter for a test flight. He replied that some of his senior pilots had begun studying the technical manuals for the aircraft last evening to determine its characteristics and to see if there was any quality that could be exploited.

"Essentially Admiraal" he replied, "the army's single wing fighter is a much *hotter machine* than our blue water bi-plane fighters. It will need a longer time to get up to flight speed as the wings of the machine have a flatter, low lift airfoil than our Sea Fury fighters and the wing loading is much higher. Although, the wings are equipped with flaps, the fighter would still need most of the flight deck just to lift off; provided that we were also doing 30 knots into a good breeze!"

"There is no tail hook of course, but the aircraft did have an extremely robust undercarriage; which is "a must" for carrier operations." He felt that the fighter's biggest problem would be landing. It was designed to use a lot of runway. It might just manage to land on the carrier but it would require at least 150 to meters to stop, even while applying full brakes without the arrestor, while risking a nose over. At this time, as is; the Army fighter is one that could be launched from our ship with full combat load and sent on a mission, but once completed the aircraft should return to an airfield as a deck landing would be too risky.

Our deck load of large wooden crates, and tarpaulin covered aircraft would generate considerable turbulence, and compromise the launch of an aircraft with unknown characteristics. The parked aircraft would have to be shifted from forward to facilitate a launch and then moved again to allow a landing on the deck aft.

Initially, this might not seem to be a problem, as we are operating our combat air patrol, but these machines are all bi-planes, which could fairly leap into the air after a twenty meter run down the deck, which was now unobstructed up forward. But we would have to clear most of the flight deck in order to launch the Fokker.

I told him to proceed with those arrangements while considering the adaption of a ship built design for a tail hook for the fighter. He was to keep me abreast of progress or difficulties and inform me when the preparations were complete.

Meanwhile I directed Captain Voorne to inform the *Johan de Witt* to provide the air umbrella for the remainder of the day as the flagship was to be engaged in the preparations of a test flight with the Army's Fokker fighter.

Shortly before eleven, Captain Voorne brought me a disturbing message. Apparently there had been a very large explosion in the canal the previous night. The incident was reported by the large Red Star Line's passenger steamship *Lapland,* then southbound in transit. Her Master; Captain Alistair McBride reported the explosion as a *"very heavy underwater detonation"* occurring at 8:43 pm local time, some 400 meters ahead of his ship, as if from a submarine mine. Much silt and muck from the bottom of the canal had been tossed up to a great height and had rained down upon his vessel, damaging the wireless radio aerials and terrifying the first class passengers upon the promenade deck!

Our squadron was fifteen hours ahead of schedule. Doing the math, Voorne realized that the mine would have gone off somewhere under our long column of ships at the time of our transit of the upper canal. Some, radical group was either trying to block the canal or stop our squadron's progress.

I ordered the squadron speed raised to 22 knots to clear these narrow waters as soon as possible. The convoy was called to second level alert, the combat air patrol was doubled and a section of Sea Harts were flown off for anti-submarine duty.

The Italian colony of Eritrea, is to be found on the east coast of Africa, and some 1000 nautical miles down the Red Sea from the entry into the Gulf of Suez. The colonial capital; *Asamara* contained an air base with an unknown quantity of bombers, but the latest intelligence from the PID Division 2, had identified two squadrons (approx. 36 machines) of CR–32 biplane fighters! These hardy battle tested machines were just a little slower than our Sea Fury Mk II fighters, but not by much, while their big Breda .50 Cal twin machine guns were far more powerful than the weaponry of the Sea Fury and a cause of great concern to me.

The Eritrean port city of *Massawa* contained a sizeable base for the *Regia Marina*. Our latest intelligence reports from OSZ had its force remaining unchanged for half a year at; three submarines of the *Perla* class, plus three large destroyers of the *Pantera* class, three smaller destroyers of the *Manin* class, the old WW1 destroyer *Orsini*, three armed merchant cruisers of the *Ramb* class and a *MAS* squadron (motor torpedo boats) operating out of the *Dahlak Archipelago*. In such restricted waters this was a formidable force indeed!

The Italian's *MAS* squadrons were arguably the most advanced, the most daring and the most efficient at this type of warfare. Two of their WWI model *MAS* boats sank the massively armored Austro Hungarian super dreadnought *Szent Istvan* with two primitive torpedoes in June 1918. Then in November of that same year they struck once again, sinking her sister ship the *Prinz Eugen* using manned torpedoes! I had to conclude that during the ensuing twenty years, the *Regia Marina's* capability had been much improved.

Even with this spectacular exploit to their credit the officers and seamen of the Royal Navy still considered their opposite numbers of the *Regia Marina* to be entirely unprofessional and referred to them as *Ice-cream merchants* or *spaghetti farmers*!

Then one night in December 1941 the British learned a sad lesson. The Italian *manned torpedoes* penetrated the defenses of Alexandria harbour and sank the last two surviving British battleships in the Mediterranean; the *Queen Elisabeth* (flagship) and the *Valiant*. These ships were subsequently raised but were not repaired until after the war with Italy was over.

Commander John Speke who was our very pleasant and efficient Dutch speaking guide on the site seeing trip to the pyramids was killed during that attack while inspecting a large fleet tanker that had also been a target.

European diplomacy in the 1930's had been redefined by the Fascist Regimes of Germany and Italy, when they introduced *undeclared war* as their tool of choice. So there was a basis for my concerns regarding the safety of the ships in my care. If the *Regia Aeronautica* was planning a surprise attack, I for one fully respected their capabilities and was going to be ready. Preparations were undertaken at once to defend against air, surface or submarine threats.

The *Dahlak Archipelago* is a group of islands lying at the southern end of the Red Sea. The sea in that area begins to narrow towards the exit into the Arabian Sea and at best our squadron could keep nine sea miles from those islands without encroaching on the territorial waters of the British protectorate of Saudi Arabia.

The Saudi Nationalists employed any incident to agitate against the British, and we did not wish to create one. The exit into the Gulf of Aden was through the *Bab al Mandab*, a channel so narrow we would pass only 20 kilometers off Eritrea and Ethiopia. One submarine at that location if undetected could devastate my squadron!

The Saudi Nationalist movement had managed to acquire a few twin engine bombers of French origin. They operated these from a remote base whose location the British had been unable to determine! On occasion they would attempt to attack British ships traveling in the Red Sea.

Their plan was to deny the use of the Suez Canal to the British and thereby deal the seaborne economy of the Empire a crippling blow. A sound plan except that their intelligence network could not determine who owned the cargos in the ships flying the flags of the other nations using the canal. Consequently when faced with their own failure they ignored it, and chose to assign guilt rather than improve their intelligence. As a result they merely killed indiscriminately.

Accordingly I gave orders that if any mysterious aircraft attempted to approach the fleet and the Combat Air Patrol (CAP) experienced any problems with identification or communication, such planes were to be shot down immediately. My ships, my responsibility, my decision, let the politicians sort it out later.

Air Operations was ordered to provide a fully armed air umbrella of ten extra fighters and fifteen bombers per ship for the time it took for our passage along the coastlines of the Italian colonies of Eritrea and Ethiopia. The deck cargos were shifted and rearranged many times to create the flight deck space that would allow for this operation, but there was nevertheless inadequate space. Finally aircraft and crates were lowered via 'B' elevator onto No.1 hangar deck and stuffed into the all available corners, with the lighter objects like replacement wings, raised up into the hangar deck-head. No 2 hangar deck had its aircraft shifted until five aircraft and all the remaining flight deck crates were stowed below.

The same arrangements were carried out aboard the *Johan de Witt.* The lower hangar was however rendered inoperable by this activity as the Fokker monoplane fighters did not have folding wings. This characteristic lack of compactness made them problematical to stow and shift below deck.

The aircraft stowage problem was alleviated somewhat a year later by adopting a simple device from the Royal Navy. The solution was a simple "L" configured cantilever beam some five meters long. At one end was a "cup-like" affair that held the tail wheel of an aircraft, the other end terminated in a 150 mm diameter shaft that slid vertically down into brackets mounted at intervals along the edge of the flight deck.

In this way aircraft were stowed athwart ships on the flight deck with the wheels lashed at its very edge and the tail section in the special beam out over the sea, a solution which freed up an extra flight deck space. This usage was abandoned in wartime where the aircraft fuselage overhang was so great that it hindered the training of the Flak guns.

As we approached the narrows the escorting cruisers and destroyers were placed on the highest alert. Ammunition was brought up to the guns, the crews were standing to stations in full battle gear. Thick anti-flash cream was readied to cover face and hands prior to going into action. News of the mining of the Suez Canal the previous evening had traveled quickly throughout all ships in the squadron and rumors were passing among the seamen and becoming ever more speculative, primarily due to embellishments added at each retelling.

The ships continued to run south at the action speed of 22 knots. I pondered the idea that my fleet's unexpected departure from Alexandria fifteen hours early may have upset the timetable of some shadowy reactionary group. They and been unable to adjust for this event due to the limited communications facilities in this barren region, and with our ships arriving ahead of schedule, the end result was the late detonation of the underwater mines. These were my thoughts at the time, and by maintaining a higher speed the effect would continue to narrow any window that an unknown enemy may have had to act against us.

I contacted our embassy in Egypt by radio to give them my evaluation, and they informed the British and the Italian consulates that as a result of the mining incident our squadron was on a *full alert* footing. Aircraft or ships that operated in our area must do so with caution, they must clearly identify themselves if challenged by our combat air patrol and not approach our ships too closely.

The British acknowledged our signal with a professional understanding and began to transmit details of all their military ships and aircraft which we may encounter. The Italians on the other hand expressed mild offense at our warning and they assured us that Il Duce would never consider taking any action against us. The day passed without incident, as all the merchant vessels which we encountered, identified themselves to us when challenged.

At approximately 15:00hrs on June 23rd, our air umbrella spotted a section of large aircraft approaching our ships from directly astern and immediately closed them at high speed to investigate. I ordered Kapt. Voorne to contact the British, French and the Italians to determine if they had any military aircraft in the area as our combat aircraft were about to challenge four bombers. The Italians assured us that they had no flights in the area, the British reply was immediate and negative while the French were confused by our request, and a little insulted.

The strange aircraft seemed unaware of the flight of Sea Fury fighters above and behind them, yet crew members were visible in the dorsal turrets and ventral Plexiglas blisters manning the machine guns and were observed to be staring at our pilots. The mysterious aircraft were well camouflaged with a uniform light sand color base coat on top with daubs of brown, a pattern well suited to blend in with the desert surrounding the Red Sea. The low flying machines were only spotted by our fighters when they left the desert and flew out over the sparkling blue waters of the Red Sea.

15:03hrs the Squadron leader, Lt. ter Zee 1e Klass (Lt. Commander) Rudy Keppler of Fighter Squadron I from the *Cornelis de Witt*, closed the formation of strange aircraft from astern and radioed his observations. He identified the planes as four medium bombers of the type Bloch MB 200, an aircraft of French origin. I immediately ordered another attempt to be made to contact the French, as I knew they had such machines based in Syria.

The bombers flew at only forty meters elevation at a speed of 150 knots. They were closing to seven kilometers behind the last ship in line, the hospital ship *Willem Usselinx*. There were old national insignia on the wings and squadron marks on the fuselage, but these has been sand blasted to almost invisibility. The pilots of these bombers neither responded to repeated hand signals from our pilots, nor did they react to radio or Morse code.

The tension ratcheted up when Lt. ter Zee 1e Klass Keppler radioed that the bombers had begun to increase speed and gain altitude. This was an ominous development as bombers cannot release their load at a low altitude for fear of colliding with debris tossed upward from the target and their own bomb splinters. The mysterious bombers were acting as if preparing to attack.

These Bloch MB 200 was a common French model of monoplane medium bomber designed in the early 1930's. They had a fixed undercarriage, a fairly slow speed but could carry a one tonne blockbuster bomb. The craft were a slightly dated design, but not by any means ineffective, and they represented an immediate and deadly threat to my ships.

I enquired if there had been any response from the French to our radio messages, the reply was negative. Perhaps a sand storm was adversely affecting the atmospherics preventing contact. The strange aircraft were carrying an external bomb load of what appeared to our pilots as two 500 kilogram bombs each. I reflected for another five seconds and then ordered them shot down at once.

Then Jagger (Hunter) Squadron I peeled away from the sides of the formation and our trailing fighters closed to within 150 meters of the strange bombers and immediately began hosing them with twenty .303 machine guns. One aircraft fell out of formation, nosed over revealing its white underside and crashed into the Red Sea as its starboard wing tip caught the surface of the water.

The remaining aircraft maintained a tight formation, and began to return fire from their dorsal mounted gun turrets. Suddenly there appeared a huge burst of yellow flame as one of the 500 kilogram bombs detonated, destroying the three remaining aircraft instantaneously. The attacking fighters were badly shaken by the shockwave and all quickly returned to their carrier.

Normally a bomb will not detonate under machine gun fire. It must have been improperly fused and had armed itself in flight. A nose propeller fuse; winds the firing pin 'in' to the detonator but only after the bomb has been released and a sufficient distance of drop has given the nose mechanism the correct number of turns required to arm the bomb.

The air burst led us to believe that the bombs were of a low quality, the type one would expect from a *backyard manufacturing operation*. Throughout the day no nation registered a protest to my action. We therefore concluded that the attack had most likely originated with the sizeable Saudi Nationalist Revolutionary Forces.

The attack came as a great surprise and caused us deep concern. I reported to it to Naval Headquarters in Batavia as an attack by an unknown flight of bombers, that would neither respond to radio communications nor visual waive off by our fighters. Instead they closed our ships on an attack heading while under fire and had returned fire, and consequently were destroyed.

Privately my impressions were that the aircraft may have misidentified us as the British aircraft carriers *HMS Furious* and *HMS Glorious* with their escorts, a common mistake as both ships were former British battlecruisers of First Great War vintage that, like my battle-carriers had been converted to operate aircraft. The entire incident; from first sighting of the bomber formation until its destruction lasted a mere seven minutes!

Later that evening we had an unexpected encounter with a famous ship, one which held a possible answer as to the mystery of why we were attacked. At 17:22hrs, our CAP sighted a group of warships to the SE, steaming rapidly north along the Asian side of the Red Sea.

The big 7.6 meter stereoscopic rangefinder of the main battery which had been sweeping the horizon that day to conduct ship identification operations reported the sighting as a large warship with a massive tripod mast, surmounted by heavy spotting tops and with three destroyers accompanying her.

The closing speed of the two formations of ships was an accumulative 47 knots so the distance between the two groups of ships was rapidly dwindling, and soon revealed to us that she was no mere cruiser.

British warships, I may safely say, have always been designed practically with aesthetic considerations brought into the process very late if at all. Every now and then the Royal

Navy produced a masterpiece of warship design; an unmatched combination of power and elegance. One such ship approached us now at 25 knots, her graceful 263 meter long hull sliced through the calm sea. She was a legend in her own time, the pride of her service and of her nation, a million visitors had trod her teak decks. All the world knew of *HMS Hood!*

The long rays of the afternoon sun passing through the east African sky illuminated her immaculate white paintwork, turning it into a rich oyster color. Her funnel caps, fighting tops and boot top were set off with black trim. A huge naval ensign streamed from her mainmast. Her eight massive 381 mm guns were trained peacefully fore and aft. The entire ship's company it seemed was turned out in crisp white uniforms lining the rail along the sheer line of both weather decks. A Morse lamp blinked out a message from her towering bridge structure. Glad to see you are all well. Congratulations Admiraal Sweers, your Battle-squadron looks very sharp." Best Regards; Admiral Sir David Browning.

I heard Kapitein Voorne order; "man the jack staff, and when the sterns of our ships pass, dip the colors smartly." *HMS Hood* then dipped her colors to my flagship. The honor just rendered was deeply felt. For centuries the ships of Holland had battled against the Royal Navy for dominance of the oceans to establish our separate trading empires. The rendered salute coming from the most renowned warship in the world and from the most reputable navy on the seas, second only to the RNLN; was quite something for the crewmen aboard the Flagship.

The naval architect in me drank in every magnificent detail of her sweeping lines. I did not take my eyes off of her for one second. Her profile lengthened as she approached and shortened as she slipped past yet from every angle her designers had achieved perfection. This ship and *HMS Repulse* were in my opinion the most graceful capital ships that were in commission with the Royal Navy. The new battleships which followed, although very good, were usually *blocky and business-like*. But soon, the moment was over. She slid past us on a sea as smooth as glass and all too soon after and sadly; forever into history. In my mind's eye forty five years on, I still see those thousands of white clad *Tars* dressing ship from stem to stern along that long sleek greyhound of a hull.

The remainder of our passage down the Red Sea was quite uneventful. The ten Royal Navy officers had been prepared their 16 mm movie equipment for another massive demonstration by the *Regia Aeronautica*. They obtained the best vantage points and waited patiently for several hours, but the Italian aircraft did not show up. They had hoped to film the Italian aircraft once more to see if it was possible to determine if any of the squadron markings matched the aircraft that over flew the Dutch fleet off Malta, and thereby confirm the ability of the *Regia Aeronautica* to shuttle aircraft from Italy to Aden via airbases deep in Libya. A capability, which if it existed could deny the Suez Canal to British shipping!

A strategic threat of that magnitude would require the formulation of entirely new war plan for an immediate and massive concentration of British aircraft to Egypt and the Sudan in case of a threat from Fascist Italy. By the spring of 1940 unfortunately; Great Britain did not, as yet have modern aircraft in any type of quantity.

However no Italian aircraft shadowed our ships. Of their Navy nothing was seen. The speed of the fleet was reduced to ensure that it passed through the narrows during the late morning. All ships were closed up and at battle stations, as we entered waters that allowed my ships no room to maneuver. Ten Sea Fury fighters provided our fighter umbrella, while our six Sea Hart bombers each carrying a 250 kilogram antisubmarine bomb flew an intense pattern around the squadron as it passed through the *Bab al Mandab* channel.

The Hawker Sea Hart bombers were beautiful looking; sleek *shark nosed* biplanes of all duralumin construction. The streamlined biplane possessed a speed of 296 km/hr. a useful range of 756 km and a reasonable bomb load. They were a desirable addition to our fleet and gave our squadron some long range heavy bombing capability. These were the original aircraft that I had hoped to obtain for my battle cruiser carriers as an interim solution until more advanced types became available.

But the British wisely held on to all of their inventory as they were still quite a useful aircraft. We were lucky to obtain what we had; just three per ship! They were acquired from the Yugoslavian Air Force at twice their original cost. The planes with their wings detached were crated up and shipped to Alexandria where they were taken aboard with our other supplies. The air-frame mechanics had assembled them all before we entered the Red Sea.

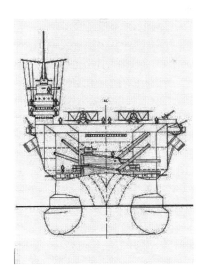

CHAPTER XV

THE BOMBARDMENT OF ADEN

Our ships put into the British Naval station of Aden at 17:00hrs, June 24th. The large ships rode at mooring buoys just inside the Cape, off *Ras Tarshine* point. The much smaller ships of the destroyer squadron with their shallower draft anchored deeper inside the harbour in more sheltered waters some two kilometers off of Slave Island.

The collection of replenishment liters and oil barges awaiting our arrival had already begun to cast off from their berths located at the north side of the Cape. These chugged along or were pushed across the harbour in our direction while jockeying to obtain the most advantageous positions along the sides of our long hulls to aid in the transfer of their cargos. I asked Kapitein Voorne to have the ship's commissary unit pay particular attention to the quality of the fresh vegetables to be brought aboard.

I soon identified a large modern steamer lying at anchor not a kilometer away. The ship recognition team made up of six officer cadets opened up the Lloyd's Register of Shipping and quickly identified her as the *S.S. Clan McGregor* an 8,000 ton deadweight refrigeration ship of the Blue Star line engaged in the Argentinean beef trade.

I asked Kapitein Voorne, to have the commissary contact her captain and enquire as to his status of ship's cargo and express our need to victual. In light of recent events I felt safer restocking meat from a British Registered Refrigeration vessel than purchase the local meat. The salted mutton at Aden was known by reputation to have an unusual slight fishy taste, which led many to believe it to be old camel!

Aden naval station is located approximately 200 kilometers to the east of the southern entrance to the Red Sea in western Yemen. The harbour is dominated by the shattered 525 meter high bowl shaped Mount Shamshan, an extinct volcano. Scattered on its jagged peaks the British maintained a radio communications center and several heavy AA gun batteries.

Lying under the mountain on the north side of the Cape was a British airbase. It had a single concrete runway some three kilometers in length and oriented along the east-west axis. It was the home to twenty Gloster Gladiator fighters of the 2ⁿᵈ Squadron of the 5ᵗʰ Fighter Group Royal Air Force and fifteen planes of Bristol Bombay medium bombers; the 12ᵗʰ Squadron of the 3ʳᵈ Heavy Bombardment Group.

The Bristol Bombay medium bomber was of similar vintage to the French model of bombers which we had earlier encountered over the Red Sea. The machine was a twin engine monoplane of a slightly dated design, having a fixed undercarriage, an indifferent payload of one metric tonne but a very useful range of some 3600 kilometers.

Aden Naval Station was only 300 kilometers from the Italian colonial territories of Eretria and Ethiopia. Consequently these aircraft represented the primary air defense between India and Africa that was available to the British within the region. When I considered the massive air power displayed over the Mediterranean Sea by the *Regia Aeronautica* so recently, I could well appreciate how tenuous the security of the British Empire was in that summer of 1939.

Our ten guests, the British officers planned to leave us at Aden and deliver a report on their transit from Gibraltar. An 18 meter wooden motor vessel arrived for my shore party, half an hour after we anchored. My party of officers and I boarded the craft in company with the departing group of British observers. I took the opportunity to casually enquire of them their thoughts regarding the strength of the Italian Air Force.

The most senior lieutenant raised his eyebrows and pursed his lips in a silent whistle, while searching for words with a slightly pained expression. "My sentiments exactly lieutenant," I replied, cutting him short. "And my flagship?" I continued. "Admiraal," he replied without difficulty, "she seems to be a very powerful, and efficiently operated warship in every way. For the life of me; I can't understand why the RN never retained these vessels with a mind to rebuild them along similar lines. These were after all British ships, British guns and British aircraft. You have demonstrated that the concept works together." I had to admit, that this reply albeit coming from a rather junior officer gave me considerable satisfaction, and perhaps an insight to what may be contained within their report.

We then motored across the bay towards the *Johan de Witt* to collect the party of Rear Admiraal van Speijk, and Commodore Heenvliet, then *putt-putted-off*, headed for a meeting with the commander of Aden naval station Vice Admiral Sir Henry Archibald Leslie-Connaught.

The Admiralty ordered an immediate air escort for the *Hood* upon learning of the bomber attack on my squadron. However, as the *Hood* was already beyond the range of Aden's Gladiator fighters, the RN's air forces in the Port of Sudan were mobilized for the task. Sadly *the force* consisted of only a single three plane wing of land based Blackburn Baffin torpedo bombers. The aircraft were equipped with a single forward firing .303 machine gun and one swivel Lewis gun in the aft cockpit. The Baffin's top speed of 136 mph precluded it from the interception role as the Bloch bombers of the Saudi forces were 40 mph. faster! Regardless of the Baffin's limited capability they were committed to act as *Hood's* escort.

Admiral Connaught realized at once that the Baffin's short range would only allow it to cover one tenth of *HMS Hood's* passage up the Red Sea. Accordingly he dispatched five Bristol Bombay medium bombers. Those planes had the range for the task at hand and although as weakly armed as the *Baffins* they looked quite impressive. By shuttling five plane wings of Bombay bombers from Aden to Cairo and back, the *Hood's* passage was covered up to Suez.

The attack on our ships by bombers belonging to a powerful, well organized, but unknown entity caused a great deal of concern to the KMN and host of nations whose ships required the use of the Suez Canal. The Dutch Office of Political Intelligence, the PID determined that the battleship *Hood* was most likely the intended target of Saudi Nationalist agitators. If correct, the incident was a result of their cavalier attitude towards ship recognition training, which precipitated the attack on the Dutch battle squadron.

The gun cameras of our Combat Air Patrol (CAP) fighters contained the film that captured the shooting down of the Bloch bombers and was studied to search for any clues as to their origin. The film hadn't revealed much except that it clearly showed the bomber's gun turrets returning fire. Our fighter pilots had observed the angle at which the bombers intersected the coastline and they approximated their airfield's location as somewhere in the *Au Namud* desert possibly near the town of *Tayma*.

The British army and Royal Air Force conducted an extensive reconnaissance effort in the *Au Namud* desert surrounding *Tayma*. Nothing was immediately located until an alert Army Intelligence Captain spotted some unusual objects decorating the camels of a small group of Bedouins that were watering at *Tayma*. The objects were aircraft engine shaft bearings. The nomads were attracted to them simply because of their precision workmanship and brightly polished nickel steel surfaces. The tribesmen were helpful and assisted the army in locating where they had found the bearings.

A motorized army column moved inland from the town for a distance of one hundred kilometers where the Bedouin announced that this was the general area where he had found the bright metal. The troops disembarked from the trucks and after a wide search located, scattered ash pits and a partially buried refuse pile. Further investigations revealed that the area had indeed been used as a temporary airfield. Although the original creators of the facility went to great lengths to eradicate all evidence of a human presence some aircraft tire impressions were found in the salt crust.

A disturbing aspect of this discovery was that the impressions were some 17 inches too narrow to match the Bloch bombers that we had shot down over the Red Sea! One had to conclude therefore that there were other aircraft in use by the revolutionaries and possibly other hidden airfields yet unaccounted for. The refuse site also revealed enough intelligence for the army to eventually to run down and destroy a large splinter cell of the suspected Saudi Nationalist Movement.

The following day while the men of the fleet worked on the aircraft transfer, the liaison group of select officers held lengthy intelligence discussions ashore with Admiral Archibald Leslie-Connaught. These sessions passed slowly, made longer by the intense heat. I was surprised at the crudeness of the base facilities. My flagship was outfitted with complete air conditioning for all the accommodation spaces. At 15:00hrs Admiral Connaught, concluded business.

A knock came at the door soon after, and Governor John Fairchild entered and introductions were made all around. The Governor then addressing the room; "I am inviting one and all, for an evening in my home atop the Mount Shamshan for 7:00 pm. My wife Hyacinth has asked me to inform you that she will not accept a refusal of this invitation, and will expect all of your senior officers!" Smiling I replied for my men, "please thank your wife for her gracious invitation, although our ship's duties are many, I could spare myself, and perhaps another twelve or thirteen officers for the evening. If you could send transportation to the jetty at 18:00hrs we will be ready. The Governor smiled and said; "done" emphasizing this with a nod.

We returned to the ships to reassign some duties and shower and dress in our number one formal evening tropical uniforms. At the appointed time six dusty Morris Army Sedans, were waiting for us as the motor launch nudged up to our assigned jetty. We quickly boarded, and the large roomy automobiles whisked us away to board the Army's cable lift that would transport us to the exclusive residences nestled at the summit of Mount Shamshan's wide fractured volcanic crater. Once there, in the comfort of the Governor's mountaintop villa we would soon escape the heat and enjoy a relaxing evening.

The military installations at the summit were not entirely devoted to combat and communications. There were a number of large comfortable villas hewn out of the rock of the north face of the mountain. These were the residences of Governor John Fairchild, General Henry Somerset and his wife Beatrice, RAF Air Commodore Sir Thomas Milford and his wife Constance, and Admiral Archibald Leslie-Connaught and wife Irene. We were warmly welcomed into the home of the Governor our host and his gracious wife Hyacinth, who had an exotic meal prepared in our honor!

Upon entering the Governor's beautiful residence; I introduced my party to those assembled: "Ladies and Gentlemen I would like to introduce some of the KMN's finest officers;"

"Rear Admiraals: Konrad van Speijk-Bronckhorst my Fleet's Deputy Commander, aboard the Johan de Witt, and Count Manfred Van Sassenheim-Heenvliet; my Cruiser Squadron Commander. Commodores: Pieter Wolfert Van Meresteyn; Cruiser Division No. 3 Commander, Derik Van Klaffens, my Chief of Staff aboard the Flagship, Dr. Peiter Berleburg; my Chief Medical Officer, Dr. of Theology; Jacob Bankert my Chief of Chaplains, aboard the Flagship, Doctor Antony Versteegen, the Chief Medical Officer, and Dr. of Theology; Rudolf Solms-Cobourg, the Chief of Chaplains aboard the Johan de Witt. Kapiteins: Daniel Voorne, Vlaggeschip commander, Abraham Van der Hulst, of the Johan de Witt, Pieter Verbeck, Chief of Staff to Admiral van Speijk-Bronckhorst, and Derik Van Rossel; Commander of my Destroyer Squadron."

Lady Hyacinth Fairchild, clapped her hands and said in good cheer, *"such a glittering company Admiraal Sweers, you have fulfilled your mission. Good Heavens Admiraal Sweers, she she exclaimed, eyeing our side arms, you have all brought guns to my party?"*

The Governor answered her; *"now 'Hye' don't fuss, it's just a precaution, there have been several incidents."* I apologized to our hostess as we continued to undo our leather pistol harness, coiled them up and placed them on the table underneath our caps.

I passed a note to General Somerset and asked him to have his mountain top military radio communications center contact my flagship on our naval wave band and transmit the message contained within, a brief coded message. The General, who heartily approved of my swift action in the Red Sea was looking very relaxed and pleased. He quickly whipped up a tall iced *Gilbys and bitters* then passed it to me, in return, in a reflex action that I quickly regretted, I offered him one of my potent *Russian* cigarettes.

Anticipating an English variation on the muffled groans and coughs that usually erupted following ones' ignition aboard ship, I tried to recover the *little* bomb of a smoke from him saying that I had just realized that the tobacco was *a bit over-dry.* But it was too late, the General lit-up and inhaled a great sulfurous cloud of the acrid smoke and exhaled with delight, tears streaming from his eyes.

"Good God Admiraal" he exclaimed gulping air, "Sweers my dear fellow, this is a rather good smoke, in an infernal sort of way!"

The General then related to me some of the family history, and his acquaintance with similar tobacco. His father Colonel Perceval Somerset III of the 4th Regiment of Hussars had brought back to England a tin keg of a similar blend from the North Indian Frontier Campaign back in 1887.

"A Sultan had attempted to flee a besieged redoubt at night during the battle for a mountain stronghold. However the Colonel surprised them with his column of Hussars just at the break of dawn and after a lightning swift action had captured the Sultan, and his men along with his personal war kit which included; various exotic liquors, the tobacco that I mentioned, tenting, silk bed clothing, crates of ammunition and seventeen painted and exotically be-decked Celestial *dancing women!*"

"The delicate booty; *les femmes' celestial,* he said winking slyly, seemed very pleased at the new prospects offered by their change in fortune. However Colonel Somerset cleared them out almost immediately before any shenanigans could develop. My father, the Colonel often recounted to me his exploits as a professional soldier, in the wilds of the mysterious Sub Continent."

"I must say Sweers, this is a dammed good smoke," chuckled Somerset who seemed to thoroughly enjoyed recounting the story. His ruddy face was turned upward and he continued to stare wistfully at the slowly rotating ceiling fan while contemplating the clouds of sulfurous smoke that drifted about. He continued to reminisce for a few more minutes and then the conversation returned to the Red Sea incident, one which revealed the increased sophistication of the SNM activities.

He asked me what the devil I thought about it all; as the Netherlands was a colonial power and must have similar problems to those of Great Britain. I forwarded the opinion that our two nations were both Empires, yours a great world power and the greatest single economy in history, and ours of a similar model, but much more modest. The Netherlands is small regional power, and yet both were on the top rung of the ladder, for good reason. Our society embraces simultaneously; a good basic education for its citizens, an elected government, a strong desire for exploration of new territories and ideas, the pursuit of personal goals, the study of the natural sciences, the applied sciences, and medicine, the development of just laws, the cultivation of a logical mind through philosophy, the expansion of the mind through literature, and a respect and appreciation of other cultures and art. Furthermore, although both our nations had strong religious beliefs, these did not intrude upon a government based on the will of the people and the needs of our nations. In the modern world a state must actively perfect all of these characteristics that I have mentioned or they will fall behind, and their people will remain unfulfilled.

It may be difficult for some of us to accept that our peoples had risen to their current position at the expense of other parties, it is nevertheless true. But that is the world in which we live, and our colonial natives will, through long exposure to our rule, benefit greatly in the fullness of time, from the association. Of course this is an easy, safe and comfortable philosophy for an Imperial power to embrace. But it is nonetheless quite true.

Any group of the *disenfranchised* within the colonies of either empire could be at the root of the recent attacks; but they would have to be exceptionally well organized and financed to undertake such adventures. These same discontented groups discount in their simplified philosophy that as rulers we have provided for their use; work where there was before jungle, roads, railways, plumbing, electrical power, just laws, modern medicine, dentistry and education for their children, and protection from lawlessness. Despite all of these modern benefits, our varied native populations commonly romanticize their old way of life, and agitate for change, with the final objective being freedom from foreign rule. Essentially they reflect the imperfect human condition.

"Also, and of great importance, we just look different. That brings into the equation an ancient primitive instinct that is rooted in millions of years of behavior, there will always be a difference and therefore a certain level of uneasiness, it is natural. We remain the *white faces* in a *brown world* of many ethnic groups, and we for the time being control finances and industries of large portions of the planet. For many of our natives, this alone is a sufficient reason for them to attempt to expel us from their soil. For others; tensions are rooted in religion; we are considered *intolerable infidels*, and our very existence is a crime. My guess is that these insurrectionists are natives within the British Empire. I am 80% sure these recent attacks originate with some type of Saudi Nationalist group, given the target, the financing and intelligence behind the attempts."

"Personally speaking; as a man of *my times* I will live out my role in the world as I understand it: duty to the Crown, to the Navy and to the family. As to the attitude of the Netherlands? She will defend the tremendous investment that is her Empire, her people, her culture, her wealth, and her Queen. We will defend these things now, as we have done over the centuries. You well must know our metal General, as our nations have crossed sabers on many an occasion!"

"Bravo Admiraal absolutely top drawer," exclaimed Somerset as he rose from his chair and advanced toward me right hand extended. Grasping my hand in a firm shake he said that Great Britain and the Netherlands had precisely the same goals in mind. *Ha! Tous pour un et un pour tous, ce n'est pas?"*

General Somerset continued; "Admiraal, I have a social theory which I will now share with you. If the present Imperial Powers had to abandon their colonies for whatever reason, I absolutely guarantee that within the space of twenty to thirty years the infrastructures and industry of those former colonies would lie in total shambles. As rulers we regularly upgraded their world, because it was necessary for the economy, and we had the knowledge to do so. Our former Native colonials, who were so eager to expel us, will in the future, be clamoring to move to Europe to enjoy the benefits of our well-ordered society. Left to their own devices they will discover that wanting is not the same as having."

We were joined by the governor at the chest high concrete wall that bounded three sides of the spacious balcony built into the cliffside. From this vantage point we looking over the deep green waters of the harbour, and the city below. At this high elevation we enjoyed, cooling breezes and a sweeping panorama of Aden as evening began to fall.

Looking down into the city and harbour I saw the ships of my squadron lying at anchor now quite tiny, like a child's toys. We were after all, five kilometers away from them and over 450 meters above sea level. Beyond the bay; the gray brown Yemeni desert stretched endlessly to the north and shimmered in the late afternoon heat, with the mountains already blushing to a rosy hue and casting long shadows.

Glancing at the Governor I complimented him on the magnificence location of his villa, its varied comforts especially the view and the coolness of the mountaintop retreat. I expressed my opinion, that this *Eden*, of theirs was the only sensible way to live in Aden. He thanked me and politely forced a chuckle at my old fashioned attempt at humor, then we turned to view the harbour far below, to mutually enjoy in silence nature's magnificence.

Governor Fairchild focused his attention on my squadron and remarked that he understood that our capital ships were a hybrid design of half battleship and half aircraft carrier and asked me to confirm that my two big ships were formerly British battle cruisers of the *Lion* class. I replied to the affirmative on both questions.

The Governor then revealed that he was a sub-lieutenant on board the *Lion* at the Battle of Dogger Bank in 1915! In that action he was wounded and eventually lost part of his left foot. Due to his wounds he was forced to leave the navy, and entered the diplomatic service. "Well then, I exclaimed, "you must come and see your old ship once again, to bring her luck!"

The current appointment he held, the Governor confided, was challenging enough but a rather dull preoccupation for his tastes. He then asked me to point out his old battlecruiser for him. His eyes locked onto the tiny object and strained to discern the details, while moving to a tripod mounted telescope located on the balcony.

The Governor continued to reflect and praise his old ship, as he studied her through the high power lens. "She was a real battler the *Lion*, right in the bloody thick of it from the start until the armistice. She was a tough lady to, for during the battles of Dogger Bank and Jutland she survived no less than thirty major caliber hits from the German heavy guns. Those damn Hun battle-cruisers though, were a terrible revelation to us! They were remarkably powerful ships for their size, far more potent than we believed, and could they ever dish it out as well as take it! When the German Fleet was surrendered at Scapa Flow, and our Royal Naval Constructors, finally managed to get aboard them, they confirmed that the Hun battlecruisers were built very sturdily, and more akin to high speed dreadnoughts."

"HMS *Lion,* was the flagship of Admiral Sir David Beatty and the proudest battle cruiser in the *big cat squadron*." I'm glad that your people saw fit to give her a new lease on life, it's a bloody shame that our own people lacked your vision."

Addressing the British Admiral, who had drifted up beside him, the Governor continued, "I dare say Archie old man; the Royal Navy would like to have those two *Big Cats* (the old nickname commonly used in the British Press for the Lion Class battlecruisers)on strength now, what?"

Admiral Connaught, slowly raised his eyebrows then nodded wistfully in agreement and said; "yes indeed, they would have made a splendid Battlecruiser division had they been modernized to burn oil. I don't know however, if the RN would have rebuilt them like you did Admiral Sweers, but I can surely see the wisdom inherent in your design.

Why you could even take out the *Hood* from 200 miles beyond the range of her big guns with that pair. Of course you would first have to obtain a more substantial bomber than that foolish little Fairy Sea Fox!"

He continued to study my ships laying in the bay like so many miniatures on a table and said, "*HMS Tiger* slipped away from us as well, possibly the finest of all our battle-cruisers. A bloody disgrace really, now that a big fight is coming. Once again more of our fine young lads will have to die fighting the enemy with second rate equipment!"

A quiet moment followed, all conversation ceased as we surveyed the harbour vista, one and all surrounded by lazily curling cigar smoke. The noise of the ice cubes cracking in the warm liquor and tinkling against the crystal of our glasses was unusually audible, enhancing the quite moment. Each man being lost in thoughts of the future that had grown with each month more grim and fraught with danger.

The staccato noise of high heels on the ornately inlaid marble floor and an exaggerated *haloooo* heralded the arrival of Hyacinth. Arms extended she reached for us locking into our proffered arms and steered us gracefully back into the villa. She announced, "men! No more talking of politics, or history, or war, or machinery, or money, come back to the party." She was the ultimate socialite; determined to mold the conversation and the evening along a gayer more carefree path. All well and good, except that we men had to now remain quiet or *change course* I suppose, as most our topics of interest were taboo to the ladies during such get togethers!

It was during such events that I really missed having my first line of defense which I could fall back on; that wily, sharp, intuitive and intelligent woman, the first commander of my heart the lovely Karen, my wife.

I smiled and turned to the Governor and reiterated boisterously that, "it would bring my ship great luck if he, a former crew member visited her, I am sure that she would be glad to see you once again; one of her valiant crew, one who had rode her into such a great and furious battle! Yes; the War Gods Governor, demand it and the spirit of your old ship calls out to you!"

Smiling warmly Hyacinth, once again took my arm and enquired as to my appetite as she steered me to the dining area. I replied that it was surprisingly quite ravenous. She attributed that to the altitude, it was actually quite cooler on the summit in stark contrast to the dry dusty heat of the lowlands. I also made a mental note to watch the gins as they would pack more of a punch for the same reason.

The meal was exotic, plentiful and with dishes from all over the world. The most discriminating pallet would have been satisfied at that table. The talk soon turned to families and children. All in the room were middle aged; with our offspring being grown and working throughout the wide extent of our two empires. However the dark clouds of war were looming on the horizon and all at the table experienced the same instinctive drive to gather their families about them.

Hyacinth turned to me and enquired of my family. So I related as briefly as possible our family history as I tended to miss them more if talking about them. I related that I had a wife Karen, and that we had been married twenty years. We had three sons; Jacob 19, Ernst 17, Michael 15 and a daughter Maja 13.

Jacob worked in Batavia as a cargo broker, Ernst also worked in Batavia in the offices of our company the *Inter Islands Steamship Company*, our two youngest; lived at home on Biliton Island in the west Java Sea and were employed on our plantation; *New Eden* learning the various aspects of the oil palm business.

Michael takes to the work well, and I feel he might stay in the family business. Maja however cannot decide to be a movie star, a famous ballerina or missionary nun. She loved a popular new American vaudeville dance team Fred Astaire and Ginger Rogers and had a thing for one of your up and coming British actors; Carey Grant.

Sometimes she would brood at length over the book *Song of Bernadette* and declare her intension to devote her life to God and to seek a position as a nurse-missionary in Borneo. I have come to expect anything from her, from a Bohemian existence in Paris, making movies in California or nursing in a contagion clinic in some remote Borneo wilderness.

Karen had departed Den Helder two months earlier for the Dutch East Indies by *British Oriental Airways* Sunderland flying boat, so that she may manage the palm oil harvest on our plantation. There we have 1300 acres of oil palms at *New Eden* with some 16,000 mature trees in all. Our native Javanese manager of long and trusted service, one Garut Sempu, had recently telegraphed us in Amsterdam that it had been an especially good year for the oil palms and he was expecting a yield of at least 2,600 tons of fine cooking oil! The oil palms incidentally were Karen's pride, she had studied Agricultural Sciences at London University, specializing in tropical horticulture and in her care the palm groves yield had been increased by 20%, for me it was all incredibly botanical, a field of science about which I knew very little.

Fortunately for my family spread out this way, Karen is able to go back and forth with little difficulty and keep the family's sense of connectivity. The new Short Sunderland flying boats of *Quantas Airlines*, *Empire Oriental Airways* and the China Clipper flying boat service operated by *British Oriental Airway's* provide a daily connection to the other side of the world. All these large aircraft provide first class passenger service and are outfitted with comfortable sleeper cabins. Sometimes the children go back and forth when out from school and then we live as a family in Den Helder. "These days," I said, "Batavia to Amsterdam is just a comfortable three day journey, barring unforeseen weather. When I first travelled to the Netherlands with my father in 1911, in those days one undertook a major voyage. The steamship on which we took passage was one of the swiftest, but with the coaling stops and cargo handling operations the trip took more than six weeks. The conveniences of flying boat service we now enjoy is truly amazing!"

I rose from my chair, to stretch my legs and excused myself to take an after dinner smoke outside on the balcony as I did not want to choke the ladies. It would have been a poor thank you indeed for such a lovely evening. I took another long look over the panorama of Aden harbour from the ideal vantage point of the balcony. The long fingers of night were slowly extending across the pink sky. The ships rested quietly below us, almost toy-like, and just out of reach on the still deep purple hued bosom of the sea. Then diamonds appeared aboard; as one by one their mooring lights were turned on. A soft desert breeze climbed the slope to bring the faintest sound of a ship's bell.

I had extended an invitation on behalf of the ship to the Governor, his wife and all present if they would allow me to return the hospitality lavished on us this evening. "Please honor my ship and company, come and join me aboard my flagship; the *Cornelis de Wiit* for dinner tomorrow evening.

By 22:00hrs the social evening was winding down and I thanked the Governor and his wife for the exceptional experience, bid good night to the other guests and so excused myself as duty compelled myself and my officers to return to the fleet. General Somerset shook my hand then introduced me to a pair of army officers; Majors Mills and Captain Hancock who were entrusted with our safe return to the ships. We boarded the gondola and with a small jolt we began the long descent down the north face of *Mount Shamshan* which terminated in the small city of *Somalipura*, nestled on the narrow plain between the cliff faces of the mountain, and the harbour at the eastern end of the airbase.

Taking in the evening view I looked to the west across the waters of the Aden bay. The clouds had now parted to reveal my ships lying starkly under a moonlight that was surprising in its powers of illumination. The slow descent would take some fifteen to twenty minutes so I surrendered myself to the enjoyment of the magical and disembodying qualities of the balmy evening. The gondola passed through successive layers of air pockets all having varying degrees of coolness and scent. I savored these last gifts from the wonderful evening before immersion in the stifling heat at sea level.

I was reaching for my cigarettes when the dull thud of a heavy explosion prompted me to glance up. I observed some three kilometers to the west where a dark mushroom cloud flickering with flame had grown rapidly out of the extreme western end of the military airfield. "Good heavens, a plane crash" I queried of our escorts? Major Mills replied, that it was unlikely as all flying was generally concluded by sundown during peacetime.

A seaward light breeze brought to my ears the faintest roll of thunder that drifted around to this side of the hill from the gulf. A storm far out to sea, I casually concluded. Even then; a little alarm bell started to go off in my head.

I enquired of Mills if there was ordinance stored at that end of the airfield? He caught my eye then quickly turned away to study the scene before answering to the negative. "Nothing is stored at that end of the runway as it would interfere with operations Admiraal." "Yes, of course it would, I hope that no one was injured by the blast" I replied thoughtfully licking my lips, with just a hint of alarm. Still looking at the tall black column of smoke from the explosion I noticed just above it actually growing out of the indigo waters of the bay; the likeness of a huge column of cotton which slowly pushed its way skyward to a height of 100 meters. There it hung suspended in silence for a brief moment, whereupon it began to collapse in upon itself, just as another dull report echoed around the sleeping harbour, followed again in some tens of seconds by a faint rumbling to seaward once again. Aden Naval station was under attack!

All being military men, we got the truth of the events more or less at precisely the same moment. Instinctively we twitched as one, then clutched the railing while looking around the gondola frantically as our minds raced through the possibilities. We stared at each other wordlessly, the whites of our eyes betraying our state; we're stuck! Impotent!

We stared around stupidly at each other in our common predicament. The cable lift had only one speed; too bloody slow! It gave the passengers a sufficient time to enjoy the view I suppose, and now, here we were suspended at least twenty meters above the steep mountain face. Rear Admiraal Van Speijk snatched the gondola phone and thrust it toward Captain Hancock and ordered him to get in contact with his people. Hancock furiously flicked the disconnect bracket for a dial tone. Having established contact with the cable lift control room, only the broken parts of his conversation with the operator at the other end of the line provided some fragments of information.

Meanwhile another tall column of water and foam grew out of the bay, this time much nearer to the ships of my squadron! "Damn it Mills" I said to the Major; "can't you make this bloody thing go faster?" I spoke the words even as I noticed that there were no controls in the gondola cabin. I had a perfect ringside seat to an attack on the Naval anchorage in which my fleet rode exposed to the shelling, and here I was suspended like a bloody puppet Admiraal on a string!

I scanned the clear night sky for planes but saw nothing. At once all the electric lights in the base winked out followed in five or six seconds by all lights on the vessels of my squadron and then all ships in harbour. I noticed that most of my big ships lying off *Ras Tarsheen* point had started to generate a smoke screen! I was beside myself with impotent fury! My ships were going into action and I was not aboard! It was the greatest nightmare to befall a commander! Godverdomme! Another column of water grew out the harbour near the cruiser *Prins te Paard*!

The intermittent deep rumbling coming from the sea and the shape of the splashes finally clicked and I realized that Aden was under attack from heavy naval guns and not Ariel bombs released from a great altitude as I had initially suspected. I estimated the shells at 250 mm or greater. Although it was evident that the base was being subjected to an unusually slow rate of fire. I had initially thought that a single Saudi Nationalist's bomber was in action over the harbour. Then I reset my train of thought and started to speculate if we were under attack by the naval forces of a European or Asian power.

Suddenly the *Prins te Paard* was instantaneously illuminated by two yellow fireballs as she loosed a full salvo from her main battery of seven 150 mm guns. The heavy report of which soon arrived, hammering the rock face of the mountain.

By now the harbour was alive with the wakes of vessels as the Royal Navy responded to the threat. A flotilla; of at least six high speed torpedo boats raced across the bay from their base on Slave Island trailing a white chemical smoke screen. Each time their flared stems slammed into a wave the little plywood boats through up huge clouds of spray.

Within a short time the torpedo boats had rounded the headland as they formed up for attack and were then lost to view around the massive dark shoulder of the mountain. More ships from my battle-squadron began to fire salvos at the enemy still as yet hidden from me by the great mass of rock. In a reflex action of frustrating impotence my right hand repeatedly clutched at the holster flap of my service revolver.

I now experienced a terrifying thought and a sinking feeling that churned my guts to jelly, I tried to locate the munitions ship *Nijmegen*. By now she would have been *darkened* and would have slipped her anchor. The attendant RN tug, was moored to her for just such emergencies would be dragging her further out to sea to protect Aden. The *Nijmegen* would be the ideal target to hit in the harbour. She carried 16,000 tonnes of high explosives in her cargo holds fore and aft. If she was struck by a shell and her cargo detonated, the blast would have completely destroyed the entire naval station and severely damaged, if not totally destroyed all the ships of my squadron, to say nothing of the loss of thousands of lives! *

---

* To put the danger into a modern perspective; her cargo had a destructive potential equal to 80% of the energy released by the Atom bomb dropped on Hiroshima in 1945!

Aden base by now had become an angry hornet nest of activity. All the ships in my squadron were evidently forcing their boilers to raise sufficient steam pressure to get underway. Below us we could see furious activity on the airbase.

Several Gloster Gladiator bi-plane fighters had already been moved from their revetments to the airstrip in preparation for an emergency sortie. Fuel bowsers and bomb towing tractors were, I observed racing down the lines of parked bombers. It seemed that the RAF would risk night operations after all!

At the east end of the airfield next to the town, I faintly made out that troops were boiling out of the barracks. Their khaki cotton uniforms standing out whitely under the moonlight whenever the clouds parted. They hastily boarded a fleet of waiting trucks which then careened off into the night carrying them to their prepared defensive positions. Due to the distance and trickery of of the winds, much of this activity was conducted in almost total silence which further added to my feelings of frustrated detachment and helplessness.

All at once, with a sudden blinding intensity, a diminutive sun materialized above the dark water of the bay right off the port bow of my flagship, and a thunderous report engulfed the inner harbour! The *Cornelis de Witt* had unleashed a full six gun salvo of her 343 mm battery towards the open sea! The dazzling effect was repeated a few seconds later by a full salvo from the *Johan de Witt*! WHAM! WHAM! the concussions smote us, now less than a mile away, starting the gondola to swing slightly and precipitating loose stones to tumble down the cliff face. Crack! Just then the *Prins te Paard* unloosed another salvo, followed immediately by the *Gueden Leeuwe* and then the *Oliphant* let loose. Crack! Crack! The *Aemilia*, our guard cruiser, with steam up, whose guns were masked by the towering bulk of the *Johan de Witt* seemed to have slipped her anchor, as she now slid into view from behind the *Johan's* stern shaping course for the harbour mouth! Within a few seconds of unmasking her forward batteries she loosed off a three gun salvo! Crack! I found myself cheering and shaking my fists in the air!

Whatever the battlecruiser-carriers could identify with their high power optics, seemed to warrant a response from the main battery! Was an enemy task force driving forward, intent on forcing its way into the harbour? "Schijt!" I yelled, pounding my fist onto the railing of the gondola. The whole fleet was in action, my flagship was slamming out the salvos and I was not aboard! Here I was returning from a nice dinner party! Just drifting through the sky gin on my breath and stuffed with pheasant which now revolted in my stomach! My ships were engaged in their first surface action, and I was not aboard! A sin of the first magnitude to a naval officer!

The RAF fighters were speeding down the runway in three plane sections, spaced only about two or three seconds apart! They leapt from the airfield and with an angry snarl banked steeply to port and disappeared behind the shoulder of the cone, hurtling into the night on a mission of cold intense fury.

Now, in frustrated anger, I started to swear quietly in a most foul manner. Van Speijk an *old sea dog* himself and quite use to blue words looked at me in surprise and shock. I apologized at once but he waved it off and turned away to look at our ships where another heavy shell had arrived with a roar. A tall spray column erupted amidships and 200 meters short of my flagship!

I turned to major Mills who was just putting up the phone. "Damn it man, in the name of all that is Holy; the bastards must have an observer close by and are directing the fall of shot! They're right on target for deflection on my flagship, and may hit her with the next shell! The accuracy of the observer leads me to believe that he is somewhere on the west side of the mountain providing range correction with a radio, the spotter is therefore inside your damn base! Get on the bloody horn Major and tell your troops in their summit positions to sweep down the west side of the bloody mountain!"

The Major taken aback at my harsh expletive carried out my directive, (even though he did not work for me), then summarized the information he had obtained over the phone. "Admiraal the base is under attack by an unknown naval force lying out to sea, our torpedo boats have been unable as yet to identify the targets but are continuing to close the muzzle flashes at 40 knots." I then thanked him. He was interrupted by a blinding flash as the *Cornelis* and *Johan* fired their twelve 343 mm guns simultaneously with a volcanic blast, one that jarred loose more boulders which crashed down the rock faces. So far, I noted with some satisfaction; the RNLN was putting on a most spectacular defense of the Base!

Perhaps I pondered; it is possible that our impressive display of firepower, was entirely unexpected, and now acted as a deterrent to the attackers? It was a comforting thought to believe that some bastards would be on the receiving end of all that raw power, for at least a hundred tons of high explosive shells had already been sent out to sea in these five minutes! Or perhaps the attackers interpreted the huge fireballs produced by our guns as secondary bursts causing damage to the base? In which case they may cease their efforts to cut and run while they still had a chance?

Mills still on the phone continued; "The torpedo boat squadron commander reports that the size of the flash of the enemy's guns would indicate that a battleship is on hand. Aircraft are up and heading out to sea, but due to the darkness and misty conditions nothing will probably be identified until the distance closes somewhat."

I turned to Van Speijk, my number two and commented on the action; "Commodore, what do you make of all this, what nation with battleships would be carrying out this attack?" He replied with a puzzled expression. "The situation is very strange indeed, Admiraal. The forces possibly arrayed against us could be a Japanese battlecruiser or more likely a German panzer ship! We know positively where the Italian battleships are; behind us in the Mediterranean Sea."

"However Sir, the targets could very well be the British and we are just in the way. Or on the other hand someone knows a great deal about our convoy, and in particular the *Nijmegen*. It may have been their plan to shell her and destroy this entire facility with the resulting detonation. You only need to achieve one hit on her to accomplish that."

I agreed with that last statement then let him continue. "Well sir, the very nature of the attack is confusing in that it seems to be a very timid attack with a low volume of shells landing in the harbour. What would be the point of such an attack unless it points to what kind of equipment is being employed if this indeed is their maximum effort? It is possible, as well that these raiders had been hit right off with a lucky shot from our heavy guns and were damaged."

"Siam could be the culprit? They have a small battleship with four 305 mm guns and our relations with them have been a bit strained of late but that ship is slow and possesses a short range and could never slip in under the watchful eyes of Air Commodore Milford's reconnaissance planes. No Sir, it just doesn't add up to them. Besides the Siamese naval officers are all ex Royal Navy, and they would not do this."

Van Speijk continued eliminating potential aggressors; "both Germany and Japan would have made a very thorough job of such an action; swift and heavy. He concluded that the attack didn't make any sense unless it was considered that our ammunition ship could be hit, the stupendous detonation resulting from such a disaster would easily take out the entire harbour. If the *Nijmegen* was the intended target it would surely explain the reluctance of the raider to approach any closer. A key link in the chain of strategic bases that support the fleet and the Empire would be broken. An occurrence that would seriously weaken the British control of the Suez Canal and would jeopardize the economy and the maintenance of colonial occupation."

"With so much to gain, the attack is actually quite amateurish and ineffectual, as it relies on a lucky hit; scored on a target cloaked in the gloom of night. Admiraal Sweers my money is on the Saudi nationalists. Perhaps they have an armed merchantman sporting old 200 mm howitzers mounted in the hold? The attack to me represents a simple show of defiance rather than one designed to achieve any sort of military victory. They couldn't possibly have knowledge of our ships or their cargos." I had to agree with him. I continued, "Commodore Van Speijk have you noticed that our cruisers have stopped firing, perhaps the targets are obscured or beyond their range?" "Perhaps", he admitted, then countered with; "or the enemy is withdrawing, we definitely gave them a warm reception as their fire has certainly slackened."

The gondola was approaching the end of its journey when sporadic rifle fire broke out close-by in the town. Immediately we all drew our service revolvers and crouched behind the steel plate side of the gondola as it entered the darkened winch building. The old pattern .45 caliber Colt Model 1917 service revolver felt comfortable in my hand. In a close action its 240 grain slugs were devastating to any attacker.

A cockney voice called to us out of the darkness, "*Allo to Major Mills and party; Sergeant Stubblefield here Sir with some of my jolly lads to escort the bloody precious toffee nosed little Dutchy Admirals, back to their pretty ships.*" Our escort then replied; "Watch your mouth sergeant! Major Mills here, with fourteen very senior officers of the Royal Netherlands Navy!

Out of the dark rang the clang of hard leather on steel decking, and from out of the gloom materialized a group of shadowy figures. We were immediately surrounded by some twenty *Tommies* in full combat kit, and with the long WW1 style bayonets fixed onto their Mk III Enfield rifles. They had the appearance of tough lean men, their professionalism was evident in the economy of their every action and their no-nonsense attitude.

Major Mills, with his heavy Webley revolver drawn hustled us out of the terminal and aboard the waiting trucks. We then we sped off through the narrow darkened streets of the old town towards the naval jetty and our waiting motor launch. The whitewashed buildings which towered over our speeding vehicles, had appeared in the afternoon sun to possess a ramshackle quaintness about them. Now these contrasted starkly with my earlier impression in those tense moments. The moonlit masonry with their gaping windows seemed foreboding, and suddenly fraught with danger. We swept the dark portals with the muzzles of our pistols as we careened past.

Mills addressed the senior NCO and then asked for a situation report. Sgt. Stubblefield replied that party or parties unknown had lobbed some 12 to 15 big shells into the base. The shelling from the sea had ceased. There was random rifle fire within the town and on the west side of Mount Shamshsan indicating a potential infiltration.

"Sergeant?" the Major addressed Stubblefield. "Were you aware that all of the officers of the Royal Netherlands Navy whom I have the honor to escort this evening speak excellent English? In fact; considerably better than you do Sergeant, and they all, heard quite clearly your ill-considered comments!" The Sergeant's piano keyboard like grin quickly faded. "Sergeant Major Stubblefield, I must say that you truly shock me! A soldier of your long distinguished service. You do realize of course that we can't have senior Sergeants of His Majesty's Army openly referring to visiting Admirals from our friendly nations, who just happen to be the personal guests of our Governor as "toffee nosed," now can we Sergeant? "Sir, no Sir!" The Major continued, "Unfortunately you will not be able to play football against the navy this weekend Sergeant. You will be getting an opportunity to demonstrate your artistic ability by washing, scraping, and then painting your barracks building, be a good man then and report to your officer at the beginning of your next three day pass so that we may find you some other duties would you?" "Yes Sir" replied the dejected Sergeant, but if I may ask Sir, why on a three day pass Sir?" "Why, three days for the first three Dutch Admirals that heard your offensive remarks, Sergeant, for a start," was the Major's reply. But do not worry so Sergeant, we will use up as many of your passes as we will require, for the Dutch Fleet Admiral had quite a large party of Admirals, Commodores and senior Captains with him!"

I was back aboard my flagship by 21:40hrs. As I clambered up the gangway I snapped a quick salute astern to the flag then was piped aboard. I noted that all hands in the AA gun tubs were turned out in good order wearing full battle gear. Their faces looking down on me from the gun tubs were smeared with white anti-flash cream, grinned skull-like in the gloom of the darkened ship. The big 343 mm kanon were trained to seaward and swung slightly forward then aft as they duplicated the movements of the 7.60 meter rangefinder to which they were slaved as it sought out a target in the darkness to the south.

Kapitein Lt. ter Zee Linus de Kroon, the *Cornelis de Witt's* executive officer met me at the gangway, saluted and then reported; "slight splinter damage to our squadron, nothing that a touch of welding and a daub of paint can't quickly remedy, and no casualties. Kapitein Lt. ter Zee den Otter of the *Zeeland* has the four destroyers of the 10th flotilla, with him at sea assisting the British naval and air efforts in locating and attacking the enemy. The last enemy shell having arrived 16 minutes ago. There had been no surface contacts up to this time with the exception of a faint submarine acoustic contact. It was unlikely given the meteorology that anything would be revealed until dawn. The enemy it seemed had withdrawn into the night. The fleet is raising steam so as to make for the open sea if required. The *Aemilia* had cleared the harbour and was underway to support the destroyers."

Glancing out to sea, I was able to distinguish, some ten kilometers away; numerous parachute flares hanging in the sky, while multiple white swords of light from the powerful searchlights aboard the warships stabbed in all directions lancing through the foreboding gloom. I made my way to the darkened battle bridge illuminated by battle lanterns and the phosphorescent glow given off by numerous radium coated instruments. The staff officers were all clustered in the command center, their faces etched with intensity shone with a pale green hue. While awaiting my return, they had prepared intelligence on the action and their recommendations, which we discussed until dawn. There we waited at action stations for the reports to come in from those ships and planes scouring the murky waters. I chose not to sortie my fleet into what I thought might be a submarine trap.

RAF Air Commodore Milford had been ordered by Whitehall to prepare a massive retaliatory attack on the enemy vessel(s) at first light with every plane that could be gotten into the air. No ship, however swift would be able to steam beyond the range of his avenging bombers in the hours remaining before dawn. Then the target would be identified and blown out of the water! Britain was to make War.

In every sea or ocean of the planet, a Royal Navy Task Force was now operational and on full alert! At the moment the culprit nation could be identified, the closest fleet would be given orders and rushed towards a coastal city of the offending nation, to demonstrate the reverse side of *Pax Britannica!*

I ordered the squadron to maintain battle stations until dawn. Steam pressure to remain adequate for 17 knots throughout the night. Those of my destroyers at sea were to cooperate with the Royal Navy till 08:00hrs, or until action is concluded, but not to venture more than 100 kilometers out. I ordered the recall of the *Aemilia.*

I took some added precautions and ordered each ship still moored in the harbour to lower their 10 meter motor launches, and embark on board them a compliment of armed marines and cruise around and through our squadron all night. All ships would ride on two or three bow anchors, while their engine rooms would maintain 15 revolutions astern on all shafts with rudders amidships throughout the night. A powerful resulting current of six knots would be generated and surround our fleet. It would stir up the harbour mud and present any enemy frogmen with zero visibility. It would also be swift enough to prevent swimmers, or small manually propelled craft from approaching the stationary hulls to attach mines.

I then withdrew to my day cabin to prepare a report to Naval Headquarters in both Den Helder and Batavia. I pondered on what news tomorrow might bring and contemplated the implications of two attacks carried out against my squadron within a few days of each other. Who was this unseen enemy dogging our passage to the East Indies? Of what use was the massive firepower of my battle-squadron if it could not be directed against such an elusive foe?

The dawn was witness to His Majesty's Forces at Aden launching a massive air and sea search including every cove and inlet for hundreds of kilometers along the Red Sea and Gulf of Arabia. The results of all the effort was for naught! The RAF however, had been unable to identify any warship out to 500 nautical miles in any direction! A number of liners, freighters and coal carriers were identified and ordered by wireless to reveal their identity and next port of call. The RN searches had not discovered the culprit, no enemy vessel lay camouflaged in a small bay.

All the shipping in the vicinity was monitored, and each ship was thoroughly inspected by the local cooperating authorities before being allowed to discharge cargo. These same cargoes were picked apart or otherwise investigated in the search for clues of the perpetrators. There were no merchantmen found to have heavy howitzers mounted in their holds. Nothing was discovered that could cast a light on the identity of the raiders. The sea was empty of potential targets. Even if the enemy had been sunk by our return gunfire a large patch of wreckage and fuel oil would have been located.

We had a genuine mystery before us, one that immediately impacted the value of the Pound Sterling. By the close of business on the first day following the attack the Imperial currency had lost 5% of its value! For apparently it was now possible for a party or parties unknown to wage warfare against the HM's Empire with no fear of retaliation! Either a battleship or ship of quite large size had just vanished completely into thin air or the entire RAF command Aden was completely inept, and the Empire a house of cards!

All of England was aroused to fury at this unprovoked flagrant attack. The Prime Minister's was in no mood to receive the Governor's report which stated that no target could be located and that the Army would require replacement aircraft as its Bristol Bombay medium bombers had a lot of time on them. Air Commodore Milford was in such a mood that he could not easily be approached. His superiors were demanding retaliation but there was no target.

A key British naval base to the Empire had been attacked from the sea and the culprits had gotten cleanly away; *Scott Free* without even being identified! Unimaginable! Unheard of! Aerial Reconnaissance by the end of the day had found nothing. Parliament the morning of the second day of fruitless searching proclaimed RAF's response to the *Aden Crisis* a national disgrace! The press had a field day and called for Milford's head!

Later that day the British Army combat engineers located and diffused a dud shell from the attackers. It was indeed a 305 mm shell. Whitehall announced that the projectile's manufacturer would be quickly identified and records would clearly indicate precisely not only what country perpetrated the attack but what ship had been issued that particular ordnance. Then suddenly and mysteriously all voices became very subdued, and the subject became *hush-hush* and *top secret*.

The whole affair slipped into obscurity and was overshadowed by the titanic events about to rip the world apart. Mankind once again; drunk with greed, armed to the teeth with stupidity, and blinded by massive ego, had staggered like a mad bull into the proverbial China shop!

Shattering events were close at hand, that would reduce half of the self-proclaimed *progressive nations* of world to rubble and destroy 100 million lives! Not until 1971 some 42 years after the attack was carried out were the veils lifted on this incident, and the entire event revealed to me.

The summer of 1971, Karen and I had spent in London. I had been rummaging through one of my favorite book-stores on Shaftsbury Street when I picked up the *"Memoirs of Brigadier General Frederick Dalton Mills."* The inner leaf held a photograph of the author whom I instantly recognized as an older and more worn visage of the Major Mills, our escort with whom I shared the gondola ride down *Mount Shamshan* on the evening of the shelling of Aden Naval Base in June of 1939.

I purchased the book and retired to our cozy London flat whereupon I settled into the big leather chair for a good read. I made a pot of Orange Pekoe; my favorite tea, and fumbled for a few minutes in my vest pocket for my Ronson lighter and my Dutch

Pantera cigarettes until I remembered that Karen made me quit smoking in 1961...Blast! I read the entire memoir in two days, between comfortable naps. Major Mills apparently distinguished himself fighting in Africa under General Wavel and then later under General Montgomery. He was involved in the defense of Tobruk and later at El Alemein where his inspired redeployment of several light anti-tank guns broke up a desperate thrust by the Italian *Centaro Armoured Divison. Freddie* was then attached to General Alexander's staff in 1944, and through the effective interrogation of some Italian prisoners of war he discovered and cracked a Saudi Nationalist spy ring working for the Nazis in Malta. The *truth drug* scopolamine was employed on several of the most stubborn of these agents and much was revealed; including to his amazed ears the details of the attack on the Aden Military Base in 1939!

Air Commodore Milford and the best efforts of the RAF, failed to find any enemy battleship that morning because the culprit was a submarine! A British craft of WWI vintage! The *M Class* boats were armed with a single 12 inch forward firing gun with twenty rounds and four 18 inch torpedo tubes. The design was intended to provide a capability to carry out a shore bombardment with stealth, and investigate the potential of the gun as an anti-shipping weapon. As the twenty 12 inch shells of the submarines magazine could be had for the price of a single torpedo, one is able to deduce that economics played a large role in the M Class submarine's development. The concept did not seem to catch on due for several reasons. The first and most serious was that it required the submarine to surface to fire, thereby making itself very vulnerable to attack. Secondly was the incredible shock placed on the small hull which compromised watertight integrity? Lastly was the one of stability. The great weight of the gun, its housing and machinery was placed above the submarine's *air bubble,* making her unusually *tender.* Consequently only three vessels were built for the Royal Navy before the Great War.

The submarine M3 was decommissioned and put up for disposal or scrapping in 1932. The M1 had been sunk in a collision in 1925 and the M2 foundered in 1931 or 1932. But the decommissioning procedure and disarming of the M 3 was somehow improperly supervised and a host of major items were overlooked and then forgotten in the glut of warships which crammed the breakers yards at the end of WW I. The empire needed new merchant ships to carry the life blood of the Empire, as several thousand now lay at the bottom of the ocean! The navy was to be scrapped to provide the steel!

The M Class boat's 12 inch gun used special shells and these were to have be emptied of their bursting charge by the naval ordinance group at Portsmouth dockyard. However the shell casings themselves were not destroyed and later the storage records went missing as did their fuses and special tools. The entire lot which had been intended for scrapping was apparently spirited away and ended up in the possession of a construction company, owned by a French oil company in Syria, owned by a family from Saudi Arabia. A branch of the same company had also recently acquired a vessel listed as an ex Royal Navy Submarine Depot Ship. The ship delivered was a (fully capable) submarine the surviving M3, last of its class. The salvage equipment of the Oil Company allowed for the recovery of a great deal of cordite propellant from the many warship wrecks laying in shallow water. Cordite, any commercial diver will tell you is particularly resistant to submerging in salt water, and still retains its explosive properties even after fifty years on the ocean floor.

That M3 was put in operational condition by the employment of some ex-U boat men who had chosen the life of; *gentleman adventurers* (the term used for piracy if you come from a good family), and the rest was history. These wellborn criminals established a base inside the hull of a sunken freighter, in a bay of *Abd Ali Kari Island* which is part of the *Suqutra Chain* of Islands off the tip of present day Somalia. These are strategically located across the lanes of sea commerce for all vessels entering or exiting the Red Sea via the southern straits.

Apparently when Whitehall had all the ordinance traced, and discovered that the attack on Aden was carried out by an ex RN vessel the curtain of silence came down and MI-6 was brought in. Further investigations revealed the magnitude of the failures of their system. Thousands of shells of all calibers and hundreds of tons of explosives remained unaccounted for. The deplorable record keeping and lax attitude evident in most of the dockyard office workers for the established procedures for the disarming and disposal of warships and armaments was not only sobering but criminal!

The entire affair was buried and Commodore Milford quickly let off the hook with his career intact due to the fact that he was a Knight of the Realm and extremely well connected. I believe his family held a 15% interest in the *Times*. No public servant regardless of position, eagerly seeks to contend with an adversary whose livelihood is made with the written word and who purchases ink by the tonne.

The cracking of the Saudi Nationalist spy ring in Malta in 1944 had catapulted the Major's career to new heights and he finished the war a General and was posted as deputy commander of the Suez and Palestine in 1947. Here his relevance to this account ends.

The threat of further attack notwithstanding; preparations continued for the next 3,400 nautical mile voyage eastward across the vast expanse of the Indian Ocean to the British Naval station of Colombo on the Island of Ceylon. Every ship took on her maximum of fuel oil and other consumables. The dry goods and foodstuffs where shuttled from the supply ship *Arnhem* which was equipped to offload cargos to rafted ships lying to port and starboard. I had requested a copy of the food testing report from the Commissariat on those goods purchased locally, to ensure that there would be no problems. The fresh vegetables were carefully tested by Lt. ter Zee 3e Klass Dietician Toering an officer who organized his unit with an eagerness of a man who had long waited longed to employ his skills.

The detailed reports he produced on the number and type of tests that he had performed on the food was very extensive. I skimmed through it noting the neatness and precision with which he had inscribed his chemical equations. The absolute fastidiousness of his work convinced me that nothing would get past the food technicians of this officer and substandard food would never be a problem experienced by my squadron.

The British Blue Star Line refrigeration ship *Clan McGregor* was contacted for the purpose of re-supplying the squadron. Her Captain Angus Ferguson informed us that his cargo was 6,000 tons of frozen Argentinean beef and 1,500 tons of Falkland Island's Mutton bound for Odessa. Our request to purchase 40 tonnes of frozen beef was radioed by Captain Ferguson to the owners of the cargo in Madras. The transaction was subsequently concluded, and the meat quickly distributed throughout my nineteen ships.

In this way we brightened up the mess menus for the remainder of the voyage. Although the Fleet Surgeon had recommended fish as our protein staple for the tropics the cooks were having some difficulty with variety. Despite their best efforts to remain creative, everyone was getting a little tired of the herring, chicken, kippers and sardine dishes. Rumors of a sardine porridge were circulated causing much dreadful anticipation. This was enough for me to tip the scales and secure the beef for the squadron. The seemingly innocent rumor deeply offended our hard working and dedicated cooks, so I requested that Kapitain Voorne grant our sea cooks an extra gallon of beer each for the remainder of the week. The ship's galley was once again a happy places to work.

All preparations were completed in the early afternoon and I ordered the fleet to light boilers and produce steam to make revolutions for 17 knots in two hours at 15:30. Once again an exotic harbour saw tall columns of smoke grow out of the stacks of our fleet. They grew to a height of seven thousand feet until they had their tops knocked over by a breeze. While I waited for sufficient steam pressure to build up I indulged the Governor.

Although the recent attack put the kibosh on the planned feting of the Colonial dignitaries, the Governor and General Somerset had taken this opportunity of a free hour and came aboard the *Cornelis de Witt* formerly the Governor's old ship the battlecruiser *HMS Lion*. A tour of the aircraft hangars, machine shops and the gun batteries seemed of genuine interest to all. The General's questions were quite technical and he kept several young officers very busy answering these. There was little recognizable of the old battlecruiser, but Governor Fairchild didn't seem to mind as he sat on a lounge chair in the shade of the foredeck's expansive canvass awning. He shared some chilled Gin with me and puffed on his briar pipe and gazed wistfully aft towards the main battery of A & B turrets which in his opinion the closest view was remaining aboard that resembled his old ship. Fairchild remarked that he still recognized her even after such extensive work, especially the view under the awning was almost identical as the canvass obscured everything above 'B' gun Turret.

The mining incident in Suez Canal, followed by the two unexplained attacks over a two day period were of great concern to all in the Fleet. In Aden I had called a staff meeting of all department heads aboard my flagship to discuss our overall state of readiness to meet all possible threats for the remainder of the voyage. It was concluded after a thorough discussion that all our ships were operating very efficiently with the exception of the two battle-carriers. These were rated at 50% of their full potential due to their anemic bomber groups, and having both flight decks crowded with crates shrouded in canvas.

In light of the recent events our fighter group's commander Kapitein Lt. ter Zee Vlieger (Commander): Jakob Van Prooijen was of the opinion that due to the rapid progress of military aviation, the light bombers of his command which were barely adequate for peacetime training was by now quite dated and practically useless for modern combat. In light of the recent events I had to agree with his assessment, for I too had lost all confidence in these units. As soon as possible they should be regulated to training duties and put ashore.

The Fairy Sea Fox *fighter bomber* continued to be our battle-carriers' greatest weakness, the machine's tiny 100 kilogram bomb load, made it almost useless, and this was aggravated by its limited ability as a fighter! The machines were therefore regulated to anti-submarine duty only. If only these had been Hawker Sea Harts we would have had a useful bomber group. The Sea Hart, an aircraft of the same vintage as the Sea Fox was an entirely superior carrier bomber design, and still suitable for service in 1939, as it carried more than twice the weight in bombs!

When I added to the Sea Fox's faults, the problem of supply for our spare parts drying up, our battlecruiser-carrier division, so recently added to our navy at great expense, was rapidly losing a large portion of its primary function; to attack surface targets on land or at sea with useful tonnages of bombs and torpedoes.

My squadron was in mid-voyage, facing an unknown hostile force(s) and our striking power was practically ineffectual! What would we do if threatened by a powerful Japanese naval force that we could neither engage on the surface with gun or from the air with bombs, nor outrun? Thank God for our squadron's 28 Swordfish Mk I torpedo planes still aboard, which had been slated for land based operations!

Accordingly I told my senior air operations officers for both battle carriers to crate up our squadrons of Sea Foxes, send them over to the supply ship and switch them out with the PZL P23 dive bombers that were sitting in the *Arnhem's* hold! It was a momentous task under these conditions. I therefore ordered that the entire ship's company to be subordinated to this task if required, but I wanted those PZL bombers on board before sailing from Aden. To support this effort I requested barges and tugs from the Royal Navy. The battlecruiser- carriers were ordered to lay alongside the supply ship as soon the tugs were made available and begin the transfer of cargos.

The Polish State Aircraft company (Panstwowe Zaklady Lotnicze or PZL) in 1937 saw an opportunity to develop new business by winning a contract to supply a heavy dive bomber for the RNLN's new battle-carriers. Accordingly the Polish design team sought to develop a prototype craft from their very successful standard army bomber the PZL P-23. The original design was stressed to allow for an increased dive angle and the wings were redesigned to fold up at the undercarriage struts. The prototype first flew in August 1937. The subsequent trials showed great promise and an order was placed for twenty eight aircraft, followed in three months by a further contract for fifty six planes with 100% spares, one hundred and forty aircraft in total. The Poles also sold us a license to manufacture these bombers but the completion of the new aircraft plant in Holland to deliver these machines was halted by the Nazi invasion in May 1940.

These stop gap bombers were obtained to fill the operational shortfall should the supply of British replacement aircraft cease and if the Americans were unable to supply us with the decommissioned biplane air groups from their carriers *Lexington, Saratoga* and *Ranger* as originally offered.

However the American planes were obtained as arranged while the Polish Government began a crash building program of military aircraft for their own Air Force. With this redirection of effort and resources, PZL had no surplus capacity for the further needs of the RNLN. The initial orders were filled as contracted. The planes had been crated up and delivered to Amsterdam just in time for our deployment. These were to follow our squadron to the Far East in the cavernous holds of our merchant vessels in the months to follow. Sailing with us we had aboard twenty eight PZL bombers plus 100 % replacements. All aircraft were loaded onto the *Arnhem* prior to our departure from the Netherlands.

I bid farewell to the Governor and his party at the clanking of the capstan. The rattle of the heavy anchor chains signaled that the final preparations for getting underway had commenced and in light of recent events we daren't tarry.

June 26th 15:40hrs, with the aircraft transfer completed, the Dutch Convoy had cleared the British naval base. Soon we were joined by the *Nijmegen* and her destroyer escort which had remained in a secluded anchorage. In short order the Fleet was steaming eastward at 17 knots into the seemingly comparative safety of the Gulf of Aden. Within a few hours I would have sufficient sea-room to maneuver the ships if threatened. Our new course would take us across the Indian Ocean and our next landfall; the mysterious and ancient Island of Ceylon.

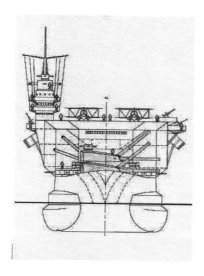

CHAPTER XVI

THE VOYAGE TO CEYLON

The port city of Aden, in southern Yemen; was one of the key naval bases of the British Empire. The city was strategically located adjacent to the most heavily used shipping lanes of that globe spanning maritime operation, those routes being from the Suez Canal of Egypt, which joined the waters of the Mediterranean Sea to those of the Red Sea, and then out into the Indian Ocean. The canal provided a shortcut that eliminated the circumnavigation of Africa, and reduced the voyage to India from Britain by several months.

Aden, guarding the gateway to India; the British Empire's greatest colony, had been bombarded at night by an unknown naval force. An *Act of War* had been unleashed upon the planet's greatest economic and military power, and the perpetrators had seemingly broken off the action at their own discretion; and had vanished into the night. The extensive and efficient Naval and Air Forces of the Empire, could locate no culprit, and their identity remained a complete mystery, and their rash act unpunished!

The attack on Aden was a direct challenge to the power and authority of *British Imperial Rule* over some 34,000,000 square kilometers of territory, and its seven hundred million subjects! The largest Economic and Imperial Power on the planet had been assaulted, the world watched and held its breath!

The inhabitants of more than fifty Crown Colonies, Mandated Territories, Dominions, Protectorates and Condominiums waited to see what their Imperial ruler would do? If Britannia's response was deemed ineffectual, millions of businesses may elect to seek more profitable markets outside of the Empire. Just as likely, hundreds of millions of subjects may reconsider paying taxes to the Crown in the belief Britain had grown weak and that self-rule was within their grasp. The *Human experience*, as contained in four thousand years of recorded history; reveals that all Empires end.

Powerful economic competitor states now evaluated Britain's perceived weakness and schemed for potential new colonies, anticipating her loss of control. The entire economy of the Empire lay in the balance. In one day the Imperial Treasury lost tens of millions of pounds sterling as its exchange rate dipped on the world markets. Lloyd's Insurance rates on British shipping jumped 17% over the course of three days! The stock value of steamship lines, and many companies that they served; with colonial holdings in mining, rubber, tea, tin, oil, grains etc. were sharply down following the attack on Aden.

The British Parliament was in an uproar. The fury was directed at the PM's Office, which in turn focused their attentions on the Admiralty, and the Royal Air Force. Air Commodore Milford, and Admiral Leslie-Connaught, the commanders of Aden's defenses were on the *hot seat*. These officers, however had acted promptly having immediately ordered; a systematic air and sea search to be undertaken using all available aircraft and ships. Yet no suspect vessel could be located out to 500 miles from Aden! The seeming impotence of HM's forces *to run to ground* the perpetrators of the outrageous attack on the base in Aden was exasperating!

Four newspaper editions per day were rolling off the Fleet Street presses, and still these could not meet the demand of an enraged population! Within their pages; Milford, Leslie-Connaught, British Arms and the PM's office were being alternately barbecued by the merciless British journalists. They were enjoying a *field day* at the Armed Service's expense. For every statement that 10 Downing Street released which rationally explained the logic of the operations which had been undertaken to defend the Empire, there were five other stories that engaged in taking wild pot shots at the Defense Ministry, and the Military Command at Aden.

In Parliament, the hawks were decrying the enfeebled state to which Great Britain's military power had been allowed to sink! In the newspapers huge headlines stated that; *the Lilliputian Dutch Navy had saved the colony and the honor of Britain.* Who, and where were the culprits? Had they been sunk by Dutch gunfire? The Gulf of Aden had been thoroughly searched. There was no evidence of flotsam, or an oil slick to support that idea that the attackers had been sunk. A true mystery was at hand. Such a mystery sells a lot of newspaper, as any and all speculations are characteristic of such an event.

The Independent Labor Party cited the inability of the massive air and sea search to locate the attackers, and railed against the waste of tens of millions of pounds on weaponry. They further maintained that the current crisis was emblematic of a misdirected philosophy, and a failed administration.

My command on the other hand had responded most spectacularly to the shelling of Aden. The awe inspiring thunder and massive bright fireballs emitted by our heavy gun salvos at night left a vivid impression on the city, regardless of how ineffective they'd been proven.

The press was unfairly contrasting the dramatic display of our massed heavy guns with the apparently lackluster response of British arms to the attack. I dare say that if the *gentleman of the press* had actually been in Aden that night and enjoyed the same perspective of the harbour which I obtained from the gondola they may have reserved their opinions.

To me, the spectacle of Aden's harbour alive with the motor torpedo boats making for the open sea at 45 knots, combined with the number of night sorties by the various fighter and bomber squadrons was a powerful and vigorous demonstration of a maximum response to the surprise attack. The only actual casualties suffered by Aden due to the entire brief action that I could discern were an empty shed at the end of the airfield, Sgt. Stubblefield's football game and his three day pass!

In my official report; I emphasized that; *British Arms had responded at once, and with vigor.* However, to the *gentleman* of the press and radio, the facts, observations, and reasoned opinions, that I and other eye witnesses had provided, constituted information which was deemed to be only of minor interest to the public. The media outrageously flogged the rumor. *Sensationalism* seemed to be the flavor of the week, as long as it sold newspapers, and radio air time!

The Government of the Netherlands had been thanked and complimented in the British House of Commons by the leader of the Labor Party; for the spirited defense of Aden! I was naturally quite proud of my squadron's response but it hardly seemed fair to Admiral Connaught and Air Commodore Milford, since our combined forces had still come up empty after an extensive search for the elusive raiders!

But the responsibility for the defense of Aden; fell squarely upon the shoulders of the His Britannic Majesty's forces; land, sea and air which were stationed at the base, and it was upon them, that the full fury of the Government and News services fell.

Only yesterday I sat across a table from these amiable senior officers and their wives enjoying their company at Governor Fairchild's sumptuous repast. We broke bread, shared culinary delights, sincere conversation and good humor. Now as a result of the attack, an unforeseen event, their stars were sinking and mine was rising, neither through their fault, nor my effort.

There were a number of newspaper cartoonists that may have a field day with lampooning my situation, trapped and ineffectual as I was during the gondola ride down the side of *Mount Shamshan*! However, it was not a Dutch Naval Base which had been under attack. The men of my battle-carrier squadron were hailed as heroes of the day, both by the people of home and abroad. The Government of the Netherlands, already alerted from the Suez mining incident, chose to show a unified front with Great Britain.

Air Commodore Milford and General Somerset, and to a lesser degree Governor Fairchild; all fine gentleman and officers, was being fed into *the meat grinder of fickle British public opinion*, for what I perceived as entertainment for the general public! Such a stupid waste of time and energy.

Our voyage to Ceylon had commenced. Above us wheeled a flight of ten modern Gloster Gladiator bi-plane fighters, an improvised combat air escort; mobilized from Aden's airstrip. After the mysterious and unprovoked attack, the Aden Naval Station's forces were on the highest level alert. Air Force General Thomas Milford provided a fighter umbrella until our ships cleared the harbour and worked up sufficient speed to launch our own fighters. Further out to sea the long range medium bombers of his command flew an intense fan shaped search pattern from dawn till dusk scouring the ocean for any warships or unusual contacts.

Ahead of us lay a voyage of some 3,400 nautical miles. Every revolution of the *Cornelis's* propellers brought me closer to my beloved wife and family. It would be good to walk through the enchanting palm groves of *New Eden* my ancestral plantation once again, with Karen on my arm. I had a thirty-day leave coming when the squadron reached Soerabaja, I was hoping that it would not be delayed due to these recent developments.

I stood on the bridge deck of the air operations island and looked aft towards the remainder of the fleet. It was strung out behind the *Cornelis de Witt,* as it cleared the mole and stood out into the Arabian Sea. To port in the distance stood the huge ragged multiple volcanic cones of *Mount Shamshan*. These crags swiftly fell behind, and slipped below the curve of the sea as my fleet sped southeast.

Our next astern; the *Johan de Witt* signaled to her escorts and then swung out of line to port turning into the wind. She began to work up to 20 knots in preparation to launch the first fighter umbrella for the day. I noted with satisfaction how her well drilled escorts reformed to screen her.

I looked aloft at the Gladiator fighters: with their enclosed cockpit they represented only a modest advance over our Sea Furies. The Gloster company also developed a naval version of this fighter for carrier operation; the Sea Gladiator Mk I. I would have liked to have had those fighters aboard as they had a reliable air cooled radial engine and twice the firepower of our Sea Fury MK II, which although a capable fighter, was a five year old design and already a dated machine, its attractive sleekness notwithstanding.

Above the fleet; our Gladiator escort resumed a tight formation, over flew the Vlaggeschip then waggled their wings and shaped course for Aden. I looked to port and the *Johan* was steaming in battle fleet formation having completed the launch of the fighter umbrella. Already the first planes had risen to the patrol altitude and had begun their search patterns. The sleek bi-planes, carefully polished by their dedicated crews winked in metallic brilliance in the bright sunlight.

Feeling a little more at ease, I turned and went back into the air conditioned spaces of the air operations bridge and sought out Chief of Air Operations Kapitein Lt. ter Zee Van Braekel. I enquired of him on the progress of preparations for the test flight of the Army's Fokker fighter that I had ordered to be uncrated; and our new PZL P23 heavy dive bombers. He replied that the aircraft were ready, all preparations had been completed in Aden as the fleet was re-supplying.

However; if the fighter design had utilized a pre-stressed duralumin skin for strength the tail hook could have been easily adapted to the skin from the outside. But as, the tail section of the Dutch fighter was made of fabric over aircraft spruce frame, it required considerable internal reinforcement. Kap. Van Braekel felt that his best attempt was not up to the task. Nevertheless he felt that with a good pilot aboard to adjust the wing flaps, the fighter could land on the flight deck without a tail-hook, provided that the battle-carrier was making 30 knots into a stiff breeze.

The PZL bombers; all told fourteen per ship were nearing full readiness and all heavy bombs had been loaded. The name the Poles chose for the naval version of their dive-bomber was Sea Eagle or Osprey. They initially carried the designation PZL P23 Osprey, they were referred to as just P23s, but later it was Osprey that was most remembered as the most common. Van Braekel had put the entire air group of 700 men to the task and a similar effort was underway aboard the *Johan de Witt*. The first PZL bomber when uncrated by the *Cornelis'* air mechanics had caused a sensation. She appeared to be a big rugged looking monoplane; brand new with all the manufactures tags still in place and not some heavily used Royal Navy cast off!

In Aden, when the 700 kilogram bombs had started to come aboard from the barges, their large size created a favorable impression amongst the air crew. These men now believed that their big warships were finally shedding the last of her milk teeth and getting some *real fangs*. The airmen felt for the first time superior to the destructive power of the ship's main battery. The gunners it was observed soon ceased their ribbing of their shipmates of the air contingent.

I certainly agreed with that sentiment. The PZL P23 was very similar in capability to the German Junkers JU 87 Stuka. It was equipped with a robust fixed under-carriage but with a radial engine instead of the Junker's oil cooled in line power plant. The 507 Kilowatt Bristol Pegasus engine's reliability and ease of maintenance were critical factors that our air staff considered as essential qualities for carrier operations.

The bomber's speed of 330 km/hr. was acceptable for the day and it possessed a good range of 700 miles. These aircraft could carry a cluster of lighter bombs for use against merchant vessels, or a single 750 kg AP (armor piercing) bomb, a weapon which contained a powerful *Cyclotol blend* of compressed TNT and RDX in a 260 kilogram bursting charge that was a real armored ship killer.

The Polish Sea Eagle gave our battle carrier division an additional devastating long range punch to augment the considerable power of our Swordfish torpedo planes. Any air group that could carry twenty-eight 750 kilogram bombs and thirty aerial torpedoes into action in one strike group, out to a range of 350 miles was capable of sinking several of the heaviest battleships in existence. Once these aircraft became operational my battle carrier division would for the first time have a reasonably balanced, fully modern powerful attack group.

However the short range of our Sea Fury Mk II fighters still posed a problem. For long range attack the bombers and torpedo planes would have no fighter escort. I had hoped to adapt the crated Fokker fighters to this role with their greater speed, twice the firepower and range of the obsolescent British plane. In light of the recent events this was to be a vital experiment.

The ships maintained their stations and kept a double lookout as we cruised southwest through the sunny afternoon across the Arabian Sea and into a clear evening. The last fighter of the air umbrella returned to the *Johan de Witt* at 21:23hrs with the aid of the ship's landing lights. Behind us our wakes stretched to the horizon arrow straight, having transited from one of white froth on royal blue, to glowing green on soft indigo. It had been a lovely day, and due to the breeze generated ship's velocity; not unpleasant.

I had spent most of the day on the uppermost platform of the air control deckhouse as long as the sun was up. I had taken my meals there and a number of my senior off duty officers took relays in keeping me company. I was thoroughly enjoying the fresh air and the magnificent view of the air group exercises, with the *Sea Harts* on submarine patrol, the *Sea Fury* fighters on CAP, and the main battery drill.

The relative calm operations of the flight deck were I am sure in contrast to the furious activity underway within the hangars. Below, lights blazed well into the night as hundreds of air frame technicians and engine mechanics worked with the aircrews to prepare twenty-eight new PZL bombers and eventually sixteen of the Fokker fighters for testing on the morrow.

I felt that unknown threats loomed close and would endanger my fleet on this voyage and therefore circumstances now dictated that I requisition the use of the Royal Army Air Force's crated fighters for my battle carriers. Any consequences resulting from my perceived breech of inter-service protocol that may arise; be damned.

The introduction of two new aircraft types to a battle-carrier at sea is a highly unorthodox affair. It put a great strain on my air technicians, mechanics, air crews and the air operations staff. To the credit of my "Air Ops" Kapitein Lt. ter Zee Konrad Van Braekel; my squadron Hoof Officier Vlieger and his opposite aboard the *Johan de Witt* Kapitein Lt. ter Zee Jan Florisz and the 1400 men of their combined groups, the preparations were completed in a first rate manner. The griping of the crews was soon quieted as they took pride in what they had accomplished, and the aircraft maintenance crews were each assigned their brand spanking new bomber.

Nevertheless I expected this level of performance from my men and more. For an even greater effort would be required of them with the ship burning and under heavy attack. We were three weeks steaming from The Dutch East Indies. I planned to have my battle squadron fully combat capable or as close to it as possible with the current equipment limitations, before I came within reach of the powerful Japanese naval and air forces.

When I pondered the unusual events of the voyage up to this point I came to conclude that my fleet may well be steaming into a war situation. After-all the Japanese precipitated an undeclared war with Russia in 1904. Their navy had launched a surprise attack on the Russian Pacific Squadron as it lay at its fleet anchorage in the colony of Port Arthur. Great success came to the Japanese as a result of this action.

Surely one would not expect her military planners to deviate from a proven method of operation. The Japanese negotiations with our Government to gain access to the raw materials of Borneo had been going nowhere for years. Over the same period of time the striking power of her navy and air forces had dramatically increased. All things considered I firmly believed that a surprise attack would be launched by the Japanese in the near future against a European Colonial power to capitalize on the confusion in Europe and thereby gain territory. But where would the blow fall; at Singapore, the Philippines, or my homeland the Dutch East Indies? England, France and America were all militarily powerful nations. In comparison little Netherlands was by far the weakest Colonial operation within South East Asia. Logic dictated therefore that it was upon the Dutch neck that the axe would fall.

I awoke to the sea air wafting through the open sidelights in the port bulkhead of my cabin. The exotic scents of an unknown ocean filled the small space. I lay for a few restful moments filling my lungs with the salty air and listening to the muffled sounds of life aboard my warship. The hiss of the foam and the rippling of the water against the hull were easily discernible through the sidelight in my cabin some fifteen meters above the sea. The deck plating vibrated slightly to the movement of some heavy equipment combined with natural forces working against the hull. Far aft and faintly a Bristol Pegasus radial engine coughed to life, unmistakable in its first deep snorts. At that moment between the world of dreams and complete alert consciousness I was one with the ship. I had become the brain of an immense mechanical, flesh and blood being, a gigantic marine cyborg. I was aware of her very component, and conscious of her moods and dreadful capacity for destruction.

The barometer on the white painted steel forward bulkhead of my cabin revealed that it was going to be a fine day and its companion chronometer accused me with 06:10hrs. I rang up the bridge and told the O.O.D. to request that the ship's Kapitein Voorne and the C.A.O. Van Braekel join me in my day cabin at 07:00hrs for a briefing and some breakfast.

The aircraft tests to be conducted that morning, if successful would allow the battle carriers to remain during the remainder of the voyage as effective units in the RNLN. If not we would be sailing into those regions which may require us to confront the Imperial Japanese Navy, gravely weakened. The vaunted *Rengo Kantai*: of 1939 was an immensely powerful, capable and numerically superior rival, one that enjoyed complete technical superiority in the air, and on the sea.

Breakfast was completed in half an hour as the ship's Kapitien and Air Chief had already eaten, and we were all anxious to begin the day's flight tests. I informed my steward that we would be taking our coffees on the Air operations platform, to which my small group now made our way.

On the flight deck below us there sat two PZL P23 dive bombers and a Fokker fighter with engines warmed up and on idle. The bombers were having their wings unfolded and looked very smart in our ship's colors, polished aluminum, with yellow upper wings and engine cowling. The Army fighter, easily distinguishable in its green and sand camouflage scheme, was sitting on 'A' hangar platform when I first grasped that the aircraft with its fixed wings could just barely make it into the hangars below. Normally with each hoisting of the ship's two hangars eight aircraft could be brought onto the flight deck every 90 seconds. These stop-gap fighters would slow our operations considerably, if they were serviced below. I made a mental note to enquire of Van Braekel as to the logistics of keeping these aircraft permanently on the flight deck, but under canvass.

The deck crews had manhandled the three aircraft to the after-deck, where they had taken aboard fuel. An airman wearing a headset came out of the operations center companionway onto our platform, snapped a crisp salute to Van Braekel, and plugged his communication cable into the bulwark receptacle, then stood by to await orders.

Air Operations while observing the activity surrounding the afterdeck, informed me that the first plane to be launched would be the Fokker. I told him to begin when ready. A yellow flag was then broken out at the flight control deckhouse. Immediately the air cooled engines of the three aircraft coughed loudly into life emitting volumes of blue-white exhaust as the pilots revved up their power plants.

The ship; now being helmed from air operations slowly began her turn into the wind with the steam sock allowing us to optimize the maneuver. I observed the dial on the air speed indicator which steadied at 43 knots of *wind down the wood*. The duty air operations officer; Hoof Officier Vliieger, Konrad van Braekel, studied his watch, and feeling that the engines of all three aircraft were running properly, ordered the yellow flag furled to be replaced by the green for execute. Immediately I noticed an increase in the snorting roar of the fighter's powerful engine as it built up to maximum power.

The pilot raised his arm, looked to the left and right then dropped it back into the open cockpit. The plane handlers holding the wheel block lanyards yanked these away, and the aircraft accelerated down the flight deck. In three seconds the fighter was abreast of the island and already airborne. Clearing the end of the deck the pilot banked to port, then began a full power climb.

Further down the platform a four man air team equipped with binoculars, headsets and clipboards established communications with the pilot and they walked him through the maneuvers he was to carry out while he fed them his report on the aircraft's performance. The procedure was repeated for "team B" and the dive bomber without a pay-load. The big dive-bomber fairly leapt from the deck, clearing it much as did the fighter, which was to be expected, bereft as she was of bombs.

The last bomber was to have a more strenuous test performed. Fully loaded with fuel and sporting a big belly mounted practice bomb manufactured aboard from the ship's supply of damage control *quick concrete mix*. The Sea Eagle pilot revved-up its engine as hoses played a spray of water across the wooden deck in front of the machine. The engine produced a deep snarling drone when the big Hamilton three bladed variable pitch propeller, set to max thrust clawed at the air.

The blocks were yanked from in front of the wheels, six deck crewmen gave it a good shove and the heavily loaded dive bomber trundled down the deck. Only two aircraft lengths had been covered when over the wetted deck a huge volume of white smoke erupted from beneath the bomber's underbelly accompanied by a startling roar that could only be likened to a ruptured superheated steam line. A visible and dramatic increase in the acceleration of the aircraft was evident and she sped down the deck to her lift-off point which approximated that of the fighter.

An underbelly rocket had been mounted on a fuselage bracket just aft of the big bomb. It had a burn time of 15 seconds which carried the plane well past the bow of the ship, then it was simply released into the sea when expended.

Team 'C' immediately began their battery of flight tests. I commented to Van Breakel that the little green rocket booster seemed to do the trick, and asked from him the Polish name for it again; to which he replied with a chuckle the *Orgorki* or (pickle). I further enquired as to our present supply of these booster rockets and learned that it was planned for these planes to have a capability of five; 750 kg bombs sorties, five; 6 x 110 kg bomb sorties and five; 3 x 225 kg bomb sorties per plane or 210 Sea Eagle sorties per ship. This represented the maximum capacity of the magazines for this type, all of which were provided with rocket assist.

At present the squadron had 440 of the rockets on inventory and we could manufacture the boosters under the terms of the original license granted by PZL. The rockets were only a standby experimental measure for normal battle carrier operations. The rocket would enable a damaged stationary ship to remain in action, and strikes to be launched from a muddy jungle airfield. The new Sea Eagle or Osprey as some preferred to call the bomber, had no trouble getting into the air from the battle-carriers when they were moving at high speed, requiring only forty meters or so with full flaps.

While watching these aircraft being put through their paces I remarked that the new fighter and bomber looked like a match set, both with radial engines and a fixed undercarriage and sporting aerodynamic, *fully-spatted* wheels. The test planes were being closely shadowed by the *tried and true Hawker Sea Hart* bombers. One loaded to the maximum with a practice bomb and the other without a payload. As the test planes were carrying out their maneuvers, their performance was being compared to the Sea Hart bombers, which were acting as their wingmen.

In addition a lone *Hawker Sea Fury Mk II* fighter was being used to shadow the Fokker. Although stripped of its machine guns and ammunition canisters the best speed that could be wrung out of the Sea Fury was 420 kph, still a good 50 kph slower than the Dutch monoplane. Nevertheless she was a nimble mount and flown by an experienced pilot. It was obvious even at this distance that the Fokker mono-plane fighter was having some difficulty in keeping the biplane in its kill zone. Clearly, from my observations the new fighter's qualities and best usage had not yet been discovered by my test pilot.

During these tests the battle-carriers still launched regular rotations of aircraft. A Sea Hart for anti-submarine patrol, our *Swordfish Mk I* long range scouts which flew a continuous circuit and two Sea Fury's per carrier to act in the interceptor roll. In this respect it was to be a typical day for the flight operations of a battle-carrier at sea under full alert.

Aboard the *Johan* there was some consternation in the afternoon when one of the Sea Eagle's 750 kg practice bombs would not release. The problem was solved when the bombardier jumped into his gondola, fully extended it below the plane's belly, then opened the machine gun port and wobbled it with his hand until it dropped off. Apparently her C.A.O. did not want to risk the undercarriage of the new plane by landing with a 750 kg practice bomb still attached...and rightly so!

The test aircraft each made several sorties, all of one hour duration. Our precious overworked *Sea Hart* bombers; a well proven design, actually complimented the performance of the PZL bomber. They were so few and highly prized. Our pilots maintained that having once dropped their bomb load they were nimble enough to act as a *second class* fighter in a pinch. Eventually all twelve of the new dive bombers and four of the army's fighters on both battle carriers completed a full range of tests for the first day.

The PZL P23 bomber offered a heavy payload, a 650 kph diving speed, a fully retractable bombardier's gondola and all round defensive protection. Sadly, it did not possess the capability to act as a second-line fighter, a quality which I greatly appreciated with our Curtiss Model 77 Helldivers that we acquired later from the Americans.

The PZL P23 bomber was a reliable, ruggedly built plane, steady in heavy wind conditions and an accurate bomber. They were well liked by both their flight crews and mechanics. As long as they were with our Battle-carrier division I had confidence in our ability to hit any enemy very hard indeed.

Later in combat when our pilots first encountered the impressive Achi D3A dive-bombers of the Imperial Japanese Navy, they commented during their debriefings how similar in appearance they were to our Ospreys. The Japanese bomber popularly known by the American designation as 'Val' was a slightly larger bird than our Osprey and with a similar speed when carrying the same bomb load. However the PZL Osprey could carry twice the weight in bombs out to the maximum range of the Val, a decisive bonus if attacking a heavily armored target. The downside in the comparison was that the Val enjoyed more maneuverability when shed of its bombs, making it a more difficult target for enemy fighters, or anti-aircraft guns.

Van Braekel was very happy with the new additions to his flock. Although the logistics of five different models of aircraft on one battle-carrier was pushing the limits of our patient hangar crews to the limit. The situation would be alleviated some-what upon reaching Batavia as the army was sure to collect their Fokker fighters.

Field Marshal Jan Baker-Dirks, the supreme commander of all military forces in the Dutch East Indies valued his modern aircraft and had fought hard to get them for his army command. I do believe that one of his son's was a fighter squadron commander stationed in Batavia and had personally recommended the machine. The Marshal would ensure that his squadrons would receive their new fighters. I wasn't about to overly delay their delivery.

July 01, 09:00 hours; our third day out from Aden our *Green 2* patrol of two Swordfish Mk I's recorded that they had spotted a flight of nine light aircraft flying at an altitude of 1500 meters on a SW heading, some 300 miles off our starboard bow.

I was very surprised upon learning of this sighting as there was absolutely nothing out there for hundreds of miles. My inquisitive nature was aroused so I directed the *Swordfish* to close the flight of aircraft and determine if possible their identity. The pilot would not have an easy task as the *Swordfish* torpedo plane was one of the slowest naval aircraft then in service, and had difficulty operating above 120 mph. Although a modern design, her engineers had decided to sacrifice speed as the price paid for great range and a heavy payload.

The personnel of the air operations station were further surprised when the mystery aircraft were identified as a type of small medium range floatplane reconnaissance light torpedo bomber of the Imperial Japanese Navy. Yet here they were flying across the vastness of the Indian Ocean!

We had just been presented with a unique opportunity to observe what must undoubtedly be a secret operation of some sort being conducted by the Imperial Japanese Navy! These float equipped aircraft processed only a few hundred miles range, and were not capable of landing on the deck of a carrier, but were of the type used by light cruisers, or surface raiders when stalking the shipping lanes. We now became involved in a very unusual encounter.

The Swordfish scout was ordered to observe these aircraft and attempt to follow them to their destination. We knew that these light machines must land soon, and we wanted to discover the nature of their rendezvous. Our unarmed bomber would not have any difficulty carrying out this snooping as she still had some seven hours of fuel in reserve could stay on station until the mystery had been solved.

Fate had handed us a rare gift; to observe and evaluate a hitherto unimagined naval capability of our soon to be deadly adversary. Our scout pilot knew his business and he trailed his quarry from behind and below with great skill from what he felt was their blind spot. After an hour and twenty minutes of observation, our *eyes of the fleet* reported that the nine plane formation appeared to be descending to land upon the sea.

Pilot W.O. Jahee's surprise was evident in his next transmission that followed some seven minutes later. He had reported that the mystery planes had been landing upon empty sea. Now, quite miraculously it seemed, several ships appeared to be in attendance at the landing site! W.O. Jahee displayed some anger and confusion at the inaccuracy of his early transmission. He requested permission to abandon stealth, to close in and get photographs. Air Ops, glanced at me and I nodded silently giving permission. The pilot acknowledged and asked his airman to get ready with his camera.

On his approach, W.O. Jahee had abandoned all caution and came in at 100 meters altitude as there was nothing that the sailors below could do now to conceal their operation. The swordfish swooped over the scene with the camera shutter clicking as fast as the air observer/telegraphist was able to operate the mechanism. W.O. Jahee noticed frantic activity aboard the ships and planes below him. He was in the process of reporting that there were two ships visible, both of an unusual configuration and an awash, overturned hull just lying on the surface when he realized to his amazement that he was looking at two immense submarines lying upon the surface of the quiet sea and another similarly huge vessel could be seen also in the process of surfacing!

These subs he reported, were of truly cruiser proportions, perhaps more than 150 meters in length, with a three deck high conning tower, and they were busily engaged in recovering the floatplanes with cranes. Manning the conning towers of the huge submarines, were several officers in white uniforms with binoculars raised, observing our approaching Swordfish. They were no doubt as surprised as our airmen at this chance meeting. Other officers were seen to be shouting at the work parties below. Collapsible cranes were made ready on the foredeck of each huge submarine. The floatplanes were then hoisted up onto the deck of each boat. The wings were then folded to lay alongside its fuselage and the aircraft were then pushed tail first down a rail system into a long tubular watertight chamber forming part of the upper hull on each huge submarine's foredeck. The third submarine had rapidly completed its surfacing operation and had begun to recover its three waiting aircraft in a similar manner. All the submarines and aircraft were painted a deep forest green and were clearly marked with the red roundel of Japan!

The Swordfish's air-telegraphist soon reported that all of the camera's film had been used up, and that some excellent shots had been obtained. I ordered the aircraft to maintain contact for as long as possible, and observe the entire process until the vessels submerged, which all three did immediately upon completing the stowage of their seaplanes. The pilot continued to transmit information and was able to observe that these large submarines descended to a depth of about a hundred meters where they were still visible as the water was unruffled and clear, and with the sun approaching its zenith allowed for deep water observation. The Japanese undersea craft then moved off in a wide V formation and shaped a course to the north east which would eventually take them close to the city of Bombay, India.

The submarines were last observed to be slowly descending and then the Swordfish lost contact with them as they had disappeared ghost like into the murk of the depths when they passed under an immense red shoal of krill. The scout plane terminated its search, and homed in on our radio transmissions using its RDF loop antenna. It returned to the ship with all due dispatch that was possible for a 120 mph machine fighting a 15 knot headwind! We were all extremely excited to see the results of the developed film.

The high quality black and white photographs revealed to us an altogether unknown capability of the *Rengo Kantai* (IJN Combined Fleet). The submarines we calculated to be immense craft of some 5,000 to 6,000 tonnes submerged displacement and carried at least three planes each and perhaps more. They were three times the size of a destroyer and approached that of our new light cruisers!

The aircraft; although of the light floatplane type were armed, and carried slung between their floats a long thin torpedo of perhaps no more than 25 cm. diameter. We had hitherto believed that the Imperial Japanese naval doctrine on the use of its submarines was in a fleet support role only. Now, however the photographic evidence suggested that that these special craft with their light torpedo armed, nine plane air group would have no chance attacking heavily armed warships, but would be ideal for hunting and sinking merchant ships.

My intelligence officers speculated that we were looking at a new type of Ariel Commerce raider, one that was capable of lying undetected beneath the waves athwart the shipping lanes? Then, with the use of hydro-phones they could identify ships up to 40 km away using just propeller noises. In this way the submarine could select which target to attack while remaining concealed. High decibels would indicate the higher revolutions of a turbine driven warship, and a ship to be avoided. But a low decibel throbbing indicated a single slow speed propeller, and the triple expansion pistons of a reciprocating steam engine. These economical drives were the type generally associated with slow heavily laden merchant ships, which were the target of choice for a raider.

The Submarine commerce raider would surface beyond the visible range of its intended victim, and launch a torpedo attack. No cargo vessel would think to veer away from or even be capable of detecting three small planes that were approaching at wave top level. Then with three fish in her guts it would be all over very quickly, as freighters, even very large ones are designed to maximize cargo space and therefore do not have more than basic subdivision, unlike warships which will have hundreds of watertight compartments.

Should the stricken ship be able to get off an S.0.S she would report an attack by torpedo-planes. Any retaliatory effort would be directed against a threat from a surface raider. No one would ever suspect the truth and be out hunting an enemy submarine aircraft carrier. Yes, such large submarines were very clever weapons indeed, and could carry sufficient supplies for several months at sea. Perhaps prize crews were quartered within their spacious hulls, thus allowing the merchant ships and their valuable cargos to be sailed back to a resource hungry Japan?

The morning of July 3rd began with the next phase of the testing the new dive bomber and fighter. Crews were selected and assigned to each aircraft for the duration of the voyage. All airmen aboard had flight time in the Swordfish, Sea Fury and Sea Fox. Some, including Van Breakel had managed even a few hours in our precious and overworked Sea Harts. Up to the time of our recent tests with the PZL Osprey, they were our only truly effective bomber. Unfortunately we had only five for each battle-carrier! All of the air officers assigned to the command center were flight qualified. Van Braekel now assigned each of his staff flight time in the new aircraft. He felt that command of an air-group required a certain minimum familiarity with the performance of the aircraft at hand.

The last day of training was devoted to flight time for selected staff officers. Indeed the carrier landings performed by these senior air officers were most revealing as some had completely forgotten a few of the procedures for landing on a carrier. Their duties had reduced them to the worst group of pilots aboard the ship, which was however understandable. But there were some interesting moments. One occasion comes to mind.

Senior Air Operations Officer Van Breakel had just touched down an Osprey in a landing that was not text book. He had climbed out of the canopy and was standing on the wing of the dive bomber jotting down a note in his flight pad when his concentration was interrupted with a loud bang that made him start and look up. The gorilla-like Flight Deck Chief Hans Brongers was glaring furiously at the perpetrator of what he considered a bad landing by a disobedient pilot!

The 2.3 meter tall, 160 kilogram Deck Chief, had run over to Van Breakel's bomber and slammed his massive open palms down on the aircraft's aluminum wing, rocking the sturdy bomber! He then shook his raised fist at the pilot and bellowed; red faced the

Dutch equivalent of; "Airman, you stupid f**king abortion, in the future if you ever again ignore an abort landing wave-off I will personally rip off your useless f**king wick and shove it up your bloody a**hole!"

At which point Van Breaker removed his flight helmet and goggles and the red faced Chief was glaring up into the visage of the Senior Air Officer. But the Chief Petty Officer did not waver, he knew that he was right in his evaluation of the landing and on the deck he owned the ass of every pilot. Deck Chief Brongers wetted his lips and was just about to speak when Van Breakel replied calmly, "right you are chief it was a terrible landing, I saw the *wave off flags*, but caught a freak down draft, and just dropped onto the deck."

Air Ops, having submitted to the authority of the Deck Chief had reinforced the concepts of discipline in the minds of many of the young sailors. Several of those *down cheeked boy sailors* aboard, still trying to appreciate their duty, had witnessed the exchange. Their imposing chief had actually reprimanded the Fleet's Senior Flight Operations himself! It was a lesson for the young sailors to remember; on the flight deck, during operations; the Chief's four chevrons could overrule even a *three striper*! News of the encounter spread quickly and grew in the retelling. The Deck Chief had now indeed become an even more powerful figure, beyond that which he already held; almost God-like in their young minds.

The fight tests were at an end and concluded with satisfaction. Each battle-carrier had on strength; one squadron of modern PZL P23 dive bombers, one squadron of Swordfish Torpedo planes, one eight plane flight of modern Fokker monoplane fighters and a full squadron of Sea Fury fighters, and all with full sets of spare parts. Fifty five aircraft in total, per battle-carrier. For the remainder of this voyage it was; *Good-bye Sea Fox*, I breathed with relief.

I was very pleased with my men who pulled off a very heavy task in one week. Over the ships loudspeakers I congratulated the Air Chief and all who had taken part. I then announced that an extra two days would be spent at Trincomalee to allow the officers and men a 24 hour leave. Sufficient time I felt; for the young sailors to… enlighten their minds with visits to the local museums and churches!

The early morning of July 5, 1939 I made my way up to the battle bridge to take my after-breakfast coffee and cigarette in my command chair. All the bridge windows were open and a cooling breeze flowed through the space. From my vantage point it was revealed, that the flagship was gently gliding across an Indian Ocean looking akin to an immense flat sheet of silver with not a ripple on its surface. The morning was unusually cool, but this would not last.

Acknowledgements exchanged with the Watch, I seated myself, lit a *Sobrani*, and had two sips of hot coffee when Kapitein ter Zee Van Klaffens, saluted and approached. He informed me that the morning was well suited for refueling the destroyers from the bunkers of the *Groningen* and *Utrecht*. These eight little ships needed fuel, as their tank capacity was very small for the massive engines that they were equipped with. The sea conditions were ideal to give the men practice in a refueling at sea operation. Once in the confines of the East Indies many islands, with our multiple shore refueling stations, there would be little chance to undertake such activities.

I agreed with my Chief of Staff's estimation. I turned to the Officer of the watch; Kapitein–Lt. ter Zee Linus de Kroon, and asked him to transmit to all ships to *heave to*, then begin the refueling operation.

The convoy was brought to a full stop within ten minutes. Aboard the fleet tankers *Groningen* and *Utrecht* their crews rigged their ships for the RAS operation. A work party of half a score sailors with a petty officer in charge of the fuel transfer deployed a heavy fuel transfer line from their sterns. Each of our eight destroyers in turn, dropped a cutter to retrieve the end of the refueling line and transfer it to the bow of their ship. In short order this was heaved aboard the bow of the destroyer where a large party of sailors dragged it amidships, and connected it to the starboard fuelling station. A flag signal was given, and the tanker began the pumping of fuel oil into her bunkers.

The Refueling At Sea operation (RAS), passed quickly, eight destroyers each being attached for about twenty minutes to a tanker had received about 200 metric tonnes. It is one of the few times that the squadron offered a really tempting target to a lurking submarine. Throughout the refueling operations, under our *full alert* two sections of bomb laden Swordfish, circled the stationary fleet. Fortunately for our vessels, with their bi-plane air-groups, take-off speed was low, and not much deck length was required. The launching and retrieval of anti-submarine patrol planes was able to be accomplished from even immobile ships.

Six days following our sailing from Aden, I had received new orders from the Admiralty at Batavia; and a message that the *Tweede Kamer*, (the Netherland's Parliament) had granted eighty two rank additional increases to the officers and enlisted men throughout my fleet, partially no doubt as a result of our involvement in what were now being officially referred to as; *The Red Sea Incident* and *The Action at Aden*. So it was then, with somewhat mixed feelings that I received my third star, and was raised to Vice Admiraal.

The new orders that I had received would delay the arrival of my convoy to the main Dutch fleet base at Soerabaja, a harbour city located on the north coast of Java. Instead the warships of my fleet would be committed to a very large multi-national naval exercise off eastern Ceylon designated; *Operation Bulwark*.

The city of Colombo on the west side of the Island of Ceylon and the even larger anchorage at Trincomalee; located on the east side of the island were the locations of the two key Royal Naval Bases of the British Indo-Asiatic Command and both were rife with spies on the payroll of Imperial Japan and Nazi Germany.

The approach of our squadron to this strategically situated big island had been anticipated. We began to encounter with unusual frequency a number large dhows that sailed across our course at regular intervals, supposedly engaged in some type of trade. These small wooden vessels of several hundred tonnes seemed to appear innocent enough, but undoubtedly some of these had agents on board who had come to observe more closely the details of the ships of my squadron.

One of these was quite easy to distinguish; as the master of the dhow was not using the breeze to proper advantage. Upon his afterdeck there were several figures clad in pressed white linen suits and sun hats. These fellows held binoculars and were constantly sweeping from one of my ships to the other.

That afternoon as the fleet approached the eight degree channel of the Maldive Island Group I ordered an increase of squadron speed to 20 knots, an action calculated to allow us to make the anchorage by 14:00hrs, on July 5th.

Our far ranging and ever vigilant Swordfish on anti-submarine patrol reported two small submarines lying *bottomed* in the shallows of Minicoy Island just to the north of our base course. The mysterious warships were lying in less than ten fathoms of clear water. Although these appeared to have been skillfully camouflaged with kelps or clever camouflage paint schemes our patrols had found them. These unidentified Onderzee boats we speculated could be vessels of Nippon. But their purposeful concealment close by our course seemed more ominous than a mere reconnaissance mission to track our location with hydro-phones. I sensed a threat.

At this point in our voyage, the daily stream of coded communications that we had been getting from Amsterdam were quite clear in their intent; assume the worst and take full measure to defend you ships. The recent events left me with few options and less patience. I decided therefore to assist these Japanese submarines with their task of confirming our arrival to this region, and to make it clear to them that we were completely aware of their presence and prepared to respond to any mischief, with a heavy hand.

Therefore I ordered two three section bomber anti-sub patrol craft to release their 250 kilogram eggs in a bracket formation of no more than 300 meters in width, making sure that the two submarines would be in the center of the triangle to get most enjoyment from the shock waves. Some of the mist from the bomb bursts still hung above the surface of the sea, when our circling Swordfish reported clouds of mud stirred up by both submarine's propellers as they quickly got underway to scuttle further down the mud bank, and into the deep emerald green gloom of the Indian Ocean. Message delivered and understood. The detonation of four hundred and fifty kilograms of AMATOL, had transcended all language and cultural barriers!

The following day we were to be met by an RAF group from Colombo airfield. The light cruiser *H.M.S. Danae* was to act as escort to guide our fleet to our assigned berths within the Royal Naval Base. I intended to use the opportunity to put on a show of strength to reassure our friends and to warn our enemies. We transmitted the details of our planned operation to our British hosts who in-turn informed us that three squadrons of RAF bombers and a fighter escort were on their way to rendezvous with our ships and that our light cruiser escort was already underway to meet us.

In what was to be our first dress-rehearsal of a maximum effort for a foreign power I ordered all the Swordfish and Osprey squadrons of both battle carriers into the air, with all Fokker fighters to act as their escort. Seventy two aircraft in total took part. All aircraft carried the maximum load of fuel but without armament in order to extend their flight time and maximize the impression for as long as possible. These squadrons would make two passes over the city. The fleet would still retain ten Sea Hart bombers and twenty eight Sea Fury fighters for patrol duties. We launched all these to act as combat air patrol in order to get as many aircraft aloft as possible and create the impression of a large and powerful naval air group.

When approaching to some fifty nautical miles from the city of Colombo the big battle-carriers turned into the wind and launched all six squadrons in just over twenty minutes. The aircraft circled their ships until their formations were complete, and then flew off in an impressive armada towards the Island of Ceylon.

I chose at this time to address the Fleet and convey my satisfaction for the hard work in preparing and testing the new air groups also for the battle readiness that was displayed so dramatically to the Governor of Aden and which earned praise in the British House of Commons. The officers and men of the 1st Battle-carrier division had made our small nation proud!

Mark Klimaszewski

The joint display of air power was also being utilized to familiarize the British and Dutch Flak gunners with the new types of aircraft that we were deploying to this theater. In our case the PZL Sea Eagle bomber and the Fokker fighter. In the case of the British, the new Hurricane fighter; a monoplane with a retractable undercarriage, a very heavy armament and capable of such a high speed that it virtually ensured air superiority in the region for at least five years.

Only some ten minutes on their way, our strike group of 72 bombers and fighters reported the approach of a large formation of aircraft; undoubtedly the RAF. In short order these resolved themselves into a tight formation of some 48 Bristol Bombay bombers; twin engine high wing monoplanes with a fixed undercarriage. These bombers cruised along comfortably at 140 knots at an altitude of 3000 meters.

The accompanying Hurricane fighter squadron was composed of some 16 machines, and was flying 500 meters above the lumbering bombers. They looked impressive, and every bit the advanced fighters that they were rumored to be!

Our 72 plane group was formed up as follows: with the 28 Swordfish Mk I torpedo planes flying in two squadrons at 2800 meters, two 14 machine squadrons of PZL Sea Eagle dive-bombers, in two formations at 3000 meters accompanied by an 8 plane wing of Fokker D. XX1 fighters and 200 meters above this formation the other 8 plane wing of the new Dutch fighter. Our naval air group and the approaching RAF formations would soon encounter one another.

The fighter pilots of the RAF on that day it seems were in a mood to play. Pilot 2nd Lt. Geoffrey Carstairs of the 17th Fighter Squadron gave an interesting account of meeting the Dutch naval air group, for the first time, inbound to Columbo; *At 11:00hours, our pilots gunned the engines of their new Hurricanes and rocketed into the air. We formed up to escort three plodding Bristol Bombay bomber squadrons at 4,000 ft. and headed west to form up with the air groups of an approaching Dutchy carrier squadron and guide them to Colombo for the big fly over demonstration for the Military Big Wigs and the Press Boys that had been planned for today. The Dutchy pilots were the 'new kids on the block', new to monoplanes, new to carrier naval aviation and were flying largely obsolescent ex-RN aircraft. We were told to be nice to 'wooden shoed' airmen. Naturally this last comment brought out the mischief in us all as we were exulting in the performance of our new fighters! These aircraft could hit 320 mph. in level flight and 400 mph. in a dive and had a massive armament for the day of eight .303 machine guns! We had privately schemed how to show the Dutchmen some real flying.*

"In a short time we spotted their aircraft deposed in three levels below us. We passed their formations on our left and circled to form up on their right. I could identify 28 planes below us and recognized the familiar shapes of the Swordfish Mk I Torpedo plane, a capable British design, one that we all knew well. Our Bombay bombers were forming up in front of a 28 plane formation of an unfamiliar type of large single engine modern looking monoplane bomber with a fixed undercarriage. In addition to these there were two 8 plane wings of a modern looking monoplane fighter also with fixed undercarriage. These were our first look at Fokker D XX1 fighters and PZL-P23 Sea Eagle bombers. Our pre-flight briefing prepared us to expect the Dutchmen to be flying the Sea Fury Mk II bi-plane fighter, another British design that we had given up a few years ago. We had planned to blow the canvass off their wings with high speed passes. But the new Fokker fighters were a complete surprise. Our lads had decided to have some fun especially if the Dutchy fighter

142

pilots were as crazy a bunch of S.O.B'S as we were. Our hurricanes rolled over and simulated a diving attack on the Swordfish below us."

"The Dutchy fighter pilots of both wings, immediately understood our invitation, and took the opportunity 'to play.' They nimbly snapped over in a tight rolls determined to intercept us, or at least we thought that. Instead only one wing followed us down the other anticipated where we would pull out of the dive and met us there. A fast game ensued, the Dutchy planes being very nimble which they happily demonstrated with very tight snap roles. It was very difficult to stay on their tails. They could out climb us although only slowly and for a while they could keep up with us in a dive for the deck but started to fall back when our Hurricanes exceeded a speed of 370 mph. We happily deduced that we enjoyed several advantages over these fighters; some 40 mph. in speed and a much heavier outfit of machine guns...eight to their two." But we also hoped that their performance would give us some indication of what to expect from the fixed undercarriage, monoplane fighters now equipping the Fleet Carriers of the IJN."

The combined RNLN and RAF air groups then passed over the city of Colombo in a stately fashion and carried out three complete circuits of the city for the benefit of the viewing of the populace. The main purpose of this display was to send the clear message that the European powers within the region were strong, united and determined not to yield the wealth of their rich colonial holdings to the resource and market starved Empire of Japan.

Early that morning we had received several coded ciphers; that Deneys Pienarr; the Governor of our Dutch East Indies Colony and the Commander in Chief of all Dutch Far East Forces; Field Marshal Jan Baker-Dirks would be in Ceylon for the next five days. They were to join the British Raj of India, the Marquee of Lithgow, at the invitation of His Excellency Lord Edward Pomeroy-Stone Hurst, Governor General of Ceylon in a hunt for white tiger seen in the remote mountainous regions, near the ancient city of Kandy.

I was to present my report on the Red Sea and Aden Incidents to the Dutch Field Marshal, who would later discuss its implications with a British Indian Army representative and Ceylon's fifteen man council of elders, engaged in the review of regional security. A council no doubt convened to examine the roots of those recent disturbing events, which my ships had experienced on this voyage.

The Fleet had received new orders from Admiraal de Veldt: *"I was to prepare the fleet for maneuvers with battle squadrons from the Colonial powers of; France, Great Britain and the United States of America: Operation Bulwark to commence in one week! The Fleet is to proceed with all dispatch under the temporary command of Rear Admiraal van Speijk Bronckhorst to the Royal Naval base at Trincomallee Harbour. Unload all surplus cargos onto Dutch merchant ships awaiting your arrival in Tambalagam Bay. Vice Admiraal Sweers to proceed at once by air to Colombo."*

I left the squadron in the capable hands of the Rear Admiral my Deputy Commander on this voyage. During my absence the *Johan de Witt* would assume the role of Fleet Flagship. I ordered that a Grumman Duck be prepared to fly me to the rendezvous in Colombo. My Chief of Air Operations Van Braekel saw to this personally and recommended, given the current tensions, an escort of three Sea Fury MK II fighters from Fighter Squadron I, each equipped with the new fuel drop tanks to extent their range, and the added precaution of another Duck to accompany the one carrying me. He surmised that in case of engine trouble and the Duck in which I was to be the occupant went down, the second Duck would land on the water, to pick me up and continue the journey. He was leaving nothing to chance.

143

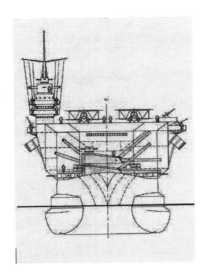

CHAPTER XVII

THE DEEPENING CRISIS, MEETING IN COLOMBO, De WINTER'S JOURNAL, THE CRUMBLING RUINS OF ANCIENT KANDY, TRINCOMALEE HARBOUR, OPERATION BULWARK, ON TO THE DUTCH EAST INDIES COLONY.

To defend herself against Nazi Germany, the Netherlands looked to France and Great Britain as the primary military allies on the European Continent. Yet during the *Czech Crisis* of 1938, these same two nations had demonstrated a complete lack of resolve to stand up to Hitler at the Munich Conference. They bowed to Hitler's demands and forced little Czechoslovakia to surrender those territories to Germany that contained her frontier defensive works, rendering her practically defenseless. Such a lack of resolve we knew would embolden the Fascists and undoubtedly lead to an expansion of their use of their rebuilt military as a political tool. The Government of the Netherlands; in light of Czechoslovakia's demise, began a sober reappraisal of its own national security, including of course the future operational capability of her navy.

The RNLN Admiralty Headquarters had, for more than three centuries been located in Rotterdam. However due to the proximity of that city to the frontier of a remilitarized and aggressive Nazi Germany, it was now; given the feeble display by our Military Allies at Munich; considered to be indefensible. The worst case scenario maintained that the Netherlands like Czechoslovakia, may also be abandoned by those same two nations in some future appeasement of Hitler.

Consequently, it had been decided, to slowly shift the entire naval command, and the bulk of our fleet to our vast, rich Dutch East Indies. The colony; made up of the *Sunda Island Chain*, to the north, and the *Lesser Sunda Island Chain*, in the south, covered an area in the Western Pacific more expansive than continental United States, and so remote, we believed, that any threat from Nazi Germany seemed shear fantasy.

The Admiralty Headquarters Unit in Batavia, located on the north coast of the big island of Java, by June of 1939 was well along its expansion into the new nerve center of our service. Also; of great logistical importance, the source of fuel oil for our fleet, the variety of gasoline octanes necessary for the army transport and aircraft were all produced at our refineries in the East Indies, all of which lay snugly under the defensive umbrella provided by the concentration of our Air and Naval Forces.

In the 1930's; France, America and the British Empire were the preeminent global world powers, and they maintained their strategic interests abroad with their large navies; whose big guns were available to punctuate policy. As modern naval vessels of that time period could steam some 700 to 800 miles per day, these nations had the ability when united; to concentrate a vast array of firepower, by drawing upon assets from all over the globe on relatively short notice.

Operation Bulwark; was a military exercise, that had been originally proposed by the Royal Navy in 1937, to the other major Indo-Pacific Regional Powers of; America, France and to the strategically located but minor powers of Netherlands, Australia and New Zealand. The operation was to serve as a demonstration of power, primarily for Japan to digest, to a lesser extent the resurgent Italian Empire, to Nazi Germany, and to the native populations of the colonies. It involved a massive concentration of naval might in Far Eastern waters, to display; *the great strategic weapon* that could be jointly wielded if these nation's commercial interests were threatened.

Since the purpose of *Operation Bulwark* was to act as a deterrent, it must have publicity. Therefore the news services of America, Great Britain, India, Egypt, France and the Netherlands were granted wide access, to provide extensive coverage of the event. All forms of media were utilized; radio, film newsreels and special editions of newspapers, to highlight the departure of the warships from their far flung bases, and follow their progress over the next few weeks until their eventual arrival at Trincomalee.

The Operation, which had originally been scheduled for the summer of 1940, had been advanced one year due to the deepening crisis in Europe, the recent attacks on the Netherlands' ships in the Red Sea, again at Aden, and the political agitation by varied nationalist groups throughout the colonies of all the Great Powers from the Near East-Indo-Asiatic to the Malaysian -West Pacific regions.

The RNLN Admiralty in Batavia had redirected my fleet to Trincomalee Harbour on the eastern coastline of Ceylon. There, over the course of the following week the Battlecruiser-carriers were to be freed of all the clutter of extra deck, and hanger cargos, mostly army equipment, and *clear for action* in preparation for the exercise. The non-combatant members of the convoy would then be detached from my command and proceed under new orders to various destinations within our East Indies Colony.

These mostly army materials would continue their journey in the cavernous bellies of naval transports that would soon be arriving from Java and Sumatra. I ordered my Assistant Chief of Staff Kapitein Kurt Rupplin to assemble all the data that we had on 'Bulwark', and to coordinate with the cruisers and destroyers in preparing for the exercise.

In the meantime I was ordered to fly on to Colombo, the major Royal Navy harbour on the west coast of Ceylon, and deliver a report on *The Red Sea Incident* and the *Action at Aden* to the Dutch Commander in Chief Far East Field Marshal Baker-Dirks who had recently arrived from Batavia.

Japan's expansion into China and then into Manchuria had led to a clash of arms with the Soviet Union. Japan had failed to successfully negotiate for the acquirement of large quantities of raw rubber, tin ore, unrefined oil, and certain rare earths from the Dutch

East Indies or Malaya. At the same time she protested to the French over rice shipments from their Indo China Colony into unoccupied China. Japan saw this food conduit as providing support to Chinese Nationalist Forces fighting her troops. This of course was true, but rice exports to central China from the Mekong delta was a thriving business one thousand years before the French had arrived. In light of these events, a gathering of regional Colonial representatives in Ceylon had been hurriedly organized in what many were seeing as a drift to war.

As one would expect; the Governor General of Ceylon Sir Anthony Mussert-Tweedsmuir skillfully downplayed any chance of alarm or panic for the public by cloaking the true nature of the meeting; for the benefit of diplomacy, under the guise of; *A Royal Hunt* for the *Rare White Ceylonese Tiger* in the interior highlands of Ceylon. His quests would include the Raj of India; the Viscount Francis Spaernwoude the Marquee of Lithgow and party; the White Raj of Sarawak Sir John Vyner Brooke and party, Field Marshal Jan Baker-Dirks of the Dutch East Indies, and the Prime Ministers of Australia and New Zealand. All these dignitaries managing the great distances involved in grand style and comfort, via the huge Sunderland flying boats of; the *Quantas Airlines, British Oriental Airways* and *Empire Flying Boat Ltd.*

By comparison, my flight to Colombo was quite unspectacular; occupying the belly of a navy Grumman Duck. It was uneventful, perhaps due to the precaution taken by having my aircraft escorted by a section of navy Sea Fury fighters.

08:03hrs July 8, 1939, the two *Ducks* followed the *Sea Fury* fighters down the sun bleached fir flight deck of the *Cornelis de Witt* and lifted lightly off. I sat in a comfortable little compartment, and so had an excellent view through the Plexiglas panels in all directions. Initially it became quite hot as my station was akin to a tiny hothouse, so I slid back the port and starboard panels for ventilation. But in short order; as the aircraft gained speed and rapidly climbed to 2000 meters it became quite cool and comfortable, so I closed these. Below lay the sea; an immense blue mystery of constantly changing hues; cobalt blue, shifting to lime green, or slate gray. Flat as glass in one spot, or ruffled by a stiff local breeze and speckled with whitecaps. The drone of the aircraft and its gentle motion tended to lull my senses and I found it quite relaxing.

The flight was somewhat shorter than I expected, as the aircraft's floats, had not slowed the bomber appreciably, and 35 minutes into it the pilot informed me that we were on approach to Colombo Harbour. Looking below, I noticed its entrance was formed by a 100 meter wide gap between two massive stone breakwaters. Each one of which was built at the tip of projecting headlands. These reached out into the sea like two great arms, for one kilometer, at some thirty degrees angle to the shore towards a common point of convergence, thereby enclosing and enhancing a natural bay that extended into the city. The deep green waters behind the stone fingers, looking no more than a kilometer square, was packed with shipping of all sizes.

Even at this altitude I detected the fragrances of the island's famous orchid gardens. Stretching to the north of the city I could make out large plantations containing neat groves of satinwood and cinnamon, commercial crops of the very highest quality, and of famous antiquity. For it was from this very island that the Emperors of Rome, and the Pharaohs of the Nile obtained the exotic woods to decorate their resplendent palaces, and spices for baths or to delight their palate. The *Duck* banked steeply to port and rapidly lost altitude. In a few minutes it touched down gently on the sun bleached concrete surface of the Army airfield, and rolled to a stop, amid a light cloud of dust. Our three escorting fighter aircraft followed the floatplane down in short order.

I was greeted by a fit, middle aged naval officer in a crisp white tropical uniform of the Administrative Corps, Commander Jacob Baker-Wassenaar of the Dutch Embassy at Colombo. He approached the amphibian and waited for the pilot to open the gondola door, snapping to attention when I emerged. He guided me to a long cream colored Mercedes Sedan which sped us off to the Embassy building, and my meeting, with Field Marshal Jan Baker-Dirks; Commander in Chief of all Dutch Forces in the Far East!

Commander Wassenaar was surprisingly easy natured, and offered his congratulations on the success of my voyage so far. He indicated that its exploits had become *big news*, and *world opinion* seemed very pleased with the display that my warships provided when defending Aden. "I was to be received as something of a hero then," I thought to myself, "there seemed little concern evident that our shells found no target!"

I was quickly ushered through the Netherlands Embassy building and into the spacious and airy offices provided for the Field Marshal while in Ceylon. The C in C Far East, a fit man of average height and receding fair hair arose from a great leather armchair, and greeted me warmly. "May I congratulate you on your promotion to Vice Admiraal," he said. "I know Fleet Admiraal Van de Velde very well, and he is no fool. He thinks that the new Battle-carrier Division, a weapon that the nation has invested so heavily in, rests in hands of a most capable officer."

The Marshal Dirks indicated, that I seat myself in one of three green Moroccan leather chairs situated in front of his massive, and ornately carved Indonesian Red Mahogany desk, he then reoccupied his chair. He seemed very pleased with the progress of the voyage of my convoy, and expressed no concern that I was not aboard my ship at the time of the attack upon Aden.

"Look at these if you would Vice Admiraal," he said, leaning forward, and lying his right hand upon a great stack of somewhat worn looking newspapers that sat upon the edge of his desk. "The *New York Times*, the *Times of London*, *La Presse* of *Paris*, the *Corriere della Sera* of Rome, the *Malta Independent News*, the *Cairo Evening Daily*, the *Egyptian Gazette*, the *Empire Tribune of New Delhi*, the *Singapore Daily News*, the *Hong Kong Business News*, the *Manila Herald*, and the *San Francisco Examiner* to name just a few. All cover your action at Aden, and praise the action of the Royal Netherland's Navy!" Smiling broadly, he passed me five or six heavy issues from the top of the stack.

Taking the proffered issues from him, I quickly flipped through the front pages of each and realized that the lead stories contained therein, were of 'The Action at Aden' which had been embellished by huge headlines and dramatic photographs of Aden harbour lit up at night by the immense fireballs produced by our warship's massed naval artillery.

"The publicity surrounding, what is now commonly referred to as the: 'Red Sea Incident' and the 'RNLN's Sterling Action at Aden' is turning out to be a perfect prelude to *Operation Bulwark* Admiraal," he intimated, "this should effectively silence most of the whining social elitists who condemn the exercise as 'sabre rattling,' and decry the cost of our 'Blue Water' Navy! These people I have discovered over the years, are the very first to board the steamships and flying boats to depart for safe regions, when the storm clouds gather! I also believe that the term *'plucky little navy,'* an expression coined by the

British Newsreel Service, and made popular in their press, will soon be allocated to the dust bin."

The Marshal continued, "On behalf of Fleet Admiraal de Velde we say well done and congratulations on receiving your third star Vice Admiraal. Get your ships ready for the upcoming exercise in which our performance must be top notch as many eyes will be on your squadron including those of a sizeable group of newsmen and photographers, from home that will be placed aboard the big ships. As you are aware, the Battle-carriers will be, for the next few years at least, in a period of transition as new aircraft are introduced. I will nevertheless be relying upon you to maintain the battle-carriers as an efficient weapon, one that is available at all times."

"On another matter, Admiraal; that of the unsanctioned use of Army material, the uncrating and experimentation with the Fokker fighter aircraft aboard your battle-carriers. Your actions were justified considering the heightened tensions following the attack at Aden and the deteriorating state of our trade negotiations with Japan. However, all these crated aircraft will be delivered to the army as planned. Those fighters that are flyable may be flown to their destination upon the conclusion of *Operation Bulwark*. Red tape and protocol be damned we will not dwell on this further." "Understood Marshal," was my only reply.

"I accept your congratulations on behalf of my men, Marshal, but I remind you that at the time of the fireworks at Aden, as I have stated in my initial report; I was ashore with a contingent of my senior officers attending a reception, arranged in honor of our arrival at Governor Fairchild's residence atop Mount Shamshan!"

The Marshal waived his hand as if swatting away a slow fly, "That is of no consequence at all to this office Vice Admiraal. You were on official business, and we are not at war. The men and ships under your command responded to the threat promptly. Think no more on that. Now let me have your complete report."

I undid my brown leather valise and handed him a thick manila folder which he opened and sifted through until he came to the photo reconnaissance package containing the images of the Japanese aircraft carrying submarines. These he studied with the aid of a large magnifying glass, while requesting that I deliver my report verbally. We discussed the implications of the events and speculated on what were the possible catalysts that had set off the Red Sea and Aden Incidents.

The Marshal listened intently as I related how our Swordfish pilot first identified the mysterious light floatplanes, as light naval reconnaissance/bombers, then how he skillfully shadowed them; until locating their gigantic submarine mother-ships, whereupon he closed in taking many high quality photos, which confirmed them as vessels of the Imperial Japanese Navy. Looking at the photos of these, he agreed with me that; the submarines seemed to be fitted out as commerce raiders. The light torpedo plane weapon he calculated, made the aircraft's submarine mother-ships all but impossible to locate!

The revelation of these new weapons, visibly disturbed him as it demonstrated just how great the gaps in our military intelligence services still were, and revealed how much we really did not know of the Japan's Navy. That such large strategic weapons as these cruiser-sized submarines, could be conceived, built and made operational without either our own intelligence services discovering it or those of the British, French or the Americans was quite worrying.

"Perhaps," he suggested; "this new type of Japanese Commerce raiding submarine that your plane discovered, provides a further justification for a major naval acquisition that your Admiraal de Velde is on the verge of completing. Only an expanded naval aviation capability can hope to combat weapons such as these."

Upon hearing this statement, I became *all ears*, as they say. The Marshal explained to me that he was about to reveal a very significant development which for the time being must remain confidential. Admiraal Van der Velde is in the final stages of completing a deal with the Brazilian Government to purchase the *Rio de Janerio*, the flagship of their navy!

The vessel, I knew; was a battleship-carrier very similar to our battlecruiser-carriers, although perhaps a little smaller, and slower. Nevertheless with an air-group of some forty five aircraft, massive artillery, and thick armor plating she was without a doubt a very powerful vessel indeed, and would greatly add to the flexibility of our naval air operations. I became quite excited as our fleet was about to add a third capital ship, making our service; a force of global significance.

Looking at the Marshal I stated confidently, "Sir, if that ship joins our fleet, it will give our naval aviation a great boost with the flexibility of three flight decks to streamline air operations. Although the navy would then have three capital ships in commission, these would actually have the capability of six; three light battlecruisers, a medium fleet aircraft carrier, and two heavy fleet aircraft carriers. When one considers that these are supported by; ten cruisers, twenty four destroyers, twenty seven U boats, plus a host of gunboats and patrol craft. That is not the description of; *a little navy!*"

"I agree with you entirely Vice Admiraal," he emphasized. Just then, an ornate green alabaster *four day clock* sitting atop the fireplace mantle began to chime. "Good heavens Marrten, the day has passed quickly! These topics deserve further evaluation, but in more comfortable surroundings I believe. May I offer you a scotch and soda at the Embassy's small but very comfortable officer's club, and then dinner; where I will introduce you to the mess? There are many of the Embassy Staff and fellow officer's looking forward to meeting you."

We arose, and the Marshal offered me a cigarette from the ivory dispenser on his desk. "Reaching into my tunic pocket I produced my silver cigarette case, popping the latch. "Try one of these Sir; a *Mahorka*, Polish Army Issue; I've grown quite fond of them, very strong."

The next morning after a restful night, I presented an informal briefing on the *Red Sea* and *Aden Incidents* to a select group of Embassy Staff, and officers stationed at Trincomalee Naval Dockyard, the Army and RAF bases. By 11:00hrs I had wrapped this up and departed for the airfield. I would fly on to meet my Battle-carriers and continue my duties as before, while the Marshal would prepare to rejoin the 'Tiger hunt' with the Raj of India and our host the Governor of Ceylon.

When I arrived at the airfield, both of the Grumman *amphibians*, and the Sea Fury fighters were warmed up and ready to go. My young pilot I noticed, was already sporting his sunglasses. I noted that his sharpness was off, and he seemed fatigued. He opened the side hatch for me to enter. I seated myself comfortably on my parachute, took a close look at his face, and gave him the *thumbs up*. The air-telegraphist-tail gunner, who jostled into his station behind me seemed equally afflicted, yet both airmen's expressions were those of deep sublime happiness. I soon realized that the other young airman from the fighters as well, had been left on their own devices in Colombo; (an exquisitely diverse city), for over 24 hours, and had seemingly *done the town.*

"Pilot, did you manage to find something to do with your time off?" "Yes Sir, the lads and I enjoyed a good dinner, then took a very nice tour of the Great Golden Budda Temple, and saw some elephants," he replied nervously. Right, I thought to myself, what a load! *Twenty something* in this port of call! "That is good pilot, very cultural, well then; you and the rest of the lads in your *tour group*, upon landing aboard ship, go straight to the infirmary for a check-up and give the Dokter all the details about it hey?"

The *Duck* rumbled down the concrete airstrip, gathered speed and soon was airborne. The big Curtis Wright radial engine droned laboriously as we climbed in a steep spiral over the city until we reached 2000 meters altitude. The handy bi-plane banked to port then took up an easterly course across the width of Ceylon, roughly on a heading for the east coast city of Batticaloa. Some 30 nautical miles beyond that city, our fleet, having rounded the top of the Ceylon at night, was making its leisurely passage south to Trincomalee.

We winged over the foothills, and below I saw that the tea plantations soon gave way to rugged jungle covered highlands of the central island, in which lay a vast fortune in ebony and calamander wood. The Kandian Hill peoples of Ceylon were originally thought to have come to the island from the Hindustani and Iranistani regions as early as 4000 B.C., although much of Ceylon's abandoned cities and temples seemed of an even greater antiquity. Today, the natives are a light coffee colored people, slightly built and of quite attractive delicate features. The majority are now Brahman Hindus, but their earlier beliefs can only be imagined when studying the crumbling facades and fantastic statuary.

As a boy I had access to the extensive library of our plantation. It contained many original records, some of these up to three centuries old! It was there; amongst the overstuffed shelving, roles of charts and dusty stacks of heavy leather volumes I discovered an aged journal bound in dry, cracked brown leather. It proved to be a record by one of my more adventurous ancestors of the 17th century, a Kapitein Pieter de Winter on my great grandmother's side of the family.

The Kapitein; a young army officer on contract to the Dutch East Indies Company and new to the region, had been tasked to pacify certain hill tribes who had slayed six Company jewel traders. These foolish men had amongst their raw stones a number of pearls which was absolutely forbidden by the ancient deities of the hill people, who upon seeing them offered for barter by the traders, slayed the offenders and returned the pearls to the sea.

The planned punitive military action did not go well for the ambitious yet inexperienced Kapitein de Winter. While he had no problem in the recruiting of a sufficient number of mercenaries to carry out his orders, his command lacked discipline. The majority of the volunteer soldiers had run off to hunt sapphires, soon after reaching the highlands. His now much reduced force, was attacked by Kandian warriors, and easily overwhelmed.

De Winter was taken captive by the natives and transported to the ancient crumbling ruins of a great temple fortress within the abandoned mountain city of Kandy. Here his journal records; he was ushered through a portal that opened the way into what he perceived as a huge lost underworld. The rather obscure entrance was flanked by a pair of gigantic stone statues of half man half elephant. What Pieter De Winter beheld in that vast unexplored region drove him mad.

The Kandian priests seeing this transition of his spirit, believed him to now be pure. His reason; having been being exchanged for absolution of his sins by their *Great Seated God.* The hill men released him and with a small dugout canoe, he found his way through those lower cavern tunnels having access to the sea on the west coast of the island. Here, with the aid of a signal fire he hailed a passing dispatch cutter, and was returned to the Dutch East India Company Fort in Colombo Bay. His condition notwithstanding; de Winter nevertheless recorded this experience in a journal, which made interesting reading due to its fantastic claims. The Company officials however thought it verified his total mental collapse. Soon afterward he was released from his contract.

In about an hour of flight at cruising speed for the bomber, we were approaching the ancient mountain city of Kandy, atop a crag centrally located in a region containing an untold wealth in rubies, garnets, amethysts and sapphires. It is no wonder, I thought; that for centuries the Portuguese, French, Dutch and British fought so many sea battles and numerous land expeditions for control of this vast treasure house.

Now the ancient city came into view, I would have an answer to a question that was more than thirty years old; was Kapitein de Winter a complete idiot, and his journal the record of a madman's nightmare? I told the pilot to fly low over the vast ruins. There! I was able to make out with complete astonishment, the field of broken masonry that was once a dome of staggering proportions. It seem many times greater than the dome of St. Peters Basilica, in fact I estimated that it could have sheltered the entirety of Vatican City! There! Amongst the great tumbled blocks I beheld the two huge statues of the dancing Gods; giant man like forms with Elephant heads!

What an amazing and unexpected revelation! Perhaps there was; the *entrance to an underworld,* as described in the centuries old journal of Kapitein de Winter. Although some portions of the de Winter's journal had been now revealed as accurate; it could not possibly be an entirely truthful account of his adventure, as it seemed just too fabulous to be believable. Nevertheless, there before my eyes; only some 100 meters below the gondola; stood the giant stone dancers awkwardly balanced on one great leg, with elbows out, wrists on hips, and their elephant heads pointed heavenwards voicing their silent song. Accurate as described every detail!

The air-telegraphist kept up frequent radio traffic with the *Cornelis de Witt,* and with the passage of another short hour we spotted the fleet. Looking below me, all seemed in order, the miniature ships appeared to be immobile on a quiet, light blue sheet, yet trailing faint white feathery wakes that indicated forward progress. The pilot, exchanged further brief communication with the ships below, and within a minute I could see that my flagship and her escorts began gracefully turning starboard, into the wind in preparation for taking our four aircraft aboard.

At 13:40hrs, the *Duck* touched down on the deck of the Battle-carrier and my pennant was hoisted shortly after the aircraft had come to a complete halt. Upon observing this, Admiraal van Speijk lowered his pennant aboard the *Johan de Witt* and the *Cornelis de Witt* resumed her role as Fleet Flagship. I made my way to the navigation bridge where I read the ship's log for the last 48 hours then returned to my quarters for the remainder of the day. The fleet prepared to pass a quiet night at sea proceeding towards Trincomalee at only seven knots which would allow us to enter the harbour in the early morning.

By dawn of July 10th the destroyer *Zeeland* reported that her artillery rangefinder aloft had identified the *Foul Point* light beacon off her port bow at a range of ten nautical miles. The fleet was now closing from the south upon the entrance to Trincomalee Harbour. Turning to Kapitein Voorne I said; "make to *Zeeland*; contact the harbour master to initiate preparations to receive our ships. Signal fleet; make all preparations for entering Trincomalee Harbour, I am retiring to my cabin." Kapitein Voorne, nodded and said "Yes Admiraal," then turning to his officer of the watch he called out; "Lt. van Hamel, signal to the fleet: request pilots, prepare ships to enter harbour."

Two hours later at 07:20hrs, the entire fleet with the exception of the munitions ship were laying within the inner harbour. The two Battle-carriers were tied up alongside the north piers of the naval dockyard, bow in, stern out and just opposite the tip of *Little Sober Island*. Behind them and rafted together were our four light cruisers; the *Gouden Leeuw*, immediately behind the *Johan de Witt*, rafted to her starboard side, her flotilla sister the *Aemilia*. Aft of these I spotted the *Prins te Paard* was tied up bow out, at a jetty, and rafted to her the *Oliphant*. The destroyers were all on mooring buoys located north of *Great Sober Island* in the *Inner Harbour*. The two fleet tankers were tied to the refueling wharfs by the tank farm located on the south side of *China Bay*, some two nautical miles west of the Flagship's berth, each taking aboard some 6,000 tonnes of Bunker oil. The *Arnhem* and the liner *Willem Usselinx* were on mooring buoys as well; floating in the middle of the *Inner Harbour*, just north of the destroyers. Here they awaited their turn to pick up tugs to move them to the fuelling wharf.

The poor lonely munitions ship *Nijmegen*, had her mooring selected by the deadly destructive potential of her cargo. She had been rafted to tugboats and piloted further inland to a mooring buoy on the west side of *Tambalagam Bay*, a remote area, four miles off the end of the *China Bay Army Airfield*. She sat two kilometers from the rail line, four kilometers away from the nearest town of *Sinnakinniya* on the south side of the bay by the narrow eastern entrance of *Naditivu Channel*. Here if the unthinkable happened, and her cargo detonated the damage to the railway, the airfield, the city of Trincomalee and its main harbour facilities would be kept to a minimum. At this point the non-combatant vessels were detached from my command, and received their direction from Naval Headquarters at Batavia.

July 15, 1939, the day of *Operation Bulwark* was at hand. The first hint of dawn illuminated a Trincomalee Harbour packed with a vast array of naval might. The warship's painted in their peacetime livery of white shone with a light shade of mauve, with their mooring lights twinkling faintly. The transition from peaceful rest to activity was a short one however, as bugles sounded, and eighty thousand feet thrummed upon decks as crewmembers formed on their warships for the morning flag raising ceremonies. Ship bands struck up their national anthems as if competing for the first rays of dawn as *God Save the King* mingled with *The Star Spangled Banner*, *La Marsiallase* and *Het Wilhelmus*!

The American contingent, of three fast fleet carriers; *Lexington* (F), *Saratoga* and *Ranger*, eight heavy cruisers; *Pensacola*, *Salt Lake City*, *Northampton*, *Chester*, *Louisville*, *Chicago*, *Houston* and *Augusta*. The entire thirty four vessels of the *Craven* and *Simms* class destroyers for a total of forty three warships and four auxiliaries; the fast fleet tankers; *Santee, Suwanee, Cimarron* and the aviation gasoline carrier *Rio Grande*.

The combined fleet of the British Empire, not to be outdone also totaled forty seven vessels. The Battlecruisers *Hood* (F) and *Repulse*, the aircraft carriers; *Courageous, Glorious, Furious* and *Hermes*, five *Kent* class heavy cruisers; three R.N., two R.A.N., six *Leander* class light cruisers; three R.N., three R.A.N., and twenty seven destroyers of the *Flotilla Leader A* through *D* classes. There were three RN fleet auxiliaries in attendance, but I do not have these names.

Next came *La Marine Nationale*, the navy of France; a contingent of thirty six vessels of very attractive design; led by the magnificent new battle-cruisers *Dunkerque* (F) and *Strassbourg*, then the slow fleet carrier *Baern*, six heavy cruisers; *Duquesne, Tourville, Suffern, Colbert, Foch* and *Dupleix*, followed by the entire *Guepard, Aigle, Vauquelin* and Le *Fantastaque* class of destroyers twenty four in total, all very fast large vessels some 60% greater in displacement than other warships of that type. Two fleet oilers; *La Dordogne* and *La Garonne* supplied their fleet's needs.

Batavia; not wanting the Royal Netherlands Navy to appear too inferior in such powerful company, had dispatched nine more warships from the East Indies to augment the Dutch contribution for the naval exercise. These were the 1st cruiser squadron, of *De Ruyter* (F) (Commandeur Doorman), *Java* and *Sumatra* and the 3rd destroyer flotilla; *Evertsen* (F) of (Kapiten ter Zee Van Mook), *Kortenaer, Piet Hein,* and the 4th destroyer flotilla; *Van Ghent* (F) of (Kapiten ter Zee J. Brouwer), *Banckert* and *Van Galen.* The new additions gave our contingent a respectable twenty three ships; two Battle-carriers, seven light cruisers and fourteen destroyers. One hundred and fifty three vessels in total packed the harbour, making *Operation Bulwark* the most powerful concentration of naval might in the Indian Ocean since 1782 when the battle-fleet of the Great French Amiral Pierre-Andre de Suffern fought the Royal Navy under Sir Edward Hughes for control of the Ceylon and the Indian Sub-Continent.

In no time Trincomalee harbour was transformed into an ordered chaos. Tall columns of smoke began to raise into the sky as hundreds of boilers were lit to raise steam. One by one in a precise prearranged timetable the warships of this vast armada began to raise their anchors or slip their mooring buoys, then squadron after squadron made its stately way to the open sea.

The naval exercise was set up neither for tactical training nor for actual combat conditions, it was meant entirely to be a display of sheer firepower, and so would take the form of a gigantic target practice; much like a carnival event where the customer is given a pellet gun to shoot toy ducks off of a wooden ledge. Consequently all the battlecruisers, aircraft carriers and cruisers would carry, newsmen, film crews and photographers, representing many nations. The light carrier *HMS Hermes* provided two Swordfish for shooting 16 mm film panoramas from aloft.

Our target vessels were awaiting for us at sea, within that 2500 square mile area indicated on the charts as a firing range for the Royal Navy. These had been accumulated over the years for just such a purpose. Many were seizures from smuggling operations or pirate vessels. Some were old schooners and square riggers, others were old derelict naval vessels, liners and cargo vessels on their last legs and purchased for scrap. The vessels with working boilers, had their boilers fired up, with as much coal as possible stuffed into the firebox, then the air draft reduced to burn the coal more slowly, Once pressure had been built up the steam valves were opened to the reciprocating machinery, but only enough to give five knots. At this setting they would move for perhaps several hours. The remote control radio gear would be activated and then all personnel removed by cutter. These were the best targets, and as they had engines could tow a string of old empty barges with light plywood upper works fitted to make the target more interesting. All the radio controlled vessels were to be guided from aloft by a Swordfish squadron from *HMS Hermes* as well.

The target fleet was actually larger in numbers than the naval vessels that were soon to destroy it. Its creation, maintenance, mobility, supply, coordination, crewing and operation represented a valuable service and a large professional effort. But the officer's and men of this fleet are never considered worthy of praise or a place in history, as they usually are crewed by those who have problems with sobriety, discipline, gambling, women, and perhaps even a petty crime on their record. The navy is an unforgiving service, with a long memory, but she will always be able to find uses for her highly capable but less than noteworthy sailors.

The two Dutch battle-carriers, due to their large size carried a mix of film crews from the Netherlands, one from Batavia, an American, an Australian and an Argentinian, as well as newspapermen and photographers. The cruisers being much smaller were limited to the latter two types respectively. The warships of the other fleets had made similar accommodations.

Therefore each fleet would proceed to sea in the following unusual arrangement. Big gun ships first in line ahead, followed by the carriers, then the cruisers. The combined fleet would head north into the Indian Ocean during the morning, with all shooting and bombing of radio controlled target ships to port, a course chosen to give the best lighting for the cameras. Then a pause for an hour and a half at midday, for mess call for the men, and a refreshments in the Wardroom for the guests, as the fleet slowly turned to port to descend upon another concentration of target ships and take them under fire off our starboard side, which again gave beneficial back lighting in the afternoon for the filming as well as allowing those ship's with batteries of guns not on the centerline of their ship's to also get in practice.

The massed flotillas of destroyers would be located on the opposite side of the firing from where they would display anti-submarine depth charge operations. The big ships would cease firing and bombing at intervals to allow massed destroyer formations to pass between the line of large warships to make torpedo attacks against the target vessels.

The *Cornelis de Witt* (F) and the *Johan de Witt* being battlecruiser-carriers equipped with heavy guns as well as a flight deck and air groups would participate in the heavy gun exercise followed immediately by aerial bombing exercises. Our position was in the tail end of the battlecruiser squadron, following; *Hood* (Flagship combined fleet), *Repulse*, *Dunkerque* (F) and *Strassbourg*, and leading the carrier line of *Lexington* (F), *Saratoga*, *Ranger, Baern, Courageous, Glorious, Furious, and Hermes*, with the cruisers following these in a long line. This was the morning steaming formation.

The film camera crews aboard my ship selected two places to set up for the artillery shoot, on the top of the flight deck *duck bill* right forward, and on the foredeck between the capstans. The main battery shoot started as usual; with the ranging shots with one gun per turret. Despite some visible agitation from both the camera crews, they toughed it out and kept filming. After a few minutes however the *Cornelis* had the range, and began discharging six gun salvos at better than two per minute. In short order the Kapitein received reports that the film crews on the flight deck, had experienced too much buffeting from the concussion of the firing and the 20 knot ship generated breeze and therefore had decided to move operations to aft of the tripod mast. The foredeck film crews, were less well off, suffering as they were from the wind and being roughed up by the concussion as well. They had packed up their cameras and relocated forward to the hawse pipes. Here they found no relief, and were getting a bit of a soaking from spray shooting up the pipes each time the bow bit into the five meter seas. The duty officer on watch, realizing the danger that they had put themselves in became entirely fed up with them. He sent a bosun's mate along to the rescue, who undogged a fore deck hatch and led the disheveled camera crews down through a forward companionway.

In the afternoon, the Capital ships in line ahead would cease operations as the cruisers would break into two columns and sail down the port and starboard side of the big ships, firing to seaward as they launched their spotter aircraft. These would each be followed by a mass of destroyers charging about. This display had limited tactical value and was set up entirely for the benefit of the news media, to show the profiles of the warships steaming and firing at high speed. After three hours of this activity, the warship's would steam away from the area for the evening to allow the destruction of any dud torpedoes that remained afloat, and the salvage or destruction of the surviving target ships.

The ships then prepared for an evening at sea. For those vessels hosting the members of media, the evening began with a fine meal, to be followed by a variety of entertainment. Aboard the *Cornelis de Witt* we entertained a contingent of twenty five film crew, journalists and radio broadcasters. Our guests enjoyed a very sumptuous meal, in the officer's wardroom served on our *Van Kempen* silver, then we adjourned to the upper hangar deck, where the ship's band, and theater troupe gave us their best. The lower hanger deck held boxing matches for the men in three weight classes, these were always gritty affairs, as the participants were crew members that happened to be at odds with one another. Our quests were free to wander the roped off areas under escort, to enjoy events on both decks to suite their individual tastes.

The final diversion was Kapitein Voorne hosting an evening of cigars and open bar on the gun deck of 'C' Turret, whose long gun barrels had been elevated five degrees to prevent cracks to our guest's skulls. Here the wardroom stewards had rolled out the piano, and arranged some twenty circular tables around each of which were set four or five chairs.

Here I sat comfortably with my senior officer's, enjoying a whiskey and a Ceylonese cigar while discussing the days exercise, at one of my favorite leisure areas aboard, due to its breezes and protection from rain by the flight deck. I congratulated Lt. ter Zee Van Ripper our expert gunnery officer. The accuracy of his big guns was most impressive, we hit the targets often and squarely. We matched the performance of the Royal Navy's 15 inch guns, reputed to be more accurate than our weapons, and even those of the more modern French 330 mm artillery. Hoof Van Officier Van Braekel also received my congratulations on the faultless, flying operations, our fighters zoomed about most impressively, while our new PZL P23 Sea Eagle bombing groups pulverized the radio controlled target ships only some three miles off our beam. Here I remained for most of the evening, enjoying the cool breezes and the peaceful magic of a moonlit sea, while I quietly chatted with whatever newsmen or officer who cared to join my table.

The following day the fleets cruised in a circular battle formation, with the battlecruisers and aircraft carriers in the center. Forming a circle around these were the heavy and light cruisers, and outboard of these two complete rings of destroyers. Each ring spaced at half a mile. This was again not an ideal ring spacing for combat, but it suited the cameras very well indeed.

Overhead the naval aircraft made an impressive show. More than two hundred fighter aircraft zoomed low over the warship's decks in sections of three, while higher aloft some twenty five bomber squadrons crisscrossed back and forth over the fleet in an impressive display. The antiaircraft batteries now showed their worth blazing away with blank rounds in a simulated air defense.

By mid-day this exercise had been concluded and the fleet stood down until the evening. Then night operations were demonstrated, with the fleet illuminated by many parachute flares which had been dropped by the aircraft at 2000 meters altitude. The AA batteries made a stunning display of night firing. Night flying was a very dangerous operation for the air groups, and great care had to be taken to avoid midair collision so the number of aircraft participating was a small section from each flattop. But it went off without a hitch, and after the massive display during the day, it was the darkness, the flashes of brilliant light that seemed to make the deepest impression upon the newsmen.

The following morning; the fleet made for Trincomalee Harbour, with the individual ships taking up their previous buoys. The warship's of the RNLN battle squadron did not return to dockside but rode at anchor for the evening. Our quests who seemed very impressed by the whole exercise departed via naval cutter back to their Hotels within the city.

July 17, 1939 the U.S. Navy contingent raised its anchors, and departed swiftly and without fanfare at sunrise, and we followed some two hours later. The British and French fleets would remain in Trincomalee Harbour for two more days then cruise to fortress Singapore; the most important city in the Asiatic Colonies of the British Empire. The combined fleets would then visit Saigon and Hai Phong in French Indo China, and then make for Manila and Hong Kong.

We were now underway once more on our last leg of the voyage to the friendly waters of the Dutch East Indies. The next land that we sighted would be the island of Sabang, laying off the northern tip of Sumatra. It was some 1900 nautical miles to this landfall, which the fleet reached in the evening of July 21st. The fleet maintained an easterly course, leaving the Indian Ocean behind us and passing through Great Channel between the Nicobar Island Group to the north and the island off Sumatra's headland, and into the Andaman Sea. The battle squadron continued east for four hours, before correcting our course to a southeast heading that took us into the Strait of Malacca, which separated the British Colony of Malaysia, from the Dutch Island Colony. The straits here are very busy and there was every type of vessel to be encountered from great liners to humble fishing dhows and junks.

The men were in a very cheerful mood, and watched with keen eyes the jungle choked coast of the island of Sumatra slipping by rapidly along our starboard side, as well as a wide variety of vessels distinctly Asiatic in appearance. Soon the aircraft would be leaving the ship, as each squadron would be flying out to their designated naval air stations on land. The activities below deck were hectic, as each hangar crew for made ready for the departure of its beloved bird.

By mid-day July 23rd, the fleet was approaching *the narrows* with Singapore off our port bow only some 40 nautical miles distant. Here the shipping became very heavy. We steamed through a myriad of small islands south of Singapore called the *Kepulauan Riau Group*. By evening we were clear of these and into the most western approaches to the South China Sea. After a quiet night under the stars, and moving only at six knots, we began the morning with the dispatch of the first of our four fighter and six bomber squadrons. Every few hours brought us within range of a different naval air station. Soon all our machines had flown off for dispersal. Feeling the end of the voyage drawing near, and anxious to arrive at the appropriate time to begin the welcoming ceremonies, I ordered an increase in speed for the final lap to our new home port; the naval base at Soerabaja.

It was during this final sprint towards the naval base that the fleet crossed the equator. The ancient seafarer ritual was once again replayed as all the young sailors were introduced to the Sea God Neptune and his lovely mermaids. Each ship had prepared a dunking tub on her quarterdeck, and the roll call was read. Each crewmen regardless of rank solemnly made his way aft to the site of the ritual. Here the initate was given a revolting brew to swallow, then he was seized by the ugliest hairy mermaids that one could imagine and dunked three times into the tank. In this way several thousand RNLN sailors were granted Royal Permission from King Neptune to enter the southern hemisphere of his realm.

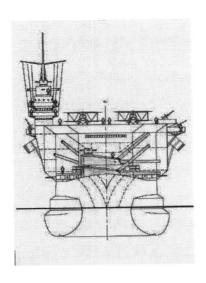

CHAPTER XVIII

THE FLEET GROWS STRONGER, ARRIVAL AT SOERABAJA, JAPANESE SPY SHIPS, A TOP SECRET SOVIET POUCH FROM MANCHURIA, SUPERIOR JAPANESE TECHNOLOGY REVEALED, OLD AIRCRAFT-NEW TACTICS, SHIP DEFENCES AUGMENTED.

Three days following the conclusion of *Operation Bulwark* our fleet was crossing the Bay of Bengal on a course that would take it into the Andaman Sea. I was sitting in my cabin and reviewing the schedule for our fleet tankers to refuel our eight destroyers when there came a knock at the door of my day cabin. "Komen," I announced and an Adjudant Onderofficer from the telegraphist office entered my day cabin, saluted and held forth a dispatch from Den Helder. The news was gratifying and confirmed a further Capital ship acquisition for our navy. The purchase of the Battleship-carrier *Rio de Janerio* from Brazil had been completed. Our rapidly growing little navy had added a third big ship to its force. The remaining reserve of some 1,400 seamen, trained for battle-carrier duty, who were currently languishing in Den Helder Naval Barracks would now have a ship. These men would exchange the chill of the North Sea, for the lush tropics of the Caribbean Sea or the Southwest Pacific Colony! The Royal Netherlands Navy was soon to be ranked the seventh most powerful in the world.

I knew some of the details surrounding the efforts of our navy to acquire the Brazilian warship, as they were revealed to me in Colombo by the Field Marshal; nevertheless I was still surprised and pleased that the negotiations had been successfully concluded.

The Battleship-carrier was to be given the name *Hr. Ms. Schoonveldt*, after the great Dutch naval victory over the combined fleets of England and France in the 17th century.

I leaned over the chart table and retrieved a copy of Jane's Warships from the book shelf and looked up the statistics on the vessel. She was a converted British *super dreadnought* of the first Great War, originally named the *H.M.S. Agincourt*. The vessel; the flagship of the *Marinha do Brazil*, (the Brazilian Navy), was singularly unique, in that it was the first commissioned *battleship-plane-carrier*, amongst all of the navies of the world.

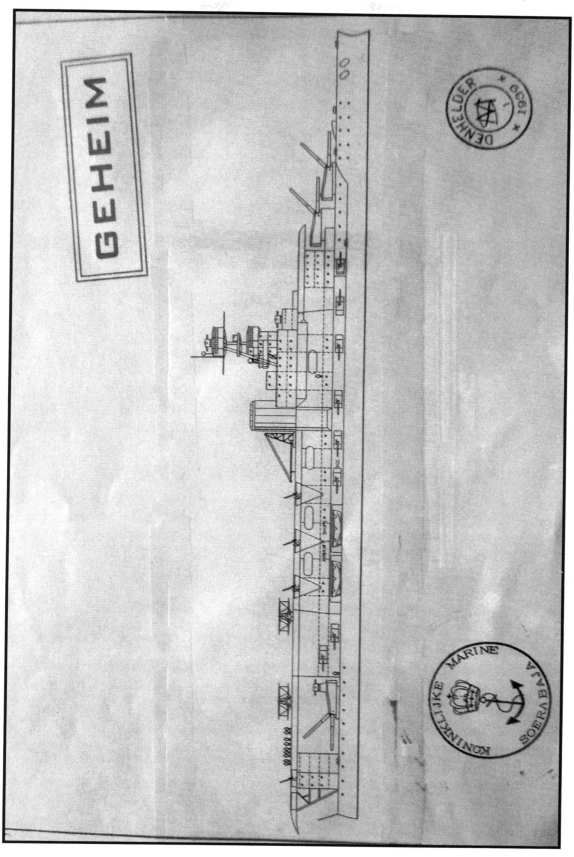

Her armament was impressive; fifty-three aircraft; thirty bi-plane bombers, fifteen biplane fighters, eight high speed pursuit fighters, six 305mm guns, sixteen 152mm guns, seven 127mm dual purpose surface and anti-aircraft guns, and sixteen 40 mm Bofors guns. Her principal particulars were; L 213 x B 32 x 9.5 meters mean draft, 36,000 tonnes displacement, speed 27 knots, 230 mm armored belt, 305 mm turret and barbette armor, 1.6 meter deep torpedo blisters, 1342 officers and men. These statistics rightly conferred upon her the elite status of *Capital Ship*. I was looking forward to having this powerful vessel join the fleet as soon as possible.

July 27, 1939 1000 hours; the end of our eventful voyage was at hand. The fleet slowly entered the constricted waters of the *Western Channel*, Madura Island to the North, with Java to the south, and just a few kilometers from the naval base at *Soerabaja*, laying off our port quarter. The unwieldy battle-carriers were to be met with the first of the navy's tugs to assist with their passage through the 100 meter wide entrance into the naval basin, and to their assigned berths. The destroyers would raft together along the new 400 meter concrete wharf just to the north and outside of the naval basin.

Kapitien Voorne, had earlier sent a thousand men to work with brushes and rags to daub white paint onto all his ship's vertical plating. In less than ten minutes they had quickly masked the flagship's rust streaks and flaked paint one would expect from forty seven days at sea. Similar activities had taken place aboard all the other naval vessels within my fleet as well.

I enjoyed an excellent location on the platform at the very top of the deckhouse and therefore was able to take in the maximum view. Around me were several of my off-duty staff officers and aides relaxing, leaning on the bulwark, enjoying a smoke and taking in the spectacle of a festive welcome. The officers and men were in good spirits at voyage end. All looked forward to some leave after months aboard ship. The problem of berthing the vlaggeschip was being directed by the officer of day from the battle bridge. There were no duties to intrude upon this moment to be savored.

It was a beautiful day to arrive at the new home port for the Battlecruiser-carrier division and their escort ships. Sunny but not overly hot. The breeze was from the west; variable, about 9-12 knots. The occasional light squall worked its way across the bay, to ruffle those waters it touched, changing them from grey green to emerald blue. The normally high humidity to be expected at this hour and this latitude was not present, and the breezes cancelled out the heat of the sun that one usually felt pressing down heavily upon the shoulders.

I was determined to make a grand entrance, after our long expected arrival. A voyage which I was aware had garnered quite a bit more publicity in the press due to all the unforeseen occurrences. Of course this was beneficial to us; as our fleet was meant to be a deterrent, and we wanted the idea of our strength to be uppermost in certain minds. The fresh white paint made the new arrivals look magnificent. Each vessel was spotlessly clean, fully dressed with colorful flags, and with all her brass work buffed to a bright polish. The Fleet made a stately, and dignified procession as they positioned themselves and prepared to *drop the hook*.

Both the East and West Channel approaches to the city were alive with activity. Flotilla's of private yachts colorfully bedecked and packed with cheering spectators had come out to gape at these massive battle-carriers. The perimeter of whose flight decks as well as the bulwarks of all the warships were lined with several thousand sailors clad in crisp white cotton *tropical uniform short*; all standing at attention to *dress ship*.

Now a series of the international flags were broken out and run up the yard of the Vlaggeschip. First was yellow field with a black ball; *altering course to port*. The great ship turned majetically into the wind; then splash, the port anchor was away. The heavy chain leapt fully two meters off the deck with a deep roar, to snake with blinding speed down the hawse hole, amid a cloud of gritty brown rust. In a few moments, it halted as the anchor settled into the silt.

At that precise moment; all my ships had released their anchors; and with the roaring of the chains as their herald, the sailors snatched up with their right hands the wide brimmed tropical straw hats from their brows and held them aloft. Then in their best yell, let out three enthusiastic; Huurrahhh, Huurrahhh, HUURRAAHHHs. This was immediately followed by wild cheering from those ashore, who appreciated the grand spectacle.

Down came flag; India, up went, the blue square with white cross flag: *my vessel is stopped and making no way through the water*, under this, the vertical blue and yellow stripes of flag: *need a pilot*, below this the red, blue, black and yellow of flag: Zulu; *request a tug*. Similar signaling operations were underway on all ships of the battle squadron.

While we rode quietly at anchor the two largest tugs in the RNLN the; *Zwarte Zee* and *Thames* had finished their preparations within the naval basin to receive our great hulls. From my elevated vantage point upon the deckhouse I could make out their masts and upperworks as they crossed its width heading for the entrance. Within a few more minutes they came around the point and approached the *Cornelis de Witte* to guide her from the straits, through the 100 meter entrance into the naval basin. Once this had been accomplished they would nudge her gently sideways towards that berth at the south end of the dock that ran parallel with *Purwa Road*. The massive profiles of the battle-carriers it is vital to grasp, were mere playthings for the fickle wind Gods of those islands. For even two such powerful tugs it would be a tricky operation given all the small boat congestion.

Our anchor was weighed and secured when the tugs had us in their power. As the *Cornelis* slowly approached the harbour mouth, certain maritime formalities were observed. The square yellow flag was hoisted up the masthead; '*my vessel is well, require free pratique*', a signal to the customs officials. Atop the small bluff, some three hundred meters off the port bow there squatted the low granite ramparts of old Fort Rotterdam. A string of *letter flags*; the reply, was now run up its towering white naval mast; V-O-E-R H-A-V-E-N (enter harbour), and below this W-E-L-K-O-M (welcome).

At that time the old fortress battery of twenty 30 Kg. Krupp muzzle loading smooth bore cannon commenced firing a 15 gun salute to acknowledge the three stars of my Vice Admiraal's pennant! Similarly; some twenty minutes when the *Johan de Witt* entered the naval basin; a 13 gun salute followed to acknowledge the two star pennant of Rear Admiraal Konrad Van Speijk. The latter salute was repeated once again for Rear Admiraal Count Gerrit Van Kerkhoven-Sassenheim of the *Gouden Leeuw*, the flagship of the cruiser squadron.

I knew that this was quite a task for the fortress's battery commander. When one considered the rate of fire for such ancient, cumbersome hand loaded muzzle loading weapons, the fortress artillery pulled it off rather smartly. The slow deliberate discharge of the big guns, seemed to enhance the dignity of the ceremony.

The white clouds of smoke produced by firing the black powder charges billowed out savagely and for a moment, in complete silence, then the thunder of their dull report rolled across the rice paddy fields, to the harbour and reached us. With their expansive energies soon spent, the cotton ball clouds were quickly caught by the lively breeze that ruffled the green water and dissipated, then replaced in a short interval by those clouds of the successive salutes.

Just then my eyes caught a movement and snapped to port. Hugging the treetops of the low hills, flying elegantly, and with a *certain wide winged magnificence*, came a huge white painted *Short Sunderland MK I* Flying boat of the *Qantas Empire Airways Co.* "Just in from Port Darwin, or possibly Rangoon," I heard myself say. She glided noiselessly down on a final approach and skimmed low over the surface of the choppy waters of East Channel, then set her elegant bulk down gracefully, creating a huge billowing cloud of mist which engulfed the entire machine briefly. A great roar developed as it reversed the pitch of its four 1000 hp Bristol Pegasus radial engines. But this soon died down as did her forward motion, then she danced lightly across the waters of *West Channel* towards the sea plane basin within the civilian harbour to pick up, her mooring buoy and discharge her passengers.

A tiny white painted steam yacht sporting a neat new green canvass awning putted quite near our port side, she was packed with smiling wildly waving gentlemen and ladies, their voices lost amid the cacophony of sound. I was worried as it bobbed crazily, in the confused waters of the busy harbour entrance, and from her tiny heart; the little polished brass trimmed boiler just managed a shrill little toot...toot. The big tugs, both pushing against the starboard side, with their view blocked by our towering hull did not see her.

The pilot aboard the Vlaageschip, who was also directing the tugs, had his hands full that day. He now became a little agitated with the small craft crowding his huge charge. I could see the signal rating breaking out from the flag locker; the flag India, followed by; the horizontal blue and yellow bars of flag Delta; *keep clear of me, I am maneuvering with difficulty,* and below this, the red checkerboard of flag Uniform; *you are running into danger.*

But then, perhaps reconsidering; the pilot chose not raise them, as the, *Commander* of the tiny steamboat, perhaps only a *Sunday Yachtsmen* may not have understood the message. The pilot did not want to run the risk of confusing the tugs with the flags, which may disengage, so he activated the ship's intercom and delivered in a greatly magnified voice a very crude order to the little steam launch hovering even closer off our towering steel side. I thought that it was a bit too descriptive myself, the citizens were after-all enjoying the enthusiasm of the moment. The ladies aboard the trim little launch, I am sure were completely aghast, upon visualizing such an appalling sexual directive! The red faced skipper, of the pretty little steamer nevertheless shoved the tiller over. He must have been deeply offended, after all he was a captain as well, and he had paying customers aboard!

Now from ashore came to my ears the growing din of many automobile horns and thousands of voices raised in greeting. Glancing over the tops of the long roofs of the warehouses and buildings of the naval base I could see a large area of pink faces and waving handkerchiefs, where a crowd was assembled under the treed bank of the river mouth along *Patiunus Street*, and the commercial wharf. A large crowd of mostly white colonists were gathered there beneath a sea of fluttering white handkerchiefs and waving arms, perhaps six thousand strong. Their cheering was soon drowned out by the hooting of steam horns erupting from the ships laying within the Commercial harbour, and those just off our starboard bow, tied up at the Warehouse jetties along the *River Mas*.

Some 500 meters away the *Arandora Star*, a 15,000 gross ton passenger liner of the Blue Star line saluted us, from within the Civilian Harbour. A tall, expanding column of white now jetted up from the foremost of her twin stacks and after a few seconds the deep bellowing of her powerful steam horn arrived.

"Admiraal," my chief of staff; Kapitein te Zee Derrick van Klaffens addressed me, while pointing and laughing; "the *Blue Star Liner* has hoisted the *Gin Pennant*! We'll drink him dry!" I raised my binoculars to confirm; yes indeed, fluttering at the foremast I was able to make out, the triangular green pennant, sporting the *Blue Star Line's*; famous inverted champagne glass. Van Klaffens, continued with a chuckle, "Is he bloody mad? Her Captain has given an open invitation to *all* ship's officers in the harbour. There must be at least several hundred ship's masters and naval officers available, for that *call to duty*!"

"I know her Captain; John Hollister very well Kapitein van Klaffens," I replied with a chuckle. "He is a most excellent fellow. I have no doubt that the head accountants, of that very prosperous shipping line, will wring their hands over her captain's generosity today, forever conflicted by their concern for the bottom line of their company's profit ledger. Not being seamen themselves they are neither able to appreciate the spirit of this occasion, nor the fabled traditions of the *Blue Star Line* that incidently make it such a popular choice and bring to it so much business!"

Turning to my right, I abandoned my position for a moment and went down the companionway to the deck below. Here were another group of the officer cadet aspirants at their ship recognition station. "Ship Information!" I called, from the bottom of the stairs. They snapped to attention looking in my direction. "The large white liner to stern to us, at the commercial jetty," I pointed.

The senior cadet officer in charge of the table, raised his binoculars; and began to read off; *Arandora Star*, reading her flag; "British registry," he called out, immediately his team grabbed the Lloyd's Register; then identifying her smoke stack scheme he called out to his fellow cadets over his shoulder; "propulsion; steam, stack logo; blue star on a white roundel, twin stacks painted red, with a single white stripe on top, black band above white stripe. White hull, green boot top, about 16,000 tons gross, I imagine." Lowering his binoculars he looked back at the other cadets.

They stood by the table, furiously working the books, and then one, snapped to attention and addressed me; "Admiraal; Blue Star Line, *Arandora Star*, class; Passenger Liner; 14694 tons gross, four steam turbines, twin screw, 22 knots. Four other ships in class; *Almeda*, *Andalucia*, *Avelona* and *Avila*, Sir." I nodded, with a grunt of satisfaction, which brought wide smiles to their eager young faces, and then I went back up top.

The ships in *Soerabaja* that morning going about their daily activity of loading and or discharging cargos and ship stores took a few moments from their routine to give us quite a reception; one that tugged at the heart strings. The hooting of ships' steam whistles erupted all over the harbour from the many and varied merchant ships, fishing vessels or warships at their berths. The *illusion of security* from Japan had at last arrived for the colonists in the form of two gigantic 40,000 warships and their powerful escorts all bristling with armament.

I ordered the fleet to return the compliment; and give them our horns for all they were worth as a thank you. I was nevertheless was more than a little startled as the *Cornelis* let go a real *ear splitter*. The chief engineer took the opportunity to vent twelve out of our sixteen active main boilers. The deck house vibrated with the released energy, as 100,000 meters^3 of superheated steam at 315°C, at 48 kg/cm^2 pressure tried to exit a single 76 mm diameter pipe all at the same moment!

I moved out onto the port bridge platform of the deckhouse and glanced up to the masthead to see my Admiraal's pennant flying proudly above the largest tri-color that we could set. Another obstacle had been mastered, and lay now behind us; the fleet had been delivered intact to *Soerabaja* as ordered. Just then a light, man-made mist fell as the huge steam cloud expanding over my ship started to cool and condense.

Turning at the noise of aircraft engines, my eyes caught the approach of several large formations of planes. A squadron of large Dornier flying boats arrayed in perfect echelon formation appeared and overflew us. These were followed by two squadrons of Army Glen Martin Bombers and one of the twin engine Fokker Fighters, all out of *Perak Airfield* no doubt. Soon to appear was a rather familiar sight; the entire air-groups of both battle cruiser-carriers in neat formations, the Swordfish, the Sea Furys, the Sea Eagles, and the Sea Harts. Noticeably absent were my modern army fighters that I had impressed for duty, these having been jealously reclaimed by our brother service.

My Chief of Air Operations, it seemed had planned his own welcome. I chuckled to myself; "There is no one so lonely it seems as; naval air crews waiting to get back aboard their true home; the ship!" It was a memorable moment, an experience that marked a milestone along the roadway of many naval careers that day.

The Vlaggeschip and the *Johan de Witt,* now securely berthed, had just begun the process of unshipping pallets of crated items destined for the repair shops on the naval base. Ship's pumps, and shafting for the lathes, electric motors for new windings and bearings, aircraft engine 500 hour rebuilds, wings and rudders for new canvas, a few washing machines, and a great volume of expended brass from the 40 mm AA batteries. Depending upon its size, weight and location, some crates were unshipped through side scuttles in the hull or were transported up from the hanger deck by using both air aircraft elevators up onto the flight deck, then maneuvered to its landward side, in reach of the dockside cranes.

Up forward the deck work parties had just begun to rig the expansive canvas foc'sle deck awnings that would cast shade to cool the teak and steel weather decks under which lay extensive enlisted seamen messes. On the foc'sle deck itself I observed all the mushroom vent caps growing magically shorter as the men below cranked them closed. No more ship generated breezes, time to air- condition the ship and give the men dry cool air for the night to ensure their continued good health. The anchor party having washed the last of the harbour mud from the massive port anchor down the hawse pipe, were stowing the hoses. Other men of the anchoring party could be seen tightening up the *big bottle screw slips* on the anchor chain. The hawser work parties had set the bow, stern and spring-lines and were busily snubbing up. The vessel was alive with *that certain ordered chaos* from transitioning a ship from sea duty to harbour station.

The bulkhead phone rang, a Lt. picked it up and then informed me that my transportation was at hand. Glancing down from the air operations deckhouse to the dock, I noticed a line of robin-egg blue, 1937 Packard four-door sedans rolling along the jetty towards the Vlaggeschip. At that moment several large cranes started to slowly crawl down their rails to pick off the crated planes. A shrill whistle and shouting which now erupted from the wharf attracted my attention as I noticed a red faced dock-master's wildly flapping his white gauntlets. Apparently the navy sedans were being a bit hasty in threading there way along the busy wharf. "Look out lads, I muttered under my breath!"

I then quickly made my way to my day cabin to collect my personal valise and carrying case. The Bosun and his work party had already removed my sea trunks from out of my cabin to the dock, my chief of staff and his aides were waiting for me in the corridor outside my cabin, then they followed me to the column of Navy Sedans, forming along the dockside; the first of which broke out the three stars of my pennant. I stepped out on to the gangway and saluted the flag astern, then was piped off the ship. My Vice Admiraal's pennant was lowered, folded and prepared to follow me ashore. My staff behind me, we trundled down the gangway onto the concrete wharf.

Slowly the procession of navy Packards made its way from the cluttered dock area to the quiet administrative block of buildings located south of the basin. Through the driver's side rear window I saw a neighborhood of grand stone houses, set amid manicured gardens and spacious lawns. These were the senior officer married residences. Some 200 meters beyond this stood the naval administrative offices, fleet engineering, combat bunkers, and hospital. Like the residences these were surrounded by lovely flower gardens and well-manicured lawns. All these shimmered whitely in the heat of the day.

My land office in the base was located in a white washed heavy stone building close to the old fortress and was surrounded by green lawns and beds of colorful flowers. The interior was delightfully cool, quite spacious, airy and of white painted wood and with a lot of glass. A large oak drafting table stood under the north side window, already stacked up with books, brown envelopes and interesting looking rolls of drawings, which seemed to beckon to me.

I turned to see an alert looking group of commissioned and non-commissioned officers snap to attention as I entered. If their smiling faces were any true indication of their feelings they seemed genuinely pleased that we had arrived, even though it would mean the end of their easy duty.

Slowly my subconscious mind came to the realization that my swaying walk indicated that solid ground was under my feet and the seven and a half week voyage was over. The tension I carried during the voyage, brought on by the known dangers as well as those imagined, in a world seemingly out of balance and on the brink of war I put behind me. These could now be eased somewhat, at voyage end. My thoughts chose to drift to that moment when I would arrive at my plantation; *New Eden,* and greet Karen and the children. The seaplane would drop me off, and thirty days leave of duty would begin. I would take Karen in my arms and…with a bang and a clatter my gear arrived from the ship, snapping me back to reality.

No sooner had the chief and his shore party manhandled the several large fireproof trunks of documents and my personal suitcases into my office than my receptionist P.O. Schrift; informed me that Lt. ter Zee 1e Klasse (Lt. Commander) Wolraven Vandermeeren of OVZ; Office van Zeeinlichtingen (Naval Intelligence Service), Batavia was awaiting my arrival with a special package. *Vloek!* I muttered under my breath. It had not taken long for complications to catch me up, as I had only been off the ship some sixteen minutes!

Saluting smartly, the Lt. Commander entered my office. "Good morning Vice Admiraal" he stated, "congratulations on your voyage". I indicated that he take a seat, as I lit up a *Panter* cigarette and said, "What do you have for me?" He then continued, "Admiraal I have two items for you. The first is that the Japanese now have several hundred additional fishing vessels, and pearling schooners operating within our waters than the same time last year. We are doing what we can to identify and remove them. We locate them with our float planes and radio their positions into the nearest customs dock and patrol boats are dispatched. But it is almost a hopeless task as they blend so well with the native boats. Just be aware of the fact that they are to all be considered as engaging in covert activities."

"Now this," he said, "a most secret item." The locked, steel reinforced attaché case carried by Vandermeeren, and chained to his wrist was emptied. I extracted an envelope and a thick manila folder stamped with a large red *GEHEIM* (secret) across the front and bound with wire crimped and sealed. I retrieved from this some 75 large, very detailed high quality black and white photographs and a heavy bundle of typed pages in the form of a technical report.

Our intelligence agents in Japan for the last five years have been slowly collecting data on the technical achievements and latest capabilities of the ever growing air arm of the mighty *Rengo Kantai*. However the obtaining of accurate intelligence was made a very difficult task indeed for at the time Nippon was a highly insular society and their security measures very tight. All foreigners in Japan were assigned agents who watched their every move. The meat of these efforts to date was rather lean, but we knew that in the last year many new types of war birds had entered service with the Japanese Army Air Force (JAAF) and the Japanese Navy Air Force (JNAF). We still as yet had little hard evidence regarding the performance of these machines. This data was absolutely crucial to the development of effective tactics to counter them.

However our agents had been able to determine that the technical ability of Japanese aviation I fear, had been greatly underrated by the British, French, Americans, and only to a somewhat lesser extent ourselves. I now had an opportunity to review with my senior staff and operational officers a series of technical drawings and reports evaluating the latest carrier-borne aircraft as well as the Japanese Army's latest twin engine land based bombers and fighters.

Operation Bulwark had concluded only a few weeks earlier, and it had left me in an upbeat and confident mood regarding our state of readiness. The contents of the pouch once revealed to me, left me feeling a little hollow. Up to this point I had believed in the combined ability of the Colonial Powers to resist Japanese aggression. Our security was based on the assumption that *European* technical superiority in aircraft design, manufacture and quality training would offset the anticipated Japanese numerical advantage in machines. This was shown to be utter nonsense.

These technical reports, now in hand, dealt with Japanese aircraft shot down or destroyed in Manchuria by the Soviet Air Force during their most recent border conflict. Several of the Japanese bombers and fighters depicted were not too badly damaged having just skidded to a stop on their bellies. Field repairs were affected to them by soviet aircraft technicians utilizing parts taken from other similar downed machines. The captured planes were then put through a series of tests by a special technical unit of the Soviet Air Force and evaluated. Copies of these detailed technical reports in Dutch translation formed the remainder of the intelligence. Naturally this material was of vital technical nature, and had tremendous value.

In the Soviet Union, not all workers were senior card carrying Communists, who had a place reserved for them at *the table of plenty*. For the vast majority of Soviet citizens, it was a life of hard work, and promises of a bright future; but little actual reward. To make life even more tasteless, the ever present watchful eye of the NKVD (secret police). Memories of the *heady days of the Peoples Revolution*, no longer gave comfort at night in a state where tens of millions of citizens just vanished, never to be heard of again! For one disenchanted official, the nights meant terror, and a constant feeling of impending doom. To this individual, the information contained in this report meant wealth, and a new passport to freedom. The government of the Netherlands was happy to provide both, in exchange for such an unexpected prize!

Readers in the 1980's (at a time this record was first seriously organized) may not realize that the speed of technological changes which they are so familiar with in that decade, had been occurring at just as rapid a pace in the field of aircraft design in the 1930's and 40's, a pace which has not slackened for over fifty years!

The Japanese aircraft design companies, had for fifteen years been operating with the maximum financial support then available from their military and had been given all the freedom and resources required to produce the very latest breakthrough designs. Many of these new aircraft were scheduled to begin production on a date so calculated as to re-equip all branches of their military at practically the same time! That being the late summer of 1941.

Every new Japanese bomber and fighter type that the Allied forces would encounter from 1940 to '42 seemed superior to the latest aircraft produced by America and Great Britain! The Japanese had not somehow *tricked everyone*, as has so often been suggested. It was the white man's prejudice against the Asiatic that had blinded us as to their true potential. In any event the warriors of Nippon now enjoyed a serious technical advantage that would take years to catch up. These completely *oriental designs* were definitely a cut above any of the naval aircraft currently aboard my battle squadron, including those biplane air groups that we would soon receive from the Americans aircraft carriers.

I was now confronted with a deep personal vexation. The battlecruiser-carrier division was largely my creation. I had sold the concept to our navy and used up the vast sum of 30 million guilders of our military budget in delivering these ship types with the assurance that they would greatly enhance our safety. The money had been spent. Seeing these excellent Japanese aircraft designs I was much less sure of my earlier claims, and realized that I had aimed too low in my evaluation!

Regardless of what the new information revealed to us of the true capability of the Japanese Aircraft Industry, I was still responsible for the solution to the technical inferiority which we now faced. As we would get few new aircraft, the only avenue open to respond to this threat was to evolve our fleet's air arm tactics to cope with these unforeseen challenges and by so doing; ensure that our efforts, monies and young lives would not be wasted.

Due to the acquisition of this invaluable technical data I now had a reasonable chance to carry it off. I asked my staff to prepare a series of experiments with our aircraft that would train our pilots to expand our operational tactics so that they would not be forced to contest with the strengths of the opposing machines; but with their weaknesses. Simply put; if for an example; the Dutch plane type 'A' can out dive the Japanese plane type 'B' then we will dive to break off action rather than snap roll away.

The detailed technical designs which we had begun to review with some initial skepticism were now shown to be completely accurate. The overall situation was sobering. Our people had to accept upon its digestion that our current defensive strategy had to be heavily modified in the light of the hard evidence that we now had in our hands.

On August 17, 1939, some three weeks after the Squadrons' arrival in East Indies waters I convened a meeting to discuss the technical impact for the Fleet and what operational procedures must we introduce into our training to offset as much as possible our equipment deficiencies visa vis the new models of Japanese aircraft. I had just turned the floor over to my chief of staff Kapitien ter Zee Derik Van Klaffens, when a Sergeant Majoor, knocked on the glass of the conference room door, looking at me and waving a sheet of paper.

I motioned him in, took the dispatch from Naval Hoofdkwartier in Batavia, which stated that yesterday; the British and French fleets which had participated in *Operation Bulwark* had arrived today at Manila after their stops in Singapore, Indo China, and Honk Kong. Something however has occurred. The British and French fleets, having been anchored at Manila for less than four hours terminated their visit to that American Colony. Both fleets took aboard maximum fuel and departed for European waters at high speed! This was an ominous development, perhaps Hitler was menacing yet another nation.

The Kapitein, who had awaited my return rose to his feet and went to the front of the staff meeting room where he reached for a series of rolled charters attached to the wall above the large blackboard. Pulling these down, he unrolled large colored drawings of each new type of aircraft that had been contained in the Soviet Union's Technical Report as well as updates on the aircraft now to be found on the IJN flattops. Using a wooden pointer he discussed each type of aircraft, its technical merits and revealed its deficiencies and how our more antiquated aircraft could cope. A summary of his presentation follows;

<u>Kawasaki K-10</u>
Type: *Carrier based biplane naval fighter with light bombing.*
Deployment and Status: *Aboard small carriers only, phasing out.*
Technical Rating: *Technical parity.*
Armament: *light machine guns, light bombs.*
Capability: *Effective against all our naval plane types.*
Countermeasure: *Freely engage with all type of Dutch navy fighter except Sea Fox.*

Mitsubishi A5M

Type: *Carrier based monoplane naval fighter with light bombing.*
Deployment and Status: *IJN; currently aboard large carriers only.*
Technical Rating: *Slightly Superior Design, and in superior numbers.*
Armament: *light machine guns, light bombs.*
Capability: *Effective against all our naval plane types.*
Countermeasure: *Freely engage with: Sea Fury MK II fighter, Snap roll down, turn inside to break off action. The Grumman F2F, and F3F fighters may engage at long range with .50 cal. mg. Dive to break off action. Monoplane fighters; use high speed strafing passes, do not engage closely. Dive or outrun to break off action. Sea Fox fighter does not engage.*

"The Mitsubishi A5M Monoplane fighter had been the new carrier plane for the last two years. We had previously thought these machines to be somewhat similar to the American pursuit fighter the Boeing P-26 *Peashooter,* but now we discovered that they were 60 km per hour faster than our old Sea Fox and more robust. But the A5M was neither more maneuverable nor more heavily armed, than our biplane fighters. Our Hawker Sea Furies were soon to be upgraded with British supplied supercharged carburetor and wheel spat kits to convert them into Mk II type fighters. The resulting 15% performance enhancement would enable them to hold their own with the monoplane. But they were too few. The Navy would have no real answer for this type of carrier fighter, until we receive our Grumman F2F and F3F fighters from the U.S. Navy. The army would just have to support us against these machines with their more powerful fighters the Fokker D. XX1 (which we so kindly recently transported for them on our decks) and their big strategic fighter the Fokker G1."

Mitsubishi A6M (Zero)

Type: *Carrier based monoplane naval fighter with light bombing.*
Deployment and Status: *IJN; currently aboard large carriers only, phasing in.*
Technical Rating: *Very Superior Design, only small numbers available.*
Armament: *light machine guns, and Cannon.*
Capability: *Effective against all our naval plane types.*
Countermeasure: *Best to engage with: mixed force of high speed monoplane fighters with highly maneuverable biplane fighters, thereby containing this enemy within a 'performance envelope' so created when machines of wide capability cooperate as a common unit; resulting in an overall superior ability. All monoplane fighters, if alone; avoid dogfight if possible. Snap roll down, and turn inside to break off action. Sea Fury Mk II or Grumman F2F- F3F, may attempt to lure this machine into a duel at lower speed, with hope of success. Sea Fox Fighters: not to engage.*

"The new Japanese naval fighter just coming into service from the firm Mitsubishi, it is designated the A6M. It is reputed to be head and shoulders above what their navy currently has. The technical report on the A6M emphasizes; high speed, long range, heavily armament and maneuverability with a high rate of climb. However they still seem to be in very small numbers at this time. The weaknesses of the A6M was that it may easily catch on fire, the pilot has no armor and they break up rather quickly when damaged. The current tactic our fighters will employ against this type will be to avoid if possible. Our high speed monoplane fighters were all outclassed by the A6M in performance. The only significant advantage which we held over that aircraft oddly enough lay in the superior maneuverability of our older biplane types, designed for the 380 to 450 kph speed range. If an inexperienced A6M pilot is encountered, he may be lured into a dogfight by pretending damage or erratic flying. If the bait is taken, he will have to slow to these speeds where his machine is vulnerable. Our fighter pilot should stick close to the A6M and by outmaneuvering he may have a chance at success."

"To support this statement we have a recent report from the Chinese Nationalist Air Force involving fighter combat against the A6M. One of their aces has made a confirmed claim of having shot down six of these new monoplane fighters in one action while flying that most famous of bi-plane fighters of the Spanish Civil War repute; the legendary Italian Fiat CR 32! That fighter is a slightly slower, but a much more powerfully armed and robust machine than our current Sea Fox fighters or even our Sea Fury's in the MK II version. Those six novice Mitsubishi pilots forgot that their new machines were not designed to outmaneuver a biplane fighter like the Fiat CR 32, at those lesser speeds at which biplane fighters are designed to dogfight. Consequently all six A6Ms were destroyed in rapid succession!"

Aichi D1A

Type: *Carrier based monoplane light dive bomber.*
Deployment and Status: *IJN; currently aboard small carriers only, phasing in.*
Technical Rating: *Technically equal to our machines. Available in large numbers.*
Armament: *light machine guns, 360 kilograms of bombs.*
Capability: *Effective against all our naval vessels.*
Countermeasure: *All fighters freely engage: but with caution as these planes are very maneuverable and rated as second class fighters. Accelerate to break off action.*

Mitsubishi Type D2

Type: *Carrier based biplane heavy torpedo bomber.*
Deployment and Status: *IJN; currently aboard small carriers only, phasing out.*
Technical Rating: *Technically equal to our machines. Available in large numbers.*
Armament: *light machine gun, large naval torpedo.*
Capability: *Effective against all our naval vessels.*
Countermeasure: *All fighters freely engage.*

"This torpedo bomber is a large bi-plane; essentially a slightly modified version of the Blackburn Shark Mk III. It was designed for the Japanese Imperial Navy courtesy of the Blackburn Aircraft Corporation of Great Britain. The plane is big and robust with a powerful torpedo. Like the Swordfish it is very slow. We are very familiar with this type of plane and its use, our AA defenses and Sea Fox fighters can deal with them."

Aichi D3A

Type: *Carrier based monoplane heavy dive bomber, second line fighter.*
Deployment and Status: *IJN; currently aboard large fleet carriers only.*

Technical Rating: *Technically superior to our machines, with the possible exception of our new Polish Sea Eagles. They are however much faster. Without bombs they are faster than all our naval fighters even the Sea Fury when up-graded to MK II, and the Grumman F3F. Grumman is supplying us with an airframe reinforcement kit and a modified carburetor supercharger that will raise the speed of an F2F fighter by 10 -12 %.*

Armament: *light machine guns, 250 kilograms of bombs.*

Capability: Effective against all our naval vessels.

Countermeasure: *All our fighter types may freely engage but with caution as these planes are second line fighters. These planes are not as maneuverable as our fighters so use close engagement tactics. Due to these faster machines we plan to add at least one wing of Brewster F2A fighters to each battle cruiser carrier, as soon as they become available.*

Nakajima B5N

Type: *Carrier based monoplane torpedo bomber.*

Deployment and Status: *IJN; currently aboard large carriers only, phasing in.*

Technical Rating: *Technically superior to all our machines, with the possible exception of our brand new Polish Sea Eagles. They are however somewhat faster. Without bombs they are faster than a Sea Fox fighter but may be intercepted by the Sea Fury when up graded to MK II, the Grumman F2F-1 when upgraded and the F3F -2.*

Armament: *light machine guns, naval torpedo.*

Capability: *Effective against all our naval vessels.*

Countermeasure: *All fighters freely engage.*

Mitsubishi G3M

Type: *Twin engine, monoplane bomber.*

Deployment and Status: *JAAF; land based, available in large numbers.*

Technical Rating: *Technically superior to our machines.*

Armament: *multiple light machine guns, rearward facing 20 mm cannon, 800 Kilograms of bombs.*

Capability: *Extreme long range and fairly fast.*

Countermeasure: *Sea Fury MK II or Grumman F3F-2 may intercept. Attack only below, or diving down at the front. But do not dive in an attack on the rear. All monoplane fighters to freely engage.*

"This new type of torpedo bomber will impose a new defensive strategy on our larger ships. Much faster long range navy fighters must be found."

Mitsubishi G4M1

Type: *Twin engine, monoplane medium bomber.*

Deployment and Status: JAAF; *land based, prototype only.*

Technical Rating: *Technically quite superior to all our similar machines.*

Armament: *multiple light machine guns, rearward facing 20 mm cannon and 900 Kilograms of torpedo or bombs.*

Capability: *Extreme long range and very fast.*

Countermeasure: *At this time there is no single naval fighter capable of stopping this plane. Only when the bomber is carrying its full load of torpedo or bombs is there a chance for a Sea Fury MK II or F3F-2 intercept.*

"For the present; the capability of this new type of torpedo bomber, requires a rethinking of our warship's defenses. For the near future; much faster long range navy fighters must be purchased."

This concluded the presentation which contained our basic intelligence on the methods that our sea borne naval attack aircraft had to master to counter the new Japanese designs. This portion of the meeting was over and I thanked Kapitein Van Klaffens.

The meeting then addressed the concerns regarding the enhanced threat on the ships themselves posed by these new types of Japanese planes. I had asked for the Executive officer, my Fleet Air Operations Senior Officer, my Senior gunnery officer and my Chief engineer from the *Cornelis de Witt*, to form a technical team with their opposite number aboard the *Johan de Witt*.

The various technical teams, now armed as they were with this latest information of the Japanese aircraft, I now tasked to investigate new tactics, and recommend countermeasures that we must develop to:

1. Prevent enemy bombers and torpedo planes from launching their weapons against the warships, especially our strategic units; the battle-carriers.
2. Develop proposals and methods which all ships of the fleet, in particular the battle-carriers may augment their defenses against the Ariel torpedoes and bombs.
3. Develop a method to destroy a torpedo once it is in the water.
4. Develop a method for the battle-carriers to reduce the effects of hits, by torpedoes and bombs.

I wanted to convene another meeting within one week to discuss the situation, and evaluate the progress. These tasks were to be a top priority so all of their current duties would be handled by their subordinates. Privately; I was now a very worried sailor. My evaluation of the hitherto unexpected air power that could be arrayed against my fleet by the JNAF and JAAF; led me to conclude that my big ships would take multiple hits from bombs and torpedoes, during a maximum assault by the enemy. How long could we survive an all-out air attack? Would we be able to carry out our extensive mission directives?

a) Oppose invasion of the Dutch East Indies.
b) Destroy the warships, aircraft and shipping of any aggressor nation, wherever encountered.
c) Maintain the sea lanes of the East Asiatic Theater to Europe, and Australia.
d) Cooperate with those forces of those nations pledged at *Operation Bulwark* to achieve the above.
e) Provide aid wherever possible and practicable to our civilian population and to those of the allied nations.

In anticipation of the results of this investigation I meditated every evening on the new difficulties my big ships would face and what solutions would I be able to devise. I knew that the torpedo hits were the most deadly form of attack. In their present configuration; five such hits would result in the outright sinking of the big ship's within half an hour of their being struck!

So the primary problem was how; to prevent a well-aimed torpedo, one that cannot be avoided by maneuver from reaching my battle-carriers? If one does detonate against the hull; then how to further minimize the inevitable ingress of flood water on a massive scale? The reader must understand that any floating structure made by man may be sunk, regardless of the measures taken.

The battlecruiser-carriers already had incorporated within their hulls four formidable anti-torpedo systems. The *Torpedo blisters* outboard, internally; the *Pugliese Crushing Cylinders*, with both systems covering 80% of the load water line to port and starboard. Then the entire unarmored bottom of the ships were protected for 80% of their length with the *Feranti Triple Bottom*. Lastly the ships were sub-divided into over 480 watertight compartments!

The sturdy steel plate blister, forced a torpedo's warhead to detonate on impact some 1.70 meters away from the hull, while the air space between it and the original hull plate, denied the torpedo the *hydraulic effect* of the sea to aid in crushing the steel shell of the hull behind it. That part of the outer blister; once blown away however; left the hull in that area intact, but unprotected.

The crushing cylinder system were designed to channel the expanding energy from an exploding warhead away from vital ship structure by diverting the energies inwards, and away from the ship's hull to crush the metal cylinders. The cylinders once crushed, were expended and no longer useful as a defense.

The triple bottom was designed to act in a similar way as the torpedo blister. But it was designed defeat attack from below the hull such as sub-surface tethered mines, and plunging shells as well as deep running torpedoes. Similar to the hull side blisters; that portion of the bottom defensive plating that was destroyed would no longer contribute to the defense of the hull.

My big capital ships, with four separate torpedo defeating systems at a time when most other naval vessels of the same size in those days used only three systems, made the Battle-carriers, in theory very tough, well protected ships.

The technical teams of both battlecruiser-carriers had assembled in the spacious meeting room in the basement bomb shelter of my headquarters building at 09:00hrs, August 27, 1939. Seated to my left was my deputy commander of the squadron; my cruiser division commander, all my four cruiser commanders were present as well as my destroyer flotilla commander; the eight destroyer commanders and the technical team from both of the battle-carriers. All together with the supporting shorthand clerk specialists to record the meeting of some thirty officers and men who were in attendance.

I opened the second part of the conference by restating the obvious, my belief that war would soon come to our Colony. The RNLN was faced with Japan, an opponent who's naval and air forces were more numerous than the earlier evaluations had predicted and according to the most recently obtained evidence from the Soviet Union, whose forces possessed attack aircraft of superior technical capability than our own!

I had to conclude that at the present level of training, and with what equipment we now had and would soon obtain from America; our battle-carriers would, in the course of a single heavy action, take multiple hits from bombs and torpedoes. These statistics were somewhat above what we had projected in our operational philosophy of the nature of a modern air/naval action. In plain talk, without heavy support from our airfields, at the present levels of preparation; our battle-carrier squadron, including escorts would not long survive an attack from a full strength Japanese Air Army or the Fleet Air Arm of the IJN.

I had ordered the specific technical teams to study all aspects of these problems and propose simple achievable solutions, however odd these may seem, any idea was to be considered. These solutions would now be presented today in open forum for debate and criticism and then adopted, modified or totally discarded.

The first problem to be dealt with; that of combating enemy aircraft was undertaken by the team of my Chief of Fleet Air Operations; Hoof Officier Vlieger (Commander Flier): Konrad Van Braekel.

His team came up with two additional defensive strategies in which our aircraft could be employed. He stated that our current air defensive measures were sufficient, barring errors to protect the core ships from air attack. But there would come a time when the defense may be overwhelmed by sheer numbers.

In this scenario the fleet commander would transmit to all aircraft a code word *FIGHTERCLOUD*. The term was both a code word and a fleet battle condition. Three things would then happen;

1.) All the battle carriers screening vessels would launch their reconnaissance aircraft. These machines would form a ring around the Fleet for the purpose of delivering enfilade fire into approaching enemy torpedo bombers, which had to fly parallel to the ocean surface and in a straight line to deliver their warhead. The reconnaissance floatplanes were also charged with providing accurate reports of enemy torpedoes in the water. But both of these methods only applied under extremely intense enemy air attack.

2) The second directive under *FIGHTERCLOUD* would be that all planes aloft would concentrate over the Fleet, regardless of their earlier mission and all remaining aircraft aboard would be launched to bolster those machines already in the air. To attack the battle-carriers enemy aircraft would have to launch an attack through a defensive screen of 100 plus machines. In doing so the enemy would enter a *Performance Envelope* having hundreds of machine guns, firing from all directions, from aircraft whose combined features presented superior performance to their own. Whereas our biplane fighters; by themselves were somewhat deficient in speed, this was rectified by the *envelope*. The simple theory behind it was that the aircraft designed for high speed combat, fights best at high speed, but not at a low one. If a high speed enemy fighter enters our *Performance Envelope*, it must maintain a high speed at all times, which is seldom impossible. When it climbs or turns sharply the speed falls, and it then may be dispatched by our biplane fighters, which have superior performance at those slower speeds.

3) The third directive would require that all land based naval fighter squadrons, so designated as *support for the fleet*, would be immediately launched to concentrate over the ships, to enhance the aerial *Fightercloud.*

In order to ensure that the latter happened; when the Battle-carriers steamed to within one hundred and fifty mile of a naval airfield, all its resources automatically came under the direct command of the Fleet Commander. Any naval base so activated could only be stood down by the Fleet Commander, or when the fleet moved beyond the one hundred and fifty mile zone, the maximum effective range of the fighters that we had available to us in 1939.

These tactics were then put to open discussion and debated for an hour. After which time I halted further debate and declared these adopted. I then directed the Air Chief Commander Van Braekel to prepare the required documents to introduce the updated information to the fleet and set up training programs.

The second problem to be dealt with how the ships may maneuver to avoid bombs and torpedoes. The technical team had to admit failure, as there was no new tactical maneuver that could be conceived beyond the methods already in place, with one exception. A fleet or vessel facing the prospect of heavy torpedo attack, and in the absence of sufficient air cover may seek to steam into shallow waters, areas over subsea banks, and reefs. In some of our patrol areas, there were many expanses where the water depth was only 16 meters. The team maintained that if the enemy planes could be forced to drop their torpedoes from above 100 meters elevation there was a good chance to believe that they would drill into the shallows and detonate without hitting the ship. I kept that one in my pocket!

The third problem facing us was how to destroy a torpedo once it was in the water? The airmen and the gunners came up with two separate reasonable solutions that were in some ways complimentary. Both had been investigated with success and were thoroughly discussed. I was satisfied that we had something here that was an achievable solution, so I ordered their development.

The pilot's solution to the third problem naturally involved the utilization of any aircraft that could be pressed into service that were not to be used for first line duty. Aboard the battle-carriers in 1939 this meant the *Sea Hart* light bombers and the *Sea Fox* fighters. The concept was built upon the knowledge that an armed torpedo will detonate when encountering a significant water pressure change, even the disturbance produced by a ship's wake.

The tactic was simple; two sections of planes, six machines total would be armed with clusters of 20 kilogram high explosive bombs, two on the fighters and ten on the bombers. These would circle over the battle-carriers at some 100 meters elevation and a 1000 meters out. Upon spotting a torpedo, its range and course would be reported to the battle-carrier, and then the plane would attack it. By dropping a single bomb in front of the torpedo the shock from its detonation would set off the warhead. In the event that the torpedo did not detonate the aircraft could direct the fire of the new Anti-Torpedo mortar batteries against it.

The gunners solution to the torpedo problem involved the acquisition of 80 mm mortars from the army, and mounting them on turntables in their own gun tubs. These were positioned underneath the AA gun tubs at the level of the upper hanger deck equally spaced along both sides between the forward bulkhead of the aircraft hangar to forward of the stack outlet. These new *Anti-torpedo batteries* would be directed against any approaching torpedoes, and by continually dropping mortar rounds in close approximation to the submerged weapon, their detonations should create shock waves that would set off its warhead.

Under a testing program; both of these innovations functioned remarkably well! The most difficult problem proved to be the directing the fire of the mortars against the torpedoes. We solved this by equipping the fire-control officers of the mortars with radio headsets equipped to pick up only two frequencies. One from the spotter planes and one from the ship's command center.

The last problem of restricting the flooding of the hull due to torpedo hits, I had reserved for myself. My solution had its faults I admit. I was haunted by keeping the battle-carrier flight decks intact and level, the ships afloat and able to fight. I tasked myself to come up with a solution to enhance this capability. I had concentrated on damage control of flood water. Dwelling on this became my bedtime mental exercise for the next week. The solution for the control of flood water, after eliminating all other concepts was so simple as to be almost embarrassing. Yet, when compared to the other solutions presented by my officers, on the following week, for the problems that I had assigned them, it seemed just as desperate, for indeed that was what our strategic situation was evolving into!

Of all the technical solutions to our equipment's shortcomings, my solution was primitive; inserting balsa wood logs into the void spaces of the blisters through their inspection manholes, then packing the space as tightly as possible with smaller blocks. To the naval architect, this would be called a reduction of the *broken stow* rating for each compartment, thereby reducing those open volumes for the sea to flood. Although, primitive, problematic and unimpressive technically, the logs; bravely designated for security reasons as: *subsurface ballistic cellulose*, worked.

My Chief Engineer; Jap Anten was very annoyed with this development; as it severely impacted the cross-ship counter flooding system which duty required him to keep the deck flight deck level for the continuation of air operations. This was a legitimate concern. However, the RNLN would never, given the scope of our duties, be operating like the Royal Navy of Great Britain or the U.S. Navy, far out at sea, thousands of miles from land. If the battle carrier took on a very heavy list then the aircraft which were aloft could return to the nearest airfields, from which they would carry on with operations.

If my Chief Engineer's commander had been a Marine Engineer as opposed to a Naval Architect he may have had his way. But I was more concerned with keeping the hull afloat than keeping its *tankage* in action. I put a very high priority on reducing those void spaces within the blisters. This was not a new concept; as the French navy during the late 19th century used to fill all the empty watertight compartments of the hull with *marine cellulose* (wood). Such material became completely degraded within four years due to the dry-rot associated in airless confined spaces; however on the short term, the oak wood packing, it was discovered; did offer some protection to the steel backing structure to some extent from splinter damage from shelling. The balsa of course could not do this, but it was an excellent material to arrest flooding, and due to its lightness, would not severely impact our draft.

2222222

After some discussion by the assembled officers on the *merits* of my solution, I ended the debate. There would be no counter flooding of the torpedo blisters until such time as the wood packing was removed. I ordered an end to further debate, and my solution be implemented.

I am sure that the Japanese spies were confused at the arrival of 5000 cubic meters of Chilean balsa logs to the naval base at Soerabaja in early November1939. The logs were treated with a copper based solution to inhibit rot and left to dry. The job of packing the blisters was made more difficult as all chunks had to fit through the 60 cm. x 30cm. access holes for each watertight compartment. Once this was completed we flood tested a section and found that the overall remaining floodable volume had been reduced from 96% to 8%! The blister was pumped out, force-air dried. All blisters were then sealed and filled with CO_2 gas to further slow the deterioration of the balsa.

The cruisers and destroyers acting as the Capital ships escorts were fully aware that they must provide AA defensive fire to the battle-carriers as a top priority even if it meant sacrificing their own safety. The Commander of each escort vessel knew that he was required to place his ship's hull within the path of a torpedo if it meant protecting the flagships.

So; armed with our odd hybrid battle-carriers, obsolete planes, new tactics and untried improvisations the Royal Netherlands Navy was fully prepared to answer the call to duty; and stand toe to toe to face down the mighty forces of the *Rengo Kantai* arrayed against us, come what may!

September 01, 1939, I had finally managed to complete the preparations that our fleet had made to adjust our capabilities in response to the information contained within the Top Secret *Soviet Pouch* from Manchuria. It had taken a month of heavy activity to get us on the right track. Naval Headquarters in Batavia was very pleased with the results of our combined efforts, and now granted me my delayed thirty day leave.

The next day I departed Soerabaja by air via Batavia, bound for my family and my home the plantation *New Eden* on Biliton Island in the west Java Sea. Through the window of the Mercedes staff car I could see that the big Dornier D24K flying boat, on which I was to travel; rested quietly on the clear green waters of East Channel, waiting for my arrival some 300 meters beyond the big newly constructed concrete wharf north of the naval basin, and clear of the muddy discharge of the River Mas. My car drove along the 400 long meter wharf where the eight destroyers of Flotilla 10 & 11 sat quietly under their sun awnings. The sedan slowed and came to a stop with a loud squeak. My luggage was quickly loaded aboard a 10 meter naval cutter. I hopped aboard, the lines were cast off and we chugged our way out to the flying boat. I judged it to be a day of fine weather. The Dornier should make Batavia in four hours. Then after refueling, it would arrive at *New Eden* five hours later in the early evening.

It was while airborne, heading for Batavia, when the radio operator walked back to the passenger compartment, saluted and handed me a message. "Admiraal, about eight hours ago the German and Slovak Armies crossed the Polish border. Wide spread fighting is reported. Emergency meetings have been called by the Allied Governments of England, Belgium, the Netherlands and France." Temporarily speechless, I merely nodded to him, while retrieving the message from his outstretched hand. I quickly read it, then stood and looked out the small window on the side of the fuselage. As it was high upon the side, I could not look down to the sea, but stared intently at the small rectangle of blue sky, as I composed my thoughts. "Good God," I muttered, "Is our world all going to shit once again?"

Britain and France had only in August 1939, not more than a few weeks ago guaranteed the security of the Polish border. They were central in the military alliance which was the basis of our security. The Netherlands held no illusions that Hitler would respect our borders if he struck westward. If those two nations went to war; the Netherlands would soon be drawn into the conflict.

Great Britain and France this time cannot sidestep Germany's direct challenge as she had done with Czechoslovakia last year. Britain's position as the planet's *preeminent moral compass, and its largest economic power* was at stake. Those of her colonies seeking self-rule, such as India would perceive such a lack of resolve as a chronic weakness, and would certainly move to oust British Rule. The same may be said of the French Empire. The rapid departure of the British and French fleets from South East Asia for home waters had now been explained.

One expected that there would be immediate losses to the merchant marines of France and Great Britain. But in shocking developments, casualties mounted rapidly for the Royal Navy's strategic weapons. Those very weapons that were the foundation of Britain's military power.

On September 17, 1939, the Aircraft Carrier *Courageous* was torpedoed in the Atlantic Ocean by a German submarine, followed soon after on October 14th by the Battleship *Royal Oak* which was sunk, also by a U-boat that had penetrated the defenses of the RN Home Fleet naval base of Scapa Flow. Both capital ships had gone down with a heavy loss of life, and represented 8% of the Royal Navy's available capital ship strength, gone in the first month of war!

Hitler was now moving with exceptional boldness. Our intelligence services had compiled a great deal of information on railway schedules, industrial manufacturing, the transfer of property and the movement of gold bullion to name just a few. All these indicators when taken together provided a clear road map for Europe's future, and it was black! The Netherlands, it appeared, was only months away from being swept up into a war against Nazi Germany.

In the Great War of 1914 to1918 the Netherlands had remained neutral. Our Intelligences Services believed that Hitler had a plan of *Continental Domination* and the Netherlands would be occupied. Government officials soon came to accept the unavoidable conclusion. As the freedom of our nation was without a doubt now in jeopardy, the shift of a number of government and financial resources to the East Indies now seemed to have been a wise move. Our great naval preparations and expenditures had been completely vindicated.

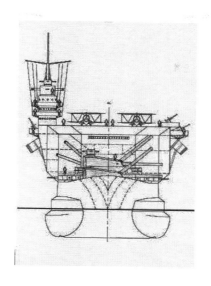

CHAPTER XIX

HITLER LAUNCHES A NEW WORLD WAR, NEW EDEN PLANTATION, HARASING THE GRAF SPEE, BATTLESHIP CARRIER SCHOONVELDT, THE NETHERLANDS IS OVERRUN, THE FALL OF FRANCE, JAPANESE TROOPS OCCUPY FRENCH INDO-CHINA, THE LAST ACTION OF THE OLD FRENCH IRONCLAD REDOUBTABLE.

The *Short S8 Calcutta* aircraft of the Empire Flying Boat Company had touched down gently in South Bay, of Biliton Island after an easy flight from Batavia. The forward movement of the graceful triple engine biplane ceased, and she wallowed gently in the light chop. A crew member opened a small bow hatch, extended his arm through as far as the elbow and clipped a light steel cable onto the mooring buoy, while the aircraft's engines were still coughing. The radio operator made his way aft down the narrow passageway and began to get my kit together, while the co-pilot, following him worked his way aft checking the cargo lashings. He moved a few parcels, then popped open the big door in the port side of flying boat's fuselage, and while looking at me with a wide grin he touched the peak of his cap and said cheerfully; "well then Admiraal, here we are home at last, eh?"

I stood up and leaned against the doorway's frame to take in the familiar sights and smells of my home. After the confinement and constant deep drone of the aircraft's engines, the gust of fresh air that entered the compartment was received with relish. The breeze brought with it the forgotten scents of the island, one being the faint musk of the thousands of *New Eden's* oil palms.

The company launch was seen to pull away from the plantation's wharfs heading directly towards us with a wide white mustache of foam growing at her bow. I waited patiently; experiencing a few moments when absolutely nothing is required of me, enjoying the very little things; that musical noise wavelets make when slapping sheet aluminum, and the gentle rocking of the flying boat as she rested on the quiet waters of the little bay.

The launch had drawn close enough so that I could make out a woman in a white blouse and wide brimmed straw sun hat waving vigorously. In another moment she recognized me standing inside the door and a familiar broad smile of white teeth appeared in a tanned face that I knew so well; my dear wife Karen. I tossed over my kit to outstretched hands, then stepped down into the boat. I caught Karen in an embrace and gave her hugs and kisses. Our launch made for shore while the flying boat began loading a few items before it departed for Singapore.

After greeting the family, *I then formed the center of a multi-legged chattering creature* that slowly and awkwardly stumbled and *crabbed* its way up the green lawns of the main house grounds. Here Karen had, in anticipation of my imminent arrival, set up a nice lunch of cold roast chicken, sliced fruit and lemonade, all to enjoyed under the shade of a nearby oil palm grove. At this special spot, the breezes tended to funnel down the long corridors of oil palms, to assist the shade in the creation of a cool and comfortable rest area.

Later, after we had eaten, and were all talked out about family matters, Karen dismissed the children. I then poured an iced coffee and lit up a *Russian Gold Tipped Imperial*. She then drew me by the hand to a pair of reclining lawn chairs further down the shaded lawn, whereupon I leaned back releasing a deep sigh of satisfaction still holding her hand. A quiet hour was spent discussing the children and the plantation business. Then I told her that we must now switch the conversation onto the serious international developments, and how they may impact our lives. Karen assembled the family once more, and I informed them of the grim news of the German invasion of Poland. There were serious ramifications for the Netherlands, if Britain and France declared war upon Germany. The Nazis would not respect the borders of the Netherlands if she struck westward. Japan the third member of the *Pact of Steel*, with Germany and Italy now became an immediate threat to our home.

We then drew up two plans, for the family to evacuate *New Eden* in case of a war with Japan. The first route considered was an escape to India via Short Sunderland flying boat. If that route was imperiled then the alternative was an escape route to Darwin Australia, by flying boat. All the details for these plans were worked out in the next few days. Finances were pre-positioned in several banks from India to Sydney. Lists of supplies were composed and duties were assigned. I handled all the aircraft reservations through my personal contacts in *Quantas Airlines, Empire Flying Boat* and *British Oriental Airways*. Once these duties were completed I felt that I could relax properly, having provided for my family's safety.

I was determined to make the best use of my leave and planned many family events among the familiar comforts of my home and plantation. I greatly enjoyed these too brief moments. Inevitably my duties followed me home as the international crisis deepened. My one month of leave passed too quickly, and I took a flying boat back to Soerabaja to resume my duties.

The battleship-carrier *Schoonveldt,* had completed her sea trials, and was commissioned into the RNLN. She was to be deployed to a Caribbean Colony of the Netherlands Antilles to guard the Royal Dutch Shell refineries at Curacao. Also in case of war the Admiralty wanted to keep her beyond the reach of the Germans. Here she would remain awaiting developments in Europe. However there was a high probability that she would be coming to the Dutch East Indies, and I was told to prepare to integrate her into our battle-carrier squadron. I therefore ordered the assembly of all data on her, to become acquainted with her capabilities.

I was familiar with this warship as she was quite famous. At the time of her completion in 1914 she created a sensation since her ordinance boasted the greatest number of heavy guns carried aboard any battleship then afloat; fourteen 12 inch (305 mm) 45 Caliber guns in seven twin turret mounts!

I recall, as a youth reading in the *Bombay Times* newspaper accounts of her in action. Eye witnesses at the Battle of Jutland spoke in awe of her shooting. Massive sheets of flame erupted along her full 213 meter length, when having crossed the 'T' of her enemy; she then loosed full seven turret broadsides straight into the van of the advancing armored monsters of the Kaiser's Imperial battle-fleet.

By 1925 however, the super-dreadnought concept was rapidly obsolescing and the flagship was marked for a major reconstruction of some type to keep pace with new ideas. The American Naval Design company; Gibbs & Cox Ltd. had a year earlier developed a radical post war concept for a new type of multi-role Capital ship for the Soviet Union; the Battleship-plane-carrier. It was a plan that involved the conversion of an existing ship, which is a far less expensive route than new construction.

The company hoped to market this design to those nations which were currently engaged in a drastic post Great War downsizing of the number of Battleships in their fleets and had instead, begun to build their first experimental aircraft carriers.

There were a number of countries that decided to take advantage of the Royal Navy's huge bargain basement sell-off in dreadnoughts to upgrade their own fleets. Several warships found their way into warmer waters and became commissioned into the navies of South America.

Brazil was one of these forward looking nations, with a modern navy. In 1920 she had acquired a surplus dreadnought the *Agincourt* from England in 1920. Five years later, her navy showed an interest in the Gibbs & Cox Ltd. Battleship plane carrier concept. The new ship type offered many economic and tactical advantages over her navy's rapidly obsolescing dreadnought. The Government of Brazil asked John Browns Shipyard of the U.K. to develop a proposal to convert the big dreadnought into a Battleship-plane-carrier.

There had already been a proposal by the Brazil's naval coast artillery command to unship some of *Rio de Janerio's* big guns and mount them in several of the coastal forts slated for upgrading. The main installations of these coastal forts protected the seaward approaches to the harbours of the cities of *Rio de Janerio* and *Sao Paulo*. These required a portion of the main armament of the battleship to replace their existing worn out Krupp guns. The decision was a good use of available resources; as the needs of the Coast Artillery could also be met by the flagship's conversion to a "battleship-plane-carrier."

The rebuilt vessel would still retain a heavy although much reduced Broadside battery. The powerful secondary artllery was to be modernized but would otherwise remain intact. A new forty plane air group for long range patrol was then added to her remaining arsenal. The peacetime economics of the warship's conversion, as highlighted below did seem to make a strong case.

The redesigned warship could now steam along the coast of Brazil and enforce her national interests over the shipping activities along a 25 mile wide strip of the sea using her guns as before. But now with the aid of her aircraft she could patrol 100 miles out to sea or over the jungle simultaneously thereby adding a 200 mile wide air corridor to her efforts. During a 24 hour cruise the rebuilt *Rio de Janerio* was capable of monitoring 140,000 square miles of Brazilian territory; an area representing an eight fold increase in what the ship had previously been able to manage! Her new propulsive machinery which had been changed from coal to oil-fired small tube boilers, generated three times the shaft horse power, while eliminating the need for 300 stokers! The elimination of the stokers made room for the addition of 450 air personnel, whose role was combat and support.

The conversion was approved by the *Marinha do Brazil*, and a contract signed in 1925 with John Browns Shipyard of Glasgow on the Clyde. She emerged from her metamorphosis in 1928 a very different looking ship than when she entered the shipyard. She was transformed into an all-round much more versatile ship, a new type of Capital ship; the Battleship-carrier, the first of her kind.

The rebuilt vessel was a slightly smaller version of the great warships that formed the heart of our squadron, yet she incorporated other variations within her design that complimented our battle-carrier division. Her striking profile displayed characteristic features that revealed the unmistakable British traits of her design. Overall she had her own unique harmonious balance, giving one the impression that she was still a Royal Navy warship.

The uniquely distinctive; massive fire-control tripod mast for example, a characteristic of British Capital ships, had become a symbol of swift justice backed by raw power. The feature some thirty years old, was well ingrained into nautical minds, and one visible on all the oceans and seas of the globe.

I was able to recall an historical reference to support this claim. The recollections of a German sailor who fought at the Battle of the Falkland Islands in December 1914. I recalled the melancholy broodings of leading seamen Hans Wirtz, of the German armored cruiser *SMS Gneiseneau*. Seaman Wirtz was one of the few survivors of the Imperial German Fleet's East Asiatic Squadron at the time of its ill-fated attack on the remote British Colony and coaling station of the Falkland Islands in December of 1914:

"The barren rolling hills of the Falkland Islands rose rapidly out of the sea as our squadron approached from the southeast at 20 knots. The lookouts in the fighting tops of our warships were soon able to identify individual features on the landscape, and even make out large flocks of sheep grazing on the hills. The men were enjoying the unfolding pastoral setting, when suddenly the alarm was given!"

"A large mass of indistinguishable tall structures stood above the hills that surrounded the inner harbour. What we had first thought to be new radio towers or masts of a merchant convoy, revealed their true nature due to a change in our angle of approach. These tall steel structures were in fact the heavy fire-control tripod masts of several British battle-cruisers!"

"Our armored cruisers executed a 180 degree turn at high speed and fled just as two 100 meter tall columns of white spray erupted out of the ocean some distance astern, with a thunderous detonation. The arrival of these heavy shells indicated that we had been observed by the alert British outposts."

"Our hearts sank, for we knew our certain death was at hand! A full long day of sunlight remained for action against ships that we could neither outpace nor outgun. Over the distant hills

could already be seen many tall black columns of funnel smoke climbing into the clear morning sky as the mighty steel monsters laying within the harbour forced their furnaces and raised boiler pressure to give us chase!"

The *Schoonveldt* had retained her tripod to support the heavy artillery fire control equipment, while allowing for the enlargement of its spotting top platform to provide an air operations control center for her aircraft. Nevertheless, the psychological impact of this highly visible and unique symbol of *Pax Britannica*: and Great Britain's ability to project its authority was not lost the naval designers of John Browns Shipyard.

During the vessel's massive conversion in 1925, the four centrally located heavy gun turrets; C,D,E & F of the original ship, had been removed to provide sufficient spaces to accommodate the newer, more powerful and yet lighter steam plant machinery. The magazines of C & G turrets were then refitted to take a variety of bombs and torpedoes. Over the main deck amidships had been constructed an accommodation space forward and machine shops aft. Then 2.6 meters above this, a 3000 square meter armoured Hangar deck of 40 mm plate. Some 8.5 meters above the Hanger deck a 200 mm teak flight deck had been laid on steel beams and girders. Two aircraft elevators were provided for; one forward and one aft sited on the centerline of the ship, these brought her aircraft up to the flight deck. One level below the hangar was 01 deck, efficiently laid out with large and well equipped machine shops to service the *air-group* as well as crews quarters. The airmen and aircraft handlers, and anti-aircraft gunners were housed in quarters immediately below the flight deck.

The *Cornelis de Witte* class vessels; were of a similar type as the *Schoonveldt*, being some 10% larger, but they lacked her powerful 152mm secondary battery. By the 1930's the 105mm guns of the *Cornelis Class* were too weak to break up destroyer attacks. Consequently those battle-carriers had to rely on their escorting vessels. The use of air groups to engage even medium range targets, was not an economical use for such expensive machines to maintain. The very heavy main battery guns mounted on these capital ships could be employed in a medium range engagement as long as the target represented a serious enough threat to justify the costs of barrel wear. The use of such large artillery usually required the ship return to base after firing 120 rounds. The main gun barrels would be removed from the turrets for re-lining, and replaced with new. For these reasons the *big guns* were best used for what they were intended, engaging heavily armored high value targets such as major warships and shore installation bombardment.

The economic impact of the lingering Great World Depression now provided an opportunity to substantially enhance our navy's strength. Brazil, South America's slumbering giant found herself with a new Government in 1938. One of its first acts was to bring in a budget that further constrained Federal spending. This directly threatened the completion of the Battleship-carrier *Rio de Janerio*, currently undergoing a midlife refit in the *Royal Scheldt Scheepswerf* in Rotterdam, as progress payments to the yard were halted.

In anticipation of such an occurrence the president of Royal Schelde; Rudolf Vandenbossche had accordingly directed his planning department to explore possible clients that would have an interest in such a warship. The obvious customer that he had in mind of course was the Royal Netherlands Navy. Consequently an unsolicited proposal was prepared and presented in late November 1938 by Royal Schelde to Fleet Admiraal

Van Der Velde of the Koninklijke Marine Ontwerp (KMOB); or Royal Naval Design Office in Den Helder, Noord-Holland.

The Naval Department; Section of Acquisitions had immediately taken an interest in the *Rio de Janerio*. The warship was a good fit to meet the needs of the navy's emergency expansion program, and its funding had allowed for the acquisition of a third capital ship. In order to ensure a first claim on the *Rio de Janerio*, the Dutch Government had made a commitment to Royal Scheldt's owners guaranteeing bridging payments to the shipyard to ensure continuation of the work, thereby removing any concerns the owners would have had in the event of a default on the contract.

President Riascos, wanted Brazil to send a clear message; of noninvolvement, in the widening European conflict as the Government of Argentina had done, and announced his nation's neutrality, and a reduction of all branches of its military. Accordingly, the shipyard was told to cease work on the vessel.

The director of Dutch shipyard, immediately contacted Admiraal Van der Velde at (KMOB). They put their heads together, hatched a plan and presented it to the Crown Treasury and the Friesland Java Bank. A proposal was made to purchase the ship and all its related equipment. The offer, a generous one, was well received by President Riascos and he quickly accepted.

The balance of two million crowns owed to *Royal Scheldt Scheepswerf* and some five million crowns to the Dutch bank was settled on to purchase the following: one newly refurbished battleship-plane carrier in first class condition, including all its air groups, their replacement aircraft squadrons, and all the warehoused spare parts for both the ship and her aircraft now stored in Brazil.

The RNLN could not believe their good luck at the timeliness of this opportunity. An additional battleship carrier would give it a very powerful vessel around which could be assembled a third battle-carrier task force. In addition, when operating with the *Cornelis de Witt* and the *Johan de Witt*, the *Schoonveldt's* third flight deck offered much greater flexibility of operations to the entire division as well as redundancy.

The *Marinha do Brazil* had like the KMN; relied on England for a continuing supply of naval aircraft for its flagship, and like us they had foreseen a supply problem due to the rise of the Nazi party in Germany. Consequently, they had sought a stopgap source of replacement aircraft to make up the shortages for the Sea Fury MK II fighter. As *Latinos*, the Brazilians naturally gravitated toward the Italians who had available for sale several biplane squadrons. The new Fiat CR 42 bi-plane Naval Fighter was of a traditional pattern but only a few years old. The Italian machine with its slow landing speed, and robust undercarriage made the CR 42 quite capable of handling the impact of a deck landing at sea. These squadrons rotated out with those flying the Sea Fury to give each type sea time.

The *Rio de Janerio* had aboard at the time of her purchase by the KMN; the original air group composed of; fourteen Hawker Sea Fury Mk II biplane fighters, with twenty six Hawker Sea Hart bi-plane light bombers. These were all stowed within the hangar. Upon the flight deck and housed under canvass was a supplemental group of monoplanes designated by the Brazilian Navy as; 'Os Interceptadores' (the interceptors) basically a rapid response unit.

The latter unit was a flight of eight modern stressed skin monoplane fighters of Italian origin. These were the *Macchi MC-200 Saetta*, and were considered to be very good machines for that period. Although somewhat under powered by American standards, these machines it was later discovered could out climb the first five production variants of the Mitsubishi A6M fighter; the infamous Zero!

The *Saetta's* twin 12.7 mm and twin 7.7mm armament was deemed quite powerful for the day, and her range of 570 kilometers which would be very limiting in the vast expanses of the Pacific was adequate for our East Indies theater, what with its many island air bases. The *Saetta* was designed to carry 165 liter drop tanks under each wing as an alternative to 160 kilogram bombs, which extended their range by one full hour when handled skillfully on patrol duty.

The *Saetta* was designed to be launched into action from the carrier and being a *hot machine* it could not return to the mother-ship as it required a much longer deck, and the aircraft's landing gear was not robust enough for this service. But the concept was an interesting one, and similar to what I had visualized earlier with our Army fighters during the Battle Squadron's transit of the Indian Ocean.

Given the speed of our naval fighters the Italian machine was still useful as a high speed interceptor, as it could be carried into theater aboard ship, then launched into battle, perform its mission and land at one of the many coastal airfields. The *Saetta's* helped our Buffalo and Grumman F3F machines with establishing the *performance envelope* when the alert condition *Fightercloud* was initiated.

The arrangement seemed to work well for the Brazilians and I could see it being adapted to our island bases. The battleship-plane-carrier enjoyed the benefit of a modern fighter group aboard, albeit for only one operation, but without the complications of servicing and repairing; the aircraft spares being reduced to a minimum aboard ship, as the fighter would be *turned around* on an airfield. I viewed it as most useful weapon to blunt aerial attack.

The *Rio de Janerio* also had ashore a 23 plane replacement squadron for each of the three types of aircraft aboard with the exception of the Italian Machines where 32 replacement aircraft were ashore.

All the British machines aboard, were reliable well proven bi-planes and of an attractive design being very sleek and shapely and with a performance that matched their looks. Our air-frame and engine mechanics were familiar with the aircraft of British origin and with the technical difficulties that plagued their earlier entry into our naval air service.

The Italian machines would be unfamiliar ones to our air pilots and technicians but an arrangement was made for the temporary loan of a group of Brazilian naval technicians and pilots to train our men. I did not therefore anticipate any technical problems associated with this new vessel's equipment during periods of intense activity.

The *Rio de Janerio's* air groups were very well maintained indeed and had already been modified for a tropical service, one just as demanding as those presented by the climate of the Dutch East Indies, so little adaption was required.

In any event the problems that were associated with the multiple types of aircraft in our naval service and their general obsolescence were ones with which the KMN was familiar. One advantage that the additional naval air-groups gave us was that they were all proven reliable machines. And so we learned to make do with what we had.

The *Rio de Janerio* with her fifty three planes aboard and sixty nine machines as reserve replacements ashore was very welcome indeed. The Fiats were of particular value as they added 124 heavy and long ranged 12.7 mm machine guns to our fleet's air defense. At the time I assumed that all the Italian machines would be land based and the *Schoonveldt's* air compliment would be matched to ours.

After-all we knew that the mighty *Rengo Kanti* (Imperial Japanese Navy) had at least 3,500 naval aircraft on strength with over 650 of these on aircraft carriers! The IJN then held better than three to one odds against the KMN, and it was further reinforced with a generous supply of replacements. The aircraft of the IJN were 90% modern with an upward trend, whereas ours naval aircraft were only 40% modern with a downward trend of improvement. These represented insurmountable odds, if encountered en-mass.

The battleship-carrier's acquisition was exciting news for the RNLN not the least of which were our new crop of young navy pilot aspirants; especially those of our East Indies natives. These men had been placed on the rotation list for aircraft and a berth on a battle-carrier, and they were the last service in the fleet that remained to be fully integrated. A circumstance arising I am compelled to reveal as much from shortages of equipment as any lingering prejudices against the native members within our service. By adding a third unit to our battle-carrier division their chances of getting the much prized posting was that much closer.

Although racial prejudice was not common, this attitude still did persist. Our native pilots, many believed were still an unproven asset. Great anxiety was felt over training and placing into their hands the preciously few strategic weapons that we had available. A number of the white officers held the opinion that the native character still contained a hefty slice of the *unmanageable primitive* that would fail under the strain of air combat operations. The *native pilot* they felt would discard discipline and training under pressure, revert to instincts and then be destroyed by the enemy.

Subsequent events would disprove any concerns some may have had as to their abilities. Their loyalty became suspect during the revolution of 1945, but it can be said that throughout the war against the Japanese they fought with grim determination, but with perhaps a different future in mind than what the Dutch had.

The Sumatran and Javanese pilots of *Fighting 5* were truly demons in the air and their record only proved once again a fact and a truth that had been revealed time and again in Spain, in Poland and Greece. Simply put; that any well trained group of men, emboldened with sufficient motivation, may in combat, inflict heavy casualties against any foe, no matter how powerful, ruthless or well-equipped they may be. And they will consistently be able do this while fighting with equipment that was not of the latest design, but merely adequate.

The acquisition of the battleship-carrier *Schoonveldt* would greatly enhance the power and flexibility of our fleet once she arrived in the Dutch East Indies. When operating with the *Cornelis de Witt* and the *Johan de Witt*, the *Schoonveldt's* third flight deck offered much greater flexibility of operations to the entire division as well as redundancy. However this required an expansion of our fleet air operations to take advantage of having this third flight deck at sea.

This new addition to our fleet presented us with a host of technical difficulties that had to be dealt with from spare parts for all the ships equipment, modern Italian aircraft types that came with her, munitions for all the varied armament and training for the thousands of personnel to man her.

Naval headquarters in Batavia set up a training facility for the men, prepared an ammunition depot and supply section for the ships stores. I was given the task of investigating the tactical implications of the new ship and set up a series of training cruises.

Consequently, the months rushed past as we all immersed ourselves in the new work. We received regular briefings on the so called: *Phoney War* in Europe. Britain and France had declared war on Germany as a result of the invasion of Poland. The French army made a limited halfhearted move up to the Siegfried Line then sat on its ass. Nazi U boats sank the Battleship Royal Oak at her berth in Scapa Flow. But beyond the submarine campaign against British commercial shipping, Britain and France were practically non-combatants.

Poland's allies had done little other than look on with *mild interest* from ring side seats at her massacre. Unfortunately for France and Britain, their military high command did not learn anything from that campaign. Their Generals saw no value in the hard won bloody education that the Polish Army received at the hands of the wheremacht during its six week campaign against the mixed combat arms of massed armor working in close cooperation with aircraft. The Allied Generals had nine months to prepare, and these lessons if absorbed would have saved them from the catastrophe that befell them the following summer.

The war in Europe was watched very closely by the inhabitants of the Dutch East Indies, and major developments were constantly discussed at every opportunity. Of particular interest to the KMN of course was the conduct of the naval war. The Atlantic and the North Sea, the Indian Ocean were up to this point the primary battlefields, with commerce raiding in the West Pacific. Ships of the RN, the RCN, RAN, RNZN, and the other minor allied navies, the Norwegians and Poles battled the Kriegsmarine.

The German Navy began the war at sea against Allied merchant shipping utilizing U-boats and large armed merchant cruisers, along with their powerful new Capital Ships. In the late summer of 1939 the German Pocket battleship, the *Admiral Graf Spee* was dispatched to the South Atlantic to await the outbreak of war. She represented a threat to the heavy British maritime trade between South America and England, the targets of highest value being the refrigeration vessels that carried frozen Argentinian beef. The Pocket battleship was a warning to England should she declare war on Germany, following its invasion of Poland. In this she failed.

Soon after war broke out the *Graf Spee* began to hunt the South Atlantic with good success. In November, the Pocket Battleship moved into the Indian Ocean, seeking prey. On several occasions Dutch vessels had been stopped and searched. Once the Germans determined that the vessels were truly Dutch, they were released to go on their way. But not before their radio sets were destroyed!

In response to the earlier heavy handed searches of Dutch vessels and this bold move by the German warship, the KMN Command in Batavia, planned an operation to teach the raider to respect Dutch neutrality and the long reach of the strengthened RNLN. RN Command in Ceylon, were informed and pledged enthusiastically to support planned the effort. (Of course it was all unofficial as the Netherlands was still at peace in the fall of 1939.)

The *Cornelis de Witt*, under my command; sortied from Soerabaja on December 3, 1939, and entered the Indian Ocean via the Sunda Strait. The press and radio services were informed of this mission. We wanted to advertise our presence in the Indian Ocean in a big way to demonstrate the deterrent of our big warships, and make the Germans reconsider their habit of not respecting the tricolor of the Netherlands. We used no screening vessels, as the distances were great and there would be no time for refueling destroyers at sea. The *Cornelis de Witt*, showed her long legs and worked up close to 32 knots. At 03:00hrs December 7th the big battle-carrier was approaching the Chagos Archipelago in the mid Indian Ocean, and very shortly it would enter the Royal Navy base on the Atoll of Diego Garcia for refueling.

The *Cornelis de Witt* would then depart for the Horn of Africa post haste to locate and monitor the movements of the *Graf Spee*. It was our intention to make her Commander squirm. My big ship had the capability to search a 1300 kilometer wide swath of the ocean with our aircraft, so finding the German ship was not a big problem for us. Once spotted, our superior speed would enable us to come up to the Pocket Battleship. After that we would operate beyond gun-range of the *Graf Spee*, while carrying out so-called 'normal training exercises.'

The German Commander clearly understood that we had no intention of attacking his ship. But he would be faced with the uncomfortable prospect of being constantly under surveillance. Our ship's normal peacetime radio traffic of ship to shore and air, would innocently give away the raider's position. There was nothing that the Pocket- Battleship could do to evade us as we were just too fast and possessed *far seeing eyes*, nor could his ship attack as we were far too powerful. Under such circumstances I have no doubt that the High Command of the Kreigsmarine (German Navy) would soon re-consider their Commerce raider's habit of violating the Dutch Flag; stopping our ships on the high seas and carrying out inspections at gun-point!

Naturally the Royal Navy thought that this plan was just lovely! If the warships of the British and French now actively hunting the German Pocket-battleship *somehow* benefitted from our radio transmissions then, such were the *fortunes of war.*

The men became aware of our increased radio traffic and reduction of speed down to 20 knots. With the RN base only two hours away there was no point in further secrecy. The crew, who had been in a great state of speculation, after more than three days at sea at 30 + knots, were informed of the mission. As many of the crew had family in the merchant marine, cheering erupted, and there was a lot of excitement at a chance to see action.

The battle-carrier entered the great interior lagoon through the North West channel and anchored within, about one nautical mile from the RN Fleet oil storage facility. The two RN, 'D' Class light cruisers; HMS *Dianna* and HMS *Druid*, were also at anchor awaiting our arrival, and their captains came aboard the *Cornelis de Witt*, to discuss our upcoming operation. Only a few hours later, in the midst of our strategy session, we received a dispatch; that the *Graf Spee* had returned to the Atlantic, where she had sunk the freighter *S.S. Streonshalh* on December 7th. The development was confirmed by the French Battlecruiser *Strasbourg*, and her escorts, who formed a hunting group in the South

Atlantic. They sailed through wreckage which proved to be of that ship. On several of the planks of her wooden hatch covers, the sides of wooden crates were scribbled; *Pocket Battleship, December 7, 1939.*

We studied our options, but soon realized that the *Graf Spee* was beyond our reach. To cover our deep disappointment, we informed the crew that the Pocket Battleship's Commander, having got wind of our approach, had run for it! The *Cornelis de Witt* departed that afternoon for Addu Atoll, accompanied by the *Dianna* and *Druid*. We anchored inside the lagoon, one kilometer off Maradhoo Beach. Each man was given a 24 hour shore leave to enjoy the lovely weather, the clean sand, and good swimming. A respectable Football match was organized between the British and Dutch crews, while other seamen, using their specialized training, formed into tactical units and expertly hunted down the local watering holes and female companionship.

December 12th, the Naval Headquarters in Batavia ordered us to return to home waters. The voyage was very anti-climactic until we learned the *Graf Spee* had been caught by a RN cruiser squadron and had been given such a bloody nose that she had run for the security of the neutral harbour of Montevideo in Uruguay, where she was scuttled by her commander who later committed suicide.

On May 10, 1940 the German Army struck westwards with an army of two million. Even though the combined armies of France, Belgium, Holland and Great Britain numbered close to six million fully mobilized troops, already in position, and complete with more tanks, guns and aircraft than the Germans, they were outthought, out maneuvered, outfought and whipped in about the same time it took Poland to fall. However Poland it should be remembered; was fighting the armies of Germany, the Soviet Union and the Slovaks, whose combined forces possessed much more modern equipment, and whose soldiers outnumbered the Polish army fivefold.

June 10, 1940 Italy declared war on France and England and its troops invaded the former's southern territory. I had long sensed a lack of true resolve in the leadership and senior officers of the French military. But it still came as a great surprise to me when France capitulated on June 16, 1940. Her huge field army of over five million soldiers had been defeated in six weeks, it seemed fantastic! It was a profound shock to the civilian population of my country, and to many officers in the Dutch Military service as well, who believed so assuredly in the combined military power of France and Britain. The map of Europe, upon the conclusion of that swift campaign now showed huge areas under German and Italian control. England looked to be so small and vulnerable.

The Dutch Colonies were of course automatically in a shooting war with the Germans and Italians. Our navy prepared plans to capture all known merchant vessels of these two belligerents, within our region. We worked closely with the Royal Navy out of Singapore and the resolute navies of Australia and New Zeeland.

In short order we secured some twenty million square kilometers of the west Pacific and cleared it of some twenty three disguised enemy ships totaling 109,000 tonnes. Following this we established a number of new naval and air bases conveniently located to facilitate movement of men and material from Malay to Perth.

Events in Europe now unraveled even further with the recognition of the *Vichy Government* of France by most members of the League of Nations. The defeat of France was a complete disaster to British Military planning. Her entire strategy for dealing with

Hitler was in a shambles. The Royal Navy; arguably the most powerful in the world at the time was vastly superior to any rival navy in Europe, and it had been backed up by the French Navy, rated the fourth most powerful fleet. After the French collapse, the Royal Navy was alone now, and was faced with the combined power of the *Kriegsmarine* and *Regia Marina*; the navies of Germany and Italy respectively. But with the conclusion of the armistice with Germany, the French Navy became a big concern for Britain. If her powerful warships fell into German hands and combined with those vessels of the Axis powers, a fleet could be formed that was powerful enough to challenge the Royal Navy.

In what many considered a rash act, Winston Churchill ordered the Royal Navy's Gibraltar Fleet Force H to destroy the French Fleet anchored at Mers El Kebir in North Africa. The British Prime Minister it seemed, would not gamble with such stakes and trust the French to ensure that their fleet would not come under Nazi control. It was an act that shocked the world and precipitated a political disaster. Following the attack, the French Government received confirmation from Hitler, that a retaliation against the British would not violate their recently concluded armistice. The French air force bombed Gibraltar and France now became a co-belligerent, with Germany and Italy against the British Empire. At this time our spirits had sunk very low indeed! With our former allies now shooting at each other, in the face of a triumphant powerful enemy! We put our faith in America and stiffened our resolve to defend the East Indies.

French General Charles De Gaulle, a proud nationalist and monarchist, was a soldier who could not live with the shame of the French defeat. Consequently he formed the Free French Army in French Equatorial Africa and offered continued resistance to the Fascists. On June 18th 1940 he spoke over the radio calling all Frenchmen to fight with his forces.

The French High Commissioner of the Pacific Theater; Lt. Commander Thierry d' Argenlieu openly supported General De Gaulle's call to arms. This would have direct consequences for the Colony of French Indo China, our neighbour laying just across the South China Sea.

In July 1940, the RNLN Battleship-carrier *Schoonveldt* arrived in East Indies waters escorting a vital convoy safely to us. During her voyage she was in action against German surface raiders that had enjoyed up until that encounter considerable success. Now with this third capital ship, our fleet was greatly strengthened and more flexible. Training could now begin with her new types of aircraft, and new flight operations could be experimented with, due to the third flight deck at sea.

One week later; Japan, concerned over the French General; Charles De Gaulle's attempt to resurrect France's pride, and fearing a shift in the attitude of the cooperative Vichy controlled French Indo China, moved to occupy the French naval base at Cam Ranh Bay. This move brought her military forces to the very doorstep of the Dutch East Indies, British Malaya, and British Borneo. The British protectorate of Hong Kong had been leapfrogged and completely surrounded, although not yet occupied. Now the entire Dutch East India colony, British Malaya and the American controlled Philippine Islands were within the range of Japanese long range bombers! America, Britain and Holland responded at once by freezing all Japanese assets. This move cut off 75% of her overseas trade, and 90% of her oil imports. Japan responded to this development by occupying Saigon, and was poised to seize all of French Indo China's rubber, rice crops and oil production.

One event occurred that demonstrated the resistance of the *De Gaullists Forces of Indo China*. Sitting in the very center of Harbour of Hai Phong, and aground on a sandbar for many decades was the old ironclad the *Redoubtable*. She was a warship of close to sixty five years, and had been transferred from the French Mediterranean Fleet to French Indo China in 1902 to act as a coast defense battleship. By 1940 she had not been seaworthy for decades, but continued to serve grounded as a stationary naval battery. Over the years brush and trees took root around her sides, and her upper works had been covered with an extensive tin roof to bring shade and make the interior more habitable. Her ancient coal fired steam plant had been disconnected from the propeller shaft in 1925 and reconnected to an electrical generator. She now provided the city with a goodly portion of her electricity. From any angle she now looked like a large four story tin sided building sitting on a brush covered island in the middle of the harbour. She became part of the city and her origin as an old battleship, it seems largely forgotten. However her original armament of eight 270 mm breech loading cannon were still intact. One in the bow, one aft, two amidships port and starboard, and four a few meters above what used to be waterline, but below within the central battery and protected by armor plating, most of which was 380 mm thick steel!

On September 5th 1940 the Japanese Government; declaring that French Indo China had become a supply route for rice and war material to Nationalist Chinese Forces, moved to occupy the French Colony. The following week a large convoy of some forty vessels anchored in the muddy waters of the Mekong River at Hai Phong, and Japanese troops and equipment began disembarking. Detachments of Japanese Marines crisscrossed the harbour in motor launches with orders to remove all French flags and replace them with the *Rising Sun*. Three boats containing some sixty Japanese marines approached a small island from all sides, of what they were told by the locals, was the city's electrical works and demanded from the administrator that the French flag be hauled down.

The boats were beached and the Japanese marines disembarked. Spreading out they advanced to the staircase that led from the flowerpot lined concrete sidewalk up into the stairway into the building. They were surprised to be confronted by men clad in French naval tropical uniforms. The commander, of the *Redoubtable*, at heart a *De Gaullist* replied that his command would not haul down its flag. The young Japanese naval officer drew his sword and ordered his men to attack. These rushed towards the staircase and were met with small arms fire. The Japanese convoy commander upon hearing the gunfire, studied the situation through his binoculars, from the deck of his troopship. Seeing the French tri-color still floating lazily in the light breeze over the Electrical Generating station, he ordered more marines to standby, those ashore to withdraw, and the river gunboat *Ohama* to bombard the building with its 100 mm gun.

To those in the Japanese convoy who had been watching this shelling, the Steam plant seemed to erupt like a volcano, reigning death and destruction onto the troops and ships of the occupation force! The old warship, still equipped with the original fifty light quick firing 30 mm cannon had returned fire, and whose ten 270 mm guns, unleashed a sporadic fire, at point blank range with tremendous blasts produced by the heavy charges of prismatic black powder! Only after a six hours of heavy confused fighting was the old *Redoubtable* taken by three battalions of marines. Four times her colors were shot away, only to be replaced. Any portion of the Japanese occupation convoy that could be sited by the guns of the old *Redoubtable* had been taken under fire. Much of the Hai Phong waterfront was burning fiercely and unusable, with its wharves and cargo cranes destroyed. In addition; the oil fouled waters were littered with the half submerged wrecks of some 11 Japanese steamships of 800 to 2200 tonnes deadweight. The Japanese invasion timetable was in a shambles!

The Japanese marines had great difficulty investing the old ship as their engineering charges were not designed to defeat such massive armor plate. Only after a fuel barge was nosed onto the beach under smoke screen and twenty tonnes of gasoline pumped into the old vessel and ignited did the remaining French sailors surrender, and these few survivors were quickly executed. The Japanese marines occupied the sand bar, throwing a cordon around the old hulk to prevent the escape of those French sailors within the blazing inferno. The flames finally managed to work into the heart of the ship, and ignited her magazines, which still contained several hundreds of tonnes of explosive, that obliterated all life on the island.

The passing of each month brought such grim news continually to us, and we responded with more training while we consolidated our forces. Soon 1940 passed, and with the coming of 1941 came more Fascist success and gloom for our battered group of widely dispersed and increasingly desperate allied nations.

In January 1941 the Kriegsmarine dispatched the modern battlecruisers *Scharnhorst* and *Gneisenau* to raid British commerce in the Atlantic Ocean. These two powerful warships represented a threat far more dangerous than had the *Graf Spee*, which was merely a pocket battleship. Each of these ships had more than 50% greater firepower, armor plate more than four times as thick, in a ship thrice *Graf Spee's* displacement. No cruiser squadron could tackle these two monsters. It would take a squadron of battleships to do them in. But of the twenty four big gunned ships available to the Royal Navy only three; the *Hood*, the *Repulse* and the *Renown* approached them in speed of 32 knots. The big guns of these British Battlecruisers could get the job done, but only the armor of the Hood could stand a heavy gun duel!

Once again panic reigned on the high seas, and normal commerce was greatly disrupted. The two German battlecruisers however never followed the Graff Spee's route into the Indian Ocean. The KMN was asked by the RN to prepare to resurrect our earlier operation to deal with the *Graf Spee*, albeit with two battle-carriers. Indeed the British Government became so concerned with the threat to their Indian Ocean shipping that they requested that the KMN base one of our battle-carriers the *Schoonveldt* permanently in Diego Garcia. We were studying the consequences of such a deployment when the German Battlecruisers, terminated their commerce raiding, and sailed into the harbour of Brest on the west coast of France, following a two month cruise, which netted them 22 merchant ships sunk.

In May 1941, the powerful new German battleship *Bismarck*, in company with the new heavy cruiser *Prinz Eugen*, broke out into the North Atlantic to begin a third great convoy raiding operation. But this time the Royal Navy was ready and she was intercepted by the Battlecruiser *Hood* and the Battleship *Prince of Wales*. After a short engagement the *Hood* exploded and the damaged POW withdrew, but not without damaging the *Bismarck*. The loss of the *Hood* was a tremendous shock as that famous ship was the greatest that the Royal Navy had.

But forces of the RN dogged the German squadron, preventing them from fulfilling their mission. The *Prinz Eugen* was detached, and the *Bismarck* finally cornered. After a battle career that lasted only nine days, the powerful German battleship, now wounded by torpedoes and shellfire, was re-engaged and finally pounded into scrap by the battleships *King George V* and *Rodney* and their escorts.

Then came the incredible news: The Army of Nazi Germany had invaded the Soviet Union on June 22 1941, expanding the war to a global scale. I now believed for the first time that Herr Hiltler had overreached his military and resource capabilities, and that his ultimate defeat was only a matter of time. One had only to study a child's globe of the earth to appreciate the vast extent of the Soviet Union, and how utterly enormous was the opponent that Hitler had selected for his next victim. I am sure that at least 200 million people around the world had reached for their Atlases upon hearing the news of the Nazi invasion. Equally sure I am, that once the maps had been studied, these astonished multitudes had voiced the question to one another; is the man barking mad?

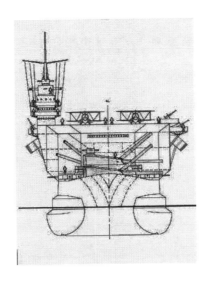

CHAPTER XX

GERMAN COMMERCE RAIDERS ACTIVE ACROSS THE PACIFIC, THE SCHOONVELDT'S DEPLOYMENT AND CONVOY ACTION.

On July 17, 1939 the newly completed Yard Project No. 718.200; a large modernized warship' had successfully completed its sea trials in the Baltic Sea and was turned over by the contractor; Royal Scheldt Scheepswerf of Rotterdam to the Royal Netherlands Navy. The Battleship-carrier was commissioned into service as *Her Netherlands Majesty's Ship Schoonveldt*. She sailed the following day for Den Helder Naval Base with a minimum crew, and her commissioning pennant fluttering proudly at the masthead.

The following day her full crew embarked, to bid goodbye to barracks living, and occupy the more confined, yet infinitely more agreeable quarters aboard their clean new ship. Immediately the process of taking aboard stores, fuel and ammunition began. Fifteen hundred pair of hands made short work of this task, and on July 23rd the big warship departed for the North Sea.

Once in open waters, her air group composed of a wing of Fighter Squadron 12, and the complete Fighter Squadron 5, and Bomber Squadron 7, flew aboard from the Royal Army airfield in Noord Holland. The battle-carrier, now fully armed and equipped, departed for the Caribbean Sea and the island of Curacao, lying just off the northern coastline of South America; in the Netherlands Antilles, on her first training cruise, and voyage as a *Queen's Ship*. (See Appendix B & C).

While this was occurring; two RNLN munitions ships had arrived in Rio de Janerio naval base, to load the ammunition and stores of the former flagship of Brazil's Navy, from the fleet arsenal. A large general cargo freighter had accompanied these vessels, to take aboard the battleship carrier's crated air groups and load the ship and aircraft stores and spares also warehoused at that base. The stores freighter, once loaded departed directly for the Dutch East Indies, via the Panama Canal while the munitions ships voyaged around the horn.

Due to strategic significance of the Panama Canal to the movement of US Naval vessels, and given the heightened political tensions in the spring of 1940, the US Government; the canal operator, not yet having completed its expanded security procedures, would not allow these two ships with their highly destructive cargos to enter the canal system. The chief concern being that an accident or an act of sabotage, resulting in the detonation of one or both of the munition ships within the lifting locks, would have rendered the Panama Canal unusable to the U.S. Navy for several years. Such an event would be a strategic disaster for America, as it would require its warships to circumnavigate the horn of South America, thereby lengthening coastal redeployments by some 15,000 nautical miles, and passing these fleets through a bottleneck region of the world's oceans where could lurk submarine ambushes.

The *Schoonveldt* was scheduled for a secretive refit in Bremerton Navy Yard, in Washington State on the US Pacific Northwest. However, until the design drawings for these installations were completed and the yard could schedule the work, the warship would carry out exercises and wait out the developments in Europe safe from any surprise attack in her remote Caribbean location. Here at the charming colonial *City of Willemstad*, she would guard the big Royal Dutch Shell Oil refinery and storage facility with her massive artillery and aircraft. Anchored in the *Schottgat*, a bay just off the picturesque city, those of her lucky crew due for shore leave would enjoy the lovely beaches during the day, while at night the exotic island ladies, the lively casinos and nightclubs would provide ample diversions. Those single officers and enlisted men of her compliment would unanimously agree that they had pulled the best duty port in the Fleet, in one of the most beautiful climates in the Dutch Empire!

On May 01, 1940, the battle-carrier disconnected from her mooring buoy and sailed for the west coast of the United States, via the Panama Canal. Nine days later, the Netherlands would be invaded by Germany.

The *Schoonveldt* entered the Bremerton Naval Yard in Washington State in mid May 1940 to officially have a new plate stem stepped onto her ram enabling more flare to be built into her bows. After these many years it is safe to say that; de-gauzing cabling was attached around the perimeter of hull below the shear line, updated communications equipment was installed that would allow coded interaction with the all allied and U.S. naval vessels. In addition an inert gas fire suppression system was fitted to the aviation fuel tanks and lines. At the time, though these installations would have drawn some protest from the Japanese Government, so they were masked by the simple hull plate work contract.

By mid-June the work was completed and after a two day shakedown cruise to calibrate the new equipment, the battleship-carrier once again took aboard her crew, began storing and taking aboard the fresh water, some 5,000 tonnes of fuel oil, aviation gasoline, aviation lubricants, shells, bombs, and all the other consumables that had been unloaded at the yard earlier, but were required for her voyage to the Dutch East Indies.

On June 17th, 1940; the *Schoonveldt* departed the Puget Sound with the morning tide, under the single star pennant of Commodore Johan Van den Kerckhoven-Polyander. Fluttering at her masthead was her new battle flag, the broad red, white and blue tricolor of the Netherlands; a nation now at war with Nazi Germany and Fascist Italy. She would be sailing in company with a US Naval force on redeployment to Manila; a naval tanker, a light cruiser and the ten destroyers of her 5th Destroyer flotilla; (DESRON 5).

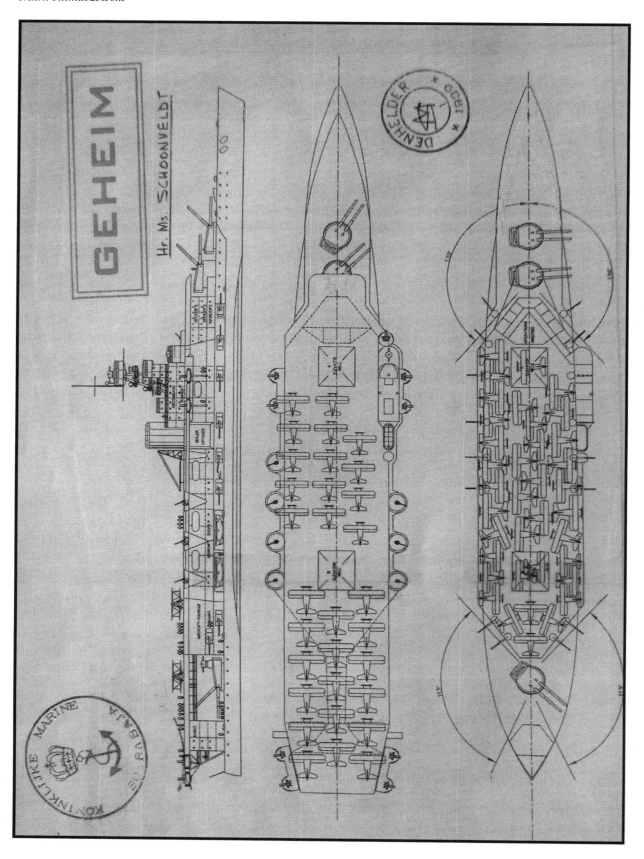

These were the obsolete *U.S.S. Dixie,* a light cruiser of the *Omaha Class,* flagship and flotilla leader. I believe that she was of late 1920's vintage. The *5ᵗʰ Destroyer Flotilla* was composed of the *old four-pipers*: *U.S.S. Gen. Robert. E. Lee, U.S.S. Gen. James Longstreet, U.S.S. Thomas Johnathan Jackson, U.S.S. Gen. Lewis Armistead, U.S.S Gen. George Pickett, U.S.S. Gen. John Bell Hood, U.S.S Gen J.E.B. Stuart, U.S.S. Gen. Richard Garnett* and the *U.S.S Gen James Kemper.* (see appendix E). These old destroyers; being quite a bit smaller than the cruiser would need a replenishment of fuel oil to operate in the vastness of the Pacific, therefore the fast fleet oil tanker *U.S.S. Lake Michigan* was assigned as support.

The destroyers represented a large class of this ship type constructed in the US for World War I, with many shipyards involved in their production. There was a practice employed in those days I understand; of choosing a name for the ship that associated it with the location of the shipyard in which it was constructed. I do recall that the names of the destroyers of *Desron 5* were of famous military men who served in the army of the secessionist Confederate states during the American Civil War. All the vessels of the *5ᵗʰ Destroyer flotilla* were built by yards in the south; Ingalls Iron Works of Decatur, Alabama, Consolidated Steel of Orange Texas, Southern Shipbuilders, of Savanna Georgia, and last of all North Carolina Shipbuilders, of Wilmington, North Carolina.

These American naval vessels, I was informed, were all manned by officers and men recruited from states in the *deep south*. Many of these men had served for years on *China Station*, either salt water duty with the Asiatic Fleet or on the *Yangtze River* in gunboats. The latter duty exposed the sailors to the worst debasements imaginable, far exceeding those fleshpots of Malta; the home port of the Royal Navy's Mediterranean Fleet, and the favorite port of call for her sailors. These former *China Station sailors*, reveled in their legendary reputation of inebriated debauchery! As the little warships they served upon were vessels built entirely in the former states of the Confederacy, paid for by the former States of the Confederacy, and named after their beloved historical figures, the men and their ships enjoyed a considerable notoriety, in the *Cotton states*.

On a fleet visit to Manila in February of 1940, I had the opportunity to socialize with officers of the USN at a party given by the Commander of the Cavite Naval Base; Rear Admiral Allister Harding. Here I was introduced to one; Captain Chester Cornfield, the commander of Fort Drum, the legendary *Concrete Battleship*. The Fort sat astride the approaches to the City's main harbour. Nothing that floated could pass her artillery and survive. The Fort, built atop a small island of solid granite was essentially a massive concrete pillbox. Its roof was formed by a massive slab of steel reinforced concrete thirty feet in thickness. The walls of the fortification were of similar construction but fifty feet thick. Fort Drum was armed with a battery of four 14 inch naval guns in pairs in two turrets sheathed in sixteen inches of armor plate. These massive pieces were backed up by a heavily armored battery of six inch naval guns, and machine guns. Captain Cornfield had once served aboard *U.S.S General Pickett,* and as an ensign he had been exposed to crew life. He gave me a humorous, account of some of their activities.

Following a night of wretched debauchery, bar fights and beer swilling on a colossal scale that was enacted along Canal St. in Galveston Texas, the destroyer crew, which had achieved the greatest tally of these debasements amongst the flotilla, was designated the *winner,* and when next at sea, the stars and stripes would be hauled down and a huge CSA battle naval ensign was run up! The ship's loud hailers would play vinyl discs of popular civil war tunes; *Dixie* or *Bonnie Blue Flag* and the crews would muster on deck and carry on with festive activity!

Several accounts of these destroyer's ribald parties had found their way into the pages of the *Atlanta Clarion,* causing a huge wave of popular sentiment in both the streets and the legislatures of the eleven formerly Confederate States. The most senior USN Admirals felt that the *heavy hand* of Navy discipline must fall upon the crews of these ships. Upon closer investigation, it was reported that recruitment in the cotton states had risen due to the *fame* of these vessels. In the past it had always been difficult to find such sailors. The Department of the Navy, after weighing the *pros and cons* had quietly dropped all current charges and only warned of *stern action* for any future breaches of discipline.

Transiting the Panama Canal some 5,000 miles to the south, just as the *Schoonveldt* was clearing Puget Sound, was a small fleet of five large Dutch merchant ships of 6,000 to 10,000 tonnes deadweight, and designated Convoy X, under the command of Commodore Abraham Crijnssen RNLN, aboard the vlaggeschip S.S. *Tjikarang* – 9500T dwt, the remaining freighters in the convoy were S.S. *Toendjeek* - 6,200T dwt, S.S. *Tjisaroea* - 7,090T dwt, S.S. *Tjinegora* – 9,230T dwt and the S.S. *Tjikandi* – 7,970t dwt. All were equipped with a Krupp 150 mm naval gun mounted aft on a quarterdeck platform. Combined they had the considerable firepower of a light cruiser. These vessels were carrying highly valuable military supplies from the US Naval Air Station San Juan Puerto Rico to the Dutch East Indies. These contained, amongst other war material; 100,000 artillery shells of mixed caliber, 40 million rifle cartridges, 4000 tires, 10,000 military boots, 2000 tents, 700 field radios, 56 tonnes of morphine and 37 of penicillin, in addition to surgical equipment, x-ray machines, some 100 new aircraft engines, air-frame and control surface parts and some 730 passengers of status. Consequently the RNLN planned that the *Schoonveldt* would affect a rendezvous with these cargo liners, somewhere east of Hawaii.

The Office of Naval Intelligence discovered that the Kreigsmarine had dispatched two large merchant cruisers the *Komet*, the *Orion* and their supply ship *Kuimerland* to the West Pacific. These were to be engaged in raiding the seaborne commerce of the Allied nations, capturing their valuable cargos, sinking the ships and disrupting trade. Upon arriving at their assigned area of operations these German merchant cruisers had destroyed the Australian Phosphate mining operation situated on Nauru Island 300 miles west of the New Hebrides. Shortly after that they sank five merchant ships two hundred miles south of that island. The German merchant cruisers had Japanese flags painted on the sides of their hulls, to dissuade allied ships from stopping them to investigate.

Codedinst (the Dutch Crypto Service) determined that at the Kreigsmarine was now operating at least three large merchant cruisers in the wide expanses of the Eastern Pacific. Codedinst believed them to be the German surface raiders; M.V. *Gull*, the M.V. *Pelican* and the M.V. *Albatross,* all large fast cargo liners formerly of the Hamburg-America Line. These vessels had been extensively rebuilt at the Krupp-Germania yard at Wilhelmshaven before the war, and were each heavily armed with a mixed battery of eight modern 130 mm U-boat deck guns, two 88 mm flak guns and powerful radio jamming gear. All three motor ships used diesel engines for propulsion, a type that were very economical on fuel, and with enormous fuel tanks built into the former cargo spaces, the raiders enjoyed a tremendous cruising range. Normally ships of this size would carry a crew of sixty to seventy men. But each vessel carried upwards of four hundred which were to be used as prize crews on captured ships. So outfitted, these modern day corsairs were ideally suited to their task; the attack, capture or sinking of unarmed and unescorted merchant vessels.

Finally two additional weapons were employed by these modern corsairs, the first; a light float equipped airplane. The machine was usually stored with wings folded in the after hold, and could quickly be deployed or retrieved by cargo boom. While these light naval floatplanes had only a modest range, they nevertheless allowed these commerce raiders to extend their search for victims out to 100 miles out from the ship. While the planes were away the corsair would deploy its little fat torpedo shaped observation balloon. Reeled out to a height of 200 meters these allowed the balloonist to view a fifty mile swath of the sea with his binoculars and report anything of interest via his gondola telephone.

These commerce raiders routinely altered their profiles with canvas and wood framing to create false deckhouses or add extra canvas funnels to appear as the ships of neutral nations. In this way they could approach an unsuspecting freighter, identify her and if she was found to be the legitimate war target, jam her radio transmissions and take her under fire. These raiders had become so good at their *game of cat and mouse* with the Royal Navy, that no victim as yet had a chance to radio her location before she was rendered helpless. Once immobilized the victim would have her cargo, if of suitable value seized, the surviving crew imprisoned. If the captured ship was found to be of value a prize crew was put aboard and she then made for Axis held territory. If vessel was old and her cargo of limited worth, she was quickly sunk.

Captured war records have since revealed that the network of German spies operating from Seattle had kept the Kreigsmarine (German Navy) informed of the *Schoonveldt's* time of sailing. The information was relayed first to Berlin and then transmitted to all their ships at sea in naval code. The *M.V. Albatross*, had received this information while lingering off French Polynesia. However this was not the case with the *M.V. Gull* and *M.V. Pelican* who were steaming some 100 miles apart, and engaged in a sweep pattern off Chile. Due to unusual atmospherics they did not receive this information.

When relaying their observations to their superiors, the Nazi agents included one critical bit of information, which was misinterpreted by the cryptologists and proved to be one of fatal consequence. The German spy reported that the Dutch battleship-carrier had no aircraft aboard. A situation that was not unusual as she had come from a refit in a shipyard. In Germany that part of the message was badly translated as; the *Schoonveldt* had sailed from Bremerton without aircraft. In those days, carrier aircraft were normally based on an airfield when the ship was tied up. Only later would they join the ship when it was well out to sea.

The *Albatross, Gull* and *Pelican* had been successful in their predations and it soon became obvious that something was amiss in the south eastern Pacific. The problem was a serious one; thirteen ships were missing. Great Britain had tiny colonial holdings in that part of the world, such as the New Hebrides, but she had no aircraft to spare to put on these islands. The Royal Navy, now a shadow of what it had been during the Great War of 1914–1918, lacked the necessary warships to patrol to these region effectively. The RN's response to the threat of the German surface raiders in remote areas of the earth was as the Kreigsmarine had expected; anemic at best.

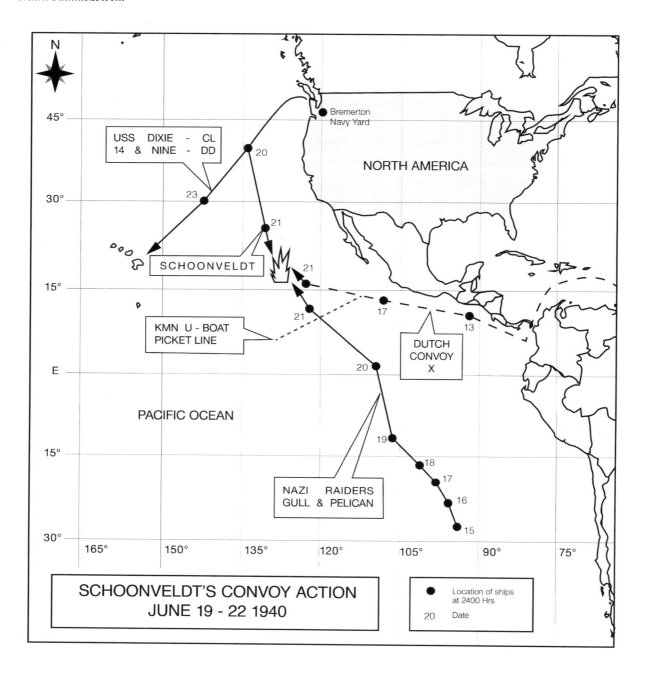

N

45°

USS DIXIE - CL
14 & NINE - DD

20

23

Bremerton
Navy Yard

NORTH AMERICA

30°

21

SCHOONVELDT

21

KMN U - BOAT
PICKET LINE

21

15°

DUTCH
CONVOY
X

17

13

E

20

PACIFIC OCEAN

19

15°

18

17

NAZI RAIDERS
GULL & PELICAN

16

30°

15

165°   150°   135°   120°   105°   90°   75°

SCHOONVELDT'S CONVOY ACTION
JUNE 19 - 22 1940

● Location of ships
at 2400 Hrs

20 Date

Ships of the neutral nations had employed as a technique of identification, the painting a large rendition of their nation's flag on both sides of the hull at amidships. The practice was a useful innovation of the Great War 1914-18 but one that may easily be exploited by Nazi commerce raiders having the intention to deceive.

The best defense that the Allied nations could prepare was a directive that all merchant ships, should, wherever possible sail in groups for mutual protection. Then if one such group was attacked, some ships, it was reasoned may survive out of the group and be able to steam beyond the range of the radio jamming equipment aboard the German raider and transmit details of the attack. In this way it was hoped, other allied merchant vessels would steer clear of the area.

Upon learning of this directive the German skippers realized that from that time forward a lone freighter would appear suspicious and cause target vessels to veer away, reducing the raiders tactics to a long, dangerous and uneconomical stern chase.

Therefore it was agreed amongst the captains to operate in unison for a time. They knew the allied instructions to their merchantmen, from captured documents and the interrogation of prisoners. There was even a slight chance that single ships may ask to join their group, which would really make life easy for them. To facilitate this deception, it was decided to request to sail 'in company' when sighting another freighter.

German spies in the Panama Canal Zone regularly transmitted reports on all shipping. The news of five large and deeply loaded Dutch cargo vessels all heading into the Pacific, and bound for the Dutch East Indies represented a target of high value. Kapitan Felix Von Essen of the *Gull* and Kapitan Heinrich Schultz of the *Pelican* were unable to resist the temptation offered by such an opportunity and so they began to hunt for Convoy X as a team.

Several advantages lay with the German corsairs. The first; they could operate spread out at 60 miles between the ships and still, by utilizing their tethered observation balloon and floatplanes, patrol easily out to 75 miles on each side of this formation creating a 210 mile wide surveillance corridor across the sea. The second; they knew the approximate location of the Dutch convoy, its estimated speed at 15 knots and the approximate course based on a great circle route (shortest distance over the surface of a sphere) laid between the head of the Panama Canal and their best guess, its approximate destination: a point in the Celebes Sea precisely 100 nautical miles south of the city of Dutch Colonial City of Davo. The third; the Dutch convoy did not know that they were being pursued, yet they suspected as much, that the commerce raiders knew of their existence and could appear from any point of the compass.

The Dutch Commodore on the other hand had made some preparations of his own. He knew that the German surface raiders could quickly overwhelm them with their longer range guns, so their defensive tactics was simple; to flee at their best speed, drop smoke floats to hamper the German gunnery and hope for a rainsquall or nightfall to break contact with their pursuers and escape. If such tactics were not possible, then the convoy would scatter in five separate directions. The Dutch Kapiteins also knew that approaching from the northeast and some ten days away was the powerful Battleship–carrier *Schoonveldt* with her long ranging aircraft and massive battery of big guns that would guarantee their safety from surface attack.

Once clear of the Swiftsure Lightship moored at the mouth of the Strait of Juan de Fuca, the *Schoonveldt* had transmitted a message to her aircraft stationed at the Naval Air Station Eugene Oregon. Her air-group consisting of; 7 – Fiat CR 42 Falcon Fighters, 14 – Hawker Sea Fury Mk II fighters and 25 Hawker Sea Hart bombers began to take off and all arrived aboard an hour and a half flight.

Commodore Maurits Van Nassau had prepared a message to Naval Headquarters in Batavia that would inform them of the *Schoonveldt's* alteration of course to rendezvous with Convoy X. The code 6 message that would include the statement, *"problems with turbine on no. 4 shaft will require shutdown for repair: expect to delay arrival Batavia by several days."* Special arrangements had been made *between* the governments of the US and Netherlands for covert naval cooperation. Commodore Arbuckle of the light cruiser *U.S.S. Dixie* (F), with her flotilla of destroyers and fleet oiler were sailing in company with the *Schoonveldt*. The *U.S.S. Dixie,* which processed a powerful new RCA radio set would transmit the Dutch Commodore's message to Batavia, and imitate the *Schoonveldt* using her call sign; S340NL. Commodore Arbuckle would do this only six hours *after* the Dutch ship had changed course and broke company with *Desron 5*. This occurred at 2400hrs June 20ᵗʰ. In this way Commodore Van Nassau expected the German surface raiders to triangulate on the direction of the *USS Dixie's* transmission, and be misled as to her location.

This information was absolutely vital for the German raiders to prepare their attack plan on the Dutch convoy. The Germans knew that the battleship-carrier was fresh from her sea trials, and only recently re-commissioned into the RNLN. It was very possible that she was having mechanical problems with some new equipment. This was a common enough occurrence, and would support the notion that the messages were not a ruse, but if fact extremely good fortune.

In order to maintain the security of the Panama Canal Zone, the U.S. Army stationed a squadron of B-17 long range bombers at Panama City. These aircraft flew a pattern around the canal out to a distance of 700 miles and reported all shipping sighted. Therefore all nations could monitor the traffic. With such security measures in place, no commerce raiders would dare to be spotted by these aircraft as their location would immediately be fixed, and the region avoided by merchant shipping. A hunt would also begin by whatever meager resources the naval and air groups of the allies could muster.

The commanders of the *Gull* and *Pelican*, set a course that would intercept the Dutch vessels well beyond the alert eyes of the B-17 bombers operating out of Panama. They planned to approach their quarry from southeast, and with the aid of aircraft and balloon, locate the convoy an hour before sunset. In such a deployment, the Dutch ships would be silhouetted by the setting sun while leaving the German ships cloaked in the gloom of the eastern sky. The *Gull* and *Pelican* would then close the range at night using their high speed. By the morning they would be in an advantageous position from which to launch an attack with artillery, and jam any radio transmission sent by their quarry before the guns had done their work.

Naval Intelligence had approximated the location of the *Pelican* and the *Gull* and had reasoned that they would attempt to intercept the Dutch convoy outbound from Panama. Accordingly they had established a submarine cordon across the path of approach which they believed that the German raiders would use. On the eighth day out from Panama, and some 1000 nautical miles beyond the range of the American B-17 patrols, the small Dutch convoy crossed this cordon. The flagship of the submarine cordon; *Hr.Ms. Dolfijn,* surfaced about a half mile to the south of the convoy, initially causing a panic amongst the merchant vessels. The *Dolfijn's* commander; Kapitein Amstel signaled Commodore Crijnssen with Morse lamp, to let him know that the submarine cordon was in place and to confirm that the battleship-carrier *Schoonveldt* was indeed at sea to the north some three days away from the current position and steaming south to rendezvous with Convoy X. The Commodore was much relieved by this information and the company. He had been aware of the friendly submarines in the vicinity, but nevertheless increased the convoy speed to 16 knots in the hope of securing the protection of the *Schoonveldt's* air group one day earlier.

June 21st at 11:15hrs, the RNLN submarine *Bluefin*, one unit making up a cordon of fifteen submarines, reported sighting smoke to the SE. This soon proved to originate from two large passenger liners approaching from the south east at some 20 knots. Their speed was such that the only the *Shark* was able to get close enough to identify them. The *Shark* blew her ballast tanks and broke surface about three nautical miles to the south and bow on to the still unidentified liners. She headed directly for what soon proved indeed to be the German surface raiders *Pelican* and *Gull!*

Through the periscope the Dutch Lt. Commander felt sure that these were the German raiders. He transmitted their position, their course as NW, including the compass bearing, and an estimated speed of 25 knots. The radio transmission, provoked an immediate response from the two large vessels. A volley of cannon fire erupted from the sides of both German ships! The *Shark* hurriedly submerged under a hail of projectiles, but not before transmitting R- R –R -R for *raider*, and her call sign. Coming to periscope depth, the *Shark* adjusted her heading to fire a spread of four torpedoes, calculated to hit into the flank of the speeding German raiders. However the bubble wakes of the torpedoes were spotted by the alert German sailors and their ships evaded this danger with a slight alteration of course to starboard. The high speed of the surface raiders soon had made as second torpedo attack impracticable.

Kapitan Felix Von Essen of the *Gull* and Kapitan Heinrich Schultz of the *Pelican* realized that their identity had been revealed and their position reported. In their exchange of ideas of how to proceed, they now agreed that it was impossible to capture the Dutch convoy and return its valuable cargos to the fatherland. But it was however, still possible to attack the Dutch ships, sink them and deny these valuable cargos to the enemy. Upon conclusion of the action, there would still remain ample time to make a good their escape due to their very high speed, and enormous diesel oil reserves, which would allow the raiders to maintain 25 knots for days if necessary. They held on their course in the hope of overtaking the Dutch merchant ships on the following day.

June 20th, 20:35hrs, some 350 nautical miles to the NW of the *Shark's* position; Kapitein Van Moote's signal was received aboard the convoy's Vlaageschip; the S.S. *Tjikarang*. Commodore Crijnssen now realized that his small convoy was being hunted. The German raiders he knew; from the *Germanisher Lloyd's Register*, were formerly large passenger liners, and had a speed advantage of at least 10 - 15 knots over his convoy, and they would overhaul him and bring his ship's under direct fire of their powerful long range guns in about 13 hours on the outside. He ordered the other four ships of the convoy by Morse lamp, to alter course one point to starboard and increase speed to 17 knots; the top speed of the S.S. *Toendjeek*. He estimated that the *Schoonveldt*, was at least a full day steaming away at this time, and heading for the prearranged rendezvous.

On June 21st, at 12:15hrs, the battleship-carrier *Schoonveldt* was still some seven hundred nautical miles to the NW of the now imperiled Dutch convoy. Her Kapitein, Jakob Polder handed a decoded radio transmission from the submarine picket flagship; *Dolfijn* to the convoy commander and said; "Commodore Van Nassau, it seems that the German surface raiders; *Pelican* and *Gull* mean to have our convoy for lunch!" Commodore Christiaan Maurits Van Nassau, turned to him and said, "Plot a course, Kapitein that will take the

Schoonveldt as close as possible to Convoy. We must get to within two hundred miles for dive bomber range within the next twelve to thirteen hours. Be aware that Commodore Crijnssen; commanding the Dutch convoy has; by pre-arrangement shaped their course to this location." The Commodore then turned away to point out the area displayed on the chart with a small circle.

Kapitein Polder, directed the watch officer to plot the new course, and ordered the engine room to make revolutions for 27 knots. He then asked the opinion of the Chief engineer if it was advisable to hang 5 kilogram weights on the pressure relief valves of the boilers to achieve flank speed?

This information was absolutely vital for the German raiders to prepare their attack plan on the Dutch convoy. The Germans knew that the battleship-carrier was fresh from her sea trials, and was only recently re-commissioned back into the RNLN. It was very possible that she was having mechanical problems with some new equipment. This was a common enough occurrence, and would justify that the messages were not a ruse, but if fact extremely good fortune.

Although the *Pelican* and *Gull* were powerfully armed raiders, and the ships themselves were large and well built, they would not wish to run afoul of the Dutch Battleship-carrier; an armored monster with very heavy guns that fired half tonne shells that far outranged their own guns. The big Dutch warship also had a *very long legs* (a good turn of speed) as well, a necessary requirement to launch aircraft. It may not even be possible to outrun her! If the *Pelican* and *Gull* crossed her path it was death and destruction for all aboard, due to the long reach of the battle-carrier's air group.

Aboard the battleship-carrier, Kapitein Polder approached Commodore Kerckhoven Polyander and said; "Sir, the ship is raising pressure on all boilers and 28 knots will be possible shortly, if we alter course three points to port we will, by maintaining 28 knots have the Dutch Convoy under our bomber umbrella within twelve hours. The duty engineer reports that a flank speed of 29 knots is possible with 15% over-pressure on the boilers, if required." "Thank you Kapitein Polder", replied the Commodore.

On morning of June 22nd, at approximately 06:30hrs Kapitan Heinrich Schultz of the *Pelican* discussed his position on the chart with his executive officer Commander Ulrich Brees. "Commander I believe that the Dutch convoy is only some seventy to eighty miles directly ahead of us, if we have enough daylight remaining, catapult the Arado and see if the pilot can spot them for us. "Jawol mein Kapitan" was Commander Brees only response. Fifteen minutes later the plane was away, launching into the clear morning, and in less than an hour the pilot radioed his mother ship that he had spotted a five ship convoy approximately sixty miles and steaming north, the quarry's location had been accurately estimated by the German raiders and the prize was now within reach. Kapitan Felix Von Essen of the *Gull* and Kapitan Heinrich Schultz of the *Pelican* altered course slightly to starboard to cut the angle, as the German raiders were advancing along a SE to NW axis, and the slight change in heading that would bring them within sight of their quarry in approximately five hours. After steadying up on the new course they both exchanged enthusiastic messages by Morse lamp, to celebrate the success of the Fatherland's armies in the field, which were trouncing the five allied armies facing them in France. Scnapps for all the crew, with Deutshland Uber Alles, played for all the crew on the ship's internal communication system. Von Essen to Schultz; *"Dammit, the war will be over soon and the army will be getting all the recognition once again!"*

The Dutch convoy was proceeding with all five ships steaming in the 'Line Abreast' formation with about 500 meters separating the vessels. The Vlaggeschip of Commodore Crijnssen; the *S.S. Tjikarang* was in the center of the formation with the *S.S. Tjinegara* immediately to starboard, and the *S.S. Toendjoek* beyond her. While to the port of the flagship; steamed the *S.S. Tjikandi*, and beyond her the *S.S. Tjisaroea*. All ships were straining to maintain 17 knots.

At 09:00hrs and alert lookout, aboard the eastern most vessel in the Dutch convoy; the *S.S. Toendjoek* spotted an aircraft astern, low on the horizon at some 15,000 meters distance and immediately reported this to his superior officer. In a few minutes the entire convoy was aware of the sighting and perhaps twenty officers located the aircraft and began studying its activities. After five minutes of observation the Kapitein of the *S.S. Tjikarang*, turned to Commodore Crijnssen, and said; "Sir, the aircraft appears to be a light float plane of limited range, and she is not proceeding on any course but is hanging back, flying a figure eight pattern, keeping us under observation, it can mean only one thing." Commodore Crijnssen, looked at his Kapitein, and said "I agree, she can only be an observation plane from one of the German raiders, guiding them to us. Make to all ships; proceed at highest possible convoy speed, order all vessels to prepare for action, make ready all smoke floats then transmit our position, course and speed and R-R-R-R for raider."

Some three hundred miles to the north of the Dutch convoy, the communications office aboard the *Schoonveldt* quickly transcribed the message and handed it to a junior telegraphist who ran it to the navigation bridge and gave it to Kapitein Polder. Commodore Merits Van Nassau after reading the message and studying the chart which now had the exact location of the Dutch convoy marked upon it. Turning to Kapt. Polder he said, "Maintain flank speed, and intercept Convoy X. We will launch a maximum air attack when we come within 250 miles of our ships. What do we have available to strike at this distance?"

Kapitein Polder turned to his Senior Air operations officer; Kapitein –Lt. ter Zee Veliger (Commander Flyer) Otto von Mossberg for the answer, who replied, "we have aboard twenty five Sea Hart bombers of which twenty two are available for immediate action. I recommend that the bombers be armed with an equal mix of our 250 kilogram HE or SAP bombs. The targets are far beyond the range of our Sea Fury fighters, but we do have seven Fiat Cr 42 fighters that are capable of escorting the bombers all the way to the target and back. The .50 caliber machine guns of these fighters would be well employed suppressing the fire from the target's Flak batteries, with which both German raiders are equipped. If we maintain flank speed, we can launch the strike in two hours and the bombers should be in attack position one hour and forty five minutes after launch. If we maintain flank all the bombers should be back aboard in one and three quarter hours after they attack. At which time we may begin to prepare them for a further mission. However I estimate that the convoy may be under heavy long range gunfire before our bombers can intervene."

Commodore Van Nassau, now addressed his senior officers, "very well gentlemen; now Commander Flyer, how would the strike play out if we launched the attack as soon as possible?" The Chief of Air Operations replied, "Commodore, in anticipation of these events I ordered all the required aircraft are on deck, fully armed and fuelled, they all can be launched in less than five minutes if their engines were warm, but it would do no good Sir. They would be over the convoy within two hours, most likely preventing any attack by sinking the raiders before they came within artillery range. The Fiat fighters had a 50 nautical mile range advantage over the Sea Hart bomber's which is 450. The bombers would now have about one hour of fuel remaining. If the strike group headed back to the *Schoonveldt* immediately after completing their attacks and have no fickle winds to contend with they could cover only 150 nautical miles. In the ensuing three hours the *Schoonveldt* would have been maintaining a flank speed of 29 knots directly towards the scene of action and as long as her machinery does not fail under such high steam pressure she would have covered roughly 85 to 90 nautical miles, and be 210 nautical miles or so from the battle. Of course Convoy X could make at least 40 nautical miles in our direction giving us a better chance, but as they may be maneuvering tactically we cannot count of their closing the range. The bombers having expended their fuel would be dropping into the sea some 60 miles short of the *Schoonveldt*, and the Fiats would get close enough for us to see them go into the drink."

The Commodore was not happy with this and his faced showed it, "Alright Commander Flyer, how does the attack play out if we launch in one hour?" The Commander who had prepared a variety of operational statistics to study answered; "If we launch in one hour sir, with the *Schoonveldt* having maintained flank speed, we would have advanced some 30 nautical miles, the convoy would be 270 miles distant, and the flight time would be reduced by 12 minutes but the planes would arrive over target 48 minutes later than if they were launched from three hundred miles. If after completing their attacks, the strike group headed back to their ship immediately the Sea Harts could fly for 180 nautical miles, and the Fiats for 230 nautical miles. The ship, still maintaining flank speed would have closed the distance to 188 miles from the scene of action. We would be able to recover the Fiats but again the bombers would start falling out of the sky. The convoy under that scenario would most likely be under attack for half an hour."

Commodore Van Nassau, was not pleased with this scenario either, and his face darkened with fury, and he turned away from his officers, to lean heavily on the chart table. He produced his cigarette tin and withdrew a *Bensson and Hedges* and lit it up, and paused to think. He knew that if he waited two hours, and launched his attack it would destroy the raiders for sure, but he would lose the valuable convoy. If he attacked now the convoy would be saved and he would destroy the raiders but he would lose his entire bomber group, which was arguably just as valuable as the convoy and its precious cargo. Neither situation was acceptable. He must delay the German attack on Convoy X, perhaps more radio transmission tricks may work. The Kapitein and the Commander Flyer, looked quietly at one another and waited on the decision of their superior officer.

The Commodore with a loud "HA", slapped his open palm loudly down on the chart over the estimated location of the German surface raiders. He motioned the Kapitein and the Commander Flyer over to the table. "Air Chief, launch the bomber attack at 250 miles from target, your recommended range, I will not sacrifice our air group, as they are of strategic value. I know Commodore Crijnssen very well; he clearly understands the situation and knows how to use his smoke floats to confuse the German gunnery. He will buy us the time that we need."

The Commodore then addressed the Kapitein; "this is what I want you to do Polder; broadcast a message to the convoy in the clear, so that the Germans can read it. Identify the source of the transmission as: *the battle-carrier, not the battleship-carrier Schoonveldt*; steaming to your position at full speed 250 hundred miles away and preparing to launch bombers to cover your convoy. Get the radio operator to dial down the power of the transmission to 18 Watts, do it now." After passing on this order, the Kapitein returned to his superior. He addressed Commodore Polyander "What are you thinking Sir?"

"I know these damn Nazis, Kapitein Polder, in fact a number of my cousins, nieces and nephews are of German origin, and some of them are real Nazis! Egomania, Kapitein is paramount in their so called; *new order*. These people constantly search for ways to demonstrate their superiority. The credit and laurels for victory in combat have always gone to their army, especially now when the Wehrmacht is kicking the schijt out of the French and British in France! What I am counting on is that; the Kapitans of those two surface raiders are egomaniacs and are desperate to grab a headline in the newspapers. I also believe that they are pursuing our ships at some 30 knots speed, and really burning fuel. I realize their ships have massive fuel oil tankage, but they will still be conscious of this high rate of consumption. They may conclude that it is unnecessary to maintain such a high speed if we help them. If they do that it could give us the thin slice of time that we need, for our air group to come within range."

"When they pick up our most recent transmission they at first will be startled, then they will evaluate it and may conclude that it was meant for them as well as for our convoy. By further studying the physical nature of the transmission, they will realize that our position is actually 300 nautical miles out from the Dutch convoy and not 250, and their communications specialist will be able to deduce that our signal was sent at the transmitting power of our old cruisers *Java* and *Sumatra*, who are equipped with ten year old and relatively weak 18 watt German radio sets. In 1937, the Brazilian Navy installed a powerful new 28 Watt Telefunken set in the *Rio de Janerio*. The Kreigsmarine is aware of this. I am gambling that the German Kapiteins will assume that our most recent transmission is composed of a series of deceptions. The first; being our distance away from the convoy, the second; from the power of the transmission they will determine that the transmission was from a cruiser's set. They may then conclude that the open identification of the ship in the transmission was a ruse as well. The Raider's Kapiteins may well conclude that the threat steaming towards them may very well be only a light cruiser; the *Java* or *Sumatra*. We know that they have cracked our naval code 6. The *USS Dixie* transmitted our bogus message on time. The Germans have had ample time to decode this. They may be led to falsely believe that the *Schoonveldt* is near the Hawaiian Islands, steaming on three shafts, and not a threat.

The German Commanders will get more comfortable with the whole game, and put the picture together. After further thought they will arrive at the scenario that I want them to: that a Dutch warship has badly missed its rendezvous point with the convoy. It is now racing south at its best speed to save it, but is still at least ten hours steaming away. The German Kapiteins will believe that the Dutch cruiser, by openly identifying itself as the *Schoonveldt,* see it's transmission as a inept ruse, one borne of panic and designed to make the raiders abandon their pursuit of the convoy and flee the certain destruction of the battleship-carrier's aircraft. Whether cruiser or battle-carrier they will realize that the Dutch ship is too far away to stop the destruction the convoy. The Commander of those Commerce Raiders will realize that he has ample time to kill the Dutch convoy and make an escape, and so will cut back from flank speed to save fuel, say 32 knots down to 23-25 knots, which is still plenty fast to intercept the target, and dispose of them. If he does this, as I think he will, it will give us enough time to close the range and launch an air attack, and still be close enough to recover our planes after the action."

Kapitein Polder's eyes began to sparkle and he replied, "It is good Commodore, it is good trick! In the meantime they will still steam north at a reduced speed to save fuel but fast enough to bag our convoy. We steam south at flank speed, a combined closing speed of almost one nautical mile per minute, and in less than two hours," smiling broadly he slammed his right fist into his left palm with a loud meaty smack.

In fact this is exactly what happened. Kapitan Von Essen ordered his observation plane that was engaged in circling the Dutch convoy to head north and scout out the source of the Dutch transmission. But the pilot of that plane reported that he would soon have to return to the *Gull* as he was running low on fuel. Kapitan Heinrich Schultz of the *Pelican* ordered that the floatplane from his ship be catapulted to confirm the nature of the Dutch ships located some 350 nautical miles to the north. The German Commanders discussed the situation by radio through their coding machines and concluded that the *Schoonveldt* was still underway to the Dutch East Indies steaming on only three shafts. Therefore the source of the transmission was the *Java* or *Sumatra*. It having failed to locate the convoy was attempting a rather shabby and ill-conceived bluff to scare off the raiders. As the Dutch cruisers had no speed advantage over the German raiders, there was no need to maintain the chase at 30 knots and waste precious fuel. If they cut back to 25 knots they would still come up to the Dutch convoy within two hours and be within gun range half an hour after that. The raiders would destroy the convoy and would disappear into the vastness of the Pacific. The drama would be completed, while the Dutch cruiser speeding to the rescue would still be at least five or six hours steaming behind them. So it was that both the raider's masters; Kapitan Felix Von Essen of the *Gull* and Kapitan Heinrich Schultz of the *Pelican* chose to cut their speed of advance back to 25 knots. It was a choice that sealed their doom.

June 22nd, at approximately 11:08hrs, the *Schoonveldt* having covered a further 58 nautical miles launched her strike group at a range of some 242 nautical miles from the estimated position of the German raiders, it consisting of 22 Hawker Sea Hart bombers of Bomber Squadrons 7 under the command of Lt. ter Zee 1e Klasse (Lt. Commander) Hernrik Bosscher, and 7 Fiat Cr. 42 Falcon Fighters of flight A of Fleet Reserve Perak Naval Air Station, under the command of Lt. ter Zee 1e Klasse (Lt. Commander) Ernst Fijenoord. If the German raiders had fallen for the deception and had continuing their pursuit of the Dutch convoy they would be sighted within the hour, and the enemy under Arial attack a half hour later!

Somewhat later, at approximately 11:10hrs, lookouts aboard the German raider *Gull* reported the sighting of smoke dead ahead, and the masts and upper-works of five ships soon poked up over the horizon. By 11:40hrs the Dutch ships were clearly visible to the Germans with the aid of a good set of binoculars. Kapitan von Essen stepped out onto the port side bridge wing and asked the rangefinder operator to call out the range. The range is now 36,000 meters Herr Kapitan, was his reply. The German raiders enjoyed a 10 knot speed advantage over their quarry and in less than an hour they would be coming within range of the deck guns.

At approximately 10:15 hours, the Pelican's Arado float plane pilot was flying at an elevation of 1000 meters and scanning the blue sea ahead of him for any sign of the enemy light cruisers. The sun which usually heats the interior of an enclosed cockpit very quickly, results in most pilots flying with it open. But the pilot was having an urge for a cigarette and he was thinking of lighting up one of the precious American *Chesterfields* tucked inside his jacket. But the wind whipping around the interior of the compartment would ruin the experience, and the wonderful tobacco burnt off too quickly and be wasted. He slid the canopy shut, reached for his packet and lit one up. He briefly put his mind at rest and scribbled some notes his logbook and entered a time. Had he not stolen these few moments and looked above he just may have seen the faint images of the 29 plane strike group from the *Schoonveldt* which was passing over him at an elevation of 4,000 meters.

June 22nd, at 12:20hrs, both Kapitans; Von Essen and Shultz ordered their ships to be cleared for action. The crew members raced around the concealed guns positions, collapsing the false deckhouse sides, and deck cargo crating. Up went the German Naval Ensign and the artillery was cleared away and elevated in preparation for its first ranging shot. The sailors carrying the long brass cased shells formed a line at each gun, awaiting the commencement of action. Kap. Von Essen remarked to his executive officer Joachim Wirtz, "The Dutch convoy has not scattered, but chooses to fight. Its Commander has played a very foolish game, and will now lose everything!" Lt. Commander Wirtz was one of the men rescued from the sea after the action. He later admitted to some feelings of unease with the Dutch Commander's display of bravado. He asked of his Kapitein; "Sir, why have the Dutch ships not scattered, we see a hopeless situation for them, why do they not see the same thing, do they know something that we do not?" The deafening crash of high explosive bombs, was his answer.

Aboard the *S.S. Tjikarang*, all eyes had been focused astern for close to an hour, ever since the two huge enemy surface raiders had crept up over the horizon. Each of the convoy's much smaller ships were armed with a single 5.9 inch naval gun mounted aft on a reinforced deckhouse platform, a location which dictated that the ship's limited combat tactics were based on the *stern chase*. The artillery mounted on the five ships of Convoy X, were taken from the old German dreadnought *Posen*, which had been scrapped in Rotterdam, upon the conclusion of the Great War. They were good weapons but their range was inferior to the lighter but more modern artillery that was aboard the German raiders. A lookout then reported that one of the raiders had fired a gun. Commodore Crijnssen signaled to all ships; *Form up line ahead on Vlaggeschip, light up two smoke floats and deploy.* These devices were released over stern and the ship maneuvered to keep the floats between them and the German raiders. The Commodore then ordered his a transmission at full wattage; Convoy X under attack, by two German raiders, give our position, and course due north at 16 knots.

The smoke float defensive weapon is very useful to confuse the gunnery of the attacking vessel during the classic '*two ship stern chase*' scenario. However it is practically useless to a single ship or a convoy of ships if they are attacked from their opposing flanks by several vessels. To clear the smoke interference for his gunners the German Kapitans decided to envelope their quarry and take them under enfilading fire, starting with their flanks and transiting to broadside fire as the faster German ships came abreast of their victims. Accordingly the *Gull* moved off to port and the *Pelican* to starboard in a Y formation to place the convoy in its crux. The maneuver would delay their cannonade somewhat but it would get his gunner clear of the interference form the Dutchman's smoke floats and ensure greater accuracy. Then the bombardment began in earnest from 21,000 meters.

Tall geysers of water began to sprout around the Dutch convoy as the German shells exploded in the sea. Commodore Crijnssen, signaled all ships to open fire. But the rounds of their return fire fell 2000 meters short. Nevertheless the Dutch ships began to weave to port then starboard in a practiced zigzag pattern to throw off the accuracy of the German guns, they were going to make it difficult for the enemy and buy some time. The Commodore responding to a sighting from one of the lookouts, raised his binoculars high into the sky and began sweeping the heavens suddenly his fixed on something and his scowl transformed into a broad grin.

June 22nd 12:23hrs, the *Schoonveldt's* strike group had arrived over the battle area at an elevation of 5,000 meters. Below them the five ships of Convoy X could be seen maneuvering, shells splashes surrounding them. Harrying them from both flanks were the two large liners firing into them. Flight A and B of Bomber Squadron 7 were flying in the typical left-hand right-hand echelon formation forming a broad V pattern with the flight leader's aircraft at the center. After viewing the situation playing out below; Lt. ter Zee 1e Klasse Hernrik Bosscher, at the head of flight A looked to his right and into the face of Lt. ter Zee 2e Klasse (Lieutenant) Benjamin Werkspoor, commander of the 11 bombers of Flight B; which were all tough experienced Chief Petty Officers. Bosscher raised his fist and then pointed with his index finger down to the raider to starboard, Lt. Werkspoor saluted and then looking over his right shoulder he spun his index finger to all the pilots in his flight which meant *follow me* then he dove straight down and began angling towards his target the *M.V. Pelican*. The maneuver was soon repeated as Flight A as Lt. Comm. Bosscher dove down onto the *M.V. Gull*.

At 12:20hrs, the pilot of the *Pelican's* Arado floatplane had just passed through a bank of clouds into the clear sky and began searching the sea once again. Below him, he was stunned to observe less half a mile away, the Dutch Battleship-aircraft carrier steaming SSE at high speed! He grabbed his throat mike and talked hastily to his radioman observer sitting behind him manning the tail gun. Otto! Otto! Transmit; aircraft carrier and give the position, but before he could complete his instructions he heard his crewmember swear and his machine gun start to clatter. Bullets started to rip into his machine from above as a full flight of Sea Fury fighters opened up on the Arado. The alert combat air patrol of the *Schoonveldt*, had pounced upon him immediately and soon two parachutes were drifting on the breeze. The German airmen now *swinging on the silk* watched in shock as their flaming Arado plummet steeply downward while several of the silver colored streamlined bi-plane fighters that had followed her down kept up a brisk fire until she crashed into the sea.

June 22nd, 12:25hrs, Kapitein Shultz of the *Pelican* had closed the range to 18,000 meters and his gunnery was beginning to have an effect. Already he had observed two hits on the closest ship and she was afire amidships, trailing a long black cloud of smoke. He would have liked to close the range further but the convoy's guns were of a heavy caliber, although fortunately of shorter range than his artillery. The Dutch commanders had acted very foolishly, if they had scattered several hours ago, they may have saved half of the convoy, now it was hopeless for them. Soon these obstinate Dutchmen must come to their senses, realize that successful resistance was futile, and then heave to and strike their colors for surrender.

He was studying the Dutch vessels through his binoculars when he was handed a sheet of paper, by the intelligence officer; "the Arado Sir, has sent this the single letter S..." Wass is loss? He turned to look at the man when there was a frightfully loud crash, and he and all around him were knocked off their feet. "Wass" he said; staggering up, just as his ship shook to her keel plates from another deafening crash! There followed a terrific detonation in the sea to port just by the hull tossing up a huge column of water that collapsed upon his head and all those manning the open bridge position. The heavy wet canvass awning practically smothered him as he fought clear, to the open sky. The great ship shook with explosions. "How could they hit us at this range?" he exclaimed as he staggered to his feet.

A biplane aircraft zoomed low over his stricken vessel, he looked four miles to port where the *Raider M.V. Gull* was afire and surrounded by immensely tall bomb splashes, while from overhead more biplane bombers dove out of the sky attacking both ships. Machine gun bullets ripped up the teak decks and the crew members of the Flak battery lay bleeding around the shattered guns, great fires roared from out of the shredded steel superstructure as more bombs slammed into the German raiders, both now heavily afire and with speed dropping.

Aboard the Vlaggeschip *SS Tjikarang* and the other four ships of the convoy; the crews were wildly ecstatic. Death it seemed had given them a reprieve. Commodore Crijnssen, smiling wickedly now, addressed his Kapitein and said; "Well now Polder, it looks like fortune has turned for us, you are an old navy man are you not as are all my Kapiteins?" Yes Sir, was Kpt. Polders reply. "Then Kapitein" Commodore Crijnssen said, "the enemy cannot work their guns in such a conflagration, signal all ships to *maintain line of battle* on the *Tjikarang*, haul around and follow me. When the bombers depart we are going to shell those Nazi bastards, to ensure that they sink. We'll give them *a taste of it* from their own German built guns!"

After half an hour of intense shelling, the Dutch convoy abandoned the effort. Each of the five ships had pumped more than thirty round into both enemy vessels at 1000 meters range. They watched as the *Pellican,* an inferno from stem to stern dipped her bows and dove under the surface of the sea amidst a great gush of steam and an upheaval of huge air bubbles as those of her remaining intact watertight compartments now collapsed from the water pressure. The *Gull* had listed heavily to port ten minutes before the *Pellican's* final plunge and now she turned turtle; completely extinguishing the raging inferno that had been pouring out of every sidelight, hatchway and rent in her steel plating. The smoke pall drifted slowly off.

At 13:15hrs, Commodore Crijnssen ordered the convoy to heave to and lower their lifeboats away to pick up any survivors. To the north, the Dutch battle-carrier continued on her course for the rendezvous, but at the more economical speed of 25 knots. Her bomber group was credited with seven direct hits on the *Gull* and eight on the *Pelican*, with the remaining bombs falling into the sea close aboard, splitting open their hulls, just as a effectively as would a torpedo. The combat air patrol of the battle-carrier having accounted for one Arado float plane, while the Fiat CR 42 fighter escort accounted for the other.

Commodore Crijnssen recovered eighty three German seamen out of a total of about six or seven hundred aboard. He asked these prisoners if there were any allied captives aboard the raiders. He was very pleased to learn that only one week before seventy three captives had been put into two captured lifeboats, and when last seen were rowing for the Chilean coast some fifteen miles away.

The Commodore then ordered a message transmitted in the clear: German raiders *MV Gull* and *MV Pelican* had been sunk. June 22, 1940 13:30 hrs. Eighty three survivors in captivity. Then the ships of Convoy X reformed and steam towards their rendezvous. Five hours later the lookout up in the foremast crow's nest of the *Tjikarang*, reported the siting of a tall heavily built tripod mast of a big warship poking over the horizon to the north west off the port bow. Soon the upper works of the *Schoonveldt* were identified. Convoy X was safe, the voyage to the Dutch East Indies would continue without further concern for enemy armed merchant cruisers.

In the afternoon of July 19, 1940 the Battleship-carrier *Schoonveldt* and the five ships of the vital Convoy X dropped anchor in *East Channel*, just off the commercial ship basin at Soerabaja to great adulation. Their exploits having brought a much needed victory to boost the low morale of the colony and nation, disheartened by the evacuation of the British Expeditionary Force from Dunkirk, followed in short order by the collapse of the French army last month. Precious Netherlands now lay prostrate under the jack-boot of the Nazi military regime, with the armies of her main allies; France defeated in the field, and Great Britain driven from the Continent!

The Royal Netherlands Navy in the East Indies now had three battle-carriers on strength. Ten days before her arrival, the escorts assigned to the *Schoonveldt*; two light cruisers, four destroyers and the fleet oiler *Marokko* had arrived in Soerabaja after a dangerous three month voyage around the horn of Africa!

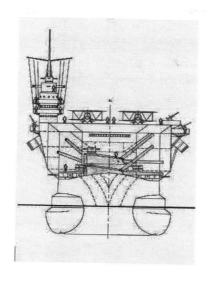

CHAPTER XXI

WAR COMES TO SOUTH EAST ASIA

By November 1941 the Imperial Japanese Army was in its fifth year of war with China. Last September it had completed the occupation of French Indo China, now twelve new military airfields, and twenty two large garrisons were in place in that occupied territory. As the Colonial Governments of England, the Netherlands, and the United States were on a perpetual state of High Alert, the region had become a time bomb with the seconds ticking rsapidly away towards detonation.

Consequently during the last two weeks of November, all branches of the military of Great Britain, the Americans and the Dutch had begun to intensify their patrol activities of the sea lanes surrounding their strategic regions. These were Burma to New Guinea and from Java to the Philippians. These air efforts were in addition to the regular long range patrols of some twenty two KMN submarines. These O-boats (Onderzee) ranged over a vast expanses of water from the Bay of Bengal and the eastern regions of the Indian Ocean to the west Pacific, beyond Australia and New Guinea to north of the Kamchatka Peninsula.

The most useful aircraft that the Dutch Forces employed for air reconnaissance missions were the Hudson light bomber, the Catalina and Dornier flying boats. These machines were well suited to this task as they were primarily quite modern, had a long range, were comfortable as that they isolated the crew within the fuselage, they were well equipped in every respect and had many hours of operational life remaining on their airframes and engines.

The Fairy Swordfish Mk I was also heavily employed in this role and possessed all the aforementioned features with the exception of crew comfort; she was an open cockpit design which tended to wear down pilots quite rapidly as they were subjected to the dehydrating effects of being exposed to the elements.

The reconnaissance flights of the three Colonial powers; all observed an increase in the number and types of merchant ships concentrating in proximity to their territorial waters. These were present in numbers that were disproportionate to the regular trading activities that were recorded for these regions. As there was no overall increase in the tonnage of cargos being handled, there was no logical economic justification for that number of ships to be operating within our zones of interest. At least four hundred fishing boats and pearling schooners were classified as *not engaged in normal activities.* Many tramp steamers were also identified as *new to our waters.*

The common evaluations at the time shared by the intelligence services of the Regional powers held that the majority of these vessels were Japanese merchantmen flying false colors and engaged in covert intelligence gathering for their military. Their nocturnal activities included; updating nautical charts to show which islands held sources of fresh water, conducting soundings of water depths, the preparing of detailed tide and current data and the locating of the best beaches on which to land troops and heavy equipment.

None of this activity could be construed as normal to vessels engaged in legitimate trade. A merchant ship does not usually drift idly, day after day. A fleet manager would dismiss any sea captain that took such a slack attitude towards the profitability of his ship. The existence of a merchant ship's viability depended on the delivery of cargo from port A to port B and back again as rapidly and as often as possible.

Our customs cutters and naval patrol boats would check out any vessel in our waters that we felt was exhibiting unusual behaviour. Using the pretext of looking for smuggled goods we would board any ship and check its cargo. But no contraband could be found. If a ship was anchored due to engine problems, then that was legitimate. If her cargo manifest was found to suit the cargo, and with her clearance forms in hand, then all was in order. But there were hundreds of new craft now in Dutch waters, effectively saturating the the ability of our men to effectively stay ahead of the influx.

Our earlier assumptions seemed to be correct, as these vessels behaved as if under Military command, perhaps carrying the troops and war equipment of Nippon. Soon these convoys were joined by torpedo boats whereupon these wide flung formations shaped new courses towards the bays along the coasts of Korea or straight east into the open Pacific. Still others; identified as large modern naval transports, arrived from the Sea of Japan then turned south to join the aforementioned vessels to assemble in the harbours and estuaries of the now occupied territory of French Indo China. The harbours of Hai Phong, Da Nang, Qui Nhon and Camran Bay soon held large concentrations of Japanese ships.

Our agents from OVZ (naval intelligence) at these locations, had observed that during the evening of December 5, 1941 these ships began to be repainted in dull olive green with light yellow mottling; the standard *Admiralty Type 3 disruptive pattern: coastal*, of the Imperial Japanese Navy!

The KMN maintained a substantial force of submarines on Far East station and had employed them with great cunning and professionalism to create an extensive chain of undersea pickets engaged in a strictly non-confrontational monitoring of all shipping. During the day our undersea boats floated in deep waters at periscope depths. A great many observations taken at this time were through this instrument. When the curtain of night fell, the undersea boats rose to the surface to engage their ship's diesel engines and made a run into the open sea to recharge the battery banks that supplied the power for the submerged propulsion system.

The night surface operations were greatly appreciated by the submarine crews who had been shut up all day in the stifling heat created by the tepid tropical waters. By sundown the stale air and body odours within the small cramped hulls had usually brought the crew to a high state of agitated claustrophobia. The men looked forward to the moment when the electric fresh air blowers would be switched on with an almost frantic anticipation. Once engaged this equipment rapidly forced fresh sea air throughout the hull and to the oxygen starved lungs within, instantly returning the crew to a functioning level of civility, and mental relief.

The submarines continued their observations throughout the night by scanning the poorly lit harbours for shipping through the use of high power light gathering binoculars and our very top secret *Naachtzicht Apparaat* (Night-sight Apparatus) or *NA Viewers*. This last mentioned optical equipment allowed us to see shapes using their heat radiation generated red band of the spectrum even in the darkest of conditions.

These devices were originally developed in 1936 by a Russian engineer working for the American company RCA, and were marketed for commercial use as *Black-Light Viewers*. But this venture was unsuccessful for the company. Our *Naval Science Branch* however immediately recognized its potential. The KMN soon purchased a *licence to build* from RCA. The KMN engineers refined the device, making it more compact, waterproof, more robust, powerful and easily manageable when mounted on a specially designed steel bulwark bracket.

NA Transmitters, on the other hand were a very simple affair. Our regular Morse Lamps were modified with an alloy steel sheet that slid in from the side of the casing in front of the lamp. The alloy was the same as a stove top element; highly resistant to electrical current. The sheet would remain a dull black while radiating 130° C. At night with the naked eye nothing was visible. But through the *NA Viewers* this alloy stood out like a beacon. The signalman would locate the other vessel at night with his viewer, and send his message by merely operating the shutter the same way as if he were sending a lamp signal using visible light. Twenty years of refinement later, this technology was very common, and known as *infra-red*.

By the end of November 1941, those of our submarines which had been monitoring the maritime activity along the coast of the occupied French Colony, had carried out their duties without any close scrutiny or interruption from Japanese long range air patrols. Now this situation changed dramatically. Our submerged O-boats were being constantly over flown by Japanese flying boats operating at such a low level that the noise from the big *Kawanishi's* four powerful engines would penetrate the small depths of water over the sub and vibrate through the hull plating with an ever increasing volume. The sound had a severe impact on the mental state of those submarine crews who were tasked with maintaining a fixed observation area. We came to appreciate this later in the war as our navy men likened the effect to the unnerving wail of the German Luftwaffe's infamous Stuka dive bomber that civilians and soldiers experienced in the European Theater of Operations (ETO).

The Japanese pilots had begun sending our submariners a strong message with each pass over flight; "we are here, we see you and your an easy target." Indeed, the first indication of war that a submariner may experience could be a deadly airborne egg.

Relief from this stress to the crew only came when the U-boot could slip into the gloom of the depths or the obscuring cloak of night.

For those readers who are not familiar with the sea and all things nautical; the airmen in those days did not have to rely entirely on locating submerged boats by spotting the tiny periscope poking up through the vast surface of the ocean, nor did they have the wide array of sophisticated instruments that are available today. The development of a *simple sea sense* was part of their indoctrination.

Submarines operating at periscope depth have only some ten meters of water over their weather deck. A pilot looking straight down from above can see the submarine as clearly as if he were looking through a sheet of glass, for the waters in that part of the world are very clear. The pilot, flying some distance away however may be drawn to the submarine's location by noticing the behaviour of the waves as they pass over the submerged conning tower only a few meters below the surface. Depending on their height, the disturbed waves may tumble and break like surf over a sunken rock or reef. On an otherwise unmarked ocean a sudden splash of white foam may attract unwanted attention to alert eyes aloft. Pilots engaged in sub-hunting were always on the lookout for concentrations of seabirds, especially over those waters that were known to be deep. The submerged hulls attract schools of small fish, these in turn attracted gulls and other diving birds. Many of these men had employed these same skills while serving in the Japanese fishery engaged in the hunting of whale or schools of tuna, where the quarry was often spotted from aircraft.

Our agents operating within the Japanese occupied *Protectorate* of French Indo China had discovered in mid-1941 that the airfield at *Long Xuyan City* was under-going a major expansion with many revetments under construction and an extended concrete airstrip suitable for large cargo aircraft and heavy bombers. New airfields although less grand were being built at the cities of *My Tho* and *Can Tho* and were close to completion. These last two locations had much shorter airstrips than those at *Long Xuyan* and were of compacted material. These characteristics suggested that small planes; machines having a high power to weight ratio were to be accommodated. Our assessment of course suggested these to be fighters.

On December 6th, our Submarine K.XIX monitoring activity at *Hai Phong Harbour* reported that the past two hours there was a tremendous amount of clanking and banging noises and the swishing sounds of many propellers were carried by the water throughout the hull of their boat. All craft in the harbour it seemed were getting underway. The boat surfaced at 23:00hrs and transmitted that the anchorage which had been filled with an estimated 100 Japanese warships and merchant steamers at sundown, was now completely empty! The naval intelligence network was able to calculate that perhaps as many as three or four large Japanese military convoys were now underway in the South China Sea, having all departed from French Indo China, with their destination(s) suspected, but as yet unconfirmed.

As I recall as late as December 06, 1941 our intelligence network became aware of the first indications of what proved to be war casualties. A handful of merchant vessels operating in the South China Sea were declared overdue having never arrived at their expected destinations, although the weather was unusually fine, and no seismic activity had been recorded.

Piratical activity; a common peacetime culprit in such occurrences and always an ever present danger in the western Pacific region; seemed to have mysteriously vanished. To us this was a harbinger of a looming cataclysm. Much as birds vanish from the sky and instinctively take to shrubbery just before the heavens release their most violent storms, the pirates with their extremely extensive and thorough network of criminal agents, were entirely aware of the Japanese military activity.

Over the course of Saturday December 6th, there developed a premonition of looming danger. Many of my men that day shared a common experience, a sense of extreme oddness, like being off-balance. Unusual incidents were being reported to our police, Coast guard, and Air control centers. These were evaluated and forwarded to my Command center aboard the *Cornelis de Witt*. Several of our Inter-Island telephone cables were out. There were a number of Customs cutters, fishing vessels and yachts that had vanished, and six private aircraft over the Sulu Archipelago, and the Celebes Sea, were reported overdue by that evening.

Our sense of foreboding deepened, when later that same day the U.S. Navy reported that a Catalina flying boat based out of NAS Manila was missing, while a RAF Lockheed Hudson based at Jesselton Airfield in the British Protectorate of Sabah; had not reported in and could not be raised on the radio.

All of these flights had vanished without having time for the transmission of the standard aircraft emergency; *Mayday*. Most of these unfortunate machines it was calculated had been approaching the extreme range of their routes when they had vanished.

In anticipation of hostilities breaking out at any moment; my ships had been hurriedly made ready for sea, and bunkered on December 5th from Dutch Navy oilers while we rode at our mooring buoys in Keppel Harbour, just south of the Malaysian Capital City of Singapore.

Thank God for small blessings; we felt fortunate indeed that these ominous developments had not transpired a week earlier, as the both battlecruiser-carriers had only recently come off the Royal Navy's massive King Alexander floating dry-dock. It was a strategic target as it was the only friendly facility in the entire Far East Theater capable of lifting our great battle-carriers out of the water. The dock had been constructed to handle the next generation of the RN's largest battle-cruisers, and giant passenger liners of up to 75,000 tons displacement!

While *in the King Alexander* both battle-carriers had their hulls scraped clean of seaweed and barnacles, the zincs had all been renewed, after which a new coating of anti-fouling paint had been applied to the prepared steel. Now, with the hulls smooth and clean and the boilers and turbines in top form the great ships should be able to really stretch their legs, 31 even 32 knots being theoretically possible.

Immediately upon refloating each battlecruiser-carrier, all hands turned out as we hastily *stored ship*, taking aboard further supplies to achieve a full deep load of consumables. Both vessels loaded a record quantity of medical supplies, food stuffs, dry consumables, anti-aircraft munitions, ship and aircraft spare parts plus additional crews from the RNLN replenishment vessel *Arnhem* then in attendance to my fleet.

Upon completing the stores transfer the *Arnhem* hurriedly departed on December 05, '41 for the relative security of the city of *Tanjon Priok* on the Island of Java, under the escort of two modern powerful gunboats of the *Florez* type. The *Arnhem,* was a highly valuable target, as she carried a great quantity of the fleet's replacement parts. But with such an escort in attendance, she theoretically enjoyed the equivalent protection, of a light cruiser as she faced the trials of the coming months.

These *Florez Klass,* vessels were rated as mere gun boats, although each was fitted with three modern 150mm guns. This made them much more powerful and hard hitting than any ships of even twice their displacement, and ensured that they would deliver a very nasty surprise for any ship that took them under fire.

16:00 Hrs December 06, 1941, my Battle-carrier division and its escorts closed up ship in preparation for getting underway. (Appendix A) Fifteen minutes later we had dropped our moorings, and departed Singapore. I ordered revolutions on four shafts to be run up for 8 knots, and our long line of ships formed up into single line ahead and headed southeast leaving the city and the protection of the massive artillery of the fortress behind in our wakes.

Deftly we negotiated our way through the congested waters. The many freighters and cargo-liners that we passed represented the shipping lines of a multitude of nations, including those of Japan. The latter I had no doubt, carried a supercargo of disguised military agents who recorded our every move.

My Battle-carrier squadron steamed slowly down Singapore Strait and approached Binlang Island to port, where the congestion of shipping eased. Once in more open waters the fleet increased to 15 knots, and adjusted course that would take us east of the Tambelon Islands by early morning.

Our direction was designed to give false information to the many Japanese spies at Singapore, who would report our ship's to be heading eastward into the Java Sea. The fleet would however, turn sharply north before sunrise, and transmit a short signal which would result in more fighter aircraft dispatched to our battle-carriers, in preparation for a *bold sweep* into the South China Sea. Consequently the airfields and naval air stations on Borneo were moved to Alert 2 status.

While we were underway from Singapore on a similar run six weeks earlier, I had experienced a singularly profound moment. One which I have never forgotten, and still am able to recall quite clearly. Its vividness has not diminished even after the passing of more than forty five years!

As we approached the Anabbas Islands, laying just off our port bow, the dawn dissipated a light sea mist and there was soon clearly revealed an immense mat of small fishing craft all loosely rafted together on the calm glass-like sea. Aboard these, toiled many hundreds of native Malaysians and Chinese all laboriously engaged in hauling up huge seine nets a backbreaking activity best undertaken in the cool of the night.

My huge flagship which loomed up rapidly had obviously interrupted their activities, the spectacle no doubt providing a welcome excuse to rest from their heavy labours. As if of one mind all seemed to pause, light up cigarettes and watch silently as our handsome ships, one by one materialized, as if by magic from out of the white vapours to sweep majestically past them, in what must have been a grand spectacle.

The blank expressions evident on their faces, which I could see clearly in my powerful binoculars, was disturbing and unfathomable. In all those men there were none that seemed impressed by our huge weapons, none that waved or cheered us on. They stood like mahogany statues, their only movement being to steady themselves as the waves generated by our swift passage violently undulated the great carpet of their small craft.

The experience gave me a very queer feeling, an odd sense of invisibility, of disembodiment and a brief flash of ridiculous insulted vanity, at this point a sprawling vision then came into my mind's eye;

A great mass of hook horned Bison rolled across the grasslands of the American West like summer thunder, causing the earth to tremble and jump under the pounding of half a million tons of flesh and bone. The shock of their hooves impact on the dry sun-baked earth shook clouds of white clay dust from their shaggy hides and humps.

Nearby and immobile on its ribbon of polished steel and hissing with impatient fury, like some huge Chinese dragon; crouched a gigantic green painted iron locomotive that had been halted in its crossing of the sea of grass by this tidal wave of flesh. Through the swirling dust, and from the crowded windows of the passenger coaches shone the white faces of fresh new immigrant farmers. They stared with frozen expressions as the sea of giant wild eyed shaggy beasts; with their long tongues hanging rumbled past in numbers that could not be imagined unless observed with one's own eyes.

After these many years I believe that I understood the hidden meaning of that unusual recollection, one that my conscious mind on that morning had been aware of but was as yet unprepared to reflect upon: *Asia stood and watched as 'Old Europe' swept past to make its grand exit from the stage. In a defiant flourish of immaculate steel ships and proud flags; 'European Colonialism' was preparing to deliver the final scene in the closing act of a long running performance entitled; Empire!*

A powerful premonition now momentarily seized me, one that I fought to shake free: *I was taking almost 7,600 fellow servicemen into a dangerous confrontation, and for many their doom.* The methodical calculations of my brain however soon overcame these animal instincts.

My orders from KMN Hoofdkwartiers, Batavia directed me that day to conduct an *anti-piracy probe* into the South China Sea. Of course, it was expected to be anything but. Some unknown widespread activity was underway within the region, so Naval Command in Batavia decided it was time carry out a reconnaissance in force while on Alert Level 2. They would *send in* a powerful battle squadron with eyes open, guns cocked and all flags flying to *display the deterrent*. My air groups would fly off and fan out as far north as the coastline of French Indo China, and as far east as the Palawan Island. These aircraft would monitor and report any unusual traffic, both ship and air.

I was quite sure that all aboard from the youngest rating to the COS all felt that this probe was anything but routine. Our collective guts gurgled and bubbled as they were twisted into tight knots by the sense of foreboding. Brigade–General (Commodore) Peiter Berleburg, the fleet Chief Surgeon remarked that our pharmacy during the last day had prescribed large quantities of ant-acid pills and anti-diarrheic, which were noticeably depleted. At the same time cigarette sales at the ship's canteen had doubled. Modern medicine and the stalwart calmness of the old chief petty officers had a most beneficial effect on the crew at this time.

The battle-fleet was designated as *Task Force Popeye* for this exercise. *TF Popeye* would proceed up the central South China Sea paralleling the northern coastline of the big island of Borneo in the region of the then Kingdom of Sarawak. In 1841 the stalwart

British adventurer; Sir James Brooke, with a handful of men and his little cannon armed sloop took on the pirates of the area and having defeated them founded a private trading Kingdom, and set himself up as the hereditary monarch.

The battle-carrier aircraft would scout out to 150 miles from the fleet. The area of coverage was a great arc of 270°, from our six o'clock to three o'clock. *TF Popeye* would proceed up the center of the South China Sea under this umbrella, as far east as the Spratley Island group; then under Japanese occupation. At which point it would turn southeast towards the north tip of Borneo, pass through the Balabac Strait, and enter the Sulu Sea. Once there we would affect a rendezvous in the vicinity of the Sulu Archipelago with the other RNLN fleet at sea at that time; *Task Force Olive* and combine. The entire force would then operate as one unit under my command, being the three star Admiraal.

Our battlecruiser-carrier's fighter outfit in peace time, was one fighter squadron made up of a 21 machines. By 1941 however; during that period of increased political tension, any cruise that we undertook north of Borneo or east of New Guinea we added two flights of extra fighters to each ship, as a precautionary measure. (See Appendix C)

Therefore at 07:00hrs December 7, 1941 one flight of seven Sea Fury Mk II fighters and one six-plane flight of Brewster F2A fighters which had departed from the civilian airstrip at Sambass City, Borneo landed aboard the *Johan de Witt*. These were soon augmented by an additional two six-plane flights of Brewster F2A fighters, (Buffalos) which had flown in from the RAF airfield at the city of Sarawak; the British Protectorate. These machines touched down on the *Cornelis's* deck at about 08:00hrs on the same day.

For the common sailor who lives in a world of repetitive monotonous routine activity; bouts of speculative musings with shipmates are much anticipated. To the more experienced hands; the arrival of the extra machines aboard was an ominous development. They knew from our training exercises that the arrival of these extra machines whose function was the replacement of aircraft casualties was an unusual measure, one indicative of a heightened alert and possibly even of a fleet action. The men were certainly eager enough. Moral was very high throughout all ships of the Task Force.

I now felt considerably more comfortable with this powerful reinforcement of fighters aboard, especially the 18 high speed, well-armed and completely modern F2A Buffalos. *Task Force Popeye* was now at 160% fighter strength. I then retrieved the little yellow tin box of Panther cigars (an anonymous gift from a fellow shipmate) and lit up one of the diminutive dark cheroots. The smoke was mild and satisfying, and it was with a sense of vigour and anticipation that I decided to take a turn about my ship.

I left the interior of the air operations deckhouse and climbed up the companionway to deck 07. The top of the deckhouse was one of my favourite vantage points. I could get from this elevated platform a clear view of the entire length of the warship. The whole expanse of the more than 7000 square meters of flight deck had become a mighty mechanism of intermeshed activity.

Several hundreds of straw hat bedecked crews were going about their duties with an obvious professionalism immediately evident to any observer. Aircraft landing crews checked the deployment of the hydraulic aircraft arrestor gear, several damage control parties, dressed in bulky heat gear examined the firefighting monitors and added spare coiled hoses to each of the armoured boxes. A group of marine engineers were up on the flight deck, keeping out of the way, and enjoying the deck activity while seemingly involved with a pressure test on the integrity on one of the inert gas lines that were employed to flood the armored aviation fuel manifolds, an effective aid in fire suppression.

The 40 mm anti-aircraft batteries were all fully manned. Their crews packed into the confines of the circular gun tubs came to refer to each other as sardines, and their tub as *the can*. All looked uncomfortable; dressed as they were with blue steel helmets, bulky cork floatation vests and with all their exposed flesh smeared with a thick layer of white anti-flash cream which gave them a modicum of burn protection.

Many of these gunners looked with envy upon the flight deck crew, who were not so encumbered. They wore no helmet but a cool wide brimmed straw hat, no floatation vest, just a colored cotton shirt that labelled their flight deck duties. The flight deck crews were generally free to move about and get in some legwork and enjoy the cooling breezes of the propeller wash from the aircraft.

The well drilled Flak gun crews, white rags in hand, oiled their weapons, spun them horizontally through 360 degrees, elevated their long black barrels and practised battery concentration or checked their ammunition canisters. The gunner's eagerness, posture and morale exhibited the utmost confidence in their ship's massive defensive high angle batteries that could hurl the incredible total of 5520 explosive cannon shells per minute towards any attacking aircraft or half of that toward a motor torpedo boat formation.

Located on the small platform in front of the AA rangefinder tower No. 1, and just aft of the bridge I observed a fire control officer with a range table in one fist talking into his headset as he scanned the skies. *'Eyes to the skies,'* everywhere that I turned, lookouts with binoculars or the little hand held *ping pong paddles* holding a transparent yellow plastic sheet, swept the sky from horizon to horizon searching for any aircraft. I was very glad to see that there were no slackers.

Looking forward I was unable to make out the tops of A & B heavy gun turrets as these lay far below flight deck level. 'C' turret located as it was completely under the forward flight deck was also similarly obscured. All six of the big guns were under director control. Undoubtedly the chief of gunnery; Kapitein Lt. ter Zee Van Riper was exercising the gun turret's efficient mechanisms, in anticipation of action.

Glancing up and back over my right shoulder I noticed that the big 7.6 meter stereoscopic range-finder was scanning the horizon. All seemed proper and correct. I stamped out the Panther's stub as I scanned the heavens. Hum, it was time for a *Balkan Sobranie*, a real smoke, a prayer and a little luck, anything to ease the gnawing feeling growing in my guts. Just as in the old days hunting pirates at night aboard the torpedo boat; I could feel the enemy close by, and sense the approach of an unseen danger.

My two "heavies" now had aboard; four fighter squadrons (and a flight of Sea Fury Fighters that were scheduled for departure) and six dive bomber squadrons totalling over 160 aircraft (Appendix C). Launching and retrieval would now get quite hectic as the normally expansive flight decks were getting rather busy.

On the flight deck aft and outboard were stowed the three flights of extra fighters, Sea Fury machines to port with the Buffalos parked to starboard. I could make out the Grumman aircrews of Fighter Squadron 2 mustering in front of the wide red engine cowlings of their stubby machines. Their squadron leader Lt. Commander Keppler conversed with the newly arrived aircrew and had introduced them to the men of Fighter Squadron 2.

Striding briskly aft down the wooden flight deck to greet the new arrivals, with his white tropical uniform whipping in the wind I observed the lean frame and familiar gait of the Air Group Commander of all the *Cornelis de Witt's* fighter squadrons the redoubtable; Hoof Officier Vlieger Konrad Van Halsen.

The new members of his warbirds, like all young men seemed awkwardly eager and excited to see action, a characteristic distinct to the uninitiated. I could easily make out their broad grins and white teeth shining in their young tanned faces from 100 meters distance, all seemed to be supremely happy to be aboard the big battlecruiser-carriers, and at sea.

Surveying the ocean from this vantage point I could see that our fleet made a brave spectacle. The Dutch navy like the Italian; documented their naval battles on film. I turned to my adjutant and ordered the photo-intelligence units of the cruisers and battle-carriers to get some of their film crews on deck to begin documenting the Fleet at sea this day of high alert.

The two huge 40,000 tonne battlecruiser-carriers, in company with the four De Ruyter Class 7,500 tonne light cruisers (ships of the very latest design), and with eight modern destroyers in escort cut steadily through the sea. All sparkled wetly in their dazzling tropical white livery; spanking along smartly at high speed. The royal blue waters of the South China Sea boiling at their sterns was piled high, the waters along their sides flecked with whitecaps, and steep white topped combers stood out from ships bows. The protesting sea roared at being flung so insolently aside, then as it passed down the ship's tall steel sides it was reduced to the soft hissing of sea foam.

I loosened the strap over my cap's visor and adjusted it up under my chin. On impulse I looked over my shoulder and up at the tall white painted steel tripod mast. I watched for a moment as the wind from our high speed passage caused the signal flags to snap with a sound like multiple pistol shots, the bright colors set against the blue sky, my three star Admiraal's pennant whipping at the mast head, and below it a spanking new national *tricolours* streamed out majestically and filled me with a deep sense completion. I am here. This is the reality for which I have worked toward my whole life. This is no dream! Only a sailor would truly appreciate that private moment, the mixed feelings of dread, awesome responsibility, worry and excitement. It was all so very clean and brave looking, a vista offered to us all so that we may fully appreciate the value of existence and the beauty of life as we confronted our own mortality.

War; the monster that sleeps, tucked away in the primitive corner of men's souls had not yet been released from its slumber. Soon; its cage door would be forced open, and it would stride forth: a colossal cyborg formed from millions of tonnes of skillfully worked metals, and by the elemental hatred and fear of hundreds of millions of souls. The gigantic military machine would spread its great arms, and with a span that girdled a planet, it would reach out towards us with its clawed misshapen paws. *War* would soon take my lovely ships into its rude grasp. Its powerful fingers of searing chemical fury would scorch their hulls and maul the steel. They would tear open and twist the armour plate to atomize the soft, delicate beings within!

More than 7,600 brave men 'stood to duty and answered the bugle call' that day to present our nation with the extraordinary gift of their lives, some very young. They represented a national treasure beyond value and one that I was tasked to expend; as I alone saw fit in the service of the nation and Crown. If we were to face the massive military power of Imperial Japan in the days to come; on this most merciless of chessboards; the sea, I must not waste even one. The heavy responsibility of this command, often imagined was now at hand. Far heavier than twenty years before as a junior officer, with the aide of my friend Lt. Hawk RN, we took fifty men armed with cutlasses and pistols and boarded the war junk *Green Dragon* of the infamous Chinese pirate *Hong Shou* (Red Hands). I was young and the fright was submerged quickly once action was joined. But now, with our Nation's future in peril, and with all its hopes riding today at sea, I felt the responsibility weighing heavily upon me. I shook myself vigorously as a dog might to rid its fur of water.

A meter above my head and just a few meters beyond my reach three slightly odd looking gulls hovered effortlessly as they rode the wind currents and matched the ship's velocity precisely. I could see their bright yellow eyes catch my glance, and they continued to study me, showing a particular interest in the brightly polished buttons on my cap and white tropical tunic. Did they just look at me with anticipation, or was that a figment of my imagination? Gulls; I thought; how they just love sailors; especially those who bob stiffly up and down; a floating feast; eyeless and uncomplaining; as the little wavelets sparkle beautifully.

Some faint tendrils delicately brushed my thoughts. I turned to stare once again with a renewed interest at the three sea birds hovering on the air currents only a few feet away, and easily keeping pace with the ship. These creatures seemed to be closely scrutinizing me. No, no, it could not be, I thought; not after all these years and the thousands of miles? The three old gulls did look rather out of place, and although the *Larus gull* is common worldwide, these were definitely of the Icelandic variety. Good heavens! Could these be the *Chancellor and his two pals* from the Tillerman Hotel in Den Helder?

Those familiar characters whose relentless squabbling had become an inseparable memory of my early morning walks to the naval base. They could easily have followed the ship I speculated. Then at sunset, they could rest in some secluded corner on our artificial steel cliffs. The good Lord knows there was enough seagull crap aboard at any time! An easy life for them with all our galley trash and the many small fish brought to the surface of the sea, laying white belly up, stunned by the incessant churning of the four great propellers of the battle-carrier.

"Ho Chancellor;" I spoke to them in fun; "do you remember the *Tillerman Hotel,* the *Tillerman?*" At the repetition of a word that they must have heard repeated thousands of time, when waiting on the slate roof of the hotel, a loud squawking instantaneously erupted from all three that sounded terribly familiar. Perhaps they associated that word with unlimited table scraps. The *Larus Gull* does enjoy a long life; three to four decades is not uncommon. Well I'll be dammed I said to myself with a smile, if these gulls are the *bloody Chancellor and his boys* that would be incredible!

Task Force Olive was centered on the battleship-carrier *Schoonfeldt.* Two light cruisers of the Tromp Class and a destroyer force completed her escort (see Appendix B). *Olive* was currently making a cruise north eastwards through the Molucca Sea under the command of Schout-bij-Nact (Rear Admiraal) Baron Johan Van den Kerckhoven-Polyander. He was one of the remaining few die hard, and occasionally still vocal; 'big gun' advocates remaining amongst the senior officers in our navy. More than a few officers tended to accept that his connection to the Royal House ensured him the command of a battleship carrier under Admiraal Van de Velde, while still remaining outspoken on the subject. Those who believed this an example of an unwarranted command, then did not know our most senior Admiraal. The Baron, a man of unreserved opinion on the matter, would never have survived long under Van de Velde unless he was an extraordinary seaman. I always felt that he secretly nursed the romantic hope to bring the heavy artillery of his battleship-carrier against an enemy in a classic gun action. A nagging suspicion that always left me a little uneasy about this particular officer.

All serving line officers in the RNLN must clearly accept that the battle-carrier's flight deck and aircraft raised the vessel to one of strategic value, a resource that could not be compromised with a gun action. Only after all our aircraft had been used up and any hope of their replacement evaporated would the flight deck cease to be of value. Only at that time I would write off all flight operations and use the ship's artillery as the primary weapon and seek surface action.

Perhaps I misjudged the man, for he seemed to willingly embrace my tactics during our fleet exercises which emphasized the flight deck as the only offensive weapon, the big guns being regulated to defensive actions only as a last resort.

Admiraal Van den Kerckhovenm-Polyander, commanding Task Force Olive; was conducting a similar *official pirate sweeping operation* as I had underway; that of monitoring shipping to the east in the Banda, Molucca and Celebes Seas and as far eastward as the American island of Mindanao. *Task Force Olive* would transit those waters to a point some 30 miles from the western shore of that big island, cruise through the Moro Gulf for half a day then shape course to the west pass through Basilan Strait and enter the Sulu Sea in the evening to affect a concentration with *Task Force Popeye*. At which time I would feel the great comfort of a fleet concentration that would give me some 200 aircraft of which almost half were fighters.

Upon entering the Moro Gulf and while closing the southwest coast of Mindanao, Admirraal de Leeuw could expect his battle group to be scouted by a friendly squadron of diminutive Boeing P-26A *Peashooters* from the 67th Pursuit Squadron of the Philippine Army Air Corps (PAAC). This fighter unit being on temporary redeployment since November 1941 to Davao airfield, located in the southern extremities of the Philippine Archipelago. The (PAAC) re-deployment was one of General McArthur's chess-piece responses to the unusual shipping activity found in waters that the USN considered vital to the national security of the Island Group. The American forces, also under a *training alert*, would be *up and looking* and were anticipating the arrival of the KMN Task Force Olive into their defensive perimeter.

Under the allied fleet agreement following *Operation Bulwark*, Great Britain, France, America and the Netherlands coordinated their military maneuvers for training purposes and alerts. The PAAC had been selected by General Dwight McAllister USAAC to provide temporary fighter support to the KMN, should it find itself engaged against the Imperial Japanese Navy (IJN) within those waters being of vital interest to the U.S.

The PAAC's little *Peashooters* would on this occasion form up with the (CAP) fighters of the battle-carrier *Schoonveldt* and carry out a series of joint tactical operations, with the *Peashooters* playing the role of a marauding squadron of IJN carrier fighters, which they looked very much like when viewed from most angles. The P-26A fighters were similar in performance to most of our machines; a mid-1930's design, only half a decade old but already out of date, a bit too slow and lightly armed. It would be foolish to discount them however as with their short wings they could easily top more than 600 kph in a diving attack, a velocity which was more than adequate to catch most types of Japanese bomber aircraft that we may encounter.

In addition to the strengths of the little fighter, the pilots of the PAAC were known to be highly skilled with their well-used little machines and completely fearless; which any combat veteran will readily admit is a very powerful combination.

By 16:00hrs December 7, 1941; Task Force Popeye was well into the South China Sea, with the Natuna Island Group laying some seventy miles to starboard when I received notification from Naval Headquarters in Batavia that Singapore had reported, two more small ships were overdue and several civilian commercial planes had vanished during the night despite the excellence of the weather. These occurrences being a repeat of the previous day's events could no longer be viewed as anything other than hostile incidents, and precursors to war. Consequently the British Commander for the Far East Theatre at Singapore; Admiral Sir Geoffrey Hollister had issued an alert to: *Standby for Matador.* A code that put all commonwealth forces on the highest alert short of war. He had concluded that an attack by Japan was imminent.

The Royal Navy; *Force X* had departed Singapore for a probe deep into the Gulf of Siam earlier that morning to officially conduct a *pirate interdiction* exercise. But in reality it was to investigate an observation by a pilot of British Oriental Airways Flight 9 on its Singapore to Hong Kong route, of unusual concentrations of vessels in the gulf. These were substantiated with a similar report from the Pan Pacific China Clipper only an hour later.

By late November '41 Great Britain had still not reinforced her fleet on *China Station* to the minimum levels as identified as in the *Fleet Exercise Bulwark.* The current situation did not represent a policy change on the part of the British naval strategy, but was rather an indication of the severe strain that the war had put on the resources of the Royal Navy. That great warship; *H.M.S. Hood* a vessel of international fame had been sunk that spring with great loss of life. She had been committed as flagship for the RN Pacific Fleet under *Bulwark,* but no longer existed. Due to more pressing operational commitments; the two new fleet carriers also committed under Bulwark, had not arrived in South East Asia.

The Royal Navy viewed the Singapore Fortress as impregnable and its naval dockyard strategic to the region, and not to be abandoned. The Royal Navy's forces in the East Asiatic Theatre had been reinforced by one new Battleship *H.M.S. Prince of Wales* and the older battle-cruiser *H.M.S. Repulse.* Make no mistake; as it then stood these two capital ships formed a very powerful unit by themselves and were supported, in theory by a RAF fighter umbrella of several squadrons. They constituted a powerful force in the area, albeit tactical in nature.

Standby for Matador, put our forces on high alert. Orders were issued to concentrate all our battle-carrier units as quickly as possible within the inland seas of the Dutch East Indies. A move that gave us the benefit from the protective ring of our airfields in case the balloon went up. While the Royal Australian Navy with those ships of New Zealand seemed to engage in small cruises out of Port Darwin. Both of these positions were rooted in political expediency and not military necessity. The US Pacific Fleet in response to *Standby for Matador*, ordered its aircraft carriers at Pearl, to sea with a heavy cruiser escort.

The combined nation fleet exercise: *Bulwark* had revealed that the minimum regional requirements for satisfactory deterrent against Japan was a large multinational naval force permanently based within the region and built around a balanced core of fleet carriers and fast battleships. The British had committed to this plan three fast battleships and two fleet carriers. A contribution recognized in 1939 by the Royal Navy as the absolute minimum to deter the mighty *Rengo Kantai*. The Americans and the Netherlands had agreed to transfer to the South Pacific ten and two capital ships respectively, and by 1941 had done so, with the US Pacific Fleet moved from San Francisco to the Hawaiian Islands, and the Dutch providing three capital ships.

Both the US Navy and the RNLN now felt deep concern for the security of South East Asia. The shortfall of three aircraft carriers left the Royal Navy at Singapore without an air canopy. France had been eliminated as an ally, and her navy neutralized. These were very serious deficiencies. The Regional Defence Plan had called for a large Naval Air Arm of 500 aircraft having the variable strike capability that can be had when operating from five flight decks at the same time. Regional security now rested heavily upon the three flight decks and 200 mostly obsolete aircraft of the Royal Netherlands Navy.

Perhaps the fact that *H.M.A.S. Australia* (a WW1 era 13.5 inch battlecruiser that had been converted from coal to oil in 1934) was now operational again after the re-tubing of her boilers and on station at Port Darwin allowed the British Admiralty to assume that sufficient forces were in the region. The U.S. Pacific Fleet having only recently re-deployed forward from San Francisco to the Hawaiian Islands undoubtedly contributed to an overly optimistic sense of security.

Her presence should have been considered only as a bonus that in no way alleviated Great Britain from her commitment to the region. Australia was not a party to the 1939 West Pacific Naval Agreement (WPNA) signed following the conclusion of *Fleet Exercise Bulwark* in late August of that year. There was no doubt that both Australia and New Zealand would become new partners in 1942 as the WPNA was designed to be revaluated every three years.

The KMN had with the addition of the battleship-carrier *Schoonveldt*, exceeded its contribution to WPNA with a third capital ship. She gave us the option of building an additional task force around her and making the operation of all seaborne aircraft that much more flexible with three decks rather than two. Our small nation, with this latest acquisition, had I say with pride, committed 150% to the mutual defence plans for the region.

The British High Command's attitude towards our acquiring a third hybrid capital ship was to some extent mystifying for such a respected service. They seemed to totally discount the vessel as entirely worthless; a view not held by the senior officers of the U.S. Navy who recognized the value of this type of warship, especially as a convoy escort. For the British this was a strange attitude indeed as *Schoonveldt's* hybrid design was originally the product of the highly acclaimed British shipbuilding industry!

This ship; the smallest of our battle-carriers at 34,000 tonnes, although well armoured (see Appendix B) could not stand for too long in a toe to toe artillery duel with any of the big gunned ships that Japan had in commission in 1941. Even with one of its smaller units, such as a *Kongo* class battleship had twice her firepower. This was a consequence not so much as a lack of heavy armour, but more due to the large un-armored spaces, of her cavernous aircraft hangars and wooden flight deck.

Yet her aircraft more than tipped the scales in favour of the Dutch warship. *Schoonveldt's* air group of 41 machines (plus 10 housed under canvas on deck in time of war) contained 20 to 25 light bombers each with a capacity of one 220 kilogram bomb, with the ship's magazines holding thirty of these plus sixty 110 kg bombs for each plane.

These weapons would allow her to sink the very largest and most powerful of Nippon's battleships. Furthermore she was able to do so at a distance of 300 kilometres from her 'big-gun' adversary with complete impunity.

No pair of the largest cruisers of the *Rengo Kantai* would dare approach her and attempt a surface attack, except with the greatest of caution. Even if she was bereft of her air group, she was after all a capital ship with comparatively thick armor, and massive gun power. Her broadside; now reduced to six 305 mm guns down from the original fourteen and the sixteen 152mm guns which had all been fully modernized with rebuilt mountings to allow for increased elevation. Coupled to these was the most modern of fire control systems. These modifications greatly increased the accuracy of these weapons while doubling their range. The combined broadside weight of 3000 kilograms was still very respectable, about equal to that of three Japanese heavy cruisers!

Of great importance to us was the timeliness of the acquisition and also the good value for the Dutch Crown. Ordinary sailor's, petty officer's and commissioned officers of her crew, alike noted that all her operations went very smoothly indeed; a characteristic which indicated to me that she was a well-balanced design with reliable equipment. Well drilled crews with smoothly operating weapons and systems are characteristics of older warships, ones that is too often discounted when comparing the capability of a mature ship with that of a new one.

Perhaps this noticeable frosty attitude displayed by the British regarding this vessel was rooted in politics, as suggested to me by one of our correspondents after the war. This seemed to make the most sense to me as none of the RN officer's to my knowledge had ever disparaged the ship. Many in fact liked her. With her big tripod mast and outsize fighting top she still looked, from all angles every bit a ship of the Royal Navy.

The U.S. Navy took note of our increased strength in the region and at some point, the Americans seemed to view the RNLN as the *senior partner* within the region. This shift in attitude was not without reason as the RNLN could operate a battle-group having at its core, a highly mobile naval air group of 200 plus carrier aircraft and 18 heavy guns on three capital ships. The Royal Navy on the other hand, by Nov. '41 had only 16 heavy guns between two capital ships, available to meet the needs of the Far East theatre. The RAN Flagship the battlecruiser *HMS Australia*, with its cruisers and destroyers, were viewed by the Americans as separate navy and were therefore not to be automatically included in the roster as part of the British contribution to the security of South East Asia Region.

I could however understand the Royal Navy's frustration. They had been carrying the lion's portion of the war against the two well-equipped Fascist navies, largely by themselves. The Royal Navy was desperately short of ships, and the three big capital ships of the RNLN were after all ex-Royal Navy. It must have been galling to the hard pressed seamen of Great Britain, in light of their mounting losses; that neither of the peace time Governments had managed to fund enough new vessels during the 1920's and 30's, or been able to refurbish and retain some of the Royal Navy's finest vessels.

The heavy losses sustained to date and the disastrous end of the French fleet at Mers El Kebir, had left the Royal Navy decidedly short of the capital ships necessary to pursue the war. The Netherlands in those dark days; had no time to waste with these concerns, nor interest whatsoever in what we saw as *sour grapes*. She had made the bold gamble to invest in a revitalized navy, and was now only focused on effective cooperation and survival.

Last November, the Royal Navy put forward their plan for the defense of the South China Sea in case of Japanese aggression. It had two components, the first designated *Clean-Sweep* would clear enemy shipping from the South China Sea, preparatory to *London Bridge*, an amphibious landing by a Free French Colonial Army to reoccupy Cochin China.

The operation was designed to deprive the Japanese of the major source of rice for their troops, and to re-supply rice to the half-starved Chinese Nationalist troops fighting the Japanese in their homeland.

The RNLN considered this a typical military operation which we would expect from the British for the following reasons. It offered a scenario that would with the re-occupation of Cochin China; utilize French troops in the jungle fighting. It placed the sea between their colony of Malaya and the proposed battle zone. Finally it would redirect Japanese focus from British territory further eastward to French Indo China. Britain wanted to seize the initiative and her strategists created a scenario in which her greatest strength; her navy stood between her colony and the land battle. In this way Great Britain's greatest weapon could be used to its best advantage.

To support the *London Bridge* operation, the Dutch battle fleet was to become the 'right hand' component of *Clean-Sweep,* and emerge from the *interior seas* of the East Indies and proceed west and north to probe for any Japanese convoys moving south along the northern Coast of French Indo China. The Royal Navy would simultaneously race up the coast of Malaya and destroy any hostile forces found within the Gulf of Siam. The RN battle squadron would then swing eastward and race up the South China Sea catching any remaining Japanese shipping between our two forces and annihilate them, thereby completing operation *Clean-Sweep*. However when originally conceived the RN fleet had contained two fleet carriers, the 'left hand' of *Clean-Sweep*. As the RN aircraft carriers were not in theater, too much of a burden would fall on the shoulders of the Royal Netherlands Navy.

Operation London Bridge, one of several joint offensive ideas proposed by the British, was one that departed radically from our more conservative KMN strategy. Our ideas centered on the more realistic scenario of defending against Japan's opening moves until reinforcements arrived, from American and Great Britain.

Under our defensive strategy we planned for the worst case scenario; which assumed that the Netherlands East Indies would find itself having to rely entirely on its own resources in the event of Japan striking south in an attack against the East Indies. A scenario where the American response to Japanese aggression in the West Pacific was delayed and Britain's response anaemic due to further attrition of her arms in the European theatre.

According to our naval theorists the Japanese Admiralty must consider the RNLN's recently acquired battle-carrier force as the primary strategic threat to any military operations due to their power and mobility. Our obvious fortress strategy allowed for the ring of airfields on our islands to act as the first line of defence to blunt all air attacks directed towards our warships. Within this *protected zone* our battle-carriers presented the enemy with a powerful but elusive foe, as it was able to manoeuvre on the east-west axis for 3000 kilometres, for 2000 kilometres on the north-south axis, and to strike against, or protect any target within a zone of 9,000,000 square kilometers!

The RNLN wanted to fight from this defensive posture, as it gave the major fleet units the best chance to survive the initial assaults while denying our oil and rubber reserves to the enemy. Whereupon the arrival of the U.S. Pacific Fleet to the Philippines and the warships of the Royal Navy's *Flying Squadron* which would provide for a massive naval and air reinforcement of its forces at Singapore. Only once all these fleets were combined; could we then even consider some joint fleet operations and take the offensive against the mighty *Rengo Kantai*.

Our intelligence section analysing Japanese radio traffic determined that elements of several fighter squadrons had begun to arrive in Cochin China at the new airfields at My Tho. These units were later identified as the *123rd Hikosentai*, of the *22nd Hikodan* of the Japanese Army Air Force (JAAF) 6th Air Army, having on strength at least forty Nakajima Ki-27 monoplane fighters. These were late model all aluminum machines which enjoyed great manoeuvrability despite their fixed landing gear. In addition to the fighters; two bomber air fleets had also been detached from the Japanese Manchurian Army for redeployment in early Nov.'41.

The bomber fleets were later identified by our Vietnamese agents as the JAAF *121st Hikosentai* newly arrived at Da Nang and the JAAF *73rd Hikosentai* deployed to Saigon. Both air fleets were equipped with Mitsubishi G3M twin engine monoplane bombers! This latest intelligence information was sobering as it meant the arrival of at least 100 long range bombers in this sector alone, machines of an advanced design having both high speed and great range! These were further supported by the fighters of the *124th Hikosentai*, also of the *22nd Air Brigade*, based at Na Drang, in French Indo China.

I had available aboard to counter these forces; 42 Grumman F2F & F3F biplane fighters, 14 Sea Fury Mk II biplane fighters and 18 Brewster F2A monoplane fighters. To these I could add 56 Curtiss Model 77 Helldivers also biplanes, which when operating without bombs proved quite capable of acting as second class fighters, adequately armed for the day with a single nose mounted 0.50 Cal mg, and a dorsal .306 Cal. mg.

There was sufficient force available to form *Fightercloud*. But only the 18 Brewster fighters had the speed to catch those twin engine Japanese bombers! If, after all these aircraft that I have mentioned were committed to act as fighter defence, the Task force could still launch 28 PZL P-23 Sea Eagles capable of carrying a total of 84 - 250 kilogram bombs on a single anti-shipping mission. The fleet therefore still retained a powerful offensive capability even under heavy air attack.

I notified all naval air squadrons at Tarakan airfield that they were now under my command which at that time consisted of Torpedo Squadron I, having on strength 20 Fairey Swordfish Mk I bombers. I also requested that the Army's high speed Heavy Fighter Group III with 30 Fokker G machines, be put on Standby alert. Their airfield was located at Tarakan Airbase on the north eastern extremity of the Island of Borneo which was well positioned to provide support as we steamed northeast towards Balabat Strait. I assigned Torpedo Squadron I to undertake a long range sweep of the South China Sea west of Palawan Island. The details I left up to their squadron commanders to work out.

I ordered that our combat air patrol be increased from seven Sea Fury Mk II fighters per flight deck with an additional flight of six Brewster F2A fighters. My Air Operations officer Commander Konrad Van Braekel coordinated with his opposite aboard the *Johan de Witt* regarding which squadrons would be utilized and in what order.

I further requested that all shore-based replacement aircraft for the fleet be put on short notice with the first echelon placed on standby to shuttle their machines to my ships when called for through our secret transit airfields near Sintang and Mamehak both of which lay deep within the interior of vast and trackless jungle wilderness of Borneo.

The Mitsubishi G3M twin engine multi-role bomber was able to drop bombs from either high altitude or attack at low altitude with both bombs and torpedoes. I knew from fleet exercises with our fairly modern Glenn Martin bombers that the use of high altitude bombing against a fast moving fleet with sea room to manoeuvre was largely ineffective. To really get hits on my warships the Mitsubishi bombers had to come in at low altitude and in order to set up a torpedo attack; fly for a time in a straight line.

All my biplane fighters and even the Curtis Helldivers would then be able to execute diving attacks against these bombers utilizing the gravity assist which would add at least 140 kph extra speed to their machines. More than enough I was sure to catch them and with luck; shoot them down. Diving attacks were at best a one or two shot deal, for climbing back up to attack altitude would consume 3 to 5 minutes, during which my fighters were most vulnerable and practically useless in defence. The enemy however would capitalize on this weakness in the fleet's defensive umbrella and press home their attacks with the utmost vigour.

The powerful defensive rearward firing automatic cannon of these Japanese bombers and their fighter escort would greatly complicate our fighter's task. However our preparations were reasonable and the defensive aircraft numerous and well drilled. So I felt with some confidence that our *Fightercloud* tactic would see us through the early stages of an air/sea battle.

17:00hrs, December 07, 1941, I gathered together my chief of staff Kapitein Derik Van Klaffens and the ship's Commander Kapitein Daniel Voorne and gave them my plan for the remainder of the day. I ordered *Task Force Popeye* to alter course and steam until 21:00hrs in *zig-zag Pattern A* at 25 knots. This method of steaming was developed to greatly complicate any attempt by a submarine to get into a suitable position for launching its torpedoes against warships.

The Combat Air Patrol was to be maintained at double strength. Two extra machines were added to the usual anti-submarine patrol. The strength was to be maintained until darkness terminated these operations.

When reaching Lat. 6 deg. N & Long. 107 deg., 30 min E which I marked with an X on the chart the Task Force was to alter course to the NE and steam for 12 hours again heading directly to the Spratly Islands (under Japanese occupation).

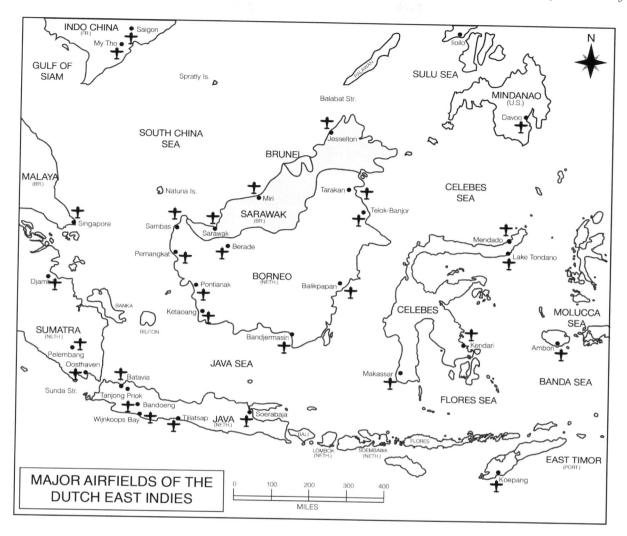

MAJOR AIRFIELDS OF THE DUTCH EAST INDIES

TF Popeye would then alter course and sail due east for the entrance to *Balabat Straat*, at 20 knots on *zig-zag Pattern A*, with the fleet passing north of British Sabah and into the Sulu Sea. An intense effort was to be made to locate, identify and determine the base courses for any type of ship and aircraft that may be encountered.

The ship's Executive Officer; Kapitein Lt. ter Zee (Commander) Linus de Kroone had assigned a battery of junior officers at the 'ship recognition station' to break out all the commercial shipping registers and naval handbooks from the ships intelligence library to aid in this effort. These books with which all sea captains are familiar contain a summation of the engineering and performance data for the world's shipping as well as a useful compendium of ship silhouettes, artist's sketches and photographs.

I then retired to my day cabin to finish work on several new damaged stability conditions for the big flagship, a task which took me into the evening, after which I sought the comfort of my bed, where I shortly surrendered to sleep with a sense that the Task Force was prepared.

231

Monday, 04:00hrs December 08, 1941. I was awakened by the harsh ringing of my telephone; which was mounted conveniently on the bulkhead bracket just adjacent to my pillow. I answered it, and the ship's commander; Kapitein Voorne tensely informed me that we had just received a Priority Class 1 message from Admiraal Van de Velde at Naval Headquarters in Batavia. It was addressed to all RNLN forces at Sea and logged in at 03:55hrs, December 08, 1941. The simple message repeated; 'Kingdom, Kingdom, Kingdom.'

Although I had expected such a development at any time, given the increasing frequency of the unusual occurrences, the shock of such news to my still sleep-dulled senses came as a stinging slap to the side of my face. Japan was on the move, somewhere in the vastness of the Pacific and Indian Oceans her forces were in action against the Netherlands or one of our allied nations. War with Japan had begun!

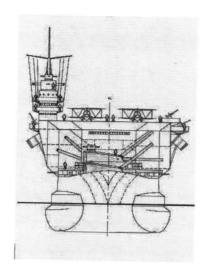

CHAPTER XXII

THE OPENING MOVES – DECEMBER 8, 1941

Upon receipt of this priority message from Batavia I ordered the flagship's Kapitein Voorne to bring the fleet to war alert, and tell the Chief of Staff (COS) to have his men assembled in the command center within five minutes. All ship to ship fleet communications were to be limited to our *Night-sight* equipment until dawn. I dressed hurriedly to the sounds of the bugle blaring through the ship's audio system calling the men to action. I collected my pocket items, my cigarette case and my code book. Before leaving my cabin I took a selfish moment and slipped over my head and under my shirt the pendant with the little gold locket that my Karen gave to me so many years ago under the towering natural columns and cathedral vaults formed by the tall trunks and long overlapping green fronds of the palm oil trees on our plantation. I then picked up the framed family photo from the corner of my desk, removed it from the frame, rolled it into a tube so as not to crease the finish and carefully put into my left breast pocket, taken last spring, while on leave it captured a very good day. It had been a blessed time and through the glass for these past months, my happy family smiled back at me.

I entered the Fleet Command Center (FCC), a 15x15 meter compartment enclosed by 76 mm of Krupp steel armor, equipped with two gas tight armored doors, and without natural illumination. My staff and senior ship's officers were all present and came to attention. The white painted compartment was filled to capacity; pale tense alert faces stared stonily in my direction. There was complete silence, with just the clicking of the ventilation unit to disturb it.

Kapt. Voorne handed me a sheaf of messages, "a Priority 1 communication for you Sir from Batavia, it has been confirmed authentic." I removed my notebook from my breast pocket and flipped to a page containing my personal codes. The first message was very short and to the point, its lack of detail seemed to enhance its powerful message and I studied it with complete intensity, then raising my voice I read it aloud:

0355 HRS DECEMBER 8, 1941.

KONINKRIJK! KONINKRIJK! KONINKRIJK!
OM ALLE SCHEPEN OP ZEE: DIT IS EEN OORLOG WAARSCHUWING!

EEN KORTE TIJD GELENDEN DE JAPANESE MARINE AANGEVALLEN U.S.
PACIFIC DE VLOOT IN PEARL HARBOUR, IN DE HAWAIAANSE EILANDEN.

DAAROM, IS NEDERLAND NU IN OORLOG MET DE JAPANNERS RIJK!

Vloot Admiraal A.K. Van de Velde
Koninklijke Marine Hoofdkwartier Batavia (KMHB)

0355 HRS DECEMBER 8, 1941.

KINGDOM! KINGDOM! KINGDOM!

TO ALL SHIPS AT SEA: THIS IS A WAR WARNING!

A SHORT TIME AGO THE JAPANESE NAVY ATTACKED THE U.S. PACIFIC FLEET AT
PEARL HARBOUR, IN THE HAWAIAN ISLANDS.

CONSEQUENTLY, THE NETHERLANDS IS AT WAR WITH THE JAPANESE EMPIRE!

Fleet Admiraal A.K. Van de Velde
RNLN Fleet Headquarters Batavia

"Well there it is gentlemen. War has come. I took a few moments to collect my thoughts, while the entire task force staff observed me in seemingly breathless silence. Noting the lack of activity within the compartment, I announced to the room over my left shoulder; "see to your duties men," and was immediately rewarded with an outburst of noisy activity. I told them to relax, and poured myself a black coffee. I strode over to the tactical table to consult the master chart of the South China Sea on which was marked our course track through the night and the latest known position of all merchant ships or vessels of war.

I glanced over to the aviation plot screen and studied its constantly changing status. The display was modeled on what we had observed during our technical mission to the *U.S.S. Lexington* some years back and was intended as a quick visual aid to locate all ships and aircraft within the fleet battle zone.

The simple but effective design consisted simply of a large clear sheet of shatter proof Plexiglas mounted vertically from the deck head in a steel frame. At its center was a black arrow representing the location of my Vlaggeschip and its heading, over it was a blue arrow representing wind direction and both were fixed with a common shaft allowing them to rotate. Radiating outward from the center was a series of lines etched into the plastic, looking much like the spokes on a wheel, each indicating five degrees of azimuth. North was always at the top and our ships heading was indicated by the black arrow. A series of circles ringed the center, also etched into the plastic. Each of these was set at 50 mile intervals out to 400 nautical miles.

Two petty officers, a telegraphist and a rangefinder-operator, outfitted with headsets constantly updated the aviation plot with colored luminescent phosphor/grease pencils, marking on the locations of ships and aircraft according to the latest data fed to them by the Air Operations Command Center. Any ship or aircraft information that was transmitted to us or we discovered within 400 nautical miles of the Battle-carrier were marked on the screen with a nomenclature which indicated bearing, course, speed and whether the objects were warships, merchant vessels, bombers, fighters, commercial aircraft and their identity. Mounted below the Plexiglas was a grey steel console that contained various bridge instrument repeaters, six headset jacks and a drawing instrument tray.

When compared to the technical standards of late twentieth century it was very basic, however it worked quite well, and required little maintenance as it had few moving parts. The few essential ingredients to its usefulness, were a continual flow of accurate data and complete dedication from the young ratings that served the plot.

I noted the location of the individual aircraft; four RAF Swordfish on reconnaissance missions out of Jesselton Sarawak flying on, radio direction fixing instruments (RDF). There was no fleet Combat Air Patrol (CAP) up as it was night, and there was no training scheduled for night air operations; although this quite possible, as all aircraft were equipped with landing lights and parachute flares to illuminate targets on the water. The flight decks of each battle-carrier, had landing lights along its full length for use at night. But to use them in a combat situation was considered too risky and against operating procedure.

One of the Ensigns tasked with updating the screen was studying a bulletin board in his hand as he marked onto the Plexiglas in green phosphorescent grease pencil the location of two large formations of ships of the Imperial Japanese Navy to our north; off the coast of French Indo-China on a southwest heading! I asked the Air Operations officer for his report on this startling development!

Van Braekel delivered his latest theater data, confirmed by submarine. An RAF Fairy Swordfish patrol out of Jesselton, had been searching along the coastline of the Japanese occupied French Indo China when they discovered at dusk two separate groups of Japanese ships sailing without lights. As of nightfall; 21:00hrs December 07'41 these were located at Lat. 11 deg. N. & Long. 110 deg. 15 min. E. of Greenwich, course SW, speed 12 knots. The first convoy consisted of some 26 troop ships, 17 destroyers and 2 battleships of the *Settsu* Class, the latter were subsequently confirmed as the *Kamamoto*, and the *Kagoshima*). The second group of ships was a naval escort for the convoy, which was located some 30 nautical miles further out to sea and steaming parallel to the first. The escort force contained one light carrier, 4 heavy cruisers and 12 destroyers, course SW, speed 17 knots!

The information was electrifying! I exhaled a cloud of blue smoke and looked with some intensity at my senior officers, studying their faces closely for a long moment.

Sunrise was 1-1/2 hours away and my ships were only an estimated 250 nautical miles from a Japanese Naval Task Force and a large invasion convoy!

Addressing my Chief of Staff C.O.S. Kapitein Van Klaffens; I ordered that this information be transmitted to all ship's immediately using the *Night-sight* apparatus, adding that it was my intention to attack these enemy concentrations as soon as possible. I further enquired of him as to why we had not been informed of this much earlier by our air patrols or submarine pickets.

He then related to me that; the Swordfish torpedo plane which had made contact late in evening of December 07, 1941, had been attacked by carrier fighters, and had its radio set damaged, with the remaining two planes of the section being destroyed. However the pilot of the surviving machine had fortunately escaped into a cloud bank just as dusk fell. The radio tech-observer-gunner had been unable to repair the set aboard the plane, requiring them to return to *Jesselton* before he could deliver his report. The distance of some 600 miles, being a rather long flight for such a slow machine as the Swordfish.

I had been informed immediately upon its receipt, and since then we had confirmed the ships as two Japanese military convoys, as he pointed towards the message log with his pencil. As for our submarine picket lines; they had not reported these vessels at sea even though they had been positioned to cover all possible approaches. Our efforts to contact our O-boots in those regions continued, but had so far been met with only the occasional *clipped* message; otherwise an ominous silence had descended over them.

I turned to the Vlaggeschip's commander Kapitein Voorne, and I asked him the status of the Task Force. He informed me that; upon receiving the fateful message from naval headquarters, had alerted the fleet, prior to calling me. Both battlecruiser-carriers, at this time have been alerted to prepare air strikes. Turning to my *Air Ops*; who preempting my request for details, handed me his clipboard to study and told me that he had, in anticipation of my wishes; ordered multiple air strikes to be prepared against both of the Japanese convoys at first light. The position of the enemy convoys had been estimated from their last known location course and speed observed seven hours earlier. The process of arming and preparing the designated aircraft is on standby and could be given the green light at your order. Two submarines in the area have been alerted to the recent developments and are moving to attack these convoys.

Turning to my Air Chief I said, "Van Breakel, we are now at war, and every second could mean life or death I commend your action and make full preparations for attack, and brief me later on the details." He then handed me his clipboard, which contained the following information.

The merchant ship convoy, the furthest away, are to be engaged by the aircraft of the flagship; *Bomber Squadron 1*; all fourteen Curtiss Helldivers committed to the attack and would be commanded by Lt. Commander Van de Groot, with all planes armed with a single 225 kilogram HE bomb. The escort would be provided by *Flight A of Fighter Squadron 1*. The seven F3F's would each carry two 55 kilogram HE bombs, and their commander will be Lt. Jacob Van Veelan. Both of these commanders were known for their skill and aggressive posture.

The *Johan de Witt* was also standing by to prepare a similar strike against the medium carrier of the *Zuiho* Type B class and the cruisers and destroyers of the convoy's naval escort. The Air Group Commander had committed to this attack; the 21 Grumman

Fighters of *Fighter Squadron 3*, to be led by Lt. ter Zee 1ˢᵗ Klasse Karl Brongers. A total of 28 Curtis Model 77 Helldivers were committed to this attack. These were *Bomber Squadron 4* under Lt. ter Zee 1st Klasse Hendrick Kool and *Bomber Squadron 5* led by Lt. ter Zee 1ˢᵀ Klasse Daniel Kruger.

The Commander Flyer; also informed me that the pilot of the reconnaissance Swordfish had been able to identify that the fighters that had attacked him were from the carrier and were of the type Kawasaki K-10. These aircraft I knew were older biplane fighters but only slightly less capable than our own machines, therefore action would depend heavily on pilot skill. The Swordfish reconnaissance plane had been able to approach the light carrier quite closely, and visible on her deck were several Mitsubishi Type 96 Torpedo bombers.

These machines were very similar looking aircraft to a Swordfish Mk I, they were after-all a license manufactured version of the British aircraft the Blackburn Shark Mk III. The reconnaissance Swordfish, flying out of Jesselton, Sarawak had obviously been misidentified by the Japanese fighter pilots and ship lookouts alike as one of *Zuiho Type B's* own lumbering torpedo planes. An understandable error given the difficult conditions one experienced at twilight.

At this point my Chief of Staff, brought me several newly decoded message from KMHB:

VICE ADMRAAL SWEERS COMMANDING TASK FORCE POPEYE;

1. DESTROY BOTH IJN CONVOYS NOW OFF COCHIN CHINA.
2. PROCEED WITH ALL DISPATCH TO CONCENTRATE WITH TASK FORCE OLIVE IN SULU SEA.
3. ASSUME OVERALL COMMAND OF COMBINED FORCES– RETIRE TO JAVA SEA VIA MAKASSAR STRAIT.
4. OPERATE IN JAVA SEA ON EAST WEST AXIS, PENDING ORDERS.

Fleet Admiraal A.K. Van de Velde
(KMHB) 04:20hrs 12.08.41.

I then asked Kapitain Voorne to prepare communications as I was going to address to the men. Then the bugler trumpeted *call to attention* into the microphone, sending it throughout the hundreds of sealed compartments of the great ship. At its close, the trumpeter stepped back while lowering his instrument, the Kapitein then presented me with the microphone, which felt extraordinarily heavy and awkward in my hand.

Then *"Het Wilhelmus"* (the Netherland's National Anthem) was piped throughout the ship. On completion, I straightened my tunic, squared my shoulders and addressed my men through the ship's loudspeaker system. "Attention men; this is Vice Admiraal Sweers your fleet commander. This morning of December 08 1941 the KMHB; has transmitted a message to us at 03:55hrs. War has broken out between the Treaty Nations of the East Asiatic Theater: the British Empire, America, the Netherlands and the Empire of Japan."

"Earlier this Sunday morning the Imperial Japanese Navy (IJN) had directed their powerful aircraft carrier battle fleet to carry out a very heavy surprise attack on the

American fleet base at Pearl Harbour, in the Hawaiian Islands. As a consequence of this rash and unprovoked act of aggression against a member of our defensive coalition; the Netherlands and all her colonies are at now at war with the Empire 'of Japan."

"The naval and air battle at Pearl Harbour is still underway at last report. We have limited information at this time other than the entire U.S. Pacific Fleet is in action. All our military forces, and civil administration throughout the Colonies have been alerted as have those of our Allies. Attacks on our nation and shipping may be expected to occur at any time, at any location and without notice."

"To the north of us there are steaming at this moment; two Japanese military convoys that naval intelligence believes are part of an invasion force. These military convoys are hugging the coast of Cochin China, and steaming on a south-westerly course having entered the South China Sea on the previous evening. Aboard our Vlaggeschip and the *Johan de Witt*, dive bomber and fighter squadrons are being prepared for action. We are going to attack those convoys and blow its ships right out of the water!"

At this point wild cheering erupted throughout my great engine of war. It swelled in force from the bridge forward, rising up into the adjoining compartments and spouting from the voice tubes that led to very bowels of my massive steel leviathan. I felt a flush of pride and rejoiced at the visceral nature of the men's response to the awful news of war.

"The coming struggle will not be easy, it will be hard. But the Japanese do not yet know the metal of the foe with whom they have chosen to contend. Take heart and remember, the great fighting Admiraals of our glorious naval history; Maarten and Cornelius Tromp, Michael de Ruyter, Jan and Cornelius Eversteen and Adrian Bankart to name just a few. Let us not forget those great brother statesmen; who are the pride of the City of Dordrecht, the founders of the Dutch East Indies Trading Company which created this colony and after whom our great Battlecruiser -carriers are named. All these men were the tigers of the sea! For more than 100 years, no nation, nor alliance of nations could stand against such sailors! They built this great Empire which today nurtures our mother country and which we must now defend. Remember the quality of fighting blood which flows through your veins and pumps hotly in your heart!"

"As an infant nation did we not free ourselves from the strangling domination of the Spanish Empire? Did we not defeat the towering war galleons of the Dons armed only with guts and our little oared fishing boats mounting their puny four gun broadsides? When they looked down upon our little boats from the stern castles of their great galleons; did they not burst out laughing and taunt us with the name 'Beggers of the Sea'? And later, that same day, as we stood upon the bloody decks of their captured galleons did the mail shod leather gauntlets of our victorious fore-fathers not roughly scrape those smirks, along with the skin and beards from their faces?"

"In the first century of freedom did we not sail the whole globe and establish ourselves as the preeminent maritime power? At a time when Japanese fishermen feared to lose sight of land, did we not dare to voyage to the lands of the frozen oceans? Did we not continue to explore and grow despite the threats of nations much larger than our own?"

"Did not the illustrious Cornelis de Witt, take command of our channel fleet and drive the Royal Navy from the sea? Did he not send them fleeing up the Medway River, whereupon their defeated navy took refuge behind a great river spanning iron chain?"

"Did not his elegant and mighty golden galleons break that chain with their sharp iron reinforced beaks, to navigate around the tricky sandbars and shake the Lion by its beard in its den? Then, after having humbled the Royal Navy's best, did he not capture their great flagship the *Royal Charles* where it lay abandoned at the Admiralty wharf, its crew having fled, and sail it home completely intact as a prize of war?"

"Did Britannia's greatest sea captains not stand; ankle deep in stinking black river muck, weaponless and with bared heads bowed in shame and curse the day they dared take to ship and cross swords with the Dutchman?" Again there rose a thunderous cheering. "Now, all of you old barracuda aboard of course know the answers to these many questions that I have posed. But for those young minnows amongst you; the answer to all these questions is yes to all those remarkable feats. For such was the quality of our forefathers!

"But those times of which I speak were the old days of glory, and now centuries past! Today Great Britain is our staunch ally, and the Royal Navy is also at sea this morning. I need not remind you of the quality of those battle hardened sailors!

"Men, you know that I speak the truth when I say that we are an old sea folk, and none too patient with those who would dare tug our beards and risk our terrible wrath. Although the Royal Netherlands Navy is much smaller than the Imperial Japanese Navy, remember that we are not alone in this struggle, we have very powerful friends indeed. The British Royal Navy and the United States Navy have today become our allies in another struggle. These represent the first and second most powerful fleets in existence! Our great battle squadron is also a very deadly weapon, and one which has been unwisely disregarded by a new enemy which has never met us in battle before. I say; woe unto them! For we are powerful, poised and now unfettered by the rules of culture, due to their unprovoked act of war!"

"I have every confidence that the future of our nation is assured as long as it rests in the unshakeable grip of the Dutch sailor! So men, let us make sure to beat the 'jack-tars' of the Royal Navy to the mark, and be the first Allied force to put Japanese ships on the bottom!"

"From this day forward our Task Force will become a great primordial sea beast, a gigantic Kraken, one having a primitive, unquenchable hunger. It smells Japanese flesh in its waters and I intend to let it glut its ravenous hunger. I want those two Japanese battleships on the bottom by day's end! I want their aircraft carrier sunk and the invasion convoys smashed!"

"Our small nation, now lies defeated under the hob-nailed jack boot of the German forces, a nation which shares a military alliance with Imperial Japan who faces us today. The spirits of our families have been brought low, but will be uplifted by the news of the victories you will provide. Your action this day will give them a hope that will sustain them until the day of complete victory. The nation will accept nothing less! Do I make myself clear seamen? Then let me hear it!"

Once again the 41,000 tonnes of machinery, weapons and armor plating that made up this great ship, echoed as the men beat their tools or bronze hammers, against the steel bulkheads and decks, and lifted up a battle roar from thousands of throats! The great steel beast bellowed, revealing its battle voice as it raced on defiantly towards the dawn!

I continued; "One day I assure you, our victorious fleet will return home, to an enthusiastic population, having triumphed over all our enemies both close and those afar in Europe. We will sit once again before the warm fires of our home hearths surrounded by our reunited families in a free and peaceful nation. Long live the Netherlands and God preserve Queen Wilhelmina! Good luck to you all in today's action."

I then handed the microphone over to Kapt. Voorne while I turned back to look at the chart table. Task Force Popeye had reached the point that I had indicated the previous day some three hours earlier and had turned N.E. heading towards the small Spratley Island group. I picked up the Command center's incident log and scanned all the Task Force transmissions and sightings from the previous evening up to the present moment.

I queried A.O. Kapitain Van Braekel about our heavy dive bombers; the Polish Sea Eagles. The fleet relied on these machines to deliver massive knock-out blows against heavily armored warships, and coastal installations. Had he considered using them to strike against the Japanese battleship escort where their 750 kg. Armor Piercing (AP) bombs would be very effective?

He replied that he had considered their use, but had judged it to be too risky. There were 40 modern JAAF fighters stationed at My Tho Airbase, Indo-China, only some 120 nautical miles from the nearest convoy that we planned to attack. In addition to that danger; that light carrier would have her own air patrol in close proximity and as many as half of her 30 machine air group may be fighters.

Once our *Helldivers* had dropped their bombs they would assume their secondary role as class B fighters and could take care of themselves. Whereas the huge wings of the Sea Eagles which enabled them to carry such large bombs made them very stable and therefore slow to respond to their control surfaces and consequently quite vulnerable to fighter attack. Van Braekel had not wanted to commit our most expensive aircraft to any mission when there could be as many as fifty five enemy fighters in opposition over the area of the target.

I replied that his appreciation of the risks involved to the *Sea Eagles* was entirely justified. I then continued, "However if we destroy the enemy light carrier before the Sea Eagles attack, the threat posed by her fighters would be much reduced, as they would be forced to withdraw. While some of the carrier's aircraft may fly to My Thoa Airbase, they could not be serviced quickly, as they were different machines from those of the JAAF."

We had the *Pezetels* aboard primarily to bust up armored ships and there were two valuable targets of opportunity in the furthest convoy. I then asked him if he had considered whether to commit the *Sea Eagles* to action with added fighter escort? He replied; "*Fightercloud* Sir, we must retain sufficient planes to form the cloud."

Air Ops; Van Braekel then continued; "Both of these convoys may actually be an elaborate trap Admiraal, one laid specifically to draw out our Task Force and destroy it. The Japanese may not be aware that we know of the recent arrival in French Indo China of the JAAF *121ˢᵗ* and *73ʳᵈ* bomber *Hikosentai's* from Manchuria. We must assume that their intelligence network is aware that our Task Force is at sea and that they will have a general idea of our location at this time, one which they will determine precisely after dawn today. The Japanese are very crafty Admiraal, Hawaiian Radio reports that they launched surprise attacks against the American fleet in the midst of their Sunday worship services. Did they not do the same thing to the Russian Fleet at Port Arthur in 1904?" To which I replied; "yes *Air Ops*, I agree a deception may be involved here as well."

Van Braekel calculated that the IJN had connived to present us two tempting targets in the hope to lure many of our aircraft away from our fleet leaving only a token combat air patrol of perhaps ten machines. Then the JAAF would hit us hard with both *Hikosentais* of 100 bombers plus, with perhaps a full fighter *Hikosentai* of 30 machines in escort to suppress our flak guns. Under those conditions, he felt that *Task Force Popeye* would be lucky to survive the day.

At this point in the conversation the Flagship's Commander Kapitien Voorne who had been listening to our conversation, spoke up. He was an officer having extreme pride in his ship. He reminded the Senior Fleet Air Operations Officer that the ships of the fleet were designed with multiple redundant systems for defense which included; subdivision of their hulls into hundreds of watertight compartments, extensive armor plate, well drilled damage control teams, flame suppressing gas systems, temperature activated fire curtains for the aircraft hangers, high speed maneuver and more than 150 automatic anti-aircraft cannon!

I shot the ship's Kapitein a quick glance and he fell silent. I then proceeded with my questioning of my Hoof Officier Vleiger, to evaluate his assumptions and preparations that related to the morning attack. "Am I correct in my estimate 'Air Ops' that once the air-strikes currently under preparation are launched and away we would still have some 44 fighters held back that would be applied to *Fightercloud*. And that these could be further augmented by the remaining Helldivers, all told aloft and aboard approximately some 58 machines?"

To eliminate confusion I began checking my notes against the *Status Table*. This was a 1:48 scale model of the flight deck on which were positioned scale wooden models of our planes. The top wings had an F or B panted on with a number for each squadron. This simple method gave us an instant appreciation of the disposition of all planes on the flight deck. Below were two shelves one for each hanger. On these shelves were wooden models of each aircraft aboard. We knew exactly what was aboard or in the air. Bins to the side, now empty would fill up with destroyed aircraft as the air-battles progressed. Later, as replacements came aboard models would be retrieved from these bins and given new squadron numbers.

To this my Air Operations Officer replied; "barring breakdowns; almost Sir. The *Johan de Witt's* strike against the enemy carrier and cruisers will involve three full squadrons. Nodding towards the small aircraft wooden models sitting on the *Status Table* he said Admiraal it is easy to miscount as the models of the Sea Hart bombers on submarine patrol look almost identical to those the Sea Fury Fighter. Our remaining fighter compliment has been reduced to 40 fighters, while aboard remain a reserve of 14 Helldivers of Bomber Squadron 2, to be used as class B fighters, under *Fightercloud* for a total of 54, with 6 Sea Harts airborne on anti-torpedo duty, for a total potential of 60 machines of varying capability."

I told Van Braekel that I would have preferred to see the entire strike go out from just one battlecruiser-carrier. In that way over the course of the day's action the launching of the second strike would be undertaken by the second ship and not be interrupted by the need to land returning damaged planes short on fuel, and possibly with wounded aboard. But the usage was still approved.

In his appreciation of the situation; the Chief of Fleet Air Operations felt that we must proceed with the air strikes against the convoys with all haste. I was confident that his *time-motion-effort evaluation* of flight deck operations had allowed him to choose the most effective procedures for utilizing two flight decks for operations given the time constraints.

Nevertheless at the earliest moment I ordered all of the Brewster fighters up with drop tanks at first light as a strengthened Combat Air Patrol before we launched the first airstrike. As an added measure I directed that all the remaining aircraft aboard other than the Sea Eagles to be prepared for standby level two which was the first stage in ordering *Fightercloud,* for like Van Braekel, I also believed that we would be hit hard by the JAAF this morning a few hours after sunrise.

I addressed a group of my most senior officers who were studying the little models of ships that were being added to the horizontal plot table to represent the Japanese convoys, the targets of our early morning attacks. KMHB (naval headquarters Batavia), being fully aware that we could not transmit radio messages without assisting the Japanese in locating our fleet, began to transmit to all ships at sea a war alert and coded instruction to all its warships. In this way we learned that Task Force Olive was speeding on its way to the Celebes Sea.

I directed my C.O.S. Commodore Derik Van Klaffens to prepare a status update; if the Task Force was fully prepared for a surface action as well as air attack, and also to determine if there had been any contact with the Australian battle-group whose last known position was in the *Arafura Sea* on a North West heading. A link up should be advantageous to both navies. I would dearly love to have a battlecruiser, two heavy cruisers and their attendant destroyers in company!

The Australian Commander Rear Admiral Sir Kevin Whitely, in light of the recent ominous developments, may be attempting to concentrate with the RN battle squadron based at Singapore. He may also be seeking out a RNLN Battle-carrier Task Force as a cruising companion for the protection that our substantial naval air umbrella provided.

Turning to my C.O.S. and his number two; A.C.O.S. Kpt. Lt. ter Zee Kurt Rupplin, I directed them to estimate the JAAF air attack scenarios based on their latest reinforcements in Cochin China. I needed an evaluation on how may the IJN and JAAF respond to our attacks throughout the day? I expected that their powerful 6th Kokugun (Air Army), imbued with an aggressive doctrine, would employ all their resources in one massive blow against us.

I directed my 'Air Ops' to get out a message to our torpedo bomber squadrons, both the land based Swordfish and our float plane Fokker's on Borneo. All these aircraft had a very long range. Van Klaffens was to give them the locations of the two Japanese convoys and tell them that I order all these naval squadrons to begin a series of torpedo attacks against the enemy ships with everything that they have, and to sustain these until there are no longer any targets or until I give the order to stand down.

I then directed the C.O.S to contact Generaal Armin van Buuren of the KNIL (Royal Netherlands 3rd East Indies Army Air force) at the airfield in Bandjermasin, Borneo. I requested that his Glen Martin medium bomber squadrons strike the fighter and bomber bases in French Indo China from which the bombers of JAAF *73 rd.* and *121ˢᵗ Hikosentais* were operating, as soon as possible if not already been so ordered. These enemy formations represent a severe and immediate threat to Task Force Popeye at our current exposed location in the South China Sea.

My C.O.S. Van Klaffens soon reported to me that Generaal Buuren's headquarters acknowledged our request and would comply, they also reported that the 3ʳᵈ Army's bomber forces had already dispatched a section of three machines to destroy the Japanese Navy radio station on Spratley Island, an observation facility which aided the JAAF with RDF signals. Popeye's Combat Air Patrol units were briefed to expect the detection of these twin engine bombers at sunrise on an approach from the southeast.

I took my C.O.S. and the senior gunnery officer; Kpt. Lt. ter Zee Tieler van Ripper aside to discuss the potential of surface threats based on recent information received. "Gentlemen; you may recall that when the *Rengo Kantai* began rebuilding its battle fleet in the 1930's to incorporate those very tall gunnery fire control towers; their naval planners had concerns how the new structures would stand up to shock and blast. Our units of the OVZ - *Office Van Zeeinlichtingen* was able to discover that the Japanese Admiralty had duplicated similar structures on a series of their older battleships that had been regulated to training status. The work was carried out behind canvas screening at their largest naval shipyards."

"Our submarines were able carry out successfully several nocturnal reconnaissance missions of the Japanese Naval shipyards. They used a combination of periscope observation, *NS viewers* and later teams of our native snorkel men were sent ashore at night. These final missions revealed that the Kure Naval Arsenal had installed the *Hiraga Type*; experimental command/communications control towers aboard the *Settsu* and *Kawatchi* type dreadnoughts. While the Yokosuka Naval Arsenal had installed similar structures incorporated on the *Satsuma* and *Aki* type semi-dreadnoughts. Similarly the *Fujimoto Type* experimental superstructures were fitted aboard the *Katori* and *Kashima* type pre-dreadnoughts in the new outfit docks of the Osaka Naval Arsenal!"

"We are now faced with a very unpleasant series of surprises, gentlemen. The RAF Fairy Swordfish reconnaissance patrols have now confirmed that the first two ships I have mentioned, which we thought would be used by the army as coastal fire support platforms, have been actually re-commissioned into the IJN as modernized battleships, and fully armored. The last four ships which we all had believed to have been scuttled under the terms of the Washington naval treaty, must now be considered as salvaged, rebuilt and commissioned back into the Imperial Fleet, as third class battleships!"

"Chief Gunner, Van Ripper; are you able to recall the armament of these new foes?" To which he replied; "Sir; all these older dreadnoughts are as well armored as our battle-carriers, and have heavy guns although slightly smaller caliber ones; The *Settsu* type; has twelve – 12" guns, the *Aki Ckass* have a mix of four-12" guns, and twelve – 10" guns and both of these types are 18 to 20 knot ships. While the *Katori Class* battleships are still older, at best 15 to 17 knot ships, and have four - 12" and four – 10" guns. It would seem Admiraal; that the Japanese have found a way to introduce at least forty six heavy guns to their fleet having a combined shell weight of some 24,000 kilograms. These do balance out the 9,800 kilos of our ships heavy guns, and those of the RN in this theater, although only about 16,600 kilos in shell weight could make up a combined broadside, due to the old wing turret arrangement of many of their heavy guns. Also, I believe that these old ships are not meant to engage in sea battles, but are to be used as fire support ships for invasion troop convoys only. By assuming all shore bombardment duty they leave the IJN Main Battle Fleet free for action. They should not present a danger to our Task Force, as we greatly outrange their guns, however if they are encountered unexpectedly, perhaps at night and at close range, they would be very dangerous and their bombardment rounds were certainly make a shambles out of our aircraft hangars and flight decks."

I stared at Van Ripper for a brief moment, appreciative of his precise, and detailed technical grasp of the implications, then replied; "thank you Kapitein–Lt."

It was clear to me that the IJN's response to expansion of the KMN fleet in the East Indies, and the threat of its eighteen pieces of heavy artillery, had been at least on paper balanced out. The only thing that prevented these ships from operating with the IJN's fast modern divisions of heavy cruisers was range and speed, their hulls it was reported, had not been lengthened, and the propulsive machinery was still coal fired. Shortcomings notwithstanding, these old battleships posed a serious threat a closer ranges.

Commodore Van Klaffens my C.O.S. now spoke up; "Admiraal, I believe that the presence of these ships is an indication that the *Rengo Kantai* may attempt to seek out a surface battle with us after our aircraft have been expended, and have suffered damage. A scenario that would leave their main fleet of most modern heavy ships undamaged to face the US Pacific Fleet."

"Thank you C.O.S.", I replied, "I agree, we will talk more on this. Now then gentlemen, we would be able to reduce that *Big Gun* threat to a more managed level today by sinking the two *Settsu Class Battleships* let us see to it!"

OVZ, (Dutch Naval Intelligence) had concluded before the war that the existence of our powerful mobile naval air arm based as it was on three battle carriers was the *Rengo Kantai's* single most important strategic naval target in the region. Detailed in our Strategic Defense Plan for the East Indies, was Case 3; a battle study which turned out to be very close to our current situation: *The naval forces of the Bulwark Coalition: RN Flying Squadron: absent. US Pacific Fleet: absent. Situation: critical; overextended and out-numbered. KMN forces at sea; within defensive perimeter.* Case 3 study proved valid except, that we were, at present, far outside our defensive perimeter and well within the reach of the powerful Japanese Army Air Force!

The Japanese High Command; was revealed as aggressive and ambitious with far reaching well thought out plans. Fear; makes one hate, which is a type of self-preservation mechanism. I never thought that I would hate anyone again. I came to hate the pirates that infested the waters of the East Indies; whether Chinese, Malay, or the natives of our own colony, because I had to fight them. Now the sheer craftiness of the Japanese enemy revealed itself in so many ways in the last few days, caused me to fear, and its old familiar cold fingers, returned to brush my neck, tickle my spine and knot my insides. Alas, I was becoming that other more harsh and brutal Maarten. I would learn to hate again, I thought with sadness, decency was being washed away by the sweat of fear.

If the intent of the IJN and JAAF was to make a maximum effort on the first day then so would the ships and aircraft of the Royal Netherlands Navy. We knew that the main carrier fleet of the *Rengo Kantai* and a large portion of their surface forces were at sea, somewhere off of Hawaii. I estimated that it would be a minimum of five days before they would be able to disengage and steam back into East Asiatic waters. An additional week would pass before these major forces would have; refueled, recovered, reequipped, repaired and redeployed from their action against Pearl Harbour. For that short period we would have local naval air superiority with as many as 200 seaborne aircraft and backed by a sizeable reserve.

For this period it was possible to operate outside our defensive ring of airfields, after which time we must retreat to those protected waters, as we could not match the combined power of Admiral Nagumo's squadron assembled around six fleet carriers and its 600 + modern aircraft. After that time we would undoubtedly become *the hunted.*

Returning to my Air Operations Chief Van Braekel, I said; "My orders are clear Air Chief, I am to seek action. I agree with your preparations for the air attacks with one exception. Once the current strikes are launched you are to organize a maximum heavy bomber strike against the two Japanese dreadnoughts escorting the invasion fleet using 750 kg. (AP) armor piercing bombs. I order all the *Sea Eagles* of Bomber Squadron 3 and Bomber Squadron 6 from the *Johan de Witt* to be launched within the hour. The two Japanese battleships are undoubtedly to act as fire support, and a central command ship for an invasion force. If we could sink or disable these, and deny their use to the Japanese, it may derail their entire invasion and win for us a Strategic victory!"

There is no question in my mind, that the lumbering *Sea Eagles* would be at great risk on this mission, but it was a calculated one which I felt was well worth it. I did not want to reduce the fighter strength of the fleet below the 61 machines to provide them with an escort, as these were being held back for defense. In my estimation, at the time the Sea Eagles arrived over the enemy battleships the flagship's first strike against the convoys would have been completed and those combat capable fighters which remained out of the original 28 machines of the Fighter Squadrons 1 and 3 would provide cover for the Sea Eagle's attack on the armored ships, and then cover their withdrawal. If this proved insufficient, there were still 42 Helldivers, from the first attack that would be flying back to their ships and would provide protection.

I understood Van Braekel's concerns for retaining a powerful air reserve to ensure the success of *Fightercloud.* He seemed quite relieved at my decision and agreed that the Grumman Fighters and Curtis Helldivers would be well located to support the Sea Eagles. The Model 77 Helldiver, it must be remembered, once shed of its bomb load, was only a little slower than the brand new Nakajima Type Ki-27 Army fighter stationed at *My Thoa* Airbase in Cochin China. The Helldiver was very maneuverable and it enjoyed a longer range, and with the nose mounted .50 cal. machine gun and dorsal mounted .30 caliber had a more powerful punch than the light twin 7.7 mm guns of the Japanese fighter.

One other aspect that figured into my battle plan was the range of the Grumman F2F and F3F fighters, which was considerably longer than the bombers, and allowed them to travel to the target convoys and back twice before landing to refuel, while the Brewster Buffalo fighters were able to do the round trip at least three times and maybe even a fourth time.

The Air Operations staff had to keep a tight record of information on the fuel usage of all these fighters to have an effective air traffic control and manage the complex flight deck operations. The heavily loaded Sea Eagle strike force could just manage the range to target and return. These unescorted machines would maintain a tight box formation where their well sighted armament of 84 Lewis guns allowed them to train 28 weapons in any direction.

It was my intention to redeploy those of the returning Grumman Fighters which had the largest quantity of fuel and ammunition remaining to provide additional escort duties for our Swordfish and Fokker floatplane torpedo planes as they passed under the air umbrella of the battle-carriers. I would have these fighters support the lumbering torpedo planes as they made the *run in* for their attacks and then cover their retreat. While all our Sea Fury Mk II fighters, would of course be retained for fleet protection in the Combat Air Patrol duty, as their much shorter range eliminated their usage as escorts for the type of aircraft that we were now operating.

I looked around my Fleet Command Center. All my officers seemed to be busily engaged in their tasks. But a sense of nervousness and tension lay like a heavy blanket over the compartment, which seemed to have become, in the last few minutes; very warm and close. All bravado aside; the staff officers knew just how powerful and numerous our enemy's weapons were.

If there was a JAAF trap laid for Task Force Popeye, then the enemy forces arrayed against our ships should all reveal themselves within the next few hours. When the heavy action that I expected, arrived with the dawn, it may rapidly develop to a crisis pitch. In such circumstances I did not want to have my multirole Helldivers seconded to submarine patrols. They were much too useful. A less capable craft could be employed for this duty. By this time I was entirely convinced that the Japanese new our position to within 50 miles. I therefore directed my C.A.O. Van Braekel to contact Tarakan airfield and send us six of the reliable Hawker Sea Harts for each battle-carrier. These were to depart their airbase with all haste, then refuel at Beraoe airfield (a secret base in the heart of Borneo) and come aboard as soon as it was determined that Task Force Popeye had steamed within range.

I further directed the C.A.O. Commander Flier Van Braekel to personally contact Task Force Olive and inform his opposite aboard the *Schoonveldt*, Commander Flier Wolraven van Hall, which of our land based air units Task Force Popeye had already started shuttling eastward as support, and requested a status report on their air group, and any NAS squadrons that they may have put in motion.

I then undid the dogs of the armored door, brushed aside the heavy blackout curtain and passed out onto the catwalk mounted on the port side of the citadel and caught a full blast of the clean sea air, still cool enough from the dark to be refreshing. Here I could now enjoy for a few private moments to collect my thoughts before the storm of Japanese steel arrived. A selfish moment to savor the hypnotic effect of the hissing foam and the beauty of the phosphorescent bow waves as they were forced out from the side of the great speeding warship.

Some twenty meters out from its steel side a large school of bottle nosed dolphin were taking advantage of the *free ride* that the pressure wave of our hull offered. There they frolicked surfing the crests, their swift darting bodies glowed greenly like a huge string of Christmas tree lights strung out under the dark green ink of the sea. Their forceful exhalations and squeaky voices sounding almost humanlike...*a sea family at play!* As they leapt above the waves some trick of reflected light allowed me to see their intelligent eyes watching the ship, full of curiosity for our rushing leviathan. With each breaching; a handful of green glowing beads shook clear of the foam and were cast carelessly upon to the water's surface. By some peculiar characteristic of *surface tension* they maintained their spheres, to roll and skitter over the backs of the waves, to finally collect spinning, glittering and tumbling in their troughs, for a fraction of a second, like a cloud of emeralds, whereupon they returned in a blink, to the sea!

I produced my silver cigarette case, popped the catch and retrieved a potent and generally unappreciated *Russian Gold Tipped Imperial*. A cheroot of a particularly pungent Turkish blend. I rolled the smoke under my nose and sniffed the aroma in perverse anticipation. Within the case, next to the *Imperials* were some *Panteras*, an *anonymous gift* from my ship's officers mess, and undoubtedly a rather heavy hint from my messmates to switch brands! Perhaps I would try one but I still had to wait for dawn to break however to light it, as flaring match could be spotted at night by an alert submarine watch keeper at a distance of ten kilometers giving them plenty of time to set up for an attack.

I had to satisfy myself with a gulp from my mug of hot coffee, my first of that day. Then removing my cap and briefly bowing me head. I prayed for God to forgive me for what I was pledged to do this dreaded day. The war up to now had been rather remote, with light duty. We conducted patrols, ran down the odd commerce raider, stopped and searched vessels, but now that had all changed. We were faced with a very powerful and aggressive foe with many times our capability. When action was joined, battles would be fought to a decisive conclusion. The men up to this point had not been tested. Real war was coming. I now required that all of the 7,800 men under my command must discard their mantles of civilization.

In order to perform their duties the men must toss aside the lifelong teachings of their mothers, priests, ministers and rabbis, they must suppress all those virtues obtained through culture and society and raise up the beast; the *joyful slaughterer*. They must open that door which sets loose the darkness that slumbers within all men. They must transform themselves from decent beings into calculating, merciless and efficient killers. Then for the remainder of their lives; they must evaluate the price now due of wearing the uniform. Many an honest soul would ponder with shame throughout the long years the breaking of the first commandment and grieve the lost treasures of their care-free youth and innocence.

I then focused my thoughts, and began to re-examine my plans for the coming battle. I must not allow these somber ramblings of a peacetime brain to intrude into this effort. In my position and under these conditions it would be criminal to do so. I redirected my thoughts to evaluate how bright the phosphorescent wakes of our task force may appear to an enemy aircraft searching the night from aloft.

This caused me to reflect on the views held by an officer of the Surgeon General for the R.N. whom I met in 1938 while a guest aboard the famous aircraft carrier *H.M.S. Furious*. The then seventy-two year old Vice Adm. Sir Harold Wooster-Axeworthy was I recall lecturing a group of young flyers on the biological oddities of the Japanese race which rendered their naval pilots; "dangerously deficient, athletically atrophied and optically overmatched."

Strolling across the hangar deck he spoke to very young and impressionable airmen; "Japanese eyes you see being *slitty-like* simply do not admit as much light to the retina as

Mark Klimaszewski

does the *normal open round eye* of the white man. Therefore it is simple to conclude that the *Jappos* are at night; half blind! Furthermore as their mother's carry them on their backs for the first year of their lives they are quite unable to develop the full sense of equilibrium that a flyer must have. So you see; young pilots do not worry about the odds, as our little yellow brothers are not to be feared in the skies!"

That type of silliness was all too common within the British armed services in those days. "You dolt" I thought. "It was the North American Indian mothers that carried their children on their backs, not the Japanese!" Sir Harold lived at a time when there were a great many more "glass ceilings" in society than there are today. The native servicemen in the R.N. were restricted to the lowest social level which prevented them from obtaining officer's commissions in His Majesty's services. Sir Harold's *prejudice based anthropology* was quite common in those days. These conclusions however, could not be held in the same regard as the truly vast accomplishments of British medical and scientific effort, as his conclusions were arrived at for political reasons, without experiment, or serious study. Sir Harold may have altered his anthropological summations had he observed any of my native pilots undergoing air combat training, an experience which may have provided him with raw data on the subject and vibrated the pillars of his comfortable world.

Aboard the battleship-carrier *Schoonveldt*; now racing through the empurpled spicy darkness of the Celebes Sea; was Naval Fighter Squadron 5. Fully half of its twenty five pilots to a man were native to Java or Sumatra. They also had an *oriental* eye *of sorts*, but seemed nevertheless to have passed all of the pilot's stiff training and medical examination with ease! All were revealed to be natural fliers. They took the squadron name of *Rangda's Arrows*; (Rangda, being a particularly hideous native demon) and they were, man for man as deadly efficient as any carrier skipper could hope for. Sir Harold; you were so full of runny schisse! How many boys will die with their heads packed with your jibberish?

Dawn, December 8, 1941 in the South China Sea. I noticed the first grey strip of light appear, forming the edge of a new horizon, I glanced at the luminescent dial of my watch; 0500 hours. I turned and reentered the FCC where the Senior Air Operations Officer Konrad Van Braekel reported that a CAP of twelve Brewster Buffalos from the flagship, and six from the *Johan de Witt* were standing by to launch. Both Helldiver bomber squadrons and their escorting fighters were fully fuelled and armed, waiting on the flight deck with their engines warmed and ready. The fighter pilots had been briefed to expect air attacks coming from both the North West and North East directions soon after dawn.

An Air Operations staff officer then reported to him that there was now sufficient light to launch our strike aircraft, the sea conditions were nominal, and the winds were favorable from the N.E. at 13 knots. Turning to the Vlaggeschip's commander I said; "Kapitein Voorne signal the *Johan de Witt*; have both battle-carriers turned into the wind, then launch the Combat Air Patrol, followed by all attack aircraft."

I proceeded up the companionway to the flight deck above, then climbed into the Air Control deckhouse and emerged out onto Deck 06. Looking aft I saw that the fighters and dive-bombers of the first strike group were neatly lined up on the sun bleached fir planked flight deck. Here they waited, for the signal to unleash maximum engine power. The pilot of the first machine of Fighter Squadron 2, sat in his cockpit with its Plexiglas

248

canopy slid back, I could clearly see, as he watched the deckhouse intently for a green light, which soon blinked; on.

At once a burst of power dragged the fighter forward. It charged down the long deck towards me. In a flash the barrel like body of the Brewster F2A Buffalo hurtled past the island with blue flames firing out of its twin exhaust pipes. The first combat mission of the day was off the deck, Monday morning at 05:08hrs December 08, 1941. The weapon had been unleashed.

I looked up into the early morning sky; an approaching weather system had disturbed the atmosphere but offered as compensation a rich combination of blues, yellows and red pastels. I jammed a *Gold Tipped Imperial* into my lips, lit it behind my cupped hand, and took in my first deep inhalation, flooding my relieved system with rich calming nicotine.

Far to the east, towering new thunderheads were already forming over the South China Sea. One of which, now colored by the dawn was entirely pink and shaped exactly like a gigantic human skull! It seemed to peek around a mushrooming billow of yellow and orange highlights, from where it leered horrifically downward, casting its great shadow onto the sea and across the course of my fleet!

Death, it seemed was at hand, hungry and hoping for a morning banquet! It hovered gluttonously over the sea and with jaws agape it waited, preparing to gather up all the young slaughtered souls!

Could it be that only I noticed this cumulus monstrosity? Frozen for a moment I watched in horror; as against this unsettling backdrop, moving across its face, there seemingly crawled and wiggled in the air currents, maggot like, the tiny silhouettes of the *Johan de Witt's* CAP fighters as they clawed for altitude. I shuddered and prayed that some wind would hurriedly dissipate this unnerving spectacle!

Now blowflies were added to its face, and became starkly silhouetted or illuminated to shine with a wet green yellow or pinkish metallic hue, as squadron after squadron left the decks of the battlecruiser-carriers and climbed into the dawn. The air throbbed with the power and effect of tens of thousands of kilowatts driving the propellers, whose steel blades beat the heavy moist air of the young day with innumerable blows.

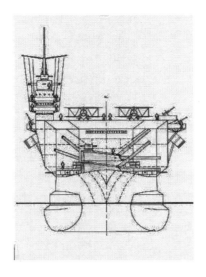

CHAPTER XXIII

THE FIRST BATTLE OF THE SOUTH CHINA SEA – DECEMBER 08, 1941.

<u>The Observations of:</u>
19 year old Air Telegraphist Gunner Jan Steen flying in the rear cockpit of a Curtiss Model 77 Helldiver, Aircraft No. B1C-8, a bi-plane dive bomber flown by Lt. Rudolf Thorbecke commander of Flight B; Bomber Squadron 1 from the flagship *Cornelis de Witt*, of Task Force Popeye, RNLN, December 08, 1941, South China Sea:

"The crews of Bomber Squadron 1 and Fighter Squadron 1 had been briefed at 04:25hrs; fourteen of our Helldivers, escorted by seven F3F-2 fighters were to launch the first strike against an enemy convoy to the N.E. Instantly wild cheering had burst from the aircrews, but a sharp remark from the our squadron leader Lt. Com. Van de Groot produced immediate silence. The A.O.O. Commander Flier Konrad Van Braekel gave us the courses to target and return, the radio frequencies to use, the communication codes, the meteorology, the data about the enemy fighter concentration at My Thoa airbase, the proximity of the IJN escorting convoy of warships and that it contained a light carrier, the payloads that were being loaded aboard our dive bombers and then described the convoy which we were to hit and our targets. Another exclamation erupted; but this time a groan of disappointment when it was understood that we must concentrate all our dive-bombing expertise to attack the merchant vessels only! Every one of us wanted the battleships and the light carrier! The A.O.O. then made us to understand the high value placed on the merchant ships as targets for they carried all the equipment and as many as twenty thousand troops of an invasion force."

<u>The Observations of:</u>
25-year old: Lt. Commander Rudy Keppler: Squadron Leader of Fighter Squadron 2, of the Battlecruiser-carrier *Cornelis de Witt*, flagship Task Force Popeye, RNLN, flying aircraft number F2C-1, a Brewster F2A monoplane fighter on a Combat Air Patrol mission South China Sea, 05:05hrs. December 08, 1941:

"My fighter would be the first aircraft to launch from the flagship, this first morning of the war in the East Indies/South East Asia. I stood on the brakes of the "Filthy Lill" and opened her up. The

big Wright Cyclone 9 cylinder radial engine began to scream as it built up revolutions. These soon climbed to 2,800 rpm, the maximum for the steel Hamilton Variable pitch three bladed propeller. The Cyclone; adequately described the roar. The unnaturally restrained power shook the sturdy air frame of the stubby fighter's barrel like fuselage. With my cockpit canopy slid back I waited for my launch-controller in the deckhouse to give me the green lamp. FLASH GREEN...feet off brakes...the trollop leapt forward...maximum pitch on the prop.....air on lean...fuel on... flaps max, watch the yellow line on the deck.. rudder....the tail lifts ...nose drops...I see the flight deck now .... yellow 1 stripe...pull back on the stick ...off the deck now....the wings flex and creak as they take the fighter's weight. I flash past the deckhouse...turn to port...crank the handle to retract the landing gear, and I am away."

"I climbed for altitude and immediately began to search the early morning sky for enemy aircraft. The Air Chief had briefed us to expect an attack to come in from the enemy carrier at first light. I scanned the skies; up for dive bombers and fighters, just above the water for torpedo planes. As my ship climbed upwards in a long spiral I looked down upon the fleet and saw a steady stream of silver aircraft flowing from off of the decks of our battle-carriers at uniform spacing of some 5 aircraft lengths."

"I glanced back over my left shoulder to observe the other aircraft of FS-2. Like the tail of a huge kite, the fighters of my squadron were all strung out behind me at regular intervals, stretching in a long line back to the flight deck of the Vlaggeschip. I glanced down between my feet to check the visibility through the belly window but its view was too restrictive to be of immediate use so early in the morning. At this altitude the aircraft were all shining in the new light of sunrise but below the sea was still shrouded in misty conditions."

The Observations of:

25 year old: Lt. Commander Konrad Van de Groot, leading Bomber Squadron 1, Curtiss Model 77 Helldiver, Aircraft No. B1C-1, flying off of the flagship; *Cornelis de Witt* of Task Force Popeye, RNLN, strike leader of combined air group designated; Striker One, 05:20hrs, December 08, 1941, South China Sea:

"The day was clear with clouds building to the east, with a fine mist, and visibility out to 80 kilometers. The entire squadron had flown off in record time...less than 10 seconds between launches! The deck crews had formed rotating teams of "pushers" and as soon as the bomber's breaks were released I put maximum pitch on the propeller just as five men on each side of the aircraft pushed hard against the lower wing, and advanced for three strides. That extra shove to overcome static friction at 'second one' shaved three seconds off the launch time. We climbed to a planned altitude of 5000 meters in long steep spirals. Looking to port and below; the fleet looked very smart and well-formed up. Upon the crowded decks of the ships hundreds of sailors looked aloft, and waved their naval issue straw hats to bid us good hunting."

"Soon all my birds were in position at altitude. My fourteen bombers were flying in left echelon formation. Looking above; the seven "Grumman F3F Flying Barrels" of our fighter escort were 200 m. above us and had taken up the same flying formation as the bombers. To starboard I could make out an identical concentration of aircraft rising up from the busy deck of the Johan de Witt. These were however flying in right echelon formation as were their fighters. We formed together into two large V formations, one above the other, and as one group we turned north towards the coast of Indo China. I had 42 dive-bombers having mixed payloads of 225 kilogram SAP and HE

bombs, 28 fighters having fifty six 50 kilogram HE bombs, 70 machines and 112 aircrew. The time to first target was sixty three minutes. The IJN was going to catch Holy hell!"

"The preflight briefing made it clear that we may expect two types of fighter opposition this day; the JAAF Nakajima Ki-27 a swift monoplane, and the IJN Kawasaki K-10 biplane. Although these two machines presented different problems, both were within the capabilities of our nimble fighters escort. As for my dive-bombers? Once they had released their bombs; the Helldiver became a very maneuverable machine indeed and although under gunned for a fighter they were a dangerous quarry for those aircraft the enemy opposed us with that day. Our 50.cal nose machine gun had for example a much longer range and six fold the destructive power of the light machine guns of either enemy fighter type that we may encounter."

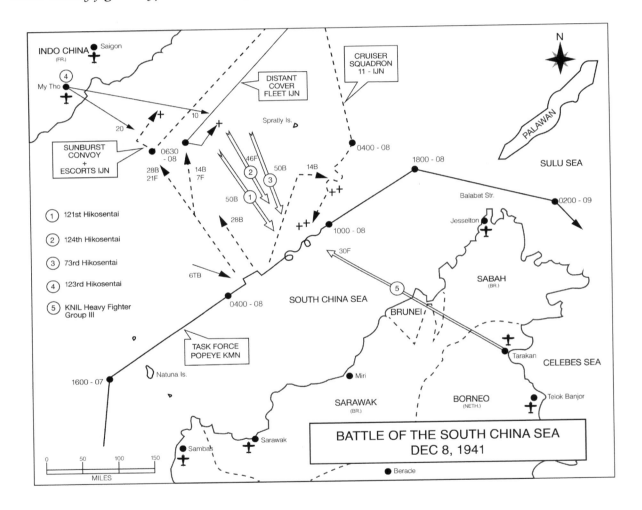

05:42hrs December 08, 1941, the preparation of the PZL-P23 Sea Eagles heavy dive bomber strike was only half complete when from out of the loudspeaker on the bulkhead a voice loudly screamed; 'ALARM TORPEDO, NAAR DE HAVEN' (Alarm Torpedo to Port)! One of our Sea Hart bombers on submarine patrol observed the wakes of six torpedoes etching green lines of phosphorescence across the surface of the sea racing up on an interception course with our fleet! These had been very cleverly launched to be concealed in our wakes, and had been launched from out of the still darkened gloom of the west! The enemy torpedoes were moving along a northeasterly course and would strike our fleet formation at about 30° from aft, as we had by then turned into the wind.

How is it, I thought that the Japanese torpedoes do not detonate prematurely when hitting the varying water pressures in our ship's wake? I felt the icy fingers of terror crawling up my spine and wrapping around my shoulders! It hit home like a 10 kilogram sledge hammer with stunning clarity; that our newly developed emergency anti-torpedo techniques of light Arial bombs and mortars had only been tested on Dutch torpedoes! We had assumed that the Japanese technology that was no better than ours, as Dutch torpedoes exploded when encountering large variations in water pressure!

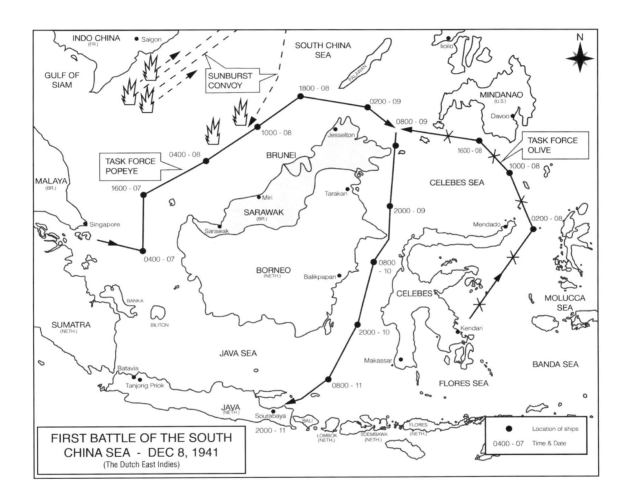

The battle-carriers had not yet completed the launching of all aircraft and were still on a northerly course, and still vulnerable to the deadly fish. Immediately the big ships and their escorts put their helms over and altered course to starboard and out of their path. The submerged war heads would now run harmlessly past our ships, angling away by 60° to port. We were out of danger for the moment.

Three destroyers in the meantime had turned westwards to search out and sink the enemy submarine(s) and had already begun their cooperative effort with the Helldiver on A.S. patrol. Two Sea Harts nevertheless were ordered to intercept the torpedoes in the first combat test of our new tactics. Each aircraft flew down the torpedo phosphorescent trail and dropped clusters of 50 kg bombs in front of their racing submerged targets. The bomb detonations would confuse the submariners, and make them doubt their equipment. In a repeat of our training exercises on Dutch torpedoes, the detonation of three of these bombs several meters below the surface caused such a hard concussion that the warheads exploded. One by one they were quickly eliminated. There had been some luck involved in their spotting, as these torpedo wakes had been very difficult to distinguish, disguised as they were in the wake of the ships! Those sneaky little bastards, I murmured just under my breath. Nevertheless a huge wave of relief came over me as I shook my shoulders in an exaggerated shiver.

The submarine's skipper, who had undoubtedly made a surface attack, perhaps, I assume having seen our numerous patrol aircraft rising from the ships at first light had decided to play it safe and launch his fish from the dark side of the dawn and at long range. Choosing the protection that the darkness offered to him, nevertheless came at the cost of his mission. He had released his torpedoes at over 6,000 meters range which gave our roving air patrols some four minutes to spot and destroy his deadly fish.

The Flagship; *Cornelis de Witte* had turned violently to starboard when the *Alarm Torpedo* signal had exploded onto our eardrums. Kapitein Voorne instantly hit the large overhead button which emitted a terrible squeal throughout the vessel, this usually allowed all hands a three second interval before maximum helm over tilted the decks as the ship's big rudders bit deeply into the tormented water and several hundred tonnes of force slammed her stern to port.

Upon the flight deck and within the two hangars the heel started loose aircraft to rock on their pneumatic tires and tools & equipment to rattle as the hull trembled, and the great vessel heeled over and took on a 3 degree list to port. The downward force of gravity acted upon the great weight of water in the starboard anti-rolling tanks combined with upward thrust of the reserve buoyancy of that port side portion of the hull forced under the water, fought against the angular velocity of the ships mass acting against its center of gravity in the high speed turn, trying to tip her over. I could see it all in my mind and I counted softly as she righted herself precisely at the right moment. Then Kapitein Voorne called for flank speed, and the great ship vibrated slightly but noticeably accelerated and steadied up on the new course.

I had been straining slightly to hold myself steady against a table as the ship maneuvered. My lips had gone dry and my stogie had burned down and was stuck to my lower lip searing it, the smoke had started to make my left eye water as I tried to spit it away, I had a coffee mug in one hand and a sheaf of reports in the other. I regained my balance then went over to the Air Operations officer and told him that I wanted the *Johan de Witt* to launch all of its remaining fighter aircraft as soon as the battle-carriers were free to maneuver for wind. Just then another urgent warning; ALARM LUCHAANVAL! (Alarm Air attack) screeched out. Multiple reports now came in to the command center, Torpedo Bombers were closing from the west and the north!

I was convinced that the maximum effort by the JAAF and IJN would soon unfold and that we were now seeing only the spoiling attacks developing, ones designed to deny us flight deck operations. Over the deck head loudspeaker the pilot of our sub hunting Helldivers on his probe to the west called in; "Falcon 1 to Mother Goose, six large biplanes approaching at wave top height out of the west; range 12,000 meters I am closing to identify." Three of our CAP Sea Fury fighters then dove to support the dive-bomber which had only one forward firing .30 cal. machine gun, and a dorsal gun. "*Falcon 1* to *Mother Goose*; I have just over flown six Mitsubishi Type D-2 torpedo bombers, course due east speed 110 knots! I am engaging".

Then; "*Falcon 3* to *Mother Goose*; six D-2 torpedo planes, and three monoplane fighters, speed 120 knots, course due south, range 15,000 meters, elevation 100 meters. I am attacking. Two air attacks were now inbound; one from the west and another from the north using the classic 90 degree enveloping maneuver; bloody torpedo bombers!

Kapitein Lt. ter Zee Van Ripper the Vlaggeschip's senior gunnery officer rang up his gunfire control center and barked sharply into the phone; "ALLES LUCHAFWEER BATTERIJEN; VOORBEREIDEN, VOORBEREIDEN, VOORBEREIDEN, MEERDER DOEL: TORPEDO BOMMENWERPER! AANVAL; NARR HET NOORDEN 15.000 METER EN IN HET WESTEN BEREIK 12,000 METER! (All Anti-Aircraft Batteries, prepare, prepare, prepare, Target; Torpedo Bombers from the north 15,000 meters and from the west 12,000 meters.

I ran through the mathematics of the closer attack, the one coming in from the west. Our ships were steaming at some 30 knots (16 meters/sec.) with their sterns presented to the enemy at that time, the enemy machine's speed of advance was only 57 meters per second. As a result the powerful but slow biplanes were closing slowly at only some 41 meters per second! It would take five minutes at least to get into a launch position... the math didn't work! They could not hit us on this heading, they had insufficient time as our fighter's would soon destroy them. Turning to my Chief of Air Operations, I was about to tell him to concentrate more fighters on the northern attack when Commander Flier Van Breakel gave the order vectoring four CAP buffalos north to aid the four Sea Fury MK II fighters of *Falcon 2*.

I then became puzzled, was this enemy primarily engaged in harassment; to disrupt our flight operations at dawn? Or just suffering from a badly timed attack plan? Were the earlier torpedoes from submarines at all or other torpedo planes? Both attacks seem to suggest to me that their torpedoes may have an incredibly long range as the Japanese aircraft were using a *stand-off technique* to deliver their weapons.

Glancing towards Kapitein ter Zee Daniel Van Braekel, I asked, "Air Ops? If we turn north into the wind to launch the remaining Sea Eagles we will present our long hulls to those torpedo bombers coming from the west and risk being hit. Are we able to launch our planes on this bearing?"

"Admiraal," the Air Chief responded; "the meteorology unit reports that the moderate northerly winds have fallen to three knots so there would be little to gain from turning into what is only a light breeze. However the ships themselves at this speed are generating more than enough wind to launch our remaining fighters, and even the last of the Sea Eagles without the *Ogorki* rocket."

I hastily barked the order, "Get them all up immediately Air Chief, from both battle-carriers! Start fitting the Sea Eagles with the pickle booster rockets to save launch time if you must, but get those bombers off the deck with the single 750 kilogram AP bombs first, then get all the fighters away and keep the bloody launch intervals as low as possible. Is that clear AO?" He replied in the affirmative, and I waved him on.

The loudspeaker once again belted out its message from *Falcon 1*; that all six enemy torpedo bombers had been engaged by CAP Buffalos, had dropped their fish at a range of 10,000 meters. These were on a course to pass north of the fleet, no doubt in an anticipation of our alteration of course to the north that would allow the launching of the aircraft to continue. So the change of course to the north was out. While Falcon 3, soon reported an air battle underway between its Sea Fury MK II fighters and enemy carrier fighters and torpedo planes who are pressing forward despite their casualties. The Japanese Kawasaki K-10 biplane fighters shortly succumbed to three to one odds against them, after a valiant effort. All the Mitsubishi D-2 bombers were shot down into the sea, without managing to release their deadly fish.

The latter was not accomplished without some difficulty as the big, robust torpedo planes stood up well to light caliber machine gun fire. The design was a licensed copy of the Blackburn Shark MK III, manufactured by Mitsubishi. If I survive this, I promised myself; the next time that I am in London I will go to the Blackburn Aircraft Company head office and punch its director right in the nose, for selling this design to the enemy.

Although; in the space of a few minutes all the medium carrier's fighters and torpedo planes had been dispatched by our fighters. I was completely shocked to discover not only how closely *TF Popeye* was being monitored by the Imperial Japanese Navy, but that they were able to operate effectively at night and put in coordinated attacks against us at first light! Nevertheless we had responded well, the attacks had been thwarted swiftly and operations continued as before. Our makeshift defense of using light bombs to destroy torpedoes in the water proved effective. Eerst bloed nar ons! (First blood to us!)

The Observations of:
25 year old Lt. Commander Van de Groot, Squadron Leader; Bomber Squadron 1; flying off the flagship; *Cornelis de Witt* of Task Force Popeye, RNLN, strike leader of combined air group designated; Striker One, South China Sea. 06:24hrs December 08 1941:

"Striker 1….to Mother Goose...Striker 1...to Mother Goose... target in sight, target in sight..., invasion convoy; 25 troop transports, 2 battleships Settsu Class, 1 oil tanker and 11 destroyer escort of Minekaze Class,.....Course SE, speed 17 knots, no enemy fighters, 4,000 meters altitude... tipping over now...first section go...spread out..all sections. Just as in a training flight pilots.. follow me down..take your time get hits...no fighters...no fighters. All Helldivers arm your bombs...diving attack.. diving attack......attack...go first for the transports…primary target the transports…and the oil tanker..tipping over…"

The F.C.C. erupted in cheers we had caught them with no fighters! Then all our ears strained to make sense of the cacophony of noise that issued from that little vibrating speaker. The scream of the air past the cockpit of the first dive bomber increased as the powerful radial engine, and the big three bladed propeller of that long-snouted diver bomber tore the machine earthward; exulting in the assist of gravity..500 kph...600 kph. "ZOOOM *what the hell was that? Schiesse, fighters!..LOOK OUT Godverdomm fighters! 760 kph!*"

Lots of swearing now issued from out of the deck-head speaker, mixed in with the rattle of automatic fire…a period of confusion now ensued, as the airmen cluttered up the radio frequency with their excited chatter, nevertheless I could sift out the commander's voice, with whom I was quite familiar;

"my bombsight is rapidly fogging up…diving through warmer air,… all strikers get something to wipe the condensation from your canopy and bomb sight fast…OK..I am back on target a fat 5,000 tonne, three hatch troopship just below…release…pull up… two eggs away!"

The Observations of:
17 year old Air Telegraphist Gunner Jan Steen flying in the rear cockpit of a Curtiss Model 77 Helldiver, Aircraft No. B1C -7, a bi-plane dive-bomber piloted by Lt. Rudolf Thorbecke commander of Flight B Bomber Squadron 1 from the flagship *Cornelis de Witt,* Task Force Popeye, RNLN, 06:26hrs Dec. 08, 1941:

"Lt. Thorbecke tipped the 'Amorous Anny' over into a steep dive (her favorite angle). I lay back on my seat and looked straight up. Over the radio I had heard that Striker leader had dove through some fighter planes but he was going much too fast in a dive to be chased. The Lt. asked if I had cleared the rear .306 gun for action? The laminar flow of air on the fuselage was now of secondary importance, as we were going into action. I replied in the affirmative, and then raced to do this."

"The big air cooled .30 Cal. machine gun was stowed deep with its barrel down and lashed to the gun ring mount located aft in my rear cockpit position. I popped off the retainer clip and freed up the receiver, then I had to push the gun up and the barrel out to port so that I could haul myself up and push down the duralumin turtle-deck sections into their stowed positions. A task that I accomplished with ease as I was floating weightless in my shoulder harness half the time as the Anny tore seaward constantly accelerating."

"The gun was deployed, I yanked back on the bolt, I was loaded and ready for action; and just in time as a monoplane fighter flashed past behind us, overshot, then corrected, and struggled to stay on our tail with guns winking. I attempted to track the machine, the muzzle of the weapon finally caught up to it and I squeezed off some wild rounds. I found it very difficult to train the barrel of the machine gun against the screaming slipstream tearing past the Plexiglas side screen at close to 700 kph! Big white blobs like cotton balls went whizzing up past my cockpit rocking the dive bomber, heavy tracer fire from below. I could see the rudder moving to the left and then the right as the Lt. corrected his dive to keep his maneuvering target in sight."

"I felt the bombs release then we leapt up and I became dizzy as the blood drained from my upper body; and rushed towards my boots. I fought the blackout as Anny started to level out over the water as we zig-zag our way out of the enemy flak which viciously ripped up the waves just behind us."

"Then I saw the target ship; a large freighter in light green and faded yellow camouflage paint. The bulwark and amidships deckhouse was packed with helmeted army personnel, oriental faces contorted in snarls of rage and fury they were blazing away at us with their small arms! One of our 225 kilogram bombs had missed the ship, falling very close to starboard sending up a huge column of dirty white spray. The other bomb passed just over the deckhouse structure from aft and had plunged through the foredeck just in front of her forward cargo mast. A huge fire-ball explosion erupted violently upwards hurling debris and soldiers skyward."

"Anny had flattened out over the sea and sped away when I noticed a straight line of tall splashes stitching the water and tracking our course. Fighters!…I swung my gun around, pressed the trigger and began to shoot…up and to my right, where at 50 meters no more…three sleek monoplane fighters with fixed undercarriage chased "Anny" with twin guns winking on top of their engine cowlings. My, but aren't you graceful little devils I thought?"

"The right hand fighter suddenly shot upwards, climbed steeply and started to smoke. Flashing over top of them coming in from their port side was the stubby body of one of the F3F flying barrels,

her heavy and light machine guns hammering! Painted on the fighter's engine cowling; a naked buxom, long legged blond leaned forward sensually and it seemed that one green eye winked at me, her amazing body so arched that the red hot exhaust fired out her perfect ass! 'Filthy Lill' to the rescue, what a babe! As we flew away I observed the troopships, several of which had been heavily hit. Above them our Helldivers were still to be seen dropping out of the sky like so many silver beads threaded onto a necklace of smoke, guns sparkled in their red painted noses as they plunged downward to deliver the dark deadly eggs tucked neatly under their fat bellies."

"Where is the main force of the JAAF fighters I asked myself? Lt. Thorbecke then turned 'Amorous Anny' around to help cover the other dive bombers yet to release their bombs. Many of our Helldivers and the Grumman fighters were mixing it up with their JAAF opposite number which seemed to be very agile, but not quite so much as our biplane fighters; the F2F & F3F's. "Perky Polly" flashed by, guns hammering, the cowling decoration, a hugely endowed slutty brunette, leered mischievously in my direction! Then our .50 cal. nose machine gun began to hammer again, we then flew through a plume of black smoke and I felt an instant flash of heat on my right cheek. Then I was blazing away at a Nakajima on our tail with a long burst."

"I imagine that was when I was hit. The next thing that I recalled was waking up slowly, still inside of 'Amorous Anny'. She was quiet now, and no longer heaved and bucked, she must be down or home; back on the flight deck of the good old Cornelis."

"I was being gently lifted from out of the rear cockpit by many hands. My neck hurt, I seemed unable to talk, my mouth was dry and my tongue swollen, any attempt that I made at movement was sluggish and required concentrated effort. My brow which ached sharply, felt hot and sticky, I found it difficult to focus my eyes and I felt very drowsy."

"I looked up into the face of a grizzled chief machinist's mate who seemed to be taking a great deal of time and care fumbling with the buckles of my parachute harness. Beside him the brutish face of the deck chief Polder looked down at me almost with tenderness and he must have been sweating as salty water droplets were splashing into my eyes. Careful Ace, he said to me gently, we've got you. I smiled lazily and was trying to formulate a rather rude and humorous remark when I drifted quietly into a warm unconsciousness."

Then, 17 year old Air Telegraphist Gunner Jan Steen was wounded in the head by shrapnel from a 5 inch anti-aircraft burst from the modernized Japanese dreadnought *Kagoshima*. The shell exploded one meter off the port wing tip peppering the side of his dive-bomber. When the surgeon removed his headgear it was revealed that a large portion of his left brow and skull had been cut clean through and folded over! He survived his wounds to the amazement of his shipmates who believed, as they later joked; because he never used it!. After a period of convalescence at the Auckland City Hospital in New Zeeland, he was demobilized due to his injuries in November 19, 1942. The young man now healthy and still adventurous had no place to turn as both the Netherlands and the East Indies were now occupied by the Axis powers. Using his remaining military pay he boarded the Pan American China Clipper to San Francisco, and from there he immigrated to Canada, to join the sizable Dutch émigré community in Montreal.

Mr. Steen was interviewed for this book in 1986 while living in British Columbia, Canada. There he operated a landscaping nursery, on the Saanich Peninsula from which he supplied shrubbery and tulips to the gardens of the Provincial Government building in Victoria. One of his former employees: Tajiro Kuboashi had served in the IJN in World War Two and had been a thirteen year old sail maker's apprentice aboard the IJN battleship *Kagoshima* at the time of the Dutch attack, and his battle station was serving a 5" anti-aircraft battery! A truly uncanny coincidence!

The Observations of:
22 year old Lt. ter Zee 2e Klasse, (Lieutenant) Jacob Van Veelan, Flight 'A' Leader of Fighter Squadron 1 from the Battlecruiser-carrier *Cornelis de Witt*, Flagship of Task Force Popeye, RNLN, flying aircraft no. F1C-1, a Grumman F3F biplane fighter, on a Dive Bomber Escort mission, South China Sea, 06:20hrs December 08, 1941:

"Six minutes earlier the right echelon machines of Striker 2 peeled away to starboard to begin their attack on the IJN warships formation below. That was my first view of a Japanese Navy medium carrier. I really envied Striker 2. I located the troopship convoy, barely visible ahead and closed the distance. I rolled "Perverted Penny" over to port to have a better view of the targets 6,500 meters below me. The ships; immediately became aware of our planes, and had begun to maneuver for room, delicate perfect wave patterns were generated; looking from above like so many snakes swimming on the surface of the pond. A few puffs of dark smoke appeared 300 meters below the Helldiver formation which confirmed that those two escorting fat battlewagons below had a several large caliber flak guns aboard. Already the Helldivers were streaming down in a steep graceful dive. Some 3000 meters below us several thin clouds drifted across the target. Flying from out of the one furthest to the north east I was able to identify five three plane sections! As I watched these enemy fighters began to climb, looking uncannily like our Dutch Army Fokker Fighters, until I saw the red roundels on each wing."

"The JAAF Nakajimas were too far away to stop the Helldivers now streaming downwards at great speed. The Ki-27 fighters may attempt to create a torrent of machinegun fire through which the Helldivers must pass but they would by then be reaching a very high velocity and should pass on down through the cone of danger in an instant."

The bulkhead speaker clearly delivered the radio transmission from one of our dive bomber units; *"Perverted Penny to all my girls; let's get down there to those fat troopships and give them all a good case of the bloody clap!"*

At this comment; my Chief of Air Operations looked at me apologetically with a little embarrassed shrug, I reassured him with a shake of my head and a suppressed grin, that it did not matter, as I recalled that I swore a lot more rudely than that, in the heat of action; hand to hand fighting the South China with Chinese and native pirates twenty years ago, half mad, with cutlass in one hand, my Colt .45 revolver in the other…covered in blood and shit.

"The F3F fighter had two nose machine guns; a heavy .50 cal. to starboard and a .30 cal. light machine gun to port. The first weapon was a much more powerful and longer ranged armament than those aboard the beautiful Nakajima fighter; which at the time was perhaps the most graceful of all the fixed under-carriage monoplane machines ever produced. It was the first of these weapons which allowed my fighters to score at once, and heavily."

"Both groups of fighters attacked one another at a closing speed of 800 kph. The range came down very fast with our machines being able to fire all the way down. The Nakajimas had to wait to fire until they were only some 300 meters below us. Already several of their lightly built machines had shed component debris and shreds of duralumin skin as each .50 Cal bullet packed a whopping six foot tons of kinetic energy! On this first exchange six Nakajimas had already broken off their

climb smoking, they turned nimbly away, to attack those Helldivers which had already dropped their bombs and were climbing for altitude, or flying at sea level, having just released their bombs."

"Perverted Penny and her girls released their bomb-lets over the convoy then plunged into a wild free-for-all with the JAAF Nakajima fighters which enjoyed at this stage a three to one superiority against the F3F escorts. We had gotten lucky with the JAAF on this first encounter. Our Helldivers had committed to their steep descent before they were spotted by the enemy fighters, after which only a ramming attack had any chance of stopping them. The nimble fighters of the enemy we soon discovered were superior to our machines only in that they had an 40 kph. speed advantage over our F3F-2 fighter in level flight and only 20 kph. over the Curtiss Mod. 77 Helldiver, when shed of its bombs!" They could not match our robustness nor the extreme maneuverability of our fighters."

"Striker 1 could not out run the Nakajima Ki-27's, we were forced therefore to outfight them, smash them up. We had to destroy the enemy fighters completely or make them break off action and flee. In a way we were trapped, if we returned to the flagship they could simply follow us to the battle-carriers where they would pose a grave danger. The Helldivers did not have time to engage in prolonged air combat, although they were for the most part itching to. They had to return to their ships quickly as the target convoy was close to the limit of their range."

"The Japanese pilots fought like 'WW1 knights of the air' preferring to dogfight at slower speeds than their machine was designed for, rather than use their advantage in that capability and make high speed passes at us. The men riding the "girls" remembered their tactical training and demonstrated it during this air battle. The lightly built Nakajima was unable to perform as tight turns as our fighters at the highest speeds but with our shorter wings the centers of lift were much closer inboard, therefore we were able to roll out of trouble much faster, nor could the Ki-27 skid its tail sideways very well to pour fire into those enemy machines in its 9 o'clock or 3 o'clock. The two types of machines although of different concept were never-the-less well matched. With the F3F-2; which many considered to be the best development of an obsolete concept combating the Ki-27, a good first effort in a more modern design concept; the cantilever wing. I was able to repeatedly put my F3F-2 into dives that the Nakajimas would be unable to follow. At such high speeds their thin cantilever wing; which was only some 300 mm thick at wing root would buckle under the 8 + Gravity turns. Our biplane wing; a stayed box beam wing was a structure almost two meters deep, with a very large inertia and was incredibly strong for its weight."

"Two Nakajimas who had tried following me down in very steep dives had to 'shallow it out' overshooting me, I then I pulled up tightly, hammering my nose guns into their underbellies. Both our Grumman and Curtiss machines enjoyed an early model of self-sealing internal fuselage fuel tanks, whereas the longer wing tanks of the Ki-27's were equally large targets. Striker 1 had shot down six Nakajima's without loss to fighter or bomber. We had peppered their wings quite a bit and they lost much of their fuel. Our heavier machines with moderate ballistic armor over the vitals had fared well. Our wings had been holed quite a bit but this was not so serious. The Grumman fighter's wing were just a fabric over a duralumin frame and contained no tanks. Nine times out of ten the repair involved simply a fabric patch, a little glue and a touch of paint. The JAAF fighters had enough of us it seemed. When we broke off our attack to depart, they did not dog our return as we had feared they might.

The 6th *Kokugun* (Air Army), had recently been deployed from Manchuria to provide support for an up-coming big operation designated Nnezumitori (mousetrap): *The Destruction of The Dutch East Indies Colonial Fleet.* The Japanese 123rd Fighter Regiment had just switched over to the Ki-27 from the venerable Kawazaki K-10; a nimble bi-plane fighter, a machine with considerably different handling characteristics.

The pilots of the *123rd Hikosentai* (Air Regiment) of fighters, were equipped with new cantilever wing, all aluminum fighter, the Nakajima Ki-27. On December 08, 1941, the unit based out of My Thoa Airbase, French Indo-China was scrambled to protect the Malay Invasion Convoy and escort vessels of General Takaguchi, now under threat of imminent air attack by the Battleship-plane carriers of the Dutch Colonial Fleet, currently cruising eastward in the South China Sea, off the coastline of Sarawak.

The Observations of:

41 year Colonel Tatsujiro Shimada, the Commanding Officer of the 123rd Hikosentai (Air Regiment) of fighters, of the 22nd Hikodan (Air Brigade) of the 17th Hikoshiden (Air Division) attached to the 6th Kokugun, (Air Army) of the Japanese Army Air Force (JAAF): (See Appendix F)

"America and Great Britain were the two nations that had greatly assisted the Emperor in his decision to transform Japan from an agrarian feudal state into an industrial world power in the space of forty years. Great Britain had financed the construction and training of our first class Japanese Navy. Then she supervised its use in its first major action in 1904 against a European Power; our attack against Russia's Pacific Fleet and its colonies to destroy the eastward expansion of Russia trade."

"After this curtailment of Russian Pacific trade had been accomplished, that gigantic country was no longer seen as an expansionist threat, being as she was totally occupied with internal revolution and economic strife. Then to our surprise, our recent passionate advocate; Great Britain no longer viewed our military expansion in a sympathetic way. In fact she aligned herself with France, America and the Dutch with their extensive trade monopolies, and chose to economically isolate Japan and let her wither on the vine."

The European Colonial Powers of the South East Asia region, refused to sell us the quantities of minerals, raw material and oil to feed the industries which maintained our strong growing Empire. They drastically underestimated our resolve to unravel the bonds that America, the European Colonial Powers had been applying through their unacceptable trade restrictions on the Japanese nation."

"Our ambassadorial service felt that the European Colonial Powers reasoned that they could bully Japan in South East Asia, they thought that we were afraid of their submarine cordon, and they felt our own military was over-extended and deadlocked in remote Manchuria, fighting the Soviet Army. They gravely underestimated the capability of the new modern Empire of Japan!"

"A crisis had been brewing in French Indo China. As the Vichy regime of France was by 1941 an ally of the Axis powers, Great Britain had been intercepting her shipping plying its trade with Japan. The French were afraid of further British violations of its administrative territories and had appealed to our Devine Emperor for protection. The Japanese Empire had agreed therefore to send troops and military equipment to garrison the threatened coastline and the Imperial Japanese Navy had been tasked to ensure their safe delivery."

"At 04:30hrs Dec. 08, 1941, the 6th Fighter Hikosentai was called into action! The Imperial Japanese Navy was at sea escorting a convoy carrying 13,000 troops of General Takaguchi's 15 th Infantry Division to Saigon. The Dutch Navy had been observed yesterday departing from Singapore and steaming into the Java Sea. However, during the evening it had changed course and

entered the South China Sea, at high speed, in great strength, on a course and in such a formation that could only be interpreted as direct attack on these Japanese convoys."

"Our pilots assembled in the bamboo main building hall at the front of which was a huge map of the South China Sea. Off of the coast of Lower Cochin China were two small Japanese flags on pins side by side in the sea. *Far to the south were affixed long menacing lines made of ribbon. The black ribbon which indicated the course track of the British Navy during the last 24 hrs. It started at the tip of Malaya and made an erratic path into the Gulf of Siam, correspondingly the blue and red ribbon represented the track of the Dutch Fleet over the same period. That ribbon ran north out of the Java Sea, then turned NE. on an obvious interception course for our ships at sea. The escorting warships of Japan were not strong enough to stop the approach of these large aggressive fleets if they attacked the troopships. The newly arrived Kokugun from Manchuria would have that honor."*

"The location of the new bases for the Bomber and Fighter Hikosentais of the 6th Kokugun (Air Army) were indicated on the wall map and these were spread out at strategic locations along the southern coastline. We felt assured that our powerful bomber groups and our new fighter Air Regiment would be a wall of safety for our Army at sea."

"The enemy fleets we were told contained powerful vessels. The British squadron had two huge new battleships with destroyer escorts, while the Dutch formation was larger still, having a host of destroyers, cruisers and two huge half-battleship half airplane carrier vessels. JAAF Intelligence reports revealed that those hybrid ships in addition to their many heavy guns carried at least 100 light attack planes and fighters and it was against this latter fleet that our bomber Hikosentais and our fighters would operate."

"A messenger entered the briefing hall, ran up to my table in great agitation and handed me a radio communication. I rose from the corner of the desk on which I had been sitting and slammed my bamboo disciplinary rod down across the table with a great bang. Instantly the room froze. I called for attentiveness and went solemnly to a wall mounted loudspeaker and turned it on to loud."

"The Tokyo radio announcer had some very uplifting news of great fortune. Japan had responded with honor to the continuous aggressive posture of the allied nations. Today our glorious fleet under the command of Admiral Yamamoto had launched a tremendous attack against the U.S. Pacific Fleet threatening us from its forward base in Hawaii and completely smashed it! The great naval victory was on such a huge scale that it could be considered even a greater victory than Tsushima! The Emperor sends his greetings and congratulations to all his subjects serving in uniform. The room exploded with wild cheers of; Banzai! Banzai! Banzai!"

"Our long range seaplanes which had been shadowing the Dutch Navy assured us that large formations of aircraft would soon be flying off from the decks of the battleship-plane carriers with the undoubted intention of attacking General Takaguchi's convoys."

The Observations of:

21 year old Master Sergeant Shintaro Sakai; flying a Nakajima Ki-27 fighter of the 133rd Chutai, (Squadron) JAAF. Operating from My Thoa Airbase in Cochin China. Dec. 08, 1941: (See Appendix F)

"05:45hrs, it was with great enthusiasm that we ran to our new fighter planes. The air mechanics had already started the engines and they were running smoothly. A red flare was seen to arch over airstrip two, the three fighters of our Shotai wingtip to wingtip gunned our engines and raced over the damp grass to be the first fighter into the air. Our light machines fairly leapt from

the ground with the grace of swallows. Our altitude for this mission was 4000 meters. We would locate the troopship convoy and the naval screen to the south, where we would make contact with the air umbrella of our IJN aircraft carrier. The plan was simple; we would fly a long looping figure eight pattern over both convoys at 4000 meters, then intercept and destroy any enemy aircraft that dared to approach the ships."

"Earlier that month the JAAF intelligence had discovered that all of the naval aircraft aboard the Dutch vessels were obsolete biplane types cast off from the American and British navies. Our very modern Nakajima single wing fighters of all aluminum construction were much more technically advanced than the machines flown by any European power in this region. Consequently our commander demanded a quick defeat of the Dutch battleship-carriers' air groups to expose them to massed air attack by the heavy bombers of the Army. The anticipated air action was eagerly anticipated by our young pilots as all hoped to achieve "Ace" status on this first mission! We had every confidence in our superior flying skills as we had seen action in Manchuria against the Air Forces of both the Soviet Union, and the Chinese Nationalist Army."

"Suddenly my wingman Sgt. Naboru Hinoki yelled; "Enemy Planes to the south at 7000 meters! Above us and two kilometers south I could see a two long lines of silvery biplane aircraft already dropping out of the sky...dive-bombers! We had not expected these machines for at least another hour! Looking below I saw the troopships in three columns sailing slowly along. The cloud cover was minor. How skillful had been the approach from the enemy!"

"Squadron Leader Lt. Tsubone then said; "133rd. Chutai; climb and attack!" We turned our machines skyward in a long steep loop and tried to single out a target. The biplane dive bombers and fighters were all shooting their nose guns at us on the way down to the convoy. I realized with dismay as their heavy slugs started to chew into my fighter plane that their weapons outranged ours by at least 1500 meters!"

"The Dutch dive bombers dove down past my fighter at such a great speed that I did not think possible for the fabric covered wings of that biplane! I could neither follow at such a speed nor prevent the attack against the troopships which, I must say with deep regret; was already well underway. But I was a Japanese pilot, I must try. A crisis was unfolding rapidly before my eyes while I was momentarily helpless!"

"The 133rd Fighter Chutai tipped the noses of their three fighters over and dove after the Dutch machines our twin 7.7 mm machine guns chattering. But these speeding biplanes proved impossible to overtake, bullets started to hit my fighter from above and the tail gunner of the dive-bomber that I was following was shooting up at me. I pulled hard to the right and out of my dive to avoid the deadly crossfire just as the plane that had been attacking me from behind flashed past; a large long snouted bi-plane of polished duralumin; a Curtiss Helldiver...the tail gunner, seeing me tried unsuccessfully to train his weapon. Then more bullets slammed into my left wing...I rolled hard to the right and put the nose down. A rain drop shaped fighter flashed past me. It was another bi-plane built of polished duralumin like the dive bombers. I made out the red painted engine cowling, with its rudder painted in red, white and blue stripes. Army intelligence had been correct; the enemy's navy operated only biplane attack groups, but they were very fast and maneuverable! So I thought with rising fury; this then was what obsolescence looked like!"

"Shintaro! Shintaro! yelled Naboru over the radio; enemy fighter on your back! Looking over my shoulder I saw the red painted engine cowling of a stubby Grumman F3F closing on me from behind with nose guns winking and matching my every move with ease. I turned hard to the right and climbed; the big 9 cylinder radial engine droned. I could it seemed out-climb my heavier attacker

as I had some slight power to weight advantage according to the Ki-27's technical manual. But ohh so slowly did the distance open between our machines, this was not working, all the while I kicked the rudder to the left and right so that I would not be an easy target for his longer range guns. I evaded my pursuer as I passed through a small cloud. Emerging; I looked wildly about, where was my Chutai? I rolled to the left and looked down on the fleet. The ocean was criss-crossed with the delicate wave patterns and long white wakes as the ships below steered with desperation to evade the bombs which I could see raised huge dirty columns of water as they exploded in the sea. Several large Marus were already hit and on fire. More bombs were striking on and around them as I watched. The destroyers and battleships were firing their flak guns furiously as they twisted and turned in a desperate efforts to protect the troopships."

"Below me I saw a number of the enemy dive-bombers flying low over the sea. Some having already expended their bombs, were slowly climbing for altitude to renew their attack with machine guns on the crowded troopships. Now they were at their most vulnerable! I chose a target and closed to the attack in a shallow dive from behind. I wildly searched the skies as I descended for any fighters that may be hunting me while I aimed my guns. The tail gunner of the dive bomber that I had selected started to shoot at me as his pilot took evasive action to the left, before I was able to put his aircraft in my sighting scope. Once more I tracked the Helldiver and had just started to fire when the nimble machine turned tightly inside my left turn. Then heavy bullets slammed into my engine with jarring impact and it started to misfire. I turned hard to the right and broke off the action. The engine vibrated very badly then it lost all power, it sounded like it had taken hits in the cylinders. My new fighter on only its sixth flight crashed into the jungle some ten kilometers south of the airbase. I had to trust to the silk as my fuel tanks had been riddled by numerous bullet holes and fire was a real danger now. If the engine had not died the Nakajima would most likely have burnt. But she glided very well and got me safely over the land."

"In Manchuria, our unit converted to the Nakajima Ki -27 monoplane fighter. We had done this to combat the Polikarpov I-16; a fast monoplane of Spanish Civil War fame, called the Rat. I looked up at the underside of my silk parachute twisting in the turbulence I thought with a great remorse; if only I had been flying my trusty Kawasaki K-10 fighter; an aerodynamically clean, beautiful little biplane of superb maneuverability, although slower that the Nakajima. With it I would have bested this enemy! I knew that our combat experienced fighter pilots could have handled the Dutch Navy fliers. How would I be able to explain this loss to Squadron Leader Lt. Tsubone? I wondered if my fellow pilots had managed to stop the enemy attack?"

The Observations of:

25 year old Lt. Commander Dirk Hollander leading Bomber Squadron 4, designated Striker 2, flying a Curtiss Helldiver, aircraft number B4J-1; *Moaning Mona* from the Battle-cruiser carrier *Johan de Witt* of Task Force Popeye, RNLN, South China Sea, 06:20hrs, December 08, 1941:

"The Air Operations Officer Commander Flier Wolraven Van Hall gave us a detailed briefing on our priority target a Japanese light carrier believed to be of the Zuiho class. Next in priioty was her powerful cruiser escort of four Moyoko Class and then the destroyers. Cheering broke out as our group drew the choicest target! We were worried that we may have been assigned the troopship convoy. Sinking the Zuiho and her cruisers would have been a real feather in our caps. She and her cruisers, like the Johan de Witt were major fleet units. Furthermore, as our target fleet was a little closer than the troopships, the target for the flagships bombers, Bomber Squadron 4 would *strike the first blows for the RNLN against the enemy! The IJN would judge our metal on how we acquitted ourselves on this first action, and their plans would subsequently reflect either caution or contempt!*

"Bomber Squadron 4, launched from the Johan de Witt in record time; only 7 seconds between planes! All my aircraft formed up on the Moaner in right echelon formation. We clawed at the sky for altitude. Above us the seven Grumman F2F-1 fighters of Lt. Gunter Harmse were also disposed in right echelon formation. We soon formed two VEE formations with fighters and bombers of Striker one and raced north. All aboard realized that this day would be decisive for us, not necessarily so for the mighty Rengo Kantai, for whom destruction of all these forces today would be merely an inconvenience. Powerful forces were arrayed against us, over which we must prevail on each occasion or perish. All the crews of 'Bommenwerper Eskadron II' knew that in a contest against the Imperial Japanese Navy we would be heavily outnumbered. In the event that we succeed in fighting our way through to the assigned target we must have accurate bombing."

"The fighters of Lt. Harmse being some 300 meters above spotted the enemy ships ahead of us first and signaled to me. In a minute I also found them and could identify the light carrier which, without a deckhouse looked just like a brick. Surrounding her and speeding to the S. E. were her escorting warships. As I watched at the prow of each ship a large cloud of white spray appeared. We had been spotted, and the enemy vessels connected full power to their propeller shafts and leapt forward cleaving the seas with their sharp prows."

"Looking to my right not 10 meters away was Lt. Commander Van de Groot smiling widely. I pointed down to the target and he nodded and gave me a sharp salute followed by the old Roman hand sign of thumbs down; death. I gripped my stick and spoke to the pilots of my Helldivers; Striker 2 break right and follow me down. Keep your spacing, get in close and make hits. If the carrier is heavily damaged before you reach her then don't waste your bombs, you will just be redistributing scrap steel on a sinking ship; go after the escorts, cruisers first."

"With that I waved to Lt. Commander Van de Groot and I began a 15 degree dive to target with the remaining 14 bombers of Striker 2 following me down in 'text book' perfect spacing. I ordered my crewman; Air Telegraphist Gunner Anton Boshof to signal the flagship; Striker 2 to Mother-goose target identified beginning our attack. Within a minute we had reached 530 kph. and would soon attain a velocity at which no fighter umbrella could overtake us. As the speed increased the wing strut stay wires produced the sound that named my bird; 'The Moaner.' Mother-goose acknowledged my transmission then the radio came alive with the excited voices of our escort: Enemy fighters diving from above! The chatter of machine guns, roaring engines and excited instructions."

"Below; the target was coming up fast due to the rapid approach of my machine. I dove steeper still with the airspeed indicator hovering at 700 kph. At 1000 meters altitude my ship passed into warm moist air and the cockpit glass and bombsite began fog over as the warm humid air entering the cockpit caused condensation to form on the chilled steel and glass of the bomb site. I slammed open the canopy vents to heat up my instruments and mopped off the front Plexiglas with a cotton rag. While the target had been somewhat obscured but I held on. White blobs of tracer from the Zuiho's powerful flak guns whipped past the cockpit shaking the machine with their shockwaves. I released my 225 kg. bombs and pulled up just as I took an explosive shell that passed through the lower port wing fabric detonating well behind us. The diver-bomber staggered and looked as if the damaged wing would collapse, a huge hole had been torn through the lower port wing. The upper wing was bent upward with the extra stresses. I dared not pull up and attempt gaining altitude.

I slowly made my way back to the Johan de Witt hugging the wave tops to gain some assist from the phenomena of "surface effect."

"My radio was destroyed and I was reduced to conversing with my crewman with messages scribbled on scraps of paper torn from my fight log. One of my bombs I saw clearly hit the small aircraft carrier on the starboard quarter near the waterline on her torpedo blister as she was engaged in a hard turn to port. The other bomb exploded in the sea just short of the nimble warship. I thought for a moment how sluggish she made the Johan de Witt appear as I had observed her carrying out the same evasive maneuver many times. Neither of my bombs would have totally impaired the fighting power of the enemy carrier as her torpedo blister was designed to defeat the effects of detonations against the hull. The ship would have been violently shaken however and red hot steel splinters would have slashed her sides."

The Observations of:
Air Telegraphist Gunner; Anton Boshof aboard the *Moaning Mona* who, with his 0.30 Caliber tail gun ready for action, swept the sky for enemy fighters and had a good view of the action astern:

"The Japanese light carrier's luck had run out. Several of our Helldivers had scored good hits as she was afire amidships, with a huge pall of dark smoke billowing out over her stern, flames were leaping from out of rents in her flight deck and rolling aft blanketing everything behind the conflagration. Yet her high speed did not seem to be impaired. An air battle raged between our F3F's and the carrier's CAP. Our Helldivers now devoid of bombs, and lightened due to burning 40% of fuel now assumed their secondary role as fighters and hurled themselves at the enemy machines which attacked with a vengeance. The Japanese fighter defense was furious as it was skilled. As we drew further away from the battle I could see that our dive bombers were still dropping out of the sky to pounce on the escorting warships. The Moyoko class cruisers must have detached in the night for they were nowhere to be seen, so our bombers pounded away at the Japanese destroyers. We rattled along so low to the sea that the prop wash sent up a cooling spray. The pilot had managed to put some distance between our laboring Helldiver and the battle, so that I could only see the tall spouts of water thrown up by the bursting bombs; looking ever so much like huge trees with dirty brown foliage spreading wide over a short white column of the trunk, then flashes of gunfire spurted from the ships, lots of black smoke and aircraft afire...falling into the sea."

The "Moaning Mona" and her brave crew did not make it back to the *Johan de Witt* on that day. Aircraft number B4J-9, *Silky Smooth Sally*, a Helldiver from; flight B of *Striker 2*, flown by Chief Petty Officer Flyer Rupp Slaghuis volunteered to escort the *"Moaner"* home;

"Some 100 kilometers from the fleet Lt. Commander Dirk Hollander waved at me and shook his head. He signaled that he was going into the sea. I nodded in understanding and radioed his 'grid reference' position to our air rescue teams. The landing went well considering the damage. On bumping the first wave top both the upper and lower sections of the port wing collapsed and she nosed in heavily. I circled the crash site until I spotted two dark heads in the foam. The green dye marker stained the sea which I knew meant that they had pulled clear the rubber boat and were ok. Then I waggled my wings and flew on towards our ships."

"I was later informed that one of our little Ryan seaplanes had managed to pluck them from the sea after a two hour bobbing on the warm waters. No sharks were seen but many aircraft were observed to the east at a great distance. The 'Moaner's' crew was retrieved alive and well but naked

as the day they were born. The Ryan floatplane is a small aircraft and it was never imagined to take three people. Fortunately after stripping off all their wet heavy clothing to save weight, with wallets clamped in jaws, wet and naked as the day they were born, both airmen struggled aboard into the single forward passenger seat to be greeted by a diminutive, and widely grinning 17 year old female air cadet Sylvia van Ommen; the seaplane's owner!"

Contrary to our earlier intelligence which suggested that the IJN light carrier's fighters were Kawasaki K-10 biplanes some were actually Mitsibishi A5M fixed undercarriage, canti-lever monoplanes. Fast and nimble monoplane fighters though they were; they were equally matched by the Grumman F3-F. The slight speed advantage of the Mitsubishi machines were more than offset by the self-sealing tanks, the longer range gun, superior maneuverability and overall robustness of the Grumman fighters. The Helldivers although able to hold their own were still a bit overmatched due to weight. As soon as all their bombs had been expended, *Striker 2* broke off action to return to the *Johan de Witt*.

Seven of the returning planes of *Striker 2* had machine gun and shrapnel damage. For the loss of four Curtiss dive-bombers and both of the Grumman F2F fighters that had been last minute substitutes. *Striker 2* had hit the light carrier with eight 225 kg and four 105 kg bombs leaving her adrift and heavily afire. Four destroyers had been hit squarely and several others damaged by splinters from near misses. Three Mitsubishi A5M fighters had been shot down, and many more aircraft destroyed in the hangar and on the flight deck of the burning flat top. The cruisers were nowhere to be seen. The Japanese fleet had lost six destroyers heavily damaged, the carrier afire and presumed sunk. The remaining escorts were seen to be withdrawing to the N.E.

The Japanese light carrier had been identified as the Suzaku. I had no doubt that it was her torpedo bombers that had attacked us at dawn, now she had been repaid in full!

06:24hrs December 08, 1941, Kapitein ter Zee Daniel Van Braekel reported that *Striker 3* was away from both ships; Bomber Squadron 3; having 14 PZL- P23 Sea Eagles each carrying a single 750 kg. Picric Acid AP bomb. These were escorted by seven Grumman F3Fs of Flight C, of Fighter Squadron 1 from the flagship. The *Johan de Witt*'s attack force was composed of Bomber Squadron 6; having 14 PZL- P23 Sea Eagles all armed with a single 750 kg Amatol AP bomb, and were escorted by seven Grumman F2F's of Flight C, of Fighter Squadron 3. Ten minutes later the speakers within the FCC erupted;

"CAP SIX! CAP S IX! Alarm! Mother Goose I am grid reference G7. I am reporting a formation of fifty plus, repeat fifty plus aircraft approaching your location from the north at an elevation of 4,000 meters! Speed 200 knots! I am engaging."

One of *Cornelis de Witt's* Buffalo fighters flying reconnisance had sighted the most dangerous of our enemies yet to appear, a massive JAAF *Hikosentai* was approaching at high speed. They were targeting us for a high level attack and intended to carpet bomb us with an estimated two hundred 250 kilogram high explosive bombs! The A.O. Van Breakel grabbed the microphone by the plot table." *Fandancer 4A & 2B* (these were our short range Sea Fury Mk II fighters) concentrate over the fleet and maintain CAP, *Fandancer 4A* climb to 6,000 meters...all CAP Brewster fighters prepare to intercept the enemy bomber formation bearing green 5 degrees, at 4,000 meters!

Turning to me the A.O. said; "Admiraal I suggest that after launching all remaining fighters we must enact *Fightercloud*." To this I replied; "A.O. negative on *Fightercloud*. That order which would have required the preparation and launch of all reserve machines, which I felt was premature, and one that would halt the mission of the Sea Eagles, as they were well in front of their *point of no return*. I continued, "I will not be forced onto the defensive Air Chief. The attacks against the convoys go in! If this Task Force is not attacking enemy shipping then all we will have accomplished today is to provide target practice for the Japanese Army Air Force! We still had available enough fighter resources to frustrate the attacks of these fifty enemy machines.

As another *Hikosentai* (a bomber regiment) could be expected, I ordered the Air Chief to bring to readiness and shuttle forward those naval fighter squadrons on Borneo that cover this sector of the South China Sea. He was then to contact Colonel Wilden of the Royal Netherlands East Indies Army Air Force (KNIL-ML) at Tarakan Army Airfield, Borneo and request long range fighter support from his Heavy Fighter Group III, as quickly as possible. He passed on the location, course, speed and altitude of what we had identified as elements of the JAAF *121st Hikosentai*, and ask how quickly and in what strength they would be able to intercept. I was anxious to see how the JAAF bombers would stand up to fire from the Fokker G1 twin engine fighters of the Royal Dutch Army, with their eight nose mounted machineguns.

The Air Chief, his assistant and their group of eighteen men were now starting to feel the stress of the engagement since new threats were rapidly appearing. The air traffic control was getting particularly complicated...the sweaty smell of nervous tension was filling the air of the Command Center. Someone turned on the cool air blowers.

But that was nothing compared to the ordered chaos below within the aircraft hangars. The ammunition magazine lifts delivered hundreds of ammunition drums and bombs up along armored shafts to the two hangar decks for waiting aircraft. Both elevators brought up four planes to the flight deck at each double decked lift. Six hundred men prepared aircraft on each ship working like automatons. They were carrying out their duties swiftly and with the greatest of caution not to overlook the slightest critical safe handling procedures. Up on the flight deck a 100 man handling team: retrieved the incoming planes, sorted them out, brought up others and lined all these planes in neat rows on each side of the flight lane according to their deployment schedules. At the same time the refueling men worked the valve manifolds expertly as they pumped tens of thousands of liters of volatile 100 octane aviation fuel into the waiting squadrons of aircraft, and their drop tanks. When the fueling was completed, that piping system with the hoses was bled and purged with inert gasses. Between fueling operations, there was not even a tenth of a liter of aviation octane above the armored decks.

06:36hrs December 08, 1941; in addition to the original CAP fighters and the Buffalos, the two battle-carriers had by this time launched; 14 Sea Fury Fighters with drop tanks and most of the remaining 28 F2F & F3F fighters. The pushers and plane handlers worked furiously and were able to reduce the launch interval to six seconds, in preparation for the anticipated action.

Then the deck-head loudspeaker in the FCC squawked; "Alarm! *CAP 21 to Mother-Goose, CAP 21 to Mother Goose*; I am at grid reference T6, altitude 2000 meters, I have just over flown four heavy cruisers, repeat...four heavy cruisers course; south, speed 36 knots! Do we have British cruisers in these waters?"

The flagship's Commander; Kapt. Daniel Voorne, turned to my C.O.S. Commodore Derrick Van Klaffens and asked if there were any friendly cruisers in the area, to which he shook his head. After last month's alert, the KMN, USN, and the RN by mutual arrangement keep each command center updated on the locations of all their major warships. The Air Chief then directed *CAP 21* to descend and identify ship class as no friendly forces were known to be in our area. One of the Air Staff officers, who had been waiting for a pause in his superior's stream of instructions, interjected to inform his chief that all our fighter aircraft were now up.

My C.O.S. looked at me and said "Admiraal it is just possible that those cruisers are the light carrier's escorts that was identified some nine to ten hours ago. At nightfall they may have broken off from their fleet and steamed at full speed hoping to reach us in the dark before we could launch our CAP at sunrise. It is certainly possible as the math works, 350 sea miles, 9 hours at 30 plus knots."

I was guessing that it had been the enemy's intention to engage the battlecruiser-carriers before dawn and destroy our flight decks with their long range guns before we could launch our aircraft, leaving us without an air umbrella to face heavy air attacks for the entire day. A very clever strategy indeed I thought; a series of coordinated massive blows coming from all directions involving surface, sub-surface and air attacks to saturate our defenses and overwhelm Task Force Popeye. We then should expect their powerful 73rd *Hikosentai* to appear at any time.

Our flight decks must remain intact, at whatever the cost. The enemy cruisers seem to be trying to force us north towards the many airfields of the JAAF Air Army and further away from our airbases or risk a surface engagement with their powerful artillery. Although not knowing our precise location, the Japanese Fleet Admiral had still ordered the surface attack, but had miscalculated the correct course to intercept us and had missed. Matsumoto's cruisers were still a long way off, and dangerously exposed to our powerful Air group, and with only a slim chance of knocking out our Fleet Air Operations.

The loudspeaker squawked; "*CAP 21* to *Mother Goose*; *CAP 21* to *Mother Goose*. I have identified four *Moyoko* class heavy cruisers, repeat, four *Moyoko* class heavy cruisers, speed 36 knots, 100 nautical miles east of TF, course due south. We are now experiencing heavy and accurate Anti-aircraft fire."

Kapt. Daniel Voorne turned me and said; "Admiraal Sweers, given that our maneuvering is reducing our speed of advance on this heading to 25 knots, when added to the speed of the enemy cruisers we have a combined closing speed of 40 knots. If those enemy cruisers remain unchecked, the Task Force will be exchanging salvos with them in approximately two hours and twenty minutes. He then turned to our gunnery officer Commander Tieler Van Ripper and said "Well Commander, how do you feel about matching your twelve big tubes to the forty 203 mm guns of those enemy cruisers?" The Commander beaming replied; "twelve 343mm and the twenty eighty 150mm tubes of our light cruisers Kapitein!"

"Not today gentlemen," I said to all. "I will not risk the destruction of our Battle-carriers flight decks and aircraft hangars simply to enjoy pulverizing those cruisers with our heavy guns! The rash acts of the Japanese Commanders have today handed us the makings of huge naval victory! For if we manage with great luck to sink four of their most modern 8 in. cruisers, two dreadnoughts, a medium carrier and destroy a convoy of troopships we will have justified the creation of this entire squadron in the first day of this war! Timing for such a complex battle reveals itself to be the entire key to its success; and the Japanese have already fumbled this! Let us not reverse this good fortune and give them exactly what they had planned for!"

The gunnery Commander van Ripper, was noticeably crestfallen so I continued; "Commander, whether we survive this day or not will depend to the greatest extent on our air defenses, which will include a supreme effort from all your anti-aircraft batteries! Regardless of my intentions; a surface battle may yet develop with those *Moyokos*. I will not turn away from these enemy cruisers. I will neither, alter course to port and move closer to the JAAF airfields of occupied French Indo China, nor will I alter course to starboard, and let our aircraft returning from their attacks on the enemy shipping drop into the sea due to fuel starvation. I have orders to rendezvous with the *Schoonveldt* battle group to concentrate in the Sulu Sea!"

Commander Tieler saluted, then returned to his action station at the other end of the compartment; at which point I said; calling after him; "Commander Tieler, take heart, you may yet still give that order of the first level that you have long dreamed of."

Turning to Hoof Officier Vleiger Van Braekel, I said; "Air Chief; those Japanese heavy cruisers are blocking our entry into the Sulu Sea. What air elements can you assign at to eliminate them?"

The Air Chief; being completely aware that I had no intention of resolving the problem with artillery, had been preparing a solution and suggested the following;

1. Immediately alert Bomber Squadron 2, arm half with a 250 kg AP and the remainder with a 250 kg HE bombs, launch ASAP and go destroy those four *Moyoko's*.
2. As Bomber Squadron 6 will soon be under the umbrella of our Fleet Combat Air Patrol it no longer has a need for a fighter escort, so have Fighter Squadron 3 reassigned to shoot up the enemy cruisers' fire-control and range-finding equipment with whatever remains of their .50 cal. heavy machine gun ammunition, before returning to the *Johan de Witt* for fuel and rearmament.
3. Contact Tarakan Naval Air Station, give them the location of the Japanese cruiser squadron, and reassign the squadron of torpedo planes already airborne, and on their way to attack the troopship convoy and divert it to attack the cruisers."

These all appeared to be satisfactory and I gave him the order to carry on.

Turning to my Chief of Staff Commodore Derrik van Klaffens I told him; "*Contact Batavia to report these four enemy heavy cruisers and transmit their course, speed and location to any submarines we may have in the area. Task Force Popeye has all its aircraft committed, heavy air attacks are inbound. The enemy troopship convoy has been heavily attacked, details to follow. TF Popeye continues to attack the Japanese convoys, and preparing an air attack against an IJN force of four heavy cruisers attempting to initiate a surface action. Signed; Vice Admiraal Sweers, Commanding; Her Majesty's Battlecruiser-carrier Task Force Popeye, South China Sea, 06:40hrs December 08, 1941.*"

Then my Air Chief raised his voice so all within the Command Center could hear; "*Gentlemen, the battle is rapidly escalating. Air Staff; it will take cool heads to get our returning planes recycled into action while we are under attack. Undamaged planes are to have top priority, get them down, refueled and rearmed and back into the air in record time. Lightly wounded pilots*

270

to be next in priority and then the more seriously damaged air-planes last, but only if the machine is not too badly damaged, otherwise they are to hit the silk, I cannot have damaged machines crashing on our flight decks. Calm cool heads will prevail today, this is the work that we have all been trained for, now get on with it."

That was a hard order for Van Braekel to transmit to the wounded airmen. But if their condition was very bad they were a hazard to operations. If they fainted and crashed while attempting to land they could neutralize our flight operations at a critical moment. All our pilots of course knew this and understood that it was their duty to ditch their damaged machines in the sea, if there was a danger of crashing aboard.

I knew, for wounded and incapacitated men, the idea of landing on a shark infested sea, in a sinking plane was a particular nightmare that many found difficult to face despite the fact that the fleet destroyers and many smaller patrol vessels now trailing the fleet would have them aboard in short order. Our considerable float plane rescue groups, stationed along the coastline of Sarawak in small groups of two or three, and made up largely of *private flying club* aircraft had been alerted, and even now were concentrating to provide support for the rear battle area.

At 06:46hrs December 08, 1941; the loudspeaker squawked once again; ALARM! "Brewster 9 to Mother Goose, Brewster 9 to Mother-Goose; I am flying at 5000 meters altitude about 20 kilometers east of Cu Lao Thu Island. I see approaching from the north at 1000 meters a formation of fifty plus twin engine bombers with a squadron of monoplane fighters 1000 meters above them. Course southwest, speed 200 knots. I am climbing for altitude and falling back to close up formation, will attack as soon as concentrated."

Air Ops turned to me and said; "Admiraal, these must be elements of the *73rd Hikosentai*, based at Hanoi, 1000 meters elevation would suggest a torpedo attack." Before Van Braekel could ask the next question that I could see his lips forming I said; "Order *Fightercloud* Air Ops. This is it then. All the JAAF units that Naval Intelligence tells us are likely assigned to this region of the South China Sea have now been committed against us. We are going to undergo shortly, massive air attacks, but we still have a little time yet. Try to refuel as many fighters as possible before the attacks come in. Please remind the plane handlers that for this action when a fighter lands, determine if the machine is battle worthy, attach the exterior drop tanks, to keep the fighters in the air as long as possible. As soon as the armorers have installed the machine gun belts then get the plane back into the air. The battle-carriers will be relying heavily on your torpedo defeating planes. We must maintain a straight course to land our planes and at that time we will be most vulnerable to attack. Co-ordinate it well Air Chief." "Yes Admiraal, be assured that my men are well trained and know their duty," was his reply.

We knew that the twin engine bombers of the enemy had great range and enjoyed the ability to linger over the Task Force for at least several hours and send in attacks, whereas our fighters must land and refuel at least twice to match their time in the air. The Air Chief would not give them that time, he concentrated *Fightercloud*, the slower fighters would climb for altitude and dive to meet the enemy with the head on attack method, he reminded the fighter pilots of our recent training exercises; to identify the target type first, recall its capabilities and how we have planned to stop that type, then attack those enemy machines with the utmost aggressiveness."

Turning to the Vlaggeschip's Gunnery Officer I said; "Commander van Ripper, your torpedo defeating mortar teams will be tested heavily today, I trust that they are fully prepared as they will undoubtedly see heavy action within the hour."

Then to my Chief of Staff; "Commodore, I trust that all the ships of the Task Force have been kept up to date on the latest intelligence. Ensure that my cruisers understand to maintain those positions and maneuvers which we have developed to provide maximum close anti-aircraft fire support to the battle-carriers under the fleet condition of *Fightercloud*.

The C.O.S. replied; "Be assured Admirral that these matters had been taken care of, all the ships of the Task Force are in their correct position and aware of the implementation of the *Fightercloud* condition and of the impending air attacks and are operating in accordance with its requirements."

Noticing a pause in the activities of my senior officers, I addressed them, "Gentlemen", I nodded to the Ship's Kapitein, my C.O.S., and the Air Chief, "please join me for two minutes up on the deckhouse platform." We made our way swiftly up to deck 06; my favorite spot for surveying deck operations. The lookouts snapped to attention as we ascended to the platform then automatically resumed their sweeping of the firmament with their yellow filter binoculars. It was a truly glorious morning and I gulped the clean air. Retrieving a cheroot from its steel tin, I lit up a *Panter*, sucking in the heavy smoke, then exhaled with a loud AHHHH!" This simple pantomime diffused their noticeable tensions. At which my officers chuckled as they lit up.

There was a lot to see, as the sky was full of our fighters, and patrol aircraft which elicited a very comfortable feeling. Already the Air Operations was bringing down the Sea Fury Fighters to top up their fuel. In an effort to extend the air time of these relatively short range machines, their pilots had practiced several experimental fuel saving flying techniques, such as shallow gliding, just under the stall speed. This surprisingly allowed the machines to stay in the air for an extra 20 minutes over the fleet, with full power being held back for combat operations when the enemy machines were close at hand. One by one the Sea Fury's came down onto the fight deck for fuel and then lightly departed, taking only three aircraft lengths to do so.

I studied a section of Sea Fury Fighters that happened to be flying close aboard and just above a pair of circling Sea Harts light bombers on anti-torpedo patrol, both types of planes shone wetly with condensation in the early morning sunlight. Noticing that my Air Operations Officer was looking at the same machines I breathed out; "Air Chief," I said, turning to Van Braekel, "the Hawker Aircraft designers certainly got it right don't you think when they produced the Sea Fury Fighter and the Sea Hart Bomber, have you ever seen more sleek looking biplanes totally complementing one other?"

"Yes my Admiraal" was his reply as he exhaled a cloud of smoke, "I agree, a more beautifully matched set of biplanes you will not find, they look like bookends. The Grumman fighters also match up nicely with the Curtiss Helldiver, but not quite so neatly as the Hawker machines. Those latter planes did after-all come from two separate aircraft manufacturers." Then we studied their graceful flight in silence for few moments as the aircraft circled the fleet to pass out of our field of view.

The bulwark telephone set buzzed and Kapt. Voorne retrieved it, then cocked his head a little while covering his ear with the finger tips of his right hand to reduce the noise from the aircraft engines roaring along the flight deck. He listened intently for a moment, smiled broadly and hung up the telephone. Turning to me with a grin he informed me that *Striker 1 & Striker 2* had completed their attacks on the enemy and report very heavy damage to both Japanese convoys. Casualties to machines and crew were light to moderate. All the Squadrons are returning. While the Helldivers will need refueling, the fighters will have at least an hour of fuel remaining although their ammunition is low. I slapped the bulwark with my fist then clamped my hand over my chin to suppress a yell.

All the officer's joined in a round of congratulations. Kapt. Voorne, picked up the phone again and asked; "With your permission Admiraal" and I nodded, Voorne flipped a switch on the set and then he addressed the ship's crew, to announce our bomber's successful attack. Immediately there was a huge roar gathering in force, a wild cheering issued up out of the cavernous steel spaces within the flagship, was it my imagination or did the very steel of the bridge vibrated with it? So many of my men were very young, and their bold enthusiasm was infectious. The men working the flight deck and standing at the antiaircraft batteries danced about shaking their straw hats and fists to the sky. The men, now with renewed confidence understood that they were not sacrificial lambs, but an effective powerful weapon, to be feared. Their blood would not be spilled in vain.

Several minutes later as Kapitein Voorne's message was relayed to the other ships, faint gusts of cheering were heard rolling across the waters with a sound like beach surf and gulls from the cruisers *Gouden Leeuw* and *Aemilia* speeding along half a kilometer off our port side. Within the Fleet Command Center the news of our successful attacks were being furiously coded for transmission to Koninklijke Marine Hoofdkwartier Batavia (KMHB) our fleet headquarters for the East Indies.

Both enemy convoys had suffered heavy damage with the light carrier and several destroyers sunk, the detonation of the invasion force's ammunition ship, six troop ships sunk outright, ten heavily afire, and with the remaining vessels reversing their course! We had stopped an invasion and won a strategic victory. I suddenly felt lighter, as if I had set down on the ground a heavy haversack. The Task Force and especially my battlecruiser-carriers had at least partially justified their existence.

My C.O.S. Kapitein Derik van Klaffens turned to me and said, "The retreating convoy will be attacked by our Swordfish later today." He then looked up to the masthead where my Admiraal's pennant whipped in the wind above our clean Tri-color battle flag and said; "Vice Admiraal on behalf of all the officers and men I wish to congratulate you on your vision that led to the creation of these great ships, with which today we are able to defend our homes and families, for adding to the long role of honors of the Royal Netherlands Navy and striking at the enemies of our Queen and country!" Unable to reply; I clasped his proffered hand in a vigorous handshake followed by the sincere expressions from the other officers.

I turned to the men and said; "Look out upon this panorama gentlemen, our proud fleet, a powerful force. Linger for a moment on the varied sounds of the sea and the ship. Remember this time and this beautiful morning. Preserve this memory as a source of strength for the future may be very difficult. We have reached a common plateau in our careers. War has come and we have just managed to acquire the weapons that we have long needed to carry out our duty. I am sure you all share similar sentiments regarding this fortunate situation. The coming battles are what we have lived, trained and paid in advance for. At last we may serve in the secure knowledge that we are no longer merely a token fleet but have the power to bloody the nose of any aggressor. Today we have laid the first brick in a great monument that will one day be raised to complete victory."

"Soon a great air sea battle will occur and plunge us into a furious all-consuming activity that will be beyond all previous experience. Our preparations have all been well-made. Fight the ships and aircraft as you have been trained to do. Now, let us see to this day."

With a final long look at my little fleet of fourteen brave warships, steaming in formation ready for action, I descended the companionway and returned to the Fleet Control Center within the cavernous vibrating hull of the huge battlecruiser-carrier.

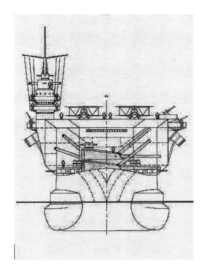

CHAPTER XXIV

NEZUMATORI-BANZAI!

December 08, 1941; Task Force Popeye was now committed to its first air-sea battle and to whatever fate the *Gods of War* may hold in store for it. The ships and men of the Royal Netherlands Navy's 1st Battle-carrier Division and its twelve escorts, answered their nation's *call to arms* and steamed resolutely forward, advancing along a northeasterly course through the South China Sea that roughly paralleled the coastline of Borneo.

Although the ships of Task Force Popeye were equipped with very powerful motive machinery, I experienced a sense that we had been seized by an irresistible force, much as a raft is helpless in the grip of a mighty current, and were being drawn relentlessly toward some great maelstrom of apocalyptic proportions. I am sure that I was not alone in this sentiment, yet I was able to observe that all aboard seemed to be filled with a grim resolve to defend our families, colonists and their Island homes, to destroy the enemy wherever we encountered him, and to carry out our part in introducing the Japanese to the horrific consequences of what they had begun.

The Dutch battle-group constituted a single great interlocking steel and bronze mechanism; a 140,000 tonne mass of animated machinery and armor plate, all skillfully fashioned to deal death to an enemy. Our high powered; stereoscopic range finding optics in their cylindrical turrets hummed and clicked as they responded to their operator's foot pedals, constantly sweeping the horizon from left to right and back again for the telltale smoke of ships and the sky for enemy aircraft. Every few moments these would freeze to focus and identify distant objects. Along the warships sides and across their upper-works bristled the muzzles of hundreds of cannon controlled by precision instruments. These ranged in size from the very heavy to light caliber, and poked ominously in all directions, ready to discharge their explosive shells, which could deliver eight tonnes of destruction twice a minute to the distant horizon or raise a curtain of white hot steel splinters around the entire squadron.

Above the warships wheeled our flock of falcons, the 'eyes of the fleet,' clothed not in feathers but in polished duralumin, with bright yellow or red division colors. Our nimble fighter combat air patrol crisscrossed the sky in thirteen sections of three. The fighter crews were eager, erecting a wall to the north, between the fleet and the JAAF bases in French Indo China. There were in addition to those, already in the air; 28 fighters and 42 dive bombers participating in our first combat strike against a Japanese Naval convoy and its escort, the majority of which would be returning to reinforce our defenses after completing their mission.

Rapidly approaching from the southeast, a powerful reinforcement was coming to our aide, the 30 Fokker G.1B twin engine monoplanes of Heavy Fighter Group III from the KNIL: Koninklijk Nederlands Indish Leger or (Royal Netherlands Army of the Indies) based at Tarakan Airfield on Borneo. These modern twin engine monoplanes were tasked with the interception of the three Japanese air regiments that were preparing to attack my fleet. I was hoping that their heavy armament of eight nose mounted machineguns, would redress to some extent the obsolescence of our naval air groups.

The great battlecruiser-carriers; the strategic component of our navy, which formed the very heart of our East Indies Fleet, steamed in echelon formation, with the *Cornelis de Witt* (F); half a nautical mile to port and one half nautical mile forward of her sister the *Johan de Witt*. Typically, while in this formation all the Vlaggenschip's aircraft would approach their landing zone from the port quarter, while the *Johan de Witt's* air groups would approach from her from the starboard quarter.

We found this echelon steaming formation facilitated an air-control plan which allowed the maximum field of fire port and starboard for the mother ship's anti-aircraft batteries at low angles of elevation while ensuring that these batteries would not be turned on any friendly aircraft attempting a landing aboard the sister ship.

Two light cruisers; the *Prinz te Paard* (F), leading the *Oliphant;* (Appendix A) were steaming in column parallel to, and a nautical mile to port of the *Cornelis de Witt, while* the two others; the *Gouden Leeuw* (F), followed by the *Aemilia* cruised to starboard of the *Johan de Witt.* All four fine new ships, modern in every way; these warships contributed a high volume of medium artillery for a surface action and with a total of forty of the 40mm Bofors auto-cannon, they contributed heavily to the battle squadron's air defense. Any torpedo planes intent on attacking the Battlecruiser-carriers would first have to overfly the cruiser's antiaircraft batteries at a dangerously low altitude to gain a launch position.

There were five destroyers arranged in a wedge formation one nautical mile forward of the battle-carriers and cruisers with the squadron leader; the *Zeeland* (F) at the apex, and in a 45 degree echelon to starboard at half nautical mile intervals from her; the *Gelderland* then *Bulhond.* In the left echelon; a similar formation with the *Jakhals,* off the *Zeeland,* followed by the *Endragt.*

Located one nautical mile behind the battle-carriers; and spaced a half nautical mile apart were three destroyers bringing up the rear of the fleet; the *Draak* (F) in the center and with the *Piet Heyn* to port and the *Zoutman* to starboard.

These eight small ships, each equipped with the latest acoustic gear that could detect, locate and identify the underwater noises produced by different types of propellers and machinery at great distance were therefore able to contribute a valuable anti-submarine component as well as a rapid fire light artillery and torpedo attack capability for surface actions, with an additional contribution to the anti-aircraft umbrella. The three destroyers stationed to the rear were positioned to pick up pilots of downed aircraft, although once the main action commenced they would not break the battle-carriers screen to retrieve pilots, but would drop flotation gear and dye markers, leaving these men to be retrieved by the small armada of light craft to our rear.

The *Battle Squadron* possessed total three dimensional capability in the air combat, the surface, and under the sea, an essential balance of weaponry required by naval forces at the end of the 1930's. Sea warfare was no longer a two dimensional battle fought on the surface of the sea as in the days of sail. A modern fleet of the twentieth century had to control the skies above its ships, as well as the waters below.

Hundreds of naval gunners waited tensely for the call to action and unleash their one hundred and forty six 40 mm Bofors guns, the most advanced anti-aircraft auto-cannon yet devised. That gun was a weapon so advanced in design that it remained in service on all Continents for more than seventy years after the events that I am presenting concluded.

Something not often spoken of up to this time was the incredible effectiveness that the squadron managed to achieve with our substantial outfit of 40 mm Bofors AA guns. The various exercise drills that these batteries practiced were: the direct fire against multi targets, inter-ship AA fire support plans and the creation of a fleet AA umbrella effective out to 6000 meters and which could be contracted or expanded to produce a dome over the entire Fleet. A dome of varying intensity, that could be created with a speed and accuracy that was astounding if not actually witnessed.

I cannot convey to the reader the effect produced by a *Fleet Barrage* that is able to hurl some 18,720 explosive 40 mm cannon shells per minute at an enemy formation! It is an experience one can only appreciate if you are standing on the open flight deck when it is unleashed! The psychological impact on enemy pilots must have been very severe given such an enormous volume of fire.

Two months before the German invasion of our homeland, several convoys of freighters had arrived in our East Indies Empire to deliver some 280,000 of tonnes of cargo. Much of these were war supplies; including vast quantities of 40 mm AA ammunition. At the outbreak of hostilities each ship was issued four times the initial wartime estimates. As we steamed into battle on that day each of the Battlecruiser-carriers had aboard as I recall some 800 tonnes of this ammunition, or some half million rounds, a quantity which allowed each 40 mm tube approximately four hours of continuous fire!

Underneath this 40 mm AA umbrella of steel we still had several tens of 20 mm Oerlikon light AA cannon and .306 Browning water cooled machine guns. Although manually aimed, their concentrated firepower against targets within 500 meters was quite substantial.

Once action commenced and the JAAF began to gnaw on the battle-fleet's giant armor plated and fire spitting body; wreckage and personnel from both opponents, living and dead would litter the ocean in the wake of the ships. All survivors were to be saved from the sea's cruel embrace. Trailing ten nautical miles behind the main fleet there was a growing flotilla of our light naval craft whose task was quite varied with many small ancillary duties. These included anti-submarine patrol and the recovery of sailors and pilots in the water. These small vessels each in turn had put out from their secluded bases along the coast of Sarawak, upon getting an alert. They would cover their portion of the battle-zone to pluck men from the sea and return them to the shore.

Approaching TF Popeye from the northeast and northwest, at some 200 knots, on converging bearings were two JAAF Bomber *Hikosentais* (Air Regiments), the *73rd* and the *121st* totaling six squadrons, all elements of the *6th Kokugun* (Air Army)! A force having between them at least one hundred of the most modern type of twin engine high speed bombers, then in existence within the Asiatic-Western Pacific theater! Stowed within their bellies waited hundreds of high explosive bombs and air launched torpedoes. Mounted aft, in the dorsal position of these machines was a rearward firing, high velocity 20 mm auto-cannon, giving that formation a deadly long range explosive punch that extended far beyond the gun range of any fighter aircraft that any nation had in the region.

Escorting this onrushing air armada; were some thirty machines of the *124th Hikosentai*, composed of the *134th Chutai* (Squadron) and *135th Chutai*, the very latest design of Japanese Army monoplane fighter, the fast and nimble Nakajima Ki-43, a machine which became more commonly identified in the Pacific theater later in the war, when assigned the code name of *Oscar*, by the Americans. Our opponent, the entire JAAF *22nd Hikodan* (Air Brigade); composed of four Air Regiments was literally a gigantic aerial flail of immense destructive power!

These enemy formations of sleek speeding, twin engine bombers and fighters in their tight attack formations bobbed up and down slightly on the early morning's air currents. The sand brown base paint with green spider web mottling scheme betrayed their earlier service in Manchuria. The aircraft looked rather out of place in the rich blue and white tropical firmament of the cloud studded South China Sea.

The highly trained airmen of these advanced machines were out for blood and revenge. Due to a miscalculation of the Dutch Fleet's base course and speed, their Hikosentai had been alerted too late, and would delay their arrival over the Dutch Fleet, and upsetting the critical timing of their elaborately laid trap. The Dutch dive bombers were now devastating the invasion convoy and naval escort of General Iwabe Takaguchi's 15th Infantry Division, a humiliating reversal of fortune and a dishonor to the Emperor!

The aircrews of the Japanese Army Air Force (JAAF) attacking us that fateful morning were grimly dedicated to erase this stain, to overcome any opposition, to seize the enemy's task force in a stranglehold and ram their deadly missiles down the very throats of the enemy!

To compound the JAAF threat; to the northwest of *Task Force Popeye* were four very powerful heavy cruisers of the IJN closing our position at high speed! These large modern warships; having detached themselves from the naval escort of General Takaguchi's convoy at sundown, had steamed all night at flank speed, some 36-37 knots with their boilers producing 10% *over safe pressure*; on a redeployment calculated to deny the Dutch Battle Squadron an escape corridor into the Sulu Sea, and the protection of the Dutch airfield system, thereby snapping shut the *Nezumitori* (mouse trap), and completing their destruction by continued attacks with bomb, torpedo and heavy gun.

However, the Japanese cruiser's bold charge required them to steam over many dangerously shallow banks in their headlong dash at their powerful adversary. Some of these shoals were less than 20 meters deep, and the corals interacted with the cruiser's entrained pressure boundary layer caused increased friction. The cruiser's velocity being slowed by several knots for brief occasions, further compounded the unexpected little errors that already crept into the complex Japanese plan to destroy our battle squadron.

Here now, facing our first day of action an attack was developing against my Battle-carrier Squadron which followed the precise scenario that I had used to justify their creation; one of combined air and surface attack! The stage was set for a major clash of naval might.

In a surface battle, the Japanese heavy cruiser squadron enjoyed a superiority in speed to the Dutch Fleet of some 5 knots and could choose when to engage, although their orders, I am sure, were to drive straight at us. Our twelve heavy 343 mm pieces still exceeded the power of the forty 203 mm guns aboard the enemy cruisers by some 30%, and their lighter weapons were a few thousand meters inferior to us in range.

Hits on our battle-carriers by a number of 203 mm shells was survivable for such large heavily armored ships, whereas a single solid hit by our heavy shell on an enemy cruiser could have disastrous consequences due to its massive kinetic shock and penetrative power. Whatever advantage these enemy heavy cruisers may have realized in volume of fire at long range was one which they would only enjoy for a short period of time, and then only if they survived our air attack unscathed. They would have to close the range to some 18,000 meters to secure the many multiple hits needed to halt our air operations. Upon achieving this range, they would come under a smothering blanket of fire from the 150 mm guns of our cruiser escort, and still face the ever increasing accuracy of the heavy main battery, as the range came down.

The gamble taken with these highly valuable ships was one that the IJN high command entirely appreciated, but felt to be worth the risk. The danger that Cruiser Squadron 11, faced from the Dutch dive bombers would; they calculated be short lived and survivable. General Hideki Oshimo, commander of the JAAF *6th Kokugan*, (Air Army) had personally assured General Tojo that the Dutch Battle-carriers, would have few remaining aircraft following the attack by the four air regiments of his 22nd Hikodan (Air Brigade). The four heavy cruisers of Rear Admiral Tamon Matsumoto's Distant Cover Fleet, were powerful enough to shake off the attacks by the enemy's obsolete aircraft, close their damaged fleet and finish them with long range torpedo and artillery.

In my operational orders I emphasized: that if an enemy surface force threatened our fleet, while the Task Force was under the threat of air attack; we may engage them with our twelve heavy guns and dive-bombers. Our light cruiser squadron would not break formation to attack them but maintain the AA and torpedo screen around the battle-carriers. I believed that the heavy cruisers posed less of a threat firing from long range than did a swarm of enemy bombers. However, if there was no immediate air threat to the Fleet, the light cruiser screen may be ordered forward to attack the enemy heavy cruiser force, and *go in under the big guns* of the battle-carriers to close the range.

Rear Admiral Tamon Matsumoto, the Commander of Cruiser Squadron 11 that provided the *heavy surface punch* component for operation *Nezumitori*, had missed the scheduled dawn attack against the Dutch Fleet. But during his post war interrogation, he stated that there still existed some chance for initiate a surface battle, although he did not expect his force to survive its headlong dash.

Nezumitori, although a complicated plan, was simple in theory. A coordinated massed air attack by long range technically superior fighters to sweep our short range and outdated machines from of the sky. Then simultaneous attacks by level bombers to destroy the aircraft hangars and flight decks of the battle-carriers, eliminating further air operations. Then torpedo bombers would launch their deadly fish to smash through the sides of the ships and sink them.

The Japanese attack; designed to completely saturate our defenses; was the very type of attack that our strategists had envisioned and one for which we had prepared.

The IJN move followed a pattern set in 1904 at Port Arthur, and at Pearl Harbour. The stroke showed complete contempt for enemy power, an attitude explained with one simple word; Samurai! I felt confident that our defensive measures and upgraded tactics were the best that we could devise, given our equipment and quantity, and that these measures should work reasonably well, provided that our guesswork and assumptions were not too off the mark and the enemy chose to press home their attacks.

In this battle we could not allow the enemy aircraft to have the luxury of circling our fleet outside of the range of our flak guns, only to dart in and attack when our planes had to land aboard for refueling. Although the JAAF formations could do so, they would be forced to attack us and destroy our aircraft hangars to halt our on-going devastation of their vital Invasion convoy. However in order to accomplish this, they must first penetrate our *Fightercloud* screen and then shrug off the battle-squadron's massive Anti-aircraft barrage! It all sounds so simple and straight forward in theory. But the reality revealed several nasty surprises to both sides!

The Japanese military strategists were faced with a gigantic gamble for the opening day of the war in the Pacific. Their widely flung forces had to hit their naval and land targets by surprise all on the same day and achieve success on that first day! The JAAF Hikosentais attacking us should have used caution and patience, but the situation demanded boldness. *Fightercloud* was a defensive measure only, now the Japanese pilots were forced to enter it, with only half the strength that they needed.

Task force Popeye had positioned itself well to undertake its duty of convoy interdiction, and had achieved some successes which had now awakened a hornet's nest. Fifty aerial torpedoes and perhaps two hundred bombs were winging their way towards us with a vengeance. To oppose this I had called for condition: *Fightercloud,* to the great relief of my Chief of Air Operations. A concentration over the fleet of all available fighters and dive-bomber's acting as second line fighters, was now underway.

Therefore, at 06:46hrs there were over the ships: 7 Sea Fury Mk II fighters, 14 Grumman F2F & F3F fighters, and 19 Brewster F2A *Buffalo* fighters; for a total of 40 aircraft on fighter duty. Added to this were 6 Hawker Sea Harts on torpedo defense missions. From the four cruisers in company each had launched 2 Fokker floatplanes and each of my eight destroyers had launched its reconnaissance floatplane.

These latter 16 machines had two LMG.'s each and the crew's had been trained to fly a circle pattern around the ships and deliver enfilade fire into any low level torpedo planes targeting the battle-carriers. Although slow they could stay aloft for a considerable time and each was equipped with four 50 kilogram *Bomblets* for anti-torpedo defense, their primary role when engaged in fleet escort duty.

Due to their slow speed, the circumference of the circle they could fly was kept to a minimum, its diameter set at no more than 500 meters from the outer ring of ships. This exposed them to a very severe threat from the fleet's Flak batteries. Accordingly all these planes were painted a bright yellow to distinguish them from enemy machines.

All told at that time there were 62 aircraft aloft on Combat Air Patrol, in close proximity to the fleet, assigned to its defense, of which 40 were actual fighters, and the remaining 22 machines able to provide enfilading light machine gun fire into enemy torpedo planes.

At approximately 07:20hrs, and less than 100 nautical miles out were the aircraft of *Striker 1 and 2*, with some 18-21 Grumman F2F and FRF fighters, and 38-42 Curtiss Helldivers, returning from their attack on the enemy troopship convoy earlier in the morning. The exact losses and condition of these returning planes were not precisely known. These aircraft were just over half an hour away. I estimated that these returning strikes would only be able to contribute no more than ten serviceable machines all tolled to the fray and all of these may be very low on ammunition.

The 7-F3F fighters making up Flight 'A' of FS-1, could if needed, be detached from the inbound *Striker 1* to provide escort to the 28 Sea Eagles on their mission to sink the two Japanese fire support battleships *Kumamoto* and *Kagoshima*.

The roughly 56 to 63 machines of *Striker 1 and 2*, would arrive over the fleet, most having an urgent need to land aboard. A fact which greatly complicated the fleet's air defense. Therefore at the beginning of the enemy's main attack; the battle-carriers would be at the disadvantage of having to turn into the wind and steam a straight course in order to recover the Helldivers, adding to our vulnerability. However, if the JAAF Air Brigade Commanders, took the time to concentrate their four air regiments, and coordinate the high level bombing and torpedo attacks, it may just give us enough time to land the returning *Helldivers*, refuel, rearm and launch them up into the air battle.

Here now was demonstrated a great advantage of bi-plane air groups. Due to their low take-off and landing speed, very little of the flight decks full 220 meter length was used. Consequently the Air Chief regulated the forward half of the flight deck for launching aircraft, and the aft half for landing operations, with each activity served by its own aircraft elevator. The *twinning of the flight deck,* had to be suspended when Buffalo fighter and the Sea Eagle bomber operations were underway as they were monoplanes and needed much greater flight deck lengths to take off and land. Fortunately for us the prevailing breezes were easterly, and we could therefore maintain our desired course to Balabat strait.

My Air Ops Officer Commander Flier Van Braekel worked the flight decks with an incredible example of coordinated activity, having made allowances for every eventuality. In an attempt to augment our CAP fighters his aircraft maintenance crews and handlers were able to later add a further 17 third class fighters from the refueled and rearmed Helldivers from *Strikers 1 & 2*, for an estimated aggregate maximum for *Fightercloud* of 89 machines protecting the fleet of which 52 were fighters.

In the coming air battle, our defending force looked on paper at least to be very powerful; at best case our 119 machines to oppose 150 of the enemy. But; of these only 19 were first class and as swift as those of the enemy armada and could be counted as equal to the 30 KNIL heavy fighters, the remainder being slower. In addition the JAAF air fleet had fuel aboard to stay over us for four or five hours of action whereas only our Grumman fighters and Buffalos could stay aloft for extended periods of between three and four hours respectively. While the Sea Fury fighters would have to land every hour for fuel and the Helldivers every two hours on the outside. The Dutch Army fighters as well would be operating far from their base at Tarakan; on the Makassar Straits, and at best could only give us twenty minutes of full action before having to retire.

As the magnitude of the disaster at Pearl Harbour began to unfold that first morning, it became clear that our long term defense plans would be seriously affected with America knocked out of the picture for the immediate future. How had the Japanese managed to achieve such complete victory and catch the U.S. Pacific Fleet in its harbour? From our perspective this was an extraordinary fiasco. Only a few days before the Japanese attack on Pearl Harbour, the RNLN, had warned the Americans of the approach of the Japanese fleet! Our most senior officers were presented with a baffling mystery!

The ships and aircraft of my command were at action stations, the men had been fed and clean undergarments donned to reduce the chance of infection if wounded. There was little more to do than sweat out the remaining interval. I looked at the clock and counted down the minutes until the arrival of the Japanese *Typhoon of steel*!

I had perhaps five minutes before the storm would fully develop, and I thought of the mystery behind the attack on Pearl Harbour. Our extensive picket submarine network had spotted the Japanese Carrier Fleet as it sailed from its temporary base in Tankan Bay in the Kuril Island Chain. Despite the fog and foul weather at the time of its departure and for several days following it; the submarines of the KMN demonstrated superb feats of seamanship and navigation by cruising on the surface to keep pace with and parallel to the Japanese Carriers designated the First Air Fleet. Throughout the great run across the Pacific, the Dutch Submarines had remained undetected. Each boat then handed off their duty to other pre-positioned cordons of submarines, much as one would hand off the baton in a track and field relay race. Eventually fuel shortages and clearing weather conditions forced the RNLN submarines to break off their shadowing operation. By that time however, Naval Intelligence was able to determine that the base course of the Japanese Carrier Fleet led directly into the very heart of the strategically vital waters of the Hawaiian Island Chain!

By November 29, 1941 complete details of the Imperial Japanese Navy First Air Fleet's movements were in the hands of RNLN Intelligence services and Lt. Generaal Hein ter Poorten personally laid it down on the desk of the most senior intelligence officers at U.S. Naval Headquarters in Washington on the morning of November 30th; a full week before the devastating attack! The Secretary of State; Cordell Hull had released this information to the press a few days later and suggested that a Japanese attack in the Pacific was imminent, but it now seemed the US Pacific Fleet took insufficient precautions! Indeed a great tragedy and crisis was in the offing.

I quickly penned a pre-action report for transmittal to Naval HQ in Batavia then sat down for a smoke. It was the first time my backside was in a chair for three hours. The steward brought me a large glass of iced orange juice which I gulped down, alternating between drags off of my cigarette. The ship's Kapitein was in the Battle bridge just forward of the Fleet Control Center, where my senior Staff officers were clustered a short distance away talking intently as they listened to the air traffic transmissions of our air groups and sifted through and logged in the various messages as they arrived to the center. The Command Center was a hive of coordinated activity, functioning now at the highest level, as the fleet was entering into; a *fully involved Air-sea battle.*

I then asked my Air Operations Officer for the latest action status reports. He calmly replied; "*Fighercloud*, Admiraal, has achieved the required mass of machines that we have estimated will be necessary to defend the fleet formation. The 30 machines of the Royal Army Heavy Fighter Group III, are approaching and not far off. Three enemy Air Regiments continue to close us rapidly but are some minutes away. Early reports indicate that our Brewster fighters which were initially engaging the *73rd Hikosentai* had suffered light damage from a new Japanese fighter which seems to be extremely fast, and very maneuverable, but lightly armed with only two light machineguns." I then replied; "I hope that our pilots keep their heads and remember our revised tactics to deal with these machines." Of course, I silently pondered; this measure would only get them so far; if you're out-classed, you're out-classed.

The Air Chief continued; "All the remaining CAP Brewster fighters, are falling back on the fleet before the advancing enemy air armada. Our F2A's, as you know Sir have the most powerful weaponry by far of all our shipboard fighters, and along with the Army's Heavy fighters have the best chance of knocking down the larger enemy planes. Our F2A's understand that wherever possible, to conserve their ammunition for the enemy bombers as they make their *run in* against our ships, while upholding their vital part in cooperating with their paired off biplane fighters to maintain *Fighterclou*d."

"We will see how the new Japanese fighters do when opposing Sea Fury or F3F fighters at the same time that they must contend with the high speed and heavy firepower of the Brewster F2A. Either way our combination of machines with their varied capabilities will not allow the Japanese fighter pilots to enjoy an advantage as they would be subjected to the deadly mathematics of the *Performance Envelope*."

"I have drilled into the brains of our Brewster Fighter pilots, not to approach the fleet too closely when the air battle develops to a high intensity over the ships. They risk drawing fire from our antiaircraft batteries, as they are our only monoplane fighter and may easily be confused as the enemy who only fly monoplanes."

"The Sea Fury Fighters have been landing and refueling at a good pace. The Flight Deck Chief, P.O. Brongers has rigged canvas water closets equipped with buckets for the pilots right on deck as their bursting bladders and bowels seem to be the pilots greatest concern of those returning from action; their moral being very high indeed. That portion of the turnaround is all going exceptionally well. Pilot rotation is minimal; it is apparent that all our fliers want a crack at Tokyo's airmen. The cooks have sent up paper bag lunches and water flasks for our deck crews and Flak Battery men."

"The Royal Army's Heavy Fokker fighters are making good time and will arrive about the same time as the JAAF 121st Air Regiment and will go straight into the attack as they are only be able to give half an hour of battle this far out. All our pilots have been made aware of their imminent arrival so they won't be blazing away at just any large two engine aircraft."

"Overall Admiraal, we are well prepared, and our chances are better than average I should think." "I am glad to hear it Air Chief, and I share your evaluation," I replied. "Check on the status of the fighters of Tarakan Naval Air Station shuttling forward to Jesselton Airfield. Expedite their refueling and dispatch them to join the fleet with all haste." He immediately turned and passed this order on to his aide, requesting a status report on these machines.

I produced a new tin of *Panter* cigarettes from my tunic pocket, sliced the paper seal along the cover edge with my thumbnail, then popped the lid and extended my arm to the Commander Flyer. Air Chief Van Breakel who hesitated for a brief moment, but then recognizing the familiar light yellow tin of the *Panter Tobacco Company* cheerfully retrieved a smoke, while striking a wooden match off his wristwatch.

I poured myself a fresh cup of black coffee, added three spoons of sugar and sat down in the Fleet Commander's chair in the Command Center. All radio reports, and orders would be received and dispatched from my senior officers at this location, and I sat at the apex of the information stream, much as an axle is to a wagon wheel. The major pieces had all been set on the chessboard, the plans and preparations for a great air-sea battle were now complete, and the opposing forces were only minutes away from locking horns. The *Crucible of Battle* would soon reveal the truths, the failures, the strengths and the weaknesses as well as the overlooked and unforeseen complexities of a modern air-sea engagement to both sides. Up to however it was the Japanese airmen who have had combat experience. Success or failure today, the lives of thousands of seamen, and the security of the entire Dutch East Indies Colony would largely rest on the decisions that I would make in the next few hours, each of which I may have only seconds to ponder.

There was nothing of strategic nature that remained for my input at this moment I would now step back and let the officers fight their ships and air groups. I took a big gulp of the hot sweet coffee, almost scalding myself. I stared at the scuffed dark green linoleum covering the steel deck, fixing my eyes on a dark scratch mark, *excluding all else*, to fine tune my hearing. The radio reports from the aircraft began steadily to increase in quantity, and detail, while on the other hand I noticed that their quality; their crispness and accuracy began to erode as they became more frequent, as our pilots aloft fought for air to give voice to their reports. They were maneuvering more often and the increasing centrifugal forces created by their high speed twisting machines squeezed their bodies, forcing the air out of their lungs.

In the distance I now picked up at first faintly, a new sound; a long unending rumble, as of heavily laden steel wheels rolling across a wooden deck. The noise now became a continuous roar that magnified in intensity as the air battle moved over the sea towards the Vlaggeschip and one by one the escorting warship's anti-aircraft batteries came into action. The JAAF Bombers went straight into the attack, penetrating into our *Fightercloud*. Our fighters dove upon them attacking with grim determination. Those bombers that survived, and had blasted their way through *Fightercloud* would soon attract a volcanic AA direct fire.

Immediately the command center erupted with an additional layer of shipboard communications: ALARM LUCHAANVAL! ALLES LUCHAFWEER BATTERIJEN; VOORBEREIDEN! VOORBEREIDEN! VOORBEREIDEN! MEERVOUDIG TORPEDO BOMMENWERPER NAAR PORT, MEERDERE DOELEN, ONAFHANKELIJKE CONTROL: SCHIET! SCHIET! (Alarm air attack, all anti-aircraft batteries; prepare! prepare! prepare! multiple torpedo bombers to port, independent quadrant control: shoot! shoot!)

Then; at 07:10hrs, with a roar and a jolt that made the steel plating hum; the portside anti-aircraft batteries; all twenty two 40 mm auto-cannon cut loose; now the *Cornelis de Witte* was in it, battling for her life! The Command Center's 76mm armor plate somewhat muffled the din. I sat on a stool, with my right arm resting upon the corner of the situation table. I kept my ears open for whatever commands I was able to sift out the flood of operational radio, and verbal traffic, listening for those items which were of strategic importance only. The telephone sets now began to ring as sections of the ship called up the battle bridge. These were snapped up by officers that hurriedly passed the messages to Kapitein Voorne. He answered steadily enough, while viewing what he could see of the battle with his binoculars.

My eyes swept the command center which became a nest of ordered but frantic activity. The young petty officers manning the plot screen carefully daubed the clear plastic with their colored grease pencils. From here I could monitor the entire battle as it developed from this remote location. A blue circle surrounded the fleet, indicating the presence of our air umbrella. A line extended from the top right quadrant of this circle, at the end of which was a box containing a set of letters: FC90-50. *Fightercloud* at the latest update, now revealed that 90 total aircraft were aloft, of which 50 were fighters. Three converging wide red arrows extending down from the north revealed that two Japanese Bomber Regiments and a Fighter Regiment had arrived. These were flagged with; JB50, JF30, JB50, which indicated that three Japanese Army Air Regiments had arrived over the fleet with 130 aircraft! The grease pencils revealed that one bomber squadron, had detached and was now attacking in two waves, while the remainder of the enemy Air Regiments circled, beyond the range of our AA batteries. A long solid blue arrow extending from our two o'clock at the edge of the display straight into the very center of the circle, indicated that the 30 heavy Fokker fighters of the Royal Army were only minutes away from engaging the Japanese. Two very short dotted blue lines were now etched on the clear plastic, originating from Jesselton, in Sarawak and pointed towards the engagement, the letters 14GR printed on the plastic indicated that the 14 Grumman F3F fighters of Flight A & B of Fighter Squadron 12, which had been shuttled up from Tarakan NAS, was on their way to us, although still half an hour away.

The men's verbal exchanges becoming more and more clipped and as the Japanese bomber waves came in. Heavy detonations erupted in the sea around us making the huge ship tremble and steel plating hum loudly as if struck by gigantic hammers. The helmsman responded to orders barked in his ear. The great ship turned sharply to Port, and began to take on a heel.

I had to watch the air action to properly gage the effectiveness of our air defenses, and told my aid to inform the Kapt. Voorne that I was going up on deck. Grabbing my steel helmet, binoculars, and flotation vest I quickly made my way to starboard out through the side of the Command Center to a catwalk at flight deck level then ran up the ladder and into the air control deckhouse. Several times I almost tripped as the two staff aid officers that always accompanied me, raced along so close behind that my heels hit their chins as we ascended the companionway.

Now the physical world grabbed me; the wind, the roaring, the flash of the guns, I took in a wide panorama and surveyed the sky above us, the F2F and F3F fighters were steeply diving upon a formation of enemy bombers, in sections of three machines abreast. Those little stubby winged fighters could reach more than 800 kph in such a maneuver and the escorting enemy machines that attempted to attack them from the rearward position were quickly left behind. Their brightly painted red or yellow engine cowlings and polished aluminum bodies grew larger by the second, as long ribbons of smoke followed them down, sparkling faintly with the ejected bright brass shell casings. I noticed with some satisfaction that as long as our Grumman fighters attacked in a dive, the maneuver negated the enemy machine's speed advantage. Our fighters seemed to be everywhere ripping into the formations of Japanese aircraft. The theoretical advantages of our *Performance Envelope* concept was proving valid, as our pilots at this point seemed to own the sky!

The first wave of bombers had attacked and had been scattered, and heavily shot up. Raising my binoculars to port I observed the second wave of some 16 bombers executing a shallow dive in towards the flagship. Within a few seconds of my observation, half of them were now trailing smoke. Flames could be seen within the engine cowlings of several. Sections of Grumman fighters, attacking from above at their flanks, continued to pass down the now ragged formation of bombers, only to pull up and away over the surface of the sea at a tremendous speed. Christ, I thought, watching their performance, you have to be young to take 10 gravities! 1000 meters above the first wave of bombers, our Buffalo fighters had their hands full tackling almost twice their number of nimble Nakajima machines, but soon received assistance from our Sea Fury Fighters.

At once a gigantic curtain of black smudges erupted around and in front of the Japanese bombers. Even at this range I could see the glint of shredded aluminum and shattered Plexiglas. The formation staggered slightly up then corrected itself, to get back in position. I could see individual aircraft being shoved and bounced by the numerous explosions of the shells. Not only were the twenty 40mm auto-cannon of the portside A, B and C Flak batteries of the flagship engaging them from head on, but so were the three port batteries of her sister ship. I could make out from the tracer shells that both the *Prinz te Paard* and *Oliphant* had taken the enemy bombers under fire, ripping into their formation from the side with their combined twenty 40mm auto-cannon! Although the Oerlikon 20 mm auto cannon batteries were below my line of sight, I could still make out their distinctive chatter, as they chewed enemy metal.

Motivation at times may achieve great wonders, but on this occasion neither vengeful flesh, nor precision machinery could withstand the devastating effects of hundreds of explosive cannon shells per second! The brave Japanese pilots and their graceful machines were literally vivisected by millions of red hot steel splinters. They either disintegrated in a cloud of smoke or dove burning into the sea to explode. Five riddled aircraft survived this attack long enough to reach the target. But only one machine released two bombs which arched slowly through the air and fell, widely bracketing the bows of the Vlaggeschip to detonate with little effect in the sea. These bombers passed across the bows of the *Cornelis* trailing long tails of flaming aviation gasoline, then made an attempt to turn away to port and exit the Task Force's AA Fire Zone along the line of axis of our base course. But as they presented their tails to the AA fire coming in from the Battle-carrier, the AA batteries of the starboard screening vessels raked them along their full length, and they slowly sank towards the waves, heavily afire, surrounded by a dogged cloud of black shell bursts, until they nosed into the sea, generating a huge cloud of spray which instantly disappeared amidst the violent detonation of their bombs. I can only assume that their bombardiers were dead or so much mechanical damage had occurred that the bombs could not be released, as four of these five bombers it was observed had their bomb bay doors closed!

The *Cornelis de Witt's* Flak guns suddenly ceased fire, and the flight deck crews and aircraft handlers who, despite the urgency of their duties had stopped to watch the unfolding drama, now erupted with wild cheering. An entire squadron of enemy 'war birds,' 16 bombers, fully one fifth of their entire force had been utterly destroyed! Not even one bomb had reached us, and beside the light casualties the exposed deck crews had suffered from the machine gunners of the bombers, casualties were very light! The thick Fir planking laid atop the 15mm armor, had absorbed the machine gun bullets without allowing the ricochet.

We were not out of the woods yet, the Japanese Hikosentai Commanders, still had 81 bombers, and would use every last one of them to destroy us. They would vary their tactics. As for the fighter action it was a different matter. The Japanese fighters discovering their inability to stop the heavily built *Grumman* machines, immediately pounced upon them as they leveled out over the sea, when their speed dropped from 800 kph of the dive to 320 kph at sea level. Here the Japanese pilots had initial success, with several F3F's crashing into the sea. But now the Nakajima fighters experienced the effects of *Fightercloud!* While it was a simple matter to attack those Grumman fighters that had finished their dive and were only a few meters above the waves, it was quite another to avoid the attacks of a flights of Sea Fury fighters, who were far more maneuverable than the Japanese machines at 300 kph. It was a deadly error for them, having entered the *Performance Envelope* the Japanese fighter pilots now found themselves surrounded by numerous enemy machines, having such combinations of speed and maneuverability that their aircraft could simply not match. Many of the Japanese fighter pilots had chosen to completely ignore the F3F and Sea Fury bi-planes all together and attack the Buffalos. Although less maneuverable than the Ki-43, the F3A was more robust, with a higher speed and could also easily outpace the Japanese machine in a dive, while its quadruple .50 Cal machine guns were much more powerful and long ranged. If, for any maneuver the Japanese machine slowed appreciably it was immediately set upon by the agile biplanes. Ten Japanese fighters were quickly shot down by this trap within three minutes of the first air assault!

I took a private moment, and looked up over my left shoulder at the flags on the mast. The broad tricolors the RNLN battle flag snapped smartly in the clear blue of the sky. Above it, streaming from the masthead, was my Vice-Admiraal's Pennant; a long triangular flag of navy blue with three gold stars. I studied this inspiring sight as I contemplated the revelations of action. The burden of command felt a bit lighter now, for I knew that the huge gamble that the Dutch Crown had made in the rebuilding of our colonial navy had not been wasted. I had seen the battle-squadron in action, Task Force Popeye was not a *Paper Tiger*. The aircraft and men aboard the ships carried out their duties efficiently. I felt confident that the various teams and individuals; whether an AA battery, a pilot, a flight deck aircraft handler or armorer, were all capable to respond to any threat with utmost effort even while under local control. I then quickly returned to the Command Center within the citadel.

Colonel Kengi Nishimura, Commander of the 121 ST Hikosentai, looked down upon the disastrous attack made by the *119th Chutai*. His complete surprise was only matched by his fury. The enemy seemed to be very strong in defensive ability! He growled a curse under his breath; "General Yamada, you cannot trap a tiger with a cursed mousetrap!"

His face grew dark with rage and sorrow, he took some relief when he formed in his mind, his next decision. He ordered his radio operator to open a frequency for the entire air armada. To all aircraft; this is Colonel Nishimura; "Banzai! I give the order that no aircraft is to return to base if even one enemy warship remains afloat!"

He knew that a large formation of Dutch naval aircraft would soon be returning to their fleet, providing substantial reinforcement to their defending aircraft, but he did not know of the close proximity of 30 heavy fighters of the Dutch Royal Army Air Force, or the approach of 14 more Grumman F3F Fighters from Jesselton Naval Air Station, that would swell the enemy Combat Air Patrol to almost 100 fighters, not counting the 35-40 other less capable machines participating in the enemy Fleet's defense. He must press home his attack now with all their remaining aircraft and thereby saturate the Dutch squadron's defenses. Although in the grip of a fury, and the passion of his order that made him tremble, Nishimura's training would not allow him to risk the men and machines of his command unnecessarily. His disciplined mind coolly calculated a workable solution to the unexpectedly effective combined defenses of the Dutch squadron.

The enemy warships had put up a tremendous anti-aircraft barrage, but it seemed to be of medium range capability only; perhaps 8 kilometers maximum. He would exploit that weakness. The Dutch Navy fliers, it was noticed seemed unwilling to venture too far from their fleet, but remained over it in an umbrella of colorful, and sparkling aluminum machines, twisting and swooping, locked in battle with the Nakajima fighters. He would use this deployment against them as well.

Nishimura ordered the 118th and 120th Chutais to withdraw 30 kilometers to the northeast, and then circle back towards the head of the enemy fleet. He would have the torpedo bombers attack in a classic 'X' pattern, with one squadron enfilading the port quarter of the Dutch warships and the other the starboard quarter. It did not matter then in which direction the enemy may turn as it would present its broadside to a shoal of speeding torpedoes.

To cover this maneuver, Colonel Masatake Goto's 124th Hokosenti of Nakajima fighters would attempt to concentrate close above the Dutch Fleet and strafe their decks with machinegun fire. From this intimidating position the fighters would seem to present the greatest danger and should distract the bulk of the enemy fighter activity away from chasing the withdrawing torpedo planes.

The last of the 14 Curtis Helldivers of Bomber Squadron 2 had just flown off at 07:05hrs to begin their attack against the enemy cruisers when the fighters of our Combat Air Patrol identified a new formation of sleek twin engine bombers speeding towards us from the northwest; the Japanese *73rd Hikosentai* had arrived.

I turned to Commander Flyer Van Braekel and said; "Air Chief, the enemy cruiser formation is now somewhat less than 120 nautical miles away, and due to our combined closing speeds will be well within range for an artillery duel in less than two hours, Bomber Squadron 2 has got to stop them at all costs!"

The Commander replied, "Yes Admiraal, the bombers are commanded by Lt. ter Zee 1e Klasse Stefan Kuntz, he understands the grave danger those cruisers pose to our fleet. He and his men are the absolute best that there is Sir, Lt. Kuntz plans to dive onto the enemy from an elevation of 3,000 meters, and he has assured me that all his bomber crews have agreed to pull out of their dives and release their bombs when the chances

Far Aft and Faintly

of a miss are zero. Otherwise they will all crash their machines straight into the decks of ships!" I was taken aback by this astounding expression of duty, and for the moment could not reply. These flyers were all very young men, with many decades of sweet life ahead. Van Klaffens stared back at me; his face stone grey, lips a thin colorless line and with black eyes unwavering. I knew that he cared deeply for all his aircrew, and that they were deadly serious, for already that morning many of our young airmen had ascended heavenward on wings other than those of fabric and aluminum. "Thank you Air Chief, I relied very humbled, I dearly hope that it won't come to that."

He nodded in agreement, then glanced down at his clipboard. "We have received a report from *Tarakan Naval Air Station*, Admiraal. Torpedo Squadrons 1 and 2 totaling 28 Fairy Swordfish MK I's took off a half hour ago, and will be attacking the Japanese shipping off Cochin China over the course of the day. Unfortunately, their limited speed will not allow them to intercept these cruisers in time. In addition to this, our six Hawker Sea Hart bombers that had departed earlier this morning on rotation to *Jesselton*, have been ordered refueled and loaded with 220 kg. HE bombs. These have just taken off and will be able to attack the enemy cruisers in a little over an hour." Nevertheless I am supremely confident that Bomber Squadron 2 will at least heavily damage the *Moyokos* allowing us to maneuver beyond the threat of their guns."

I then was approached by Kapt Voorne and the Van Breakel. The Air Commander said, "Admiraal; our aircraft report that a new JAAF Bomber Regiment is moving into a position to deliver a shallow diving attack with three full squadrons, while the two remaining squadrons of the 121st Bomber Regiment that had been circling, have moved ahead of us and are preparing a torpedo attack against the port and starboard bows with the X formation from head on as well! Our Army fighter support have just arrived and at this very moment should be engaging the enemy aircraft."

Kapt Voorne, turned to duty officer Kap. Lt. ter Zee Linus de Kroon and said; "Alert the senior gunnery officer to stand by with his anti-torpedo mortar teams". Then saluting me, he said; "Admiraal I will be returning to my action station." I returned the salute and he hurried off to the battle bridge. At least Voorne will have windows I griped to myself, while I've got to sit in this bloody armored box!

The main attack of the enemy had been unleashed against Task Force Popeye. It quickly reduced one's ability to think clearly due to the shattering noise, shaking, jolts and bangs that overwhelmed the senses. You could have discharged a revolver in the room and not have been able to distinguish it! With our senses overwhelmed, our training took over. We worked instinctively as automatons without hesitation, carrying out functions, receiving information and scribbling down orders as speech was completely impossible.

The Observations of:
25 year old Lt. ter Zee 1e Klasse Stefan Kuntz: Squadron Leader Bomber Squadron 2, Battlecruiser-carrier *Cornelis De Witt*; Vloot Vlaggeschip, Task Force Popeye Dec. 08,'41:

"When the call to action stations had roused us out of our bunks early in the morning, to be informed that we were at war with the Nippon; the men became hot for action. Two Japanese Fleets were the targets. Imagine our exasperation when Bomber Squadron 2 was held back as reserve! My men pressed me to get the Senior Air Officer to reconsider. I went to the Command center, and as I waited for an opportunity to speak with him I surveyed the situation developing within the large

compartment. *The big plastic situation board revealed to me that we were in for a heavy day! The constant radio traffic, frantic decoders, huddled knots of senior officers were a clear indication that the SAO would be in no mood to listen to the whining of my airmen! To hell with this I concluded! I hastily returned to my crews, and responded to their protests with; Don't worry boys, from what I could determine; everybody get busy and fill out your last will and testament form as there will be ample opportunity for each of you to lose your lives today. We are undergoing an air attack by three Japanese Army Air Regiments, and a surface fleet is charging down upon us from the northeast! There was no more whining for action from these men for the remainder of the day!"*

"*06:40hrs, Action notice! A quick briefing by the Air Chief; a Squadron of enemy Heavy cruisers was racing towards our fleet from the east, and would be upon us in a matter of hours! 06:46hrs Alarm Status Fightercloud. For a moment there was great confusion; do we cancel the bomber mission to answer the emergency call for maximum CAP? The Air Chief overrides Fightercloud, the bombing mission is a go! Our orders were simple;* **sink the enemy cruisers at all cost!** *After the enemy ships are destroyed; join the CAP over the fleet so that the Sea Fury fighters can land and refuel. Our machines had already been fueled and the .50 Cal and .30 Cal machine gun magazines re-filled with belts of ammunition. Fat orange nosed 225 kg Amatol AP bombs was quickly affixed to the 'A Frame Bracket' under the belly of each dive-bomber and the whole squadron brought up from the lower aircraft hangar onto the flight deck in less than three minutes! The dive bombers were quickly arranged on the flight deck by a small army of aircraft handlers. The pilots began to fire their Kauffman starters with loud bangs, and the big Curtis Wright Radial engines one by one snarled and coughed to life, briefly venting clouds of blue-white smoke. While the engines warmed up to optimal, my crews went through their 'mission profiles', then began to check their navigation, the cockpit instruments and control surface cabling. While above us we impatiently viewed our cap fighters zooming around combating enemy fighters. The deck crews shouted and pointed out to us in the distant northeast, where a dark band was now visible against the morning sky, indicating the arrival of a large formation of enemy bombers!*"

"*07:00hrs, I checked the engine temperature, and fuel mixture; and asked for a report from all my pilots, READY 1, READY 2, READY 3, ...until all were finished, I radioed the Air Chief that we were set; I waved the wheel blocks away, and revved up the engine waiting for a green light... there is is..feet off the brakes...full pitch on the propeller...maximum revolutions...and a shove for good luck from the aircraft handlers...were off!*"

"*The* **Frantic Fiona** *rolled down the flight deck and within four seconds was airborne. Immediately she began creaking and the wires hummed as the wings took the weight of the ship and its load. I shook my head in mirth, those bloody Yanks and their silly names for aircraft! Unfortunately, it is very bad luck for a machine to be renamed, even if mustered out of one navy and into another! I found myself unconsciously stroking the side of the fuselage as if it was the soft inner thigh of the disheveled scantily clad blonde dish adorning the fuselage. I banked slightly to starboard and upon looking behind me, I made out the 14 Curtis Model 77 Helldivers of Bomber Squadron 2 strung out in neat intervals like yellow beads on a long string that reached right back to our great Vlaggeschip. All the machines were away. Although I had seen them many times during operations the two massive Battlecruiser-carriers still looked very impressive from the air, dangerous and ready for action. The three main battery turrets were trained, port, starboard, port, with the long gun barrels elevated. The Helldivers took up right and left echelon formation on my machine and we steadied up on an azimuth of 8 degrees. The Air Chief now radioed to wish us good hunting* *and inform us that we have lost our fighter escort to the Combat Air Patrol due to the Fightercloud emergency condition."*

"Looking up and to my port I could see two monoplane Nakajima fighters at 800 meters range turning sharply in our direction preparing to attack. Nothing like an easy target of heavily laden bombers, slowly climbing for altitude. I knew that we could not jettison our bombs, as our mission was vital. But as the Japanese machines attempted their maneuver; their speed dropped rapidly down and in a flash three Sea Fury fighters and a Grumman F3F pounced upon them! The Japanese pilots tried to evade the dogged pursuit of the biplane fighters on their tail which lacerated them all the while with machinegun fire. The Nakajima fighters, twisted and then dove, but to no avail, they simply could not match the bi-plane fighter's performance at that lower speed. The entire drama played out in less than half a minute, when both Nakajimas exploded into flame and went plunging into the Sea."

"There! Only forty minutes into our mission; and the enemy cruiser squadron was in sight! At this distance all that I could make out were four tiny black pyramids, each sitting at the tip of a long ribbon of white, advancing abreast over the sea with ominous intent. Their four long arrow straight wakes stretched back to the horizon, diminishing in width with the distance until vanishing into the blue haze where sea and sky met. My radio operator gunner; Air Telegraphist Gunner Pieters signaled the Vlaggeschip to report: "Mother Goose, Mother Goose, Sparrow 2, elevation 2,000 meters, visibility 60 nautical miles, 07:55hrs, commencing attack on enemy cruiser squadron".

"We would commence our attack from behind, up their wakes. I thought to myself these are bloody BIIIIG cruisers! They sported massive control towers and looked like battlecruisers. I estimated them as having twice the displacement of our new light cruisers, and man: were they ever moving! I put their speed at 36 to 37 knots! Whether we lived or died depended to a large extent, if the enemy could bring our battlcruiser-carriers under fire and destroy our flight deck operations. WE WOULD NOT LET THAT HAPPEN!"

"I called the Squadron to action: Helldivers arm your bombs! By sections of three, we will each dive down on an enemy cruiser beginning with the starboard cruiser, then work to port, each section hitting the next ship over. I will lead the first attack. Aim for the funnels amidships, that part of a ship moves the least in any maneuver. Stay on target and hit them hard. The last two Helldivers will remain aloft until all sections have attacked, these will then bomb those cruisers that appear to be least damaged. When you pull out of the dive, fly away down their bows to mask their flak guns. Aircraft without bombs assume fighter escort duty, these cruisers carry float plane fighters. Here we go men; Section 1, follow me down!"

"I dropped the long nose of Frantic Fiona, slid my bombsight back towards my eye, located the first cruiser and centered her waist in the crosshairs focusing on the forward stack. Our velocity rose sharply from 300 to 760 kph as screaming with the fury of a betrayed lover, the long nosed bomber plunged downward at an angle of some 85 degrees towards the sea. The details of the ship's structure rapidly came into focus as we closed her at some 580 feet per second! I could now make out the white blobs moving over her brown linoleum decks, the shoulders and round caps of individual sailors. The flak batteries of all calibers were flashing continually under a haze of smoke. The tracer anti-aircraft rounds appeared as huge glowing cotton balls that hovered motionless above the smoke for an instant and then zipped past the dive bomber, shoving it around with the shockwave of their passing. I fought to keep the racing ship in my crosshairs as she snaked over the sea. My left and right feet were constantly flapping the rudder controls and my hand gripped the bomb release lever with painful pressure. I yanked hard on the release lever, felt the bomb bracket deploying, enabling the bomb to clear the propeller and then at the moment of release the aircraft

lifted, and I yanked her nose hard up and to the right, not believing for an instant that I would have time to pull out of the dive and recover control of Fiona. I knew that the 225 kg AP bomb could not miss from that distance, and the Helldiver had barely responded when a deafening crash and shock wave slammed into us from behind. Gunner Pieters, machine gun had been hammering away even before the pull out, a tactic he employed that would still allow a stream of bullets to hit the target in case he blacked out during the pull-out. Fiona raced off over the waves, and I brought the Helldiver around for a look at what we had accomplished. Her speed had not dropped noticeably in those few seconds but a huge black mushroom cloud was growing out of the warship at amidships. Just then, plunging downward into my field of view, and angling in off her port quarter in an attempt to avoid the fireball; the second plane of my section; flown by Lt. ter Zee Versteegen had reached its release point. The bomb detached and the Lt. pulled away to his starboard. His Amatol egg dropped to the deck and disappeared through it just between the D and E gun turrets of her main battery. An incredible bright fireball erupted from inside the cruiser engulfing the entire aft half of the ship. Her aft magazine had gone up! Quickly looking aloft I saw the remaining pilots of Flight 'A' break off their attack to avoid being engulfed by the tremendous fireball. I banked Fiona to port and crossed the bows of another cruiser. I searched the sea and sky but could find no sign of Versteegen's bomber, it could not have survived as the aircraft had only been some 20 meters from the ship when her magazine went up. I was momentarily overcome with guilt and anger, the youngest officer in my squadron had taken it upon himself to make the ultimate sacrifice to guarantee a hit on the target. Did he not realize that his act was pre-mature so early in the action? Quickly the anger faded when it came to me that, with so many variables at play in the attack he could not have planned that result. They were a gallant aircrew!

"The cruiser squadron had launched eight float plane fighters that we were not aware of until they raced in to attack from above. The Japanese floatplane fighter pilots had been drawn into the main air battle only a few minutes away which now involved more than 200 machines. The floatplane fighters were actually Mitsubishi zeros and would have been able to easily defend the cruisers against a formation of twin engine Glen Martin bombers or Swordfish torpedo planes, but with their outfit of a massive centerline float and two small under wing floats their performance suffered considerably. They were not well positioned when the Dutch dive bombers arrived on target, being five kilometers off to our port side, and they were only able to line us up and engage at long range with their cannon. The Helldiver; in a dive does over 800 kph. Only at the bottom of their dive are they vulnerable. The Japanese pilots soon discovered this and as they were unable to stop the attack, so they lingered in an ambush position. However, the Helldiver, once free of bombs was transformed into a tricky little dogfighter in its own right, and only a few knots of speed separated their performance from the massively encumbered floatplane fighters. The zero pilots were determined and they only had to have a Helldiver in their sights for a split second, to unload a stream of 20 mm cannon fire into an intersection with the target. Two of our dive bombers were lost this way."

"The dive bomber attack continued against the enemy cruisers and played out in much the same manner as the first attack. Of the 14 dive bombers involved, seven had obtained solid hits on their decks and superstructures of the remaining three Japanese heavy cruisers. One of these aircraft had its pilot killed at the point of release and the aircraft and bomb slammed into base of the raked funnel. The five others Helldivers managed very near misses, which caused severe hull shaking and strain. When the attack was finished, the heavy cruiser whose aft magazine had exploded, had lost her stern and had rolled over to port turning turtle, a second enemy cruiser was heavily afire, stopped with a huge slick of fuel oil surrounded her and looked to be completely devoid of life. Her *two remaining squadron mates were in a similarly disabled state; afire and circling very slowly trailing oil. But they were not dead ships as their frantic air gunners directed a brisk barrage at all aircraft within range, including their own Zero floatplane fighters! Here and there bits of wreckage floated in the vicinity on which one could make out a few white clad crewmen."*

"The ten surviving aircraft of Bomber Squadron 2 were immediately locked into air combat with the Japanese Mitsubishi float plane fighters and had to battle their way back to the their ship. However within a few minutes fighter support arrived from those Fightercloud machines that had been chasing the enemy torpedo bombers northward but losing the contest of speed. Our stubby F2F and F3F fighters dispatched these dogged Japanese machines, whose awkwardness became quickly apparent against the more agile Grumman Machines."

The Japanese high command had made a risky gamble with its heavy cruiser squadron to ensure the success of *Nezumatori*, and lost. In seventeen minutes the action had been decided. Crusier Squadron 11, of the Imperial Japanese Navy was in a shambles. One cruiser had its bottom blown out and was afire and sinking, a second was going down by the stern, and heavily aflame after a magazine detonated. The two remaining heavy cruisers were severely damaged, and reported as 'wreathed in smoke and circling very slowly.'

When this action report came in and was handed to me at 08:30hrs I stood and called for the Kapt. Voorne and my Van Braekel. "Air Chief," I smiled, you've earned your sardines and beer today! Cancel the diversion of the land based torpedo bombers unit assigned to attack these cruisers and redirect them to go after the remains of the Japanese convoy and its escorts." However, within a few hours, I was to learn the error of this last order.

Turning to Kapitein Voorne, I continued; "Bomber Squadron 2 has eliminated the cruiser threat! Two sinking, two heavily damaged, afire and drifting! Taking the message from my hand he read it, laughed and congratulated the Air Chief, who responded; "the six *Sea Harts* should be bombing those survivors any time now." "Good! Good" I replied, "Kapt. Voorne transmit this news to the crews. In a short time I was rewarded with a lot of back slapping and cheering. The day was turning out to a great naval victory for the Netherlands. Task Force Popeye was proving to be too big of a bite for the Japanese strategists who had planned the operation!

Kapitein Voorne then addressed one of his aids; "Warrant Officer please fetch Commander Van Ripper to the Command Center. In short order the Chief Gunnery officer arrived and saluted. "Guns" Kapitein Voorne began, "the enemy heavy cruiser squadron, now 60 nautical miles out is still approaching us from the northeast to cut our escape route through Balabat Strait. The enemy has been heavily damaged by our dive bombers, we believe two have sunk and the remaining pair are afloat, in bad shape but still very dangerous. Due to the needs of *Fightercloud*, all the available Helldivers will be assigned to combat air patrol. We only have six *Sea Harts* available to finish these cruisers, and they may not be sufficient. So coordinate with the *Johan de Witt* and prepare your main batteries for surface action. The target will appear off the starboard bow."

Commander Van Ripper paused to glance at his watch; then looking up at the plastic Status board said; "given their damaged condition and estimating a combined closing speed is 40 knots, in one hour Kapitein Voorne we should be able to range them with the main battery stereoscope." The Kapitein Lt. ter Zee, saluted crisply and rushed away. The greatest moment of his career was at hand; to atomize enemy warships with the Battlecruiser-carrier division's massive 343mm artillery!

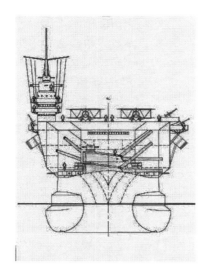

CHAPTER XXV

AIR ATTACK ON THE DREADNOUGHTS KUMAMOTO AND KAGOSHIMA, JAPANESE SIXTH AIR ARMY ASSAULT, SURFACE ENGAGEMENT WITH HEAVY CRUISERS, DAMAGE CONTROL, WITHDRAWL INTO THE SULU SEA, FLEET CONCENTRATION, LICKING OUR WOUNDS.

At approximately the same time that the 22nd Air Brigade of the 17th Air Division of the JAAF was hurling its four Air Regiments at the warships of Task Force Popeye, and that great air-sea battle was reaching its crescendo, Strike Group 3, from the two besieged Battle-carriers, composed of 28 PZL P-23 Sea Eagle heavy dive-bombers had flown without fighter escort, completely unmolested to their target: the retiring remnants of General Takaguchi's Malaya Invasion Force.

The Observations of:
20 year old Air Bombardier Gunner Jan Steen flying in the belly gondola of a PZL P-23 Sea Eagle, Aircraft No. B3C-1, flown by Lt. Commander Jakob Van Prooijen, Commander of Bomber Squadron 3, from the Vlaggeschip *Cornelis de Witt*, Dec. 08, '41, South China Sea:

"8:40hrs Dec. 08 '41. The flight to our target had been uneventful, beyond the stressful takeoff, as our Task Force had been under severe air attack throughout the entire squadron's launch. Lt. Commander Van Prooijen was the first to spot our targets and ordered the Strike Group to prepare. I abandoned for the moment my current position at the bomber's ventral Lewis gun, to turn around and assume the bombardier's position. Through the Plexiglas bubble of the bombardier's belly gondola, I had a fine view of the sea 2000 meters below. In the distance, some forty kilometers ahead lay the southern coastline of Cochin China, far off to the west the Gulf of Saigon, while ahead hanging above the broad blue expanse of the South China Sea was an immense cloud of heavy black smoke. Descending from this vast pall were ten tornado-like funnels that reached down to touch the sea. It was there at that point of contact, where bright yellow shifting blobs confirmed that ten Japanese troopships were still furiously burning! This was the hard evidence our air group's work

earlier in the morning. I was able to detect on the unruffled, oil befouled sea, extending from this area of disaster a number of long straight line disturbances on its surface that pointed the way to an invisible convoy of ships steaming eastward. In another ten minutes they came into view."

"I began to study the two largest warships with my binoculars, both ships were identical, and from their chunky appearance; dreadnoughts. As we drew closer I was able to distinguish a number of their main features; six big twin gunned turrets, of which four were laid out in the now obsolete hexagonal arrangement; two turrets to port and starboard with one forward and one aft on the centerline. The ships each had a single, unusually double curved trunked funnel, and a very tall forward leaning control tower. After quickly flipping through the pages of my International Warship Recognition Manual, I confirmed that these squat compact warships as the 23,000 tonne battleships of the Settsu Class. Their funnel rings confirmed; two white on the closest as the Kagoshima, and the leading vessel with three rings the Kumamoto; both vessels of Great War vintage, but which had undergone extensive modernization."

"I was also able to identify six undamaged freighters of 3,000 to 5,000 tonnes and fifteen destroyers, three of the latter type seemed to be damaged and under tow, and all were survivors of our air attacks earlier today. These vessels had reversed their original course and were making their way north eastward, possibly to a safe harbour up the coast of Japanese occupied French Indo China as fast as possible. I reported my observations at once to my pilot, and the air telegraphist/ gunner quickly radioed this report back to the Cornelis De Witt."

"During our mission briefing, the importance of our targets was explained. Our high priority targets, were the two modernized dreadnoughts. Although, no longer considered worthy of inclusion into a modern 'line of battle' by 1941 standards due to their low speed, we knew that they had been rebuilt to provide support for their army's amphibious landing operations. With a massive armored fire control tower and communications outfit, these ships were designed to act as a command and control center, as well as to provide heavy shore bombardment capability. Protected as they were with thick armor plating, and with their twelve 305 mm big guns and thirty smaller cannon of mixed caliber, they could sit off a beach and reduce the heaviest coastal defense installation to rubble. These two specialized vessels were of high importance to the Japanese. If we could destroy them, we may deprive their Army of several vital pieces of invasion equipment, thereby unhinging their plans."

"In another minute we had been identified as hostile aircraft by the ships below, as they now began to weave back and forth, looking ever so much like snakes swimming on a pond, then the heavy flak guns aboard the two battleships opened fire on our formation. Lt. Commander Van Prooijen, acutely aware of this danger, and seeing no fighter cover over the convoy, decided to attack immediately, and chose to dive straight down upon the twisting targets, thereby giving them precious little time to shoot. He selected the leading ship; Kumamoto as his target and signaled flight A to follow him down. Flight B was to hang back, and observe the results. If the battleship was destroyed they were to bomb the merchantmen, then the destroyers. Bomber Squadron 6 from the Johan De Witt, under the command of Lt. Commander Marthinus Steyn, carried out a similar operation against the Battleship Kagoshima."

"Our bomber nosed over into an 85 degree dive. I engaged the arming mechanism for the 750 kilogram picric acid Armor Piercing warhead. The target rapidly began to fill my optical sight as our speed rose to 500 kph. In a very short time the green light indicted the deadly egg was 'armed for release,' (fully armed three seconds after release) and I turned the control over to the pilot, who was busy keeping the maneuvering target in the cross-hairs of his scope while calling out the

altitudes. The robust bomber bounced and shuddered in response to the course corrections and heavy buffeting as the big five inch AA rounds whizzed past the fuselage. I could now clearly see the white clad forms of the Japanese sailors on the battleship's wide deck, frantically working their guns, and then at a point where I was sure that we would crash into her, the pilot released the bomb and we pulled rapidly to starboard."

"I struggled to return to my ventral machinegun against the G-forces of our maneuver. By the time that I had done this, the aircraft had already flown a kilometer from our target. I had a perfect panoramic view of the battleships from the belly gondola. The unique silhouettes of each battleship were highlighted darkly against the spectacularly tall white splashes of the 750 kilogram bombs. Each vessel slowly became an inferno. The flashes of their heavy flak guns were repeatedly engulfed by spectacular dark mushroom clouds as multiple heavy bombs detonated one after the other deep within their hull. It was immediately obvious that our AP heavy bombs had defeated the obsolete deck armor arrangements of the old warriors and both vessels were clearly doomed!"

"Our aircraft climbed up to 1000 meters altitude while it circled the stricken Japanese Battleships. 'Flight A' had hit the Kumamoto with five out of seven bombs. The tall control tower was leaning backward over a cavernous inferno, the funnel was gone and a huge flap of deck plate was folded over the starboard side, the ship was still underway however, circling slowly to port and burning fiercely. The Kagoshima had also been put through the meat grinder. Commander Van Prooijen, seeing that the two old dreadnoughts were finished, ordered the unengaged bombers to attack the merchantmen. This was soon accomplished despite the heavy flak thrown up by the defending destroyer escorts, and all six went down quickly, being large relatively slow moving targets."

"Five aircraft of Bomber Squadron 3 still had bombs and proceeded to go after the weaving destroyers. While those attacks were developing, I reported that at 9:20hrs the Kumamoto had rolled over to port and gone down, and the Kagoshima was heavily afire amidships, down by the bow and settling rapidly. I was momentarily amazed as these warships, so powerful in a surface battle, had succumbed so easily to our air attack. We were very fortunate that the Japanese Army fighters, at My Thoa Airbase had not been on hand, or it would be a Japanese sailor pondering our quick demise. The Sea Eagles then assumed a defensive box formation, and made off as rapidly as possible, for we greatly feared that at any moment a squadron of vengeful enemy fighters would pounce upon us."

The attack against the *Kumamoto* and *Kagoshima* group of ships had met with great success. For the loss of three bombers, and four damaged; two dreadnought battleships, six freighters, the three crippled destroyers had been sunk and another destroyer had been heavily damaged by near misses. Eleven destroyers had escaped our attentions. I knew that these would be subjected to torpedo bomber attack later that day, and may suffer further losses. 'Striker 3', broke off the attack after twenty minutes having expended all bombs, and then shaped a southeasterly course to rendezvous with the Battle-carriers.

While Striker 3 was completing its mission, the great air battle over the fleet had been decided. The four Air Regiments of the *22nd Hikodan*, had been soundly defeated. The JAAF had lost 62 of 100 bombers, and 26 fighters. A large portion of the *121st Hikosentai*, an estimated 16 bombers had been destroyed in their first attack! Many of the retreating bombers were heavily damaged, and lucky to get away.

The tactic of *Fightercloud*, with the timely support of the KNIL's (Royal Netherlands Army) 30 machines of the Heavy Fighter Group III from Tarakan Army Airfield, and backed by the massive anti-aircraft capability of the fleet, had proved too much for the two Japanese bomber regiments. When the 14 Grumman F3F Fighters inbound from Borneo to reinforce the Dutch fleet were identified by the Japanese airmen, and the information transmitted to General Yamada's headquarters at Hanoi, he ordered the withdrawal of the remaining aircraft of the *22nd Hikodan*. Although his air brigade had suffered heavily, he felt confident that he had inflicted crippling damage upon the enemy. He knew that a surface battle was soon to take place, but was not yet aware of the decimated condition of Rear Admiral Tamon Matsumoto's command, and that it had been reduced to two damaged heavy cruisers.

TF Popeye, now had a chance to catch its breath, news of the Dutch Battle Fleet's successful defense was transmitted to naval headquarters in Batavia and was received with great relief and adulation. It was also a time for an assessment of the Fleet's activities.

The repeated combinations of level bombing and frontal attacks by torpedo bombers from the port and starboard, and bombers releasing clutches of bombs from above was very difficult to evade. The Japanese airmen masterfully coordinated the timing of their deadly attacks. At the height of the battle, the two huge battle-carriers were drawing the attentions of at least half of most of the torpedo bombers. The improvised anti-torpedo mortar teams had been constantly firing to create their shock waves barriers in front of those torpedoes. The great ships so far had not been struck by these weapons. Our after action reports concluded that these mortar teams had caused thirteen torpedoes to detonate prematurely, four of which would without a doubt have hit home. Wave after wave of Japanese bombers would form up and carry out coordinated attacks. Our fighter aircraft whose formations were getting progressively more ragged, would respond, and tear into them, scattering the bombers. Our fighter pilots, had completely mastered the tactics of *Fightercloud*, the coordination of high speed monoplanes, with the high maneuverability of the slower biplanes. There was no maneuver or trick that the enemy pilots could use to evade their fire. Then once again; the very determined Japanese Pilots would form up and repeat the process, secure in the knowledge that it was mathematically impossible for our fighters to get it right all the time. Each attack when closing within range of the Flak guns, would have a black cloud formed by hundreds of exploding cannon shells raised across its path. These attacks it was observed had cost the enemy dearly, as at no time during the extended air battle of over one hour, was the sky not marked with burning aircraft falling from the sky. Of every five aircraft that plunged into the sea, four were Japanese.

All the Japanese bombers sprayed their targets with machine gun fire when attacking and with cannon fire when withdrawing. The latter causing most casualties amongst those crew serving unarmored equipment, in the exposed antiaircraft batteries, the flight deck crews and the like.

The final air attack on the fleet beginning at 08:20hrs proved to be the most destructive, as our victory today did not come without serious casualties. The destroyer *Eendragt*, the Vlaggeschip of Destroyer Flotilla 11, had taken a direct hit from a 250 kg bomb on her fantail, which detonated her depth charges, destroying her propellers and blowing off her stern. The Flotilla Commander, Kapitein Lt. ter Zee Guus Slootweg, transferred his flag to the *Zoutmann* to continue with the fleet. A tow was then rigged by her Flotilla mate the *Draak*. Once achieved the pair was able to manage a speed of 20 knots for half an hour.

But the structure of the weakened hull began to leak badly, so her Kapitein; Lt. ter Zee 1e Klasse Albrecht Fosen decided to abandon ship. The *Eendragt's* crew was removed to the *Draak*, which then sank the wounded destroyer with a torpedo. The *Draak* sped on to take up her station in the fleet. Several other destroyers had been severely shaken by very near misses and were consequently suffering casualties from splinters, damage to light structures, leaking pipes, steam lines, and electrical shorts.

The light cruiser *Prins te Paard*, Vlaggeschip of Cruiser Division 4, under the command of Commodore Egmond Borsselen; had a 250 kg bomb detonate on the top of 'A' Turret; which ripped open the 25 mm armor, killed the gun crews, dismounted the two guns and completely destroyed the turret transverse mechanism. A fire ensued which could not be fought, the flames and smoke of which required the abandonment of the control tower and bridge. The crew abandoned the magazine and shell rooms and the spaces were flooded, but not without the loss of 37 men. The ship, although shaken was otherwise in good condition and maintained her speed, her position within the cruising formation, and with all her remaining guns in action.

Those Japanese bombers that had already dropped their bombs, circled our fleet at 1500 meters range spraying explosive rounds from their dorsal 20 mm auto cannon onto the decks and upper works of both battle-carriers. The accuracy of this barrage was not very good as they had hoped. As each bomber engaged in this activity became immediately targeted by typhoon of Flak and were destroyed. Nevertheless, this fire did cause casualties amongst those men in exposed areas and small fires to break out on the Flight decks as well as within the upper aircraft hangars, as the wooden planked flight deck, although 150 mm thick, could not stop cannon fire. These fires were all small and easily smothered.

I was atop the air control deckhouse at the time that the flagship experienced a moment of grave danger. A seamen manning an observation post just behind me shouted and pointed, I turned and looked to port. Coming through a bank of heavy black smoke, was a lone JAAF twin engine bomber flying at very low level, one which had been missed by our CAP, and had not been detected by our AA batteries either, due to the confusion of battle, and much smoke over the water from the burning aviation fuel of downed aircraft, and the massed AA batteries of the fleet.

In a heartbeat, the portside 20 mm Oerlikon batteries, and light machine guns erupted to blaze away at the visibly disintegrating bomber in a ragged concentration. The daring pilot having approached to within 300 meters of the flagship chose survival, and he immediately climbed steeply for altitude to clear our flight deck that stood some 23 meters above the water. He then flew over the foredeck to instantly become hotly engaged by those starboard Flak Batteries that could bear. The bombardier, just prior to this had released a clutch of four 200 kilogram bombs when some 50 meters from the Vlaggeschip. As these round black bombs arched gracefully through the air towards my ship, all I had time to do was lower my binoculars, clutch at my pistol and say; oh Schisse!"

One bomb slammed into the hull just abaft 'C' Turret and below the main deck level, where it detonated outside, against the 155 mm armor plating, forcing it in locally, about 100 mm. The ship shook and rang to the impact of a great hammer, and many including myself were thrown off their feet. A small fire broke out in the adjacent compartment, which was quickly extinguished, the armor had kept the bursting effects of the bomb outboard.

The second bomb passed just under the lower edge of the flight deck forward and glanced off the armored roof of 'C' Turret showering it with life rafts dislodged from above. Bouncing up; it cleared the starboard side of the ship about 6 meters above the deck and detonated 30 meters to starboard lacerating that side of the ship and Flak gun positions with white hot splinters, riddling the light plating and wounding me in the right shoulder. The main battery 'C' Turret was temporarily out of action with an electrical problem due to the two jarring impacts. While above the damage control parties raced to clear away the detritus from the turret and deck.

The third bomb flattened the twin 40 mm mount in the forward gun tub of the port side Flak Battery 'A' crushing three men, and wounding two more. Bouncing off the mount it landed on the forward flight deck, where it then skidded along the steel armor, trailing picric acid foam from its cracked body, then spun out over the starboard side splashing into the sea some 30 meters out. It quickly sank but then detonated some ten seconds further aft along the starboard side, as the ship was advancing at 15 meters per second. The underwater shock rattled the great ship slightly, and made her hull ring with a dull boom like a great drum. Otherwise there was no damage other than giving the men working the guns of the B and C starboard Flak batteries a good soaking. The fourth bomb had passed over 'A' Turret and detonated in the sea, again rattling the ship, but causing only splinter damage.

While picking myself up off the deck, a seamen saluted me and said; "you are wounded Admiraal." I quickly surveyed the scene of the bomb impacts on the ship where the smoke of fires were catching hold, and then hurried below to listen to the damage control reports, and have a medical orderly dress my shoulder wound.

Entering the Command Center, I grabbed a coffee and lit up a cigarette taking a deep drag, then unbuttoned and removed my tunic and sat down. The damage to the ship was reported as localized, with a few small electrical fires put out, and then smoke vented from the affected compartments. A seaman 1st Klasse Hospital Corpsman was immediately summoned and began tending to my shoulder. He then paused, looked up at me from daubing the blood from the wound, he saluted me smartly then coolly took the cigarette from my lips, crushing it out. I was momentarily stunned, and before I could say anything he spoke up with professional admonishment; "you have been wounded Admiraal, it is more than just a scratch, I won't have you slipping into shock while under my care because of a cigarette. It is strictly against medical procedure!" The corpsman went back to work on my shoulder, while I looked over at Kapt. Voorne, who had been watching the mini-drama unfold. I struggled vainly, while searching for a suitable reprimand. Clearly, I thought; the corpsman should have asked me to snuff out the smoke! But Kapt. Voorne looked at his clipboard, shook his head and suppressed a tiny smile at my conflicted expression. I then lowered my head, resigned myself to the situation without further attitude and was quickly stitched up. To the overworked corpsman, the wounded had no rank.

The *Johan de Witt*, had not come through the day's first action unscathed. In addition to the small fires topside from the attacking bomber's cannon, a Japanese aerial torpedo struck her starboard side, aft of amidships and some thirty meters forward of the funnel.

The ship was greatly jolted. Aircraft, equipment and men were tossed up off the deck, and steam pressure to her outboard shaft began to drop rapidly. The superheated dry steam at 315 ° C that fed the propeller shaft turbines, is completely invisible, and its release through a fractured pipe instantly killed 15 men in the starboard turbine room before the main valve supplying steam to that shaft could be shut down.

The torpedo had struck the outer 19 mm plating of the hull blister, which was designed to defeat torpedoes. The soft balsa wood packed around the crushing cylinders in the void space behind the impact zone was completely powdered, but did not impede the air space, while the torpedo was unable to transmit its massive hydraulic load to the hull plating, which remained intact.

As I had calculated; the balsa wood packing that had not been crushed by the shock wave, greatly limited the flooding of the adjacent blister spaces. The battle-carrier did not take up a noticeable list. However for some 15 meters along the hull in the area of the destroyed and flooded blister, there no longer remained any torpedo protection for the hull plate. Accordingly, upon a receipt on the extent of the damage report on that torpedo hit the *Johan de Witt's* Commander; Kap. ter Zee Van der Hulst ordered that the fuel oil wing tanks adjacent to the damaged blister be pumped out to other tanks to create an empty void behind the hull shell plating, essentially creating an *Ersatz Torpedo Blister*. The *Johan de Witt* was able to maintain a speed of 24 knots on her three remaining shafts, and the Task Force adjusted, to allow her to remain in formation.

Our Sea Hart bombers had not been able to deliver the *coup de gras* to the remaining pair of enemy heavy cruisers, as they had run afoul of two Mitsubishi float plane fighters that had survived unnoticed. The Sea Harts bombers were forced to jettison their bombs into the sea and then proceeded to fight off the Japanese machines, but not before they reported that they were unsuccessful and the two *Moyokos* were underway once more.

Although the big Japanese cruisers evidenced significant upper works damage, their man gun batteries were reported as trained to starboard with all guns at high elevation, fires no longer spouted from the bomb craters in their decks, as both warships were making approximately 20 knots in the direction of our ships. Our Helldivers carried bombs less than one third the weight of the Sea Eagles; still these cruisers' survival came as a surprise. It was not until after the war that it was discovered that this class of Japanese heavy cruiser was protected with deck armor that was up to 130 mm in thickness in strategic locations, a level of protection superior to older battleships of that time!

Rear Admiral Tamon Matsumoto, the Commander of the Cruiser Squadron 11, attached to Vice Admiral Tomoshige's Distant Cover Fleet, could not believe his good luck! Half his force had survived the Dutch Air attacks and the surface battle that he had been commanded to seek out, would now occur.

Captain Sengi Kozu of the *Yakushi*, had signaled earlier that the damage to his heavy cruiser had been shored up, and its fires were extinguished. The Flagship the *Tokachi*; had also taken a heavy bomb hit, and was shaken by several near misses but had survived these, due to their first class deck armor arrangement. The *Senjo's* amidships 127 mm AA magazines had been penetrated by a bomb and she had exploded and sank. While the *Hotaka* had lost her stern. Of the original ten big guns on each of these two surviving cruisers sixteen had been put right and were cleared for action.

Admiral Matsumoto believed that the Dutch Fleet had already sustained heavy damage, as the Japanese airmen had reported that both enemy battle-carriers had taken multiple bomb and torpedo hits. Now he must block their attempt to escape into the Sulu Sea, and the protection of Dutch airfields. Then the JAAF could complete their destruction, and the primary strategic objective of 'Operation Nezumatori' would have been accomplished, and his losses for the most part justified.

Two of his powerful cruisers had survived and were still capable of giving battle. The ship's highly trained damage control parties had put out the fires, had shorn up the weakened structures with timber and relit the fires to the boilers. What damage remained was still serious, but not fatal. The guns were cleared away in preparation for a surface action that could not be avoided. These would be under local turret control, as the main fire control computers and their stereoscopes were all smashed. A surface battle would now occur. Regardless of the odds stacked against him, his ships were as dangerous as wounded tigers.

Admiral Matsumoto, would begin his attack against the Dutch fleet by launching his *Long Lance torpedoes* from the remaining undamaged starboard torpedo tubes beginning at a range of 35,000 meters. The enemy fleet's position and course was being constantly updated by his single remaining observation plane. Such a long range was well within the capability of the torpedo but still more than ten kilometers beyond the range both of his guns, and that of the enemy's 343mm weapons. His ships would continue to launch their submarine missiles while constantly correcting for course variations, until they were all expended. At the same time he would be closing at high speed to engage the enemy with his guns. The *Long Lance Torpedo*, was the best kept secret in the considerable arsenal of the mighty *Rengo Khantai*, for it had twice the destructive power and four times the range of torpedoes possessed by any other nation. The Dutch Fleet would not even be aware that they were in the water, undoubtedly believing that his 203 mm guns were the only danger blocking their escape through Balabat Strait.

The report that two of the Japanese heavy cruisers had survived our air attacks, and were continuing to close us, came as a most unpleasant surprise to me. The 8 inch guns of these ships now became, the primary surface threat to our continued operations. We had just received the news about the success of our *Sea Eagle* squadrons against the retreating Japanese convoy. The Japanese invasion fleet of the coast off French Indo China had been eliminated, although eleven destroyers had escaped. The surviving destroyers were not worth the risk as I knew they were difficult targets to hit. Of more concern were the six other Japanese Air Regiments of heavy bombers, newly arrived from Manchuria. These based further north along the west coast of French Indo China on the newly constructed airfields at Da Nang, Qu Nhom and Na Trang. My fleet was well within their range, and they could hit us at any time.

My orders had been carried out. The two Japanese invasion fleets had been turned back with crippling losses. Further damage to the fleet was not warranted. I would withdraw my ships into the Sulu Sea as ordered. My fleet needed to repair its damage in security behind the fighter protection of the British Air Base at Jesselton, the Dutch Air Base at Tarakan, and the PAAC (Philippine Army Air Corps) Base at Davao, on the Island of Mindanao. There I would join with *Task Force Olive* to await further orders. However, our escape route to the Sulu Sea was now blocked by two enemy cruisers, and this was no time to begin a gun action as the flight decks of both battle-carriers were rapidly filling up with returning aircraft; most of these critically short of fuel and ammunition, many were shot up and had wounded fliers aboard.

Fightercloud had fulfilled its mission, and had decimated those enemy bombers that attempted to pass through such a hornet's nest. But of the 80 or so aircraft operating in the Combat Air Patrol as fighters, 18 had been destroyed. The Royal Army heavy fighter group had lost 6 of its machines, with as many damaged. Our Curtis Helldivers losses stood at 9 with 16 damaged. Our Sea Hart light bombers lost 5 machines, 7 damaged. The destroyers, recovered only half of their little yellow float planes. The Sea Eagles seemed to have gotten through the day with the loss of 4 bombers. The fleet had lost close to 40 of its aircraft, with 55 damaged and in need of repair, of these 8 became write-offs. The Aircrew suffered 62 killed or missing, with 80 wounded, leaving the total Air Group with only 34% effectives! The 14 F3F Fighters from Jesselton were a great boost, and had by this time landed aboard the Vlaggeschip for immediate refueling, as the *Johan de Witt* was still fighting her fire in the after elevator well.

The JAAF fighter opposition had been very heavy, estimated at two Army Air Regiments, and 8 IJN float plane fighters from the heavy cruisers. Fortunately for us the *124th Hikosentai*, had lost many of its fighters at the hands of the Dutch Army twin engine Fokker fighters, whose approach from the enemy Fighter Group's six o'clock position, was mistaken by their pilots as the arrival of an additional JAAF bomber Regiment; the *63rd Hikosentai* operating out of Binh-dinh Airfield Indo China. There was no question in my mind that this one incident was of huge significance to the air battle's successful outcome, as it completely disrupted the enemy attack, inflicting heavy losses and instilling a certain level of confusion amongst the Japanese airmen for the remaining battle. Good fortune had been with us today.

Trailing in the wake of the fleet bobbed the detritus of a sea battle, burning wreckage from the ships, burning patches of aviation fuel, life rafts with wounded airmen, and the still bodies, all to be patiently sifted through by the flotilla of rescue craft, and military and civilian float planes, following behind and those that had been dispatched from Miri, in Sarawak and the emergency airfields in Sabah.

Turning to ship's Kapt. Voorne and the Senior Air Operations Officer Commander Flier Van Braekel, I said, "Air Ops, the Japanese attacks seem to have lessened appreciably, please verify if the JAAF formations have withdrawn. If this is the case; stand down from *Fightercloud*, but maintain a strong Combat Air Patrol. Continue to land those aircraft returning from their missions, refuel all the flyable machines and get them off the ship as quickly as possible. Then shut down all pumping of aviation fuel, bleed the lines, and fill them with CO_2, it seems for a time that we will be involved in a surface battle!"

Then at 09:05hrs addressing the ship's Kapitein I said, "Kapt. Voorne maintain present course and speed, prepare the fleet for surface action. Destroyers to stay in formation to screen the Battle-carriers, make to all cruisers: make full speed to intercept the Japanese heavy cruisers approaching us on the port bow and sink them. The Battle-carriers are to open fire when in range, and over the heads of our light cruisers, ceasing fire only when each of the enemy has been definitely hit hard, and when our cruisers are well engaged. I am going up on top of the deckhouse to observe." He saluted smartly, and gave the orders. Pausing at the companionway I looked over at the corpsman busily slinging the arm of my Chief of Staff. I was hoping to catch his eye, but he did not have time to notice me. I jammed a cigarette between my lips and left the compartment.

Returning to my position atop the deckhouse, I noticed just after 9:30hrs, while looking above me, that the *Cornelis's* big stereoscopic rangefinder had obviously locked onto something. I turned and trained my binoculars upon the *Johan de Witt* now steaming half a nautical mile off our starboard quarter. She also had her main battery *slung out* to port pointing in the same direction as our heavy guns. I raised my binoculars to the horizon but was only able to detect a small smudge of smoke. Our four light cruisers were now pulling ahead of the fleet at 31 knots and in a short time they all had formed up into a *Line of Battle* behind the *Gouden Leeuw* (Golden Lion), Vlaggeschip of Schout-bij-Nacht (Rear Admiraal) Count Manfred Van Sassenheim-Heenvliet, Commander of Cruiser Squadron 3.

As these graceful light cruisers swept past the Vlaggeschip, with their great battleflags streaming in the wind, under Count Sassenheim's Rear Admiraal pennant, they looked quite magnificent. Across the waters I could hear faint bugle calls, an ancient tradition from the days of sail, alerting the men to the impending surface action!

All the cruiser men aboard these hurrying warships were acutely aware that they were at the cusp of an historic action that would be remembered by our Nation for centuries to come. All aboard knew that they were on the threshold of the single defining moment of their navy lives. The Dutch Fleet was locked in a life or death struggle with a powerful enemy that had launched a surprise attack. The two great battle-carriers, the very heart of the fleet were wounded and needed their cruiser escort to *clear the way* to safer waters!

The citizens of our beloved Native land desperately needed a great naval victory to boost their spirits. The Fleet Admiraal had called upon his cruiser escort to protect the battle-carriers. Never before had these cruiser men been more conscious of their value and their duty. Upon this *gun action* could rest victory or defeat. The future of the Netherlands lay within their hands!

As I watched these brave ships rush furiously forward, with the foam piled high against their sterns, I recalled somewhat inaccurately those famous lines from the 19th century English poet Lord Thomas Babington; *Horatius at the Bridge.* His inspiration was the heroic efforts of a handful of Roman soldiers who blocked a gate into the city of Rome against a large detachment of infantry from the army of Alba, a neigbouring city, some 2800 years ago.

At a desperate moment the commander spoke to his heavily outnumbered men defending the bridge over the moat:

> *Then out spoke brave Horatius, the Captain of the Gate;*
> *To every man upon this earth, death cometh soon or late,*
> *And how may men die better when facing fearful odds;*
> *Than for the ashes of their fathers, and the Temples of their Gods.*

Eventually, with all his brave band cut down, *Horatius* was alone, pierced by arrow, and suffering many sword cuts. Feeling his strength ebbing he set fire to the bridge. Once the blaze was well established he lept into the moat with full armor. He was such a powerful individual that he swam to the other side, even so heavily encumbered. His actions were so incredible, that the soldiers of Alba, paused to cheer his escape!

The question had been raised in the past on many an occasion, mostly by the very young who poccess at best a limited experience of life: *Do we not live in a time when such loyalty is obsolete?* Looking at the now distant fantails of my hurrying cruisers, turrets trained to port, guns elevated to the maximum, I thought not.

Chief Petty Officer Rangefinder Anton Steeple, squinted through the powerful optics of the main battery stereoscope of the *Cornelis de Witt*. He had been watching a smudge of smoke about 30° off the port bow for the last minute. Then he stiffened and gripped the focus knob of his instrument. There! Coming rapidly up over the horizon two squat slate black little pyramids. At a closing speed of some 40 knots the details of the enemy cruisers could soon be identified, and he reported the sighting, range and bearing to the battle bridge at 09:33hrs. The main battery was loaded, elevated, and correcting the bearing on the targets.

Then Kapitein Voorne gave the sharp order; "Main batterie, target; port 30 degrees, range 30,000 meters; commence! commence! commence!" I was atop the deckhouse on the starboard side when the three strikes of the firing gong coming over the bulkhead mounted speaker brought me out of my thoughts. The six 343 mm Kanon spoke with one thunderous report. The ship lurched and I staggered, dropping my coffee. I clutched the bulwark to steady myself. A massive yellow fireball erupted from the ships bows, which transformed into a vast cloud of dark brown smoke, billowing out from the side of the ship over the sea. There was a flash of heat on my face and arms, then dark shadow, and the smell of burnt cordite, as the great brown clouds blew back over the flight deck. The familiar sound of ripping linen filled the air as 3.7 tonnes of shells arched towards the enemy! Looking quickly over at the *Johan de Witt*, I saw that she had let loose her six gun salvo!

I took up my glasses and attempted to spot the fall of shot, there was time as we were shooting at an extreme range. At this distance I was unable to make out anything but smoke on the horizon. I moved to port and looked back upon the busy flight deck, engaged in retrieving the many aircraft that we had put up that day. Then men paused in their duties to raise their straw hats and cheer, at the familiar heartening thunder! The burden of the battle it seemed had now been lifted from their exhausted shoulders, and transferred to the men manning the heavy guns!

I once again looked towards my cruiser squadron now several thousand meters ahead, still racing onward. I could see now at this great distance a flash of yellow erupt from the two dark little pyramids sitting on the edge of the horizon, just as the great tall geyser like plumes of the first salvos from my battle-carriers struck the water. I then knew that the enemy cruisers had opened fire upon us. I waited, counting down some thirty seconds, until the salvos, a long line of shells plunged into the sea, several thousand meteres off the vlaggeschip's port bow. It was plain enough to see that most of the enemy cruisers twenty big guns were still in action.

CRASH, stagger, heat, flash, smoke, the *Cornelis* had fired again. The enemy cruisers were still too far away for me to make out any detail. Once again, regularly following the vlaggeschip by some 15 seconds; the *Johan* let loose a full six gun broadside with a thunderous report. Lifting my binoculars I located our light cruiser squadron some 8,000 meters ahead of us. Tall spouts thrown up by the Japanese cruiser's secondary battery shells were falling all about them, in front and behind. Watching my light cruisers intently I was rewarded with multiple bright flashes rippling along their sides, as one after the other; the ships of the 3ʳᵈ Cruiser Squadron opened fire. *Now we have them*, I thought, six against two! But there was no great pride to be taken from this action, just murderous work!

Flag Lt. Hesse, approached me and said "Admiraal, you don't look well, I will keep you informed of any developments." I then realized that I was quite dizzy as I hadn't had taken any nourishment; only cigarettes and coffee for the entire day. I departed once again for the Command Center. Here a steward was going around with a tray of food, I grabbed a ham and cheese sandwich, and a bottle of fruit juice from the platter. I went over to the aviation plot to study the screen, and sat.

At once the CAO, came up to me and extended his hand with a message. I said, "Just read it," while I busied myself with the wax paper wrapping of my breakfast. Swallowing a big mouthful of juice while I chewed, I nodded to him. "A decoded message from Striker 3 Admiraal, *"09:20hrs, Japanese Dreadnoughts Kumamoto and Kagoshima, six freighters, four destroyers sunk, three aircraft lost, returning to ship. Lt. Commander Jakob Van Prooijen, Commander of Strike Group 3.* "Congratulations Admiraal Sweers, the Chief Air Officer added with a smile." Immediately there was a ripple of cheerful comments coming from in the Command Center. I congratulated him; "Well done *Air Ops*, well done, there will be an extra sardine for your toast at supper tonight!"

The senior officers in the room came over to me and warmly offered their congratulations. I spoke up loudly to the men within hearing; "my congratulations to you men, well done for the days successes." Turning to Kap. Voorne I said, "Inform the men of the vlaggeschip, and transmit the news to the other vessels." He saluted, and within a few moments the *Cornelis de Witte* rang to the sound of wild cheering.

The men and ships under my command that day have fulfilled the orders we had been given from Naval Headquarters in Batavia. Now we must avoid the retaliatory wrath of the JAAF and escape into the Sulu Sea to lick our wounds and join up with *Task Force Olive*. We must assess the battle, discover our mistakes, and prepare for the next round, which was sure to follow. Our mighty foe would leave us bloody little time to do this. The last remaining obstacle, the two enemy cruisers before us, must be swept aside as quickly as possible.

Kap. Voorne approached me with another message; "Admiraal Sweers; a message from Task Force Olive;" *Present Air Group; 28 Fighters, 28 Bombers, Location: Chart 11, Grid Square 16, Course West, Speed 27 Knots.* Admiraal, this places Task Force Olive, exiting the Celebes Sea, some 100 nautical miles south of the city of Davao on the island of Mindanao. *TF Olive* would be able to enter the Sulu Sea, north of Jolo Island at 06:00hrs December 09ᵗʰ, putting our link-up at about 08:30hrs December 9ᵗʰ."

"We must maintain this course Admiraal until we recover our *Sea Eagles*, as they will be at the limit of their range, then we may head directly towards *Balabat Strait* and put some distance between our fleet and the eight other JAAF Bomber regiments in French Indo China. Despite the great potential strength of the Manchurian Air Army Admiraal, the many reports that we have received seem to suggest that many of their Air Brigades are heavily engaged elsewhere. After all they are making war on America, the British and the Dutch simultaneously. Their targets on this first day of war include, Pearl Harbour, Hong Kong, and twelve targets in the Philippines including the city of Manila, and the US navy base in Cavite, eight points in Malaya, including Singapore, as well as fourteen bases and cities in our colony, besides our Fleet. It is my understanding that our Royal Army's Glen Martin bomber squadrons will be carrying out retaliatory strikes on four JAAF airfields beginning in the evening. It is my opinion that the JAAF Bomber Regiments are overextended. The 6th Army Air Force commanders had calculated on a single massive blow to destroyed our fleet. In light of their tremendous miscalculation, I believe that the likelihood of another air attack on our fleet today is about 30%."

"Barring unforeseen circumstances Admiraal we should rendezvous with *TF Olive* in less than twenty four hours. The *Schoonveldt's* fighter support will be very welcome, and we will be behind the fighter screens from Jesselton, and Tarakan air bases."

The surface action played out largely as expected. At regular intervals I could discerne the many tall columns of water thrown up by the enemy cruisers' shells marching ever closer to us over the sea, like a great white picket fence. For a time these salvos came well grouped and with regularity, but always short, never closer than 1000 meters. Seven minutes after opening fire, the gunners of the battle-carriers had reported the first of five solid hits from our 343 mm artillery upon the enemy heavy cruisers. In another ten, it was reported that our light cruisers were now hitting the enemy regularly, with full salvos. I returned to the deckhouse top to observe the conclusion of this one sided surface action. On the horizon I could make out with my binoculars that the two enemy cruiser were very heavily engaged and afire. Nevertheless, sporadically now, their main battery guns were still searching for us.

The few heavy hits from our big guns so severely damaged the two Japanese heavy cruisers that their ragged fire which was gradually walking across the sea to our fleet suddenly ceased. Our light cruisers smothered these dying steel monsters repeatedly with their concentrated salvos that was pumping sixty rounds a minute into their rent hulls and shattered upper works, few of which missed. I went to the voice tube and hailed Kapitein Voorne in the command center; "Kapitein; This is Admiraal Sweers; Check Fire, Check Fire, Check Fire main battery both battle-carriers, signal to *Johan de Witt.*" When the last Japanese gun was silenced, the Dutch cruisers checked their gunfire and closed to 3000 meters range to finish the enemy with torpedo. At 10:17hrs the tough Japanese warships began to sink, with the ammunition from their AA rounds continually exploding amongst the raging fires, the red hot plating hissed at it submerged. Little could be seen of any survivors, and with their scorched battle flags, fluttering from their twisted broken spars, 26,000 tons of glowing twisted scrap metal slipped under the sea, overhung by a vast pall of dark greasy smoke.

Within minutes of that dramatic event we, received reports of torpedoes passing through the formation from directly ahead, so our destroyers began search patterns for submarines, and three Sea Hart bombers flew out ahead of the fleet.

The Sea Hart bombers on anti-submarine patrol had no difficulty locating the underwater missiles as they were thirty feet long, black and running only a few meters below the surface. The Sea Harts began targeting these with clusters of small bombs, soon reported that thirty plus of these were heading in our direction, well spread out in four discernable waves. Then the *Cornelis de Witt's* anti-torpedo mortars in constant contact with their air observer, and which had proved so effective during the air battle, began popping away furiously to a target on the port quarter, occasionally a very heavy detonation was heard indicating that an enemy torpedo had been prematurely set off.

I was observing this ominous development, with my binoculars. The mortars had erected and were maintaining a wall between the side of the ship and a subsea threat some two hundred meters off. The six meter tall splashes of the mortar bombs were replaced within seconds by more rounds, but the fence nevertheless crept ominously closer. A huge geyser of water erupted a hundred and fifty meters high as another torpedo detonated. The *Cornelis* was making a high speed turn to starboard to avoid a torpedo, a maneuver that causing her to heel a few degrees to port as well.

Suddenly there was a great shock, we had been hit squarely amidships by a very powerful torpedo! The entire 40,000 metric tonnes of the *Vlaggeschip* seemed to be momentarily lifted and then dropped back into the sea. There was a great deal of crashing, as equipment tore loose from their mountings. Everyone, on top of the deckhouse platform had been thrown down, I staggered to my feet to look back at the flight deck, only to be knocked flat by tonnes of water cascading down from above that had been tossed up by the torpedo. Half drowned and paddling around in two feet of water, I raised myself up to observe the flight deck. Most of the deck crews had been knocked off their feet, and were in the process of picking themselves up off the deck. Many of these were marines serving the 40 mm Flak batteries who had been hurled out of their gun tubs landing 10 meters away on the flight deck. There were those that lay still, and a number that dragged themselves on broken legs. In less than a minute after regaining my feet, I was relieved to see that the medical staff were already on deck to attend to these casualties. Many aircraft sitting on deck being serviced or stowed, had been tossed about with some overturned. Smoke was soon billowing out of the aft aircraft hangar. The ship had been severely shaken and had settled back onto the sea, but was still underway although I could feel her speed rapidly falling off. Black clouds of smoke containing burning material was venting out of the starboard stack.

I went to the voice tube, and hailed Kapitein Voorne in the battle bridge. There was no answer so I made my way rapidly down the companionway, and through the corridors to that location. Everywhere there was a light haze of smoke in the air and alarms and startled men busily carrying out their duty. Arriving at the command center, the senior ships officers greeted me and expressed their joy at my survival. Kapitein Voorne, approached me with preliminary damage reports;

"Admiraal we have taken a torpedo amidships on the portside blister, which has been completely destroyed for about 10 meters. Counter flooding does not seem to be required at this time, as the hull shell plate remains intact. Fires have broken out in the aircraft machine shops and on the lower hangar deck. These are being fought by Engineer Schaupp's damage control teams and he reports that they are well contained, as the three asbestos isolation curtains broke free from their restraint and dropped down in the lower hangar."

"Chief Engineer Jap Anten reports that the main steam line to the port propeller turbines is fractured and the cross over valve is also jammed. Four of the boilers were snuffed out by dust and he has ordered that the fires be banked on eight remaining port boilers until the crossover valve can be replaced. The steam line to the steering gear has broken and the ship cannot maneuver under steam until this is repaired. Speed will be reduced to 15 knots for at least two hours. A number of

Mark Klimaszewski

piping systems have reported small leaks, and these are being repaired as well. Casualties in the black gang amount to two killed, seventeen wounded mostly with burns."

"The remainder of the ship is sound, the bulkheads are watertight, and there are no hull leaks or seriously weakened structures. The main battery, and Flak batteries with the exception of the Port B battery are at 100%. That Flak battery has some damage to its ammunition hoists. The Air Operations Officer reports that air operations continue, with no further casualties to the aircraft, other than a big shake up. Fire damage to the aircraft machine shop will have to be assessed. Casualties for the aircrews and flak crews from this hit amount to eight killed and twenty six wounded. I have sent a party to the Manual Steering compartment so that we may be able to get the Vlaggeschip under local control and back on course." "Very good Kapitein, have a repair party check the command center communication line to the top of the deckhouse."

My staff officers, and senior ship's officers were all assembled and I expressed my happiness that all seemed unhurt. "Gentlemen we are in a serious situation, the *Cornelis* is damaged but still in action and serving as the Task Force Vlaggeschip. However we are by no means out of danger, as more Japanese air attacks are possible. With our reduced capability we cannot put up much of a *Fightercloud* after the last four hours of action. We must enter the Sulu Sea and rendezvous with the *Schoonveldt* as soon as possible to have her fighter aircraft for protection. I will neither reduce the fleet speed to 15 knots, to match our current speed, nor let the Vlaggeschip fall behind. Commander Flyer Van Braekel, you will immediately evacuate all the aircraft from the hangars that are not presently flyable but have intact engines, to the flight deck port side and forward of Elevator B. Arrange them as we have trained in the Baltic to provide motive power to the ship. Then you will identify as quickly as possible the remaining aircraft that are in good order and ready for action, those that can be easily repaired. I must know what the Air Group's strength and capability is at present. Co-ordinate with the *Johan de Witt*. Prepare the hangars and men to receive replacement aircraft tomorrow morning. As soon as you have arranged the cripples on deck, tell me how much accumulative horsepower they can contribute to driving the ship. Finally, identify the useless machines, and set them aside for scrapping, and have their useful parts return to ship stores." The Air Operations Officer saluted quietly and went off to carry out these orders, I knew that he hated this directive as it was very bad for the aircraft engines, but he knew that our situation was very serious, and we must quit the area rapidly.

The light cruisers, which had by now returned to their stations within the fleet showed slight scars of battle, black blistered paint, splinter damage, as they had not been ignored by the enemy's guns. While the Japanese heavy cruisers concentrated their heavy guns against the battle-carriers, their powerful batteries of dual purpose 127 mm Flak guns that had not been destroyed by the bombing, fired at the attacking Dutch light cruisers. Our cruiser men, had been greatly alarmed at seeing the *Johan de Witt* still smoking and the *Vlaggeschip* afire and circling out of control! But steering control was soon achieved using the manual helm, (requiring twelve men), and we resumed our planned course. The internal fires were extinguished, within half an hour.

Thirty aircraft of all type were brought up and lashed to the flight deck in single file along the port side, noses forward. The cockpits were manned by the deck crews many of which were rated to start aircraft engines, and move aircraft under power. The engines coughed to life and were soon running smoothly at full power, and propellers set at

308

maximum pitch. Their cumulative horsepower was some 20,000 kilowatts. The water hoses were brought on deck to create the cooling mist, required for these air cooled power plants. The noise was deafening, but the added thrust from these machines, and the two starboard shafts running at at 300 revolutions, allowed the *Cornelis de Witt* to reach 24 knots, which she maintained for two hours until the damage to her steam fittings serving the port shaft turbines were repaired and all boilers relit to give full power. The men working on the flight deck enjoyed the cooling effect of the mist, and it visibly relaxed them. The men generally were in good spirits, after the action, it was good to see them joking around, morale obviously was still very good.

At 11:30hrs, our Combat Air Patrol reported a large group of aircraft approaching from our 7:00 o'clock position. These soon revealed themselves to be our Sea Eagles. Both Battle carriers turned into the wind and took their bombers aboard, which were all very low on fuel. By this time the *Cornelis* had made repairs to her steam piping and had reconnected her two starboard shafts. Two more bombers had been lost as their fuel tanks had been leaking fuel and they had gone into the sea, but the airmen were later rescued and returned to their ships. The recovery of Strike Group 3 was completed despite the damage to both battle-carriers.

We left the scene of battle behind us, where the sea was covered with a great deal of detritus; splintered charred wood, torn canvas, wooden boxes, and the occasional empty lifeboat. Our rescue craft eventually made it to that area to retrieve any Japanese sailors or airmen that remained alive. Those that were discovered and offered succor, usually raised fists at their rescuers. A few of the more shattered souls were recovered, smeared with oil and in miserable condition, but only a handful of crewmen from a cruiser squadron that may have mustered 2400 men.

Task Force Popeye, with all its combat air groups now recovered, and her escorts in place shaped a direct course for Balabat Strait. We cracked on the speed as we watched the sky behind us with great caution. While below decks in the aircraft hangars, some seven hundred men toiled to restore their damaged work areas, and to refurbish and rebuild the many crippled aircraft. The wakes of the battle-carriers were littered with discarded wings, aircraft rudder parts and masses of scorched detritus.

The dead were collected on the port side of the foredeck, put into a peaceful posture, and placed under white canvas shrouds. The *sail makers* then sewed these into a tight canvas sack, around each body, and then strapped a small steel ingot under their feet. At 14:30hrs Kapitein Voorne, held the *Burial for Service at Sea* ceremony. Once the prayer had concluded, the honor guard came to attention, and the roll call of the dead was read out. Then their shipmates upended the ten flag draped planks and our valiant heroes slid out and over the deck edge of the ship, to plunge into the sea, released into God's care. The ceremony was solemnly repeated until all 76 of the Vlaggeschip's dead were buried. Similar services were held aboard all ships of the fleet. Our total casualties for TF Popeye, so far this one day 313 dead, 537 wounded, not including sixty two missing airmen.

Task Force Popeye steamed on through the evening, tending to the wounded and repairing her battle damage, while at the same time making preparations to renew the battle. Fortunately, the night was peaceful and without further incident. At sunrise next day, both battle-carriers launched seven fighter planes for the Combat Air Patrol, which departed at 06:00hrs. Two of these scouted ahead for Task Force Olive.

Half An hour later a message arrived aboard from a Brewster F2A fighter that he had encountered the Sea Fury Combat Air Patrol of Task Force Olive, and in the distance he could make out the *Schoonveldt* and her six escorts steaming towards us at flank speed. The fleet concentration had been achieved by 08:15hrs December 09, 1941. Task Force Olive soon became visible from the bridge of the *Cornelis de Witt*, Morse lamp signals were exchanged and the battleship-carrier and her escorts fell in behind the ships of Task Force Popeye. I had signaled her welcome, and asked my SAO to inform the *Schoonveldt* to take over all CAP duties. Once this had been accomplished, the aircraft of the *Cornelis* and *Johan* were recalled to their ships. The combined fleet of three battle-carriers, six cruisers, and eleven destroyers maintained course due east at 24 knots; the Vlaggeschip's best speed.

The Chief Medical Officer, Brigade Generaal (Commodore) Peiter Berleburg, entered the *Cornelis de Witt's* command center accompanied by a small medical team to report on the condition of our ship's wounded men. He had been called to the command center by Kapt. Voorne. Seeing my bandaged shoulder and arm in a sling, he approached, saluted and asked me how I felt. Noticing my color, gave me a quick examination, read my diagnosis card, tied to the bandages. "You are suffering from a shock Admiraal, you should be in hospital. Although your wound does not appear large on the surface, it is quite deep, since the splinter grazed the bone as it passed through your shoulder." He gave me an injection, then handed me a small white pill and made it clear that I take a rest or he would ask Kapitein Voorne to relieve me for medical reasons. The wound was throbbing with a burning sensation, so I was not in the mood to argue. I asked him if I could take a look at his triage station set up in the lower hangar deck, and visit the recovery ward in the post-surgery, to which he replied, "All is well down there. First for you; immediate bed rest." Then to one of his medical attendants he said; "assist the Vice Admiraal to hospital, and return."

Turning to Kapitein Voorne I said; "Kapitein, I am going to hospital at the order of the Brigade Generaal Doctor, until I am discharged fit for duty, contact the Johan de Witt and inform Rear Admiraal van Speijk-Bronckhorst that I am transferring command of the combined fleet to him." Kap. Voorne gave the order and saluted. "Admiraal leaving the Bridge," Kapt. Voorne called out. All present came to attention and saluted me. I reluctantly abandoned my battle station for the hospital, below the armored deck. Here, I quickly fell into a deep sleep several hours, while the combined battle-squadron raced toward Makassar Strait. For the time being at least, within range of our own air bases, I felt that *Task Force Popeye* was relatively safe.

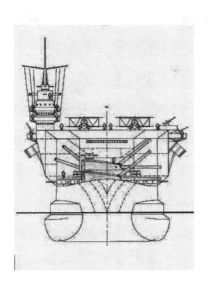

CHAPTER XXVI

WITHDRAWL TO SOERABAJA, CONFERENCE IN BATAVIA, JAPANESE BOMBING, REPORT ON PEARL HARBOUR, DESTRUCTION OF FORCE Z, IN ADVERSITY: DEFIANCE, STRATEGIC SITUATION, NEW ORDERS.

The rendezvous in the Sulu Sea between *Task Force Popeye*, and *Task Force Olive* had been achieved. The *Schoonveldt* took up station a half nautical to behind the *Johan de Witt* and the Combined Fleet then turned due south, exiting the Sulu Sea on a heading that took the warships between Tanjong Hog headland of Borneo and the Island of Twai Twai. The fleet skirted the western rim of the Celebes Sea heading for the mouth of the Strait of Makassar, and the perceived security of the *interior waters,* situated well within our circle of airbases. The day had turned grey and misty, which reduced visibility, making aircraft identification more difficult.

The men of *TF Popeye*, needed resting after some twenty eight hours at their battle stations which included combat operations. The luckiest men could now remove their combat gear, tend to their minor wounds of scratches, abrasions, and sprains, clean up the detritus at their battle station, then get below for a shower, a hot meal and some rest. The not so lucky lay below in hospital, being attended to by our medical staff and the Chaplain. I was more fortunate, having been discharged from the ship's hospital at 0900hrs Dec 10th. I returned to my cabin for a shave, shower and a change of uniform, before returning to duty. I telephoned the command bridge and asked for the duty officer. He gave me the status of the ship and the fleet and informed me that there was no signs of enemy activity. I decided then to visit the hospital.

I made my way down into ship. The 100 bed hospital was located two decks below the lowest hangar deck and upon the main deck. Here the motion of the ship was very muted and allowed wounded men to rest. I walked between the rows of beds and their sleeping bandage swathed occupants accompanied by a medical orderly. Those men who were awake and seemed strong I thanked for their service and told them that the Netherlands had a great naval victory. I then met with the Brigade Generaal and asked him how they were handling the casualties. He told me that there were 93 patients, four had died in the night. The medicine supply was sufficient for another two weeks at this rate. The Chief Medical officer then explained that there were thirty surgeries scheduled for today, and as he only had five surgeons, his skills were needed so he couldn't stay and talk. Peiter asked me how my shoulder felt. To which I replied, "Fine." He then requested that the air-conditioning unit for the hospital and surgery be repaired as soon as possible so that the wounded my rest comfortably, and to keep the ship's motion to a minimum whenever possible. I thanked him for his service and told him that I would pass on his needs. With that, I went on to the command center.

Once the Dutch Fleet had entered the Makassar Strait, all naval air operations were turned over to the undamaged battleship-carrier *Schoonveldt* and the capable hands of her Chief of Air Operations Commander Flyer; Heer Willem de Valk van Lothringen. He also now commanded the support of those airfields along Borneo's coastline; Tarakan, Telok-Banjour, Balaikpapan, down which we were presently steaming, and Makassar on the Island of Celebes. The fleet's Combat Air Patrol were provided by the 14 Hawker Sea Fury MKII fighters, and 6 Grumman F2F Buffalos of Fighter Squadron 5, Commanded by Lt. ter Zee 1e Klasse (Lt. Commander): Ernst Fijenoord.

These 21 fighters, flying from the undamaged battleship-carrier, supported by fighters from the airfields at Tarakan, Balikpapan and Makassar gave our Battle fleet the time and security it needed to lick its wounds and return the flight decks to operational status. We fully expected that the JAAF would pursue our wounded squadron until its destruction and the attacks would continue unabated; however in this, we were lucky.

On three occasions aircraft sightings were reported and the fighters of the CAP immediately went into action, while the ships of the combined Fleet went to action stations. The Sea Furies hovered over the ships, while the speedier and more heavily armed Brewster fighters flashed off to investigate these dangers.

The first sighting; was of a large aircraft flying west to east across our path, which proved to be a four engine flying boat that was at identified as a Kawanishi H6K, Japanese Navy long range reconnaissance aircraft. The sighting was amended a few minutes later, as it turned out to be a civilian flight; a Short Sunderland Flying Boat of *Quantas Airlines*, on her way from Singapore to Australia via Sarawak and the Portuguese Island of East Timor. She was carrying twenty-two terrified officials from the *Communications Bank of Hong Kong* who were escorting a shipment of gold bullion. (That news made me personally happy as *New Eden* had a very large account with CBHK.) Our aggressive fighters it seemed had given them a damned good scare by closing to within *spitting range* until we could see the white faces of the crew and passengers!

The second sighting; was a very large and ominous looking formation; which proved to be 20 float planes flying out of Lake Tonado Naval Air Station, 24 bombers flying out of Balikpapan NAS on Borneo, escorted by 21 Grumman F2F and F3F's fighters from Kendari NAS, on Celebes. These fighters were to have come aboard the *Johan de Witt* as replacements today, but when news of their ship's torpedoing was reported, Naval HQ had this unit shuttled over to Mendado NAS to provide additional fighter support for the torpedo bombers operating off Lake Tonado. This 65 plane naval formation was conducting a sweep of the Celebes Sea for Japanese warships, merchant ships and fishing vessels reported in the area. After the fury of the last 24 hours, and experiencing the power of *Japanese Arms*, it was heartening to see that powerful Strike Group passing overhead and flying in the direction from which we had just come.

The last sighting; was of a pair of monoplane fighters, which upon closer investigation, revealed themselves to be a pair of curious Albatross, a large gull like seabird with a very large wingspan, often reaching 2.5 meters. This misidentification, elicited a few choice remarks from the Chief of Air Operations, as the warships had sounded the bugle call for battle stations, sending more than 6500 men racing to action stations.

Aboard each battle-carrier of TF Popeye, some six hundred aircraft technicians had worked feverishly throughout the night, to put the aircraft hangers in order, then repair our damaged aircraft. By 12:00hrs of December 09, 1941, as the combined Fleet was crossing the Celebes Sea, Air Operations was able to report that out of the original 162 aircraft prior to yesterday's battle the two battle-carriers had presently available for duty 100 effective aircraft, 11 cripples lacking spares, with 8 effectives recovered by our cruisers and destroyers. Task Force Popeye's air group losses were in effect 54 planes or 33%! At this rate we would only have two or three battles of similar magnitude remaining before the RNLN was incapable of taking an air group to sea!

Of even greater import was our lack of airmen. Unfortunately flesh does not heal as quickly as our machines could be made right, and our available aircrews fit for duty that morning could only man 65 of these machines, although many of the wounded airmen were very keen and insisted that they could fly. The strength of the air groups of TF Popeye had in reality been halved. I made a mental note for future action that our shipboard pool of reserve airmen be increased from fifteen to forty. For now we would draw the airmen that we required from our hangar crews at least 30% of which were qualified to start and run aircraft engines. At least 15 C.P.O.'s aboard the *Cornelis* held private pilot licenses.

Four KMN submarines took up position to close the narrows behind us as the Combined Task Force withdrew southwards past the Tanjung Mangklihat headland, of eastern Borneo. To the south and east a similar force erected a cordon between the Island of Celebes and Flores, blocking the entrance of any surface force from entering the Banda Sea. The native population had been informed to tie up their boats, and await permission to sail. Any small fish boats or pearling schooners that were at sea, were confronted by a surfaced O-boat and its deck gun. These two cordons were checking about two boats per hour, as many boats tried to flee Dutch East Indies waters.

A more complete damage report on the condition of Task Force Popeye was now transmitted to Batavia. Acting upon this information Naval headquarters decided that upon reaching Soerabaja Naval Base, the undamaged ships of Task Force Popeye were to take aboard consumables and replacements then be reassigned to support *Task Force Olive* which would immediately proceed eastward to take up station in the Flores Sea.

The damaged vessels of Task Force Popeye, now under the protection of land based aircraft, would enter the Bali Sea and make for the repair facilities of Soerabaja straight away. The flyable aircraft aboard my two damaged battle-carriers, would depart for the Royal Naval Air Station at Perak to the west of the city. Here they would reinforce the Army and Navy air defenses. The entire East Indies region we were discovering, lay within the great range of the latest types of Japanese Army Air Force heavy bombers now operating out of newly completed airfields in French Indo China.

TF Popeye had just steamed past Balikpapan to our starboard when the Combat Air Patrol of the *Schoonveldt* reported a group of fifteen junks and schooners, each of between 50 to 100 tonnes displacement, proceeding northward up Makassar Strait in our direction. These vessels were operating in mid-channel, and would get a very good look at our fleet's composition and condition as we sailed past. All commercial vessels had been warned three days ago to stay in harbour or face the consequences. While most small vessels lacked radio, the warning had been distributed by more cumbersome but equally effective methods, billboards, telephone messages to all harbours and villages, via our various administrative networks that we knew worked well. No legitimate commercial vessel was to be at sea. If these were encountered they were to be dealt with as pirates or Japanese.

I immediately ordered the four warships of Destroyer Squadron No. 3, ahead at flank to investigate these curfew violators, to approach bow on, so as make the distinctive silhouette of the Dutch destroyers more difficult to identify.

The tactic worked, as fully half of these ships quickly began to run up the red disc on a white field, the crew's loyalty had been established, and several of these boats had started to begin radio transmissions. Commander Captain Van Rossel then ordered Destroyer Squadron No. 3 to sink all ships. The destroyers raced along the lines of fish boats, with the sixteen 40 mm Bofors flak guns, and 24 heavy machineguns firing into them from as close as 300 meters. There was light arms return fire, but it quickly subsided as the flak batteries reduced these mostly wooden vessels to matchwood.

Upon entering the Bali Sea, all serviceable aircraft were flown off the two damaged battle-carriers. The *Cornelis de Witte* and the *Johan de Witt* entered their berths at the Naval Base in Soerabaja at 08:10hrs of December 12th without any further incidents. Immediately upon securing the ships, divers were put overboard to inspect the torpedo damage, and a small army of workers from the naval dockyard, with their assorted equipment came aboard to put things right. While this effort was underway a fleet of ambulances and flatbed trucks began lining up to transport the wounded to our base hospital.

The cruiser *Prins te Paard*, was the first of my damaged ships to be berthed at the repair facility. A dockyard crew had been prepared and on standby, and immediately upon the running out of her gangway, they came aboard the cruiser to inspect the damage to 'A' Turret. The magazine was pumped out of water, and the bodies of the dead were gently removed to shore for a burial service. Then the men began the removal of the damp cordite and the shells. The entire mounting it was soon discovered was a complete write-off, as it would require months of work to repair in even peacetime conditions. It was decided therefore to remove the mounting entirely. The open top of the mount was then plated over with two 19 mm layers of mild steel with salvaged 25 mm armor cut from the scrapped turret welded atop these.

I ordered my pennant hauled down and turned command of the Battle-carrier over to her Kapitein, who would stay aboard to oversee her repair. Similarly, Rear Admiraal Bronckhorst hauled down his pennant from the *Johan de Witt's* masthead placing her under the command of Kapitein Van der Hulst.

I now assembled all of the damage reports for the Vlaggeschip, and those of the other ships. I next informed Batavia that the Task Force Popeye had arrived at Sourabaja, and that repairs were underway. I then went ashore with my staff to join the senior officers of the fleet urged on by air raid sirens.

Japanese bombers were dropping parachute flares over the city and the sea to illuminate targets. But this proved to be a mistake, for above them were waiting two squadrons of the Royal Army's Fighter Group II. The flares now descending slowly lite up Soerabaja, but silhouetted the Japanese bombers perfectly as the Fokker Fighters and Curtis monoplanes dove down upon them. The Mitsubishi machines broke formation and fled closely harried.

My Adjudant Officier brought me a message from Naval Headquarters. Admiraal Van de Velde now summoned both Battle-carrier Admiraals and our Chief of Staffs to a conference in Batavia. A Glen Martin bomber was standing by at Perak Army Airfield and we were to depart at first light. A great many things were happening, and the situation was getting more confused every hour.

Rear Admiraal Bronckhorst, and I, with our C.OS.'s in tow quickly got our kit together; document valises, and vital material together then hurried to a big Mercedes Naval limousine that whipped us through a city heavily shrouded in smoke. On three occasions we were stopped by Army checkpoints. Faces on all sides probed the sedan's interior. We produced our identification papers, were soon waved us on. Through the half open window I could see rubble in some of the streets and destroyed vehicles. The smell of burnt wood was in the air. The city had changed, since I had left it only nine days ago. The cab of the car was stifling, we were quiet and subdued, with the occasional somber face illuminated briefly by the dull orange glow of our cigarettes.

The sedan passed a damaged airdrome and swerved around a bomb crater pulling to a stop with a screech on the airfield concrete. We piled out of the sedan in disorder, grabbed our kit and hurried out to the aircraft just as it started to sprinkle. The twin engine machine was warmed up and ready to go. We had only just taken our seats when the pilot gunned the engines. The aircraft quickly gained speed, and raced down the darkened runway to lift off just as the first light of dawn lanced our tired eyes though the bomber's Plexiglas nose. The flight would take some two and a half hours so we made ourselves as comfortable as best we could to get some sleep as we would undoubtedly be very busy when we landed.

Some violent maneuvering of the bomber tossed us about, bringing our dosing party sharply awake, thinking we were under attack. Looking out the Plexiglas bubble on the port side I soon became aware that we had an escort. Three Brewster monoplane fighters and three Grumman F3F fighters. I could see from the squadron markings that the aircraft were from the *Cornelis de Witt*. "We are in good hands gentlemen," I said pointing with my thumb through the bubble. Just then the telegraphist gunner came forward with a thermos full of coffee, "Admiraal, sorry about the tossing about, just some unusual downdrafts, we will be landing in about half an hour." Once out of the confines of the bomber I removed my right arm from the sling which I then folded and stuffed into my stained tunic.

Naval Headquarters in Batavia was a hive of ordered activity. Lt. Commander Steeple, the Adjudant of Fleet Admiraal Van de Velde had met my party at the main door, and led us into the big conference room on the first floor of the east wing. All the windows were heavily sandbagged, and there was a thin layer of plaster dust over the floors and furniture. Here there were assembled about twenty five to thirty senior officers from all branches of the Netherland's military, as well as officers representing the RN, RAN and RNZN. Immediately upon our party being announced we became the center of attention, and all within the room were standing, looking at us and smiling. Admiraal de Velde strode over with a broad smile and grasped our hands in a firm shake and congratulated us on a great naval victory. A victory that the reeling and confused Colonial Powers needed desperately to keep up their spirits.

The financial implications of victory were critical to maintain confidence in the British Pound, and the US Greenback. If these nations looked to be losing the war, world finance would dump their currency. While the economy of America and perhaps even still that of the British Empire, could ride such a move out, bankruptcy and total financial collapse now stood at the Netherlands elbow.

Then turning to address the men in the room the Fleet Admiraal said with a brave voice; "On the morning of December 8th, off the coast of Cochin China, an engagement occurred between; a Japanese invasion armada of 58 ships bound for Malaya and 14 ships of the Royal Netherlands Navy. The invasion force contained 25 merchant ships carrying the men and equipment of the Imperial Army's 15th Infantry Division. These vessels were supported by a powerful IJN Task Force of 33 warships, and four Air Regiments of the Japanese Army Air Force's Sixth Air Army. Opposing these forces was the Battle-carrier *Task Force Popeye*, Commanded by Vice Admiraal Marrten Sweers, whose fleet was well supported by the *Royal Army Heavy Fighter Group III*, Commanded by Colonel Wilden from Tarakan Airfield, as well rescue units from Sarawak."

"After a long morning of action of some four hours duration, that included, three naval airstrikes against the enemy invasion convoy, and an airstrike against the enemy heavy cruiser squadron, repeated heavy attacks against the Dutch Fleet by the JAAF bombers and torpedo planes that went on for two hours, and a surface battle against a pair of heavy cruisers, the Japanese were, completely, and most assuredly whipped in the air, and on the sea!"

At this point smiles broke out all round and a number of men gave us boisterous congratulations. Admiraal Van Der Velde, waved them quiet as he had more to say. "Japanese Arms have lost during the *Battle of the South China Sea,* as a result of our resolute action: two modernized dreadnoughts, a light carrier, with an unknown portion of her air group, four heavy cruisers, six destroyers, twenty five troopships, an army of 14,000 men, with all their equipment, and some 100 army aircraft of all types!" The hall erupted with a joyous clamor. The Fleet Admiraal quieted them and continued, "The ships and air groups of *Task Force Popeye*, did not escape without serious damage, or casualties. But we have a without any doubt; a smashing great victory for the Royal Netherlands Armed Forces!"

The Fleet Admiraal then asked us to his office to deliver my comments on the action we had fought less than 76 hours ago. I started with; "by the grace of God and a great deal of good fortune, and miscalculation on the part of the Japanese we were victorious!" There were a few more details, than had earlier been available, I gave the current assessment of the condition of the battle-carriers and their air groups. The ships could still be fought, but they needed their structural damage repaired, all the piping systems, especially those carrying aviation fuel and bunker oil had to be thoroughly checked for tightness. The battle-carriers alone needed 8,000 hours of repair work, or a minimum three weeks in the dockyard, to get them seaworthy.

I was then asked for any impressions of the battle and the Japanese Army Air Force. I replied that all men and ships of our fleet had fought exceptionally well, with great professionalism and high morale. The cruiser escort performed excellently in screening the battle-carriers and in their aggressive attack on the Japanese heavy cruisers.

Our heavy artillery fire from the battle-carriers proved its worth, securing a number of solid hits on each heavy cruiser which greatly reduced their ability to return accurate fire. The effectiveness of our Flak batteries came as a great shock to the enemy, as time and again I saw attacking sections of three and four bombers literally vivisected, as they closed to attack.

The Japanese aircraft, I discovered first hand were much more technically advanced than earlier imagined. The concept of *Fightercloud,* our *stop-gap* measure to deal with them, actually worked quite well, and this I have seen with my own eyes. But the attrition rate to our fighters was high, as we were engaged against superior aircraft. "In the future we need to carry as a minimum; an additional high speed fighter Squadron on the decks as a permanent outfit for each ship, to give more balance to the *Fightercloud* formation."

The wood packing within the torpedo bulges of the Battle-carriers, the most simple of our stop-gap innovation does indeed limit the flooding after a hit and has proved to be a worthy compromise. The crushing of the soft balsa actually deadens the shock of a torpedo.

As a result of our experiences during the surface battle, and the observations of our light cruisers and aircraft, we now suspect that Japanese warships are equipped with a new type of very powerful torpedo that has an exceptional range, of at least 35,000 meters. We must capture one of these intact and evaluate it.

I emphasized that the battle-carrier force had adequate cruiser protection but a formation of such a size required at least twenty destroyers to provide an effective screen.

"The JAAF twin engine bombers were not nearly as maneuverable as smaller carrier based single engine bombers that would have had more success against *Fightercloud.* The Japanese airmen seem to be highly skilled and pressed home their attacks with great determination, but our Flak batteries, took a dreadful toll. I got a very good look at the enemy aircraft, and they seem to be exceptionally well made and airworthy, not the *bamboo and paper airframes attached to an engine with twine,* so often made light of in the British newspapers. One of our greatest handicaps is the lingering impression that the Japanese military equipment, and the race are inferior."

"Fleet Admiraal, my heartiest congratulations to the men of the Royal Netherlands East Army Air Force, Heavy Fighter Group III, at Tarakan Army Airfield. I believe that they were instrumental in our victory for several reasons, not the least of which was the heavy firepower of their eight nose mounted machine guns, which I personally observed to have a devastating effect on the Japanese aircraft, but also because of their skillful use. I will request a unit citation for Group III."

In response to this he said; "We have recovered several downed enemy airmen and they gave us some interesting information. An indication of the strength of your ship's defenses was that both of the Japanese Bomber Regimental Commanders requested to be reinforced, by the *113th Hikosentai.* The Japanese airmen were completely unaware that we had heavy twin engine fighters and believed that our Fokker machines were actually the expected JAAF bomber regiment reinforcement."

I ended with; "I am preparing a much more detailed report with a long list of bravery citations. The men performed with great skill and self-sacrifice. Finally, and this is of extreme importance, we had been very lucky on December 8th. Our success was largely due to the fact that the Japanese bombers were inadequate in number to contend with our heavy Flak defenses and the *Fightercloud* swarm. We need more fighters that can stay in combat longer, like the Brewster F2A." This greatly simplifies flight deck operations.

The Fleet Admiraal then debriefed the other members of my party in further discussion, regarding the battle, the damage, repairs, replacement personnel and the like.

I was dismissed by the Fleet Admiraal, and went back into the operations room. Lt. Commander Simon van Ruyuen, a staff officer to Admiraal Van der Velde approached me with a cup of coffee and a tray of sandwiches. He began telling me of the other events that had transpired since we had sailed from Singapore: "The afternoon of December 10th had been a busy one at Naval Headquarters. Seeing that I was completely done in, he began to read to me certain select reports and supplemented these with his comments;

ITEM: *Japanese bombers are active from Singapore to Manila again today, with the airfields at Jesselton, Sarawak, Tarakan being hit.*

ITEM: *The Royal Navy sailed this morning. Force Z; composed of the battlecruiser HMS Repulse, the new battleship HMS Prince of Wales and four destroyers as escort, from Singapore to repel another Japanese invasion force off of Malaya.*

ITEM: *The RAN battlecruiser HMS Australia and her escorts of cruisers and destroyers had been ordered to Singapore to concentrate with the RN Force Z. These would form the 'big gun surface battle component' to offset a squadron of four Japanese battlecruisers that had been reported in the Gulf of Siam.*

ITEM: *The US Navy is redeploying to Batavia; the old light cruiser USS Dixie, and her flotilla of nine old 'four piper' destroyers from Manila. The US Naval base at Cavite, on the Island of Luzon, is constantly being bombed and has become too hot for them. The fleet sailed the night of Dec. 9th, and headed east into the Pacific to get clear of the heavy JAAF air activity over the Philippine Islands. When this is accomplished, they will then steam south east of Mindanao and make for the Molucca Sea. Along this route, they will get air support from the PAAC (Philippian Army Air Corps) 26th Pursuit Squadron at Davao airfield on Mindanao, and our airfields at Mendado and Kendari on Celebes on the final leg of their run. The Schoonveldt will rendezvous with the USS Dixie and her destroyers about noon of December 16th to provide them with an escort.*

ITEM: *The KNIL Netherlands Royal Army Air force would be making a maximum effort again for the next three days, carrying out night bombardments of the JAAF bases in Indo China, at My Thoa, Hue, Na Drang and Saigon.*

"The reports from Pearl Harbour had come in and they were absolutely devastating. We at first believed that the US Fleet had sortied, from its harbour and was giving battle to the IJN on the open sea. But we soon after learned the extent of what is a disaster!"

ITEM: *The US Army Air Force on Hickam Field in Hawaii, had been all but wiped out, caught napping on the ground. The US Pacific Fleet has taken a very heavy blow. The fleet actually was caught at its berths within the harbour, in the middle of Sunday Services. Consequently six Battleships; Arizona, Oklahoma, Nevada, California and West Virginia were sunk in the harbour. The Arizona is a total loss, as her forward magazines exploded, there are losses of lighter warships as well, casualties both military and civilian 3 to 4,000. The Battleship Pennsylvania was in the graving dock and survived the attack, as the torpedoes could not reach her. Fortunately, the big fleet carriers; Lexington and Enterprise were not in harbour and escaped destruction. These two aircraft carriers and the battleship, are the only USN Capital ships left in the Pacific, and the Pennsylvania is being withdrawn to San Francisco!*

"When this report was decoded at Naval Headquarters in Batavia it had caused a deep gloom to take hold on those present, one that grew only worse, because bad news kept coming in:"

ITEM: *The Royal Navy Aircraft Carrier HMS Indomitable, on its way to Singapore has struck an uncharted rock in the Indian Ocean, and must return to Alexandria in Egypt for dry-docking. Consequently the RN at Singapore will have no naval airpower at sea!*

"While I was scarfing a ham and cheese sandwich and spooning down a bowl of hot chicken and rice soup, more messages arrived from the decoding room. These were handed to Admiraal Van de Velde, and I could see the old warrior was visibly shaken, as he read them. Then raising his voice he read to the assembled personnel."

ITEM: *Soerabaja is presently under air attack and the warships and merchant vessels, had put to sea and were maneuvering to avoid offering a stationary target. They were not being targeted however, as the Japanese bombers seemed to be only concentrating on destroying the dockyard facilities, fuel tanks, and Perak Airfield.*

ITEM: *The US Army Air Forces throughout the Philippine Islands was wiped out while it sat unprotected on its airfields. The losses are estimated at over 100 bombers and fighters, or 90% of their entire force available!*

Then Admiraal Van de Velde paused, as if to gather his will, and delivered devastating news; "I hold in my hand a confirmed report from Royal Navy Headquarters in Singapore dated 12/10/1941, that has just been decoded:"

ITEM: *RNHQ Singapore 12/10/41, 14:15hrs: Force Z, while maneuvering at sea today, in an effort to repel a Japanese invasion force reported off Kuantan Malaya, was engaged at 11:40hrs by elements of two Japanese Army Air Force Regiments composed of bombers and torpedo planes. After an heroic action in which both capital ships were repeatedly struck by bombs and torpedoes, the battlecruiser HMS Repulse went down at 12:33hrs, and the Flagship, the battleship Prince of Wales followed at 13:20hrs. Loss of life was very heavy including that of the Fleet Admiral Sir Tom Phillips.*

"The room fell silent and nothing was heard for several moments but the whirring of the overhead fans, the faint rustling of papers, and somewhere in the anteroom a female rating began to sob. The deepest shock imaginable emphasized the power of the enemy we now faced, and a heavy gloom seemed to settled over those assembled. Another massive knockout blow had been delivered by the enemy to stagger the British, already reeling from earlier setbacks! Everyone at that moment withdrew into their private world of gloomy thoughts, sadness, and worry."

The year 1941 had been a very hard one for the Royal Navy. In May the battlecruiser *Hood* had been sunk in the Atlantic by the German battleship *Bismarck*. At the same time the evacuation of the British Army from Crete was underway, with the *Luftwaffe* inflicting more heavy losses on the Royal Navy; 3 cruisers and 6 destroyers sunk, with the battleships *Warspite*, *Barham*, and the aircraft carrier *Formidable* heavily damaged and knocked out of action, as well as 6 cruisers and 7 destroyers damaged. The losses kept mounting; the aircraft carrier *HMS Ark Royal* sunk in the Mediterranean on November 14th to be followed by the battleship *HMS Barham*, only eleven days later! The prospects of substantial reinforcements coming to South East Asia from either Britain or America now seemed nonexistent! Of all the warships assembled for the display of the *Great Armada* during *Operation Bulwark*, it was upon the small fleet of the Netherlands that the greatest burdens would now lie."

"It was at that moment when we had all retreated into a deep gloom that Admiraal Van de Velde's voice boomed out with a great roar snapping everyone back to reality. "Three of your loudest cheers for the gallant sailors of *Force Z,*" he yelled, raising his huge fist! When the Hurrahs were completed, with tears, red eyes and renewed anger, he referred to Task Force Popeye; "The sinking of *Force Z*, a powerful fleet, manned by seamen we know to be of the highest quality, and by the same JAAF air regiments that *Task Force Popeye* has so recently defeated, smacks of the magnitude of our victory in the *Battle of the South China Sea*, and the quality of the men and ships of the Royal Netherlands Navy! I give you Admiraal Sweers, and his officers of Task Force Popeye! Three cheers!" When the Hurraahs died out we all felt much better, the old Admiraal knew sailors, and fighting men by God! I had no idea that simply yelling as loudly as was possible could change one's mood!"

The Fleet Admiraal, now entered the room with the remainder of my officers, strode over to me and said, "One bit of good news Admiraal Sweers; our coastal forces have reported picking up 33 of our airmen, from the South China Sea, 23 of which are no worse for wear. These will be returned to their squadrons as soon as flights may be arranged. Vice Admiraal, I believe these would be mostly your lads," handing me the decoded dispatch with a smile.

The destruction of Force Z, was an immense disaster that had immediate consequences. The surface component around which the Royal Navy had planned to build up a large fleet, had been destroyed! The Battlecruiser *HMS Australia* and her escorting vessels, had been immediately ordered back to home waters by the Australian Prime Minister. This was a black day for the RNLN. The worst case scenario of our battle studies was at hand. With the main naval power of our Allies: Great Britain, France and the United States destroyed, the little RNLN had for the near future to shoulder the seaborne defense of South East Asia and face the full military might of Imperial Japan!

In three days of war; the Japanese Naval and Air forces had sunk eight allied battleships and battlecruisers, and damaged two of the three largest ships in the RNLN. The entire naval strategy for the defense of the Pacific and South East Asia had become unraveled. The only other naval forces of any appreciable strength in the Central Pacific, were the remainder of the US Navy; a battle group of two fleet aircraft carriers in Pearl Harbour and their escorting cruisers and destroyers.

In the West Pacific-South East Asia region it was a battle group composed of the RNLN, and the RAN, having between them four Capital Ships, of which two were damaged, and the remainder a scattered force, (also containing damaged ships) made up of cruisers and destroyers of the RN and USN. These two widely separated forces had to face the IJN of more than twenty Capital Ships, supported by more than six hundred modern warships! When intact, the RNLN was by far the strongest of the remaining Allied Fleets in South

East Asia, with three battle-carriers at is core. The RNLN must therefore gather all the orphans about it, and cobble together a new defense plan.

Indeed Admiraal Van de Velde had immediately began working on just such a plan, and was preparing a request through the Netherlands legations to the Governments of Great Britain, America, Australia and New Zealand to have all their warships placed under the command of the RNLN in Batavia, and concentrate these ships in East Indies waters.

The capability of the Japanese Military had been woefully underestimated. Their aircraft and pilots were of high quality and available in great numbers. Even after completely destroying a large Japanese invasion convoy and sinking its escorting vessels, the loss had not seemed to have slowed them in the least. Japanese troops had landed December 11th at Khota Baru in northern Malaya and in Siam at Singora.

Batavia, Soerabaja, and Singapore had already been attacked by JAAF bombers without much success however, as the Allied nations could still put up substantial fighter aircraft to resist. But we knew that these attacks would increase. At Singapore the JAAF concentrated their bombing on the King Alexander Floating Dry Dock. By the afternoon of December 10th, it was completely wrecked. In retrospect it was a foolish hope to believe that this facility would be available to us in the event of war with Japan, as the strength of their attacks were at once powerful and widespread.

As a consequence of these attacks the Dutch battle-carriers would now be unable to be lifted from the water to repair their torpedo damage, as there was no other facility within the hemisphere to lift such large ships. Therefore cofferdams; hollow water tight chambers must be constructed around the damaged underwater portions of each hull as they sat in the water. Within these chambers some of the preliminary repair work could begin. The work would be difficult and could not be undertaken if the ships had to continually steam into the open sea and maneuver to avoid Japanese bombers. The vessels had to remain stationary for several weeks.

As to addressing the question of how quickly the damaged ships could be ready for action with their damaged hulls, aircraft hangers and depleted air groups; the Battle-carriers could still fight, but only at 50% strength. The survival of the Dutch East Indies Colony, now depended on our ability to play for time, to be evasive, shuttle back and forth within the ring of our airfields, while preserving our battle squadron's strength until our Allies could regroup and strike back at the Japanese Navy.

Admiraal Van de Velde in short order grasped the situation. He said to me, "Admiraal Sweers, due to the strategic nature of our Battle-carriers, I believe that the JAAF will be hunting your two cripples with a vengeance. They will also continue to bomb the dockyard and facilities of the Soerabaja and Singapore. So I do not believe it will be possible to repair the two battle-carriers at any naval base."

Motioning us to follow him, my Deputy Commander Rear Admiraal van Speijk-Bronckhorst, and I strode over to a big chart mounted on the back wall. The Fleet Admiraal took his pencil and tracked eastward towards Portuguese Timor. "Here" he said, circling with his pencil a tiny island that lay in the Savu Sea, "this small uninhabited island of Palalua is remote, and has a deep protected lagoon, it is an extinct volcano, one where the caldera, exploded eons ago, then collapsed inwards, leaving a ring scarcely a mile across. I dropped the hook in there on a sailing vacation some twenty years ago.

The channel to its interior is narrow but deep, scarcely 150 meters in width. The sides of the cone are tall and steep, and should give you adequate protection from detection and attack from the air if by some chance you are discovered."

"Carry out what repairs you are able to do, at the dockyard, to make your ships seaworthy. In two days you will take both battlecruiser carriers to this location, establish a remote repair station and put your ships in order as soon as possible. You will sail at night, unescorted and at high speed. I will have patrol craft divert shipping from your path. If you sail by way of Lombok Strait, there is little traffic through those waters now and the shore on both sides has been cleared of natives and is now occupied by the Army. Nobody will report your ships entry into the Indian Ocean. Lay up along the south coast of Lombok island during the day, here in this small bay south of the village of Selong. The water depth is ten to twelve fathoms and the seabed is muck, so your anchors should hold well. I will ask the army to evacuate any natives living between the road and the south coast. Work out an effective camouflage system to transform your ships into what an aircraft would likely report upon sighting as; foliage covered islands."

"I replied; camouflage may be effectively accomplished Admiraal by adapting the Army's method for disguising their airstrips, to my flight decks. It is however, very labor intensive, and I will need to take my hangar deck crews and the aircraft maintenance men with me, as they left the ship to support their aircraft which are now sitting on Perkak Airfield. When my ships are fully repaired, and their air-groups will come aboard, the ships will then be combat ready, if all the hangar crews are aboard."

The Fleet Admiraal replied; "You may take these men back to the ship, as Perak Airfield has plenty of ground crew to handle the needs of both the Army and Navy aircraft. Many hands makes for quick work, and the cutting of palm fronds will take a lot of hands. I will send ahead at once, the repair ships *Poolster* and *Pelikan,* the captured Italian freighter *Tripoli,* with 4,200 tonnes of construction material, and the supply ship *Arnhem,* with her gunboats. Later on I will dispatch to you, replacements, several gate vessels, a large fuel barge with two tugs, and within a week, ten minesweepers when you are ready to sail again. You will also need a fresh water barge as the island has no potable water, the very reason why it remains uninhabited and such a good location. There is also a small grassy plain on the opposite side of the island to the entrance, no doubt form ages ago during a lava flow. It is large enough to handle small biplane aircraft. But we want to keep activity on the sea around that island to a minimum, so as not to attract the attentions of enemy reconnaissance aircraft. The passage should take you two nights. If you have no questions, I want you to leave immediately."

"I understand Fleet Admiraal," I answered. "Good luck then men," he replied, placing his massive hand upon my right shoulder, causing me to wince. He was momentarily startled at my expression of pain then said, "what is the matter Admiraal, have you been wounded?" "Yes Fleet Admiraal, I replied, a small wound to the shoulder, during the action of December 9th, I took a bomb splinter. "Vice Admiraal;" he asked sternly; "are you fit for duty?" "Yes Sir," I answered without any hesitation. "I was treated in the *Cornelis de Witt's* surgery and discharged by the Chief Medical Officer." "Very well Admiraal Sweers," was his reply. We exchanged salutes and I went off to collect my men.

While my small group was collecting themselves, I stopped by a desk and ordered the rating to hand me the telephone. I told the operator to connect me with a number, my home plantation on Billiton Island. By the grace of God I made a quick connection, and Karen answered. After a flurry of questions. I asked her how everyone was and was relieved to learn all were well. The family was at home and things were peaceful, although the news was alarming. I then explained to her that I had been in a battle but came through alright. I told her that the Japanese presented a real threat and that she must get the family together and evacuate the plantation within the next few days.

Karen and I had made several different plans of action if war broke out and how hostilities may develop. There was money set aside under the Plantation accounts in *The Communication Bank of Hong Kong*, at the main branches of New Delhi, and Rangoon, and the *Lloyd's Bank,* in Singapore, Darwin and Sydney Australia. In my top desk drawer there was a folder containing legal documents giving her all the account numbers and bankers names. The key to it was in my shaving stand. I also gave her the names of several pilots that I knew personally, who flew for *Quantas Airlines, Empire Flying Boat Inc.* and *British Oriental Airways,* and whom I trusted completely.

I informed her that Singapore was being routinely bombed as were Batavia, and Soerabaja and many other cities, and that Japanese troops had already landed on the northern Malaya Penninsula. In my opinion, the plan for taking a Sunderland Flying Boat to India through Singapore and Burma was too dangerous. I suggested the quickest route to safety was to board at Batavia a *Quantas Airlines* flying boat bound for Darwin Australia, where our plantations two steamers had a warehouse, wharfs and even a small apartment/office as well. This would give the family a place to live, as there may be a lot of refugees.

I explained that, she and the children must fly out tomorrow for Batavia, and that I had already arranged for a ten passenger float plane from *Java Airways* to pick the family up at *New Eden* tomorrow evening. I know the owner Rudy Moone very well, and that we have a contract with him to service the Plantation. If the plane for some reason does not make it to you, his number is Banda3467. Avoid using the inter-island steamer, as all commercial shipping was at risk.

"Karen, now listen clearly, no time for questions. Start to prepare, take the immediate family only, no servants. Travel light, take all the cash, identification papers, family inoculation records, prescriptions, deeds to the plantation, the first aid case, the quinine pills, salt tablets, maps, compass, etc. all according to our plans. Take the two Colt .45 cal. revolvers, my 7.92 mm Mauser Army rifle and take several boxes of ammunition for each weapon. The rifle bandoliers may still be in the saddle shop where I sent them for cleaning. Give these to our sons, as they are all familiar with these firearms. I will contact you in Darwin as soon as possible. Tell the workers to release the animals from the stables, and to take care of themselves. Get out now, no delays. The situation is very serious."

Karen heard the urgency and desperation in my tone. She ceased her questions and then agreed to our plan. I bade her goodbye then rushed to join my small group at the waiting sedan. Reaching into the pocket of my tunic, I retrieved my sling and eased in my arm, the throbbing within my shoulder soon eased to a great degree.

My officers now struggled to pack our kit into the rear of a big Packard sedan. We had picked up two extra passengers; Army officers bound for the same destination. Eventually the overloaded boot was secured with a length of rope. The navy sedan sped off to the airfield where our refueled Glen Martin bomber was waiting with engines warmed up for our return flight to Soerabaja.

There I would, complete patchwork repairs on both battle-carriers, load all the structural plate and rolled sections with welding equipment; acetylene, oxygen bottles, that I would need to replace about 50-70 tonnes of damaged hull steel structure. Other consumables were also required to replenish the ships properly; fuel oil, aviation gas, food, fresh water, medicine, and spares to prepare the Battlecruiser carriers for sea and the dangerous voyage to the remote uninhabited Island of Palalau, an extinct volcano on the southern rim of the Savu Sea. Even there we would not out of the range of the JAAF bombers based in French Indo China. If we were lucky to remain undetected for several weeks, our ships would be made fit again and ready to renew the battle. In the meantime our air groups would stay in the fight, and operate from our well distributed naval air stations.

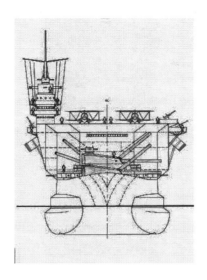

CHAPTER XXVII

NIGHT EVASION INTO THE SAVU SEA, THE REPAIR FACILITY, DAMAGE ASSESSMENT, THE COFFERDAMS, JAPANESE AMPHIBIOUS LANDINGS IN NEW GUINEA AND THE ESTABLISHMENT OF JAAF AIR BASES, THE FLEET ADMIRAAL ASSUMES COMMAND.

All the whole day of December 12th, the divers and ironworkers of the Naval Dockyard in Soerabaya labored to cut away the collapsed steel of the *Crushing Cylinders*, and the torn and twisted steel plating and framing from out of the damaged torpedo blisters, of the two battle-carriers. When this had been completed, there was revealed a similar pattern of destruction for both ships. The Japanese torpedoes had destroyed an area some 18 meters long by 8 meters high, all of it sacrificial structure. The internal shell plating behind the torpedo damage was slightly *dished in* on both ships due the air blast of the detonation, and scratched by shrapnel, but otherwise intact, the compartments behind the damaged areas; having been air tested, remained watertight. The blisters, had done their work and detonated the torpedoes some 1.5 meters from the hull plate, while the crushing cylinders had collapsed as designed, thereby absorbing a tremendous amount of the energy released by the weapon's warhead. The blister had to be rebuilt in these areas to create the necessary dead air space, and new crushing cylinders had to be fabricated from large diameter pipe and installed to restore the hull to its original level of underwater protection.

The ship carpenters of both battle-carriers, now got to work to plank over the area of missing blister plating by using teak from the dockyard stores. The 300 mm by 75 mm planks were attached longitudinally at the extreme ends of the damage by steel sockets welded to the blister shell. The natural bend of the planking, reinforced behind with heavy wood frames; created a curvature that closely approximated the shape of the original steelwork. The planks were caulked, tarred and a second layer covered the first at the seam, and fixed together with long bronze screws. The ends were then faired into the hull plating with plate. The heavy wood planking was covered in tar and sheathed in sheet metal and nailed fast.

Half of this excellent effort was carried out under water, and often at night, and was considered a difficult task even in times of peace. When the stop gap repairs to the torpedo bulges had been completed, the flooded spaces were pumped out, and a team of hull technicians and I entered the bulge through the manhole at its top to inspect the overall water tightness. The work looked so sturdy that I contemplated for a moment just not bothering to replace it. But when I considered the shock of near misses from bombs, and that a big torpedo may actually penetrate the wood planking and detonate against the hull, I resigned myself to the work ahead. There was no doubt in my mind that the woodwork was sufficiently strong to allow both battle-carriers to make the full speed passage to the Island of Palalau. While this work was being carried out, the upper aircraft hangar had been converted into a mould loft where the new hull steel was being layed out and cut.

There was by December 12th, quite a number of confiscated, Japanese owned fishing vessels already tied up along the west bank of the Maas River outside the Naval Base. These had been emptied of their crews by the Royal Army, and were placed under the guard of a company of native infantry. Kapitein Voorne had sent a shore party on a tug assisted barge over to these vessels with the intention to take off the fishing nets. These items were to be divided up between the battle-carriers and later proved to be of great value in fabricating our camouflage matting for the big ships. While carrying out this work the naval sailors aboard the Japanese fishing vessels discovered a few hidden radios that were missed earlier by the army. These were given to our intelligence units aboard the *Cornelis de Witt*.

Kapitein Voorne, two days later, recounted an incident involving one of our crewmen, a Chief Petty Officer. The sailor, who had only been with the Vlaggeschip a few days, had transferred from a destroyer under repair in the US not a week before the outbreak of hostilities in South East Asia. He was the leader of the shore party that had been sent over to the fishing vessels. The company of native infantry, guarding the fish boats, had gone through these boats to get souvenirs for themselves, amongst these items were the familiar Japanese flag of red disc on a white field, and a number of beautiful silk banners emblazoned with Japanese heroic phrases. While leading a work detachment of sailors along the quay, the CPO passed by the corner of a brick storehouse and ran suddenly right into a group of native infantrymen, standing in the shade, inspecting their souvenirs. One of the sailors shouts in Javanese good naturedly: *"lookout lads; the Japanese Army, we are dead!"* The bored Colonial Native Infantry instantly played along with the navy shore party, and screamed fiercely Banzai, Banzai, brandishing their rifles with fixed bayonets; at our sailors, while laughing. The Javanese being Asians, are practically indistinguishable from Japanese soldiers, and the CPO, who must have seen native sailors in their white tropical uniform aboard ship, had never seen them in their brown Army uniforms. The soldiers who were outfitted with puttees, and webbing that was not all that different from that of the enemy. Perhaps if the men had been wearing their distinctive *Dutch Pattern* steel helmet, which is the same model used by the navy, the Petty Officer would have grasped the situation, but instead these were hung on their belts, and the soldiers were wearing their service field caps with the neck flap. Upon seeing the Japanese Flags, then the Asian faces of the soldiers, the new CPO was undoubtedly very startled, but when several of his men raised their hands in mock surrender, his instincts snapped and he dove headlong into nearby shrubbery! Of course this caused a tremendous outburst of laughter, from the sailors and soldiers alike. Then a huge bellow of curses interrupted the fun, as a Seargent of the CNI detachment, having observed the entire incident, and who it seemed did not find the joke amusing, rushed over to his infantrymen cursing loudly. He told his men to put away their bloody Japanese booty or he would have it confiscated. Cursing loudly he reminded his men that misidentification of troops in the heightened tension of war, even for a few seconds may cause death, and then ordered them back to their duties. The Seargent, also a native Indonesian, asked our sailors if the man in the bushes was armed. When he was told that the CPO had no weapon, he went to the edge of the bushes and called out in perfect Dutch that the soldiers were of the Royal Dutch Army, 23rd Regiment. The CPO emerged, evidently with great embarrassment, for he knew the incident would dog him for the rest of his service in the Asiatic Fleet .

At the same time that the fish nets were being acquired, the aircrews of both battle-carriers had been put to work collecting hundreds of tons of foliage from local plantations, these palm fronds were bound into tight bails, loaded onto the Army's heavy trucks for transport to the Naval Dockyard, where the men transferred these to the upper hanger deck of the battle-carriers, through the ship's side scuttles along with a great deal of bamboo in bundles, all in preparation for the great task ahead.

Perak Airfield was now packed with aircraft, and became for the JAAF a very dangerous target to attack. In addition to the Royal Army Air Regiment of 40 Fokker D.XXI Monoplane Fighters and the 200 biplane fighters and dive bombers on inventory as replacements concealed in revetments; there were now 100 aircraft recently flown off the battle-carriers that were available. The combined fighter strength of over well over 150 machines frustrated six attacks by the JAAF bombers, and managed to keep them away from the Dockyard for the 36 hours it took to repair the torpedo blisters for sea.

I signaled Naval Headquarters in Batavia that I planned to sail at 20:00hrs December 13, 1941. Destroyers patrolling to the north and south of Lombok straight had closed it to shipping so all was in preparation for a high speed dash at night. A full load of fuel was pumped into both battle-carriers. A last check of all equipment, spares, and material needed to put the ship in top condition was made. A team of dockyard iron workers, and pipefitters were taken aboard. All aboard were anxious to clear the harbour, and repeatedly watched the sun's progress to the ridge of hills, waiting for nightfall. The Dockyard officially turned the ship over to the navy and my Vice Admiraal's pennant was hoisted at 18:00hrs. The tugs had moved the *Cornelis de Witt* out of the Naval Basin into the Maas River as evening fell, followed shortly by the *Johan de Witt*. We dropped our pilots at 19:57hrs and proceeded northeast at six knots.

I looked around the darkened navigation bridge, at the group of tense faces of the officers which were dimly illuminated by the phosphorescence of the bridge instruments. Addressing Kapt. Voorne, I said: "Kapitien; an interesting exercise this will be; a high speed night passage on compass and knot meter. Normal Coastal Navigation methods are out, as our lighthouses and navigation buoys have been deactivated throughout the colony, to confuse the Japanese. All the lookouts would sweep the seas using the *Night*

Sight Apparatus, to avoid encounters with other vessels. Please make for Lombok Island at our best speed, and signal the *Johan* to follow." "Yes Admiraal," he replied, then turned to pass on these orders. At the ringing of the engine telegraph that signaled for full ahead, I moved into the confines of the red-lit command center, behind the navigation bridge.

Here, I poured myself a cup of hot coffee, then retrieved my little yellow tin of *Panter* cigarettes from my tunic, I lit up, took a deep drag then exhaled, followed by a swallow of coffee. I positioned myself on a tall stool beside the big chart table, to study our course laid out in pencil; one hour at 32 knots, alter course two points to starboard, 5 hours at 32 knots, alter course seven points to starboard, through Lombok strait, at night at 32 knots, no navigation beacons for 1.75 hours, alter course to port 32 knots for 1.5 hours, slow to 5 knots, enter the mouth of Ekas Bay, nine hours after departing Soerabaja. Somewhat lost in my thoughts I looked around at the small group of officers, who were silently studying my face. I spoke up loudly, "an interesting night ahead gentlemen, loosen up and smoke if you wish."

In a few minutes the main steam valve to all the turbines was opened, and all thirty boilers, equipped with super heaters were brought up to maximum pressure. The great ships began to really stretch their legs, the tip of the needle on the knot meter repeater in the Command Center vibrating over the 32 knot mark. It was to be a blacked out high speed run across a dark sea that was during times of peace; congested with traffic. I trusted our instruments; the clock, the knot meter, the chart, and the Night Site to get us through, and that our patrol boats had cleared the way ahead of us from wayward large vessels. If a native wooden fish boat sneaking out after curfew to lay her nets at night, crossed our path, even one of several hundred tonnes, if struck at this speed would be reduced to matchwood in seconds. I retrieved my linen sling from a pocket in my tunic and gently slid in my right forearm, which instantly eased the ach in my shoulder.

Below the hangar; air crewmen, numbering in their hundreds turned out to tackle the great pile of heavy fish nets. One side of each net was cut open from the mouth to the *Cod End.* The others were prepared in the same way then woven together to form eventually; eight great mats roughly 100 meters by 50 meters. These were then coiled up for loading onto the aircraft elevators, to be brought up onto the flight deck in the morning. Our sister ship, was performing the same tasks as we.

The night was tense, and muggy in the hangar deck as all the ventilation openings had been sealed to darken the ship, and the blowers had malfunctioned. Nevertheless, the intensity of the work at hand made it passed quickly. There was sufficient cloud cover to effectively mask our transit, yet allow us to distinguish the headlands and Capes from the water as we approached them. The early morning found both Battle-carriers moving slowly with bows pointed down the length of Ekas Bay, a well protected body of water ten kilometers in length by four in width, with a narrow entrance from the south less than a kilometer across. The Fleet Admiraal had sent to that location four 600 tonne fishing trawlers, under naval command, to assist us with anchoring. The vessels although not as powerful as tugs nevertheless had powerful engines for dragging nets. These assisted us with gentle nudges to a protected location behind the small headland to the east. As they were not naval vessels they would not be a topic of idle chatter amongst the residents of the island. Here under two bow and one stern anchor the Battle-carriers would wait out the day, hopefully unobserved by the enemy.

While this precise maneuvering was underway, all hands turned out to spread the heavy fishing nets over the ship. One by one the coils of netting were brought up on the two aircraft elevators and positioned along the centerline of the flight deck. When the anchors were dropped and the fish boats clear, these nets were unrolled on the flight deck with the ends hanging down into the water on each side. In this way each ship was entirely shrouded. The men placed bamboo posts on deck, much like tent poles, propping the net some two meters above its surface. Then the palm fronds and foliage were poked through the netting above the deck and also fixed to the netting down the sides to the waterline.

Our attendant vessels, having viewed the finished job from several angles, signaled that both battle-carriers were well disguised, and then departed for the day so as not to draw any attention to the area. The massive camouflaging operation which had now completely transformed our vessels was accomplished in less than half an hour by twelve hundred pairs of hands!

The day passed without incident, distant aircraft engines were heard on several occasions but these machines never came into view. I learned at a later date that the towns of *Mataram* and *Praja* laying fifty and thirty kilometers to the west on Lombok were buzzed by lone aircraft, but these were soon shot down by a section of Army Fokker fighters that had been dispersed to a hidden airfield on the Island of Bali.

The *Cornelis de Witte* lowered a 15 meter motor launch with a detachment of marines aboard. This vessel steamed to the mouth of the bay to intercept any traffic that may approach. Here we passed the day, the off-duty men laying on the warm wood of the flight deck under the shade of the camouflage nets had a peaceful comfortable rest, sleeping, writing letters, playing cards and the like. Not so with the dockyard workers however as they returned to the business of pre-fabricating the necessary hull structure that would eventually replace the plank patches to the hulls.

As evening approached, the labor intensive camouflage process was reversed; the nets were pulled out of the water and rolled up like great carpets, to be positioned fore and aft along the center of the flight deck and secured. Pulling the nets up the side of the ship was difficult due to the weight and all the obstructions on which they snagged, nevertheless it was done smartly. Our fishing boats appeared just as our anchors were being drawn up. Each ship was nudged away from the shallows and steam put to her turbines. Another night passage at high speed was ahead of us.

The battle-carriers cleared the mouth of bay at a 21:30hrs December 14, 1941 and steamed due south into the Indian Ocean in line ahead formation, with the *Cornelis de Witt* in the lead. After half an hour the ships altered course six points to port, on a direct route to Paulau Island. The Chief Engineer, Jap Anten, who had every confidence in his boilers, hung 20 kilogram weights on their blow-out safety valves to give us more boiler pressure which yielded 112,000 kw, and 335 revolutions on each shaft, for an extra 1.25 knots. The knot meter repeater quivered all night hovering over the 32 knot mark. I had never seen this old lady move out so smartly, I therefore went out through the gas tight door in the starboard side to look at her cleave the water.

A massive bow wave system was formed and flung aside, all glowing like green emerald in the dark. Soon to arrive were the dolphins who loved surfing on the bow waves while playing in the green glow. Those intelligent creatures seemed to greatly appreciate the beauty created by a ship's passage at night, but they preferred only steamships or ships under sail due to the quiet. They seldom approached diesel powered vessels which emitted a great deal of underwater noise, which I am sure they found very discomforting. Looking back at the down-curving stack, I did not see any sparks at all, the combustion of our fuel was evidently very efficient.

I returned to the bridge and asked Kapitein Voorne to pass on my compliments to the Engineers, the ship was performing exceptionally well, especially with the wooden patches on their sides. I assumed my position in the Command Center, to watch the progress being marked on our chart. The passage proved to be uneventful, merely a night of cigarettes and coffee. At 01:00hrs, I returned to my cabin for two hours rest.

The telephone next to my berth awoke me, with a start. Picking it up I heard, "Paulau Island off our port bow Admiraal, preparing to enter the bay." I replied, "Very well, proceed in, and have the camouflage parties fall out in preparation to disguise the ship as soon as we have anchored." I then hung up the phone and undogged a port light, the sunrise was half an hour off. My steward then began to lay out my tropical short uniform, and I told him to put together a breakfast tray for me from what was available in the officer's wardroom: scrambled eggs, some melon, toast, orange marmalade, juice, black coffee. I will take it up at the navigation bridge. Then I proceeded with my morning ablutions at a hurried pace.

Arriving on the Bridge Deck I was greeted by Kapt. Voorne, an officer who seemed to be always on duty when I went to that station. The island looked to be something out of a Jules Verne novel; with tall steep crags perhaps 200 meters in elevation enclosing a circular bay perhaps a little more than a mile in diameter. To the south, a narrow entrance. At the north end a deep fracture splitting the crag from its top down to perhaps 50 meters above the surface of the sea. The vegetation was waist high saw grass running to shrubbery on the steep slopes of the inside, the exterior of the cone was as any other island, palms covering the lower reaches running down to the sea, with grassy slopes running up to the summit of the crags giving them a soft quality. The charts indicated that a shallow shelf of some eight fathoms encircled the entire interior of the bay, and projected some 100 meters from the shore. Then the seafloor fell away into a deep abysmal pit.

As the navigation bridge cleared the walls of the entrance, a lookout reported the presence to our port of the small flotilla of support ships that the Fleet Admriaal had promised. The Repair ships; *Poolster* and *Pelican* were moored one behind the other some 300 meters apart, with the *Tripoli* behind these. On the other side of the Bay lay the *Arnhem* and her two gunboats *T-102*, and *T-104*. In short order two 15 meter motor launches approached our ships from the *Pelican*. Kapt. Voorne went to the Starboard Bridge platform to communicate with them. The first launch approached, and hailed us with a megaphone. Anchorages had been selected for us.

The *Cornelis* was rafted up with its torpedo damage against the hull of the *Pelican*, and the *Johan* with her damaged side to the *Poolster*. I could see now what was happening; the repair ships had already begun construction of the cofferdams along their sides, the hull of the Battle-carriers would provide the other side, and a watertight chamber would be created in which the steelworkers and ship fitters could repair the hull blisters. I was happy to see the preparations advanced to date.

The battle-carriers slowly made their way into the Bay. As once before we relied upon our crippled aircraft to help with the final positioning of the ships. Two pair of Helldivers were lashed athwart ships at the bow and stern ends of the Flight Deck, and with powerful engines, and their variable pitch propellers; gave the big ships the sideways maneuverability that they needed. Fortunately, very little wind could find its way into the interior of the island's cone, as breezes caused us some difficulty, even while at three point anchor because of our massive profiles. Soon both vessels were snugged up against a repair ship. Steel clips were welded to both hulls, and by driving in wooden wedges, hundreds of tons of force was generated to press the vessels tightly together against the wood and rope packing of the cofferdam. Work immediately began to construct a watertight floor to enclose the space. Ten divers aboard the *Pelican*, who were already suited up, and sitting on a bench at the ship's waist, were assisted with the donning of their round bronze helmets, their air hoses were laid neatly out and they climbed down the rope ladders dangling from the ship. The work space was illuminated by electric lighting, and the pumps kept the minor leaking to a manageable level. It had taken all of two days to complete the cofferdam and I was glad that so much of the replacement steelwork and piping had been prefabricated in the few days that we had between our arrival and departure from Soerabaya.

Turning to my C.O.S I said, "Commodore Van Klaffens the ship is now in the hands of the *Pelican,* and our repair crews. Please call a conference aboard the Vlaggeschip of all ship commanders, for noon today."

The *Conference of Commanders*, was a relaxed exchange of all information following a good lunch in the wardroom. We discussed the repair work at hand, the materials needed, and if there were any shortages. Then we laid out a timetable. We moved on to a discussion of security for the bay, and assigned several more launches to the minor tasks, and the two gunboats with their combined six 155mm guns were to defend our position from surface attack. The Gunboats Captains had created three lookout posts on the top of the crater, from here was reported our approach. The means of communication employed was flag signals. The Vlaggeschip's Brigade Generaal Joost Wittgenstein; Commander of our Marines, suggested that he could facilitate this effort by supplying these lookouts posts with three field telephone sets from the Marine's stores we had aboard. He could run the lines right into the Command Center, of the *Cornelis de Witt* if we wished. Work during the night was to continue, but special precautions had been made so that no lights could be seen from the air. I was satisfied with all these preparations. The camouflage netting was deployed to cover each battle-carrier and its attendant repair ship. The lookouts on the crater rim confirmed that the results were very effective. The work continued unabated under this huge shroud, which only had to be rolled back when the Arnhem needed to use her cranes, for lowering the steel weldments down into the cofferdam for installation.

When I was informed that the Vlaggeschip's cofferdam was completed, I chose to personally inspect the underwater chamber to see if it was safe enough for the men. The *Pelican* being a much smaller vessel than the great Battle-carrier allowed it to fit comfortably under the overhang of the flight deck, and the gun tubs of the Flak Batteries, and the two ship's hulls had been warped tightly together leaving a gap of four meters between them, for the fabrication of the cofferdam and the repairs. The narrower the cofferdam the stronger it could be made, which was needed as the watertight shaft would descend 8.5 meters below sea level, and therefore the wooden ends of the space must resist water pressures of roughly 4.8 tonnes per square meter.

I changed into my white denim cotton coveralls, took a pair of work gloves and wore my peaked cap to distinguish myself from the other men then descended down the rope ladder to the very bottom of the shaft. The men working within the damaged blister were a little surprised to see me, but as there was no room for standing to attention I just told them to carry on cutting and welding. The cofferdam was made of two layers of heavy teak planking, bolted to an internal steel *H section* frame. The ends of the planks were bolted to plate tabs welded against the hull plating. The same method was used to build the floor of the cofferdam. The entire outside of the cofferdam was covered with heavy canvas whose perimeter had been left long, rolled up and pounded into the cracks between the planks and the steel of the hull; a very difficult task as it was performed by divers who had to swing their caulking mallets underwater! There were a dozen little leaks and drips, and the bottom was always under 15 centimeters of water, but a small pump kept it from rising further. The cofferdam was very substantial, and looked quite strong. I noticed that the repair crews showed no fear of it collapsing, which I greatly appreciated as the work progressed rapidly. The *Johan de Witt* was fitted with similar cofferdam, and worked progressed quickly on her underwater damage as well. I told the men that I would get them more forced air ducting to improve the venting of the welding fumes. Then, as I was satisfied with these arrangements. I climbed back up to the main deck scaffolding and asked Kapt. Voorne to pass on my well done to the repair parties.

The port and starboard sides of hull of the original Lion Class battlecruisers had ten coaling doors between 'A' Turret and 'C' Turret of the main battery. These were of 25 mm steel, one meter by one meter, and side hinged, which facilitated the transfer of sacks of coal from a collier into the warship at main deck level. The Battle-carriers were by 1941 powered by oil fired boilers so all these doors were not needed. Seven had been replaced with welded plate inserts, but three had been extended; cut down to main deck level to act as doors. These were now opened up and their gangways were passed through to the weather deck of the *Pelican*. On the second day after tying up to the repair ship, I made my way down to the main deck to evaluate the men's activity. Through the open door, the gangway over to the *Pelican* beckoned to me. I turned, retrieved a bulkhead telephone and rang up the bridge to inform them that I was going ashore. I then stepped through the 25mm thick side door of the hull and crossed over the gangway. On the *Pelican's* opposite side; another gangway to starboard led down onto a small barge, which in turn was connected to the grassy slope of the crater by several long wooden planks. Behind me, followed my shadows; two junior officers; of Luitenant ter Zee 2de Klasse rank. These men were outfitted with camera, flashlights, clipboards, rubber boots etc. As I conducted my inspection of the ship, these men would take note of my comments, snap photographs or venture into the more filthy recesses that required youthful flexibility. Once upon land I paused for a moment to get my bearing; then pushed off and began to climb up the long slope of the ancient cone along the faint pathway of flattened grass to the nearest of our Marine observation posts. The steep climb was good for me as it taxed my wind, but the view from the rim of the crater was worth it.

The two marines on duty, had their backs to the crater as they scanned the sea with their field glasses. On hearing my labored breathing they turned to see the Fleet Commander sweating his way up the slope, and immediately dropped what they were doing and hurriedly put on their tunics and came to attention. I asked these marines to report their observations, and was informed no activity at all air or water, I then sat down heavily on the turf and took in a beautiful panoramic view of the blue sea and soft green grass covered slopes of Paulau Crater. I removed my tunic and shirt to bare my torso to the sun and enjoy that perfect balance of breeze and heat. I asked a marine to pass me the field telephone, taking the receiver from him I then cranked the handle of the unit three times. Putting the phone to my ear I heard it picked up in the *Cornelis de Witt's* Command Center on the second buzz. "Lookout post no. 1 to Vlaggeschip, I am reporting that your camouflage is very effective, Admiraal Sweers over and out." I looked at my young officers and the two marines, and said, "Come now lads you won't let your Fleet Commander take the sun by himself?" "No Admiraal," was their reply. The shirts came off, and I lit up another Panter. From this vantage point, I swept the cloudless sky and royal blue sea, for signs of any activity. A few tiny boats could be made out to the north, at a great distance but otherwise all was quiet. In the interior of the crater, small wavelets had been ruffled in places by the gentle breezes and these sparkled hypnotically in the sun. There atop the crater's rim I evaluated the combat lessons that we had learned and pondered the adjustments that the Commanders of the JAAF would be making to negate our Battle-squadron's air defenses. I spent an hour at this peaceful location, enjoying the warmth of the sun upon my skin and turning a little pink. From this vanatage point I surveying the beautiful seascape through my glasses. Then returned to the *Cornelis de Witt* feeling quite refreshed from my little outing.

One week into our repairs both ships were looking very much better and close to completion. A great deal of work may be accomplished in a short time when you have available several hundred skilled metalworkers, motivated by a sense of urgency. What would surely have been months of work at a commercial yard were put right in a fraction of the time. The new steel framing for the hull, was passed down to the men in the cofferdam in manageable sections, fitted in place and welded up. The curved plating of the blisters outer shell were, *rolled to suit* in the machine shops within the hold of the repair ships. When completed these plates were lifted by the repair ship's cranes and lowered into the cofferdam for final fitting and welding. The skills of the metalworkers aboard were excellent and I would challenge a fully equipped shipyard to have made the repairs to the damaged hulls more rapidly than the repair ships had.

The same skilled attention was applied to repair the bomb damage of the port 40 mm Flak Battery A, and the lingering effects of the bomb hit to the hull adjacent to Main Battery 'C' Mount. The slight damage to the aircraft hangers was put shipshape in short order. The repairs to the *Johan de Witt*, were accomplished with the same care and speed.

Towards the evening of our sixth day in our secret repair facility, our lookouts reported that an aircraft was circling the island. All welding and use of electric lighting was shut off as we waited under our camouflage netting. All ships within the cone had improvised their disguises quite effectively, and I felt confident that all would pass muster of a cursory glance from a high flying aircraft. The strange aircraft however dropped lower in altitude and lined up on the entrance to the small bay, then proceeded to land on the water! The machine was soon identified as one of the Navy's Grumman Duck Amphibians. Once landed she coasted into the waters of the bay and proceeded to the camouflaged side of the battle-carrier. A party of sailors upon the flight deck hauled up on a few lines and the netting in front of the seaplane was raised 7 meters to reveal a small docking barge rafted to the side of the battle-carrier. Two sailors stationed on it grabbed the lines thrown to them from the plane and she was quickly snugged up against the dock, and the camouflage netting lowered behind her. The door of the seaplane was popped open and out stepped Fleet Admiraal Van de Velde and two staff officers from Naval Headquarters in Batavia!

I was in my cabin, when Admiraal de Velde boarded the *Cornelis de Witt*. I asked Kapt. Voorne to have the Fleet Admiraal's party escorted to our Main Conference Room, and activate the Air Conditioning Plant for that space. I made my way there, before the Fleet Admiraal and his small group arrived. I summoned a Steward and asked him to prepare a tasty cold lunch, with lots of iced lemonade, and tea. The Fleet Admiraal soon arrived and greeted me. He asked how the repairs were going and I replied; "All the welding should be completed by tomorrow evening or noon next day at the latest, then metal preparation for painting. Then we will need half a day to remove the cofferdams and burn off the steel tabbing on the hulls. The same may be said of the *Johan de Witt's* progress. In three days Fleet Admiraal we will be ready for sea."

"Maarten," he said that is very good news to hear. Not too soon either as the strategic situation is becoming ever more critical. Please assemble the staffs and senior ships officers of both Battle-carriers for a briefing, I have much to tell you." Turning to his staff officers he said, "Prepare your material." These officers occupied a corner of the great table and began unpacking their gear. They produced a large chart, which they quickly unfolded and tacked it to the bulkhead, over one corner of the Great Wall Map of The Pacific and South East Asia. I noticed at once that it was a map of New Guinea, on which were marked large red arrows at the extreme west end of the Island which was Dutch territory, with red dots laying inside the Great Bay of Cederawasih, and a big red dot on the end of the Island of New Britain, in the Bismarck Archipelago.

The room rapidly filled with officers, from the vlaggeschip, and these men poured themselves coffee, and speculated on the reason for the Fleet Admiraal's arrival, while we waited for the officers from our sister ship to arrive. The Air Conditioning unit kicked in with a rattle, and the Fleet Admiraal, said loudly to all, "smoke if you wish gentleman." He advanced the opinion that this location could be expanded into a permanent wartime facility. I replied that the idea was a good one, and could work. We had seen no aircraft or ships approach the island. The effects of wind and wave on the island's bay was not noticeable, and with no heavy motion to impede repairs the work progressed rapidly and under safer conditions.

In a short time my senior officers were all assembled. In addition to myself, five other operational officers and five staff officers from the Vlaggeschip were present, with a similar group from the *Johan de Witt*.

"Now Gentlemen," Admiraal Van de Velde said loudly, "The reason for my visit. Four days ago I attended a meeting of the Allied Command in Singapore; now designated *Joint Command* for the American, British, Dutch and Australian armed forces in South East Asia/West Pacific. The news I am afraid is not good." This admission caused a murmur of concern among the officers assembled. The Fleet Admiraal continued; "The Japanese are pressing the forces of the British, Americans and the Netherlands very heavily on land, at sea and in the air." He turned to the bulkhead behind him and moved over to the big wall map that showed the South East Asian Theater of Operations. He picked up the wooden pointer off its ledge and turned on the overhead map lighting. "Here," he said pointing, "Japanese troops are pushing the British Army down the Malay Peninsula at a pace it was not thought possible through such dense jungle. The enemy have large quantities of light tanks, the British have none, and little in the way to defend against them other than artillery and mines of which they do not have much of a supply either. The British troops have been reduced to improvised defences. The Japanese have heavy air support and command of the sea, while the British have limited air capability remaining, with the RN practically swept out of the South China Sea."

Pointing to Borneo on the wall map, he continued; "There have been enemy amphibious landings here along the coast of Sarawak, and British North Borneo. The Japanese troops have moved inland and have captured the airfield at Miri from which they are now operating a Fighter Group. The defenses around Jesselton are collapsing, and the air squadrons there have been pulled back to Tarakan. The airfield facilities at Jesselton have been demolished to deny them to the enemy. Japanese troops are marching westward along the coast road from Miri and are threatening the capital city Sarawak and its air base. The Royal Netherlands Army has moved eastward from Borneo into Sarawak to throw up a defensive line in front of the Japanese troops. The airfield at Sarawak (Kuching) is a good one and has long airstrips of hard compacted coral. If the enemy captures these; he will place bombers on them and be able to double the rate of their air attacks against targets in Java, Borneo, Celebese and all the inland seas. At present the Royal Netherlands Army is confident that it can hold these troops in the mountainous region that divides the territory of Sarawak from Borneo and keep them out of our Colony."

He then pointed to the American Protectorate of the Philippines. "The Japanese Army Air Force Bombers have been raiding all points throughout these islands. Their armies have landed on the north coast of the Island of Luzon, at Laoag and Apari and are marching south down both coastal roads, heading of course towards the Capital City of Manila. For some incredible reason, General McArthur did not put the Philippines on a war alert when Pearl Harbour was attacked, and as a result 90% of his aircraft were destroyed on its airfields, when the JAAF attacked! This comment caused gasps of amazement from my officers! Pausing only momentarily, the Fleet Admiraal continued, "The US Army had stopped them for several days by throwing a defensive line across the northern tip of Luzon from the town of Vigaan on the west coast to the town of Lagan on the east coast. But yesterday the Japanese Army unhinged this defense by carrying out an amphibious landing behind them, further down the coast at the town of Baguio, and the US Army then was obliged to fall back to avoid entrapment."

The Fleet Admiraal continued; "But all is not bad news. The Americans have responded to this disaster not only quickly but if I may say spectacularly. The old USS Langley, a former aircraft carrier, now converted to an aircraft transporter was loaded with thirty crated fighter aircraft to be delivered to the Philippines. After her departure from San Francisco three days ago, it was decided by the US Naval strategists to mount an additional effort using their Fleet of Rigid Airships, whose commanders were desperately looking for an operation that would utilize them."

"The Commander of the USN Airships, effectively argued to the US Secretary of the Navy, that the voyage to South East Asia would take the USS Langley five weeks, with no guarantee of success, and her aircraft would arrive in the combat theater in crates. However, a similar effort could be mounted, as a supplementary operation with the USN Rigid Airship Squadron No. 1 based at Akron Ohio. Airship Squadron 1, could land its current compliment of parasite Goblin fighter aircraft, and after only minor adaptions take aboard fifty P-40 Warhawk fighters ready for combat, and deliver these to Davo airfield on Mindano in four to five days! The entire airship armada of the US Navy would be involved, composed of the ships; *Sacramento, Long Beach, Milwaukee, Biloxi, San Clemente, Poughkeepsie, Mobile, Knoxville, Tallahassee* and *Chattanooga*. Each airship will be modified to carry five of these fighter planes slung from their bellies on modified steel brackets. They could approach the Philippine Island from any direction, at night and release the fighter aircraft to reinforce any airfield or multiple airfields. The Rigid Airship Squadron can cover 2400 miles a day, and with their ten day supply of fuel, are capable of repeating these deliveries twice a month!"

"Approval was granted for the project, and the USAAF assigned a Fighter Regiment to begin loading onto the Airship Squadron. I am pleased to inform you that USN Airship Squadron No. 1, with fifty P-40 fighters left the Army Airfield at Akron Ohio this morning bound for the Philippine Islands!" This news brought smiles, to faces of my men for the first time in weeks. The Fleet Admiraal then added, "Yes, indeed, leave it to the *bloody yanks* to do something so imaginative and magnificent!"

"However Gentlemen, I did not fly all this way to give you an update on the war but to prepare you for your next mission." Van de Velde then went over to the map of New Guinea that his staff officers had tacked to the wall. "Here and here," he said, pointing to the red arrows and dots that marked up this map. "These are the locations of Japanese activity that gives us great concern." The Admiraal's pointer slashed across the map. It is now plain to Joint Command SEAWP, that the Japanese plans are more ambitious and wide reaching that we had ever thought. Pointing to the Island of New Britain laying to the east of New Guinea. "Our submarines have reported, that the Japanese engineers are developing massive naval facilities in the harbour of Rabaul, here on the tip of the Island of New Britain, in the Bismarck Archipelago, and also on a string of airfields in the Islands of the New Hebrides. Once completed, Japan's Army bombers and naval aircraft will be in a position to sever the sea lanes between Australia, and America, effectively cutting the whole planet in half! The Pacific to the north is blocked to shipping by the ice of the Arctic. And by putting submarines off the entrance to the Panama Canal and off the tip of South America the Japanese could block these shipping choke points and deny Allied entry into the Pacific! Under these circumstances; America would have great difficulty in continuing the war with Japan!"

Then pointing to the western end of the big Island of New Guinea, the Fleet Admiraal said, "The Japanese have landed forces on the western regions of New Guinea, here in the big Bay of Cenderawasih. The minelayers of the Imperial Japanese Navy have sewn extensive fields across the top of the Bay, closing the channels between the islands of Biak and Numfoor at the western approaches and Biak and Yapen on the eastern approaches,

336

leaving channels open between the main island and those of Numfoor and Yapen. Safe behind this barrier, a great concentration of auxiliary shipping is amassing. Our two submarines in those waters have carried out extensive night reconnaissance in the areas of the landings and report that large airfields are being constructed at the towns of Wasior, Bawe, Nave, and Napan. Once these have been completed, Japanese long range bombers will be able to hit all points in north and eastern Australia, and attack all our airfields, naval bases and cities of the Dutch East Indies from the rear and our flank. We have no chance of defending our vital regions from massed bomber attacks coming from all directions, and that is how Japan plans to knock the Netherlands out of the war, and cut the US - Australia lines of Supply."

"The effect of these alarming developments were the topics of ABDA (American, British, Dutch, and Australian) Joint Command meeting at Singapore from which I have come. Here is what has been decided is the appropriate ABDA response; to divert enemy pressure in the west, we are going on the offense in the east! In a short time; date to be finalized; the RNLN will concentrate all its battle-carrier strength in the Banda Sea; they will be supported by six light cruisers and twelve destroyers. There the ships of the RNLN will be joined by the *Task Force Wombat* from the Royal Australian Navy, composed of a battlecruiser, two heavy cruisers and six destroyers, and *Task Force Stonewall* of the United States Navy, composed of a light cruiser and nine destroyers. The entire force will be code named *Task Force Linebacker*, and will have forty surface ships of which I will have overall command, and hoist my Pennant on the *Cornelis de Witt* as my Vlaageschip, Vice Admiraal Sweers will be my deputy commander. Looking up at me he said; "I will supplement your staff Vice Admiraal, with two officer's from Batavia, otherwise your staff will become mine." Each battle-carrier will form its own Task Group under their current commanders, details to follow. Fifteen submarines from the RNLN, the RN, and the RAN have been dispatched under the Command of Commodore Bert Flowers RAN to coordinate with us on attacking the shipping in those areas around New Guinea and New Britain that I have already pointed out. The battle-carriers will each take aboard one extra fighter squadron for this mission giving the fleet some 250 aircraft, these will be kept on deck. Yes it will be crowded aboard the battle-carriers, but we may run into heavy opposition, and will need every aircraft."

"Our *Coastwatcher's* on New Guinea have reported that there are now over one hundred freighters and as many specialized vessels moored in Cenderawasih Bay at the four separate locations that I have mentioned, supporting the construction of those four airfields."

"On the date appointed, *Task Force Linebacker* will move across the Banda Sea at night and pass through Dampier Strait south of Wagieo Island and round the western tip of New Guinea at dawn. At that time all available bombers will launch a massive air strike at the shipping within the bay. Four hours later, the entire Task Force will proceed into the bay along a course through the minefields, currently being mapped by our submarines. Two flotillas of destroyers with a light cruiser as flotilla leader will detach from screening the heavy ships and attack the enemy shipping and complete its destruction. If any ships attempt to escape eastward, they will run into our cordon of submarines laying in wait at the minefield's exit corridor. After detaching a destroyer to screen the seaward side of each capital ship, the cruisers and the remaining destroyers will attack the shipping with gun and torpedo. The three battle-carriers will bombard the construction site and facilities at the airfields at *Wasior, Bawe* and *Nave*. The battlecruiser *Australia* will bombard the airfield and construction facilities at *Napan*." This news caused great exitement all round. The Fleet Admiraal continued; when we have completed our mission, *Task Force Linebacker* will withdraw to the Java Sea via the original route."

The Fleet Admiraal continued, "While we are bombing, torpedoing, shelling and causing as much havoc and discomfort to the enemy as we are able, some seven hundred miles to our east a Task Force of the USN composed of two to three fleet carriers, and four heavy cruisers and their destroyer escort will be carrying out a similar operation against the enemy shipping and facilities at Rabaul in New Britain!" Once again the assembled officers found it difficult to contain their enthusiasm. The Fleet Admiaal then said," Yes, gentlemen we are taking the fight to the enemy, and as always the navy leads!"

Settling the men down; the Fleet Admiraal began speaking once again, "There is of course the mighty *Rengo Khantai* to worry about, nine aircraft carriers, ten modernized battleships and six hundred other warships, who will not be sleeping. Our Naval Intelligence people have told me that heavy forces may well be in the area, of our upcoming operation, but these will not be strategic in nature. They are absolutely certain that at the time we kick-off our attack against the airfields in New Guinea; Admiral Nagumo, will sortie from his current position at the Ellice Islands, with six fleet carriers, four fast battleships, and a host of light escorts, to strike at the RAN Fleet now concentrated at Sydney. Following the attack, the IJN First Air Fleet will then proceed south of Tasmania, and move into the Indian Ocean to attack shipping, there and in the Bay of Bengal. Kondo's objective will be to draw out and destroy the Royal Navy now assembling a new *East Asiatic Fleet* at Diego Garcia in the Central Indian Ocean. So far the Royal Navy has concentrated at that base four old 'D' Class cruisers, four old 'R' Class slow 15 inch battleships, and three new aircraft carriers. But these are far from ready to meet the Imperial Japanese Navy on the open sea. When we confirm for the RN the movement of Nagumo's Fleet into the Indian Ocean their ships will retire to Aden. Japanese Naval Intelligence believe that their bold thrust into the Indian Ocean may be carried out without concern for their 'rear' as they believe that the USN will be too cautious to venture far from Hawaii, and that the two Battle-carriers of the KMN are badly damaged, and now without drydock facilities.

TF Wombat, the combined warships of the RAN and RNZN around the Battlecruiser *HMAS Australia* is now based at Sydney. Our submarines have been very effective to date, in monitoring the movement of Admiral Nagumo's Fleet. When he moves against the fleet at Sydney, *TF Wombat* will retire westward, refuel two days later at Perth, and then make for the Banda Sea to concentrate *TF Linebacker*. As soon as the Australian Air Force long range patrols out of Freemantle confirm that Admiral Nagumo has moved past Australia's southern coast into the Indian Ocean, our combined fleets will strike the airfields at New Guinea." Once again the men stifled their excitement with some difficulty.

Fleet Admiraal van De Velde, having concluded the presentation, took a few questions then dismissed the assembly. Turning to me he said; "Maarten, do you have anything to add?" I replied, to Fleet Admiraal, "the *Joint Command Operation* is an excellent opportunity to strike at the enemy. As to your accommodations aboard; each Battle-carrier was outfitted as a cruising vessel for state visits. I will have the stewards prepare the *Royal Quarters* for you. "Thank you Maarten," he replied. As we walked off he patted my wounded shoulder with his palm and was startled at my wince. "Admiraal Sweers, does your shoulder still cause pain?" he asked with some incredulity. "Your brow, I now see has a slight film of sweat, yet it is cool in this compartment. You also look a bit pale. Report to the Chief of Surgery today. All my officers must be in the best of health for the upcoming operation. Now do you have any of those excellent strong Russian cigarettes?"

December 23rd, I was standing on the shaded flight deck under our camouflage netting, inspecting the abrasion of the rope against the bamboo posts when a warrant officer came up to me and saluting said; "Vice Admiraal Sweers, the Fleet Admiraal requests that you attend him in his day cabin." I made my way aft then to the side of the flight deck and down a short ladder into a gun tub, from there into a passageway and knocked on the door of the Royal Quarters. I then entered the chamber when beckoned. Stepping over the sill, I saluted the Fleet Admiraal, then removed my cap. I was surprised to see present the ship's Chief Medical Officer Brigade Generaal (Commodore) Peiter Berleburg. Admiraal Van de Velde turned to me and said in an official tone; "Vice Admiraal Sweers, I have just finished reading your medical report from our chief of surgery here, it is not a good one." He retrieved a dark vellum sheet from the report which I immediately recognized as an X-Ray photograph. Turning to the Chief Surgeon he said, "Doctor if you would please explain." The Brigade Generaal took the X-Ray photograph from the hand of the Fleet Admiraal and handed it to me. He then pointed with a pencil to a bright spot and said; "There Admiraal, you see a very small metal fragment embedded in the shoulder blade. It has become infected, hence your slight fever. Again with the pencil, there is also a dark mass here beside the infection that could be a cyst or something more serious. It should be explored at once and removed." I asked, "Is it possible to do the operation aboard ship, as I don't want to be off her as we prepare for the upcoming operation." To which he replied, "Yes I can do the surgery here, but if the mass is not a cyst, you would need a biopsy, and possibly a specialist. I am essentially a trauma surgeon, not a disease specialist. Sometimes cutting into diseased tissues causes the effects of certain maladies to spread very rapidly. In that event I would not want to transport a delicate post-surgery case by air. So I am recommending that you fly to Darwin, Australia and admit yourself to the Royal Darwin Hospital. It is the oldest and finest within the region and is recognized as the best disease treatment center in the country. I have radioed The Royal Darwin's Chief of Surgery; Dr. Devon Fitzgerald, I know him well. You would receive the finest of care, and may rest without the worry of duty. Dr. Fitzgerald's reply was that they have a bed already waiting for you. Here is a bottle of penicillin pills, take one every four hours for the next week."

Feeling a bit stunned and quite *boxed in* by this unexpected turn of events, I turned to appeal to the Fleet Admiraal. But preempting me he said; "Maarten, it is for the best, you need leave to recover. I want you back here as soon as possible as our attack on the Japanese airfield construction sites on New Guinea may commence within a month. Your experience is indispensable to me. Also I have learned that Karen and your family are safe in Darwin, and I have sent them a message telling of you imminent arrival. Think of it Maarten, Christmas with your family! Your steward is at present packing up your personal kit. In one hour you will be boarding a Grumman Duck for a flight to Darwin.

You will be escorted by two Brewster F2F fighters currently on their way to us from Naval Air Station Makassar as we speak."

"In the event that you will be unable to rejoin the ship, who of your present command do you recommend as your replacement?" To which I replied, "all of the officers that have served under me for these last years have given excellent service, but my replacement should be my deputy commander, Schout-bij-Nacht (Rear Admiraal): Konrad van Speijk-Bronckhorst, as he is next in line." Very well Vice Admiraal", the Fleet Admiraal replied. He then without further exchange of words retrieved the medical file from the hand of the Chief of Surgery and stuffed them into a larger brown envelope which he sealed and handed to me. "These are your orders, leave papers and medical records. That is all Vice Admiraal, you are dismissed."

Then Adriaan Van de Velde; stepped out from behind his desk, and came forward to shake my hand warmly, saying, "Good luck to you Maarten get well, take the opportunity to rest up, we need you." I replied: "Fleet Admiraal Van de Velde, three years ago I took command of a *Battlecruiser-carrier Division*, an unproven hybrid combination of big guns and air groups. I present it to you today, a powerful, efficient and proven weapon. You may have complete confidence in the soundness of the ships, the flexibility of their combined arms and the professionalism of the men." I then saluted and left the day cabin. My posting as Commander of the Battlecruiser-carrier Squadron, the most sought after command in the RNLN had come to an end.

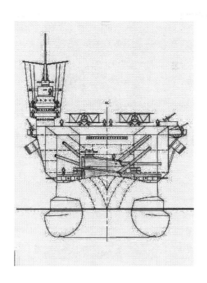

CHAPTER XXVIII

DARWIN HOSPITAL, FLEET CONCENTRATION, USS LANGELY SUNK, USN RIGID AIRSHIPS DELIVER FIFTY P-40 WARHAWKS TO MINDANAO, TASK FORCE LINEBACKER ATTACKS THE JAPANESE BASES ON NEW GUINEA, AFTERMATH.

I left the Fleet Admiraal's Day Cabin, and made my way forward to return to my quarters. My steward was waiting with all my gear packed except my personal items. These he had left for me. I asked him to fetch a glass of water, while I seated myself at my desk. I opened the small tin of antibiotics, selected one small white tablet, and washed it down with one mouthful. How much time would pass, I speculated before I would once again occupy this cabin? I was feeling a bit hard done by I suppose, but there is no room for personal sentiments in military service, especially in times of war. All command thought and action must be based on clear ice cold logic.

I gathered up my family photographs from the top of my desk, removed the personal letters and writing material from its drawer along with my silver fountain pen, and bottle of ink, my rings, extra watch, silver cigar and cigarette cases, compass etc. Then packed these away in my leather valise along with my personal set of binoculars. Looking around the room, it was now entirely devoid of my presence. "My God", I thought, "I love this duty and this ship!" Turning to my steward I said, "I have enjoyed serving with you Benjamin, you will be staying aboard to attend the next occupant of this cabin, please have my belongings transported to the Flying boat, I will be along in a few minutes." There was still some fresh coffee in the cistern, so I poured half a cup, and then removed a new tin of *Panter* cigarettes from my tunic, broke the seal with my thumbnail and lit one up. I had been negligent in ignoring the ache in my shoulder I suppose, there was no use in hiding the sling any longer. I fished it out of my tunic pocket and eased in my right arm. Well, I thought; that's it then, I slapped the desk with my open palm, stood up and stubbed out the butt of the *Panter* in the brass ash tray. I made my way down to the main deck where an escort of my senior officers, I discovered were awaiting my arrival.

Mark Klimaszewski

These men accompanied me to the ship's side. They formed up on either side of the passageway leading to the gangway, ship's operations to forward, staff officers aft and I passed between them to leave the Vlaggeschip. The last in the line, her Kapitein Daniel Voorne carefully handed to me my Vice Admiraal's Pennant, now neatly folded into a triangular pattern with the three stars up. He then stepped back in line, and saluted. I walked to the deck edge, turned aft to salute the jackstaff of the *Cornelis de Witt,* and then looked back to my escort to return their salutes which they had been holding. I addressed my officers with a full heart, "Gentlemen, of my staff and operations; I hope to return to my duties here within three weeks, if however, that is not meant to be then I thank you for your service. It has been an honor to serve with you, I wish you all a safe and Happy Christmas." I turned about, and stepped off the deck, to proceed down the gangway.

I fought to keep my thoughts clear, and forward looking. I would soon enjoy the company of my family for Christmas, who were all safe thank God! In this I was a very lucky man, for many had already lost loved ones. These rationalizations did not dispel the feeling of great emptiness that now engulfed me. The door to the Grumman Duck floatplane stood open, looking ever so much as a coffin waiting for me to enter. I turned for one more look back to see my great ship, and then entered the aircraft compartment. The pilot closed the door with a muffled thump and I settled in for the flight. I calculated that the shoulder operation would require at least three weeks to knit, and I might just make it back to my *mistress* before *the New Guinea Operation* kicked off. However, I did not realize it at the time, but my love affair with that *Seductive Lady* was over. I would neither trod her decks at a future time, nor would I ever see her again. Eighty three months ago, this great ship and her sister were reborn as I drew my first tentative line on a piece of paper while sitting at my drafting table, and now the relationship was at an end.

The Grumman Duck pointed her nose toward the collapsed section of the cone that provided the exit from the hidden bay and gunned her big radial engine. The trim little craft accelerated across the smooth waters without any delay. Through the sidelight in the door I could see the spray streaming past. Then all became quiet, just the steady droning of the engine and the creaking of the Duck's wings as they took the weight of the plane. The aircraft rose into a clear sunny day, and before we even reached cruising altitude our Brewster Buffalo fighter escort had joined us. The flight across the Timor Sea was uneventful and the Duck touched down three hours later in the waters off East Point, just a half mile off the water front of the city of Darwin.

My shoulder was scheduled for operation within a few days after my arrival at the Royal Darwin Hospital. However, the proceedure was delayed until the penicillin had destroyed the infection, therefore I entered surgery somewhat later on January 5, 1942. When the metal fragments were removed from the bone, the surgeons decided to explore the wound to discover the sources of several other spots on their X-Ray photographs. They soon discovered some unusual masses on the scapula other than what a surgeon would expect as the results of an infection. The doctor took a number of biopsies and the wound was then closed. The uncertainty and wait for results of the biopsies, resulted in a longer convalescence than I had expected. The navy would not allow my return to duty without a 100% clean bill of health. As a consequence of this, I did not return to the *Cornelis de Witte.* She and her sister sortied to begin the operation against the Japanese shipping and construction facilities on western New Guinea without me.

342

The USN Rigid Airship Squadron No. 1, had successfully delivered its P-40 Warhawk fighters to Mindanao. The Airships approached to within fifty miles of Davao Army Airfield at night. The fighter pilots then descended into their machines and started their engines. When these were sufficiently warmed up, beginning from the front of the airship, each pilot pulled the release lever above his head on the airship's fighter bracket and the planes dropped gracefully away. As the last P-40 disengaged the great Rigid Airships came about and set course for San Francisco and open up the throttles to achieve full speed 180 kph. and put some distance between them and the Japanese dominated airspace.

The P-40 fighter pilots had received their position and bearing information from the airship before detaching, and the eighty kilometers to the airfield was accomplished in fifteen minutes time just as dawn appeared on the eastern horizon. They immediately spotted a JAAF Bomber Regiment, a few kilometers off, flying at 1000 meters altitude, which was preparing to bomb Davao airfield. The P-40's formed up fifty machines strong and tore into the Japanese formation, causing them to drop their bombs and flee for their lives. The excited Warhawk pilots, who were itching to tackle the enemy, could not believe their good luck having flown right into combat, to decimate an enemy bomber regiment less than half an hour after detaching from their airships! The P-40 pilots were surprised when they were challenged by six little obsolete monoplane fighters with fixed undercarriages, and wire stayed wings; the remaining Boeing P-26 *Peashooters* of the Philippine Army Air Corp (PAAC), *7ᵗʰ Pursuit Brigade*. The *Peashooter* pilots waved excitedly to them and guided the newcomers down to the camouflaged airstrip, just as the dawn began to hit the trees of the jungle.

Unfortunately four weeks later, the USS Langley mission met with disaster. She was sunk by Japanese bombers off the south coast of Java, as she attempted to run in and unload her crated up fighters.

Admiraal Van de Velde had kept the battle-carriers at their secret location for several more days until a Grumman Duck delivered to him the minefield charts completed by our submarines, which indicated the clear channels into the Bay of Cenderawasih. By which time the Battle-carriers were ready for sea, and had taken aboard a full load of all consumables; from high octane aviation gasoline to tinned sardines, and more than 1000 tonnes of munitions. Still he waited for the right moment to sortie, to have his aircraft fly aboard, and to coordinate the concentration of Task Force Linebacker. In the meantime the picket submarines of the RNLN kept on performing their invaluable service of monitoring the movements of the Japanese First Air Fleet Battle Group, with the aid of excellent hydrophone equipment during the day, and at night running on the surface with the aid of the *Night Sight Apparatus*. By the time the Japanese Fleet had steamed between New Caledonia and New Zealand, *Task Force Wombat* had already departed Sydney, and was half way to its refueling stop at Perth on the west coast of that Continent.

Thirty six hours following our last submarine sighting; a Short Sunderland long range flying boat on its reconnaissance flight out of New Zealand reported the presence of the Japanese Fleet 400 miles SE of Tasmania, before it was shot down. The Japanese Admiral realizing there was nothing further to be gained by stealth cranked on the speed and made a sweep along the south coast of Australia hoping to catch the warships of the RAN especially their Flagship; the Battlecruiser *HMAS Australia* lingering within the region. Finding few targets he proceeded onward into the Indian Ocean to hunt down and destroy the fledgling British East Asiatic Fleet, and paralyze the shipping in the Bay of Bengal. A ship of the *Catalina Flying Boat Squadron* based in Freemantle reported the departure of Nagumo's Fleet from Australian waters, on a heading west. This information was the *starting-gun* that Fleet Admiraal Van de Velde had been waiting for.

According to the *Joint Command* plan; *Task force Wombat* departed Perth after refueling, and made for the south coast of Java at 20 knots, feeling very exposed with limited land based air cover. Here they were to be first met by the *Schoonveldt,* carrying an expanded air group of 29 Sea Hart Bombers, 14 Hawker Sea Fury Mk II bi-plane fighters, and 14 Brewster F2F fighters, for a total of 57 machines. Escorting the Dutch Battle-carrier were six cruisers and twelve destroyers. This mass of ships now moved eastward.

At the time this event was transpiring, the assigned air groups for the *Cornelis de Witte* and *Johan de Witt* Battle-carriers began shuttling towards their main jumping off airfields at Makassar and Perak. The Fleet Admiraal anticipating the approach of the combined fleets, then sortied from Palalau at dawn. The battle-carriers sailed west at twenty knots and within an hour, their compliments of Helldivers, Sea Eagles, Grumman F2F and F3F fighters began to land aboard. The last to arrive aboard were the Buffalos, what with their great range lingered, providing the air cover. Two extra full strength Brewster Fighter Squadrons 12 and 14, (14 machines ea.) newly formed from the reserve machines and concentrated at Makassar Naval Air Station, came aboard. In total ninety aircraft landed aboard each battle-carrier, that morning!

By this date *Task Force Stonewall* had managed to sail safely into the Java Sea where it undertook the patrol of the region east Java Sea to the waters of the western Flores Sea under the protection of the Naval and Army fighters based at Makassar and Kendari on the island of Celebes and those at Perak Airfield. In preparation for the New Guinea Operation, these ships now passed through Lombok Strait at night and rendezvoused on the morning of January 03, 1942 with the now fully equipped battle-carriers of Fleet Admiaraal Adriaan Van de Velde. He then moved his combined fleet west until he effected the rendezvous with the *Schoonveldt* and *HMS Australia* group, which was achieved at 16:30hrs. *Task Force Linebacker,* was now successfully concentrated. The four Capital Ships having between them; 124 Fighters and 113 Bombers on three flight decks, 20 – 343 mm guns, 6 -305 mm guns, and 28 – 152 mm guns. The escorts contributed some 12 – 203 mm guns, 172 pieces of medium artillery ranging from 120 to 152 mm. The forty ships of Linebacker carried more than 255 Flak guns varying from the heaviest; 7 – 127 mm, to 17 – 76 mm, and 230 – 40 mm bofors guns. There were many other smaller caliber AA weapons as well, but the Bofors guns alone could throw up 27,600 explosive cannon shells per minute! There had never been such an Armada in Dutch East Indies waters at a time of war, it was indeed a formidable concentration of power, for any navy.

The operation against the Japanese presence on the Dutch half of the Island of New Guinea was correctly coordinated with the USN Carrier strike against Rabaul, and launched on the morning of January 05, 1942. It did not go as cleanly as planned however, as the crafty enemy and their mighty fleet had prepared the defenses of their facilities on New Guinea more carefully than we had imagined. A nasty surprise was the intervention of an IJN heavy shore bombardment squadron composed of four modernized semi-dreadnoughts, which precipitated a close range surface battle. Our move against the

Japanese installations on New Guinea had been anticipated, but the strength of our attack had been underestimated.

The Airstrikes went off as planned, and our dive bombers succeeded in inflicting tremendous damage on the Japanese shipping. Three hours later Task Force Linebacker, smashed its way through the Japanese screening vessels and flooded into the bay. The destroyers and cruisers had a field day racing through the concentrations of fleeing vessels torpedoing and shelling the enemy at will. The heavy ships pulverized the airfields and their construction equipment for half an hour reducing the airstrips and buildings to a lunar landscape, and any object larger than an oil drum to atoms. Then the Fleet Admiraal formed up his ships and withdrew in good order.

It was during the afternoon of January 5th, when *Task Force Linebacker* was withdrawing towards Sela Dampier Strait at the western tip of New Guinea that the crisis developed. The Japanese had only a few days earlier concentrated a fleet of four modernized semi-dreadnoughts in the small Kepa Island Atoll, laying some 50 miles to the north of the Bay of Cenderawasih. These *Satsuma Class* shore bombardment vessels due to their slow speed had been deployed forward for the upcoming operations against the east coast of Australia, primarily the bombardment of Sydney Harbour. These ships had lain for 36 hours under excellent camouflage, rafted together within the lagoon, and as a consequence had been misidentified by our reconnaissance aircraft as an island. Upon receiving the alarm from the Japanese picket vessels screening the path through the minefields, guarding the Bay of Cenderawasih, these modernized battleships had raised steam and sortied to intervene.

These four old *Satsuma Class* semi-dreadnoughts had been upgraded by the Japanese to carry out shore bombardment duties only, and were therefore not fitted with modern fire control instruments that could calculate the range of a swiftly moving target, from a moving platform. However, if they could get close enough, the combination of their old Barr and Stroud *one meter* stereoscopes, and their massive firepower of 16 – 305 mm and 48- 250 mm heavy guns presented a tremendous threat to the ships of *Task Force Linebacker.*

Our Airmen concentrating so heavily attacking the shipping within the bay only discovered these battleships moving to intercept our fleet some four hours after sunrise, when our first air attacks were launched! Air attacks were prepared, and launched with success but too late to prevent a surface battle. The Japanese bombardment squadron had closed the range dramatically as the Allied Fleet was transiting the constricted waters between the coastline and the enemy minefield, and our ships could not turn away to open the range.

At a critical moment, the destroyers were ordered forward to deliver a torpedo attack with their remaining weapons against the oncoming Japanese battleships, which were already exchanging main battery salvos with the ships of *TF Linebacker.* Kapt. Voorne, related to me the end of *Task Force Stonewall;*

"The old light cruiser USS Dixie CL-14 swept bravely up our starboard side, with two gigantic Stars and Stripes Battle Flags streaming from her fore and main masts. I held my breath as she loosed off a full salvo! With the tune; Bonnie Blue Flag blaring from her loudspeakers she led her nine 'old four pipers' against the armored might of the Japanese Battle squadron. Those hulking gray monsters could now clearly be seen approaching with unaided vision through the intermittent

breaks in the smokescreen at a range of 17,000 meters, their dark sides alive with the flashes of gunfire. As the antiquated American warships; with all their little guns popping away furiously, began to vanish one by one into the smoke, I saw them raise up to their main masthead the old Confederate Naval Ensign! A lump came to my throat for I knew the fearless reputation of their crews, and that I was looking at these brave little ships for the last time!"

The destroyer attack was launched well within the range of the massive secondary batteries of the Japanese fire-support battleships, so when the little destroyers sped clear of our smokescreen they faced a murderous fire. Having expended most of their torpedoes against the Japanese freighters and naval auxiliaries, the destroyers commanders chose to close to a range where they could not miss with the few torpedoes that they had remaining between them. Those ships of *Desron 5* without torpedoes chose to remain with their sisters to absorb some of the enemy fire, and consequently suffered heavy casualties for their bravery. Nevertheless, the resolute charge of these antiquated American warships caused the enemy battleships to turn away, which allowed *Task Force Linebacker* to sail clear of the narrow channel through the minefield, and gain the *sea room* that it needed to fight the enemy, and its eventual withdrawal to the safety of the Java Sea!

It was during this phase that the Fleet Admiraal was killed. Kapt. Voorne who was with him inside the aviation deckhouse at the time related to me what transpired. *"An unidentified squadron of Japanese bombers appeared and began to attack the ships of TF Linebacker. The Fleet Admiraal, who was of the old school, shunned the enclosed battle bridge and its armor, and instead preferred to command the battle from atop the deckhouse. The old warrior's blood was up, and he had become rather fierce. A clutch of bombs slammed into the armored deck and deckhouse, there was a great shock, and I was thrown off my feet. The next thing I knew, I was being shaken by my shoulder. The Fleet Admiraal was standing over me as I was laying on the deck, my thoughts still addled. I got to my feet and steadied myself. The Admiraal said; "Kapitein are you wounded?" I replied that I did not think so. He continued, "That is good, now call for a medical aide and a damage control team to clean up this mess!" I noticed that the front of the Admiraal's white cotton tunic was blackened, torn and stained with blood and that the hose of his Gas mask had been severed and was hanging below his groin. I said to him; you are wounded Admiraal, to which he replied, yes I know but not seriously, now let us get back to commanding the battle. Just then; there came a very loud hissing whistle, like a kettle of water boiling on a stove and a distinctive but muted buzzing. There behind a fallen steel beam we spotted rolling around on the deck, to the gyrations of the ship, an undetonated 250 kilogram bomb that was furiously expelling picric acid foam through a crack in its casing. We both instantly realized the threat of its imminent detonation. Shoving me towards the door onto the flight deck the old Admiraal, stepped over the twisted steel beam, stooped and grasped the heavy object in his great arms, then hoisted it to his chest, with apparent difficulty and pain. The Fleet Admiraal straightened to his full height, took a deep breath and paused for a moment as if in somber reflection, he turned to me, his face as white as wax and said through his gritted teeth; "See to your ship Kapitein, she needs you!" He then pushed powerfully off the torn steel deck edge and through the gaping hole in the outboard side of the deckhouse to topple twenty three meters into the sea! I was shocked at this, but soon came to realize that the Fleet Admiraal had in fact been mortally wounded, as neither of us had been carrying a gas mask. The old sailor gallantly, and without hesitation, performed his last service to the ship! I returned to the fight, with a renewed fury, and a deep desire for vengeance!"*

At approximately the same time that these events were transpiring, I was abed in the *Post Operation Ward* of the Royal Darwin Hospital recovering from my surgery. While still unconscious, I was experiencing a vivid dream; I was at sea, aboard the *Cornelis de Witt*, and she was engaged in a heavy action. I had been blown off the ship into the sea. Fighting my way to its surface I touched a floating object and dragged myself into what appeared to be a native canoe of sorts. The sounds of battle receded, as I watched my great Vlaggeschip, her flight deck afire, vanish into the gloom of the evening, with all her heavy guns flashing regularly. Then with the coming of the full moon I believed that I saw the pale faces of thousands of men swimming back towards me from the direction in which my ship had vanished! I called out to them as they silently drew near, but there was no reply on the freshening breeze. A number of these pale objects now pressed up against the bulwark of the canoe and I reached over, drawing one from the ink black waters. The object proved to be a wide brimmed sailor's straw sun hat, of the type used by all our enlisted men. Squinting in the moonlight I read the name on the hat band; *Cornelis de Witt*! There were thousands of these hats sailing lightly across the waves propelled by the breeze, hurrying away from the resting places of their wearers! I screamed aloud at the horrific implication; the great ship had gone down with her thousands of men! At that moment; I awoke from my medicated sleep, with a terrible feeling of dread that my beloved ships were in danger.

I recovered from my wounds, and discharged from Darwin Hospital on January 26, 1942. I was assigned to a staff position in the newly established Joint Allied Command Headquarters in Sydney. The strategic situation in South East Asia had reached a critical point. Japanese military pressure was heavy and unrelenting. Malaya was now mostly occupied, with the fall of Singapore imminent. The Dutch Military Commanders realized that the East Indies Colony may soon be lost, and that the colonists, Government personnel and Military Command must relocate to Australia.

Admiraal Nagumo's powerful Aircraft Carrier and Fast Battleship fleet did not locate the main force of the Royal Navy in the Indian Ocean as planned, although it did manage to discover and sink the light carrier *HMS Hermes*, and the heavy cruisers; *HMS Cornwall* and *HMS Dorsetshire*. Thereafter it hurriedly returned to the Pacific, following the news of General Doolittle's bombing of the Japanese mainland on April 17, 1942. Admiral Somerville's Asiatic Fleet, was unable to close the enemy for a night air attack utilizing its radar equipped torpedo planes. The air groups of his three aircraft carriers were less than one third of that of the six fleet carriers of his opposite number Admiral Nagumo, and therefore he had to withdraw before such a superior fleet.

Japanese troops completed the conquest of the Malaysian Peninsula, then Singapore was put under siege. The city fell on February 15, 1942, General Percival and 90,000 soldiers went into the sack, inflicting upon the British Army, what many consider to be, the greatest military defeat of its long history. Manila likewise was invested by the Japanese army and fell, and the remainder of the Philippines was soon after completely occupied. The US Army was pushed off the Bataan Peninsula and squeezed onto the fortified island of Corregidor. Here they held on grimly, subjected to continual air and artillery bombardment, finally succumbing on May 06, 1942. After a long siege, General Wainwright and a garrison of more than 12,000 went into captivity. The Japanese continued their victorious expansion throughout South East Asia, to eventually threaten

India, and isolate Australia. Their progress was checked by the key naval battle of the Coral Sea in May 1942 and then a few weeks later the mighty Rengo Kantai was heavily defeated at the naval battle of Midway. Finally, the wave of Japanese victories ended in the Solomon Island chain at a place of death called Guadalcanal.

The New Guinea Operation was sound, but contained within it a seed of miscalculation. The naval bombardment inflicted upon the enemy airfields and facilities a great deal of damage. The destroyers and cruisers attacking the shipping within the bay sank sixty-two naval auxiliaries, dredges, crane vessels, and freighters totaling 230,000 tonnes! The picket and support vessels of the Imperial Japanese Navy also lost a light cruiser, six destroyers, and four modernized semi-dreadnoughts. Eighteen bombers, and twelve fighter aircraft of the JAAF were also shot down. *Task Force Linebacker* did not get away without suffering; two battle-carriers damaged by bombs and shellfire, two light cruisers, three destroyers and one submarine sunk due to gunfire, torpedo or mine, 18 aircraft lost. Most of our sailors were recovered from their stricken ships, but the price in men was high, including our most senior Admiraal.

The Japanese Combined Arms Operations against the Dutch East Indies, was so powerful and well-coordinated that they were not appreciably checked by the set back at New Guinea. Nevertheless the destruction of the unfinished airfields simplified the air defense of the Dutch East Indies and bought us some time - two months perhaps, which was much less than the six months that we had hoped for. Despite all our preparations, planning, and sacrifice we were defeated.

When the Dutch East Indies fell in March 1942, the effect of *Linebacker's* attack on the Japanese construction sites in New Guinea was downgraded, and for two years assumed to be a strategic failure. But it was still viewed as an important tactical victory for the destruction of what was estimated as fully half of the enemy's seaborne construction capability. However, by the end of 1943, it became apparent that *Linebacker's* sacrifices had a far reaching effect, and were not in vain. Many of the enemy's airfields planned for Imperial Japan's newly seized territories had still not been completed, due primarily to the destruction of the specialized personnel, pieces of construction equipment and support ships at New Guinea. In that way Linebacker's New Guinea Operation did contribute to the success of the *American Island Hopping Campaign* in 1944-45.

The story of the Battlecruiser-carrier Fleet of the Royal Netherlands Navy does not end here. They remained in action, where their combination of big guns and air-groups continued to frustrate the enemy. However, as I was neither present with *Task Force Linebacker* during the New Guinea Operation, nor for any of their future activities; it is not my place to record a further, detailed history. I feel that it is up to an officer from one of the battle-carriers that continued to *soldier on*, who must relate those events.

THAT IS ALL

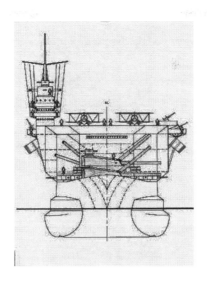

APPENDIX: A

ORDER OF BATTLE: RNLN 1ST BATTLE-CARRIER DIVISION - DEC. 08, 1941

TASK FORCE POPEYE

Battlecruiser-carriers – Two: Cornelis de Witt Class

Cornelis de Witt - Battlecruiser-carrier, Task Force, Division Vlaggeschip.

- Length: 245 meters, Beam at W.L.: 32 meters, Draft: 8.5 meters
- Flight Deck: 189 x 35 meters, Displacement: 38,000 tonnes standard
- Armour Plate Max: 230 mm at W.L., Main Gun Turrets: faces; 250 mm sides 200 mm, tops 200 mm, Barbettes; 230 mm. Secondary Battery; 100 mm, Main Deck: 100mm, Gunnery Citadel; 200 mm, Air Command Center: Vertical 50 mm, Deck: 50 mm. Torpedo Blister; 35 mm shell armor.
- Torpedo Protection: 200 mm W.L. armor, 3 internal longitudinal 30 mm armor bulkheads P&S, Pugilese Crushing Cylinders, Ferranti Triple Bottom, and Admiralty Type 2 Hull Blisters: subdivided and cellulose packed.
- Boilers: 30; Oil Fired, Admiralty-Yarrow, w/ Superheater; Power 94,000 KW;
- Machinery: Curtis–Brown geared turbines, 4 – Shafts.
- Range 11,000 nm at 15 knots, Maximum Speed: 30 Knots.
- Aircraft: 21 fighters (+ 14 at war)*, 42 dive bombers.
- Main Kanon: Armstrong Whitworth; MK V, BL; six – 343 mm, range 30,000 meters.
- Secondary Kanon: Elswick Ordnance, ten – 104 mm, range 11,000 meters.
- Anti-aircraft Kanon: Bofors; forty four - 40 mm automatic, range 7,000 meters.
- Anti-aircraft Kanon: Oerlikon; ten – 20 mm, automatic, range 3,000 meters.
- Heavy Machinegun GP: Breda; ten – 12.7 mm.
- Machinegun GP: Browning; ten - .30 cal water cooled.

- Anti-torpedo Batterie: Stokes/Brandt; eighteen – 81 mm mortars.
- Crew: 190 officers and 2037 men.

* Stored on flight deck under canvas.

Most Senior Line and Corps Officers:

Vice Admiraal (Vice Admiral): Maarten Danielszoon Sweers – Fleet Commander
Commanduer (Commodore): Derik Van Klaffens – Chief of Staff
Kapitein – Lt. ter Zee (Commander): Kurt Rupplin – Assistant Chief of Staff
Kapitein – ter Zee (Captain): Daniel Voorne – Ship's Captain
Kapitein – Lt. ter Zee (Commander): Linus de Kroon – Ship's Executive Officer
Hoof Officier Vlieger (Commander Flier): Konrad Van Braekel – ("Air Ops") Fleet Air Operations Senior Officer.
Kapitein – Lt. ter Zee (Commander): Tieler Van Ripper – Gunnery Officer
Brigade – Generaal (Commodore): Joost Wittgenstein – Commander of Marines
Hoof Officier van den Marine-Stoomvaartdienst 1e Klasse, (Chief Engineer); Jap Anten.
Hoof Officier van den Marine-Stoomvaartdienst 2e Klasse, (Fire Fighting Officer): Ernst Schaupp.
Brigade – Generaal (Commodore): Peiter Berleburg – Chief Medical Officer.
Brigade – Generaal (Commodore): Jacob Bankert – Chief of Chaplains.

Johan de Witt - *Battlecruiser*-carrier, Task Force Secondary Vlaggeschip

- Length: 245 meters, Beam at W.L. : 32 meters, Draft 9.5 meters
- Flight Deck: 189 x 35 meters, Displacement: 38,000 tonnes,
- Armour Plate Max: 230 mm at W.L., Main Gun Turrets: faces 250 mm, sides 200mm, tops 200mm, Barbetts 230 mm, Secondary Battery 100 mm, Deck: 100mm, Gunnery Citadel; 200 mm, Air Command Center 50 mm, Deck: 50 mm, Torpedo Blisters: 35 mm shell armor.
- Torpedo protection: 200 mm. W.L. armor belt, 3 internal longitudinal 30 mm armor bulkheads P&S, Pugilese Crushing Cylinders, Ferranti Triple Bottom, and Admiralty Type 2 Hull Blisters, subdivided, cellulose packed.
- Boilers; 30 – oil fired, Admiralty-Yarrow, w/superheater; Power 94,000 KW,
- Machinery: Curtis Brown Geared Turbines; 4 – Shafts,
- Range 11,000 nm at 15 knots, Maximum Speed: 30 Knots.
- Aircraft: 21 fighters*, (+ 14 at war)* + 42 dive bombers.
- Main Kanon: Armstrong Whitworth, MK V, BL; six – 343 mm, range 30,000 meters.
- Secondary Kanon: Elswick Ordnance, MK II, BL, ten – 104 mm, range 11,000 meters.
- Anti-aircraft Kanon: Boffors; forty four - 40 mm, automatic, range 7,000 meters.
- Anti-aircraft Kanon: Oerlikon; ten – 20 mm; automatic, range 3000 meters.
- Heavy Machinegun GP: Breda; ten – 12.7 mm.
- Machingun GP: Browning; ten -.30 cal water cooled machine guns.

- Anti-torpedo Batterie: Stokes/Brandt; eighteen – 81 mm mortars.
- Crew: 170 officers, 2017 men.

* Stored on flight deck under canvas.

Most Senior Line and Corps Officers:

Schout - bij –Nacht (Rear Admiral): Konrad van Speijk-Bronckhorst Task Force Deputy Commander.
Kapitein – ter Zee (Captain): Pieter Verbeck – Chief of Staff
Kapitein – ter Zee (Captain): Abraham Van der Hulst – Ship's Captain
Kapitein – Lt. ter Zee (Commander): Arnold Mussert – Ship's Executive Officer
Hoof Officier Vlieger (Commander Flier): Wolraven Van Hall– Chief Air Operations Officer.
Kapitein – Lt. ter Zee (Commander): Wiliam Visser t' hoofer – Gunnery Officer
Kapitein – ter Zee (Captain): Pieter Oosterveer – Commander of Marines
Hoof Officier van den Marine-Stoomvaartdienst 1e Klasse, – (Chief Engineer): Anton Seyffard's
Hoof Officier van den Marine-Stoomvaartdienst 2e Klasse, (Fire Fighting Officer): - (Fire Fighting Officer): Michael Tschritter
Brigade – Generaal (Commodore): Dr. Antony Versteegen – Chief Medical Officer
Brigade – Generaal (Commodore): Rudolf Solms - Coburg – Chief of Chaplains

Light Cruisers – Four: De Ruyter Class

Schout - bij –Nacht (Rear Admiral): Count Manfred Van Sassenheim-Heenvliet; Cruiser Squadron Commander, attached to 1st Battle-carrier Fleet.

Gouden Leeuw - Cruiser Squadron Vlaggeschip, Vlaggeschip Cruiser Division No. 3, attached to Cornelis de Witt.

- Length: 173 meters, Beam at W.L.: 15.6 meters, Draft 5.8 meters.
- Displacement: 7,800 tonnes.
- Armour Plate Max: 76 mm W.L. belt, Turret faces: 100 mm, sides 70 mm, tops 70 mm, Main Deck: 35 mm.
- Boilers: 6 – oil fired, Yarrow: Power; 49,000 KW.
- Machinery: Parsons all geared turbines 2 – shafts.
- Range 4,500 nm at 15 knots, Maximum Speed: 32 Knots.
- Aircraft: two – Fokker reconnaissance.
- Kanon: Krupp; seven – 150 mm, range 22,000 meters.
- Anti-aircraft kanon: Boffors; ten - 40 mm, range 7,000 meters, automatic.
- Heavy machinegun GP: Breda; six – 12.7 mm.
- Machinegun GP; Browning; ten - .30 cal water cooled machine guns.
- Crew: 40 officers, 415 men.

Commanduer (Commodore): Pieter Wolfert Van Meresteyn – Cruiser Division No. 3
   Commander.
Kapitein – Lt. ter Zee (Commander): Pieter Sieppert – Chief of Staff
Kapitein – ter Zee (Captain): Maarten Van Leeuwen – Ship's Captain
Kapitein – Lt. ter Zee (Commander): Adolf Dierker– Ship's Executive Officer

Aemilia - Cruiser Division No. 3, attached to Cornelis de Witt.

- Length: 171 meters, Beam at W.L. : 15.6 meters, Draft 5.8 meters
- Displacement: 7,500 tonnes.
- Armour Plate Max: 76 mm belt, Gun Turrets: 100 mm faces, 70 mm sides, tops 70 mm, Deck: 35 mm.
- Boilers: 6 – oil fired Yarrow: Power: 49,000 KW.
- Machinery: Parsons all geared turbines 2 – Shafts.
- Range 4,500 nmi at 15 knots, Maximum Speed: 32knots.
- Aircraft: two – Fokker reconnaissance.
- Main kanon: Rhienmetal; seven – 150 mm, range: 22,000 meters.
- Anti-aircraft kanon: Boffors; ten - 40 mm, range 7,000 meters, automatic.
- Heavy machinegun GP: Breda; six – 12.7 mm.
- Machinegun GP: Browning; ten - .30 cal water cooled machine guns.
- Crew: 35 officers, 400 men.

Kapitein – ter Zee (Captain): Rupert Gruninger – Ship's Captain
Kapitein – Lt. ter Zee (Commander): Daniel Van Setters – Executive Officer

Prins te Paard - Vlaggeschip Cruiser Division No. 4 attached to Johan de Witt.

- Length: 171 meters, Beam at W.L. : 15.6 meters, Draft 5.8 meters
- Displacement: 7,500 tonnes,
- Armour Plate Max: 76 mm WL belt, Gun Turrets: 100 mm faces, turret sides 70 mm, tops 70 mm, Deck: 35 mm.
- Boilers 6 – oil fired, Yarrow: 49,000 KW.
- Machinery: Parsons all geared turbines 2 – Shafts.
- Range 4,000 nmi at 15 knots, Maximum Speed: 32 knots.
- Aircraft: two Fokker reconnaissance.
- Kanon: Krupp; seven – 150 mm. with 22,000 meters range.
- Anti-aircraft kanon: Boffors; ten - 40 mm, range 7,000 meters, automatic.
- Heavy machinegun GP: Breda; six – 12.7 mm.
- Machinegun GP: Browning; ten - .30 cal water cooled machine guns.
- Crew: 33 officers, 403 men.

Commanduer (Commodore): Egmond Borsselen – Cruiser Division No. 4 Commander.
Kapitein – ter Zee (Captain): Frank Schoonderbeek – Ship's Captain
Kapitein – Lt. ter Zee (Commander): Bob Zollner – Ship's Executive Officer

Oliphant - Cruiser Division No. 4 attached to Johan de Witt.

- Length: 171 meters, Beam at W.L.: 15.6 meters, Draft 5.8 meters.
- Displacement: 7,500 tonnes, Armour Plate Max: 76 mm belt.
- Turrets: 100 mm faces, 70 mm sides, Deck: 35 mm.
- Boilers 16 Babcock–Wilcox: 39,000 KW. Machinery: Parsons Geared Turbines 2 – Shafts.
- Range 4,000 nm at 15 knots, Maximum Speed: 32 knots.
- Aircraft: two – Fokker reconnaissance.
- Main kanon: Krupp; seven – 150 mm, with 22,000 meters range
- Anti-aircraft kanon: Boffors; ten - 40 mm, range 7,000 meters, automatic.
- Heavy machinegun GP: Breda; six – 12.7 mm.
- Machinegun GP: Browning; ten - .30 cal water cooled machine guns.
- Crew: 35 officers, 400 men.

Kapitein – ter Zee (Captain): Michael Veermeeren – Ship's Captain
Kapitein – Lt. ter Zee (Commander): Arnold Tjeerdema – Executive Officer

Destroyers – Eight: Zeeland Class

Kapitein – ter Zee (Captain): Derik Van Rossel – Commander Destroyer Squadron No. 3, attached to 1ST battle-carrier Fleet.

Zeeland – *Squadron* Vlaggeschip, Vlaggeschip Destroyer Flotilla No. 10, attached to *Cornelis de Witt*.

- Length: 105 meters, Beam at W.L.: 10.3 meters, Draft 3.5 meters.
- Displacement: 2,200 tonnes.
- Boilers: 4 oil fired -Yarrow; Power; 33,000 KW.
- Machinery: Parsons Turbines; 2 – Shafts.
- Range 3,200 nmi at 15 knots, Maximum Speed: 33 knots.
- Aircraft: one – reconnaissance.
- Kanon: Rheinmetal BL; five – 120 mm, range 14,000 meters.
- Anti-aircraft kanon: Boffors; four - 40 mm, range 7,000 meters, automatic.
- Heavy machinegun GP: Breda; six – 12.7 mm.
- Machinegun GP: Browning; six - .30 cal water cooled.
- Torpedoes: eight – 530 mm tubes.
- Mines: twenty four; charge – 200 Kilogram AMATOL.
- Crew: 18 officers, 136 men.

Kapitein – Lt. ter Zee (Commander): Frans Kuysterman - Ship's Captain
Lt. ter Zee 1e Klasse (Lt. Commander): Ed Loonskin - Ship's Executive Officer

Gelderland - Destroyer Flotilla No. 10.

- Length: 105 meters, Beam at W.L. : 10.3 meters, Draft 3.5 meters
- Displacement: 2,200 tonnes.
- Aircraft: one - reconnaissance.
- Boilers: 4 oil fired -Yarrow; Power; 33,000 KW.
- Machinery: Parsons Turbines; 2 – Shafts.
- Range 3,200 nmi at 15 knots, Maximum Speed: 33 knots
- Kanon: Rheinmetal BL; five – 120 mm, with 14,000 meters range.
- Anti-aircraft kanon: Boffors; four - 40 mm, range 7,000 meters, automatic.
- Heavy machinegun GP: Breda; six – 12.7 mm.
- Machinegun GP: Browning; six - .30 cal water cooled.
- Torpedoes: eight – 530 mm. Tubes.
- Mines: twenty four, charge - 200 kilograms of AMATOL.
- Crew: 15 officers, 133 men.

Kapitein – Lt. ter Zee (Commander): Deneys Zanbeek - Ship's Captain
Lt. ter Zee 1e Klasse (Lt. Commander): Tieler Vanooyen - Executive Officer

Jakhals - Destroyer Flotilla No. 10.

- Length: 105 meters, Beam at W.L. : 10.3 meters, Draft 3.5 meters
- Displacement: 2,200 tonnes.
- Boilers: 4 oil fired -Yarrow; Power; 33,000 KW.
- Machinery: Parsons Turbines; 2 – Shafts.
- Range 3,200 nmi at 15 knots, Maximum Speed: 33 knots
- Aircraft: one - reconnaissance.
- Kanon: Rheinmetal BL; five – 120 mm. with 14,000 meters range.
- Anti-aircraft kanon: Boffors; four - 40 mm, range 7,000 meters, automatic.
- Heavy machinegun GP: Breda; six – 12.7 mm.
- Machinegun GP: Browning; six - .30 cal water cooled.
- Torpedoes: eight – 530 mm Tubes.
- Mines: twenty four; charge - 200 Kilograms AMATOL.
- Crew: 15 officers, 133 men.

Kapitein – Lt. ter Zee (Commander): Frederik De Leenheer - Ship's Captain
Lt. ter Zee 1e Klasse (Lt. Commander): Lothar Neubauer - Executive Officer

Bulhond - Destroyer Flotilla No. 10.

- Length: 105 meters, Beam at W.L. : 10.3 meters, Draft 3.5 meters
- Displacement: 2,200 tonnes.
- Boilers: 4 oil fired -Yarrow; Power; 33,000 KW.
- Machinery: Parsons Turbines; 2 – Shafts.
- Range 3,200 nmi at 15 knots, Maximum Speed: 32 knots

- Aircraft: one - reconnaissance.
- Main kanon: Rheinmetal BL; five – 120 mm, with 14,000 meters range.
- Anti-aircraft kanon: Boffors; four - 40 mm, range 7,000 meters, automatic.
- Heavy machinegun GP: Breda; six – 12.7 mm.
- Machinegun GP: Browning; six - .30 cal water cooled.
- Torpedoes: eight – 530 mm. Tubes.
- Mines: twenty four, charge - 200 kilograms TNT.
- Crew: 15 officers, 133 men.

Kapitein – Lt. ter Zee (Commander): Isaak Meulenbroek - Ship's Captain
Lt. ter Zee 1e Klasse (Lt. Commander): Hans Otterdyks - Executive Officer

Eendragt - Vlaggeschip Destroyer Flotilla No. 11, attached to *Johan de Witt*.

- Length: 105 meters, Beam at W.L. : 10.3 meters, Draft 3.5 meters
- Displacement: 2,200 tonnes.
- Boilers: 4 oil fired -Yarrow; Power; 33,000 KW.
- Machinery: Parsons Turbines; 2 – Shafts.
- Range 3,200 nmi at 15 knots, Maximum Speed: 32 knots
- Aircraft: one reconnaissance.
- Main kanon: Rheinmetal BL; five – 120 mm, with 14,000 meters range.
- Anti-aircraft kanon: Boffors; four - 40 mm, range 7,000 meters, automatic.
- Heavy machinegun GP: Breda; six – 12.7 mm.
- Machinegun GP: Browning; six - .30 cal water cooled.
- Torpedoes: eight – 530 mm. Tubes.
- Mines: twenty four; charge – 200 Kilogram TNT.
- Crew: 15 officers, 133 men.

Kapitein – Lt. ter Zee (Commander): Guus Slootweg - Ship's Captain
Lt. ter Zee 1e Klasse (Lt. Commander): Albrecht Fosen - Executive Officer

Zoutmann - Destroyer Flotilla No. 11, attached to *Johan de Witt*.

- Length: 105 meters, Beam at W.L.: 10.3 meters, Draft 3.5 meters
- Displacement: 2,200 tonnes.
- Boilers: four oil fired, Krupp Vulcan; Power - 33,000 KW.
- Machinery. Thornycroft; 2 – Shafts, Speed: 33 Knots.
- Range 3,200 nm at 15 knots, Maximum Speed: 33 knots.
- Aircraft: one - reconnaissance.
- Main kanon: Rheinmetal BL; five – 120 mm. with 14,000 meters range.
- Anti-aircraft kanon: Boffors; four - 40 mm, range 7,000 meters, automatic.
- Heavy machinegun GP: Breda; six – 12.7 mm.
- Machinegun GP: Browning; six - .30 cal water cooled machine guns.
- Torpedoes: eight – 530 mm. Tubes.

- Mines: twenty four; charge – 200 Kilogram TNT
- Crew: 15 officers, 133 men.

Kapitein – Lt. ter Zee (Commander): Dick Skaalrud - Ship's Captain
Lt. ter Zee 1e Klasse (Lt. Commander): Benjamin Krikken - Executive Officer

Piet Heyn - Destroyer Flotilla 11, attached to *Johan de Witt*.

- Length: 105 meters, Beam at W.L.: 10.3 meters, Draft 3.5 meters.
- Displacement: 2,200 tonnes.
- Boilers: four oil fired, Krupp Vulcan; Power - 33,000 KW.
- Machinery. Thornycroft; 2 – Shafts, Speed: 33 Knots.
- Range 3,200 nmi at 15 knots, Maximum Speed: 33 knots.
- Aircraft: 1 reconnaissance.
- Main kanon: Rheinmetal BL; five – 120 mm. with 14,000 meters range.
- Anti-aircraft kanon: four - 40 mm, Boffors; range 7,000 meters, automatic.
- Heavy machinegun GP: Breda; six – 12.7 mm.
- Machinegun GP: Browning; six - .30 cal water cooled.
- Torpedoes: eight – 530 mm. Tubes.
- Mines: twenty four; charge – 200 Kilogram TNT
- Crew: 15 officers, 133 men.

Kapitein – Lt. ter Zee (Commander): Ruud Strieker - Ship's Captain
Lt. ter Zee 1e Klasse (Lt. Commander): Otto Lentz - Executive Officer

Draak - Destroyer Flotilla 11, attached to *Johan de Witt*.

- Length: 105 meters, Beam at W.L.: 10.3 meters, Draft 3.5 meters.
- Displacement: 2,200 tonnes.
- Boilers: four oil fired, Krupp Vulcan; Power - 33,000 KW.
- Machinery. Thornycroft; 2 – Shafts, Speed: 33 Knots.
- Range 3,200 nmi at 15 knots, Maximum Speed: 33 knots.
- Aircraft: 1 reconnaissance.
- Main kanon: Rheinmetal BL; five – 120 mm. with 14,000 meters range.
- Anti-aircraft kanon: Boffors; four - 40 mm, range 7,000 meters, automatic.
- Heavy machinegun GP: Breda; six – 12.7 mm.
- Machinegun GP: Browning; six - .30 cal water cooled.
- Torpedoes: eight – 530 mm. Tubes.
- Mines: twenty four; charge – 200 Kilogram TNT
- Crew : 15 officers, 133 men.

Kapitein – Lt. ter Zee (Commander): Eelke Drebble - Ship's Captain
Lt. ter Zee 1e Klasse (Lt. Commander): Alfred Van Allen - Executive Officer.

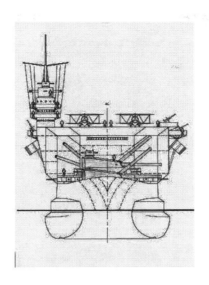

APPENDIX: B

TASK FORCE OLIVE

Battlship Plane Carrier: One - Schoonveldt Class

Schoonveldt – Battle-carrier Task Force Vlaggeschip.

- Length: 207 meters, Beam at W.L. : 32 meters, Draft 9.5 meters
- Flight Deck: 161 x 33 meters, Displacement: 35,000 tonnes,
- Armour Plate Max: 229 mm at W.L., Main Gun Turrets: 230 mm, deck; 60 mm
- Boilers; twenty, oil fired Babcocks Wilcox, superheated, Power: 56,000 KW.
- Machinery: Westinghouse; shaft all geared turbines; 4 – Shafts.
- Range 9,000 nmi at 15 knots, Maximum Speed: 27 Knots.
- Torpedo defense: 200mm waterline armor, 35mm armor internal longitudinal bulkhead P&S, British Admiralty Type 1 Hull Blisters, 30 mm armor, cellulose packed.
- Aircraft: 14 fighters, 23 dive bombers. (+ 6 fighter's war).*
- Kanon: Woolich Arsenal MK XIII; six – 305 mm; range 26,000 meters.
- Kanon: Elswick Ordnance; sixteen – 152 mm, range 17,000 meters.
- Anti-aircraft kanon: Elswick Ordnance; eight – 127 mm, range 12,000 meters.
- Boffors Eighteen – 40 mm, range 7,000 meters, automatic.
- Oerlikon; ten – 20 mm cannon, range 3,000 meters, automatic.
- Heavy Machine gun GP: Breda; ten– 12.7 mm,
- Machine gun GP: Browning; ten– 0.306 cal., water cooled.
- Anti-torpedo Batterie: fourteen; Stokes/Brandt; – 81 mm mortars.
- Crew : 134 officers, 1583 men

* Stored on flight deck under canvas.

Most Senior Line and Corps Officers:

Schout - bij –Nacht (Rear Admiral): Baron Johan Van den Kerckhoven-Polyander – Task
  Force Commander
Kapitein – ter Zee (Captain): Arnold Rommens – Chief of Staff
Kapitein – ter Zee (Captain): Rost Van Otterloo – Ship's Captain
Kapitein – Lt. ter Zee (Commander): Gideon de Vries – Ship's Executive Officer
Hoof Officier Vlieger (Commander Flier): Willem de Valk van Lothringen – Chief Air
  Operations Officer
Kapitein – Lt. ter Zee (Commander): Lothar ter Poorten – Gunnery Officer
Hoof Officier van den Marine-Stoomvaartdienst 1e Klasse – (Chief Engineer): Julius
  Frost
Hoof Officier van den Marine-Stoomvaartdienst 2e Klasse (Damage Control Officer):
  Michael Luedtke

Light Cruisers: Two Tromp Class

Commander (Commodore): Erik van Steekelenburg - Commander of Cruiser Division
  No. 5.

Prins Van Oranje - *Squadron* Vlaggeschip.

- Length: 132 meters, Beam at W.L. : 12.4 meters, Draft 4.6 meters
- Displacement: 4,200 tonnes.
- Armour Vert. Max: 30 mm WL belt, Gun Turrets: 30 mm faces, 17 mm sides, tops
  25 mm, Deck: 25mm
- Boilers: 6 - oil fired, Krupp Vulcan; Power - 43,500 KW.
- Machinery: Parson's geared turbine; 2 – Shafts, Speed: 32 Knots.
- Range 3,200 nmi at 15 knots.
- Aircraft: one - reconnaissance.
- Kanon: Krupp Germania; six – 150 mm. with 22,000 meters range.
- Anti-aircraft kanon: Boffors; eight - 40 mm; automatic, range 7,000 meters.
- Heavy machinegun GP: Breda; six – 12.7 mm.
- Machinegun GP: Browning; six - .30 cal water cooled machine guns.
- Crew: 52 officers, 400 men.

Kapitein – Lt. ter Zee (Commander): Hans Ulriksen – Chief of Staff
Kapitein – ter Zee (Captain): Jacob Van Ostenbrugge – Ship's Captain
Kapitein – Lt. ter Zee (Commander): Klaus Fjaagesund – Executive Officer

Groot Hollandia

- Length: 132 meters, Beam at W.L. : 12.4 meters, Draft 4.6 meters
- Displacement: 4,200 tonnes.

- Armour Vert. Max: 30 mm WL belt, Turrets: 30 mm faces, 17 mm sides, tops 25 mm, Deck: 25 mm.
- Boilers: 6 - oil fired, Krupp Vulcan; Power - 43,500 KW.
- Machinery: Parson's geared turbine; 2 – Shafts, Speed: 32 Knots.
- Aircraft: one - reconnaissance.
- Kanon: Krupp Germania; six – 150 mm. with 22,000 meters range.
- Anti-aircraft kanon: Boffors; eight - 40 mm, automatic, 7,000 meters range.
- Heavy machinegun GP: Breda; six – 12.7 mm.
- Machinegun GP: Browning; six - .30 cal water cooled machine guns.
- Crew: 38 officers, 380 men.

Kapitein – ter Zee (Captain): Maarten Van Kempen – Ship's Captain
Kapitein – Lt. ter Zee (Commander): Dieter Kristianson – Executive Officer

Destroyers: Four Perseus Class

Kapitein – ter Zee (Captain): Albrecht Van Rooyen – Commander Destroyer Flotilla No 15. Attached to *Schoonveldt*

Perseus - Squadron Vlaggeschip

- Length: 105 meters, Beam at W.L.: 10.3 meters, Draft 3.5 meters.
- Displacement: 2,200 tonnes.
- Boilers: 4 - oil fired, Krupp Vulcan; Power - 33,000 KW.
- Machinery: Thornycroft geared turbine; 2 – Shafts.
- Range; 2,500 nmi. at 15 knots, Max. Speed: 36 Knots.
- Aircraft: 1 Fokker reconnaissance.
- Main kanon: Krupp Germania; five – 120 mm. with 14,000 meters range.
- Anti-aircraft kanon: Boffors; four - 40 mm, automatic, 7,000 meters range.
- Heavy machinegun GP: Breda; six – 12.7 mm.
- Machinegun GP: Browning; six - .30 cal water cooled.
- Torpedoes: eight – 530 mm. Tubes.
- Mines: twenty four – 200 Kilogram TNT
- Crew: 15 officers, 233 men.

Kapitein – Lt. ter Zee (Commander): Wiliam Jennissen - Ship's Captain
Lt. ter Zee 1e Klasse (Lt. Commander): Luis Van Arragon - Executive Officer.

Prometheus

- Length: 105 meters, Beam at W.L. : 10.3 meters, Draft 3.5 meters
- Displacement: 2,200 tonnes.
- Boilers: 4 - oil fired, Krupp Vulcan; Power - 33,000 KW.
- Machinery: Thornycroft geared turbine; 2 – Shafts.
- Range; 2,500 nmi. at 15 knots, Max. Speed: 36 Knots.

- Aircraft: 1 reconnaissance.
- Main kanon: Krupp Germania; five – 120 mm. with 14,000 meters range.
- Anti-aircraft kanon: Boffors; four - 40 mm, four – 12.7 mm,
- Heavy machinegun GP: Breda; six – 12.7 mm.
- Machinegun GP: Browning; six - .30 cal water cooled machine guns.
- Torpedoes: eight – 530 mm. Tubes.
- Mines: twenty four – 200 Kilogram TNT
- Crew: 15 officers, 233 men.

Kapitein – Lt. ter Zee (Commander): Derik Krassman - Ship's Captain
Lt. ter Zee 1e Klasse (Lt. Commander): Frederik Osgoode - Executive Officer.

Polyphemus

- Length: 105 meters, Beam at W.L.: 10.3 meters, Draft 3.5 meters.
- Displacement: 2,200 tonnes.
- Boilers: 4 - oil fired, Krupp Vulcan; Power - 33,000 KW.
- Machinery: Thornycroft geared turbine; 2 – Shafts.
- Range; 2,500 nmi. at 15 knots, Max. Speed: 36 Knots.
- Aircraft: 1 Fokker reconnaissance.
- Main kanon: Rheinmetal; five – 120 mm. with 14,000 meters range.
- Anti-aircraft kanon: Boffors; four - 40 mm, four – 12.7 mm.
- Heavy machinegun GP: Breda; six – 12.7 mm.
- Machinegun GP: Browning; six - .30 cal water cooled.
- Torpedoes: eight – 530 mm. Tubes.
- Mines: twenty four – 200 Kilogram TNT
- Crew: 15 officers, 233 men.

Kapitein – Lt. ter Zee (Commander): Stefan Falkenberg - Ship's Captain
Lt. ter Zee 1e Klasse (Lt. Commander): Anton Mossring - Executive Officer.

Argonaut

- Length: 105 meters, Beam at W.L. : 10.3 meters, Draft 3.5 meters
- Displacement: 2,200 tonnes.
- Boilers: 4 - oil fired, Krupp Vulcan; Power - 33,000 KW.
- Machinery: Thornycroft geared turbine; 2 – Shafts.
- Range; 2,500 nmi. at 15 knots, Max. Speed: 36 Knots.
- Aircraft: 1 reconnaissance.
- Main kanon: Rheinmetal; five – 120 mm. with 14,000 meters range.
- Anti-aircraft kanon: four - 40 mm, four – 12.7 mm.
- Heavy machinegun GP: Breda; six – 12.7 mm.
- Machinegun GP: Browning; six - .30 cal water cooled.
- Torpedoes: eight – 530 mm. Tubes.

- Mines: twenty four – 200 Kilogram TNT
- Crew: 15 officers, 233 men.

Kapitein – Lt. ter Zee (Commander): Rost Kohlmann - Ship's Captain
Lt. ter Zee 1e Klasse (Lt. Commander): Linus Mossring - Executive Officer

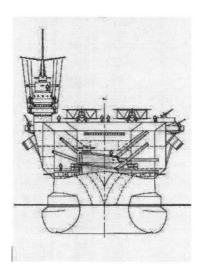

APPENDIX: C

ORDER OF BATTLE: AIR GROUPS AT SEA – DEC. 08, 1941

Our intense war training revealed that ship borne naval air groups may be heavily attrited during a period of intense action. Therefore in order for the fleet to recover its downed airmen and maintain its ability to project power the aircraft and crew losses had to be made good as soon as possible.

Naval aircrews for the RNLN Battle-carriers were espensive to qualify, difficult to replace and our pool of reserves was unfortunately somewhat shallow. Therefore the RNLN sought to devise a method to would rapidly recover airmen who had been shot down or otherwise forced down into the sea due to technical problems and return them to active duty with minimal delay.

Preparations were undertaken to rescue these aircrews from the sea on a large scale. The waters dividing our island colonies had already been provided with a grid like network, by the navy, each with a number and letter combination. The general location of a downed aircraft was usually radioed in by the pilot, from reports of accompanying aircraft or deducible from the aircrafts flight plan.

These regions were patrolled by a variety of radio equipped light high speed boats, or by picket vessels, gun boats and submarines. These; when taken together numbered in the hundreds. All the available second line non – combatant seaplanes such as the Fokker T.1Va and the training squadrons with float equipped Ryan STM-S2 were subsequently pressed into service for pilot rescue.

In addition to the military, many of our island living citizens and businesses were in possession of light float planes. The Civil defense Korp, supported these efforts, and could mobilize thirty or forty machines anywhere from Java to New Guinea given two hour alert.

The rescue floatplane usually had no difficulty spotting the downed pilot as he was equipped with a variety of helpful items not the least of which were his small bright yellow life raft, yellow lifejacket, flare pistol and to discolour a large patch of water at his location and thereby assist the spotting process a yellow dye marker. In action they proved to be very effective with a record of over 70% sea recovery.

The pilots once recovered were flown to the nearest airbase for a medical check. Those who were found fit to return to duty were debriefed, given cigars, schnapps, food and rest. There they waited for return to the battle carrier squadron.

The return flight was usually carried out by versatile PZL – P23 Sea Eagle, which when it had its bombadier belly gondola extended could carry up to four extra men sitting on their parchutes.

We also were fortunate enough to acquire eight of the highly prized Grumman Ducks. These powerful bi-planes equipped with a large central float which incorported robust retractable landing gear and had been designed specifically for the USN to carry passengers from land or water to the deck of an aircraft carrier. So they were perfectly suited for the needs of our Battle cruiser-carriers as well.

All the RNLN duck pilots had been carrier qualified on these machines for this service, and as we could squeeze seven men into these they became invaluable to provide a means to replace our warship's losses and fly out the casualties when at sea. But there were never anough of these.

A normal period of rotation for this process was 36 to 48 hours from the rescue of the downed airman to his delivery aboard the battle-cruiser carrier. An interval that we improved upon after hostilities had commenced.

The details of replacement airplanes for the battle-carriers; their type, aircraft numbers, their commanders and locations on airbases are dealt with in Appendix D.

NAVAL AIR GROUPS ABOARD SHIPS DEC. 08 / 41

Cornelis de Witt Air Groups

Aircraft squadron colours: Yellow, natural Aluminum, red white and blue Horizontal stripes on red rudder.
Air Operations Commander: Hoof Officier Vlieger (Commander Flier): Daniel Van Braekel.
Air Group Commander Fighters: Hoof Officier Vlieger (Commander Flier): Konrad Van Haslen.
Air Group Commander Bombers: Kapitein – Lt. ter Zee Vlieger (Commander): Jakob Van Prooijen.

Fighter Squadron 1

Outfit: 21 – Grumman F2F-1, F3F-1 and F3F-2 Fighters
Squadron Leader: Lt. ter Zee 1e Klasse (Lt. Commander): Rudy Keppler.
The squadron was divided into three seven plane flights.
Aircraft numbers: F - designates fighter, C - first letter of ship's name followed by aircraft number.
Deployment: Bomber Escort, Combat Air Patrol (CAP).

Flight A:

Flight leader: Lt. ter Zee 2e Klasse (Lieutenant): Jacob Van Veelan.
All pilots: Adjudant - Onderoficier – Vlieger (Warrant Officer Flier) or Lt. ter Zee 3e - Klasse (Ensign).
Aircraft Numbers: F1C - 1 to F1C – 7.

Flight B:

Flight Leader; Lt. ter Zee 2e Klasse (Lieutenant): Dag Sandkuist.
All pilots: Adjudant - Onderoficier – Vlieger (Warrant Officer Flier) or Lt. ter Zee 3e - Klasse (Ensign).
Aircraft Numbers: F1C – 8 to F1C – 14.

Flight C:

Flight Leader; Lt. ter Zee 2e Klasse (Lieutenant): Pierre Van Paassen.
All pilots: Adjudant - Onderoficier – Vlieger (Warrant Officer Flier) or Lt. ter Zee 3e - Klasse (Ensign).
Aircraft Numbers: F1C – 15 to F1C – 21.

Fighter Squadron 2

Outfit: 6 – Brewster F2A (Buffalo) Fighters, 7 – Hawker Sea Fury Mk II.
Squadron Leader: Lt. ter Zee 1e Klasse (Lt. Commander): Rudy Keppler.
The squadron was divided into two flights;
Aircraft numbers: F - designates fighter, C - first letter of ship's name, then aircraft number.
Deployment: Fleet (CAP) Combat Air Patrol.

Flight A

Outfit: 6 – Brewster F2A (Buffalo) Fighters.
Flight Leader; Lt. ter Zee 2e Klasse (Lieutenant): Piet Sinke.
All pilots: Adjudant - Onderoficier – Vlieger (Warrant Officer Flier) or Lt. ter Zee 3e - Klasse (Ensign).
Aircraft Numbers: F2C - 1 to F2C – 6.

Flight B

Outfit: 7 – Hawker Sea Fury Mk II.
Flight Leader: Lt. ter Zee 2e Klasse (Lieutenant): Bob Rotering.
All pilots: Adjudant - Onderoficier – Vlieger (Warrant Officer Flier) or Lt. ter Zee 3e - Klasse (Ensign).
Aircraft Numbers: F2C – 7 to F2C – 14.

Bomber Squadron 1

Outfit: 14 Curtiss Model 77 helldivers.
Squadron Leader: Lt. ter Zee 1e Klasse (Lt. Commander): Konrad Van de Groot.

The squadron was divided into two seven plane flights.
Aircraft numbers: B - designates bomber, C - first letter of ship's name, followed by
    aircraft number.
Deployment: Sea and land targets; Bomber Escort.

Flight A

Flight Leader; Lt. ter Zee 2e Klasse (Lieutenant): Ruud Filon.
All pilots: Adjudant - Onderoficier – Vlieger (Warrant Officer Flier) or Lt. ter Zee 3e -
    Klasse (Ensign).
Crew: Vliegtuig Telegrafist Schutter (Air Telegraphist Gunner).
Aircraft Numbers: B1C – 1 to B1C – 7.

Flight B

Flight Leader; Lt. ter Zee 2e Klasse (Lieutenant): Johan Mohrman.
All pilots: Adjudant - Onderoficier – Vlieger (Warrant Officer Flier) or Lt. ter Zee 3e -
    Klasse (Ensign).
Crew: Vliegtuig Telegrafist Schutter (Air Telegraphist Gunner).
Aircraft Numbers: B1C – 7 to B1C – 14.

Bomber Squadron 2

Outfit: 14 Curtiss Model 77 helldivers.
Squadron Leader: Lt. ter Zee 1e Klasse (Lt. Commander): Stefan Kuntz.
The squadron was divided into two seven plane flights.
Aircraft numbers: B - designates bomber, C - first letter of ship's name, followed by
    aircraft number.
Deployment: Sea and land targets; Bomber Escort, CAP.

Flight A

Flight Leader; Lt. ter Zee 2e Klasse (Lieutenant): Eelke Toering
All pilots: Adjudant - Onderoficier – Vlieger (Warrant Officer Flier) or Lt. ter Zee 3e -
    Klasse (Ensign).
Crew: Vliegtuig Telegrafist Schutter (Air Telegraphist Gunner).
Aircraft Numbers: B2C – 1 to B2C – 7.

Flight B

Flight Leader; Lt. ter Zee 2e Klasse (Lieutenant): Michael Van der Lay.

All pilots: Adjudant - Onderoficier – Vlieger (Warrant Officer Flier) or Lt. ter Zee 3e - Klasse (Ensign).
Crew: Vliegtuig Telegrafist Schutter (Air Telegraphist Gunner).
Aircraft Numbers: B2C – 8 to B2C – 14.

Bomber Squadron 3

Outfit: 14 – PZL P-23 Sea Eagles.
Squadron Leader: Lt. ter Zee 1e Klasse (Lt. Commander): Jakob Van Prooijen.
The squadron was divided into two seven plane flights.
Aircraft numbers: B - designates bomber, C - first letter of ship's name, followed by aircraft number.
Deployment: Sea and land targets.

Flight A

Flight Leader; Lt. ter Zee 2e Klasse (Lieutenant): Adrian Van Veelan.
All pilots: Adjudant - Ondeoficier – Vlieger (Warrant Officer Flier) or Lt. ter Zee 3e - Klasse (Ensign).
Crew: Two - Vliegtuig Telegrafist Schutter (Air Telegraphist Gunner) and Adjudant Ondeoficier – Bombardier (Warrant Officer Machinist).
Aircraft Numbers: B3C – 1 to B3C – 7.

Flight B

Flight Leader; Lt. ter Zee 2e Klasse (Lieutenant): Jan Klootwijk.
All pilots: Adjudant - Onderoficier – Vlieger (Warrant Officer Flier) or Lt. ter Zee 3e - Klasse (Ensign).
Crew: Two - Vliegtuig Telegrafist Schutter (Air Telegraphist Gunner) and Adjudant - Ondeoficier – Bombardier (Warrant Officer Machinist).
Aircraft Numbers: B3C – 8 to B3C – 14.

Support Squadron 1

Outfit: 4 – Sea Hart Bombers, A.S. Patrol, 2 – Grumman Duck Floatplanes.
All pilots: Adjudant - Onderoficier – Vlieger (Warrant Officer Flier) or Lt. ter Zee 3e - Klasse (Ensign).
The names of the men and aircraft numbers unavailable.

Johan de Witt Air Groups

Aircraft squadron colours: Red and Yellow, natural Aluminum, red white and blue vertical stripes on a yellow rudder.
Air Group Commander Fighters: Kapitein – Lt. ter Zee Vlieger (Commander): Erik Schalk.

Air Group Commander Bomber: Kapitein – Lt. ter Zee Vlieger (Commander): Daniel Banckert.

Fighter Squadron 3

Outfit: 21 – Grumman F2F-1, F3F-1 and F3F-2 Fighters.
Squadron Leader: Lt. ter Zee 1e Klasse (Lt. Commander): Karl Brongers.
The squadron was divided into three seven plane flights.
Aircraft numbers: F - designates fighter, J - first letter of ship's name followed by aircraft number.
Deployment: Bomber Escort, combat air patrol (CAP).

Flight A:

Flight leader: Lt. ter Zee 2e Klasse (Lieutenant): Gunter Harmse.
All pilots: Adjudant - Onderoficier – Vlieger (Warrant Officer Flier) or Lt. ter Zee 3e - Klasse (Ensign).
Aircraft Numbers: F3J - 1 to F3J – 7.

Flight B:

Flight Leader; Lt. ter Zee 2e Klasse (Lieutenant): Jan Jawijn.
All pilots: Adjudant - Onderoficier – Vlieger (Warrant Officer Flier) or Lt. ter Zee 3e - Klasse (Ensign).
Aircraft Numbers: F3J – 8 to F3J – 14.

Flight C:

Flight Leader; Lt. ter Zee 2e Klasse (Lieutenant): Tomas Bertijn.
All pilots: Adjudant - Onderoficier – Vlieger (Warrant Officer Flier) or Lt. ter Zee 3e - Klasse (Ensign).
Aircraft Numbers: F3J – 15 to F3J – 21.

Fighter Squadron 4

Outfit: Mixed Type Fighters.
Squadron Leader: Lt. ter Zee 1e Klasse (Lt. Commander): Nicholas Verschoor.
The squadron was divided into one seven and one six plane flights.
Aircraft numbers: F - designates fighter, J - first letter of ship's name followed by aircraft number.
Deployment: Bomber escort, Combat Air Patrol (CAP).

Flight A:

Outfit: 6 – Brewster F2A (Buffalo) Fighters.
Flight leader: Lt. ter Zee 2e Klasse (Lieutenant): Wiliam Klepper.

All pilots: Adjudant Opper-Oficier Vlieger (Chief Petty Officer Flyer).
Aircraft Numbers: F4J – 1 to F4J – 6.

<u>Flight B:</u>

Outfit: 7 – Hawker Sea Fury MK II Fighters.
Flight leader: Adjudant – Onder-Oficier – Vlieger (Warrant Officer Flier): Christian Fischer.
All pilots: Adjudant Opper-Oficier Vlieger (Chief Petty Officer Flyer).
Aircraft Numbers: F4J – 7 to F4J – 14.

Bomber Squadron 4

Outfit: 14 - Curtiss Model 77 helldivers.
Squadron Leader: Lt. ter Zee 1e Klasse (Lt. Commander): Hendrick Koole.
The squadron was divided into two seven plane flights.
Aircraft numbers: B - designates bomber, J - first letter of ship's name, followed by aircraft number.
Deployment: Sea and land targets, bomber escort, CAP.

<u>Flight A</u>

Flight Leader; Lt. ter Zee 2e Klasse (Lieutenant): Anton Boshof.
All pilots: Adjudant – Onder-Oficier Vlieger (Warrant Officer Flier) or Lt. ter Zee 3e - Klasse (Ensign).
Crew: Vliegtuig Telegrafist Schutter (Air Telegraphist Gunner).
Aircraft Numbers: B4J – 1 to B4J – 7.

<u>Flight B</u>

Flight Leader; Lt. ter Zee 2e Klasse (Lieutenant): Luis Botha.
All pilots: Adjudant – Onder-Oficier Vlieger (Warrant Officer Flier) or Lt. ter Zee 3e - Klasse (Ensign).
Crew: Vliegtuig Telegrafist Schutter (Air Telegraphist Gunner).
Aircraft Numbers: B4J – 8 to B4J – 14.

Bomber Squadron 5

Outfit: 14 - Curtiss Model 77 helldivers.
Squadron Leader: Lt. ter Zee 1e Klasse (Lt. Commander): Piet De la Rey.
The squadron was divided into two seven plane flights.
Aircraft numbers: B - designates bomber, J - first letter of ship's name, followed by aircraft number.
Deployment: Sea and land targets, bomber escort, CAP.

Flight A

Flight Leader; Lt. ter Zee 2e Klasse (Lieutenant): Daniel Kruger.
All pilots: Adjudant - Onderoficier – Vlieger (Warrant Officer Flier) or Lt. ter Zee 3e - Klasse (Ensign).
Crew: Vliegtuig Telegrafist - Schutter (Air Telegraphist - Gunner).
Aircraft Numbers: B5J – 1 to B5J – 7.

Flight B

Flight Leader; Lt. ter Zee 2e Klasse (Lieutenant): Erik Schalk.
All pilots: Adjudant - Onderoficier – Vlieger (Warrant Officer Flier) or Lt. ter Zee 3e - Klasse (Ensign).
Crew: Vliegtuig Telegrafist Schutter (Air Telegraphist Gunner).
Aircraft Numbers: B5J – 8 to B5J – 14.

Bomber Squadron 6

Outfit: 14 – PZL P-23 Sea Eagles.
Squadron Leader: Lt. ter Zee 1e Klasse (Lt. Commander): Marthinus Steyn.

The squadron was divided into two seven plane flights.
Aircraft numbers: B - designates bomber, J - first letter of ship's name, followed by aircraft number.

Flight A

Flight Leader: Lt. ter Zee 2e Klasse (Lieutenant): Albrecht Hertzog.
All pilots: Adjudant – Onderoficier – Vlieger (Warrant Officer Flier) or Lt. ter Zee 3e - Klasse (Ensign).
Crew: Two; Vliegtuig Telegrafist - Schutter (Air Telegraphist - Gunner) and Adjudant - Onderoficier – Bombardier (Warrant Officer Machinist).
Aircraft Numbers: B6J – 1 to B6J – 7.

Flight B

Flight Leader; Lt. ter Zee 2e Klasse (Lieutenant): Deneys Spionkop.
All pilots: Adjudant - Onderoficier – Vlieger (Warrant Officer Flier) or Lt. ter Zee 3e - Klasse (Ensign).
Crew: Vliegtuig Telegrafist Schutter (Air Telegraphist Gunner) and Adjudant - Ondeoficier – Bombardier (Warrant Officer Machinist).
Aircraft Numbers: B6J – 8 to B6J – 14.

Support Squadron 2

Outfit: 4 – Sea Hart Bombers, A.S. Patrol, 2 – Grumman Duck Floatplanes.

All pilots: Adjudant - Onderoficier – Vlieger (Warrant Officer Flier) or Lt. ter Zee 3e - Klasse (Ensign).
The names of the men and aircraft numbers unavailable.

Schoonveldt Air Groups

Aircraft squadron colours: Blue, natural Aluminum, red white and blue rudder.
Air Group Commander: Kapitein – Lt. ter Zee Vlieger (Commander) – Otto von Lossberg.

Fighter Squadron 5

Outfit: 14 – Hawker Sea Fury MK II Fighters, 6 – Grumman F2F Buffalo Squadron Leader: Lt. ter Zee 1e Klasse (Lt. Commander): Ernst Fijenoord.

The squadron was divided into two seven plane and a six plane flight.
Aircraft numbers: F - designates fighter, S - first letter of ship's name followed by aircraft number.
Deployment: Bomber escort, Fleet (CAP) Combat Air Patrol.

Flight A:

Outfit: 7 – Hawker Sea Fury MK II Fighters.
Flight leader: Lt. ter Zee 2e Klasse (Lt. Commander): Adrian Stuyvesant.
All pilots: Adjudant Opper-Oficier Vlieger (Chief Petty Officer Flyer).
Aircraft Numbers: F5S – 1 to F5S – 7.

Flight B:

Outfit: 7 – Hawker Sea Fury MK II Fighters.
Flight leader: Adjudant – Onder-Oficier – Vlieger (Warrant Officer Flier): Abraham Smit
All pilots: Adjudant Opper-Oficier Vlieger (Chief Petty Officer Flyer).
Aircraft Numbers: F5S – 8 to F5S – 14.

Flight C:

Outfit: 6 – Grumman F2F (Buffalo) Fighters.
Flight leader: Lt. ter Zee 2e Klasse (Lt. Commander): Bruno Falke.
Aircraft Numbers: F5S – 15 to F5S – 20.
Deployment: Bomber Escort, Fleet Combat Air Patrol.

Bomber Squadron 7

Outfit: 23 – Hawker Sea Hart Bombers.
Squadron Leader: Lt. ter Zee 1e Klasse (Lt. Commander): Hernrik Bosscher.

The squadron was divided into two flights.

Aircraft numbers: B - designates bomber, S - first letter of ship's name, followed by aircraft number.

Flight A

Flight Leader; Lt. ter Zee 2e Klasse (Lieutenant): Ernst Storck.
All pilots: Adjudant Opper-Oficier Vlieger (Chief Petty Officer Flyer).
Crew: Vliegtuig Telegrafist - Schutter (Air Telegraphist - Gunner).
Aircraft Numbers: B7S – 1 to B7S – 12.

Flight B

Flight Leader; Lt. ter Zee 2e Klasse (Lieutenant): Benjamin Werkspoor.
All pilots: Adjudant Opper-Oficier Vlieger (Chief Petty Officer Flyer).
Crew: Vliegtuig Telegrafist - Schutter (Air Telegraphist - Gunner).
Aircraft Numbers: B7S – 13 to B7S – 23.

Support Squadron 3

Outfit: 4 – Sea Hart Bombers, A.S. Patrol, 2 – Grumman Duck Floatplanes.
All pilots: Adjudant - Onderoficier – Vlieger (Warrant Officer Flier) or Lt. ter Zee 3e - Klasse (Ensign).
The names of the men and aircraft numbers unavailable.

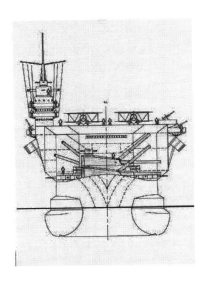

APPENDIX: D

ORDER OF BATTLE: RNLN AIR GROUPS AT AIR BASES - DEC. 08-09, 1941

The RLNN aircraft supporting the fleet were located at Naval Air Stations (NAS) at Mendado, Makassar and Kendari on the big Island of Celebes, the airfields at Tarakan, Bailkpapan and Bandjermasin on the big Island of Borneo and the airfields at Tanjong Priok, Batavia and Sorebabaja on the big island of Java. Most of these shared the facility with the aircraft of the Independent Air Arm (ML) of the Royal Netherlands Army (KNIL).

These were the principal airfields utilized for the *shuttle method* that the RNLN regularly employed, enabling the shifting of replacement naval air groups to support the operations of the fleet at sea. There were, of course many other minor airfields in use by Marine Luchtvaart Dienst (MLD) Naval Air Service throughout the East Indies Campaign as this force sought safety through dispersal.

MENDADO NAVAL AIR STATION

Fighter Squadron 6

Location: Island of Celebes.
Outfit: 21 – Grumman F2F-1, F3F-1 and F3F-2 Fighters.
Squadron Leader: Lt. ter Zee 1e Klasse (Lt. Commander): Christian Broekoff.

The squadron was divided into three seven plane flights.
Aircraft numbers: F - designates fighter, J - first letter of ship's name followed by aircraft number.
Deployment: Priority rotation to *Johan de Witt,* and bomber operations from base.

<u>Flight A:</u>

Flight leader: Lt. ter Zee 2e Klasse (Lieutenant): Bruno Schalk.
All pilots: Adjudant - Onderoficier – Vlieger (Warrant Officer Flier) or Lt. ter Zee 3e - Klasse (Ensign).
Aircraft Numbers: F6J - 1 to F6J – 7.

<u>Flight B:</u>

Flight leader: Lt. ter Zee 2e Klasse (Lieutenant): Guus Winckel.
All pilots: Adjudant - Onderoficier – Vlieger (Warrant Officer Flier) or Lt. ter Zee 3e - Klasse (Ensign).
Aircraft Numbers: F6J - 8 to F6J – 14.

<u>Flight C:</u>

Flight leader: Lt. ter Zee 2e Klasse (Lieutenant): Stefan Rinkhuysen.
All pilots: Adjudant - Onderoficier – Vlieger (Warrant Officer Flier) or Lt. ter Zee 3e - Klasse (Ensign).
Aircraft Numbers: F6J - 9 to F6J – 21.

Fighter Squadron 7

Location: Island of Celebes.
Outfit: 21– Grumman F2F-1, F3F-1 and F3F-2 Fighters.
Squadron Leader: Lt. ter Zee 1e Klasse (Lt. Commander): Jeroen Brouwer.
The squadron was divided into three seven plane flights:
Aircraft numbers: F - designates fighter, C - first letter of ship's name followed by aircraft number.
Deployment: Priority rotation to *Cornelis de Witt,* and bomber operations from base.

<u>Flight A:</u>

Flight leader: Lt. ter Zee 2e Klasse (Lieutenant): Peter de Hoop.
All pilots: Adjudant - Onderoficier – Vlieger (Warrant Officer Flier) or Lt. ter Zee 3e - Klasse (Ensign).
Aircraft Numbers: F7C - 1 to F7C – 7.

<u>Flight B:</u>

Flight leader: Lt. ter Zee 2e Klasse (Lieutenant): Hook Van Holland.
All pilots: Adjudant - Onderoficier – Vlieger (Warrant Officer Flier) or Lt. ter Zee 3e - Klasse (Ensign).
Aircraft Numbers: F7C - 8 to F7C – 14.

<u>Flight C:</u>

Flight leader: Lt. ter Zee 2e Klasse (Lieutenant): Thomas Van Der Heiden.
All pilots: Adjudant - Onderoficier – Vlieger (Warrant Officer Flier) or Lt. ter Zee 3e - Klasse (Ensign).
Aircraft Numbers: F7C - 15 to F7C – 21.

Bomber Squadron 8

Location: Island of Celebes.
Outfit: 16 – PZL P-23 Sea Eagles.
Squadron Leader: Lt. ter Zee 1e Klasse (Lt. Commander): Johan Bezemer.
The squadron was divided into two eight plane flights.
Aircraft numbers: B - designates bomber, J - first letter of ship's name, followed by aircraft number.
Deployment: Priority rotation to *Johan de Witt,* and bomber operations from base.

<u>Flight A</u>

Flight Leader; Lt. ter Zee 2e Klasse (Lieutenant): Willem Klassen
All pilots: Adjudant - Onderoficier – Vlieger (Warrant Officer Flier) or Lt. ter Zee 3e - Klasse (Ensign).
Crew: Two; Vliegtuig Telegrafist - Schutter (Air Telegraphist - Gunner) and Adjudant - Ondeoficier – Machinist (Warrant Officer Machinist).
Aircraft Numbers: B8J – 1 to B8J – 8.

<u>Flight B</u>

Flight Leader; Lt. ter Zee 2e Klasse (Lieutenant): Peter Hendrikse.
All pilots: Adjudant - Onderoficier – Vlieger (Warrant Officer Flier) or Lt. ter Zee 3e - Klasse (Ensign).
Crew: Vliegtuig Telegrafist Schutter (Air Telegraphist Gunner) and Adjudant – Onderoficier – Machinist (Warrant Officer Machinist).
Aircraft Numbers: B8J – 9 to B8J – 16.

Bomber Squadron 9

Location: Island of Celebes.
Outfit: 16 – PZL P-23 Sea Eagles.
Squadron Leader: Lt. ter Zee 1e Klasse (Lt. Commander): Manfred Schiel.

The squadron was divided into two eight plane flights.
Aircraft numbers: B - designates bomber, C - first letter of ship's name, followed by aircraft number.
Deployment: Priority rotation to *Cornelius de Witt,* bomber operations from base.

Flight A

Flight Leader; Lt. ter Zee 2e Klasse (Lieutenant): Stefan de Waal.
All pilots: Adjudant - Onderoficier – Vlieger (Warrant Officer Flier) or Lt. ter Zee 3e - Klasse (Ensign).
Crew: Two; Vliegtuig Telegrafist - Schutter (Air Telegraphist - Gunner) and Adjudant - Ondeoficier – Machinist (Warrant Officer Machinist).
Aircraft Numbers: B9C – 1 to B9C – 8.

Flight B

Flight Leader; Lt. ter Zee 2e Klasse (Lieutenant): Eugenie Janssen.
All pilots: Adjudant - Onderoficier – Vlieger (Warrant Officer Flier) or Lt. ter Zee 3e - Klasse (Ensign).
Crew: Vliegtuig Telegrafist Schutter (Air Telegraphist Gunner) and Adjudant – Oneoficier – Machinist (Warrant Officer Machinist).
Aircraft Numbers: B9C – 1 to B9C – 16.

KEDARI NAVAL AIR STATION:

Fighter Squadron 8

Location: Island of Celebes.
Outfit: 21 – Grumman F2F-1, F3F-1 and F3F-2 Fighters.
Squadron Leader: Lt. ter Zee 1e Klasse (Lt. Commander): Hans Beerckamp.
The squadron was divided into three seven plane flights.
Aircraft numbers: F - designates fighter, J - first letter of ship's name followed by aicraft number.
Deployment: Priority rotation to *Johan de Witt*, and bomber operations from base.

Flight A:

Flight leader: Lt. ter Zee 2e Klasse (Lieutenant): Jacob Van Mook.
All pilots: Adjudant - Onderoficier – Vlieger (Warrant Officer Flier) or Lt. ter Zee 3e - Klasse (Ensign).
Aircraft Numbers: F8J - 1 to F8J – 7.

Flight B:

Flight leader: Lt. ter Zee 2e Klasse (Lieutenant): Mijke Den Boggende
All pilots: Adjudant - Onderoficier – Vlieger (Warrant Officer Flier) or Lt. ter Zee 3e - Klasse (Ensign).
Aircraft Numbers: F8J - 8 to F8J – 14.

Flight C:

Flight leader: Lt. ter Zee 2e Klasse (Lieutenant): Jacob de Winter.
All pilots: Adjudant - Onderoficier – Vlieger (Warrant Officer Flier) or Lt. ter Zee 3e -
 Klasse (Ensign).
Aircraft Numbers: F8J - 15 to F8J – 21.

Fighter Squadron 9

Location: Island of Celebes.
Outfit: 21 – Grumman F2F-1, F3F-1 and F3F-2 Fighters.
Squadron Leader: Lt. ter Zee 1e Klasse (Lt. Commander): Timoty Skanderup.
The squadron was divided into three seven plane flights.
Aircraft numbers: F - designates fighter, C - first letter of ship's name followed by
 aircraft number.
Deployment: Priority rotation to *Cornelius de Witt,* and bomber operations from base.

Flight A:

Flight leader: Lt. ter Zee 2e Klasse (Lieutenant): Andrew Van Dulm.
All pilots: Adjudant - Onderoficier – Vlieger (Warrant Officer Flier) or Lt. ter Zee 3e -
 Klasse (Ensign).
Aircraft Numbers: F9C - 1 to F9C– 7.

Flight B:

Flight leader: Lt. ter Zee 2e Klasse (Lieutenant): Pieter Tazelaar.
All pilots: Adjudant - Onderoficier – Vlieger (Warrant Officer Flier) or Lt. ter Zee 3e -
 Klasse (Ensign).
Aircraft Numbers: F9C - 8 to F9C – 14

Flight C:

Flight leader: Lt. ter Zee 2e Klasse (Lieutenant): Cornelius Haff.
All pilots: Adjudant - Onderoficier – Vlieger (Warrant Officer Flier) or Lt. ter Zee 3e -
 Klasse (Ensign).
Aircraft Numbers: F9C - 15 to F9C – 21.

Bomber Squadron 10

Location: Island of Celebes.
Outfit: 14 - Curtiss Model 77 helldivers.
Squadron Leader: Lt. ter Zee 1e Klasse (Lt. Commander): Piet Van Genechlen.
Aircraft numbers: B - designates bomber, J - first letter of ship's name, followed by
 aircraft number.
Deployment: Priority rotation to *Johan de Witt,* and bomber operations from base.

<u>Flight A:</u>

Flight Leader; Lt. ter Zee 2e Klasse (Lieutenant): Gunter Frost.
All pilots: Adjudant - Onderoficier – Vlieger (Warrant Officer Flier) or Lt. ter Zee 3e - Klasse (Ensign).
Crew: Vliegtuig Telegrafist - Schutter (Air Telegraphist - Gunner).
Aircraft Numbers: B10J – 1 to B10J – 7.

<u>Flight B:</u>

Flight Leader; Lt. ter Zee 2e Klasse (Lieutenant): Christian Van Geelkerken.
All pilots: Adjudant - Onderoficier – Vlieger (Warrant Officer Flier) or Lt. ter Zee 3e - Klasse (Ensign).
Crew: Vliegtuig Telegrafist - Schutter (Air Telegraphist - Gunner).
Aircraft Numbers: B10J – 8 to B10J – 14.

<u>Bomber Squadron 11</u>

Location: Island of Celebes.
Outfit: 14 - Curtiss Model 77 helldivers.
Squadron Leader: Lt. ter Zee 1e Klasse (Lt. Commander): Adrian Hoeden.
The squadron was divided into two seven plane flights.
Aircraft numbers: B - designates bomber, J - first letter of ship's name, followed by aircraft number.
Deployment: Priority rotation to *Cornelis de Witt,* and bomber operations from base.

<u>Flight A:</u>

Flight Leader; Lt. ter Zee 2e Klasse (Lieutenant): Gerard Franeker.
All pilots: Adjudant - Onderoficier – Vlieger (Warrant Officer Flier) or Lt. ter Zee 3e - Klasse (Ensign).
Crew: Vliegtuig Telegrafist - Schutter (Air Telegraphist - Gunner).
Aircraft Numbers: B11C – 1 to B11C – 7.

<u>Flight B:</u>

Flight Leader; Lt. ter Zee 2e Klasse (Lieutenant): Daniel de Vries.
All pilots: Adjudant - Onderoficier – Vlieger (Warrant Officer Flier) or Lt. ter Zee 3e - Klasse (Ensign).
Crew: Vliegtuig Telegrafist - Schutter (Air Telegraphist - Gunner).
Aircraft Numbers: B11C – 8 to B11C – 14.

BANDJERMASIN NAVAL AIR STATION:

Fighter Squadron 10

Location: Island of Borneo.
Outfit: 14 – Hawker Sea Fury MK II Fighters.
Squadron Leader: Lt. ter Zee 1e Klasse (Lt. Commander): Ernst Van Genechlen.
The squadron was divided into two seven plane flights.
Aircraft numbers: F - designates fighter, S - first letter of ship's name followed by aircraft number.
Deployment: Priority rotation to *Schoonveldt,* and bomber operations from base.

Flight A:

Outfit: 7 – Hawker Sea Fury MK II Fighters.
Flight leader: Lt. ter Zee 2e Klasse (Lt. Commander): Konrad Kohlbrugge.
All pilots: Adjudant Opper-Oficier Vlieger (Chief Petty Officer Flyer).
Aircraft Numbers: F10S – 1 to F10S – 7.

Flight B:

Outfit: 7 – Hawker Sea Fury MK II Fighters.
Flight leader: Lt. ter Zee 2e Klasse (Lt. Commander): Adrian Scharroo.
All pilots: Adjudant Opper-Oficier Vlieger (Chief Petty Officer Flyer).
Aircraft Numbers: F10S – 8 to F10S – 14.

Bomber Squadron 12

Location: Island of Borneo.
Outfit: 24 – Hawker Sea Hart Bombers.
Squadron Leader: Lt. ter Zee 1e Klasse (Lt. Commander): Hendrik Colijn.
The squadron was divided into two flights:
Aircraft numbers: B - designates bomber, J - first letter of ship's name, followed by aircraft number.
Deployment: Priority rotation to *Schoonveldt,* and bomber operations from base.

Flight A

Flight Leader; Lt. ter Zee 2e Klasse (Lieutenant): Ernst de Geer.
All pilots: Adjudant Opper-Oficier Vlieger (Chief Petty Officer Flyer).
Crew: Vliegtuig Telegrafist - Schutter (Air Telegraphist - Gunner).
Aircraft Numbers: B12S – 1 to B12S – 12.

Flight B

Flight Leader; Lt. ter Zee 2e Klasse (Lieutenant): Julius Kinderdijk.

All pilots: Adjudant Opper-Oficier Vlieger (Chief Petty Officer Flyer).
Crew: Vliegtuig Telegrafist - Schutter (Air Telegraphist - Gunner).
Aircraft Numbers: B12S – 13 to B12S – 24.

BALIKPAPAN NAVAL AIR STATION: - DEC. 08, 1941

Fighter Squadron 11

Location: Island of Borneo.
Outfit: 14 – Hawker Sea Fury MK II Fighters.
Squadron Leader: Lt. ter Zee 1e Klasse (Lt. Commander): Gunter Smit.
The squadron was divided into two seven plane flights:
Aircraft numbers: F - designates fighter, S - first letter of ship's name followed by aircraft number.
Deployment: Priority rotation to *Schoonveldt,* and bomber operations from base.

Flight A:

Outfit: 7 – Hawker Sea Fury MK II Fighters.
Flight leader: Lt. ter Zee 2e Klasse (Lt. Commander): Adrian Den Helter.
All pilots: Adjudant Opper-Oficier Vlieger (Chief Petty Officer Flyer).
Aircraft Numbers: F11S – 1 to F11S – 7.

Flight B:

Outfit: 7 – Hawker Sea Fury MK II Fighters.
Flight leader: Lt. ter Zee 2e Klasse (Lt. Commander): Michal de Bronigne.
All pilots: Adjudant Opper-Oficier Vlieger (Chief Petty Officer Flyer).
Aircraft Numbers: F11S – 8 to F11S – 14

Bomber Squadron 14

Location: Island of Borneo.
Outfit: 24 – Hawker Sea Hart Bombers.
Squadron Leader: Lt. ter Zee 1e Klasse (Lt. Commander): Visser Breuhese.
The squadron was divided into two flights.
Aircraft numbers: B - designates bomber, S - first letter of ship's name, followed by aircraft number.
Deployment: Priority rotation to *Schoonveldt,* and bomber operations from base.

Flight A

Flight Leader; Lt. ter Zee 2e Klasse (Lieutenant): Johan de Gelder.
All pilots: Adjudant Opper-Oficier Vlieger (Chief Petty Officer Flyer).
Crew: Vliegtuig Telegrafist - Schutter (Air Telegraphist - Gunner).
Aircraft Numbers: B12S – 1 to B12S – 12.

Flight B

Flight Leader; Lt. ter Zee 2e Klasse (Lieutenant): Christian Durlache.
All pilots: Adjudant Opper - Oficier Vlieger (Chief Petty Officer Flyer)
Crew: Vliegtuig Telegrafist - Schutter (Air Telegraphist - Gunner).
Aircraft Numbers: B12S – 13 to B12S – 24.

TARAKAN NAVAL AIR STATION: - DEC. 08 / '41

Fighter Squadron 12

Location: Island of Borneo.
Outfit: 21 – Grumman F2F-1, F3F-1 and F3F-2 Fighters.
Squadron Leader: Lt. ter Zee 1e Klasse (Lt. Commander): Egmont Wolfert
The squadron was divided into three seven plane flights.
Aircraft numbers: F - designates fighter, C - first letter of ship's name followed by aircraft number.
Deployment: Priority rotation to Cornelius de Witt, and bomber operations from base.

Flight A:

Flight leader: Lt. ter Zee 2e Klasse (Lieutenant): Simon Van Meer.
All pilots: Adjudant - Onderoficier – Vlieger (Warrant Officer Flier) or Lt. ter Zee 3e - Klasse (Ensign).
Aircraft Numbers: F9C - 1 to F9C– 7.

Flight B:

Flight leader: Lt. ter Zee 2e Klasse (Lieutenant): Pieter Braunfels.
All pilots: Adjudant - Onderoficier – Vlieger (Warrant Officer Flier) or Lt. ter Zee 3e - Klasse (Ensign).
Aircraft Numbers: F9C - 8 to F9C – 14

Flight C:

Flight leader: Lt. ter Zee 2e Klasse (Lieutenant): Chritian Haff.
All pilots: Adjudant - Onderoficier – Vlieger (Warrant Officer Flier) or Lt. ter Zee 3e - Klasse (Ensign).
Aircraft Numbers: F9C - 15 to F9C – 21.

Torpedo Squadron 1

Location: Island of Borneo.
Outfit: 20 – Fairey Swordfish Mk1.
Squadron Leader: Lt. ter Zee 1e Klasse (Lt. Commander): Kurt Winkleman.
The squadron was divided into two ten plane flights.

Aircraft numbers: R - designates reconnaissance bomber, followed by aircraft unit number.

Deployment: Priority support to fleet, then reconnaissance and torpedo bomber operations from base.

Flight A

Flight Leader; Lt. ter Zee 2e Klasse (Lieutenant): Karl Frederiks.
All pilots: Adjudant Opper - Oficier Vlieger (Chief Petty Officer Flyer).
Crew: Vliegtuig Telegrafist - Schutter (Air Telegraphist - Gunner).
Aircraft Numbers: B12S – 1 to B12S – 12.

Flight B

Flight Leader; Lt. ter Zee 2e Klasse (Lieutenant): Visser t' Hoofr.
All pilots: Adjudant Opper - Oficier Vlieger (Chief Petty Officer Flyer).
Crew: Vliegtuig Telegrafist - Schutter (Air Telegraphist - Gunner).
Aircraft Numbers: B12S – 13 to B12S – 24.

LAKE TODANO NAVAL AIR STATION: - DEC. 08, 1941

Location: Island of Celebes.
Outfit: 20 – Fokker T. V111-W Floatplanes.
Squadron Leader: Lt. ter Zee 1e Klasse (Lt. Commander): Gerhard Polder.
The squadron was divided into two ten plane flights.
Aircraft numbers: R - designates reconnaissance bomber, followed by aircraft number.
Deployment: Priority support to fleet, and reconnaissance and torpedo bomber operations from base.

Flight A:

Flight Leader; Lt. ter Zee 2e Klasse (Lieutenant): Johan A. Trip
All pilots: Adjudant - Onderoficier – Vlieger (Warrant Officer Flier) or Lt. ter Zee 3e - Klasse (Ensign).
Crew: Two; Vliegtuig Telegrafist - Schutter (Air Telegraphist - Gunner) and Adjudant - Ondeoficier – Machinist (Warrant Officer Machinist).
Aircraft Numbers: R – 1 to R – 10.

Flight B:

Flight Leader; Lt. ter Zee 2e Klasse (Lieutenant): Rost Van Tanningen.
All pilots: Adjudant - Onderoficier – Vlieger (Warrant Officer Flier) or Lt. ter Zee 3e - Klasse (Ensign).
Crew: Two; Vliegtuig Telegrafist - Schutter (Air Telegraphist - Gunner) and Adjudant - Ondeoficier – Machinist (Warrant Officer Machinist).
Aircraft Numbers: R – 11 to R – 20.

Torpedo Squadron 3

Location: Island of Celebes.
Outfit: 20 – Fokker T. V111-W Floatplanes.
Squadron Leader: Lt. ter Zee 1e Klasse (Lt. Commander): Gerhard Polder.
The squadron was divided into two ten plane flights.
Aircraft numbers: R - designates reconnaissance bomber, followed by aircraft number.
Deployment: Priority support to fleet, and reconnaissance and torpedo bomber operations from base.

Flight A:

Flight Leader; Lt. ter Zee 2e Klasse (Lieutenant): Johan A. Trip
All pilots: Adjudant - Onderoficier – Vlieger (Warrant Officer Flier) or Lt. ter Zee 3e - Klasse (Ensign).
Crew: Two; Vliegtuig Telegrafist - Schutter (Air Telegraphist - Gunner) and Adjudant - Ondeoficier – Machinist (Warrant Officer Machinist).
Aircraft Numbers: R – 21 to R – 31.

Flight B:

Flight Leader; Lt. ter Zee 2e Klasse (Lieutenant): Rost Van Tanningen.
All pilots: Adjudant - Onderoficier – Vlieger (Warrant Officer Flier) or Lt. ter Zee 3e - Klasse (Ensign).
Crew: Two; Vliegtuig Telegrafist - Schutter (Air Telegraphist - Gunner) and Adjudant - Ondeoficier – Machinist (Warrant Officer Machinist).
Aircraft Numbers: R – 32 to R – 42.

PERAK NAVAL AIR STATION

Fleet Reserve Aircraft

Location: Island of Java.
Outfit: 80 – Grumman F2F-1, F3F-1 and F3F-2 Fighters.
     21 – Machi 200 Fighters, 40 – Fiat CR-42 Fighters
     86 – Curtis Model 77 Helldivers.
     36 – Sea Fury MK II – Fighters.

KONINKLIJK NEDERLANDS INDISH LEGER – (ROYAL NETHERLANDS ARMY OF THE INDIES)

TARAKAN ARMY AIRFIELD: - DEC. 08-09 '41

KNIL – HEAVY FIGHTER GROUP III

Colonel Flyer: Paul Van der Wilden

Heavy Fighter Squadron 1

Location: Island of Borneo.
Outfit: 15 Fokker G.1B – twin engine, monoplane.
Squadron Leader: Kapitein: Willem Moone.
The squadron was divided into two 7 plane flights, and a squadron leader plane.
Aircraft number: 340
Deployment: Army: support ground attack, Army: Photo Reconnissance, Army: bomber escort, Naval: fleet air support, anti-shipping.

Flight A

Flight Leader; Lieutenant: Rost Van Tonningen.
All pilots: Warrant Officer Flyer.
Crew: Vliegtuig Telegrafist - Schutter (Air Telegraphist - Gunner).
Aircraft Numbers: 341 to 347.

Flight B

Flight Leader; Lieutenant: Karel Detloog.
All pilots: Master Seargent or Seargent Flyer Rank
Crew: Vliegtuig Telegrafist - Schutter (Air Telegraphist - Gunner).
Aircraft Numbers: 350 to 356.

Heavy Fighter Squadron 2

Location: Island of Borneo.
Outfit: 15 Fokker G.1B – twin engine, monoplane.
Squadron Leader: Kapitein Aaron Deloon.
The squadron was divided into two 7 plane flights, and a squadron leader plane.
Aircraft number: 400
Deployment: Army: support ground attack, Army: Photo Reconnissance, Army: bomber escort, Naval: fleet air support, anti-shipping.

<u>Flight A</u>

Flight Leader; Lt. ter Zee 2e Klasse (Lieutenant): Rudolf de Langeboom.
All pilots: Master Seargent or Seargent Flyer Rank.
Crew: Vliegtuig Telegrafist - Schutter (Air Telegraphist - Gunner).
Aircraft Numbers: 401 to 408.

<u>Flight B</u>

Flight Leader; Lieutenant: Jake Den Otter.
All pilots: Master Seargent or Seargent Flyer Rank.
Crew: Vliegtuig Telegrafist - Schutter (Air Telegraphist - Gunner).
Aircraft Numbers: 410 to 416.

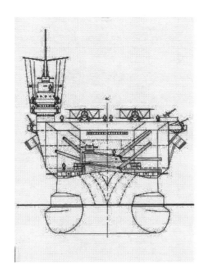

APPENDIX: E

ORDER OF BATTLE: ALLIED NAVAL FORCES SUPPORTING RNLN BATTLE-CRUISER CARRIER TASK FORCE: LINEBACKER – JAN. '42 TO FEB. '42

ROYAL AUSTRALIAN NAVAL FORCES: – TASK FORCE WOMBAT

Battlecruiser: One: Tiger Class

HMAS Austrailia – Task Force Flagship.

Rear Admiral: Sir Kevin Whitely Task Force Commander.

- Length: 216 meters, Beam at W.L. : 32 meters, Draft 9.5 meters
- Displacement: 32,700 tonnes.
- Armour Plate Max: 229 mm at W.L., Main Gun Turrets: 230 mm, deck; 60 mm
- Boilers; twenty, oil fired Yarrow Small Tube, superheated, Power: 80,600 KW.
- Machinery: Brown-Curtis single geared turbines; 4 – Shafts.
- Range 6,000 nmi at 15 knots, Maximum Speed: 28 Knots.
- Torpedo defense: 200mm waterline armor, 35mm armor internal longitudinal bulkhead P&S, British Admiralty Type 1 Hull Blisters, 30 mm armor, cellulose packed.
- Aircraft: Two – Supermarine Walrus
- Kanon: Woolich Armstrong Whitworth, MK V, eight – 343 mm; range 30,000 meters.
- Kanon: Elswick Ordnance; twelve – 152 mm, range 17,000 meters.
- Anti-aircraft kanon: Elswick Ordnance; twelve – 114 mm, range 18,000 meters.
- Pom Pom; twenty – 1 kg automatic cannon, range 3,000 meters,.
- Machine gun GP: Browning; ten– 0.306 cal., water cooled.
- Crew: 124 officers, 1183 men

Most Senior Line and Corps Officers:

Captain: James Keough – Ship's Captain
Captain: Cooper Tennant – Chief of Staff
Lt. Commander: Steven Morant – Ship's Executive Officer
Lt. Commander: William Beardmore – Gunnery Officer
Chief Engineer: Clyde Fairfield
Damage Control Officer: Lt. Commander Scott Laird

Heavy Cruisers: Two: Territory Class.

Commodore: Leslie D. Hawthorne - Commander of Cruiser Division No. 5

HMAS Queensland - Division Flagship - Captain: Thomas Conder – Ship's Captain

- Length: 164.9 meters, Beam at W.L. : 17.4 meters, Draft 6.2 meters
- Displacement: 8,380 tonnes.
- Armour Vert. Max: 50 - 76mm WL belt, Gun Turrets: 51 mm faces, 38 mm sides, tops 25 mm, Deck: 51mm
- Boilers: Six Admiralty – 3 Drum - oil fired,; Power – 59,680 KW.
- Machinery: Parson's single reduction geared turbine; 4 – Shafts, Speed: 32 Knots.
- Range 8,400 nmi at 14 knots.
- Aircraft: one Supermarine Walrus reconnaissance.
- Kanon: Woolich Arsenal; six – 203 mm. with 26,000 meters range.
- Anti-aircraft kanon: eight - 102 mm; automatic, range 12,000 meters.
- Heavy machinegun GP: Breda; six – 12.7 mm.
- Machinegun GP: Browning; six - .30 cal water cooled machine guns.
- Crew: 68 officers, 570 men.

Most Senior Line and Corps Officers:

Commander: Oliver Boyd – Executive Office
Lt. Commander: William Harris – Gunnery Officer
Chief Engineer: Angus McTaggert

HMAS New South Wales - Captain: Ian Carlisle Jr. – Ship's Captain

- Length: 164.9 meters, Beam at W.L. : 17.4 meters, Draft 6.2 meters
- Displacement: 8,380 tonnes.
- Armour Vert. Max: 50 - 76mm WL belt, Gun Turrets: 51 mm faces, 38 mm
- sides, tops 25 mm, Deck: 51mm
- Boilers: Six Admiralty – 3 Drum - oil fired,; Power – 59,680 KW.
- Machinery: Parson's single reduction geared turbine; 4 – Shafts, Speed: 32
- Knots.
- Range 8,400 nmi at 14 knots.
- Aircraft: one - reconnaissance.

- Kanon: Woolich Arsenal; six – 203 mm. with 26,000 meters range.
- Anti-aircraft kanon: eight - 102 mm; automatic, range 12,000 meters.
- Heavy machinegun GP: Breda; six – 12.7 mm.
- Machinegun GP: Browning; six - .30 cal water cooled machine guns.
- Crew: 62 officers, 560 men.

Most Senior Line and Corps Officers:

Commander: Reginald Bolton – Executive Office
Lt. Commander: James E. Taylor – Gunnery Officer
Chief Engineer: Dwight McFerson

Destroyers: Six: Town Class

Captain: Jack T. Preston – Commander Destroyer Flotilla No 15. Attached to Battleship-carrier *Schoonveldt*

HMAS Campbelltown - Captain: Terry Cummings; Ship's Captain

- Length: 97.5 meters, Beam at W.L. : 9.9 meters, Draft 2.65 meters.
- Displacement: 1400 tonnes.
- Boilers: 3 – Admiralty 3 Drum Power - 25,360 KW.
- Machinery: Parsons geared turbine; 2 – Shafts.
- Range: 2,500 nmi. at 15 knots, Max. Speed: 36 Knots.
- Main kanon: Elswick Ordnance; five – 119 mm. with 14,000 meters range.
- Heavy machinegun GP: Breda; six – 12.7 mm.
- Torpedoes: eight – 533 mm. Tubes.
- Crew: 17 officers, 142 men.

HMAS Darwin - Captain: Bert Waggoner; Ship's Captain

- Length: 97.5 meters, Beam at W.L. : 9.9 meters, Draft 2.65 meters.
- Displacement: 1400 tonnes.
- Boilers: 3 – Admiralty 3 Drum Power - 25,360 KW.
- Machinery: Parsons geared turbine; 2 – Shafts.
- Range; 2,500 nmi. at 15 knots, Max. Speed: 36 Knots.
- Main kanon: Elswick Ordnance; five – 119 mm. with 14,000 meters range.
- Heavy machinegun GP: Breda; six – 12.7 mm.
- Torpedoes: eight – 533 mm. Tubes.
- Crew: 15 officers, 140 men.

HMAS Elisabeth - Captain: – Conner Duff; Ship's Captain

- Length: 97.5 meters, Beam at W.L. : 9.9 meters, Draft 2.65 meters.
- Displacement: 1400 tonnes.
- Boilers: 3 – Admiralty 3 Drum Power - 25,360 KW.

- Machinery: Parsons geared turbine; 2 – Shafts.
- Range; 2,500 nmi. at 15 knots, Max. Speed: 36 Knots.
- Main kanon: Elswick Ordnance; five – 119 mm. with 14,000 meters range.
- Heavy machinegun GP: Breda; six – 12.7 mm.
- Torpedoes: eight – 533 mm. Tubes.
- Crew: 15 officers, 140 men.

HMAS Wanneroo - Captain: Bart Nolan; Ship's Captain

- Length: 97.5 meters, Beam at W.L.: 9.9 meters, Draft 2.65 meters.
- Displacement: 1400 tonnes.
- Boilers: 3 – Admiralty 3 Drum Power - 25,360 KW.
- Machinery: Parsons geared turbine; 2 – Shafts.
- Range; 2,500 nmi. at 15 knots, Max. Speed: 36 Knots.
- Main kanon: Elswick Ordnance; five – 119 mm. with 14,000 meters range.
- Heavy machinegun GP: Breda; six – 12.7 mm.
- Torpedoes: eight – 533 mm. Tubes.
- Crew : 15 officers, 140 men.

HMAS Toowooma - Captain: James Smith; Ship's Captain

- Length: 97.5 meters, Beam at W.L.: 9.9 meters, Draft 2.65 meters.
- Displacement: 1400 tonnes.
- Boilers: 3 – Admiralty 3 Drum Power - 25,360 KW.
- Machinery: Parsons geared turbine; 2 – Shafts.
- Range; 2,500 nmi. at 15 knots, Max. Speed: 36 Knots.
- Main kanon: Elswick Ordnance; five – 119 mm. with 14,000 meters range.
- Heavy machinegun GP: Breda; six – 12.7 mm.
- Torpedoes: eight – 533 mm. Tubes.
- Crew: 15 officers, 140 men.

HMAS Woolongong - Captain: William Shears; Ship's Captain

- Length: 97.5 meters, Beam at W.L. : 9.9 meters, Draft 2.65 meters.
- Displacement: 1400 tonnes.
- Boilers: 3 – Admiralty 3 Drum Power - 25,360 KW.
- Machinery: Parsons geared turbine; 2 – Shafts.
- Range; 2,500 nmi. at 15 knots, Max. Speed: 36 Knots.
- Main kanon: Elswick Ordnance; five – 119 mm. with 14,000 meters range.
- Heavy machinegun GP: Breda; six – 12.7 mm.
- Torpedoes: eight – 533 mm. Tubes.
- Crew : 15 officers, 140 men.

UNITED STATES NAVAL FORCES– TASK FORCE STONEWALL

Light Cruiser: One: Omaha Class

Commanduer (Commodore): Erik Fletcher - Commander of Destroyer Squadron No. 5.

USS Dixie CL. 14 (F)- Flotilla leader Flagship, Captain David Howard Rice

- Length: 167 meters, Beam at W.L.: 16.9 meters, Draft 4.1 meters
- Displacement: 7,194 tonnes.
- Boilers: 8 - oil fired, Babbcock and Wilcox; SHP- 67,140 KW.
- Machinery: Westinghouse geared turbine; 4 – Shafts.
- Range; 3,500 nmi. at 15 knots, Max. Speed: 34 Knots.
- Aircraft: 2 reconnaissance.
- Main kanon: Rheinmetal; ten – 152.4 mm. with 14,000 meters range.
- Anti-aircraft kanon: eight - 76 mm.
- Machinegun GP: Browning; six - .30 cal water cooled.
- Torpedoes: six – 533 mm.
- Crew: 800 officers and men.

Destroyers:

USS General Robert E. Lee - DD 40 - Nine: Flush Deck-Four Stack Class.

Ship's Captain: Lt. Commander Eethan Phillpot

Length: 94.5 meters, Beam at W.L. : 9.3 meters, Draft 2.4 meters
Displacement: 1,125 tonnes.
Boilers: 4 - oil fired, Normand; Power - 14,920 KW.
Machinery: Curtis geared turbine; 2 – Shafts.
Range; 2,500 nmi. at 15 knots, Max. Speed: 32 Knots.
Main kanon: Rheinmetal; four – 102 mm. with 8,000 meters range.
Anti-aircraft kanon: one - 76 mm.
Machinegun GP: Browning; four - .30 cal water cooled.
Torpedoes: twelve – 530 mm. Tubes.
Crew: 130 officers and men.

USS General John Bell Hood - DD 41

Ship's Captain: Lt. Commander Ransom Caldwell

- Length: 94.5 meters, Beam at W.L. : 9.3 meters, Draft 2.4 meters
- Displacement: 1,125 tonnes.
- Boilers: 4 - oil fired, Normand; Power - 14,920 KW.
- Machinery: Curtis geared turbine; 2 – Shafts.
- Range; 2,500 nmi. at 15 knots, Max. Speed: 32 Knots.

- Main kanon: Rheinmetal; four – 102 mm. with 8,000 meters range.
- Anti-aircraft kanon: one - 76 mm.
- Machinegun GP: Browning; four - .30 cal water cooled.
- Torpedoes: twelve – 530 mm. Tubes.
- Crew: 130 officers and men.

USS General James Longstreet - DD 42

Ship's Captain: Lt. Commander Henry Cleamson

- Length: 94.5 meters, Beam at W.L. : 9.3 meters, Draft 2.4 meters
- Displacement: 1,125 tonnes.
- Boilers: 4 - oil fired, Normand; Power - 14,920 KW.
- Machinery: Curtis geared turbine; 2 – Shafts.
- Range; 2,500 nmi. at 15 knots, Max. Speed: 32 Knots.
- Main kanon: Rheinmetal; four – 102 mm. with 8,000 meters range.
- Anti-aircraft kanon: one - 76 mm.
- Machinegun GP: Browning; four - .30 cal water cooled.
- Torpedoes: twelve – 530 mm. Tubes.
- Crew: 130 officers and men.

USS General James Kemper - DD 43

Ship's Captain: Lt. Commander Dwight Beaumont

- Length: 94.5 meters, Beam at W.L. : 9.3 meters, Draft 2.4 meters
- Displacement: 1,125 tonnes.
- Boilers: 4 - oil fired, Normand; Power - 14,920 KW.
- Machinery: Curtis geared turbine; 2 – Shafts.
- Range; 2,500 nmi. at 15 knots, Max. Speed: 32 Knots.
- Main kanon: Rheinmetal; four – 102 mm. with 8,000 meters range.
- Anti-aircraft kanon: one - 76 mm.
- Machinegun GP: Browning; four - .30 cal water cooled.
- Torpedoes: twelve – 530 mm. Tubes.
- Crew: 130 officers and men.

USS General George Pickett - DD 44

Ship's Captain: Lt. Commander Jeffrey Arbuckle

- Length: 94.5 meters, Beam at W.L. : 9.3 meters, Draft 2.4 meters
- Displacement: 1,125 tonnes.
- Boilers: 4 - oil fired, Normand; Power - 14,920 KW.
- Machinery: Curtis geared turbine; 2 – Shafts.
- Range; 2,500 nmi. at 15 knots, Max. Speed: 32 Knots.

- Main kanon: Rheinmetal; four – 102 mm. with 8,000 meters range.
- Anti-aircraft kanon: one - 76 mm.
- Machinegun GP: Browning; four - .30 cal water cooled.
- Torpedoes: twelve – 530 mm. Tubes.
- Crew: 130 officers and men.

USS General Lewis Armistad - DD 45

Ship's Captain: Lt. Commander John W. Cornell

- Length: 94.5 meters, Beam at W.L. : 9.3 meters, Draft 2.4 meters
- Displacement: 1,125 tonnes.
- Boilers: 4 - oil fired, Normand; Power - 14,920 KW.
- Machinery: Curtis geared turbine; 2 – Shafts.
- Range; 2,500 nmi. at 15 knots, Max. Speed: 32 Knots.
- Main kanon: Rheinmetal; four – 102 mm. with 8,000 meters range.
- Anti-aircraft kanon: one - 76 mm.
- Machinegun GP: Browning; four - .30 cal water cooled.
- Torpedoes: twelve – 530 mm. Tubes.
- Crew: 130 officers and men.

USS General Richard Garnett - DD 46

Ship's Captain: Lt. Commander Kevin Rutger

- Length: 94.5 meters, Beam at W.L. : 9.3 meters, Draft 2.4 meters
- Displacement: 1,125 tonnes.
- Boilers: 4 - oil fired, Normand; Power - 14,920 KW.
- Machinery: Curtis geared turbine; 2 – Shafts.
- Range; 2,500 nmi. at 15 knots, Max. Speed: 32 Knots.
- Main kanon: Rheinmetal; four – 102 mm. with 8,000 meters range.
- Anti-aircraft kanon: one - 76 mm.
- Machinegun GP: Browning; four - .30 cal water cooled.
- Torpedoes: twelve – 530 mm. Tubes.
- Crew: 130 officers and men.

USS General Thomas Johnathan Jackson - DD 47

Ship's Captain: Lt. Commander Efram Barksdale

- Length: 94.5 meters, Beam at W.L. : 9.3 meters, Draft 2.4 meters
- Displacement: 1,125 tonnes.
- Boilers: 4 - oil fired, Normand; Power - 14,920 KW.
- Machinery: Curtis geared turbine; 2 – Shafts.
- Range; 2,500 nmi. at 15 knots, Max. Speed: 32 Knots.

- Main kanon: Rheinmetal; four – 102 mm. with 8,000 meters range.
- Anti-aircraft kanon: one - 76 mm.
- Machinegun GP: Browning; four - .30 cal water cooled.
- Torpedoes: twelve – 530 mm. Tubes.
- Crew: 130 officers and men.

USS General Nathan Bedford Forest - DD 48

Ship's Captain: Lt. Commander James H. Perdue

- Length: 94.5 meters, Beam at W.L. : 9.3 meters, Draft 2.4 meters
- Displacement: 1,125 tonnes.
- Boilers: 4 - oil fired, Normand; Power - 14,920 KW.
- Machinery: Curtis geared turbine; 2 – Shafts.
- Range; 2,500 nmi. at 15 knots, Max. Speed: 32 Knots.
- Main kanon: Rheinmetal; four – 102 mm. with 8,000 meters range.
- Anti-aircraft kanon: one - 76 mm.
- Machinegun GP: Browning; four - .30 cal water cooled.
- Torpedoes: twelve – 530 mm. Tubes.
- Crew: 130 officers and men.

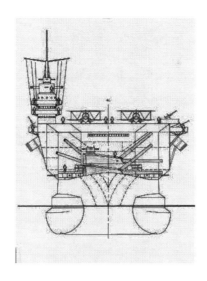

APPENDIX: F

ORDER OF BATTLE: IMPERIAL JAPANESE NAVAL FORCES AT THE 1ST BATTLE OF THE SOUTH CHINA SEA - DEC. 08, 1941

MALAY INVASION FLEET CODE NAME : SUNBURST

Rear Admiral: Matome Toyoda - Invasion Fleet Commander.
General: Iwabe Takaguchi – Commander of the Imperial Japanese Army 15 th Infantry Division.

15th INFANTRY DIVISION CONVOY - Twenty Six Ships – 14,600 soldiers.

Sutzuki Maru – 3400 Tonnes dwt. Equipment, 16 howitzers, 640 Soldiers.
Tsubami Maru – 2700 Tonnes dwt. Equipment, 26 trucks 530 Soldiers.
Hirata Maru – 3100 Tonnes dwt. Equipment, 270 Mules.
Irako Maru – 4100 Tonnes dwt. Equipment, 770 Soldiers.
Kashiwarita Maru – 2400 Tonnes dwt. Equipment, 440 Soldiers.
Inagi Maru – 3600 Tonnes dwt. Equipment, 26 trucks, 27 Tanks, 240 Soldiers.
Ashi Maru – 1400 Tonnes dwt. Equipment, 240 Soldiers.
Hayo Maru – 5400 Tonnes dwt. Equipment, 32 trucks, 1140 Soldiers.
Iwo Maru – 3400 Tonnes dwt. Equipment, 16 howitzers, 640 Soldiers.
Honan Maru – 3400 Tonnes dwt. Equipment, 16 howitzers, 325 soldiers.
Kii Maru – 3400 Tonnes dwt. Equipment, Artillery shells, 640 Soldiers.
Jintsu Maru – 3400 Tonnes dwt. Equipment, tents, 6 bulldozers, 600 Soldiers.
Kyo Maru – 3400 Tonnes dwt. Equipment, tents, field hospital, 640 Soldiers.
Manju Maru – 2800 Tonnes dwt. Equipment, gasoline in barrels, 340 Soldiers.
Chin Yen – 2700 Tonnes dwt. Equipment, small arms, ammunition,470 Soldiers.
Matsuo Maru – 5000 Tonnes dwt. Equipment, 300 Mules, 100 Soldiers
Irako Maru – 6100 Tonnes dwt. Equipment, 17 tanks, 40 trucks, 770 Soldiers.

Momi Maru – 4400 Tonnes dwt. Equipment, machine guns, rafts, 940 Marines.
Kozu Maru – 3600 Tonnes dwt. Tanker, 320 soldiers
Kuri Maru – 1500 Tonnes dwt. Equipment, 200 Soldiers.
Miyo Maru – 3700 Tonnes dwt. Fuel oil tanker, 500 soldiers.
Iwato Maru – 3400 Tonnes dwt. Equipment, 16 howitzers, 540 Soldiers.
Moroshimo Maru – 7400 Tonnes dwt. Equipment, 1800 soldiers.
Oshima Maru – 3400 Tonnes dwt. Equipment, Artillery Shells, 510 Soldiers.
Sutzuki Maru – 3400 Tonnes dwt. Equipment, Artillery Sheels, 540 Soldiers.
Tsubami Maru – 2400 Tonnes dwt. Equipment, Rice, 320 Soldiers.

(Commanders unknown)

CONVOY CLOSE ESCORT

Battleships: - Settsu Class - Two

Kagoshima - Flagship Battleship Division 6, Invasion Command Center, Fire Support.

Rear Admiral: Matome Toyoda - Invasion Fleet Commander.
General: Soema Takaguchi – Commander of the 15 th Infantry Division.
Rear Admiral: Masataki Oshimo - Battleship Division 6 - Commander.
Captain: Takeo Ugaki – Ship's Commander.

- Length: 160.32 meters, Beam at W.L. : 25.68 meters, Draft 8.2 meters
- Displacement: 23,000 tonnes.
- Armour Vert. Krupp Max: 127 - 305mm belt, Turrets: 279 mm faces, 155 mm sides, tops 105 mm, Deck: 51mm.
- Boilers: Sixteen Mirabara - oil fired, Power; 18,650 kw.
- Machinery: Curtis single reduction geared turbine; 2 – Shafts, Speed: 21 Knots.
- Range 2,700 nmi at 10 knots.
- Kanon: Woolich Arsenal: twelve: 305 mm with 18,000 meters range. Broadside: 3.24 tonnes.
- Anti-aircraft kanon: Osaka Naval Arsenal: six – Type 89, 127 mm, range 16,000 meters.
- Anti-aircraft kanon: Kure Naval Arsenal: six - 76 mm, range 5,000 meters.
- Machinegun GP: Browning; six - .30 cal water cooled machine guns.
- Crew: 168 officers, 970 men.

Kumamoto - Fire Support.

Captain: Hideki Kurita – Ship's Commander

- Length: 160.32 meters, Beam at W.L. : 25.68 meters, Draft 8.2 meters
- Displacement: 23,000 tonnes.

- Armour Vert. Krupp Max: 127 - 305mm belt, Turrets: 279 mm faces, 155 mm sides, tops 105 mm, Deck: 51mm
- Boilers: Sixteen Mirabara - oil fired, Power – 18,650 kw.
- Machinery: Curtis single reduction geared turbine; 2 – Shafts, Speed: 21 Knots.
- Range 2,700 nmi at 10 knots.
- Kanon: Woolich Arsenal; twelve: 305 mm with 18,000 meters range. Broadside: 3.24 tonnes.
- Anti-aircraft kanon: Osaka Naval Arsenal; six - Type 89, 127 mm, range 16,000 meters.
- Anti-aircraft kanon: Kure Naval Arsenal; six - 76 mm, range 5,000 meters.
- Machinegun GP: Browning; six - .30 cal water cooled machine guns.
- Crew: 168 officers, 970 men.

Destroyers: - Fubuki Class – (Modified Tpye A): - seventeen.

Captain: Isoruko Honda - Destroyer Squadron Commander

Mashima: - Destroyer Squadron Flagship, Convoy Escort,

Commander: Chuichi Kondo – Ship's Captain

- Length: 118.4 meters O.A., Beam at W.L. : 10.36 meters, Draft 3.2 meters
- Displacement: 2,100 tonnes.
- Armour: none.
- Boilers: Sixteen Mirabara - oil fired, Power; 37,300 kw.
- Machinery: single reduction geared turbine; 2 – Shafts, Speed: 34 Knots.
- Range 2,700 nmi at 10 knots.
- Dual Purpose Kanon: Osaka Naval Arsenal; six – Type 89, 127 mm. in two turrets, 16,000 meters range.
- Machinegun GP: two – 13 mm.
- Torpedoes: nine – 610 mm, three triple tube mounts.
- Crew: 197 officers and men.

Squadron Mates:

Nissho, Nowake, Oki, Sagi, Naruto, Ninaki, Mutsuki, Kozu, Kiri, Maki, Hishi, Kisso, Miyuki, Momo, Wakabi, Tochi.

Ship Commanders: Unknown.

CONVOY DISTANT COVER FLEET

Aircraft Carriers: - Zuiho Class Type B: - One

Suzaku: - Flagship – Distant Cover Fleet.
Vice Admiral: Tomoshige Sakonju - Distant Cover Fleet Fleet Commander.

Captain: Raizo Samejima – Ship's Commander

- Length: 217.0 meters O.A., Beam at W.L. : 18.39 meters, Draft 6.63 meters Flight Deck: 118.00, Aircraft Elevators – two.
- Displacement: 11, 800 tonnes.
- Armour: 25 mm Longitudinal Bulkheads, 25 mm deck.
- Boilers: Six Mirabara - oil fired, Power; 37,300 kw.
- Machinery: single reduction geared turbine; 2 – Shafts, Speed: 28 Knots.
- Range 2,900 nmi at 10 knots.
- Dual Purpose Kanon: Yokosuka Naval Arsenal eight – Type 89, 127 mm. Single mounts, 16,000 meters range.
- Anti-aircraft kanon: Kure Naval Arsenal: fifteen - 25 mm, range 3,000 meters.
- Machinegun GP: six – 13 mm.
- Aircraft: 15 - Mitsubishi Type D2 - biplane torpedo bombers, 15 - Kawasaki KI -10 biplane fighters.
- Crew: 925 officers and men.

Heavy Cruisers: - Improved Moyoko Class: Four

Tokachi: - Flagship – Distant Cover Fleet – Cruiser Squadron 11.

Rear Admiral: Tamon Matsumoto - Cruiser Squadron 11, Commander.
Captain: Saburo Kamimura – Ship's Commander

- Length: 164.9 meters, Beam at W.L. : 17.4 meters, Draft 6.2 meters
- Displacement: 13,380 tonnes.
- Armour Vert. Max: 100 mm WL belt, Gun Turrets: 76 mm faces, 40 mm sides, tops 25 mm, Deck: 76 mm
- Boilers: Twelve Miraba - oil fired, Power; 104,440 kw.
- Machinery: Komatsu reduction geared turbine; 4 – Shafts, Speed: 35 Knots.
- Range 8,400 nmi at 14 knots.
- Aircraft: 3 - reconnaissance.
- Kanon: Osaka Naval Arsenal; ten – 203 mm. with 26,000 meters range.
- Anti-aircraft Kanon: Yokosuka Naval Arsenal: eight - Type 89, 127 mm; range 16,000 meters.
- Anti-aircraft Kanon: Kure Naval Arsenal: six – 25 mm, automatic.
- Torpedoes: sixteen; 610 mm. four quadruple mounts.
- Crew: 92 officers, 690 men.

Hotaka:

Captain: Kichisaburo Rusaki – Ship's Commander

- Length: 164.9 meters, Beam at W.L. : 17.4 meters, Draft 6.2 meters
- Displacement: 13,380 tonnes.

- Armour Vert. Max: 100 mm WL belt, Gun Turrets: 76 mm faces, 40 mm sides, tops 25 mm, Deck: 76 mm
- Boilers: Twelve Miraba - oil fired, Power; 104,440 kw.
- Machinery: Komatsu reduction geared turbine; 4 – Shafts, Speed: 35 Knots.
- Range 8,400 nmi at 14 knots.
- Aircraft: 3 - reconnaissance.
- Kanon: Osaka Naval Arsenal; ten – 203 mm with 26,000 meters range.
- Anti-aircraft Kanon: Yokosuka Naval Arsenal: eight - Type 89, 127 mm. range 7,000 meters.
- Anti-aircraft Kanon: Kure Naval Arsenal: six – 25 mm, automatic.
- Torpedoes: sixteen; 610 mm. four quadruple mounts.
- Crew: 82 officers, 693 men.

Yakushi:

Captain: Sengi Kozu – Ship's Commander

- Length: 164.9 meters, Beam at W.L. : 17.4 meters, Draft 6.2 meters
- Displacement: 13,380 tonnes.
- Armour Vert. Max: 100 mm WL belt, Gun Turrets: 76 mm faces, 40 mm sides, tops 25 mm, Deck: 76 mm
- Boilers: Twelve Miraba - oil fired, Power; 104,440 kw.
- Machinery: Komatsu reduction geared turbine; 4 – Shafts, Speed: 35 Knots.
- Range 8,400 nmi at 14 knots.
- Aircraft: 3 - reconnaissance.
- Kanon: Osaka Naval Arsenal; ten – 203 mm with 26,000 meters range.
- Anti-aircraft Kanon: Yokosuka Naval Arsenal: eight - Type 89, 127 mm. range 16,000 meters.
- Anti-aircraft Kanon: Kure Naval Arsenal: six – 25 mm, automatic.
- Torpedoes: sixteen; 610 mm. four quadruple mounts.
- Crew: 81 officers, 693 men.

Senjo:

Captain: Masuo Hundai – Ship's Commander

- Length: 164.9 meters, Beam at W.L. : 17.4 meters, Draft 6.2 meters
- Displacement: 13,380 tonnes.
- Armour Vert. Max: 100 mm WL belt, Gun Turrets: 76 mm faces, 40 mm sides, tops 25 mm, Deck: 76 mm
- Boilers: Twelve Miraba - oil fired, Power – 104,440 kw.
- Machinery: Komatsu reduction geared turbine; 4 – Shafts, Speed: 35 Knots.
- Range 8,400 nmi at 14 knots.
- Aircraft: 3 - reconnaissance.
- Kanon: Osaka Naval Arsenal; ten – 203 mm. with 26,000 meters range.

- Anti-aircraft Kanon: Yokosuka Naval Arsenal: eight - Type 89, 127 mm. range 16,000 meters.
- Anti-aircraft Kanon: Kure Naval Arsenal: six – 25 mm, automatic.
- Torpedoes: sixteen; 610 mm. four quadruple mounts.
- Crew: 82 officers, 690 men.

Destroyers: - Minikaze Class – twelve.

Captain: Masanori Ito - Destroyer Squadron Commander

Tozan: - Destroyer Squadron Flagship, Convoy Escort,

Commander: Hirama Futami – Ship's Captain

- Length: 105.4 meters O.A., Beam at W.L. : 9.8 meters, Draft 3.2 meters
- Displacement: 1,300 tonnes.
- Armour: None
- Boilers: ten Mirabara - oil fired, Power – 28,900 kw.
- Machinery: single reduction geared turbine; 2 – Shafts, Speed: 37 Knots.
- Range 2,700 nmi at 10 knots.
- Dual Purpose Kanon: Osaka Naval Arsenal: four – Type 89, 127 mm. single mounts, 16,000 meters range.
- Machinegun GP: two – 13 mm.
- Torpedoes: six – 533 mm, three double tube mounts.
- Crew: 147 officers and men.

Squadron Mates:

Tateho, Sumida, Shoko, Tatshura, Suwami, Ooshio, Nokaze, Seki, Umigiri, Toshi.

Ship Commanders: Unknown.

JAPANESE ARMY AIR FORCES DEPLOYED AT THE 1 ST BATTLE OF THE SOUTH CHINA SEA - DEC. 08, 1941

6th KOKUGUN - (AIR ARMY) - Headquarterd at Hsingking – China

General: Hideki Oshimo – 6 th Air Army Commander.

17th HIKOSHIDEN - (AIR DIVISION) -

Based at Hanoi Airfield, French Indo China.
General: Kanji Tomadzura– 17 th Air Division Commander.

22nd HIKODAN - (AIR BRIGADE): - Four Air Regiments

Headquartered at Hanoi Airfield, French Indo China.
General: Hairo Yamada – 22 nd Air Brigade Commander.

73rd HIKOSENTAI (AIR REGIMENT):

Based at Hanoi Airfield, French Indo China.
Colonel: Tamon Yubara – 73 rd Air Regiment Commander.

115th Chutai (Squadron)

18 – Mitsubishi G3M, twin engine, long range medium bombers.
Squadron Commander unknown.

116th Chutai (Squadron)

16 – Mitsubishi G3M, twin engine, long range medium bombers.
Squadron Commander unknown.

117th Chutai (Squadron)

16 – Mitsubishi G3M, twin engine, long range medium bombers.
Squadron Commander unknown.

121st HIKOSENTAI (AIR REGIMENT):

Based at Hue Airfield: - French Indo China.
Colonel: Kengi Nishimura – 121st Air Regiment Commander.

118th Chutai (Squadron)

18 – Mitsubishi G3M, twin engine, long range medium bombers.
Squadron Commander unknown.

119th Chutai (Squadron)

16 – Mitsubishi G3M, twin engine, long range medium bombers.
Squadron Commander unknown.

120th Chutai (Squadron)

16 – Mitsubishi G3M, twin engine, long range medium bombers.
Squadron Commander unknown.

123rd HIKOSENTAI (AIR REGIMENT):

Based at My Thoa Airfield – Cochin China.
Colonel: Tatsujiro Shimada – 123 rd Air Regiment Commander.

130th Chutai (Squadron)

16 - Nakajima Ki-27 monoplane fighters, with fixed undercarriage.
Squadron Commander unknown.

131st Chutai (Squadron)

15 - Nakajima Ki-27 monoplane fighters, with fixed undercarriage.
Squadron Commander unknown.

133rd Chutai (Squadron)

15 - Nakajima Ki-27 monoplane fighters, with fixed undercarriage.
Squadron Commander unknown.

124th HIKOSENTAI (AIR REGIMENT):

Based at Na Drang Airfield – French Indo China;
Colonel: Masatake Goto – 124 th Air Regiment Commander.

134th Chutai (Squadron)

16 - Nakajima Ki-43 monoplane fighters.
Squadron Commander unknown.

135th Chutai (Squadron)

15 - Nakajima Ki-43 monoplane fighters.
Squadron Commander unknown.

136th Chutai (Squadron)

15 - Nakajima Ki-43 monoplane fighters.
Squadron Commander unknown

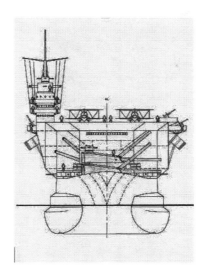

APPENDIX: G

LIST OF PHOTOGRAPHS:

9. The KMN Battlecruiser-carrier Squadron in the North Sea in 1939.
10. Similar and accompanying to photograph number 9.
11. KMN Cruisers and Destroyers in the Bay of Biscay June 1939.
12. *USS Dixie* CL 14 and nine destroyers escorting the KMN Battleship-aircraft-carrier *Schoonveldt* accross the Pacific in June 1940.
13. Similar and accompanying to photograph number 12.
14. Similar and accompanying to photograph number 12.
15. Japanese Naval Intelligence photograph of the KMN Battleship-aircraft-carrier *Schoonveldt* steaming the Pacific in June 1940.
16. KMN Battleship-aircraftcarrier *Schoonveldt* after sinking the German Commerce Raiders *Gull* and *Pelican* in June 1940.
17. Japanese Army Air Force Intelligence photograph of KMN Fleet from the air, June 1941.
18. Japanese Army Air Force Intelligence photograph of KMN Battlecruiser-carriers *Cornelis and Johan de Witt* off Singapore, April 1941.
19. Japanese Intelligence photograph of KMN Battleship-carrier *Schoonveldt* off Singapore, April 1941.
20. Japanese high altitude Intelligence photograph of the KMN De Ruyter Class Light cruiser *Prins te Paard* in South China Sea.
21. Dutch Naval Intelligence (OVZ) high altitude photograph of the modernized Battleship *Kagoshima* at Osaka.
22. Dutch Naval Intelligence (OVZ) high altitude photograph of the modernized Battleship *Kumamoto* at Osaka.
23. Battleship *Kagoshima* steaming in the Gulf of Tonkin, December 1941.
24. Cruiser Squadron No. 11, IJN at anchor in the Gulf of Tonkin, December 1941.

25. Malaya Invasion Convoy of General Takaguci carrying the 15th Infantry Division off the coast of Cochin China December 1941.
26. Similar to photograph number 25.
27. IJN Battleship Kagoshima escorting troopship and small tanker.
28. Japanese Troop transports Under Air Attack, Battle of South China Sea, December 1941.
29. Troopship *Iraku Maru* Burns after Dutch air attack.
30. Japanese Battleship *Kagoshima* under Air Attack in the South China Sea on December 1941.
31. Japanese Battleship *Kumamoto* under Air Attack in the South China Sea on December 1941.
32. PZL-P23 Sea Eagle heavy dive-bombers returning to the Battle-carriers.
33. The Japanese Light Carrier *Suzaku* in the South China Sea on December 1941, turning hard to starboard.
34. The Japanese Light Carrier *Suzaku* and three destroyers under Air Attack in the South China Sea, first bomb hit on December 1941.
35. The Japanese Light Carrier *Suzaku* and three destroyers under Air Attack in the South China Sea, stopped and afire on December 1941.
36. Her damage control teams have restored steaming pressure to the turbines of the Japanese Light Carrier *Suzaku,* she is underway again but the fires in her aircraft hangar still burn fiercely on December 1941.
37. The Japanese Light Carrier *Suzaku* continues to burn.
38. The Japanese Light Carrier *Suzaku* is seen here as she begins to lose the fight and she sinks deeper as the flooding due to damage cannot be contained.
39. The Heavy Cruisers of Squadron 11 of Rear Admiral Tamon Matsumoto race throughout the night in an attempt to engage the Dutch Fleet with gunfire at dawn of December 08, 1941, come under air attack.
40. An unidentified Japanese Heavy Cruiser describes an 'S' pattern on the surface of the South China at 37 knots as she dodges the bombs of the KMN Dive bombers, December 08, 1941.
41. Two Japanese Heavy cruisers afire and sinking in the South China Sea, on December 08, 1941.
42. Task Force Popeye under Air attack on the morning of December 08, 1941.
43. The Flaggeschip of the KMN *Task Force Popeye*; the Battlecruiser-carrier *Cornelis de Witt* executes a helm hard to port while under air attack during the Battle of the South China Sea, December 08, 1941.
44. The *Cornelis de Witt* continues to maneuver at high speed.
45. Two Japanese Heavy cruisers of Squadron 11, survive the KMN air attacks and attempt to engage the Dutch Battle-carriers in a surface battle.
46. A photograph of a Japanese Heavy cruiser maneuvering at high speed as she executes a turn to port.
47. Two KMN De Ruyter Class light cruisers of the Battle-carrier screening force race forward to intercept the enemy threat.
48. The Japanese Heavy cruiser *Yakushi* is pounded by the guns of the Dutch Fleet, Battle of the South China Sea, December 08, 1941.

49. Gun camera photo of *Yakushi*'s ordeal by fire.
50. The Heavy Cruiser *Tokachi* is blown out of the water by the heavy guns of the KMN Vlaggeschip.
51. The Dutch Fleet is seen here steaming in the Celebese Sea in good order following the Battle of the South China Sea, December 09, 1941.

The Koninklijke Marine Nederland (KMN) or Royal Netherlands Navy Battlecruiser-carrier Fleet in heavy weather in the North Sea 1939. The Battlecruiser-carrier *Johan de Witt* is flanked by three De Ruyter Class Cruisers, most likely *Gouden Leeuw* (top left) *Aemilia* (top right) of Cruiser Division No. 3, and *Oliphant* (foreground) of Cruiser Division No. 4. The destroyers in the distance are most likely *Jakhals* and *Bulhond* of Destroyer Flotilla No. 10. (Photograph Courtesy of The Maarten Danielszoon Sweers Private Collection).

The KMN Battlecruiser-carrier Fleet in heavy weather in the North Sea 1939. The KMN Battlecruiser-carrier *Cornelis de Witt* is flanked a De Ruyter Class Cruiser, most likely *Prins te Paard* (foreground) the Flagship of Cruiser Division No. 4, and the destroyer is most likely *Zeeland* Flagship of Destroyer Flotilla No. 10. (Photograph Courtesy of The Maarten Danielszoon Sweers Private Collection).

Two cruisers of the De Ruyter Class accompanied by two destroyers of the Zeeland Class, steaming across the Bay of Biscay in June 1939, on their way to a tropical deployment in the Dutch East Indies. The light cruiser *Gouden Leeuw* (foreground) leads her division mate *Aemilia*, while the destroyer *Zeeland* (top) leads *Gelderland*. (Photograph Courtesy of The Maarten Danielszoon Sweers Private Collection).

The Omaha Class Light Cruiser *USS Dixie* CL 14, and the antiquated destroyers of *Desron 5*, escort the KMN Battleship-carrier *Schoonveldt* across the Pacific June 19, 1940. Note the wing of the reconnaissance aircraft in the foreground. (Photograph courtesy of *The Battleship-carrier Schoonveldt Veterans' Association*).

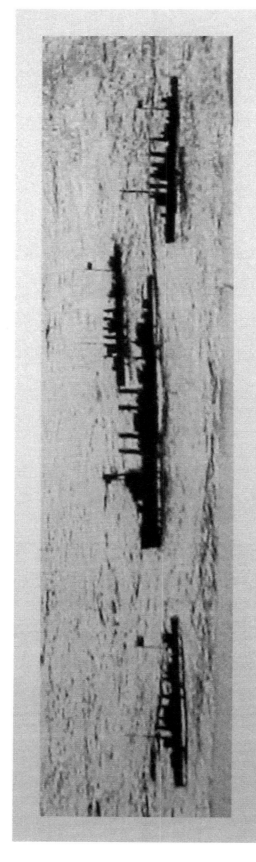

The Light Cruiser *USS Dixie CL14*, escorted by the antiquated 'four stacker' destroyers of *Desron 5*, on their deployment from Bremerton Washington to Cavite Naval Base in the Philippines, June 1940. (Photograph courtesy of The Battleship-carrier Schoonveldt Veterans' Association).

Scene from the same voyage as previous photo; the KMN Battleship-carrier *Schoonveldt* is escorted by the old four stack USN destroyers of *Desron 5* as they cross the Pacific in June 1940. The destroyers are headed to Cavite Naval Base in the Philippines, while the Dutch warship will divert on the following day and race south to destroy the Nazi surface raiders *M.V. Gull* and *M.V. Pelican* thereby saving the valuable Dutch *Convoy X*. Although the image is quite small, the six gun main battery layout of the Battleship-carrier is still visible, with the 'A' & 'B' superimposed 305 mm Main Battery turrets forward and 'C' Turret mounted aft on the quarterdeck under the flight deck. (Photograph courtesy of The Battleship-carrier Schoonveldt Veterans' Association).

The KMN Battleship-carrier *Schoonveldt* seen crossing the Pacific on July 4, 1940. The photograph was taken by a Japanese fishing vessel and was the first indication for the Imperial Japanese Navy that the Dutch Fleet in the East Indies was being reinforced by a third battle-carrier.

(Photo recovered by the Allied Military Commission in Tokyo in 1946 from seized documents that had been set aside for burning but were discovered abandoned.)

The Battleship-carrier *Schoonveldt* steaming to Java after her successful operation against the German surface raiders *M.V. Gull* and *M.V. Pelican*, July 1940. Note that her after aircraft hangar deck elevator is down and 'C' Turret is trained to port. The old French pattern domed spark screen on top of her stack is evident, this was removed at the dockyard in Soerabaja in August 1940. (Photograph courtesy of the Maarten Sweers Military Collection.

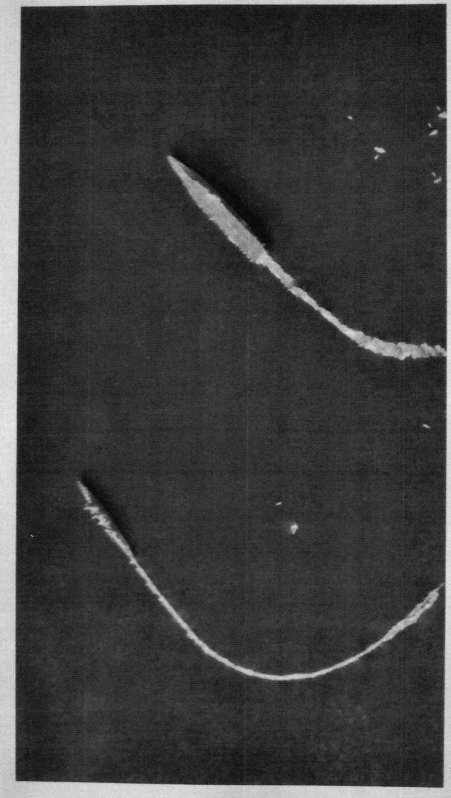

The Light Cruiser *Gouden Leeuw*, Vlaggeschip of Cruiser Division No.3 keeps perfect station abreast of the Fleet Vlaggeschip *Cornelis de Witt*, while maneuvering on the Java Sea, June 1941. (Photograph courtesy of *The Maarten Sweers Naval Collection*.)

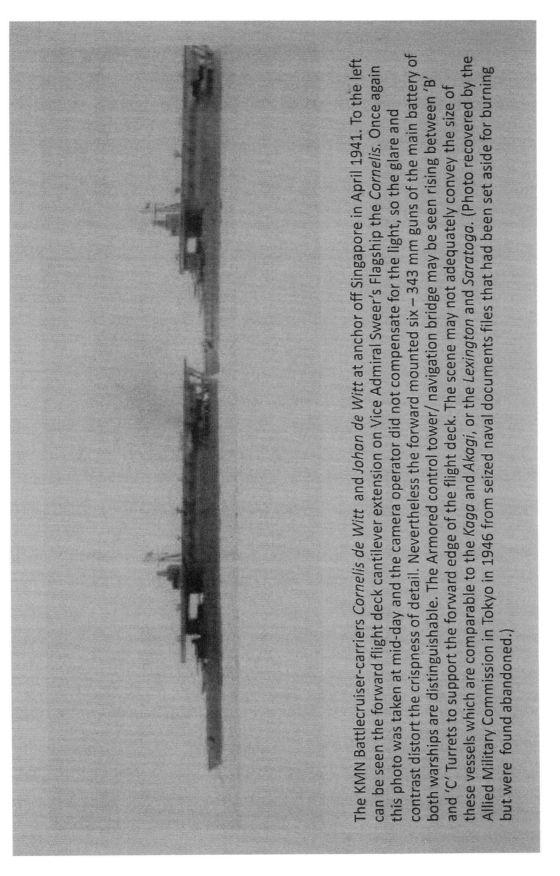

The KMN Battlecruiser-carriers *Cornelis de Witt* and *Johan de Witt* at anchor off Singapore in April 1941. To the left can be seen the forward flight deck cantilever extension on Vice Admiral Sweer's Flagship the *Cornelis*. Once again this photo was taken at mid-day and the camera operator did not compensate for the light, so the glare and contrast distort the crispness of detail. Nevertheless the forward mounted six – 343 mm guns of the main battery of both warships are distinguishable. The Armored control tower/ navigation bridge may be seen rising between 'B' and 'C' Turrets to support the forward edge of the flight deck. The scene may not adequately convey the size of these vessels which are comparable to the *Kaga* and *Akagi*, or the *Lexington* and *Saratoga*. (Photo recovered by the Allied Military Commission in Tokyo in 1946 from seized naval documents files that had been set aside for burning but were found abandoned.)

The RNLN Battleship-carrier *Schoonveldt* at anchor off Singapore in April 1941. To the left can be seen the port quarter of the RNLN Battlecruiser-carrier *Johan de Witt*. The photo was taken at mid-day by the same camera operator as the previous photo. Nevertheless the six – 305 mm guns of the main battery are visible, 'A' and 'B' Turrets forward, 'C' Turret on the after deck, under the flight deck. Of note; the old raised *French style* spark arrestor screen on the funnel has been replaced. (Photo recovered by the Allied Military Commission in Tokyo in 1945 from seized naval document files that had been set aside for burning but were found abandoned.)

Japanese Army Air Force High altitude photographic reconnaissance of the KMN Fleet captures an image of a De Ruyter Class Light cruiser, probably the *Prins te Paard* maneuvering In the South China Sea. Her aircraft is seen sitting aft of the funnel.

(Photograph courtesy of the Allied Military Commission of 1946 in Tokyo.

An Imperial Japanese Navy Battleship of the *Satzuma* Class. The Office Van Zeein-lichtingen (OVZ), The Naval Intelligence Service of the Dutch navy, first became aware in 1938 that two units of the old dreadnoughts, (evidenced by the wing turrets of the main battery) had been modernized as evidenced by the massive *Hirga* style fire-control tower, and returned to active duty. This battleship is believed to have been re-commissioned as the *Kagoshima*. The photo was taken at high altitude during a reconnaissance mission of Osaka Naval Anchorage, hence the stark contrast to determine details.

(The photograph is Courtesy of The Maarten Danielszoon Sweers Private Collection).

Another OVZ Dutch Naval Intelligence High Altitude photo- graph of a modern- ized battleship of the *Satzuma* Class taken on the same intelligence gathering mission.

This unit is believed to have been recommission- ied as the *Kumamoto*. Both of these warships are of some 23,000 tonnes displacement and mount twelve - 12" Woolich Arsenal Naval Guns, and are protected by up to 305 mm of Krupp armor plate.

(The photograph is Courtesy of The Maarten Danielszoon Sweers Private Collection).

The Old Battleship *Kagoshima*; Flagship of Battleship Division No. 6 and Rear Admiral Matome Toyoda, the Invasion Fleet Commander steams serenely across the gentle swells of the Gulf of Tonkin to collect the convoy of troop ships carrying the 15th Infantry Division on December 04, 1941. (Photograph Courtesy of the Maarten Sweers Private Collection.)

IJN *Cruiser Squadron 11*, under the command of Rear Admiral Tamon Matsumoto, provided the heavy gun support for Vice Admiral Tomoshige Sakonju's Distant Cover Fleet.

Tokacki (F) top, *Hotaka* below, *Yakushi* second from bottom and *Senjo*. The are ships seen here on December 03, 1941, laying peacefully at anchor on the Gulf of Tonkin off Hanoi, as General Takaguchi's Troopship Convoy assembles for Operation Sunburst.

(Photograph Courtesy of *The KMN Battlecruiser-carrier Museum*, Surabaya.)

The Japanese Malaya Invasion Convoy of General Takaguchi on the morning of December 07,1941 making its way west off the coast of Cochin China transporting the men and equipment of the 15th Infantry Division. (Photograph Courtesy of Konrad Van de Groot).

Elements of the Japanese Troop Convoy of Operation 'Sanbasuto' (Sunburst) off the east coast of French Indo China on the evening of December 07, 1941, steaming south on its way to invade Malaysia. Seen here are the Battleship escorts; *Kagoshima* (top left) is the Flagship of Battleship Division 6 under the Command of Rear Admiral Matome Toyoda, her sister ship the *Kumamoto* follows astern.

(Photograph Courtesy of Konrad Van de Groot).

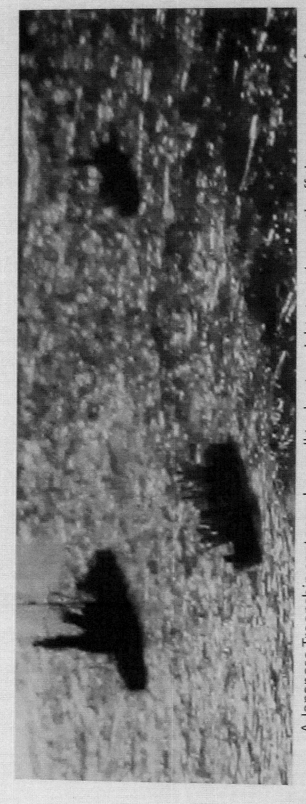

A Japanese Troopship center and a small tanker top right steaming south off the east coast of French Indo China on the evening of December 07, 1941, and escorted by the old battleship *Kagoshima* (top left). (Photograph Courtesy of Konrad Van de Groot).

Troop Transports of Invasion Convoy 'Sunburst' under air attack by the Helldivers of the RNLN *Task Force Popeye* · December 08, 1941. The 5,400 tonne *Iraku Maru* begins to burn, while the 4400 tonne *Momi Maru*, narrowly escapes a bomb off her stern. Destroyers *Nowake* (left) and *Tochi* race between the columns of freighters to provide anti-aircraft defense. (Photograph courtesy of the *Cornelis de Witt Battlecruiser-carrier Veteran's Association.*)

The 5,400 tonne *Iraku Maru* continues to burn, while a Japanese destroyer races past off her starboard Bow. Both of the vessels in this photograph would not survive the day. December 08, 1941. (Photograph courtesy of the *Cornelis de Witt Battlecruiser-carrier Veteran's Association*.)

The modernized dreadnought *Kago-shima* is seen here in this dramatic photograph moments after she hit in rapid succession by two 750 kg AP bombs.Although these alone were enough to finish her, she continued to be pounded by the PZL-P23 Sea Eagles of Heavy Dive Bomber Squadron No. 3, commanded by Lt. ter Zee 1e Klasse Jacob van Prooijen and Squadron No. 6, commanded by Marthinius Steyn of Task Force Popeye, December 08, 1941.

The sea is seen to be deeply furrowed by the high speed maneuvering of her escorts. A dark patch of heavy oil (lower right) released from a stricken tanker, spreads thickly over the water. As the ships of the convoy start to sink and the soldiers and sailors go into the water, this oil will kill more men than the attack.

(Photograph courtesy of *The Maarten Sweers Private Collection*.)

The Japanese Battleship *Kumamoto* has become the target of the PZL P-23 Sea Eagle Heavy Diver Bomber Group composed of Bomber Squadron 3 (Cornelis de Witt) and Bomber Squadron 6 (Johan de Witt), December 08, 1941. She is seen burning from a 750 kg. AP bomb strike at the base of her tripod mast. Several wide misses are evident. The once calm seas are now heavily furrowed by the steep waves of racing warships and many heavy detonations. (Photograph Courtesy of *The Maarten Danielszoon Sweers Private Collection*).

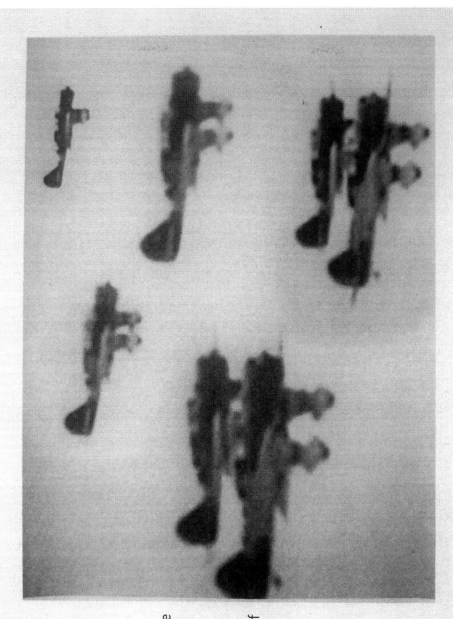

PZL-P23S Sea Eagle Heavy Dive bombers of the Royal Netherlands Navy returning from sinking the Japanese Battleships *Kagoshima* and *Kumamoto*. (Photo courtesy of the *Cornelis de Witt Veterans Association*.)

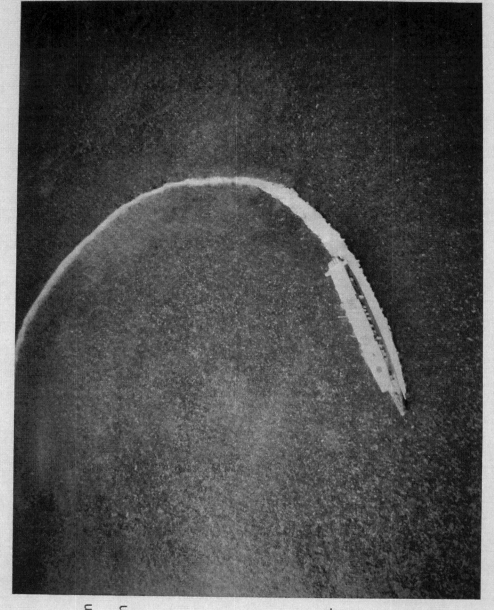

Japanese Light Carrier *Suzaku* takes evasive action and puts her helm hard to starboard at 33 knots! The RNLN airmen upon returning from their attack expressed their surprise at the agility of this light carrier. She was very hard to hit. The IJN made wide use of multiple rudders and destroyer turbines in their ships, thereby allowing for very rapid accelerations. December 08, 1941.

(Photograph courtesy of *The RNLN Battlecruiser-Carrier Naval Museum, Surabaya*).

Japanese Light Carrier *Suzaku* is bracketed by bombs from the anti-quated Curtis biplane dive bombers of 'Task Force Popeye' on December 08, 1941. The dark bomb burst would indicate a hit. The one off the port bow is close enough to cause serious damage. Note how quickly the calm seas of the two previous photos may become deeply furro-wed by many powerful racing warships.

(Photograph Courtesy of the RNLN *Battlecruiser-carrier Museum, Surabaya*).

The Imperial Japanese Navy Light Carrier Carrier *Suzaku*, Flagship of Operation Sunburst's 'Distant Cover Fleet' burns in the South China Sea, after being hit aft by a 220 kg. bomb from a RNLN biplane Helldiver of 'Task Force Popeye', December 08, 1942. Destroyers *Umagiri* (foreground), *Suwami*, and *Ooshio* stand by. (Photograph Courtesy of The *Hr. Ms. Johan de Witt Battlecruiser-carrier Veterans' Association*).

The carrier *Suzaku* burning, photograph was taken by an Air telegraphist gunner of a RNLN Curtis Helldiver from *Bomber Squadron 4*, of the Battlecruiser-carrier *Johan de Witt* during the air attack launched by the Royal Netherlands Navy Task Force Popeye, on the morning of December 08, 1941. The photograph is courtesy of *The Martin Danielszoon Sweers Private Collection*).

Fires engulf the stern of the Japanese Light Carrier Carrier *Suzaku*, Flagship of Vice Admiral Tomoshigue Sakonju. Aft of the recognition flag painted on the fight deck, the deck plating is crumpled from an attack earlier in the morning by dive-bombers of the Battlecruiser-carrier *Johan de Witt*. The photo was taken by a plane of the stricken carrier's own air group as it waited to land. This photograph was recovered by the Allied Military Commission at Tokyo in 1946. (Photograph courtesy of the KMN Battlecruiser-carrier Veterans' Association.)

The doomed light carrier *Suzaku*, Flagship of Operation Sunburst's Distant Cover Fleet. Seen here her fires rage out of control and she is sitting noticeably deeper in the water. The photo was taken from her escorting destroyer the *Ushio*. (Photograph courtesy of *The Johan de Witt Battlecruiser-carrier Veterans' Association*.)

IJN *Cruiser Squadron 11*, under the command of Rear Admiral Tamon Matsumoto is shown running the gauntlet of *Task Force Popeye's* formidable air group. In this dramatic photo they scatter under air attack, as they attempt to engage the Dutch Fleet with gun and torpedo, on the morning of December 08, 1941. Their objective was to destroy the flight decks of the two Battle-carriers and end the Dutch Fleet's ability to maintain air cover and their offensive air operations against the IJN Invasion Forces of *Operation Sunburst*. With their flight decks made inoperable, the entire Dutch Task Force may have been destroyed by the bomber regiments of the *6 th Hikodan*. (Photograph Courtesy of the *RNLN Battlecruiser-carrier Museum, Surabaya*).

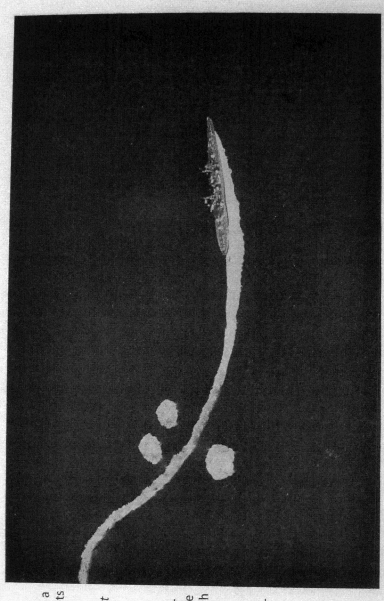

An unidentified Japanese Heavy Cruiser of Squadron 11, attempting to close the Dutch Fleet and initiate a surface battle maneuvers at 37 knots in the South China Sea to avoid the Curtis bi-plane dive-bombers of the Battlecruiser-carrier *Cornelis de Witt* on the morning of December 08, 1941.

This phase of the IJN's Operation *Sanbasuto'* was based on bad inteligence and the impetuous dash of the Japanese warships towards the Dutch Fleet was not properly coordinated with the air attacks of the JAAF *6 th Kogugan*. Consequently the Heavy Cruisers of Rear Admiral Tamon Matsuomoto, would pay the ultimate price.

(Photograph Courtesy of Lt. ter Zee 1e Klass Konrad Van de Groot (R).)

The Dive bomber pilots of the Dutch Battlecruiser-carriers were skilled and determined. By 08:15hrs the Hotaka (top right) is down by the stern and will soon sink.

Her sister, the Senjo with a heavy fire amidships, is hit again by another 220 kg. AP bomb.

(Photograph courtesy of *The Vice Admiraal Maarten Sweers Private Collection.*)

KMN *Task Force Popeye*, during the morning action of the 1st Battle of the South China Sea. The 'Heavy Hand' of the Japanese Army Air Force *6th Kokugun* (Air Army) begins to be felt, December 08, 1941. The Dutch Fleet chose a very tight steaming formation when under air attack, where it was hoped their tremendous fleet barrage would destroy the enemy. In practice however the heavy pounding administered by the bombers of the 73rd and 121st Air Regiments broke up the Dutch formation, and it became widely spaced to allow for drastic ship maneuvering. Seen here the Low level bombing by the *73rd Hikosentai* (Air Regiment) yields results; the *De Ruyter Class* Light cruiser *Prins te Paard* (middle) takes a bomb on her 'A' Turret mount at 8:31hrs destroying it completely. Ahead of her is the cruiser *Oliphant*. Behind them is the Battlecruiser-carrier *Johan de Witt*. The destroyers are (foreground) *Eendragt* leading the *Zoutmann*, (within a few moments she will lose her stern as a well aimed bomb detonates her depth charges). The destroyer following the *Prins* is the *Piet Heyn*, a bomb narrowly misses her stern, and above her the *Draak*. The ships were subjected to an Air assault that involved the release of some six hundred bombs and torpedoes! The intensity of the bombing shown here continued for over an hour. Evident are three high explosive contact fuse detonations, four near misses by delayed action armor piercing and one hit on the light cruiser. (Photograph Courtesy of *The Maarten Danielszoon Sweers Private Collection*).

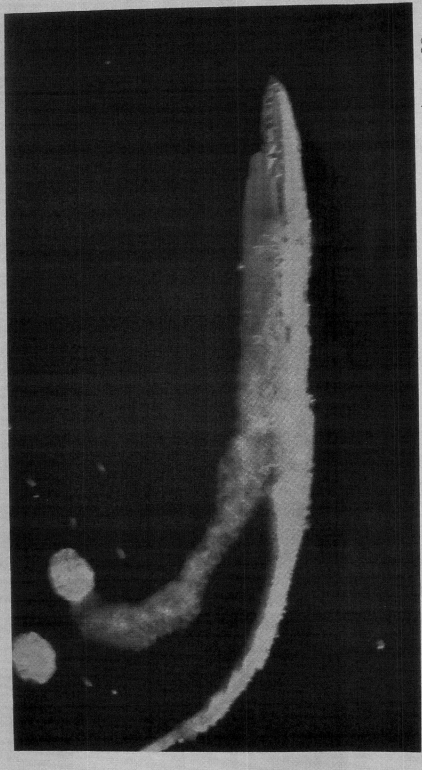

The Vlaggeschip of the KMN East Indies Fleet; the 40,000 tonne *Cornelis de Witt* is shown here at 30 knots with all starboard Flak batteries blazing away. Her Kapitein; Daniel Voorne has ordered; *Roer hard nar port*, as she fights off the massed air attacks of the JAAF 73rd Hikosentai (Air Regiment) on the morning of December 08, 1941. (Photograph courtesy of the Allied War Commission Tokyo in 1946, from the captured records of the JAAF *117th Chutai* (Squadron).

Stuurboord twintic! *(Starboard twenty!)*. The Flaggeschip completes a standard 'figure 8' maneuver to get back on her original course after frustrating a Japanese Army Air Force attack during the *Battle of the South China Sea*, December 08,1942. (Photograph courtesy of the *Maarten Sweers Private Collection*).

Two Imperial Japanese Navy Heavy Cruisers of the 'Improved Moyoko Class' steaming at high speed in the South China Sea on a heading for the Dutch Fleet to block their escape through Balabat Strait, the southern entrance to Sulu Sea from the South China Sea on the morning of December 08, 1941. The ships the *Yakushi* (top) and *Tokachi* ; Flagship of Rear Admiral Tamon Matsomoto, commanding Cruiser Squadron 11, attached to Operation Sunburst's Distant Cover Fleet. The photograph was taken by the pilot of CAP 21, a Brewster F2A Fighter from the RNLN Battlecruiser-carrier *Cornelis de Witt*, Flagship of *Task Force Popeye*. (The photograph is courtesy of *The Cornelis de Witt Battle- cruiser-carrier Naval Museum, Surabaya*).

A photograph of a Japanese Heavy Cruiser maneuvering at high speed while under air attack, *Battle of the South China Sea*, December 08, 1942. The lack of fire coming from her Flak Batteries at this moment is a mystery. (Photograph Courtesy of Lt. ter Zee 1e Klass Konrad Van de Groot (R).)

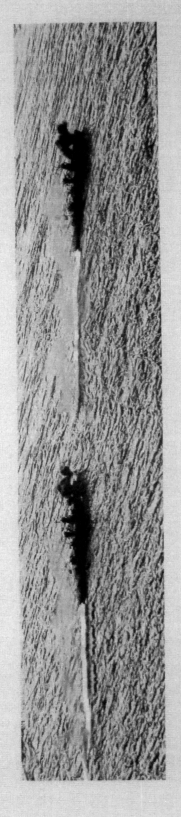

"09.05hrs; all Cruisers forward and attack!" Vice Admiraal Martin Sweers "throws away the book." He orders his light cruisers to temporality abandon their screening duties to the Battle-carriers and 'open the way' to Balabat Straits and allow his damaged Task Force to escape the fury of the massed bomber regiments of the Japanese 6th Air Army operating from airfields in French Indo China. Of the four RNLN light cruisers participating, the Gouden Leeuw and the Aemilia of the De Ruyter Class are shown at the moment they open fire with their forward turrets on the Japanese Heavy Cruisers Hotaka and Tokachi. (Photograph is courtesy of the Maarten Danielszoon Sweers Private Collection).

Heavily afire and deluged by shells the Japanese Heavy Cruiser *Yakushi* engages in a hopeless 'slugging match' against her powerful opponents; of RNLN *Task Force Popeye*, 09:40hrs December 08, 1941. As Vice Admiraal Sweers later commented; "there was no joy in destroying such a resolute ship and her crew, just relief that it was over." (Photograph courtesy of the *Cornelis de Witt Battlecruiser-carrier Veteran's Association*.)

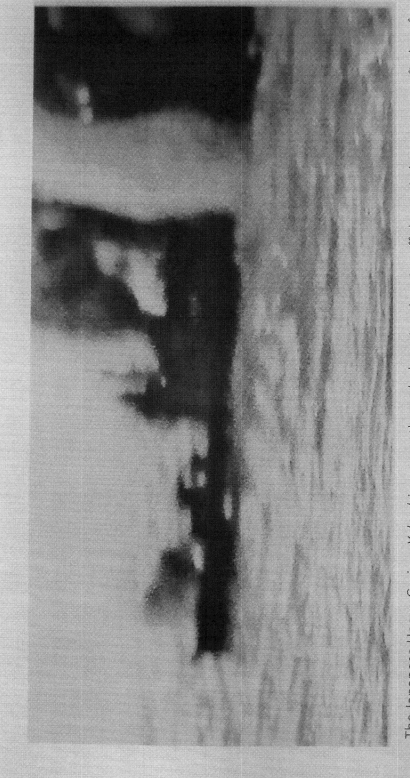

The Japanese Heavy Cruiser *Yakushi* as seen through the misted optics off the main battery range finder of the Battlecruiser-carrier *Johan de Witt*, December 08, 1941. The ship is heavily engaged but continues to shoot from a forward turret. (Photograph courtesy of *The Johan de Witt Battlecruiser-carrier Veterans' Association.*)

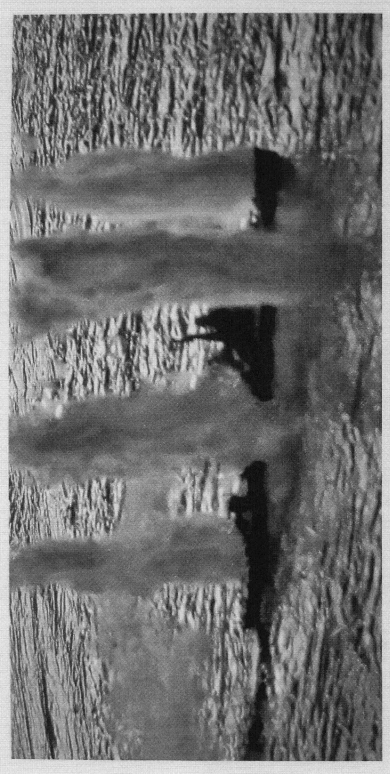

09:36 hrs December 09, 1941, the power of the 343 mm naval guns are dramatically demonstrated in this photo, as the 14,000 tonne Japanese Heavy Cruiser *Tokachi* is blown out of the water by a four gun salvo! The distinctive curve of her stem is shown clear of the water. And her upper works covered in foaming sea water from near misses. This dramatic photograph that were taken at high magnification using the camera of the main battery seven meter stereoscopic rangefinder of a Battlecruiser-carrier. (Photograph courtesy of Kapitein – Lt. ter Zee Tieler Van Riper, Gunnery Officer).

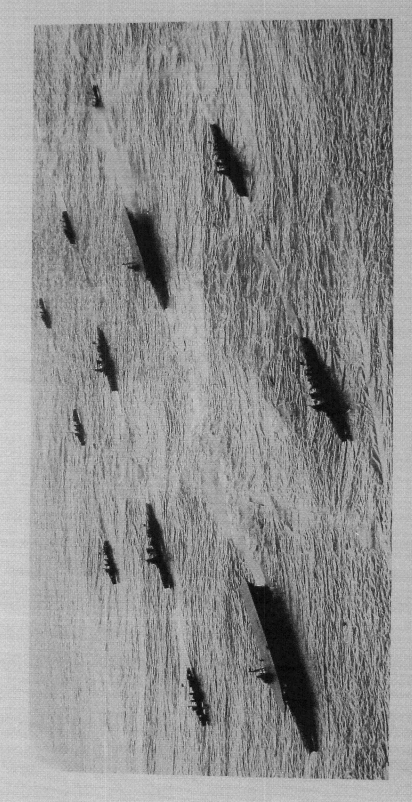

Task Force Popeye in the Celebes Sea, looking none the worse for wear after surviving the ordeal of the 1st Battle of the South China Sea. December 09, 1941. Not apparent from this peaceful looking photo is a much weakened Task Force with only 50% of its air groups remaining effective, the bomb and torpedo damage to the two Battle-carriers, to the cruisers and the missing destroyers. Nevertheless the protracted battle was a stunning victory for the Royal Netherlands Navy, on the first day of the war in the Pacific. (Photograph Courtesy of The Maarten Danielszoon Sweers Private Collection).

ABOUT THE AUTHOR

Mark Klimaszewski has worked in the shipbuilding industry in North America for thirty-five years, including ten years working on warship projects for the navies of the United States and Canada. He is a member of The Society of Naval Architects and Marine Engineers, and The American Society of Naval Engineers. He lives in Medicine Hat, Alberta, Canada.

92255122R00265

Made in the USA
Middletown, DE
07 October 2018